JOHN TWOPENNY

JOHN TWOPENNY

T. R. Wilson

HEADLINE

First published in Great Britain in 1995 by
HEADLINE BOOK PUBLISHING

10 9 8 7 6 5 4 3 2 1

British Library Cataloguing in Publication Data

Wilson, Timothy
John Twopenny
I. Title
823.914 [F]

ISBN 0-7472-1194-9

Typeset by
Letterpart Limited, Reigate, Surrey

Printed and bound in Great Britain by
Mackays of Chatham PLC, Chatham, Kent

HEADLINE BOOK PUBLISHING
A division of Hodder Headline PLC
338 Euston Road
London NW1 3BH

Characters

MR ADDY *Foreman at S. Twopenny & Son's.*
DR JAMES APPLEYARD *An elderly and dedicated London physician.*
TOM BIDMEAD *An impoverished clerk.*
BOBBS *A carter at S. Twopenny & Son's.*
MR BOWERMAN *Senior partner in the City firm of Bowerman & Dillen.*
MR BREAM *A Nonconformist minister.*
MR EDWIN CHIPCHASE *A businessman of Hales-next-the-sea.*
MR DILLEN *Junior partner in Bowerman & Dillen.*
ADMIRAL GEORGE FERNHILL *A retired naval officer, of Buttings Court.*
AUGUSTUS FERNHILL *The admiral's son, a fashionable young man.*
MR ARTHUR FLOWERS *A country solicitor.*
MR MARCUS GOODWAY *A wealthy gentleman, of London and Beacon House.*
MR HANKEY *A prize-fighter, resident in Jolly Butcher's Yard.*
OLD MEACHAM
ETHAN MEACHAM } *Father and Son, tailors at Saltmarsh.*
SERGEANT PARADINE *An officer of the Metropolitan Detective Police.*
UNCLE POMEROY *An elderly and much-admired relative of Mr Spikings.*
CALEB PORTER *A simple-minded man, manservant to Saul Twopenny.*
PHILIP REVELL *Boyhood friend of John Twopenny.*
MR RANDAL ROSE *An inmate of the King's Bench prison.*
'THE SOLDIER' *An eccentric beachcomber at Saltmarsh.*
MR ALFRED SPIKINGS *Of Montagu Place, Verity Deene's employer.*
KNIGHT SPIKINGS
TANCRED SPIKINGS } *The Spikings' sons, Verity Deene's pupils.*
DR FRANK SPRUCE *A young physician, former friend of Dr Twopenny.*
STUFFINS *Parlour-boarder at Mr Wenn's Academy.*
WALDO TUTTLE *A cheap-jack, or travelling seller of miscellaneous goods.*
JOHN TWOPENNY
DR ROBERT TWOPENNY *John's father, a physician at Saltmarsh.*
SAUL TWOPENNY *John's uncle, proprietor of S. Twopenny & Son's.*
WILLIAM TWOPENNY *Only son of Saul, a downtrodden young man .*
MR WENN *Headmaster of an Academy for boys at Norwich.*

MRS ADDY *The foreman's wife, a kindly lady.*
MRS APPLEYARD *Elderly and strong-minded mother of Dr Appleyard.*
MISS JEMIMA APPLEYARD *Dr Appleyard's sister, a charitable lady.*
MRS ELIZA BIDMEAD *Tom's wife.*
MRS BREAM *The minister's wife.*
VERITY DEENE *An orphaned poor relation of the Fernhills.*
MRS FERNHILL *The admiral's adoring wife.*
CATHERINE FERNHILL *The admiral's beautiful and charming daughter.*

CAROLINE FLOWERS } *Mr Flowers' little daughters, motherless.*
JANE FLOWERS
MRS GRACE GOODWAY *Mr Goodway's invalid wife.*
ARABELLA PECK *Waldo Tuttle's long-lost sweetheart.*
MRS REVELL *Philip's widowed mother.*
MRS FELICIA SPIKINGS *Wife of Alfred, and a devoted mother.*
HONORIA SPIKINGS } *The Spikings' daughers, Verity Deene's pupils.*
SERAPHINA SPIKINGS
TETTY *Maidservant to Dr and Mrs Twopenny.*
MISS THIMBLEBEE *A friseuse, or hairdresser, of Fetter Lane, London.*
TRIPP *Nursemaid to the Spikings children.*
MRS EMMA TWOPENNY *John's mother, a beautiful and accomplished woman.*
SAR'ANN TWOPENNY *Saul's daughter, a shrill woman of inquisitive habits.*
MRS WENN *The headmaster's wife, a musical lady.*
MRS WINCH *A poor resident of Jolly Butcher's Yard.*

For Ann Sylvester

Book One

CHAPTER ONE

The Work of a Moment

He was born in a strange place, John Twopenny: a place between the sea and the land. Though a map would have shown the place squarely on the coast, the sea was often quite out of sight there; and though the place boasted high cliffs, the cliffs did not descend into the sea, nor to a beach, nor to a harbour. And you would have looked in vain for a boat, from one end of the parish to the other.

It was a place of salt marshes – a place of remoteness and emptiness, of strange wading birds that left footprints like arcane writing across the sand, and of purple sea-lavender blooming where nothing else bloomed. A place of mists, too – swift, penetrating mists, that came from nowhere and reached, like clammy pickpockets, into every cranny of your clothing in an instant; mists like the one that was descending over young John as he walked home across the marshes one December twilight; and it was a place also of numerous little winding creeks, like the one into which John inadvertently plunged his right foot, with a sound somewhere between a splash and a suck.

'Oh, you idiot!' he said aloud, for he thought he knew these marshes well enough to navigate them blindfold. As indeed he did; but he had been daydreaming, and when John really set himself to daydream, you could have ridden a coach-and-four over him and he would never have noticed it. Recovering his balance, he drew his foot out – but not before the cold brackish water had poured in over the top of his boot, communicating a most unlovely sensation to his stockinged foot.

John sat down upon the damp ground, untied his boot, and emptied the water out of it. His stocking was so sodden, however, that he could not help but smile at how little he had gained by this action, and how comical he must have looked if anyone had been watching.

'Well, all it needs now,' he said to himself as he retied the boot on to his chilled foot, 'is for this bootlace to break, and then I shall be in a pretty pickle.'

He tightened the knot he had made, and the bootlace snapped in two. John regarded the frayed ends in stupefaction for some moments before dragging the boot off again with some impatience, and attempting a repair job with what remained of the lace. It was no easy task, in that intensifying cold, for his ungloved fingers – he was a few months short of his nineteenth birthday, and would as soon have thought of 'wrapping up warm' as of carrying an ear-trumpet and promenading in a bath-chair – and several fruitless, fumbling minutes had passed before he was roused from his concentration by a thin cry near at hand.

John started up at once, dropping the boot. He knew well the cries of all the curious birds that visited that unique shore, and did not need to hear the sound repeated to know that it came from a human throat. He faced about in the mist which, stirred by a breeze from landward, seemed in its stealthy movement to be circling round him like a host of ghostly waltzers; and, cupping his hands to his mouth, shouted: 'Hallo-o!'

His call was answered – faintly, as if there were scarcely enough breath left in the voice to pierce the curdled air – and John set off towards it at a run, quite forgetting his unshod foot, and springing across rills and channels, and over thorn hedges and scrubby dunes, with all the sureness of a lifetime's acquaintance; and with a conviction just as firm, that the voice must belong to a stranger, whose unfamiliarity with this enigmatic terrain had brought him to grief.

A stranger's face it was that turned to behold John leaping out of the mist towards him – a face at about the level of John's knees; for the stranger had slipped into one of the deepest of the creeks that branched across the marsh, and he was in the pungent water up to his neck. The coarse vegetation of the creek-side had been plucked up in the stranger's efforts to haul himself out, and strands of it hung still from his clenched hands; but it was plain at a glance that his strength was unequal to the greedy pull of the silt at the bottom of the creek, and that cold and exhaustion were rendering the contest increasingly one-sided, moment by moment. It was plain too, that had John been but a few minutes further on his way and out of earshot, the man's shouts would surely have gone unheard for all eternity.

The stranger let out a cry of relief on seeing help at hand; but uttered no word more until after John, flinging himself down at the creek-side and seizing the man's arms in his, had dragged him out and helped him to set his feet on firm ground. Though his clothes were drenched, and he gasped and shivered as hard as any man in such a situation might reasonably be expected to, the stranger very quickly displayed a complete self-possession, and the marks of a strong constitution in the way he pushed back his wet hair, briskly shook himself, and thrust out his hand to John.

'I am the most fortunate man alive,' the stranger said, fetching his breath and shaking John's hand with a firm grip. 'I was just telling myself that of all the spots in the world in which to get in such a fix, this was the worst; that the chances of anyone happening along were a thousand to one; in short that I had – Phew! – pretty well done for myself. I was quite a fool to venture out on foot so late, with no knowledge of the country. I'm sorry you've been put to such trouble, but I must confess I'm glad of it, too, if you see what I mean.'

'Oh! not at all,' said John. 'These marshes of ours can be chancy places if you don't know them, especially when the mist comes down so quickly. You're not hurt, sir?'

'I dare say I shall catch the cold I deserve for my foolishness,' answered the stranger, clapping his arms across his broad chest, and smiling, 'but beyond that, no. I thank you . . . You speak, I think, as a native of this place?'

'Yes, I was born here. My name is John Twopenny. My father is the doctor at Saltmarsh – we live just at the top of the village, below the cliff.'

'Then we are neighbours – or near enough, I dare say, in this rather underpopulated corner of the world. You know, I think, Beacon House, on the road to Hales-next-the-sea?'

'Why, yes – it has been empty for some years.'

'It has been empty for some years, as you say, my friend, but it is empty no longer. My wife is in indifferent health, and her doctors recommend sea air, and so we have taken Beacon House for an indefinite period. A rather unorthodox way for new neighbours to meet, but no matter: my name is Goodway.'

Thus the stranger, cordially shaking John's hand again. He was a fresh-coloured, upright, genial-looking gentleman in his later thirties, with a crop of curly hair and whisker just touched with grey, a strong Roman nose, bright penetrating eyes, and a voice of singular force and musicality, which John seemed rather to feel in the marrow of his bones than to hear. Mr Goodway appeared, indeed, to have wholly recovered from his mishap, and to be quite as at home now, out on the foggy marsh, as by his own fireside; and as he stood before John in his sturdy bracing way, like an urbane lion, it was as much as John could do to fend off an attack of unaccustomed shyness, and to rid himself of a passing impression that it was he who had been rescued by Mr Goodway, instead of the other way around.

'And now I observe,' Mr Goodway went on, his quick glance lighting on John's feet, 'that I have cost you a boot as well as a wetting. Has it come off in the mud, do you suppose . . .?'

'Oh, that!' said John with a laugh, recollecting. 'No, no, I parted company with it earlier – I got into something of a scrape myself.'

'We are a fine pair,' Mr Goodway said, laughing too. 'Shall we look for it?'

'Well, it must be just over – just over there . . .' John turned around, and turned around again; but the mist had so closed in on them, effacing such scant features as the marshland possessed, that he could no more have located the spot where he had shed his boot than he could have numbered the hairs on his own head. 'I'm sorry,' he said, wondering at the same moment why he was apologizing, 'I – I really don't know where I lost it. Oh! well, it doesn't signify. I can make my way home like the John in the nursery rhyme – one shoe off and one shoe on.'

'I hope it isn't far,' said Mr Goodway, smiling but frowning too. 'I may catch a chill and serve me right, but I shouldn't wish you to share in it.'

'Oh, no, no,' said John, who no more supposed that he would ever be ill than that he would ever be old, 'I shall be home in a pig's whisper. But you,' he added in sudden concern, 'you're soaked through, and have a long way to walk. Will you come home with me? My father, I'm sure, will lend you dry clothes.'

'I wish I had an excuse to accept such a hospitable offer,' said Mr Goodway. 'But I am not so forlorn as you suppose. I have my horse stabled at the Dun Cow, and I can get dry there. I would be riding him now, if I had not taken a fancy to see a little of our new home afoot, and thought myself a very clever fellow for finding my own way about the marshes. No, lead me on to the village, my friend, if you will, and I shall trouble you no longer.'

John complied readily, and a few minutes' walking brought them to the landward limit of the marsh, where the cattle grazed on the reclaimed land, and where human habitation began abruptly with the coast road and the village of Saltmarsh climbing up on the other side of it to the heather-crowned cliff.

'Well, here we must part, John,' Mr Goodway said as they drew near to the Dun Cow, which appeared as a cluster of ruddy lights glowing against the sombre cliffside. 'I seem to recollect now, some natives of the Indies – whether the East or West I'm not sure, but natives of somewhere – who have a custom whereby a man who saves another man's life must then follow him everywhere, and they must never be separated till the end of their days. Rather a deterrent to heroism, one would have thought, but no matter . . . What I was about to say was that, though I shall lay no such burden on you, I shall positively insist that you and your family – you mentioned your father, I think?'

'Dr Robert Twopenny,' said John. 'And then there's my mother, and just me.'

'Well, that all three of you will do us the honour of visiting us at Beacon House, and help us welcome the festive season. Mrs Goodway's health does not permit her to go about as she would wish, but we like to keep Christmas in the old way nonetheless, and if your parents will consider such an unconventional invitation – I might send a note, perhaps?'

'Surely – just direct it to Dr Twopenny at Saltmarsh. I'm sure my parents will be delighted.'

'Till we meet again, then.'

Thus they parted: Mr Goodway betaking himself to the Dun Cow, and John setting off at a limping clip through the village towards his home. He was by now so chilled, tired, and hungry, that the episode of his meeting with Mr Goodway was soon shunted to the back of his mind by thoughts of banked fires, clean clothes, and veal-and-ham pie; and though by the time he reached his father's house he was painfully aware of his unshod foot, the loss of his boot did not seem to him to be any great matter.

It was, indeed, a trivial thing; and with his youth, and his elasticity of temper, and his ardent belief in the stirring experiences and noble challenges that lay ahead of him on that long path of life which he was preparing to climb as energetically as he now climbed the path to his father's house – with all this tending to fix his eyes on the furthest horizons, it was no wonder that John Twopenny did not suppose that such a trivial thing as a broken bootlace could set momentous events in train just as surely as a declaration of war, a standard of revolt, or the death of a king.

CHAPTER TWO

An Encounter with a Mermaid

Almost the first objects that John could remember seeing, in his earliest infancy, were the two stone lions that stood on either side of the front door of his father's house, up at the heathery top of Saltmarsh.

They were not very large lions – the reason, perhaps, for his remembering them so well, for they were just of a height for a toddling child to rest its arms upon – and they were not very fierce lions, either; for salt wind, mist and rain had done their work on them, so that in their eroded state they resembled nothing so much as two rather ingratiating pug-dogs, sitting up on their hind legs to beg a titbit. John's father said that they had come with the house, and so he had kept them, and that now they made him laugh so much he couldn't part with them.

The lions, or pug-dogs, were there as always to greet him when John came hobbling home from the marshes that evening, and mightily glad he was to see them. And there to greet him too, when he went in, were the faces that figured even before the lions in his early remembrance. Before everything, there were for John these faces, and they seemed not only to have been always familiar to him, and never seen for the first time, but also never to have changed one jot from the first day of his existence to this.

'Home from school just one day,' said old Dr Twopenny from his chair by the hearth, 'and already he's neglecting us. How goes it, my boy? The marshes, I suppose, were in the same place as you left them in September?'

'I'm afraid I've brought some of them in with me,' said John, pausing on the threshold of the firelit parlour, and indicating the condition of his clothes. 'Will you excuse me a moment while I go up and change?'

'Whatever has become of your boot?' his mother said.

'Ah – it's on the marshes somewhere, I'm afraid,' John said. 'I'm very sorry – it's rather a story: I'll explain as soon as I'm changed.'

John was not long about his dressing, for he performed the simplest tasks, as his father said, as if he had the devil at his heels. Within that time, however, someone called at the house seeking Dr Twopenny's professional services, and when John came down he found only his mother in the parlour.

'I have solved the mystery of the missing boot,' his mother said, ringing the bell for candles. 'You met a one-legged man on the marshes, and he was in dire need, and so you gave him your boot.'

'Not quite as curious as that,' John said, sitting down beside her, and admiring the sheaf of watercolour sketches with which she was occupied. 'Why, Mother, this one's torn right across!'

'I have just been looking over some of my old work,' Mrs Twopenny said, 'and throwing out what is not fit to keep. Which, I fear, is not only most of it, but practically the whole.'

'You don't do yourself justice, Mother. You should see the drawing-master at Mr Wenn's. All *he* can draw is ladies in high-waisted gowns, walking in profile, and looking like a lot of ninepins.'

7

'Well,' his mother said, 'it's as well to be reconciled to one's limitations. And I am quite reconciled to mine – at least I hope I am,' she added with a sigh, laying the drawings aside. 'So: tell me the tale of the boot. Wait, though – best postpone it till your father's here, else you'll have to say it all over again. He's only gone to his consulting-room – the Meachams again. We'll have supper soon. Ah, here's light.'

The candles were brought in by Tetty, the general servant, a smart young woman of formidable correctness, reliably reputed to be able to see round corners. The candles revealed to John, once more, how beautiful his mother was; and he felt almost guilty as he recalled the mothers of his fellow-pupils at Mr Wenn's Academy in Norwich, whom he had glimpsed at half-holidays, and who all seemed to be, if not quite Gorgons or Harpies, at least something that any self-respecting mythological hero would have thought it worth his while to slay.

'You haven't long to go at Mr Wenn's now,' Mrs Twopenny said. 'Shall you be sorry to leave next year?'

'Sorry, but glad too, because then my real studies can begin. Though of course, if I'm to go to Edinburgh as Father recommends, that means I shall be a long way from home and shan't be able to see you so often – which inclines me to studying in London, but even then I shall be a good way away . . . I suppose I want the best of both worlds.'

'We all do,' said his mother gently. 'Well, wherever you go, we shall still be here, you know.'

'Do you ever wish you had lived somewhere other than Saltmarsh, Mother?' John said, springing up to replace a coal that had fallen from the grate.

'Whatever makes you ask that?' his mother said after a moment.

'Oh! I don't know . . . You have such talents, and there are so few people here to appreciate them. I do love our coast, but there's no denying it's rather a barren spot.'

'True . . . but then your father has talents too.'

'Ah, but it's different for father. He was born in these parts, and chose to come back here to practise. This is his element.'

'It's mine, too, now. Oh, yes, it was different in London when I was a girl, I suppose . . . but my family weren't well-off, you know. And these talents of mine, as you call them, would make a pretty poor showing in society – no more than thousands of women possess.' His mother seemed suddenly to become aware of her melancholy expression, and smiled. 'No, I would rather have old Mrs Bream tapping her stick in time when I play the piano, than a lot of high-toned folk pretending to be charmed and wondering how much my father was worth.'

John returned his mother's smile in the pier-glass over the mantelshelf, seeing reflected around her the well-loved parlour that was as evocative of his parents' personalities as a page of their writing: the bookcase with its worn volumes, his father's great stuffed chair, the table crowded with letters and sewing and more books and sheet-music and pipes and spills and the Chinese tobacco-jar, the flowered wallpaper which as a child he had always suspected, for some reason, of continuing underneath the dado to the floor, the mahogany wall-clock with the lazily swinging pendulum which old Tib the cat, ensconced on her cushion, could not help winking at, as if she knew it was nothing worth pursuing, but just had to make sure, and his mother's piano which had engaged the interest of half the village when it had made its laborious ascent to the house, mounted on the carrier's cart and protesting with shuddering discords at every pothole. Reflected there too was the open door to the dining-room, and John remembered now how strangely frightening that reflection had been to him, when he had been only of a height to place the tip of his nose above the mantelshelf; and it was curious to consider that the little hands which had struggled to grasp its slippery marble, and these long-fingered hands which rested so easily on top of it now, were one and the same.

'It's good to be home, Mother,' he said with a rush of affection. 'I can't imagine Christmas anywhere else in the world.'

There were voices in the passage, and Dr Twopenny flung open the door with the words, 'My dear, here's the Meachams, wishing to give you the compliments of the season before they go.'

A little old man followed the doctor into the room, nodding his head rapidly to all present, and giving the high-pitched titter with which the Meachams did not signal amusement, but rather a general desire to be as agreeable as possible. This was Ethan Meacham, who was such a very little old man, and so shrunken, that his legs appeared no thicker than those of Mr Punch, and scarcely more capable of supporting his weight; and whose head had sunk so far below his shoulders that he was obliged to tie the ends of his neckcloth at the back, and look perpetually ready for dinner. He was one half of Meacham & Son, Tailors, of Saltmarsh; and it was a tribute either to the healthful properties of the North Norfolk air, or of tailoring as a profession, that Ethan Meacham was the Son of the partnership – for creeping along behind him, and grasping his sleeve, was an even littler old man, who was his father, and who was known very reasonably as Old Meacham. This venerable man, indeed, made his son appear a mere sprig; and besides having no teeth, was bald to his very ears, which were as long as a bloodhound's, and had among the unkinder boys of the neighbourhood earned him the nickname 'Lugs'.

'Good evening, Mr Meacham. Good evening, Mr Ethan,' John's mother said. 'I hope it's nothing serious that brings you to the doctor this cold night.'

'Evening, Messes Twopenny: no, no, nothen serious – hee, hee, hee!' said Mr Ethan. 'Thass only Dad's pills we come for – only your pills, warn't it, Dad?'

'Run out of 'em – run out of 'em just today,' said the elder man, who with his see-sawing Norfolk accent rendered yet more piping by age, could hardly be said to speak at all, but rather to sing his every remark like a character in an opera. 'I'm not a great believer in physic as a rule, but without Doctor Twopenny's pills, I should be a poor thing – a poor thing. Hee, hee, hee!'

'Well, my friends, it's a cold night, as my wife says,' said John's father. 'What do you say to a hot toddy to set you on your way? Let's call it Christmas now – what's three days, after all, between friends?'

Mr Ethan looking respectfully to his father, the elder man accepted cheerfully. 'I don't indulge in strong liquors as a rule, but at your invitation, Doctor, and as thass – hee, hee, hee! as thass all but Christmas, as you say, I'll not say no.' Adding in a shrill whisper, as John's father began mixing the drinks, 'Not too strong for the younker, mind – ' with a jerk of his head at Mr Ethan – 'do that go to his head, and make him unmanageable.'

'Please, Mr Meacham, Mr Ethan, sit down and be cosy,' said John's mother; but before John could place chairs by the fire, old Meacham quavered out, 'No, no, don't trouble for us, thank ye: we're a-dewing as we are, aren't we, Ethan?'

'We're a-dewing, Dad,' agreed Ethan, 'we're a-dewing'; and indeed it was such a performance for the two aged men to lower themselves into chairs, and then to lever themselves out again, that they were as well to continue standing. However, in token of making themselves more comfortable, they advanced a few mazy steps into the room, and then stood there amiably trembling and quivering, like the last two shrivelled leaves on the oldest tree in creation.

'John, you'll have a toddy, too, I hope?' said Dr Twopenny, bending over the fire, his big florid face shining with the pleasure of hospitality – the thing he liked best in all the world.

'What, is that young John Twopenny there?' trilled Old Meacham before John could reply. 'Why, I had no idea – no idea as the boy was home!' For the Meachams, whether because of their age, or of endless sewing by candlelight, or both, were very short-sighted; and being not much taller than a walking-stick,

9

tended to acknowledge their acquaintances by shuffling up to within a few inches of their lapels, and, tailor-like, recognizing them that way. Thus John, to save Old Meacham the trouble of moving, went up to the old man, and presented the breast of his coat for inspection.

'I'm very glad to see you again, Mr Meacham,' John said to the hairless dome of skull that filled his view, 'and I'm glad to know you're as hearty as ever. And you too, Mr Ethan.'

'Why, John, you're as tall as your father, or very near,' Old Meacham said, locating John's hand, and shaking it. 'That run in the family, I reckon. Your uncle over at Hales – he's a big man, too. What a difference there is in folk! None of the Mcachams seem to do much in the way of growing. You wouldn't remember Ethan's mother, rest her, but there warn't much of her, either. I bring to mind the time she tippled over and fell into the dolly-tub on a washday, and was very near drowned. Very near. She was going down a third time, when I came in from fetching a penn'orth of soda, and pulled her out. She reckon to have heered the Angel Gable calling her as she sunk, but I b'lieve that was only the water singing in her ears. Ah! Thank you, Doctor,' he said, receiving his glass of toddy, and by a very gradual ascent getting it to his lips. 'Your very good health; and likewise yours, ma'am; and yours, young John. So, you'll be going out in the world soon, I dare say, John: what will you be, I wonder? Tall enough for a guardsman, I declare, although – ' he gestured across John's chest, as if wielding an invisible tape-measure – 'mebbe not so broad.'

'I hope to begin studying medicine next year, Mr Meacham,' said John, 'and become a physician.'

'Follow your father's profession, eh? You couldn't do better, couldn't do better,' said Old Meacham, making a sudden sideways scuttle which gave the momentary impression of his being about to leave, but which was merely a vagary of his uncertain legs. 'I always say there edn't a better man for physicking atween here and the Wash. Mind you, in my young days there was a fellow at Hales who'd cure anything that ailed you, and cut your hair into the bargain; though he was rightly a horse-doctor by trade, and they do say he was a mite heavy-handed when it came to midwifing. Well! I hope you'll study hard, John, and be a credit to your father and your mother, though I can't say as I should fancy the 'prenticeship myself, for there's a deal of cutting up bodies involved, so I hear, and I mightn't have the stomach for it.'

'Well, I don't know how I shall bear up when it comes to the anatomy lessons,' said John smiling, 'but I do want very much to be a doctor.'

'Dose yourself with brandy before you go in, my boy,' said his father. 'That's what I did. So did we all, I believe. The surgeon in charge took one sniff of the air and remarked that he hardly needed to have the body pickled.' And John's father gave his mighty roar of laughter; while the Meachams wheezed out the longest and shrillest of titters, and sounded like two ancient tea-kettles.

'Heyo,' said Old Meacham, setting his empty glass on the table at last by getting both hands round it and forcing it down, 'we'd best be skipping off home. Thank ye for the toddy, Doctor Twopenny; and the compliments of the season to you, ma'am, and young John.'

'And a happy new year!' quavered Mr Ethan, on his own initiative.

'Boisterous,' his father said, shaking his head, and taking hold of Ethan's sleeve, 'always boisterous in his cups'; and the two old men, after an erratic tour of the room, at length urged their legs in the general direction of the door, and took their leave.

'Father,' John said when they had gone, 'you're surely not still giving Old Meacham those pills.'

'Certainly I am,' said Dr Twopenny, with a rumble of laughter, mixing more

10

toddy, 'an excellent remedy – never known to fail.'

'But there's nothing in them – they're just baked meal!'

'I know that. You know that. But Old Meacham doesn't. As far as he's concerned, they make him feel better; and as long as he thinks that, I'm happy to go on giving them to him. Anyhow, they won't hurt him; for his age, the man's as healthy as a horse.'

'It's no wonder, after all that meal,' Mrs Twopenny said, and set the doctor off on his great roaring laugh again. If ever there was a man who relished a laugh, it was Dr Robert Twopenny; who in his sixtieth year was still a giant of a man, with a great head crowned with neatly groomed silver hair, full red lips, and boyish blue eyes. He had of late added weight to his height, and could be a little clumsy in consequence; but the clumsiness did not extend to his hands, which were very gentle – never more so than when, as now, he lightly caressed his wife's fair hair, as if to reassure himself of her reality. Emma Twopenny was more than twenty years his junior, but the doctor retained in many aspects the character of a young man – in his energy, which was particularly prodigious in the matter of entertaining and merrymaking; in his freedom from the rigidity of habit, and easiness of welcome to anything new; in his sincere repentance the next morning when, as happened not infrequently, he drank a little more than was good for him; and, perhaps less propitiously, in his ready optimism about money, which enabled him to be less than pressing about his fees and yet at the same time take up quixotic projects for the improvement of the house – such as the garden-room at the rear which had never got further than a few struts and beams of wrought-iron and timber, like a highly ornamental gallows.

Deeply as he loved his father, and strongly as he respected the instinctive skill of those large hands, John had rather more exalted notions of a doctor's vocation – which, as his father freely admitted, he had entered into merely because it seemed preferable to the law or the church. Dr Twopenny cured where he could, and where he could not cure he tried to relieve; but he had too keen an enjoyment of the good things in life to bother himself with the great questions of public health, sanitation and housing – questions on which John had once or twice waxed so eloquent that one of the more conservative masters at his school had him marked down as a mad Radical. Yet it was typical of the roomy tolerance of Dr Twopenny's mind that he accepted the difference between his son's aims and his own. That was why he had sent John to Mr Wenn's Academy, which for all its faults had not the classical, gentlemanly bias of the grander schools, and even dabbled in such new-fangled things as the physical sciences.

'Ah, well, folk are more idealistic about medicine nowadays, and it's a good thing, in truth,' said Dr Twopenny, lighting his pipe and resuming his seat by the fire. 'At Cambridge I wasn't the most serious of students, but there were fellows worse than me: a bit of dog-Latin, a lordly air, and never go near a sick person if you could help it seemed to be the general rule. Well, their time's nearly over. Whether you choose Edinburgh, my boy, or one of the London teaching hospitals, you'll be a fitter man for the profession than those overstuffed noodles. Well, well, now that we are cosy, let's have the story of the missing boot.'

'I'm afraid it will be a disappointment after such a wait,' said John; but as he told the story, the encounter took on in his mind a strange and dreamlike hue, perhaps because there was such a disparity between the scene on the marsh and the enveloping, untidy comfort of this warm parlour. Most dreamlike and unconformable of all, indeed, was the image of that poised and cool gentleman he had rescued, with his piercing eye and strong grip; such that John felt it no more likely that Mr Goodway could walk into this room and sit in one of the chairs, than that the stone lions at the front door could come trotting in from the cold and bask on the hearthrug.

11

He could convey nothing of this to his parents, however, without seeming inordinately fanciful; and they were chiefly interested in Mr Goodway as a newcomer to a neighbourhood where novelty was in short supply.

'Beacon House, eh?' said his father. 'He must have a long purse. The last fellow who took it had to give it up after half a year – the expenses were too much for him. Well, I've certainly no objections to a little Christmas junketing, at Beacon House or anywhere – the more of that, the better . . . What do you say, my dear?'

'I look forward to it – I've never been inside Beacon House,' said John's mother who, like her husband, dearly loved a party.

'Supper's laid ma'am,' said Tetty, putting her head round the door; and John, who could eat the table bare and never put on an ounce, jumped up with alacrity, dismissing Mr Goodway from his mind once more. Dr Twopenny was quite as eager, but first offered his arm to his wife with his invariable tender gallantry. John, following them into the dining-room, observed them fondly. A stranger, looking at the couple thus, might think them somewhat ill-assorted. His mother, with her fairness, her slenderness, her quiet grace, appeared beside the robustness of her husband as a silky cat might appear beside an Old English sheepdog; and the simile also held true, to a degree, in the matter of temperament. A stranger, however, could know nothing of their mutual devotion, a devotion founded on companionship – and from living with Robert and Emma Twopenny, John knew how undervalued that word was, and what a world of warmth it could contain; albeit his own private notions of love, while vague, were altogether more ardent.

A broad bay-window filled one end of the dining-room: parting the curtain to peep out, John saw that the mist was dispersing, driven before the first marauding gusts of a nor'-easter from the sea. The house, on its bare eminence above the marshes, was right in the path of the wind, which he knew from experience could come swarming ashore with the ferocity of a Viking raid; placing his hand against the window-glass, he could feel the faint shudderings and inward thrusts of the diamond panes as they were buffeted. But the house was built with barnlike solidity, of flint and pantile, and had withstood many a gale, and so John let the curtain fall and turned back to the table, certain that there was nothing out there to trouble about, and no force at large in that bleak night which could lay low these homely walls.

John's schooling, as his mother had said, was drawing to its close. After the Christmas holiday he was to return to Mr Wenn's Academy, where he was a boarder, for another half-year – chiefly to be crammed in those subjects in which, in his easy-going way, John had let the will stand for the deed. He was determined, on his return, to buckle down; for his medical studies came next, and John was eager to demonstrate to his father, who was going to support him through the long training, that it would not be a wasted investment. He had set his heart on medicine from an early age – from the time, indeed, when he had been small enough to ride in front of his father on Dr Twopenny's old black mare, and had watched him set a carter's broken bone in the middle of the field – and though John was in many ways not a very serious young man, he was very serious about his ambition to be a doctor.

For now, however, he was gloriously at leisure; he was home for Christmas, and intent upon renewing his acquaintance with everything that made Saltmarsh a beloved memory in absence. The tramp across the marshes had been a beginning; and the morning after his singular adventure there, he had a happy reunion with another landmark of his childhood and youth in that out-of-the-way spot – though in this case the landmark, to his sorrow, was not going to be there for much longer.

Philip Revell came to call. Philip Revell, John's friend from boyhood; with the same round spectacles as always, and the same short curls, and the same mild, almost sleepy expression on his round face, like an untroubled Schubert; with his

12

unassuming manner, and soft voice, and stocky limbs which had never gone through the gawky stage of his contemporaries; Philip Revell, shaking John's hand and placidly murmuring, 'British reserve and all that, but still – awfully glad, you know, John – awfully glad. And just how tall, now, do you plan on growing? Only I'd appreciate an estimate, you know, so as to prepare myself the next time. Only an estimate – to the nearest yard, say.'

There was a certain unsteadiness in their laughter over this; for it was unlikely, as both of them knew, that there would be a next time, at least in the foreseeable future. Philip was going to India. His late father had been an unpretentious clergyman at Hales-next-the-sea, and had been able only to leave his widow a small annuity. The chance of a position with the East India Company, which had been procured for Philip by a relative in the City, was too good to miss, for his mother's means were unequal to setting him up in any profession; and so he was to sail for Bombay in the New Year.

The separation would be a sadness to both of them. Accordingly, they accommodated the coming event by speaking of it only in the most cheerful terms, as if it were the most hilarious thing that had ever happened to them.

Here was Philip now, at any rate, tucking his hands under his coat-tails, and proposing an expedition with the same dimpled diffidence as when they were boys. At Hales-next-the-sea – which was five miles down the coast road, a distance they were both accustomed to walking – a travelling raree-show had set up on the quay, and was advertising as its principal attraction a real mermaid, in a glass bottle. 'It doesn't say whether it's a *live* mermaid,' Philip said, 'but I'm inclined to suppose that it isn't. Not in a bottle, you know. It would pine, I fancy, in a bottle. Start shedding its scales, and never combing its hair, and letting itself go rather. Anyhow, it might be worth a visit. What do you say?'

John said yes, very readily. He paused only to say goodbye to his parents, who were sitting over a late breakfast, and then set out with Philip into the bright cold morning. Everything that met the eye had a brilliant pearly look, as if last night's wind had swept and scoured it. Even the gulls, shabby, seedy enough fellows when you saw them up close, looked like reformed characters as they rode the onshore breeze with sun on their white breasts, and appeared to have taken a vow never to quarrel over fish-heads again.

The two struck out along the higher path which, passing at the foot of the doctor's garden, climbed amongst the gorse and red sorrel of the clifftop, and afforded a view of the peculiar topography of Saltmarsh. Here they were two hundred feet up, with at their backs the dark sandy woods that extended inland; below them, the red roofs of the village tumbled down to the lower road, which ran parallel with a dyke; beyond the dyke the green zone of reclaimed marsh sheltered behind its shingle bank; beyond that stretched the marshes, with their unearthly colours of vegetation, with their creeks and lagoons glittering like steel in the winter sun, and their strange tenantry of birds flittering in and out of the reed-beds; and at last, beyond the dunes, the sea itself, stealthily retreating across the tidal mud with a sullen, excluded look, as if it coveted its lost domain, and might decide to take it back one day.

There was scarcely a stick or stone here without its tender associations for John. Here he had grown up, with as little trouble or sorrow as was compatible with being human; on these bright roofs and smooth flint walls, barnyards and stables, thorn hedges and wind-racked trees, on track and marsh and meadow he had looked with the eyes of infant and child, youth and young man; even the monstrous great church, scarcely capable as its grey tower seemed of inspiring affection, had played a part in his development. For inside, many of the pews were adorned with graffiti of sailing-ships, executed by long-perished hands in the days when Saltmarsh had been open to the sea, and a sailor's life the dream of all the village boys who idly carved there; and it seemed to John that those same crude ships had been the vessels of his own very different dreams. It was on them that his drowsing eyes had rested through many a tedious sermon, until the ships had seemed to plunge and tack and veer like their real counterparts, and, cramming on sail, bear his thoughts off on long hopeful voyages into a far-off land called the future: a land in which he was a physician of daring and renown, penetrating the cloud of mystery that hung about the commonest of diseases, and passing like a flaming sword of righteousness through the pestilential haunts of the poor and weak. And if he sometimes perceived, even then, that the voyage might be long and fraught with hazard, he certainly never entertained the possibility of shipwreck.

Up the cliff path they toiled, and exchanged news once they had breath enough. John told again the story of his meeting with Mr Goodway, and was not a bit surprised that Philip, who knew everything before everyone else, knew all about him.

'He's a wealthy man, I hear,' Philip said. 'There's some sort of shipping firm in the City that his family have long had a stake in, and he's got other property too, I believe. His main residence is in London – Dorset Square, I think I heard – but it's let for now, while he lives at Beacon House. Mrs Goodway's a charming woman, so they say, but not strong: nerves, apparently, and town got too much for her. I wonder if your father might be able to help her.'

'Oh, Father's a mite sceptical of nervous conditions. "Nothing a little more wine and a little less religion won't cure", as he said of one lady in Norwich.' John suddenly pointed ahead. 'I say, Philip – I dare you.'

They both laughed at this echo of a phrase from their childhood, always associated with the place they were now approaching – a derelict cottage on the clifftop known as the Hanged Man's House. Who the Hanged Man had been, and where he had been hanged, and what he had done to deserve or not deserve it, no one knew; it was a tale that went back further even than Old Meacham's earliest memories. Certainly no one had ever chosen to live there, even though the flint walls were quite intact, and the gaping roof might have been repaired easily enough. It was, to be sure, an unwholesome-looking place, the rotted shutters at its two main windows giving from a distance the appearance of hooded eyes, and the brambles that had grown up about its door, unchecked except by capricious winds, suggesting in their twisted shapes rearing serpents, and upraised whips, and ghastly bonds. It did not require a very active imagination to trace a resemblance between the rust-red stain of damp that crept down from the timbers, and blood; nor to conclude that the heath hereabout was barer, and the birdsong quieter, and the song of the wind more hollow than on other parts of the clifftop.

Certainly, as boys, both John and Philip had regarded this shell of a house with mingled fascination and dread, and had urged each other to tremendous dares concerning it; and now they paused to enter it together again, for old times' sake. Why a house with such large holes in the roof should be so very dark inside was a curious question; and why the two of them should have such a sensation of intruding, in a place that contained nothing but bare walls and barer floor was another; but John all at once felt not particularly inclined to answer them, and was just about to suggest that they go on, when Philip startled him by crying: 'John! Whatever is that on your coat?'

John looked down at the breast of his coat, whither Philip was pointing from the other side of the room, and saw that something was discolouring it – something that ran like a dark sash from shoulder to hip. He had put up a hasty – almost frantic – hand to wipe it off, when recognition dawned, and he looked upward. It was as he thought: the sun shining with sudden brilliance through the decayed roof had laid the shadow of one of the great timber cross-beams directly across his body, with an effect that both he and Philip had taken for some nameless and disfiguring

14

mark. John stepped forward out of the diagonal shadow with a laugh. 'It's all right,' he said. 'See?'

'Good heavens – I shall have to change my spectacles,' said Philip, laughing too; but the experience was disquieting, and they left the Hanged Man's House very quickly, agreeing that it was just a dull old ruin after all, and that you needed the eyes of childhood to see anything in it.

'Isn't that the Soldier down there?' said Philip, pointing down at a figure on the marshes.

'That's him,' said John. 'Let's go and see him.' And, both glad enough to get away from the vicinity of the Hanged Man's House, they scrambled down to sea-level by a track that wound through the heather and, crossing the dyke by a duckboard bridge, made their way across the flats towards the Soldier.

He was given that name because of the red coat he wore; and if he had any other name, or any other coat, no one knew about it. No one knew, either, whether he had at any time been a soldier, or whether he had merely picked the coat up at second- or third-hand somewhere. Certainly no other part of his dress would have caused anything but astonishment on the parade-ground, consisting as it did of wide canvas trousers or slops, extensively darned and patched; a pair of fishermen's boots; a moleskin waistcoat; and several neckcloths of various colour and pattern, all tied round his neck together; whilst the red coat itself was much stained with sea-water, and sported strange little attachments of leather and watch-chain and string, whose purpose was known only to the Soldier himself. His age was equally a matter for conjecture, for much of his face was hidden by a profusion of thick hair and whisker that might have been grey, or blond, or any combination of the two bleached by exposure to sun and salt air; but John always felt that he was rather young than old, and he suspected, too, from something in the Soldier's accents, that he was a man of some education. He lived in an isolated hut along the clifftop, and he kept bees, and beachcombed, and dug lugworms to sell for bait, as he was doing when John and Philip approached him. If somewhat eccentric, he was not really a hermit or a hater of mankind – in his way, he was always glad enough to see you – but everything about him proclaimed one stark and simple choice, made for whatever reason: he liked to live alone.

Of course, even the least inquisitive person must have felt a curiosity to know his history. But even if someone had been sufficiently insensitive to start questioning him, they would not have got much out of the Soldier. He scarcely ever addressed a person directly. Instead he diverted all his conversation through his sole and constant companions – several tame mice which ran about his clothing, and could be continually seen peeping out of his sleeves, or over the tops of his boots. And it was through the mice that he relayed his greeting to John and Philip, remarking as they came up, 'Here's a couple of friends, see, mice: Mr Philip Revell, and Mr John Twopenny; and very nice to see them it is, and I'm sure you'll join me in wishing 'em good morning.'

'Morning, Soldier,' Philip said. 'How's the bait business?'

'We were just saying, weren't we, mice,' said the Soldier, continuing with his digging, 'as how that's a tidy order we've got, for five hundred lugworms, over Sheringham way. And how we ought to have got on with digging for 'em earlier, only we got held up by something we found, washed up at the high-tide mark.'

'Something interesting?' said John, who was an amateur beachcomber himself, and had spent much of his boyhood eagerly convinced that he was going to find a bottle containing an eloquent parchment message from, if not Robinson Crusoe, then at least someone in the castaway line.

'I don't know whether interesting's the word we'd use, do you, mice?' said the Soldier, with a shake of his shaggy head. 'It might have been interesting once upon a time, when it stood on its legs, and walked and talked, and sang – yes, for all we

15

know, mice, it might have sung comic songs, and made itself specially agreeable at musical evenings and such . . . But we don't know,' he said doggedly, as if the mouse currently poking its nose out of his waistcoat-pocket had raised some objection. 'That's what I'm saying – it *might* have, for all you or I know about it. There was no way of telling. No way of telling much, except that it was a man. Or *had* been a man, then,' he added, as if the mouse had challenged him again, 'when it was alive.'

'Ah,' said John.

'Had the – had it been in the sea long, do you suppose, Soldier?' said Philip.

'There, mice,' said the Soldier, 'he's asking the very question we asked ourselves, ain't he? And we came to the conclusion that it had very likely been in the sea for quite a time. Why,' he added, as if the mouse had objected again, 'on account of its not being in the freshest of conditions, of course. Don't tell me *you* cared for the smell of it. Or for the little sea-creatures making themselves at home in it, and going in and out of places that were never meant to be doors.'

'It's not . . .' Philip licked his lips, and gave the impression of not wanting to look over his shoulder. 'It's not anywhere hereabouts, I suppose?'

'Now, it's funny, mice,' said the Soldier, leaning on his spade a moment and wiping his brow, but still not bestowing a glance on the two young men, 'we were just saying as how our friends here, being local-born, would understand why we had to throw that object back into the sea, like it was a sprat not worth the catching, and let it be carried along Shipden way by the tide.'

John and Philip both nodded, solemnly: they understood. This whole stretch of coast yielded drowned sailors not infrequently; and once recovered, the bodies had to be buried at the expense of the parish, which was no light matter for a small place of slender means like Saltmarsh. Accordingly, it was seen as no disrespect to the dead, but rather a respect to the living, to return any such tragic beachwrack to the waves, and send it along to the harbour at Shipden, a fishing-town ten miles to the east, which had a bigger churchyard and more ratepayers.

'It may be,' pursued the Soldier, peering into his bucket of lugworms and seeming to make a mental calculation of their number, 'that it's on account of that thing we threw back into the sea – very well, mice, that dead body, if you will insist – that there's been such strange noises coming from the Hanged Man's House of a night just lately. Noises like a crying, or a screaming, or a something unpleasant and not-quite-right, that can't be accounted for. Leastways, without falling back on the belief of the people hereabouts, that those noises coming from the Hanged Man's House mean one thing, and that thing is Death. Now that may be, or that may not be; it's not for you or I, mice, to pretend we know for certain, because we don't. But if it *does* mean Death, then I'm sure we all hope that that unpleasant object that we threw back into the sea, was what the noises were referring to, and not anybody who's currently walking upright.'

'Yes, let's hope so, indeed,' murmured John; and though the glance he exchanged with Philip was not quite easy – especially as they had just been in the Hanged Man's House themselves – there was also scepticism in it, for the eccentricities of the Soldier were well known, and unkinder people might have said that his wits had turned.

'Well, well,' said the Soldier, spitting on his hands and turning to with the spade again, 'what with one thing and another, mice, we're forgetting our manners, and we haven't asked our friends how they do, and where they're off to this fine morning, and is it somewhere nice, or perhaps somewhere nasty?'

'I suppose that remains to be seen,' said John. 'We're on our way to Hales-next-the-sea, to see – well, to see a mermaid.'

'In a glass bottle,' added Philip.

'To see a mermaid in a glass bottle, eh?' said the Soldier, lifting his head and

16

meeting their eyes for the first time, very briefly; smiling, too, underneath the whiskers, and giving John a sudden haunting impression that he had once been handsome. 'Now that's a thing, mice, that I wouldn't mind seeing myself, and I'm sure you wouldn't either. A mermaid in a glass bottle!' he repeated, chuckling, and seeming to relish the phrase very much.

'Why not come with us, Soldier?' said John. 'I dare say it may be a monstrous fraud, but—'

'But then again, mice, it may not be, as I'm sure you'll agree. Very often things aren't what you expect them to be. Very often what you think's poor and false turns out nót to be; and very often – more often, maybe – what you think's right and true turns out not to be. Why? I couldn't say, mice. Maybe it's on account of something not being quite right in this odd world of ours, right from the start – a flaw in the glaze, as you might say. But never mind. The point is, mice, we're invited to go along and see the mermaid in a glass bottle – and the pity is, we can't, on account of we've all this bait to dig, and we're already behind-hand.'

'We could help you dig . . .' began John, but the Soldier was already vigorously shaking his head; and John recalled that never, under any circumstances, would the Soldier accept any help, or put himself under an obligation to anyone.

'Kind, mice,' the Soldier said, 'kind, but can't be. Never mind. We wish our friends joy of it, anyhow. Mermaids, and bodies, and noises in the night; this is an odd world of ours, ain't it, mice?'

The Soldier fell abruptly silent, and applied himself to his digging; and John and Philip, recognizing this as a signal that he had had enough of company for now, bade him goodbye. But they could hear him behind them for some time, repeating with a chuckle of enjoyment, 'A mermaid in a glass bottle! A mermaid in a glass bottle, mice!'

They had gone on some way in silence, when Philip at last mildly remarked, 'It's a funny thing, you know, about the Other Side. It never has anything cheerful to say. Whether it's ghostly noises, or lights, or phantom horsemen, or nuns, or ladies in white satin, it always means Death – or so people take it. I wonder if we're getting hold of the wrong end of the stick altogether, and what it really means when a chap strolls by with his head under his arm, is that your rich aunt's going to send you a present, or we're in for a spell of dry weather, or Maccabaeus is going to win the Derby. What do you think?'

John was glad of the opportunity to laugh, and rid himself of a peculiar feeling of oppression at his breast; and in a moment he was himself again, and soon swapping scandalous anecdotes with Philip. But privately he resolved that when he walked home later, he would take the lower path, and give the Hanged Man's House a wide berth.

With the sun moving round behind the coastal hills on their left, John and Philip followed the marsh tracks until they came at last to Hales-next-the-sea, where Philip's late father had been Vicar, and where his mother still lived. 'I'd say let's call in at my house and refresh ourselves before we go mermaiding,' Philip said as they entered the town, 'but Mother's not in the brightest frame of mind, and – well, you know how it is.' John nodded sympathetically, and no more needed to be said, for Mrs Revell was a severe woman, with a sort of acid grudge against the world in general, and a face which, John secretly thought, was sufficient incentive in itself to send a man to India.

Hales-next-the-sea was not large in extent; but a good deal of town had been concentrated in its small compass, like a well-packed trunk. There was something purposeful and businesslike about its tight maze of streets and yards and lanes, in which the narrowest needle's-eye of an alley led directly somewhere, and a blind wall or a dead-end would have seemed an affront to dignity and sense. Other towns might straggle and meander – that was up to them; Hales-next-the-sea was having

17

none of it. It was a thriving port on its own stubborn terms too. What if the open sea was two miles away from the waterfront, and the cargo ships had to get to the quay by sailing up a narrow channel through the marshes? If other ports had the sea lapping at their doorsteps, that was their affair; Hales-next-the-sea carried on its thriving trade in corn, malt, coal, fish, and other hard-headed articles quite well without it.

Amongst those who were engaged in this trade was Dr Twopenny's elder brother – John's uncle Saul. But paying a social call on his uncle while he was here was not something that occurred to John even as a possibility. The two families were not on the best of terms, Dr Twopenny and his brother being polar opposites in temperament; and besides, no one really paid social calls on Saul Twopenny, who was a fierce, pious and unclubbable old martinet. He was, however, one of the town's wealthiest men, and he had put his mark on it. His was the giant granary on the quayside, with a gantry like a masterful arm projecting over the road, so that everyone in the town had to pass through its shadow; his too were the biggest of the flint-built maltings and warehouses, directly overlooking the waterfront, with his own jail-like dwelling-house attached; and repeated in large whitewashed letters over the whole series of buildings were the words S. TWOPENNY & SON, the invariable effect of which on John was to make him feel curiously abashed.

'Your uncle, I suppose, is as gracious as ever?' Philip said as they passed under the gantry.

'I imagine so. You probably see as much of him here as we do. I think he wrote Father a letter on his birthday, exhorting him to lead a Christian life before it was too late, and adding that the cholera epidemic was God's just punishment for allowing the Catholic hierarchy in England. That was quite a temperate little note by Uncle Saul's standards.'

'They say your cousin William don't please him, and there are some proper knock-down rows after business hours.'

'That doesn't surprise me,' John said. 'William could never do anything right as far as Uncle Saul was concerned. Poor William – I wouldn't change places with him for all the tea in China, or all the money in Uncle Saul's vaults, for that matter . . . Well! It looks as if the mermaid has quite a few callers.'

There was a sizeable crowd on the quayside, gathered about a large canvas booth with a rickety dais before it, on which hung a sign inscribed in flamboyant characters thus: 'IMPRISONED within a VESSEL OF CRYSTAL, and laid entirely open to the Eyes of the COGNOSCENTI and the CONNOISSEURS of the Curious, the Marvellous, and the Educational; a genuine MERMAID!!! seized from her Aquatic Domain by a crew of intrepid BRITONS, off the Peninsula of KAMCHATKA, and here exhibited for your ENTERTAINMENT and INSTRUCTION; with diverse other WONDERS of the DEEP.'

'Vessel of crystal?' said John in Philip's ear.

'Well, I'll bet it *is* a glass bottle.'

They joined the crowd, and waited before the unopened booth for some time, until suspense became impatience; when all at once a man threw open the canvas flaps and mounted on to the dais, followed by a very fat woman with a muslin cap tied under her chin – their mutual indifference proclaiming them as husband and wife. The showman, having enjoined silence with a sweeping gesture of his arms, then held them aloft in a dramatic pause – a pause which gave John time to observe that the mermaid was not keeping very good company. The fat woman, with her fishy stare and blubbery constitution, might have been a Wonder of the Deep herself; whilst the showman's face was so inflamed as to resemble a vast raspberry, and taken together with his palsied hands, bloodshot eye, and grubby linen, suggested that he pretty much lived in a bottle himself.

'Ladies – gentlemen,' the showman croaked out at last, after waving his arms

18

about some more. 'It is not my habit, as if often the case with the less reputable members of my profession, to weary my patrons with excessive preamble. The prodigies herein presented, are such as require no words to adumbrate their sublimity, even if . . . even if . . .' The showman here tailing off into a glazed silence, he was given a hard poke in the ribs by his wife with a copper-stick apparently carried for that purpose. 'Even if words existed capable of doing justice to them. I will merely remark, that the exhibit you are about to see was admired by the Austrian emperor, and that . . . and that . . .' Falling silent again, he was given another poke in the ribs, just as if he were an item of rusty clockwork, who needed a jolt to be set going. 'And that testimonials to its authenticity, signed by the most eminent professors of Natural History, are deposited in a safe place, and may be inspected on application.'

The showman waved his arms, and seemed about to start his speech all over again; but he was promptly taken in hand by the fat woman, who plucked him down from the dais and propelled him on his rusty legs in the direction of the dingy caravan that was drawn up nearby, where he was shortly to be seen, through the decayed shutters, oiling himself very liberally.

His wife meanwhile stationed herself at the entrance to the booth and sold the tickets. John and Philip, as latecomers, had to wait around at the back of the queue. A few waterside urchins had gathered to see what was afoot; and John's attention was caught by two of them who had gone into a furtive huddle in the midst of the crowd, close to the skirts of a young lady whose back was turned. He had just started forward to see what the mischief was, when a small dog burst out from between the two boys, yelping piteously, and pelted off across the quayside. They had tied an old tin mug to its tail, and the faster the dog ran, the more the tin mug clanged and clattered on the stone flags of the quay; and the poor creature's fear and confusion were compounded by the boys, who chased after it with whoops of delight.

Cruelty to animals had always been John's special aversion; and where his feelings were engaged, he was the hastiest of young men. He was conscious only of a rush of blood to his cheeks, and then he was sprinting after the two boys. Catching a grimy collar in each hand, he hoisted the boys up off the ground and held them there like two wriggling eels; then, spotting a stone horse-trough by the moorings, he carried them over to it, and plunged them both into the icy water – one accepting this with stoicism, but the other crying, 'He's murderen me! Help! I'm a good boy! I goo to Sunday-school!' as he went under.

The dog meanwhile had with canine obtuseness taken refuge underneath the horse-trough, and thus got a soaking to add to its miseries; and it was whimpering dismally when John, with Philip's help, took it up in his arms and tried to soothe it.

'Gelert! Gelert, what did they do to you?'

It was the owner of the dog; a young lady in a sea-green walking-dress, who came running up in a state of great agitation. The dog – a spaniel – gave a squirm of eagerness, and would have leapt into the young lady's arms if John had not tightened his grip.

'He's safe, miss, but very wet, I'm afraid,' said John, mindful of the sea-green costume, 'and rather muddy.'

'Oh, that doesn't matter!' cried the young lady, gathering her pet into her arms, and immediately getting paw-prints all over her. 'As long as he's all right – Verity! Look, here he is, safe and sound!'

'And with rather more to him than there was before,' said a second young lady behind her, indicating the tin mug which still dangled from the dog's tail.

'I'll untie it, if you'll hold him, miss,' John said; and swiftly did so, rather tinglingly conscious of the proximity of the sea-green dress, and of the regard of the

19

most brilliantly blue pair of eyes he had ever seen in his life.

'There, Gelert,' said his mistress, 'it's all better. Aren't you going to thank the gentleman? No? Well, I will – you're very kind, sir.'

'Not at all,' said John, reaching out to pat the dog's head, finding the young lady's hand in the way, and scratching his own head instead. 'I – I'm sure he's come to no hurt.'

'Oh, but he might have – and I don't know what I'd have done,' said the young lady, whose eyes seemed if anything to become bluer by the moment. 'You know, people were actually laughing, and no one offered to help. Thank goodness everyone isn't so cruel!'

'Oh . . . well . . .' Lest John should enjoy his hero's moment too much, fate at that moment assumed the form of one of the urchins he had dunked in the horse-trough, who, climbing out, pitched such a well-aimed stone that it sent John's hat fairly flying, and then took to his heels with a few parting reflections on John's parentage.

'Why, the little brute!' said the young lady in sea-green, quite concerned; but her companion, a dark, slight young woman with slanting eyebrows, seemed rather inclined to laugh as the hat rolled at her feet, and handing it to John remarked: 'Dear me, this never happened to St George, did it?'

Usually John would have laughed at himself too, very heartily; but something about the blue eyes that were luminously regarding him over the top of the spaniel's head turned him quite inside out, and he supposed he would simply have gone on colouring up to the roots of his hair and gaping like a stranded fish, if Philip had not chipped in with, 'Ah, well, no harm done. You're here to see the mermaid, I take it?'

'Yes – just as soon as my brother arrives. It was his idea, you know, and now he's late. Where can he have got to?' said the young lady in sea-green to her companion.

'Lost, perhaps,' said the dark young lady.

'Oh, surely even Augustus couldn't get himself lost in Hales,' said the other, though with something less than perfect conviction; but at that moment a young man hallooed at them from the other side of the quay, and hurried over. He hobbled and limped so painfully that John was quite stricken with pity, until a nearer view revealed that there was nothing wrong with him except a pathological devotion to fashion, which had squeezed him into such an unthinkably tight pair of checked trousers, and such a Lilliputian pair of pointed boots, that he would scarcely have suffered more if he had been fitted with a ball and chain.

'I say, where have you been? I've been looking everywhere,' said the young man. 'We said we'd meet on the quay, you know.'

'This is the quay, dear,' said his sister.

'It damn well is, as well,' said the young man, looking round with an air of fascinated discovery. He had a pleasant pink face, made only a little less pleasant by his habit of leaving his jaw open when he had finished speaking; and his fashionable outfit was completed by a pilot-coat, so roomily cut that he could practically turn himself round inside it, like a man in a barrel. This he proceeded to do, presenting a blissfully unmeaning smile to John and Philip in turn, and then crying, 'Good heavens, Kitty, what a mess Gelert's made of your frock!'

'Some boys were teasing him, Augustus – and they tied things to his tail, and chased him and frightened him ever so!'

Augustus, about to break into a laugh, saw from his sister's face that that would not do, and looked grave instead.

'And these gentlemen very kindly helped rescue him,' his sister concluded. '*These* gentlemen,' she added, as Augustus showed strong signs of having forgotten that anyone was there.

'Oh!' Augustus said with a start, turning about again, and nudging his coat round after him. 'Capital – capital. Splendid business. I had a dog once,' he remarked vaguely to John. 'Got him as a pup, from old Southwood – you know. Not his brother, the other one. Queer old cove. Had half a finger missing. Gave me a whipping for stealing greengages. No?' Seeming mildly surprised that John did not share these entirely personal memories, Augustus sucked the ivory head of his cane for a moment, as a refresher to his intellect; murmured, 'Used to bite my knees,' presumably in reference to the dog rather than the breeder, and then brightening cried: 'Well, girls, well! Now that you've finished keeping me waiting, let's go and see this mermaid creature.' And linking arms with both young women, he bore them off at speed towards the booth; his sister just managing to crane her head over her sea-green shoulder and mouth the words, *Thank you! Goodbye!*

'Extraordinary,' said Philip when they had gone.

'My thoughts exactly,' John breathed.

'He's a Cambridge man,' Philip said. 'Gown, I mean, not town. I know that for a fact. A Cambridge man. Makes you think, doesn't it?'

'You know those people, then?' John said, with a tremendous effort at casualness.

'Only by sight, but they're pretty well known in Hales. *He* is Augustus Fernhill, and the lady with the dog, whom you were making such sheep's eyes at, is Miss Catherine Fernhill. The name of the dark lady with her I don't recollect, but she's some sort of companion or poor relation or such.'

'Catherine Fernhill . . . Here, what do you mean, sheep's eyes? I never even – I scarcely even—'

'Their father is a retired Admiral,' went on Philip, quite unperturbed. 'They live at Buttings Court, just inland from the town – have lived there for about a year, at any rate. The house belonged to a reclusive relative of the Admiral's who was a long time a-dying, and the old salt had to wait a good while to come into it; but now he has, he's making quite a palace of it, so I hear, and kicking up his heels.'

'Admiral Fernhill,' mused John. 'No, I've never heard of him.'

'Well, apparently he had quite a famous name in the Service, on account of never having been anywhere near a sea-fight in his life . . .' Philip beamed through his spectacles. 'His daughter's very charming, though, isn't she?'

'Yes – yes, I dare say she is,' said John gruffly.

Again, if he could have heard that tone in his voice, John would have laughed at himself – under normal circumstances. But normal circumstances had ceased to prevail. He didn't know what it was that he felt, except that it bore no resemblance to the feeling of being conventionally smitten. There lurked somewhere, indeed, amongst the complex shadows of his emotion, something that could only be described as sadness – a troubled, haunted sadness, that made him want to run away and do something of which he had no clear idea except that it would be significant. All this was so very different from John's normal state of feeling that he was quite disoriented, and would not have been wholly surprised to find that the sea and sky had changed places, or that the celebrated mermaid was all she was claimed to be.

The mermaid, alas, was not. John and Philip bought their entrance tickets at last; and while John's interest had waned somewhat, and he was more preoccupied with peering over the heads of the crowd that filled the booth in hopes of seeing a sea-green costume, the mermaid was by any standards a disappointment. She was rather a small mermaid, to begin with, and the glass bottle in which she reposed seemed to have once borne a label, and gave off an odour which brought pickles to mind; but that might have been forgiven if the mermaid had had long hair, or a figure – in short, if she had not been quite so obviously constructed out of half a stuffed monkey and a cod's tail, to such generally ghastly effect.

21

No one, however, complained, except one testy old gentleman, who made quite a fuss about being defrauded; but the fat woman merely informed him, with a certain harsh justice, that if he expected to see a real mermaid on Hales quay for sixpence, then he was an even bigger fool than he looked.

The old gentleman, however, would not be satisfied until he had repeated all his complaints at length – buttonholing John and Philip for this purpose, as they happened to be standing close by; and as a consequence they were almost the last to leave the booth, and the Fernhill party had long gone on their way by then. Philip confessing to a damnable thirst, they repaired to a tavern for ale and beefsteak, where John drew pictures on the wet table-top with his forefinger, alternated bursts of merriment with profound silences, kept glancing over his shoulder as if to see something or someone that was never there, and was generally, as he admitted, not very good company.

Walking home alone, he found he was not very good company for himself either. The strange mixed mood that had come upon him had resolved itself now, and what was left at the bottom of the crucible was dissatisfaction – dissatisfaction with himself. In fact, John had no more nor less cause to be dissatisfied with himself than anyone else. Along with his father's height he had inherited his mother's fairness of colouring which, added to a freshness and mobility of expression, a good-humoured mouth, and grey eyes that crinkled readily in amusement, made him a pleasant person to look upon; and if bodily he was still somewhat on the high-strung and gangling side, he was as lithe and agile as a cat. He possessed abundant energy; he was a thoroughly sociable young animal who would dance till the candles burnt themselves out; and he had seldom done anything mean or petty. As for his weaknesses and defects of temperament, they were more potential than actual, insofar as they had not yet been tried by circumstances; and such hastiness and rashness as he had shown, for example, and such tendency to think in extremes, and believe in a thing because he wished to believe in it, had not been productive of any dire consequences, any more than the cracks in the timbers of a ship that has never had to weather a gale.

He was, in sum, an attractive young man of spirit and promise – but you would have had your work cut out to have convinced him of it that afternoon. He was despondent about himself on account of the beautiful young lady in the sea-green costume, though what logical process lay behind this state of mind he could not have said.

'I am the laziest fellow at Latin there ever was,' he reproached himself as he passed by the pine-woods and dunes below the town of Hales.

'I go into the most foolish, crack-jawed laugh at the feeblest things – I know, because I've caught myself doing it,' he said to himself, as he scrambled over the fossilized limbs of ancient trees that poked up through the sand at low tide.

'As for my feet, they are an abomination – surely the biggest, clumsiest feet that ever disgraced the legs of man,' he told himself, as he came in sight of Saltmarsh with the sun sinking at his back, and his shadow racing a dozen yards ahead of him.

'I am a wretch,' he concluded, as he ascended the sandy path to his father's house; and the most curious thing of all was, that he found himself quite as cheerful as he had ever been in his life, even as he spoke these despairing words.

He found his parents in good spirits too. They had had a visitor: Mr Goodway himself had called, bearing an invitation to an evening party at Beacon House on Christmas Day.

'Friendly of him to come himself,' Dr Twopenny said. 'Most men with his means would have sent a servant over. Well, well, I fancy he'll liven the district up, you know. It'll make a pleasant change, not having to do all the entertaining ourselves hereabouts. Not that *I* mind, but my banker's none too keen.' For Dr Twopenny, besides keeping a very good table, regularly invited half the county to

22

it. 'Seems there'll be a deal of company there, anyhow – anybody who is anybody, and me as well,' he went on, rubbing his hands and laughing. 'Doing the thing in style – man after my own heart. You know, I reckon we ought to throw a new year's party in return – what d'you say, my dear?'

'I'd say yes, with pleasure,' smiled John's mother, 'but then I'm not your banker.'

'Oh, pooh – I'll butter him up. He's been extending me credit for so long, I think it would quite shatter his mind if I suddenly turned solvent. Well, John, my boy, how did you like her?'

'Who?' said John with a start.

'Why, your mermaid, of course. I must say, you look as if she knocked you back a bit.'

'Oh! The mermaid,' said John, and gave an account of the raree-show which made the Doctor laugh uproariously. John's thoughts, however, were elsewhere. He was thinking of the party at Mr Goodway's, and his father's words – 'a great deal of company' and 'anybody who is anybody' – kept revolving themselves round and about in his head, until they were skipping along in waltz time. *I wonder*, thought John, *I wonder*, and soon those words were waltzing too, and kept up the dance steadily until he went to bed; and they were still waltzing on the evening of Christmas Day, when they began to whirl faster and more giddily with each turn of the gig-wheels that bore the Twopenny family towards Beacon House.

CHAPTER THREE

Good Tidings

It was a bitter night, but still, and a few patches of frost – rare on this salt coast – sparkled on the road, like stars jostled out of the overcrowded sky. The prevailing cold blue tones of the landscape made the gig-lamps appear in comparison as red as blown coals, with an effect prettily appropriate to the season. John's mother softly hummed a carol as they went along. She was wearing a gown of azure watered-silk beneath her wrap, with her bright hair in a simple chignon, and in her mature and quiet beauty looked quite the equal of any deep starry night that ever was. The doctor, too, as always when going out, had dressed with care, and with his white hair neatly combed and his big face full of genial animation, looked the one man any party – but especially a Christmas party – could not do without.

As for John, though his dressing had – most unusually for him – taken him an age, he was repeatedly seized by an apprehension that it was incomplete in some way, and was once or twice even visited by a dreamlike conviction that he was not wearing any trousers. But even when he had finally convinced himself that he was wearing everything he ought to be, the dreamlike feeling persisted, along with that waltzing speculation, *I wonder . . . I wonder . . .*

Dreamlike, too, was the sight of Beacon House, as his father turned the gig into the drive. Perhaps it was because he was used to seeing it empty and shuttered, and now here it was one mass of lights. And yet he realized what really surprised him was that it was the home of Mr Goodway, and it did not seem to accord with his image of that bluffly urbane gentleman at all. Beacon House had been built sixty-odd years ago for a retired Norwich merchant, on a sheltered clifftop site, in the Gothic style then coming into fashion; and the lights now burning within accentuated the shadowy massiveness of the buttresses, and sharpened the angles of the gables, and made of the pointed window-frames something resembling fiery mouths filled with sharp teeth. And though the house was of modest dimensions, it looked very large, perhaps because Mr Goodway had had many of the trees that surrounded it chopped down, so that it rose out of the Norfolk heathland more like a castle than the glorified villa it really was. The general impression was one of power; and it revived in John, with regard to Mr Goodway, that peculiar uneasy shyness that had suddenly afflicted him on the marshes.

But this was swiftly succeeded, as the gig drew up in the drive, by all that waltzing, whirling, tingling, exhilarating anticipation that had tormented him for the last two days, and which now tuned itself up to such a pitch that when he stepped down from the gig his feet touched the ground with the woolly indistinctness that characterizes a dream; and the open front door rushed at him with a dream's swiftness, and swallowed him up into a dreamlike hubbub; and everything began to present itself to his consciousness with a dream's fragmented immediacy.

Here is a cold tiled hall, and a maid taking his hat and muffler from him with as much snatching sharpness as if he had stolen them and were guiltily bringing them back. Here is a big reception-room, which is so much warmer than the hall, that to

24

cross the threshold from one to the other is to feel your cheeks turn painful scarlet in an instant, and be conscious of presenting a rather startled face to the company. Here is a great gathering of people, like a human hothouse; the ladies in their vast, gaily-coloured skirts appearing as the species in full flower, and the gentlemen in their narrow black tailcoats the wintry stalks. Here is Mr Goodway himself, coming forward to greet them with his frank smile of welcome, and his observant eye, and his handshake that John finds a little perplexing – seeming, in its heartiness, as if it commits him to some bargain that he knows nothing about.

'Welcome, welcome, and a merry Christmas,' says Mr Goodway, who is very well turned out, with his white shirt-front making the most of his broad chest. 'Quite a crush, I'm afraid – but then nothing can be worse than a half-empty room, and everyone staring at each other across an acre of carpet . . . There, I've begun by apologizing. I shall stop at once, and merely say how very welcome you are, Dr Twopenny; and Mrs Twopenny, I'm honoured; and my friend Mr John Twopenny, who will excuse the familiarity, as we met so informally I don't think we could ever be ceremonious with each other if our lives depended on it.' Much comradely twinkling on the part of Mr Goodway, much inexplicable awkwardness on the part of John. 'So: let me introduce you all to Mrs Goodway, who has been greatly looking forward to meeting you.'

They are guided to a settle by the fire – John in the meantime glancing quickly over the company, and looking out for the young lady in the sea-green costume. She is not here. The waltz abruptly stops spinning, and John tastes dust and ashes while pretending to himself that he isn't really that disappointed, and goes forward to meet his hostess trying hard not to look as moony as he feels inside.

'Grace, my dear, here are what I must call our neighbours, but hope soon to call our friends,' says Mr Goodway, introducing them to a lady who, though beautifully dressed, and indeed beautiful, is quite plainly ill, or has been ill recently. She is delicately made, and there are smoke-coloured shadows under her eyes.

'Marcus has told me a good deal about you,' Mrs Goodway says, in a voice surprisingly deep and low; and her eyes light very intently on John as she adds with the faintest of smiles, 'And I believe it is you I have to thank for my husband's being here at all, instead of at the bottom of the marsh.'

'Oh, not at all,' says John – or says something of that kind, at any rate; for he is suddenly distracted by the sight of an auburn head turning, over at the other end of the room. Fool, fool! To be looking for a sea-green walking-dress at an evening party! To suppose that the young woman whose image he has carried in his mind would never wear anything but a sea-green walking-dress, and to suppose that because the sea-green walking-dress is not here, then *she* is not here! For she *is* here, after all!

Thus lifted from depression to buoyancy in an instant, John cheerfully repeats, 'Oh, not at all,' and thinks Mrs Goodway a charming woman, and Mr Goodway a fine fellow.

'Speaking as a neighbour, not a doctor, ma'am – for all doctors, as you know, are humbugs,' says Dr Twopenny, 'how do you find yourself? Is the Saltmarsh air beneficial?'

'I feel stronger by the day,' says Mrs Goodway, 'though I wish I were strong enough to go out and return my neighbours' courtesy, instead of obliging them to come to me. I hope to do so, soon.'

'Indisposition is a terrible thing, isn't it!' cries the lady who is keeping her company on the settle, and who suffers from a chronic though benign form of it. This is young Mrs Bream, the Nonconformist minister's wife, who is so often in what polite society calls 'an interesting condition' that it has ceased to be interesting at all, and she is merely assumed to be pregnant unless she specifically states otherwise. 'It puts one under such obligations, and makes one feel quite a nuisance all in all. But then, as Mr Bream says, if we were never ill, we would never appreciate what it's like to be well, so it's a dispensation, really.' Thus young Mrs Bream, a smiling, doll-like piece of vacancy who seems to exist only to echo her husband's opinions, and to add perpetually to the shoal of little Bream.

'My dear, would you like the screen?' says Mr Goodway, indicating a painted fire-screen in the chimney-corner. 'There's quite a blaze now.'

'I would, thank you, Marcus,' says Mrs Goodway. It is unusual, and touching, to hear a married couple address each other by their Christian names in company, in that intimate way: touching, too, is Mr Goodway's tender concern for his wife, and the little caress he gives her hand as he moves the fire-screen close to her. Not forgetting his duties as host, he adds, 'And are you quite comfortable, Mrs Bream?'

'Oh, very comfortable, thank you! Ever since my first, you know, I've always been prodigiously healthy, right up to my time,' says Mrs Bream. 'I'm quite blessed in my constitution – but then, as Mr Bream says, we are all showered with so many blessings, we could hardly begin to count them all.' And Mrs Bream gives a smile of surpassing stupidity, and returns to the contemplation of her teeming womb.

More new arrivals surrender their garments to the righteous maid, and make the disconcerting transition from icy hall to hot room, and John and his parents are detached from their host and hostess, and take a plunge into the body of the guests. They are a lively set, perhaps because of the season, perhaps because of the punch and negus which are already circulating; and the guests as a whole evince that readiness to enjoy themselves that comes from a consciousness that all this must have cost a pretty penny, and is not costing them anything.

John is simultaneously aware of all this, and aware of nothing but the fact that the young lady named Catherine Fernhill is here; and is altogether in such a light-headed state that he fairly jumps when a hand touches his arm, and his name is spoken.

Philip Revell: looking more than ever, in his evening clothes, like a shrewd, kindly mole, but with a slight shadow thrown across him by the presence of the lady on his arm – his mother, who looks more acid than ever. Mr Revell died ten years since, but his widow still dresses in full mourning – not so much to commemorate the dead, as to make the living feel miserable.

'Well, my dear fellow, and how do you do? Not much of a showing, is it? – hardly anyone worth meeting,' says Philip. 'Hold on, though – there is someone. You'll never guess – those same people we met on the quay at Hales. Now isn't that remarkable? I waded in and made myself known – you know what I'm like – because we never were properly introduced that day, you know. And they were most anxious to be introduced properly to you, or one of them was, in particular. Anyhow, shall I take you over there now? Great bore, I know, but still.' And so John goes with him – telling himself, not for the first time, that Philip is the best friend anyone ever had, in the intervals of dreadful hallucinations that his feet are getting bigger by the moment.

And then, before he knows it, he is in amongst the Fernhill family, and the girl who wore the sea-green costume, and who is looking even more dismayingly beautiful in a lavender ball gown with a lace bertha, is recounting his rescue of her dog in such glowing terms that the waterfront urchins might have been fire-breathing dragons with two heads apiece. Even the readiness of youth to think well of itself is abashed by this exaggeration, and John is about to make some modest disclaimer when it is abruptly done for him – the dark slight young lady who was also present at the memorable occasion remarking in a cool voice: 'Yes, the villains were thoroughly vanquished; and one can only hope that their clothes weren't quite ruined by the soaking, for I suspect they were the only ones they owned.'

26

Giving John a look as cool as her voice, from under her slanting eyebrows.

John uncomfortably reviews the incident in this light, and is somewhat at a loss for words, when he is forestalled by a chuckle from Augustus. For he is here – or, at least, a suit of fearsomely fashionable evening clothes is here, which is so very crisp and starched and stiff that it might easily stand there on its own, the divine Augustus peeping his pink face over the collar being no more than a dispensable detail. 'Damn me,' says Augustus, with another chuckle, 'I must say it sounds jolly amusing – I wish I'd been there to see it.'

'You were there, Augustus,' says his sister patiently. 'Don't you remember? The day we went to see the mermaid.'

Augustus wrinkles his forehead, what there is of it, and then, snapping his fingers, cries, 'Good Lord, so I was. I remember now. Made me laugh uncommonly. And so help me, *you* were there, too – I'd stake my life on it,' he says, shaking John by the hand for the second time in five minutes. And John exchanges a glance with Miss Fernhill – Catherine, as he must learn to think of her – in which there is confusion, amusement, embarrassment, and on her part at least a renewed conviction that the rescue was as heroic as she has made it out to be.

However, Catherine Fernhill was not born out of the sea, like Venus, but is part of a family of Fernhills; and it is with them as a body that John must converse – in particular her father, the admiral, who monopolises the attention of anyone who joins the circle. Preoccupied though he is with Catherine, John has ample opportunity to observe Admiral Fernhill, especially as the old gentleman greatly likes the sound of his own voice, and is seated right in the centre of the group. The admiral is not a very large man, or a very handsome one; but he has a tremendously shining nut-brown bald head, just fringed with grey tufts, which gives him an appearance – as an unknown, ageless lady on the edge of the group admiringly remarks – so thoroughly naval. Certainly Admiral Fernhill seems to think so too, and makes great play with this naval head of his, and generally flourishes it as if it were a wooden leg or a set of medals. But he seems amiable enough, if a little inclined to turn red to his bald crown if he finds himself contradicted. A little inclined, too, to take umbrage if anyone mentions the existence of poor people in the tight little island, and to assert that He For One Glories In The Name Of Briton, with as much querulous indignation as if someone has said he doesn't. John, of course, is a little prejudiced in his favour, as he can hardly suppose that the father of Catherine is a complete fool; but he cannot help reflecting that if Admiral Fernhill were a woman, she might well be dismissed as a vain, talkative, petulant idiot.

As for Mrs Fernhill, she is all that a man like the admiral could wish in a wife – an admiring listener, with the faded remains of a pretty face carefully wrapped up in lace and artificial flowers, and her head perpetually on one side like a stuffed bird. They are so complementary a couple, indeed, that whereas the admiral is complacently convinced that he knows everything, Mrs Fernhill is quite as satisfied that she doesn't know anything; insofar as the most untaxing interrogative, such as Catherine's asking her where Augustus has gone to, elicits the response, 'I really don't know, my dear – I don't know anything about it, I'm sure!'

But here is the admiral coming out of his monologue and, semaphoring condescension to John with his shining head, remarking that he believes Mr Twopenny's father is a medical man? John answers yes, and adds with a certain pride that he hopes to become a physician himself.

'Indeed, indeed, a physician yourself, eh? Then perhaps you can tell me something – something I've often wondered,' says the admiral, with such a waggish parade of building up to a joke that the unknown ageless lady spontaneously declares he is a Pet, and Mrs Fernhill inclines her head to such an adoring angle that she looks as if she has hanged herself with her headdress. 'Now what I want to know is this – what, precisely, did Alexander the Great die of?'

John, surprised, confesses that he does not know.

'Aha!' cries the admiral, looking even more pleased with himself, if that is possible. 'Well, then, let me ask you this. What did Shakespeare die of? The poet, you know,' he adds helpfully.

Again John confesses his ignorance.

'Well, well! Let's try this, then. Columbus, now. Come, I have hopes of you yet. What did *he* die of?'

'I'm afraid I haven't the remotest idea,' says John.

'Neither have I!' cries the admiral. 'But whatever it was, the doctors couldn't cure it! Eh? The doctors couldn't cure it!' And he leads the laughter at his joke, repeating it for the benefit of anyone within earshot. However, the admiral adds that he means no harm, and as a token of reconciliation indicates that his punch-glass is empty, and grants John the privilege of fetching him some more.

Visiting the punch-bowl, John observes that his parents are in conversation with Mr Goodway, and seem to be getting on famously; and for some reason a cloud of doubt crosses his mind, and he wonders whether he is being rather a fool about this Catherine Fernhill, who probably thinks of him as no more than the young man who helped out when her pet dog was in trouble. Suddenly gloomy, he looks up to see his gloom reflected across the punch-bowl in the face of Mr Flowers, the solicitor – though this is a matter of physiognomy rather than temperament, for Mr Flowers, not yet forty, has a bloodhound sort of face; a kind, laconic, easy-going bloodhound, that is, keener on a blanket by the fire than a long run across country.

'Heyday, John. Merry Christmas to you. Cold night, isn't it? Tum-te-tiddle-de-tee,' sighs Mr Flowers, who is Dr Twopenny's solicitor, as he is to most of the district. 'Left Wenn's for good now?'

'No, I'm going back for one more term before I start medical studies.'

'Oh, yes, of course. Your father was saying. Clean forgot. Rum-pum-pum, ta-dah.' It is Mr Flowers's habit to punctuate his conversation with these musical snatches, though he does not so much sing them as murmur them, as if he were reading them off a notice.

'How are your little girls, Mr Flowers?'

'D'you know, they grow at an alarming rate. Like sunflowers. It can't be normal. Children are supposed to be small, aren't they? You know, like lapdogs. Part of the appeal, I thought. Oh, well. Inevitable, I suppose.' Mr Flowers is a widower with two delightful and intelligent little daughters, to whom he is as devoted as he pretends to be indifferent. 'Goodway's done wonders with this house, hasn't he?' Mr Flowers goes on, lifting his heavy eyes in brief, unexcited admiration. 'Still, he's got the wherewithal, I suppose. Wealthy family. Your father finished that garden-room yet?'

'No,' John says, 'the project seems to be suspended.'

'Ah? Just as well, really. Tiddy-om-pom-pom.' Mr Flowers dips his jowls in his punch-glass. 'Rather good punch. So, you're to go in for medicine, I hear? University?'

'Well, Edinburgh is supposed to be the best place to study. But there are also the teaching hospitals like Guy's, in London.'

Mr Flowers nods. 'World all before you. Splendid thing . . . Piece of advice, John – kindly meant – don't take it amiss. Just this: live within your income. Sounds trite, I know. But try and live well within it, if you can. After all, you never know. Diddle-de-diddle-de-dee.'

John, not at all offended, assures Mr Flowers that he will; and indeed, his material wants are few, and he has no intention of jeopardizing the career he feels summoned to by getting into debt. So he parts with Mr Flowers on cordial terms, and bears the punch back to Admiral Fernhill, who is too busy describing a sea-battle to thank him.

However, the battle is welcome to rage for as long as the Admiral's memory, or imagination, can sustain it; for he has got to his feet in order to make the necessary illustrative gestures, and in the general redistribution of seats, a space has opened up right beside Miss Fernhill. And John, before he has had time to think twice, or even once, has claimed it in an instant. Wild exultation, as Miss Fernhill greets him warmly with a smile that he has already come to recognize as peculiarly her own – a friendly, ingenuous smile, with something a little droll in it, her lower lip slightly protruding in a way that John finds particularly heartbreaking. Wild dismay, as he realizes the necessity of finding something to say, and the apparent impossibility of saying anything except an incoherent burble. At last, desperately resorts to their only common theme, and asks after her dog.

'Oh, he's quite recovered, thank you. Though he got very mournful when he realized he wasn't coming with me this evening, and I had to whistle to him for a full fifteen minutes before he would be reconciled to staying at home.'

'Er – whistle to him?'

'Yes – tunes, you know,' says Miss Fernhill, as if this were the most natural thing in the world. 'They send him into a sort of trance. His favourites are "O ruddier than the cherry" and "Believe me if all those endearing young charms", though I have quite a job to reach the high notes in that one and sometimes nothing comes out but a sort of puffing noise like a pot boiling over. Do you like music?'

'I like music very much,' says John, with a dreadful consciousness of displaying no more conversational powers than a parrot.

'You wouldn't,' says Miss Fernhill, in a solemn confidential voice, 'if you heard me. My governess gave up the music lessons altogether after a while, saying something about Mozart being buried in a pauper's grave and his widow selling off his manuscripts but what I was doing to him was even worse. She said in Venice, his grave, I mean, but I think she must have meant Vienna because he could hardly have been buried in a canal, could he?'

'I can't sing, either,' says John, with a feeling rather as if something were being plucked out of his breast and laid in Miss Fernhill's lap, except not so gory.

'I'm very glad to hear it. I wish nobody could sing. Well, no, I don't mean that, that's just envy coming out. Verity – ' with a motion of her eyes to the dark young lady – 'Verity can play, and sing, like anything. She can read French and Italian too. She's wonderfully accomplished, and I'll bet her pupils will turn out quite geniuses . . . She's going to be a governess, you see. Or it looks as if she will have to be. Her poor father was Papa's cousin's cousin, or something like that, and he died, and she was left with no money. And so she's staying with us until she finds a situation. Well, I wish she were staying with us permanently, but Papa says it's only a temporary arrangement, and I mustn't suppose otherwise. But then perhaps I can talk him round,' says Miss Fernhill, a little wistfully. John rather doubts, even on so short an acquaintance, that the admiral is a man who can be talked round to doing anything he doesn't want to do; but there is something in Miss Fernhill's expression which convinces him that she resists thinking badly of people, an impression which is confirmed by her next words. 'You mustn't mind about Papa – you know, what he said about doctors,' she goes on in a whisper. 'He's only teasing. I think it must be a splendid thing to be a doctor, and I've heard what a fine reputation your father has in these parts. And so you are studying medicine? It must be dreadfully hard.'

'Well, I – I haven't begun my studies as yet,' says John, who feels peculiarly shy of confessing that he has not yet finished schooling. 'Very soon. Though I have often helped my father informally, and he has taught me the rudiments as far as his time allows.' This is true, and it has given John a very solid practical grounding in the profession. 'However, I hope to . . .'

29

'Yes?' says Catherine, who has nothing of the languorous young lady about her, and is eager to know everything.

'Well, I hope to specialize in the infectious diseases, with regard to sanitation and housing, rather than practise as a general physician. It is in the living conditions of the poor that the great challenge to medicine lies, and it is up to medicine to demonstrate what our government refuses to acknowledge. And they *must* acknowledge it at last, because pestilence won't consent to stay out of sight in the slums and rookeries – they will find it creeping into the Palace of Westminster itself if they don't take heed, and then there really will be a to-do . . . I'm sorry. This is dry stuff for a Christmas party,' he says, conscious of getting on to his favourite hobby-horse, and feeling it about to run away with him.

'I don't think so. This is the time when we're supposed to consider the poor and meek, isn't it? I suppose, then, that your work will be in London when you're qualified?'

'I imagine so, yes,' says John, with all the casual confidence of someone who has been to London precisely twice in his life. 'That is where the main problem lies. And too often it's a matter of the simplest health measures, if only concerted action can be taken . . .' The hobby-horse is getting skittish again, and John reins in with a jerk. 'Well, I must qualify first, before I start setting the world to rights. And finish my schooling,' he adds, with a sudden, desperate frankness. 'At Mr Wenn's Academy, in Norwich.'

Miss Fernhill, however, is not the sort of young lady to give a hitch of her chin, look at him askance, and declare that he is a mere Boy. She simply says, 'Oh, we are often in Norwich! Mama has family there. Just think, we've probably passed each other in the street, and not known it!'

These words, the vision that they conjure up, and the glowing look that accompanies them, pretty well undo John completely. Passionate and illogical assertions, to the effect that he would know her anywhere even if he didn't know her, spring to his lips; but he is fortunately prevented from uttering them by a burst of music. The young man who has been engaged for the purpose has stolen to the piano, and announces the commencement of the dancing with such a thunderous volley of chords that Mrs Fernhill gives a little shriek of alarm, and Augustus's eyeglass, which he has only just managed to screw into place, shoots out of his eye like a champagne cork.

The shock over, however, couples soon begin forming up, first amongst them being John's mother and father. It is, of course, the most natural thing in the world that John should stand up with Miss Fernhill; but a sort of burning consciousness of this fact seems to paralyse them both, so that they sit licking their lips and looking awkward for some few moments – crucial moments, as it turns out, for it is just then that they are descended on by Mr Bream the minister.

'Miss Fernhill, I do declare! And Mr John Twopenny, unless my eyes deceive me! This is a pleasure – this really is a pleasure!'

Hearty, manly handshakes are bestowed on both of them; and Mr Bream, who has been making a tour of the room, dosing everyone in turn with his dreadful optimism, now positions himself between them, and all hope of their joining this dance is gone.

'This is a delightful occasion, is it not? The true Christmas spirit! You will find some amongst my brethren, you know, who would not countenance merrymaking on the nativity. Not I. Even the consumption of intoxicating liquors I find a forgivable indulgence at such a time, though I forbid it to myself; but then, my spirits are so continually elevated I hardly find myself in need of artificial stimulants. Do you not find it so, Miss Fernhill? Are we not surrounded by so many evidences of Providential dispensation, that we simply cannot repine? I could not help but remark to my boys the other day, when we were walking to

Blakeney on a sick visit, and our journey was enlivened by a shower of rain: boys, I cried, is this not a remarkable instance of Providential dispensation, that the shower should clear, just having rained enough to replenish the earth, freshen the air, and add variety and zest to what would otherwise have been a certain monotony of fine weather? And they took the point, you know! Even though Georgy, the youngest, murmured something about being soaked to the skin, in a voice which if I did not know him better I might call mutinous, I interpreted that as merely the inconsequence of the infant mind – and all in all, I think they were pretty struck by the point, you know – I think they were!'

Thus Mr Bream, beaming at them in turn. He is not a young man, Mr Bream, but there is a perennially young look about his square-jawed face, with its great eyes terribly open, and its black eyebrows terribly lifted; and he has curiously young-looking hair – reputed by some to be a wig, though it is more likely that Mr Bream's hair simply grows like that. He is often to be seen briskly walking the cliff-paths, numerous offspring in tow, his square shoulders and turned-out feet giving him the semblance of some huge earnest duck. His home, and his flock, are at Hales-next-the-sea, but he makes forays all along the coast in search of strayed sheep; and if they are inclined to doubt that this is the best of all possible worlds, he shepherds them to the extent that they often regard the wolf as an eligible alternative.

'Mr John, I have been talking with your excellent father,' pursues Mr Bream, who with his monumental obtuseness seems to have no idea that there is any dancing going on, 'and he informs me that you are to follow him into the medical profession. That is an excellent avocation! We must go to the Apocrypha for scriptural endorsement: "Honour the physician with the honour due unto him", but I am no stickler for textual authority: let us, indeed, honour the physician, for as the verse continues, "the Lord hath made him." Isn't that so, Miss Deene?' – to the dark young lady, who is passing by him at that moment.

'I suppose so, sir,' answers Miss Deene, out of the back of her head. 'Just as He made the diseases, as well.'

'Now isn't that remarkable? That, Mr John, touches on precisely the point I was about to make to you: that it is very probable that you will come across many distressing sights, and circumstances perplexing to a believer in divine benefi-cence. Oh! yes – I am a realist, you know, Mr John; this world of ours seems often enough to be in a sad condition, almost enough to make a man despair. But do you know what? Shall I tell you something? I am full of hope! Now isn't that a curious thing? And do you know why I am full of hope?'

John, suppressing a number of disrespectful replies, shakes his head.

'It is because God will not let me be otherwise! There is simply no help for it!' cries Mr Bream, in his most booming, eyebrow-raising, madly-staring way. 'Mr John, I want you to consider, just for a moment, the feelings of Noah upon beholding the return of the dove to the ark – Would you oblige me? – just by considering, for a moment, that enchanting scriptural episode? And now I want you to consider my own comparable feelings, on visiting a poor family of my acquaintance, who had lost their first two children in infancy. The couple had been blessed with a third child; yes! and it had lived. And most wonderful of all, though the child lacks the use of its legs, through some congenital infirmity, its honest father is by trade a carpenter, and thus is easily able to construct those admirable contrivances, with wheels and struts and so forth, which afford a measure of mobility to the halt and lame. Now! Now you will comprehend why the heart of Noah on beholding the dove can hardly have soared higher than mine, when I saw this affecting piece of heavenly work; and now tell me that we do not live in an age of miracles! Good heavens – ' Mr Bream, having talked all through the first dance, suddenly becomes aware that the second is beginning – 'I

31

do believe there's dancing. Miss Fernhill, you must not miss it; please, let me offer myself as a partner for this most civilized and festive amusement.' And so saying, he whisks Miss Fernhill off like some fairy-tale enchanter, who is going to put her in a castle and cheer her up for ever more: John meanwhile trying so hard not to look crestfallen that his face quite aches with the effort.

The admiral and his wife have stood up for this dance, too, leaving only Miss Deene and Augustus of the party. Augustus, whose dress inhibits him from dancing, or from doing anything much beyond turning himself stiffly about like a man in a suit of armour, at once buttonholes John and says affably, 'It's Twopenny, ain't it? Glad to see you, my dear fellow. I say, can we talk confidentially?'

John says he will be honoured.

'Nice of you – nice of you. Now the thing is this . . .' Augustus is distracted for some moments by his insecure eyeglass, which has produced such painful effects on his face that it looks as if someone has attacked him with it. Having hammered it in place again, he goes on: 'Had much education? Classical, in particular, I mean. Greek, and – what's the other fellow?'

'Latin?' suggests John.

'That's the one. Thought you'd know about it. Devilish difficult customers, aren't they?'

'I've never found them easy,' says John, 'Greek especially.'

'Ah. Now let me tell you something,' says Augustus, drawing John closer, and lowering his voice earnestly. 'About that Greek. Do you know what? *The letters aren't the same*. You know – A, and B, and what's that other chap, jolly old C. Different in Greek. Little squiggly fellows. That's where I've been going wrong, I find. Quite a turn-up, ain't it? Thought I'd let you in on it, anyhow.'

John manages to thank him.

'Not at all, old fellow. Don't mention,' says Augustus, giving John a slap on the shoulder, and dislodging his eyeglass again. 'Education, eh? Curious business altogether. Hanged if I can see the use of half of it. Ha! Remember old Dr Luckey? – oldest master in the school, but he had an arm as strong as a man of twenty – made my back look like a regular butcher's shop once. You know the one – wore powder on his hair – kept his cane in a flute-case. No? Oh, well. Glad to see you, anyhow, Twopenny. Come and see me at Buttings some time, won't you?' And just as if he had bumped into John in the street, Augustus shakes his hand and goes creaking away.

Left alone with the dark young lady, Miss Deene, John feels the necessity of conversing with her, but finds it difficult to know how to begin. His constraint proceeds not only from her evident self-possession and tart tongue, but from a vague, unsettling feeling that she does not like him. She forestalls him, however, by speaking herself, noticing the direction of his gaze and remarking, 'Catherine dances very well, doesn't she?'

'Er – yes, indeed,' says John, a little embarrassed at having been so obvious. 'Very well.' It is true: even with Mr Bream as a partner, Miss Fernhill is so naturally graceful she seems hardly to be in contact with the floor.

'However, it is Mr Bream she is dancing with, and not you,' says Miss Deene, 'and so you will have to endure talking to me for the present.'

'I'm sure I shall enjoy, not endure,' says John, though he is not sure of anything of the kind.

'Oh, you needn't bother with that flowery talk on my account. You've nothing to gain by winning *me* over. And besides, I don't butter up as easily as the admiral or Augustus.'

This accusation that he has been currying favour with Miss Fernhill's family is so stinging that he can only reply in kind. 'I wouldn't dream of buttering you up,

Miss Deene,' he says. 'As any cook knows, butter and vinegar don't mix.'

Miss Deene, however, only gives him her sidelong look, and discomfits him even more. Distant as he knows the connection to be, John, observing her, cannot trace any family resemblance at all between Verity Deene and Catherine Fernhill. Miss Deene, though her figure is trim and well-made, does not look as if she might take to the air when dancing: her feet seem to be in very close contact with the ground. And John cannot conceive of anyone gazing with adoration into her face – not indeed because it is ugly by any means, but because those cool grey eyes beneath their slanting brows seem to see altogether too much, and that wry mouth seems very little concerned to hide its expressions, or restrain the caustic tongue within it.

'Anyhow,' says John, with an obscure sense of putting himself at a further disadvantage, 'I don't suppose Augustus was showing anything more than common politeness when he invited me to Buttings.'

'Probably not – but I'll bet that won't prevent you taking the invitation up.'

'I hope nothing will ever prevent me from returning civility with civility,' says John, hoping to sound incisive, and realizing with dismay that he sounds priggish instead.

'My dear Mr Twopenny,' says Miss Deene, laughing, and seeming to invest his name with an enormous fund of mockery, 'it really is of no account to me that you have fallen for Catherine. It is quite understandable, indeed. But it's simply no use you wishing I would fly away on a broomstick, because I won't. Not here, and not at Buttings either. When you come, that is. I shall be there to get in your way, I'm afraid. I refuse to spend my life tactfully withdrawing.'

'Thank you for the warning. As for the broomstick, you reserve that for nocturnal expeditions, I suppose?'

Miss Deene gives an appearance of wanting to laugh, but whether with him or at him John cannot tell.

'And as for those two boys at Hales,' he adds, remembering her earlier remark, 'I am indeed sorry if I spoiled their only clothes – but that still doesn't excuse them being cruel.'

'What an easy person you are to provoke,' says Miss Deene calmly.

'Not really. But if you go out of your way to provoke, you're bound to score a few hits here and there.'

'And I think I have just scored another one,' says Miss Deene, calmer still.

John is conscious of wanting to say something, but being able only to make spluttering sounds; conscious too that the dance has just ended, but that to turn and look for Miss Fernhill's return will make him even more ludicrously obvious in Verity Deene's eyes. Once again, however, she forestalls him.

'Yes, Catherine is coming back,' she says, looking over his shoulder. 'Though it will be a slow business, because I think Mr Bream is telling her some long, uplifting story. Ah, well, third time lucky, perhaps, Mr Twopenny.'

The admiral is returning too, and makes a great fuss because his chair has been moved in his absence, by a full three inches. John, meanwhile, waits in intolerable suspense for the return of Miss Fernhill; and when a shadow falls across him, leaps out of his seat, only to look into the hangdog eyes of Mr Flowers.

'Sorry, John. Didn't mean to startle you. Rompity-tompity-tom,' says Mr Flowers, with a bow to Miss Deene. 'I can't positively promise not to trample your toes, Miss Deene, but leaving that aside, may I have the next? Oh – ' with an apologetic glance at John – 'unless . . .?'

'Oh no! Mr Twopenny hasn't asked me,' says Miss Deene, giving John a devilish look, 'don't suppose that for a moment. We've just been having a chat. Thank you, Mr Flowers, I shall be very glad.'

A feeling of having been taken down several pegs, without knowing quite how or why, remains with John after Miss Deene has stood up with the solicitor . . . but all at once it is gone. Miss Fernhill is here, and the next dance is theirs, because he has asked her for it in a sort of urgent babble; and presently the young man at the piano strikes up again like twenty musicians, and John is leading Catherine Fernhill on to the floor.

Only a dance at a Christmas party, after all – so, John supposes, he might think if he were twenty or even a dozen years older; but to him it is the crossing of a bridge from one life to another. Even his nervousness leaves him, and he stops conjuring up visions of himself treading on the skirts of her gown with terrible tearing sounds, and simply gives himself up to admiration. The shape of her face, for which only the worn simile of a heart is appropriate; the fun in her eyes, which give the lie to the association of blueness with coldness; the freshness of her skin, North-Sea-breeze freshness rather than that sickly roses-and-snow freshness beloved of poets; even her stature, which is somewhere between middle height and willowy, and impresses him so forcibly as an ideal standard that he wonders he has never thought of it before. And then he realizes that he is staring like an idiot, and launches himself into frantic conversation which the figures of the dance make even more fragmented and nonsensical, so that at last Miss Fernhill cannot contain her laughter, and he laughs too and gives it up.

But he must give her up, too, when the dance is over: etiquette and plain neighbourliness prohibit him from simply ignoring everyone else in the room. He forlornly tries to signal this complex message with his eyes, as he relinquishes her; and then suddenly asks, without quite knowing why, 'What do you think of Mr Goodway?'

Miss Fernhill, being herself rather inconsequential in her manner of talking, does not seem surprised at this abrupt question, and answers, 'I don't know him well, but he seems a very agreeable gentleman – very frank and open, you know, the way Dr Johnson was supposed to be, though in truth I think Dr Johnson sounds the rudest old man that ever was and probably never said half those pithy things.' And then she is snatched from him by her mother, who wishes to introduce her to someone, and John cordially wishes the someone at the bottom of the sea.

Just then, however, he finds himself face to face with his host; who has been indefatigably making the rounds of the guests, but who still gives that impression that you are the one person in the room he wishes to see. 'Well, John, we shall all suffer for this in the morning, no doubt; but who gives a hang about that – take some more punch,' is all Mr Goodway says, in his relaxed way; yet there is something in his glance which convinces John that Mr Goodway sees all through him – something in his glance which says, in effect, 'So, you are quite smitten with Miss Fernhill, and are thinking of nothing but dancing with her again: I understand, my friend, I quite understand, and will say no more about it!' It is not patronizing; it is not even indulgent; and John cannot imagine why it makes him so uncomfortable. But it does, all the same.

However, Mr Goodway soon moves on, and so John crosses the room, and finds his mother and father.

'Well, my boy, this is something like Christmas, eh?' cries the doctor, who is all heated with punch and dancing, and seems to shed good cheer around him like a ruddy light. 'We must match this, in the new year: I've half a mind to go round everybody in the room and invite 'em here and now.'

'Mr Flowers seems to be taking a good deal of notice of that dark young lady in grey,' says John's mother. 'I don't believe I've ever seen him dance since his wife died. Who is the lady, do you know, John?'

'Aye, you seem to know that party, my boy. The old man's Admiral something-or-other, isn't he? Will you introduce us?'

'Er – yes, I've met them,' says John, who finds himself curiously embarrassed

34

about this simple fact, in front of his parents. He is very proud, however, to introduce them to the Fernhills; and though the admiral puffs and preens, and seems for a moment on the verge of repeating his joke about doctors, it passes off pretty well. Soon, indeed, to John's mingled alarm and delight, Dr Twopenny is throwing out an invitation to the Fernhills to come and celebrate the new year at Saltmarsh; the admiral, half flattered vanity and half pompous pride, indicates that he may condescend to grace the occasion; and then there is dancing again, and Dr Twopenny – who can be as thick-skinned as he is warm-hearted – gallantly asks Miss Fernhill if she would object to taking the floor with an old fossil, and leads her out. And John just intercepts a glance of amusement from his mother – who misses nothing – and then she in turn is claimed by Mr Goodway, and he is left bereft again.

Here is another glance of amusement – from Miss Deene, who always seems to see him at a disadvantage, and never at his best. It is a challenge of some sort, he decides, and for that reason – or for some reason, he cannot tell what – he boldly goes up, and asks her to dance.

'Why?' says she.

'Why not?'

Miss Deene raises an eyebrow. 'You wouldn't ask me, if Catherine were not already taken.'

'You wouldn't refuse me, if you had not decided to mock me at every opportunity.'

'Whoever said I was refusing you?'

'Well . . . you did.'

'Oh! I wasn't aware of it. But if you say so, I shall not argue with you. Thank you, anyway, for asking.'

John finds he is breathing hard, and making that spluttering sound again; and so retires in defeat, mentally resolving that he will get the better of her one day.

'Sometimes I wish my father were not quite so infernally sociable,' he says despondently to Philip Revell.

'Oh, your turn will come again,' replies his friend. 'Besides, Miss Fernhill likes you, so there's nothing to worry about.'

'How can you tell?' The gloomy indifference with which John says these words betrays nothing of the joy leaping up inside him, or so he thinks.

'Don't be an ass,' says Philip chuckling. 'I say, I've just been upstairs. You never saw such luxury – well, not on this coast, anyway. Goodway must be worth a mint of money.'

'Philip, do you . . . do you really suppose she likes me?'

'You are an absurd fellow,' says Philip. 'She won't have much opportunity to decide whether she does or not if you lurk about here. Go in and win.' And, the dance just ending and Miss Fernhill leaving the floor, Philip gives John a hearty push in her direction.

Does she like him? The question becomes academic as the evening proceeds, and John dances with her again, and again, and talks with her at delicious length, and forgets all his tortuous doubts in the simple pleasure of her company. If this is not liking, then it is an unusually delightful form of politeness; whatever it is, he feels that he could rest content with it for a very long time.

But even a party like Mr Goodway's must come to an end at last, and it is this apprehension which smites John as he is leading Miss Fernhill out for the final quadrille, to such visible effect that she looks alarmed, and asks him what is wrong.

'Oh! nothing – I just wish tonight didn't have to end.'

'So do I,' says she warmly. 'I never enjoyed an evening so much . . . Dear me, you look pale – are you sure you are quite well? I noticed there was some cold duck at supper, and Papa was fearfully ill with that once, and Mama said he came up in

35

great weals all over his back, though I was quite a child at the time and didn't understand the word weals and I cried till I was fit to burst because I thought Papa was turning into a waggon or a hackney-coach or something—'

'Miss Fernhill,' says John, 'Augustus has asked me to Buttings.'

'Oh, good, I'm glad!'

Seized with gloom as he is, John does not heed the eagerness of these words for a moment. 'But should I come? I mean – I can't pretend that I would be coming just to see Augustus.'

'Oh,' she says; and then with a dawning smile, 'oh, I see . . . You're very scrupulous.'

'No, I'm not really,' he says, smiling too, with gloom flying before a victorious tumult of happiness. 'As long as I can see you again . . .'

'Well, we are coming to you in the new year, besides,' says Miss Fernhill. 'I'm sure Papa will accept your father's invitation. Isn't he a charming man? – your father, I mean. I'm sure I would rather be attended by him if I were ill, but we always have Dr Digley from Hales because Mama swears by him; but though I'm sure he is a good doctor, I'm never quite easy with him because he smells of horehound and has the most frightful hair growing out of his ears . . . So we will – I'm sure – see each other again,' she concludes, with a look that is grave, shy, and humorous all at once.

John can only return her look: grinning like an idiot, he supposes, but he doesn't care.

'Well, you are not so pale now – that's good,' says she. 'It can't have been the duck after all.'

The couples form up for the last quadrille. John surveys the room, seeing Philip whispering something wickedly amusing in the ear of a young lady in pink; seeing Mr Bream cornering Philip's mother, and vainly hurling uplifting thoughts at her granite misanthropy; seeing Miss Deene listening with her sidelong look to some lawyer-like anecdote from Mr Flowers; seeing Augustus, whose head for drink is not of the strongest, dozing in an upright position on a settle, and periodically starting awake with a look of vacant alarm; seeing the admiral regarding the pier-glass with his reflection in it, as if it were a particularly fine painting; seeing his parents sitting out at last, and in conversation with their host – Mr Goodway leaning over the sofa on which they are sitting, and resting his hand on Dr Twopenny's shoulder as they roar with laughter at something John's mother has said; seeing Catherine Fernhill smiling into his eyes; and seeing nothing within his whole view that has the slightest suggestion of a shadow about it, or promises anything but fair.

CHAPTER FOUR

A Little Learning

'Mr Twopenny.'

The lawn and shrubberies visible from the schoolroom window were all spangled with frost. So exquisite was the scene that it seemed scarcely possible that something as prosaic as the weather was responsible for the transformation. It was easier to imagine that the garden had been placed under an enchantment like the Sleeping Beauty's castle, and that it would require some far more magical agency than the sun to return it to normality.

'Mr Twopenny.'

It was a pity, the way you stopped noticing these things once you left childhood behind. Dew on spider-webs in the early morning, sparkling all along the hedgerows: now that had always been a wonderful thing to see, when he was a boy! And then somehow you stopped seeing such things, and went around in blinkers. Though as a matter of fact, he seemed to have begun noticing them again just lately. Probably it was because of—

'Mr Twopenny!'

'Sir!' John snapped to attention.

'Well, I am relieved to find you know your own name, at any rate,' said Mr Wenn. 'It would, I suppose, or should I say I fear, be too much to hope that you might also know, or at least be on nodding terms with, the theorem we were discussing?'

'Er – yes, sir,' said John, bending over his book. Mr Wenn's sarcasm was sometimes so elaborate that he could only reply yes or no at random.

Mr Wenn sniffed his dry sniff. 'Returning, then, to geometry, which the greatest thinkers of the greatest civilization in the world's history seem, unaccountably, to have found a more improving occupation for the mind than staring out of the window – a lapse of taste in the Greeks for which I am sure Mr Twopenny will forgive them; we observe . . .'

Mr Wenn's remark about John knowing his own name was, at it happened, rather apt. He knew his own name, but that was all he did know about himself for certain just at the moment. He was a stranger to himself, full of mysteries. His former selfhood – the old John – had been a fairly predictable fellow who had never given him much trouble. The new John was not like that. The new John would not be content with one emotion at a time, but insisted on feeling five or six at once, and got torn apart in the process. The new John had been dreadfully cut up at saying goodbye to Philip Revell, who had sailed for India last week, just as the old John would have been; but the new John had stubbornly managed to have other things on his mind at the same time, and was curiously distracted about the leave-taking, and then felt guilty afterwards, and bemoaned the fact that he would never again have such a friend as Philip and didn't deserve him in the first place, in a very maudlin fashion.

The new John, moreover, had fantastical notions about his appearance. He was curiously obsessed with the fact that he only needed to shave every other day,

37

instead of every day, and had even begun submitting his innocent chin to a daily scrape with a razor, as if this might constitute a self-fulfilling prophecy. The new John entertained terrible suspicions about the back of his head, and if he got between two mirrors, expressed wild horror at its shape, and did violent things to himself with hairbrushes. Likewise, the new John pronounced himself disgusted with the old John's wardrobe, and said it was only fit for a scarecrow.

Most disturbingly, the new John had continually to be prodded into applying himself to his studies, even though he knew quite as well as the old John how important they were. He was, in fact, rather a mess; and if he was happy, more happy indeed than the old John had ever been in his life, it was in a messy sort of way, and the happiness was all jumbled up in such a heap of contrary thoughts, plans, visions, memories and feelings, that neither of the Johns could really lay his hand on it, and say, 'Here it is!'

However, both of them had to settle down together, and get on with that jogging, trundling, everyday life that takes no account of emotional turmoil; and everyday life meant returning to Mr Wenn's Academy in Norwich, in those first frosty weeks of 1851, for one last spell of captivity. Not that it was the most oppressive of captivity, for John was now a parlour-boarder, living in Mr Wenn's own house, and taking his meals, seasoned with rarefied sarcasm, at Mr Wenn's own table; and when he was not being crammed with indigestible mathematics, he had a good deal of time to himself. The Academy was situated on the outskirts of Norwich; it was an austere Georgian building fenced about with iron railings as thin, sharp, cold and unapproachable as Mr Wenn himself, and with precise regular views of the cathedral and castle from its symmetrical windows, like architectural elevations. One wing housed the school, which included a long dormitory always very bare and cool, like a great scholastic larder; in the other wing Mr Wenn entertained the parlour-boarders, and nurtured his family. The family consisted of a baby with a philosopher's forehead, a serious-minded little girl who talked about the Heptarchy at breakfast, and Mrs Wenn, a tall aquiline lady proficient in music. For a few guineas extra per term she gave music lessons to the senior boys, always making her stately progress to the music-room with a bust of Handel clutched in her right hand; partly for inspiration, but also as a suitable instrument with which to club down any boys who might attempt familiarities – for the Academy was strict in its moral tone. They were not in the business, as Mr Wenn often acidly remarked, of turning out rakes; and if this accounted for a certain dryness and dullness in its atmosphere, it also accounted for the Academy's solid reputation amongst people who wanted their sons to be educated men rather than fine gentlemen. Indeed Mr Wenn – a chalky, fleshless, elongated man dressed in unvarying black, who was rumoured to sleep standing up like a horse – had very earnest and individual views about education, and even took his boys to view buildings under construction and iron foundries at work, with stern injunctions that they should take all knowledge as their province.

Not, of course, that the old Adam could be entirely suppressed in Mr Wenn's students, as John's own case showed. Catherine Fernhill was so much in his secret thoughts that he did not quite trust her to stay there, and he could not deliver up his copybook to Mr Wenn without a dreadful suspicion that instead of the prescribed Latin verses he had submitted the rather fulsome poem which he had composed in his room late at night; a poem which sang her praises very exhaustively, but which was somewhat disfigured, he felt, by the lack of a rhyme for 'Fernhill'. The other parlour-boarder, Stuffins, after some thought suggested 'Colonel'; but though John was grateful for the suggestion, he couldn't work it in somehow, perhaps because of its associations with red cheeks and moustaches.

For it was Catherine Fernhill, of course, who was responsible for the change in John; Catherine Fernhill's the one dominating image he had brought back to Mr

Wenn's with him; and as far as his memories of his Christmas vacation were concerned, they were hazy where they did not include her, and intolerably vivid where they did. He knew, for example, that he had helped his father on several professional visits to sick fishermen's families at Shipden (Dr Twopenny charged no fee for these); but he recalled the circumstances only as one recalls a dream later in the day, whereas the New Year's Eve dinner that his father had given was so fresh in his memory that he could have accurately accounted for every minute of it. Thus: seven-thirty, Catherine arrived . . . seven-thirty-six, Catherine first caught his eye across the drawing-room, and smiled . . . eight o'clock, Catherine took his arm to go in to dinner . . . eight-twenty-five, he and Catherine so deep in talk at the table that they had hardly had anything to eat . . . nine-thirty, he and Catherine still so deep in talk, in the drawing-room now, that even Mr Bream could not drive his wedges of optimism between them, and had to seek other victims . . . ten o'clock, Dr Twopenny suggested an impromptu carpet-dance, and John and Catherine were the first to spring up . . . eleven-thirty, John's mother was relieved at the piano by Miss Deene, and other couples began to weaken, but John and Catherine were still on the floor as if they meant not only to dance the new year in, but dance it out as well . . . He could remember everything, in fact, right down to the moment that the Fernhills' carriage took them away from Saltmarsh; and after that the mists closed in again.

The mists opened again only to reveal Buttings Court, the home of the Fernhills, which he had visited shortly before his return to the Academy. It was a Jacobean house, not quite a manor, tucked away in the wooded country behind Hales-next-the-sea. John had learned a little more about Admiral Fernhill now, and gathered that his chief renown – apart from that shining naval head – lay in inheriting money, and marrying the daughter of an admiralty lord, which showed a grasp of strategy he had never demonstrated at sea; but in the fitting up of Buttings Court, the admiral had certainly not been inhibited by modesty. Busts of great seafarers, friezes of dolphins and Neptunes, model ships mounted on plinths, framed navigational charts, glass cases full of medals and citations and tattered ensigns and fragments of cannon-shot, all contrived to give an impression that Admiral Fernhill had, at the very least, won the Battle of Trafalgar single-handed; and the main hall was dominated by a vast oil portrait, representing the admiral pointing to a map with his other hand buried in his waistcoat, while in the distance behind him a tremendous sea-fight raged – though John was unsure whether it was incapacity or irony on the part of the artist that made the ships all look like toy boats in a bathtub.

But no matter. No matter that the place was a brazen monument to one man's ego; no matter that Mrs Fernhill, though civil enough, kept calling John Mr Halfpenny, or Mr Threepenny, or any numismatic name except his real one; no matter that Augustus not only remembered inviting him, but actually supposed there was no one else there he had come to see, and spent an unconscionable time showing John his new outfits; no matter that, when he at last contrived a walk around the gardens with Catherine, he had to accept the presence of Miss Deene as chaperone. It was all one to him, as long as she was there.

And, of course, as long as she was glad to see him. He had passed through the initial phase of wanting nothing more than to contemplate her existence, and had reached the crucial stage of falling in love – the stage in which some reciprocal feeling is not merely hoped for, but seems necessary to one's very sanity. Unfortunately, this is also the stage in which one doubts the evidence of one's senses. A plain signal – or wishful thinking? A secret glance – or a look of mistrust? Warm smile – or cool politeness? John certainly ran through every excruciating doubt that ever lover tormented himself with; but he was in better case than many, because it was about Catherine Fernhill's feelings that these anxious questions hovered, and it soon became clear that Catherine Fernhill could no more hide her feelings than she could climb a steeple. And when at last John's visit to Buttings came to an end, and he said goodbye, her doleful expression unmistakably proclaimed that she did not want him to go. Even the imps of doubt could not place any other interpretation on that look, and admitted defeat; and John walked home to Saltmarsh without his feet touching the ground once.

These, then, were the memories that he took with him back to the Academy, and which kept interposing themselves between him and his studies. And as if that were not distraction enough, there was the daily ordeal of the post, for at Buttings he had taken advantage of a few minutes alone with Catherine to ask permission to write to her. The correspondence, tentatively begun, had soon become compulsive on both sides; but John's being a parlour-boarder meant that he had to wait until Mr Wenn handed him his letters at the breakfast-table. And Mr Wenn, perhaps with some clairvoyant perception of what was going on in John's heart, always chose to point the occasion with some of his chilliest irony.

'Oh dear me – I had quite forgot,' Mr Wenn would say, noticing the letters that had lain by his plate for a full fifteen minutes, 'the post. How very remiss of me. Let us see what we have here. Hum, hum.' He would then read the directions on the letters with leisurely attentiveness, while John tried to swallow his bread-and-butter and his impatience at the same time.

'Ah, yes. A letter for Mr . . .' Here Mr Wenn held the letter closer to his eyes, and then held it at arm's length, and then held it sideways. 'Mr Stuffins. The calligraphy, if my eyes do not deceive me, of your honoured father, Mr Stuffins. Will you have the goodness, Mr Stuffins, to present my compliments to your parent when you return to him that prompt reply which I know your filial duty will dictate?'

'Yes, sir,' said Stuffins, who in his crushed way could never quite look Mr Wenn in the face, and seemed to answer the teapot instead.

'I am obliged to you, Mr Stuffins,' said Mr Wenn pleasantly. 'On the subject of your esteemed father, my dear sir, I believe I have lately omitted to inquire after the progress of his gout. Will you be so good as to enlighten me? Does it improve?'

Stuffins muttered that it did not, with his eyes on the bread-knife; and then addressing the sugar-bowl, added that the old fellow's foot was swelled like a pumpkin last time he saw him.

'Like a pumpkin! Dear me! I am most distressed to hear that, Mr Stuffins, though I am compelled to admiration at the vividness of your simile. Like a pumpkin! Dear me, dear me.' And Mr Wenn seemed to become lost in ruminations on mortal frailty for some time, his hand resting lightly on the other letters; whilst John bolted down more bread-and-butter, until he felt quite sick with it.

'Hum! Whatever was I thinking of,' said Mr Wenn, rousing himself at last, and observing the other letters under his hand with amiable surprise. 'Here, I believe, is a letter for Mr Twopenny. Oh! My dear – ' to Mrs Wenn – 'I think Mr Twopenny's cup is empty. Will you take some more tea, Mr Twopenny? Do oblige me by taking another cup. I hope it is not stewed – please, my dear sir, say the word if so, and we can have a fresh pot made directly. I always think there is nothing worse than tea that has been standing too long. No? You're sure the beverage is entirely to your liking?'

John would probably have said yes if the tea had been hemlock; and he felt that Mr Wenn knew it.

'Very well. Here is your letter, sir. From, I perceive, your father likewise.'

John thanked him, trying not to look at the remaining letter by Mr Wenn's plate, and feeling guilty for feeling disappointed.

'Now here is an opportune conjunction,' said Mr Wenn brightly. 'Mr Stuffins' father has gout, and Mr Twopenny's father is a physician. What, I wonder, would be Dr Twopenny's suggested remedy for the elder Mr Stuffins' condition? Does he favour cupping? Or is that old-fashioned? I should be most interested to know.'

'My father has no specific for gout,' said John rapidly. 'Only a less indulgent diet.'

'Indeed, indeed?' said Mr Wenn. 'Mr Stuffins, I wonder if your father's physician concurs in such a prognosis?'

Stuffins, addressing his own sleeve, said that the old fellow had been told time and time again that his toping would be the death of him, but he wouldn't leave off.

'Well, well. Mr Stuffins' answer, leaving aside a certain Saxon robustness of expression, would seem to indicate an encouraging unanimity amongst the members of the medical profession. Would that scholars would so readily agree! I am reminded of an amusing controversy surrounding the interpretation of those Old English relics contained within the volume known as the *Exeter Book*, in which two highly respectable dons of Oxford almost came to blows over a disputed palimpsest, and . . . Mr Twopenny, I hope I have your attention?'

John, gripping his knife as if he had it in mind to commit murder (which indeed he did), tried to look fascinated; but he could not stop his glance alighting momentarily on the remaining letter, and Mr Wenn saw it.

'Oh! My dear sir – of course, you wish to have your other letter. Here it is.' Mr Wenn held the letter just short of John's outstretched hand, feeling its weight. 'Well, well, you are fortunate indeed to have so voluminous a correspondent. People often lament, nowadays, that the art of letter-writing has decayed, but here is evidence to the contrary, judging by thickness and frequency, at any rate. The style and matter of the epistle, of course, are not for me to inquire into.'

And Mr Wenn smiled his bloodless smile, and handed the letter over, his eye falling upon John with such a sardonic gleam that John felt he might as well have advertised the fact that he had a love letter by papering it all over the dining-room walls.

The devouring of the letter had to wait until after supper, when John retired to the room he shared with Stuffins, ostensibly for further studies before the taking away of the candles at eleven o'clock. The room, though very clean, was somewhat spartan in its furnishings, Mr Wenn frowning on frivolous ornament; and though John had got used to this, young Stuffins refused to submit to such a prohibition. That is to say, he went to his trunk every evening once they were alone and, drawing from it a number of plates cut from illustrated papers, stuck them all over his side of the room. There they stayed until the approach of the maid at eleven, when he hastily took them all down, and put them away in his trunk again. Stuffins performed this ritual every night without exception, and John felt there was a certain heroism in it, even though the pictures themselves were somewhat monotonous in their appeal. They were all engravings of Beauties, whether of the Society kind or the other kind; and though they all looked much the same to John, Stuffins never got tired of them. He was a raw-boned, sandy-haired young man with a pinched face and perpetually red eyes, as if he had got soap in them at some remote date and never got it out; he was in a permanent state of resentment of Mr Wenn, of the Academy, of education, of his father, and of his father's plans for him, and his solace was these large-armed ladies and the very different sort of world they conjured up.

'I tell you, Twopenny, I shall live in a pretty fast set when I come of age, and nothing the old cuss can do will stop me,' Stuffins said. 'I shall be in London then – and let me tell you, there are some uncommonly fast women in London. Once get me among them, and you won't see *me* with my nose in a law-book, I can tell you that. My way of living will be a deal too fast for that, mark my words.' 'Fast', indeed, was Stuffins' touchstone: anything that might be described as fast, such as horse-racing, cards, tobacco, slang, liquor, debt, jewellery, France, boxing, or getting up late, had his wistful admiration. Even John's corresponding with Catherine Fernhill he managed to see in a fast light; and when John was poring over one of her letters of an evening, Stuffins would always contrive to catch John's eye across the room, and then wink, and raise his eyebrows, and say 'Letter from the lady, eh? Pretty fast I call it, Twopenny – pretty fast,' and blow on his fingers as if they were hot, and tap the side of his nose, and thrust his tongue in his cheek, and generally enjoy himself.

'But look here, Twopenny,' he said one night, after running through this expressive repertoire several times, 'what's the game where the lady's concerned? What's it to be? Elopement, perhaps? I reckon that would be pretty fast. That's what I'd do, if I was you. As soon as we're free of old Wenn, scoop her up and off to Gretna. And as for the father, give him an uppercut and lay him out, and settle him that way.'

It was Stuffins' fixed belief that Catherine's father was an inveterate enemy of John's, and was going to have to be 'settled' in some dramatic way; and try as John might to explain the real facts of the case, he would not be reasoned out of this romantic fantasy.

'Or,' pursued Stuffins, 'you could call him out. I'd be your second, if you wanted. I thought about doing that to old Wenn, but I decided he ain't worth the formality. Just a couple of jabs, a sharp right hook, and lay him out – that's all the formality Wenn's going to get from me, I can tell you that.' For another of Stuffins' fancies was that he was going to commit some act of exemplary violence on Mr Wenn before their time at the Academy was up. These bloodthirsty imaginings were not as disturbing to John's mind as they might have been, however, because anybody could have seen that Stuffins was terrified of Mr Wenn, and no more capable of these defiant acts than a rabbit of squaring up to a snake.

However, Stuffins' question had echoed a question in John's own mind. What, indeed, *was* the future to be? He must bear in mind that he was scarcely nineteen, and she no older, and that all his prospects lay in the profession for which he was preparing, for his father had little to leave him. With this consideration before him, he realized that some of the visions he had been entertaining were quite as fanciful as Stuffins' idea of dropping the admiral with a blow to the chin and bundling Catherine into a swift carriage; and there was another realization waiting to be admitted, if he let it in – the realization that a handful of meetings, and a boxful of letters, were not a very substantial foundation on which to build quite such a lofty Spanish castle as John had been constructing these past weeks.

But dwelling on practicalities, he found, could no more deject him permanently than could trigonometry, irregular Greek verbs, or Mr Wenn's asperity. He was, quite simply, enjoying being in love too much for that.

How it came about that his dedication to medicine was intensified by his being in love he could not tell, but so it was. Somehow he found time between penning huge letters, mugging up his studies, and dreaming, to read such medical treatises as Mr Wenn's library afforded, and on his free afternoons to visit the Norfolk and Norwich Hospital, where he talked often with the consultant surgeons, and where he gained first-hand knowledge of the diseases of the poor who were crammed into the yards and courts of the ancient city. Indeed, if there were any doubt that love had made a complacent lamb out of John, that was quickly dispelled by the fierce dispute he had with the doctor who attended the boys at the Academy. He was a physician of the old pompous school; and his views on epidemic diseases, which were based on a purple-faced, double-chinned conviction that the poor were naturally idle, dirty and improvident, whipped John up to such a fury that he was almost ready to follow one of Stuffins' more colourful prescriptions, and thrust the buffoon head-first up the schoolroom chimney. 'I am going to have to watch that hasty temper of mine,' he admonished himself later; and he made light of the incident when he wrote to his father about it, for Dr Twopenny had often gently advised him that people, unlike soup, were not improved by being hot and peppery.

John's letters home, indeed, though they had never been solemn, became even less so that last term; perhaps he made them brighter and more facetious in compensation for the fact that they were less frequent. His lurking guilt about this was mollified by the knowledge, gleaned from their own letters, that his parents were enjoying life greatly. They had become, it appeared, very good friends with the Goodways at Beacon House; card-parties, dances, dinners and excursions filled their letters, and suggested that Robert and Emma Twopenny had entered on a new lease of life since the arrival of their convivial neighbour. John was glad. Dullness, he knew, depressed his father's health as well as his spirits; and he had often wished that his mother might have more varied company, and more opportunity for her warm, canny and humorous personality to blossom. Less straightforwardly pleasing was the news that his father had embarked with fresh energy on his plans for the house, and had not only had the garden-room finished at last, but had laid new carpets throughout and begun the building of a coach-house. John could not help wondering where the money was coming from – or rather, when it would be paid back, for lowering a bucket into the well of credit and hoping it was not dry was, he knew, his father's habitual method of finance. But then John reproached himself. His father had, after all, been managing that way for thirty years, and he surely knew what he was doing; and there was always the restraining influence of his mother, who kept her feet on the ground, and was unlikely to have her head turned by a new extravagance in their manner of living.

So, he satisfied himself that all was well at home, perhaps a little more casually than he would have done before – for there was the preoccupation of Catherine, besides his studies, and no one can perform the miracle of the loaves and fishes with his heart, however big it is. Hence John's agonized confusion as spring approached, and with it the half-holiday. Mr Wenn was parsimonious with these, and doled out a meagre few days even to the parlour-boarders; and John's original plans for the short break – spend it at Saltmarsh, and thus see his parents and, all being well, Catherine too – were thrown into doubt by a letter from Catherine herself. Her family were coming to stay at Norwich with relatives, for precisely those four days that he would have free; and though she was shy of directly proposing that they meet up in the city, hints to that effect were all over her letter, which featured the word 'Norwich' in practically every sentence right down to the postscript.

A meeting in Norwich! John passed in a rapid moment from delightedly considering the idea to urgently insisting on it. It must be done – it must be arranged – he could not live without it. Yet was he then to remain in Norwich the whole half-holiday, and not see his parents at all?

This division of loyalty was new to him, and perplexing. He solved the dilemma at last, however, by a plan that would please everybody, just as long as his energy was equal to it. First day, go to Saltmarsh, stay there second day, return to Norwich as early as possible third day, leaving this and fourth day free to meet Catherine. Yes: that was it. The only obstacle was the slowness of transport between Norwich and Saltmarsh. Work had just begun on extending the railway to Hales-next-the-sea, but in the meantime there was little coaching that way, and he would have to make do with the lumbering pace of the local carrier's van. However, there was no help for that. Swiftly the arrangements were made, Catherine agreeing to meet John in Norwich's Chapel Field on the third day (chaperoned, of course, by Verity Deene – a social necessity that would have been less irksome, John felt, if it had been anyone else but that infuriating young woman); and John leapt from his bed before dawn on the first day of his half-holiday, to be ready for the carrier who left Norwich market-place at seven.

Was there anything at home, during the two days he spent there, that impressed itself with unusual force on his mind, to be recalled with special emotion in after days? So he sometimes asked himself, in those same after days, in circumstances far different from those that prevailed in the snug house on the cliff at Saltmarsh. If there was one overriding impression that he took from that all-too-brief stay, it was of love: the love that his parents bore him, their love for each other, and his love for them, binding them together more closely, it seemed, than ever before. Certainly the first sight of his mother and father, waiting for him at the open front door in company with those ridiculous stone lions, filled him with as profound a feeling as if he were returning after an absence of years from beyond the furthest seas. Certainly the warmth of the initial greetings did not subside into a casual cordiality, but continued right through his stay, so that there was scarcely a minute when they were not talking animatedly, or laughing together. Certainly the prospect of saying goodbye to them again was a sad one, even though it was something as compelling as Catherine Fernhill that was calling him away.

But whether or not there had been a change in him, there was no mistaking the change at home. Dr Twopenny had undertaken more improvements since his last letter; he was having an upstairs lumber-room converted into another guest bedroom, and had ordered a new chaise from a coach-builder in Norwich to replace the old gig. 'Well, you know, we go about a good deal more these days, with the Goodways,' he explained to John, 'and the old gig was draughty for your mother – she takes cold easily.' The name of Goodway, indeed, was often on his father's lips – somewhat less so on his mother's – and it was plain that the coming of Mr Goodway had acted as a piquant relish to the doctor's taste for the good things in life, and had sharpened his appetite.

And again, John thought the association with the Goodways a good thing – and yet he could not, for the life of him, be easy with Mr Marcus Goodway himself. Why, he could not have said. That gentleman called, on the second day of his stay, and was as pleasant as ever to John in his greetings and inquiries about his studies; and yet John found that he could not reply with any naturalness. Somehow, faced with that athletic frame and understated manner, John seemed to feel the years fall away from him, and he was twelve again, awkward and resentfully self-conscious.

A possibility suggested itself to John: was he, in some curious way, jealous of Mr Goodway? Did he see Mr Goodway as an intruder in the cosy, intimate little world that the three of them had had together? He was an only child, after all, and had never had to share his parents with other siblings. Perhaps his feelings were really no different from those of a boy peeping enviously into the new crib.

Whatever the reasons for his dislike, he could say nothing of it: it definitely would sound like jealousy if he began carping about his parents' boon companion. Or at least, his father's. He noticed that his mother was not quite so talkative when Mr Goodway was there, and he thought he saw her give her husband a covert glance when yet another grand party, with cards and music, was mooted; but in the main she seemed to be enjoying their revivified social life as much as the doctor, and it was not until the night before he was due to depart that John received any hint to the contrary. Even then he was not sure about it; but it was the enigmatic words his mother spoke that night that in aftertimes returned to him most hauntingly, and stood forth from the glow that was his memory of his half-holiday at Saltmarsh.

Dr Twopenny had been called out to a patient after supper, and John had gone with his mother to look over the newly finished garden-room. The afterglow had long vanished from the sky, and when John lit candles the broad windows of the room, though they overlooked the garden, showed them only their reflections swimming in greenish darkness, as if the sea had finally reclaimed Saltmarsh, and the house were at the bottom of it.

They had been talking for some time in the desultory, muted fashion of perfect ease, and it was in the same casual spirit that John said, regarding the elegant pillars of wrought-iron, 'Well, what a pretty penny this must have cost Father! He's really going the pace with this Mr Goodway, isn't he?'

His mother's back was turned to him, but he could see her face, lowered though it was, in that dark drowning reflection in the glass; and he saw trouble stir in it, like a guttering in a candle-flame.

'Yes,' she said at length, 'yes, he is.'

'Mother – what's wrong?'

His mother smiled, momentarily catching his eye in the glass. 'Nothing, my dear. Just . . . John,' she said, in a sudden urgent tone, 'I was very young when I married your father – a girl almost. And he was a mature man. But the kindest man, generous to a fault . . . So I married him. And I never regretted it. Some people said . . .'

Her voice had sunk almost to a whisper. John, surprised and disturbed, studied her face in the glass; but her eyes were hidden from him by the lowered lids, and the reflection floating in blackness appeared like a sculpted mask, noble in its expressionless beauty.

'Well,' she said, pulling her mantle close about her shoulders as if she were chilled, 'I never regretted it. And – and I am loyal, I am loyal to him and I shall remain so, it doesn't matter what . . .'

'Why, of course, Mother – I know it,' said John. There was something about the look of their two reflections, fixed in that teeming darkness, that he did not like. He moved with a wrench, as if breaking a spell, and went over to her, putting his arm about her shoulders. 'It's none too warm in here. Let's go back to the parlour, eh?'

She patted his hand, looking up at him and faintly smiling. 'You're very like your father, when he was younger.'

'Well,' he said, trying to speak lightly, 'I take that as a compliment.'

'Yes . . .' The smile lingered, but it seemed to have something of a wince about it. 'Yes, I meant it so. Come. Let's light the lamp in the porch, for when your father comes home.'

And that was all. And though John was a little troubled, it was not a sense of trouble that he took away with him next morning. It was, rather, that sense of love – love embracing, powerful, and invulnerable, enclosing the house at Saltmarsh like a stout wall; and he could not conceive of any trouble strong enough to breach it. He left very early in the morning, and though he had insisted that they mustn't lose their sleep, both his parents were astir likewise, to see him off; and they stood arm-in-arm at the front garden gate, his father's silvery hair and his mother's fairness both catching the spring sunlight, waving cheerfully to him as he descended the road to the village, until the road turned and the red roofs blotted them from his sight.

It was past midday, and John was beginning to wonder whether the carrier had once taken a whimsical vow to visit every last village and hamlet in the county of Norfolk, and had chosen today to fulfil it, when at last the cathedral spire of Norwich came in sight. Into sight, too, came rainclouds. Concern about whether he was going to be late for his meeting with Catherine overrode concern about whether it was going to rain; and after stowing his bag at the coach-office of the White Swan where the carrier put up, he set out for Chapel Field at a lick, too preoccupied with baleful scenarios involving Catherine consulting her watch, losing patience, and washing her hands of him for ever, to take much heed of the raindrops, which now began to spatter on the cobbles as if they meant business.

No, all was well, and all manner of things would be well: she was there, waiting for him, and with a smile that had no impatience in it – rather, pleasure and shyness in equal proportion. All was well: at least, if one ignored the fact that Verity Deene was with her. And though he had managed to ignore that fact very well in his anticipation of this meeting, he found it could not be ignored so easily now. Worst of all, the more he tried not to wish Miss Deene would fall down a deep hole, the more it was written all over his face that he did. Miss Deene's cool glance certainly showed that she read it there, and that she strongly declined to act on the suggestion.

However, here the three of them were, in the public gardens of Chapel Field; a pleasant green spot with the tower of St Peter Mancroft peeping benignly over the trees, and the bustle of the old city held at a comfortable distance. A pleasant spot, indeed, for a leisurely walk, when the weather was fine; tolerable, perhaps, when not fine, if you had an umbrella, as both Catherine and Miss Deene had, and if the rain was not heavy. John had no umbrella; and the rain was now coming down so hard that the spring flowers were drooping their heads to the earth, as if they regretted ever having come up. But if anything was more remarkable than the way the rain seemed to concentrate itself on John, and plastered his hair to his skull, and coursed down his face, and dripped from his nose, and turned his grey coat black and his white trousers grey, it was the way he betrayed no consciousness of the rain at all, and contrived to give the impression that he was promenading the gardens under the balmiest sky that ever summer gloried in.

Catherine, of course, had an umbrella, and they would surely have shared it – if they had been alone. But to have done so with Miss Deene present would have been such an underlining of that lady's supplementary role that they both baulked at it; and so they carried on as they were. But that Catherine was conscious of a certain awkwardness about the proceedings was clear from the way she burst into a tremendous flow of talk, as if to assert that she was quite as comfortable as John pretended to be.

'Well, and how did you leave your excellent parents . . .? I mean, of course, how were they when you left them, not how did you leave them in the sense of on foot or by coach or anything of that kind. How very confusing the English language must be to foreigners! I remember the mistress who taught me French – she was a very charming person, even though she had to take brandy rather often for her nerves on account of being stabbed in the neck with a knitting-needle by a mad aunt when she was a girl – well, she spoke the most fluent English but I remember her quite losing her patience with the language once and saying it was full of inexplicable expressions, like "Bring to table" and "It is coming on to rain" . . .' Catherine broke off in perplexity at this reference to something they had both been striving to ignore, and said hesitatingly, 'I think, by the way, the weather is turning a little inclement—'

'Oh, it's nothing of consequence,' said John, holding out his palm in a careless manner while the water poured from his eyebrows. 'And thank you for the inquiry – my parents were very well when I left them. I hope your family are the same?'

'Papa's a little troubled with rheumatism. He often is at this time of year – I believe it's the damp weather . . .' Catherine looked perplexed again, but as John smiled back gamely through the curtain of water, she went on, 'Mama is a little headachey too, but I think that's because of the smell of plaster and whitewash at home, for we've had decorators in, indeed that's partly why we came away to stay in Norwich, because Mama couldn't bear the upheaval and one of the workmen kept singing a song about a waterside lady and some sailors, and it was rather a pretty tune but Mama said it was more than a Christian woman could bear.'

'Augustus?' said John, suppressing an almighty shudder as a gout of rain infiltrated his shirt-collar and made a startling progress down his spine.

'He's spending the vacation with a friend from Cambridge. I think he said it was Southampton he was going to, but as he writes me that he can't see the sea

46

anywhere, I think he must have ended up in Northampton instead, and whether that's where he meant to go in the first place I'm not quite sure, he only answers "Don't fuss Kitty" when I ask him . . .'

They were by now the only people left in the gardens; and such deep puddles were forming across the path that when John stepped in one the water shot up to his knees, and he had to pass off his shout of surprise as a particularly interested 'Oh!' in reply to something Catherine said. Now, it was noticeable that throughout this Miss Deene appeared to be in some discomfort, if not actual pain: there was a hectic colour in her cheeks, and she was continually biting hard on her lower lip; and when John began trying, very creditably he thought, to shake the water out of his trouser-leg without impeding their pace or disrupting the conversation, Miss Deene's condition took a definite turn for the worse, and with tears starting from her eyes she let out a muffled yelp.

'Verity! My dear, are you ill?' Catherine said in concern.

'I'm afraid I might be, quite soon,' Miss Deene said, hiding her face in her handkerchief. 'Oh, dear . . .! There – that's better. No, Catherine, really, I shall be quite all right. But I think I shall have to go away from you for a while. No – truly, that will be the best restorative for me.' Catching sight of John's dripping fringe, she seemed to suffer another attack; but she recovered, and assuring them that she would be better soon, arranged to meet them in half an hour's time at St Peter Mancroft, and left them.

'She can be quite an unaccountable creature sometimes,' said Catherine, turning to John, 'but at heart she's . . . Oh, dear, you're soaked!'

'Not at all,' said John, 'not a bit of it.' And then, giving it up and abandoning himself to laughter, 'Yes, I am a little wet, now that you come to mention it.'

Catherine laughed too; and when she said that he must come under her umbrella, as if it were possible for him to get any wetter than he was, they laughed again, until they were out of breath. But they shared the umbrella, anyhow, and though the rain did not stop, they did not stop walking round the gardens either, and probably would have continued in their circuit until they had worn a hole in the path, like horses turning a mill.

Their time, however, ran out all too quickly. Nothing of great moment was said under the umbrella, for they were enjoying themselves too much for that; but as the moment of parting drew near, John recalled the dizzy imaginings that he had entertained on the way here, and felt that some sort of leap from the steady ground they had hitherto occupied must be made. But then as he stood there licking his lips, his tender years rose up before him, challenging him to count them, and refusing to add up to more than nineteen; and the years to come before he was qualified and able to support himself, let alone a wife, rose up likewise, and invited him to note how many they were, and what tough customers they looked; and the sheer absurdity of his standing before Catherine like something dredged up from the bottom of a pond, and beseeching her to get engaged to him in the middle of Chapel Field gardens, descended on him with a dampening effect that could not have been surpassed by twenty cloudbursts. And yet – and yet—

'John,' said Catherine, looking wonderingly up into his face, 'are you all right?'

It was the first time she had used his name thus. 'Catherine,' he burst out, 'I've missed you so!'

'Oh, I've missed you too,' she said brightly; then, frowning, 'Oh, I didn't say that right, did I? I meant to say it sadly, because it *is* sad – not seeing you, I mean; but seeing you makes me happy again, and when I'm happy that's what comes out, instead of . . . But I *am* sad now, because we've got to be parted again, and . . .'

He extracted her from this complexity with a kiss. Its effect on her seemed quite powerful, though he suspected this was partly attributable to his hair discharging its burden of water full in her face as he bent down. However, once she had dried herself with her handkerchief, they managed to laugh again; and John returning to the attack said, 'Catherine, what do your parents think of me?'

'I'm sure they think very well of you indeed, John,' she said warmly. 'I'm sure anyone would.'

Gratifying as this reply was, John grasped at a passing intuition that Catherine would always tend to give the answer that pleased, because she could not bear to give the answer that pained; and whereabouts between the two lay the truth, in this case, was difficult to guess. 'What I mean is, if I were to ask to – to pay my addresses to you—'

'Oh, John, that sounds just like someone in a play, like the one we saw in London last year where the farmer's son wanted to marry the squire's daughter and he went away to sea because he couldn't, and he became a buccaneer and came back with a Spanish bride and one leg . . .' Noticing John's somewhat despairing expression, she stopped and said in an altered tone, 'I'm sorry, John – I do know what you mean; but you see, I thought you already were. Paying your addresses, I mean. At least, you've made your feelings clear – about me, I mean: and as far as my feelings go, they're the same – about you, I mean; and so . . .'

Well, what of addresses, and engagements, and money and a profession and the years to come and all the rest of the dismal practicalities? Here, in these halting words and this soul-shaking look, was quite enough for John to be going on with; indeed, how could those dismal practicalities do anything but shrink into insignificance, after such words, and such a look, and such a kiss (first putting up her hand to his hair, and wringing it out like a dishmop) as she now gave him?

And besides, one day of the half-holiday remained to him, and they could meet again tomorrow – a fact they had both been forgetting in the luxuriousness of emotion. It was true that tomorrow seemed like an unreachably distant shore, when John retired to the parlour-boarders' room at Mr Wenn's that night; but still his uplifted spirits must have been obvious to Stuffins, who had declined to make the journey home for the half-holiday, 'on account of the old cuss gave him such a Dutch welcome, he was as well where he was.' After watching John arranging his wet clothes before the fire, and after bestowing on him some of his most suggestive winks and grimaces, Stuffins at last said, 'Look here, Twopenny: no one's ever called me a peach.'

John, in his absent state, could not for a moment work out whether Stuffins was merely offering this as a somewhat unsurprising statement of fact, or complaining of the omission; and so he settled for 'Eh?'

'You're a sly one,' said Stuffins admiringly. 'Sly, old man. I like it. Pretty fast, I call it. But come – you know I don't peach, don't you? Least of all to old Wenn. Oh, no. It's not peach *he'll* be getting from me, I'll tell you that, but it'll be . . .' Stuffins cast about for a suitable figure. 'But it'll be juicy, I can tell you that. Oh yes! Pretty juicy.' He was so pleased with this that he repeated it several times, making a few boxer's feints as he did so. 'Well! You see what I mean. I'm not a fellow to go tattling tales to Wenn, am I? So: what I want to ask is – bearing in mind, Twopenny, that I don't peach, and you can tell me in confidence – did you meet the lady today?' This with such a strenuous wink that Stuffins quite made his own eyes water.

'Yes, I did,' said John readily. 'And we're going to meet again tomorrow.'

Stuffins let out a long, hushed, almost inaudible whistle. 'Thought so,' he said. 'Have to admit, I thought as much, but even so . . . damned fast I call it, Twopenny. Devilish strong stuff. I like it. Meeting twice in two days, eh? Phew. Twice in two days, eh? Well, well, this will be a pretty memorable half-holiday for you, old chap, and no mistake.'

John did not doubt it; and as he gazed at some bewitching visions of the future that had got themselves into the fire, and did a merry dance for him down among the flames, he did not suspect the memories of these past few days as having any potential for pain, or that they might be the last of their gentle kind.

CHAPTER FIVE

No Place

'Ho, miss – so this is where you are! With your nose in a book, as usual.'

The speaker was Admiral Fernhill, coming into the library at Buttings Court where Verity Deene was reading. He stumped over to the table where the newspapers were set out, and taking up one that he often commended for its sound common sense, meaning that it pandered to his prejudices, he glanced at the spine of the book she was reading.

'Milton, eh?' he said, wagging his lustrous head with as much complacency as if he had ever read a line of him. 'Heavy stuff for a Saturday morning, isn't it?'

For a woman, you mean, Verity silently corrected him; providing herself meanwhile with the deferential smile that the admiral expected to see on the faces of young ladies whom he honoured with his company.

'I'll tell you something about Milton,' said the admiral. 'You've heard, I dare say, of the Civil War of England? Oh, yes, we had a Civil War, you know, many years ago . . .' This with particular smugness, as if a Civil War were like a constitution or a steam-engine, and there was a certain pride attached to having it first. 'It was between the king and parliament,' the admiral went on, taking his ease in his own amply cushioned chair, 'or, if you like, between the Cavaliers and the Roundheads. That's a simpler way of putting it, you know, my dear.'

Verity looked her gratitude for his kindness in thus framing his lecture in terms fir for her feminine brain.

'Now your precious Milton, miss – and here is something that I think will surprise you – was of the Roundhead party. The followers of Cromwell, you know.' There was so much condescension in the admiral's explanatory tone that he turned the great man's name into Crom Well, and made him sound like a Scottish beauty spot. 'What do you think of that?'

Good heavens! I never knew! How clever you are, Admiral! And there was I thinking that the author of Paradise Lost *was the Queen of Sheba's butler!* Verity's habit of internalizing the replies she really wanted to make was so ingrained that they sounded in her ears quite as plainly as if she had said them out loud; but she took care that her face betrayed nothing of what was going on within her, and merely added a look of genteel surprise to the smile.

'In fact,' continued the admiral, 'the Civil War, I regret to say, culminated in the execution of the king. And I am afraid that your precious Milton – and I think this will surprise you, my dear – was one of those who put his name to the king's death warrant.'

It took all Verity's considerable resources of self-control not to scream out at this idiotic falsehood, fly at the admiral with the anchor-chain mounted on the wall above her, and throttle him with it. But even though she mastered this urge, she still could not help saying, as politely as possible, 'Well, I have read a little about Milton, sir, and I have never seen that fact mentioned.'

The admiral's chin went up sharply, as if he saw Contradiction tacking into view on the horizon, and were preparing to blow it out of the water.

'And I understand,' Verity went on, 'that he lived well on into the Restoration, which hardly seems likely if—'

'Now, now, my dear,' said the Admiral, very red, 'I think you're muddling yourself now. The Restoration, now, that's an entirely different period. That, you know, was when we all became Protestants, which is a different thing altogether.'

Verity was too dumbfounded to say anything; but she had wild visions of painting the word REFORMATION on a wooden sign, and then beating the admiral over his shining head with it. Admiral Fernhill, meanwhile, taking her silence to mean that she submitted to his superior knowledge, settled his chin in his cravat again and said, 'Yes, that's what it is, my dear. You're getting a little muddled. You must have been reading about some other poet, you know. Shakespeare, perhaps.' In his renewed condescension he renamed the poet Shakes Spear, as if he were a stage direction.

'Yes,' said Verity, clenching her fists, 'that's probably what it was.' Her anger subsided into mischief. 'Yes, that's what it must have been. I'm very fond of Shakespeare – *She Stoops to Conquer* is my especial favourite.'

'Well, now,' said the admiral, pompously considering, 'I don't feel that's his greatest work, you know. Not of the highest class, as Shakespeare goes – but certainly, excellent as a lighter specimen, for ladies' reading.'

'Oh, yes, indeed. Well, I shall lay the Milton down. I cannot continue to read a book written by a regicide, can I?' She gave the admiral a straight look, daring him to admit that he did not know what the word meant. He did not, of course; but still, even his stupidity could not miss the challenge in her look. She was under no illusions about Admiral Fernhill's feelings towards her, and it would have been too oppressive to her spirit, which loved truth above everything, not to have let the antagonism out into the light now and then. 'Please excuse me,' she went on, 'I have letters to write.'

'Ah? Good, good,' said the admiral, who was now so dreadfully red in the face that he might have been hanging up by his heels all morning, and just that moment been cut down. 'You mentioned, I believe, an agency in London which undertakes to find suitable positions for young ladies in your circumstances?'

'For young ladies who are to be governesses,' she said. 'Yes.'

'Good, good. Well, I am sure, my dear, you are neglecting no opportunity of furthering your prospects in that direction, so I won't keep you from your letter-writing.'

'Thank you, sir.' As she went to the door she smiled ruefully to herself; for though she could beat the admiral in every contention short of fisticuffs (and would not have minded having a try at that), he always held the weapon of her humiliating dependence in reserve, and she was helpless against it.

Milton and King Charles . . . Shakespeare and *She Stoops to Conquer* . . . Whatever would her father have said, she wondered, to these latest imbecilities of the admiral's? But she swiftly concluded that her father would not, alas, have said anything, at least not to Admiral Fernhill's face. The late Mr Deene had been a scholarly man, a generous man, and an admirable man; but he had also been a timid man, who had entirely lacked the thrustfulness of his distant nautical relation, and had spent his whole life as a clerk for the Excise, dying at last at his desk and probably, Verity thought with a wry pain, apologizing with his last breath for spilling the ink. Timidity would have inhibited him from telling Admiral Fernhill what a ridiculous booby he was, just as dependence inhibited Verity; but she was also compelled to admit that her father would not even have inwardly mutinied as she did, so strongly developed were both his tolerance and his humility. 'We must make allowances,' was his repeated injunction, 'we must always make allowances, my dear'; and dearly though she had loved her father, and acutely though she missed him still a year after his death, she held to the firm opinion that there was a strong link between the making of allowances and the taking of liberties.

However, there was nothing to be done but swallow her feelings down; though she occasionally turned to another method of relieving them, which was to invent an appropriate punishment for whoever had roused her anger, and spend a therapeutic few minutes contemplating it. This she did as she crossed the hall, pausing for a while before the huge portrait of Admiral Fernhill as if lost in admiration, but actually imagining the original of that likeness being placed a short jacket and pantaloons and sent to the strictest, most brutal school that his beloved country boasted, there to be caned daily, set horrendous exercises, and so relentlessly tormented as a dunce by the boys that his life was a burden to him. Having refreshed herself thus, she went in search of some place at Buttings where she would be welcome. Her own room, being hardly more than a garret, was not encouraging; and she knew better than to intrude upon the sitting-room where Mrs Fernhill received her morning visitors – the assembled old hens laying their addled eggs of gossip with an intolerable amount of clucking, and Mrs Fernhill tending, if she noticed Verity at all, to greet her with an absent 'Oh! you're here, are you?', while the rest of the coop fixed her with their beady eyes, and seemed to mark her down as a broiler whom the farmer was going to come for very soon. So she sought out Catherine, whom she found still finishing her unpacking, in typically disorganized fashion, for they had come back to Buttings from Norwich early yesterday.

'I sent the maid away,' Catherine confided to her, removing a bundle of papers from one of her boxes, 'because I didn't want her to see these.'

'What on earth can they be?'

'Why – John's letters, of course.'

'Oh! I see. For a moment I thought, judging by the length, that it was a manuscript translation of the Bible, with notes and commentary.'

'Now don't be satirical, Verity,' Catherine said, 'because I know you don't mean it. John writes such charming letters! I hate to imagine what he thinks of my scrawls.'

'You know as well as I do that he puts them all under his pillow, though how he manages to rest his head on such a heap I don't know.'

This was said in Verity's usual pawky fashion; and yet there was a harsher note in it too. Catherine heard it; and looking up in surprise she said, 'Verity – do you think we're *very* foolish?'

'I don't think you're foolish at all,' said Verity quickly, pressing her hand. 'And as for John Twopenny – well, he has fallen in love with you, and there's nothing very foolish about that. Quite the reverse.'

Catherine looked shyly pleased; but stealing another glance at Verity's averted face she said hesitantly, 'Do you – do you really not like him, Verity?'

'Good heavens, it's of no consequence what I think,' said Verity, taking up some crumpled lace of Catherine's and smoothing it. 'I'm not being maudlin, my dear – just truthful – when I say that my opinion, however you look at it, is entirely irrelevant.'

'It isn't to me,' Catherine said gently.

Verity met her eyes and smiled. 'I'm sorry. I shall cut off my own head with this sharp tongue of mine one of these days, and serve me right. But you're too soft with me, Catherine – you are! When I get in these ill humours, you ought to take the longest, sharpest pin from your dressing-table, and stick me with it.'

'Oh, I couldn't do that,' said Catherine seriously. 'It would hurt, you know. But I do value your opinion, Verity – you know I do: you're clever, and you see things clearly . . .'

'Do I?' said Verity, in an almost inaudible murmur.

'Yes, you do; and I would hate to think that you don't like John. And sometimes I think that you don't like him, and I can't tell why.'

Verity was silent for a moment, mechanically smoothing the lace; and then answered, 'Well, you shouldn't worry about it, Catherine, because I *don't* like people, as a rule. Oh, no, I don't,' she added crisply, as Catherine was about to protest. 'I used to try to like them, because it seemed to be expected of a person, and I thought I had better make the effort; but I soon found it wasn't worthwhile, except in special cases. And you wouldn't believe how much easier life is, once you've made that decision, and are not continually burdened with the duty of liking people! And as for John Twopenny, he amuses me – he amuses he very much, you know, and that's quite near enough to liking, by my standards.'

Catherine's look seemed to suggest that she was not quite convinced; but she merely said, 'Well . . . I'm glad you don't hate him, at least.'

'Hate him? How could I hate a young man with whom I can have such splendid arguments? And besides, Catherine – and I am being quite serious now, and not bemoaning my lot – you know that my opinion really *won't* matter for very much longer, simply because sooner or later I shall have to go away.'

'Oh, Verity, don't say that!' cried Catherine; but after a glance at Verity's sober face, she nodded. 'I know,' she said. 'I know that's what – what's been agreed. And I know you're ready to do it. But perhaps – perhaps I can make Papa see—'

'No, no,' said Verity, holding up a hand. 'It's not up to you to make your father see anything. I have no claim on him, except the claims of a distant kinship which he is quite right in feeling he has already fulfilled, in giving me temporary shelter; and besides, round about the time I decided that I wasn't going to go out of my way to like people, I also took it into my head to be a proud little baggage, and though some might say I've little enough to be proud about, I've stuck to it, and there it is. And besides again, there are worse things than being a governess, you know, Catherine – it's not as if I'm to be a chimney-sweep; and your father has undertaken to give me very good references.'

'But still, we shall be away from one another,' said Catherine sadly, 'unless—'

'Unless a position can be found nearer to Buttings,' said Verity. 'Which would be very nice. But truly, it looks as if my best chance is in being thrown on the London market, because it might be an age before any position becomes vacant in this part of the world, and your father . . . well, your father of course wants to see me settled.'

'I wish I were married!' said Catherine, after studying Verity with beautiful melancholy for some moments.

'Why, my dear? – apart from the obvious, I mean.'

'Well, when I marry I come into some money from my grandfather; and so if I was married I could give the money all to you, and you wouldn't have to go and be a governess.'

'Thank you for the kind thought,' Verity said laughing, 'but I think you had better consider first what your husband would say to your giving away your fortune to a poor relation.'

'Oh, Verity, you don't mean to suggest that John—'

'No, no,' Verity said emphatically, 'that is one thing I definitely acquit him of. In fact I would take my oath that your wealth or otherwise has never even entered into his head. I suspect he's altogether too . . . romantic for that. But what's this, what's this? I mention husbands, and immediately the name of John Twopenny springs to your lips. Speak out, now, Catherine: consider yourself in the witness-box. Was a proposal, or anything of that kind, offered under the shelter of that umbrella?'

'Oh – well, no . . . not really . . . I mean, we're very young, and I couldn't consider anything like that at present,' said Catherine, becoming suddenly very brisk about the unpacking of the bundle of letters, and dropping the whole lot in the process.

'Here, let me,' said Verity. 'Oh, don't worry, I shan't look at them. Well, my dear, if we *were* in a court of law, you would certainly be held to have convicted yourself out of your own mouth.'

'I do like him,' said Catherine.

'Of course,' said Verity; and something very different from Catherine's smile of uncomplicated excitement passed momentarily over her face, and over her spirit too. 'Well!' she went on, shaking the something off, 'as you say, you are both young, and have lots of time before you.'

'Yes . . . but I've been wondering whether I ought to tell Mama, at least, about John and I writing to one another. Not the meeting, perhaps – but the writing. I suppose she ought to know.'

'Well, if you want to be *very* proper about it. But really, with such a very . . . enthusiastic correspondence, I would be surprised if your mother didn't know already.' Though now she came to think of it, Verity thought it quite likely that Mrs Fernhill hadn't noticed a thing; for that lady's head was not of the roomiest, and anyone attempting to squeeze any idea into it between adoration of her husband and concern over her dress would have had to work like a beaver.

Catherine persisting in her uneasiness over this, however, Verity at last agreed that something should be said to Mrs Fernhill which would remove any taint of secrecy from the lovers' proceedings, and went with her to offer moral support. The hens had by now fluttered off to their several roosts, and Mrs Fernhill was discovered alone, gone broody over the latest fashion-paper from London, and cropfull of longing for a new bonnet – or rather, newer than the one she had bought last week. It was as Verity had feared: once Mrs Fernhill had established that what Catherine had to say did not refer directly either to herself or the admiral, she became serenely vague.

'I'm sure I don't know, my dear,' was her reply when Catherine asked her whether corresponding with a young man, known to the family and of unimpeachable reputation, was as a general rule reprehensible. 'I really don't know anything about it, I'm sure!'

'Well, Mama, if I was to correspond with Mr Twopenny – you remember, we dined with his family – that would be all right, wouldn't it?'

'My dear Catherine, I really don't know why you're bothering me in this way, and talking to me about Mr Fourpenny – I don't suppose for a moment *he's* going to help me to a new bonnet after the fashion shown here, and neither will the milliners in Norwich, I'll be bound! Really, sometimes one might as well be living at the North Pole, for all the little comforts one can procure in this county!'

'I think what Catherine is trying to say is that she wouldn't wish to do anything that you might disapprove of,' put in Verity, 'and if, for example, in your day—'

'Oh! In my day everything was quite different, my dear,' Mrs Fernhill cooed, with an airy wave of her hand. 'You may not believe it, but we wore the most tremendous leg-of-mutton sleeves, and I went to my first evening party in a gown that fell straight as a candlestick with absolutely no fullness at all—'

'But, Mama, is it all right?' said Catherine. 'The – connection with Mr Twopenny, I mean.'

'My dear, I really don't know anything about it, I'm sure, and I mustn't be bothered in this way, or I don't know what will happen!' cried Mrs Fernhill fretfully, fanning herself with the fashion-paper. It was her habit, when threatened by intimations that life consisted of more than clothes and complacency, to retreat into these sibylline hints of disaster; though as far as Verity could see, nothing ever did happen, except that whoever was bothering her gave up and beat a retreat. As Catherine did; though it was quite typical of Catherine likewise that she did not consider the encounter unsatisfactory, and said brightly to Verity afterwards, 'Well, I'm glad that's cleared up; I shall feel easier in my mind now.'

Verity could not help feeling fond of Catherine, even if there was occasionally an element of despair in the affection; and there was little to dislike in Augustus, who was generally as benign as his dimness allowed him to be. But in essence it was Catherine alone who made Buttings Court tolerable to her; and even had Admiral Fernhill not made it so plain that the home offered her here was only a temporary expedient until she could provide for herself, Verity would still have considered it as something to be escaped from, and the sooner the better. She was quite ready to admit that her upbringing had made of her a too awkwardly-shaped peg to fit into any conventional hole: losing her mother early, she had been raised entirely by an intellectual father who had educated her himself, and educated her far more fully than was considered needful for young ladies; whilst of the practical side of life, which Mr Deene had never comprehended, she had early been mistress by necessity. In her memories of her first spelling-book, A was certainly an Apple-pie, but B, in the Deene edition, was a Bill, and an unpaid one at that; and she had a hazy recollection that B had also been, at one time, a Bailiff. Not that she would have changed anything about her earlier life; but she recognized that it had made of her a curious compound which was not wholly to the tastes of polite society, and which she had to adulterate with watery convention in order not to be thought – as Mrs Fernhill had once referred to her – 'a peculiar bluestocking sort of girl – no conversation!' So, she was accustomed to feeling out of place; but she had never felt more so than at Buttings Court.

There was her lowly status, for one thing; and though the admiral had not gone so far as to make her wear around her neck a placard saying POOR RELATION, she sometimes suspected that only his own vanity had conquered the inclination. She would have eaten her diet of humble-pie with a more ready appetite if she could have found anything in her benefactor, or in the way of life to which he was allowing her temporary access, which elicited esteem and respect; but, Catherine's kindness of heart and sweetness of temper excepted, Verity saw nothing at Buttings Court which justified her existing in a permanent state of grovelling thankfulness. Admiral and Mrs Fernhill had been so successful in continuing to live while their close kinfolk died that they had garnered, by diligent inheriting, a fair fortune; which added to the rewards tendered to the admiral by his grateful countrymen, enabled them to live in style – the country style, at present. For though the Fernhills had of necessity resided long in London – and even, very occasionally, at sea-ports – it was the life of a country gentleman of leisure that had always attracted the admiral, and which he had eagerly taken to on acquiring Buttings Court. And so it was the values, beliefs and manners of county society that prevailed there, and those same values, beliefs and manners that enfolded Verity Deene like a suffocating cloud, and made her feel that the life of a governess was not such a bad prospect after all.

It was not the country itself that she objected to. The fresh air, the proximity of the sea, the landscape – all these she appreciated; and there was nothing about farming, or sea-fishing, or the people who carried on these occupations, that repelled her, or roused in her anything but interest and respect. But country living as practised at Buttings, she found, did not include these things. When the admiral and his wife mentioned a certain hamlet along the coast, and remarked that there was no one there, they did not imply that it was a ghostly deserted settlement; they meant that there was no one there who had a billiard-room, or paid calls, or shot game, or went out for that peculiar purposeless thing called a 'drive', which entailed dressing up like a peacock, having the carriage made ready, having the horses groomed, getting into the carriage, rattling slowly up and down such of the local lanes as were fit for wheeled traffic, coming back, having the whole apparatus put away, having the horses groomed, and then changing clothes all over again.

But it was a ritual, and sanctified; as sanctified as those everlasting dinners, where 'the poacher' was the one great theme of conversation, coming in, as it were, with the fish, and remaining on the table even after the desserts and the ladies had been taken away, and being picked at by the gentlemen over their port until there was nothing left of him. Sanctified, too, were the cards after dinner, the ladies being granted the inestimable privilege of watching the gentlemen play – an occupation which Verity privately compared, in point of entertainment, with watching a dog chew a bone. Sanctified likewise, the ladylike sewing after breakfast, and the resolute avoidance of such awkward questions as what was to be done with these little fandangles of embroidery when they were finished; sanctified, most sanctified of all, the endless leisure, unfilled, unappreciated, and turned to no worthwhile account whatsoever.

About the morning walks which Verity and Catherine took there was somewhat less of sanctity, perhaps because walking might be taken to mean that you lacked the means to ride; but Verity liked them better than anything at Buttings. Often they walked into Hales-next-the-sea, a distance of only a mile or so, but a world away in its atmosphere; for here all was purposeful activity, and from its smoking chimneys and busy shops, from its coal-drays and beer-drays, from its warehouses and granaries and its tall ships loading and unloading, Verity took refreshment and heart.

Catherine liked going there too; though Verity did not have to follow the direction of her eyes to know that those whitewashed signs bearing the name TWOPENNY which adorned the town had much to do with the attraction. It was part of Catherine's charm, however, that she believed herself to be as opaque as she was transparent; and when she at last remarked on the signs, she spoke as if she had only just noticed them.

'Oh, look – S. Twopenny and Son,' she said casually. 'That must be John's uncle, I suppose.'

'Why do you suppose that?' said Verity.

'Hm? Oh – well, I think he mentioned to me that he had an uncle at Hales. I wonder if he is like John's father in looks? The two families don't get on, apparently. The uncle's quite a fierce solitary old man, very strict in his religion, and dreadfully hard on his children, his son especially—'

'Quite detailed, for a mention,' said Verity.

'Now, Verity, don't be dry. I can't help but be curious . . . Though I must confess I can't imagine such a grim person resembling Dr Twopenny at all. John's father's such a kind, gentlemanly man – isn't he?'

'He certainly seems so.'

'There – not even you, who can be so hard on people, can find anything to say against Dr Twopenny,' Catherine said triumphantly.

'No,' said Verity, 'no, I can't.'

'You know, it's curious seeing John's name written up everywhere in such large letters,' said Catherine as they took the road out of the town. 'And yet not, in a way because I – you'll laugh at me, but somehow it seems . . .'

'It seems as if you are always seeing his name written in large letters, everywhere you go,' supplied Verity.

'Why, yes! That's exactly it . . . How did you know?'

Verity smiled, and pressed her hand. 'Because I know everything, my dear,' she said briskly, 'I learnt it all from books.' And she made Catherine laugh all the way home, with an account of the hunting young gentleman who had sat next to her at dinner yesterday, and who had asked her in a serious voice whether Italy was in Rome, or Rome in Italy; and by being as salty and lively as she knew how, she got the rising melancholy down again, and nailed the trapdoor shut.

Yes, the walks, and the company of Catherine, were sweet; but much in Verity's current mode of life was not so, and left such a bitter taste that she looked forward to quitting it, and taking up that traditional occupation of dispensable young ladies. She had already registered her name and references with an agency office in London, which dealt wholesale, retail and for export in governesses, tutors and nursemaids; and she awaited the issue of her destiny with tolerable composure.

That is to say, she tried to; and was, on the whole, successful. Only sometimes when she lay sleepless at night, in her room at the top of the house where the wind howled and the timbers creaked and the night was black and lonely, did she allow herself to dwell on other visions of what might have been and what might be – or rather, was unable to stop herself doing so, no matter how hard she hammered down that trapdoor. And then she was restless, and the stoical philosophy that had always been her standard revealed itself as a little tattered and threadbare. It had long been her conviction that if the moon was to be obtained at all (a doubtful proposition in any event), it was certainly not to be obtained by crying for it; but in those sleepless hours the argument lost its force, and she even found herself making that lunar transaction, and enjoying the silvery goods in her dreams. She reproached herself very much for this; not only because such fancifulness was foreign to all her beliefs, but because its principal effect on her was to make her extremely unhappy.

After all, she pursued, what place could the heart, with all its vulnerable vagaries, be expected to have in the life that lay ahead of her? No place, came the firm answer. There was no place for it at all. And so she really must look smart with the hammer and nails, whenever the trapdoor showed the slightest signs of lifting. The dreams and fancies of the night did not belong – had no place, in fact – in the grey, commonplace daylight that was to be her perennial lot.

Yet even leaving aside her hopeless secret – which made her avert her eyes from those giant whitewashed letters as pointedly as Catherine looked at them – there was something else that complicated matters, and prevented her from wholly reconciling herself to the schoolroom and the stipend. There was always, of course, a theoretical alternative for women in her position, and that was to marry; but Verity had never regarded herself as a fascinator, and was besides, as she often half-playfully asserted, very difficult to please, and did not expect to come across a man who could meet her standards. Moreover, hard-headed as she undoubtedly was, the idea of considering marriage in the cold light of a financial prospect guaranteeing so much security per annum was repugnant to her. But she had not expected this theoretical alternative to present itself to her in practice – but such was undoubtedly the case, as spring ushered in summer, and ushered in a suitor in the shape of Mr Flowers, the solicitor.

Suitor, perhaps, was rather a romantic word. All that had happened, since that Christmas party at Beacon House when he had danced with her, was that Mr Flowers had focused his general amiability on her – had been, in the mincing phrase of society, particular in his attentions. When he called at Buttings – which was frequently – he sought her out: when they were both present at social occasions, he sought her out likewise. He did not act the lover; but as a man who was usually as prosaic and detached in human relations as his profession would suggest, he left no room for doubt about what this exception to his rule signified. Verity knew it; and Catherine had observed it too, and sometimes gently rallied her about it.

'Mr Flowers was very complimentary about your playing again,' she would say. 'And it was not empty compliment either – he really seemed quite transfixed as he listened to you tonight!'

'I saw him with his chin on his hand,' Verity said, 'and I rather fancy he was asleep.'

But she could not laugh it off, and she saw that it would not do to laugh it off. Mr Flowers, in his sleepy-eyed and phlegmatic way, was serious. Why he had fixed on her she did not know. They certainly did not pour out their hearts to each other in wild torrents of words, Mr Flowers being content in the main to let her make the conversation, and throw in the odd laconic remark here and there; but it was plain that he listened, and that whatever he heard he liked sufficiently to contemplate hearing it on a permanent basis, and in a permanent relation. For when he did talk, he talked much of his house at Sheringham along the coast, and of his domestic circumstances, and of his two little daughters, and of how he would like Verity to meet them. It would be too much to say that in speaking thus he was advertising a vacancy, and suggesting that the post was hers if she cared to apply – Mr Flowers was not so prosaic as all that; rather, what he was doing was carefully laying before her all the facts of the case, like an honest lawyer, and she, like an honest jury, was to be left to consider her verdict.

The facts of the case were straightforward. Mr Flowers was a widower of forty, an educated man whose manners were unassuming and pleasant, whose integrity was a byword, and whose facial resemblance to the less excitable canine breeds was by no means without a certain worldly charm. He was in possession of a good income, and owned a modest house overlooking the sea which all who had seen it were agreed was a model of discreet comfort and taste. All these he was prepared to bestow – he had not yet said so, but had made it clear that he was going to unless given unequivocal discouragement – on Verity Deene, who was a girl with no money or influence. And with no graces either, as Mrs Fernhill and her assembled poultry would surely add; and they would call the little minx very fortunate to get him.

The matter of love was not amongst the facts of the case, and probably counted as inadmissible evidence. Verity knew as well as she knew her own name that she did not love Mr Flowers, not in the way that poets sang of love and Cleopatras died for it; she had, alas, her own all too cogent reasons for knowing that. As for the depth of Mr Flowers' feelings for her, she could not tell. He was not at all demonstrative, and gave no sign of being unable to sleep at nights for thinking of her; but then much could be hidden behind an unemotional façade. She had, alas, her own all too cogent reasons for knowing that too.

Catherine, at any rate, greatly liked Mr Flowers, and was deeply interested in the possibility of a match. 'After all, you know, Verity,' she said one day after Mr Flowers had called, 'it's only right that you should be admired, because you deserve it; and Mr Flowers is an intelligent man, and a man of taste – just the sort of man who should appreciate you. And it's so plain that he does, my dear – I wonder when he will ask—'

'Oh, Catherine,' Verity burst out, 'please, don't say any more about it.'

Catherine looked into Verity's face. 'Oh, Verity . . . are Mr Flowers' attentions not – not welcome? I'm sorry – here have I been prattling on about him, and—'

'No, no,' said Verity, 'it isn't that. Oh, I don't know what to think. I like Mr Flowers very much, and of course a lot of girls would say that the – the life he can offer, compared with scraping a living as a governess, would be heaven, and that anyone who would pass up such a chance must be a fool. And I dare say they'd be right.'

'And I know he would appreciate you, really,' Catherine said. 'He's as true as steel. And you would be able to live life to the full, and use and enjoy all your talents. It's not as if there would be anything second-best about the arrangement, is it?'

Verity was silent for some moments: silent as she had been earlier when Catherine had read out to her an amusing passage from John's latest letter. 'No, it's not,' she said at last; but her love of truth cried out within her at this perjury, and proclaimed the lie at the heart of her situation – the lie, the lie, that she could not let out.

CHAPTER SIX

A Little More Learning

How it had come about John did not know, for there had been distractions enough, during his last term at Mr Wenn's Academy, for him to have gone backward in his education rather than forward; but as the summer matured, and the breaking-up approached, Mr Wenn pronounced himself satisfied with John's attainments. He even went so far as to say that if Mr Twopenny performed as creditably in the wider world as he had at the Academy, then a distinguished career lay ahead of him.

'Always assuming, Mr Twopenny,' Mr Wenn added, as if regretting that he had been betrayed into warmth, 'that you do not allow your intellectual and moral fibre to slacken and degenerate at this crucial juncture. It happens, sir, all too easily. Young gentlemen, on the premature assumption that they have entered upon man's estate, often take a plunge into dissipation, and forever endure the consequences.'

Even if John had contemplated a plunge into dissipation, however, he scarcely had the means to do it. Though he received a monthly allowance from his father, by way of Mr Wenn, it had not been forthcoming this month; but he had a little left over from the previous sum, and supposing the matter to have slipped Mr Wenn's mind, he thought little of it.

John's only indulgence, indeed, was to spend more time at the Norfolk and Norwich Hospital, where he had begun making notes for his own use on the treatment of typhus. Now that his enrolling as a medical student was in sight, his enthusiasm took fresh fire within him; and in his dreams he was already hurling down medical officer's reports before parliament like a scientific Moses, and striking those complacent authorities dumb with the force of his arguments.

Trailing fragments of such dreams behind him, he came down to breakfast one brilliant summer morning in such high spirits that even the long wait for Mr Wenn to hand over his letters seemed a tolerable prospect. He was confident that there would be letters, for Catherine's correspondence was unfailing, and it was besides some time since his last letter from home. An unusually long time, indeed, though he had thought little of it; and longer since his mother had written, such communications as he had received from Saltmarsh being penned solely by his father. But he had thought little of that too.

No letters: a glance at the space beside Mr Wenn's plate confirmed the disappointing fact. A glance at Mr Wenn's face, and John's disappointment became puzzlement. His tutor bent a heavy frown upon him, and his greeting was barely audible; and John wondered whether he had transgressed in some way – whether, perhaps, he had taken a plunge into dissipation without knowing it.

Stranger still, Mrs Wenn lacked her usual aquiline self-possession, and spilt some tea in pouring; whilst the infant she-Wenn, after lisping a few tentative remarks about the Augustinian conversion, lapsed into silence, and to John's astonishment looked as if she were going to burst into childlike tears. What could it mean?

58

Mr Wenn ate even less than usual; and he very soon pushed away his plate, and in a tone of voice of which John could make nothing except that it was quite unlike him, said, 'Mr Twopenny, after you have breakfasted, will you step into my study, and favour me with a word or two? No hurry, my dear sir – no hurry. At your convenience, Mr Twopenny.'

Greatly wondering, John declared himself ready at once, and followed Mr Wenn into his study; and just before the door was shut behind him, he was certain that he heard Mr Wenn's daughter break into a sob – a sound he no more expected to hear from that firm-minded little girl than a donkey's bray. What could it mean?

'Please, Mr Twopenny, be seated. Be easy, sir,' said Mr Wenn, still in that tone of voice which John could not place; and as John sat, his bafflement was compounded by Mr Wenn's reaching out his long, bony hand, and patting his shoulder.

'You may have wondered, Mr Twopenny,' said Mr Wenn, not sitting himself, but pacing about in an uncharacteristically vague fashion, 'at the fact that there is no correspondence for you today.' Mr Wenn stopped pacing, and stood hunched over his desk. 'In fact, there is a letter for you. It is here.' He placed his finger on a packet that lay on the desk. John stared at it; then stared at Mr Wenn. 'The letter . . . the letter is from your father. It was brought here by a person from the village where your – the village that is your home. There is a covering letter with it, addressed to me by your father, and entreating me as a kindness to take you aside, and prepare you, before delivering the letter into your hands.' Mr Wenn paused, licking his pale lips. 'This office . . . this duty . . . I hope I can discharge. John . . .'

Unthinkable, the austere and lofty Mr Wenn calling him by his first name! So commented John's mind inconsequently, as it began to slide into the abyss, and as Mr Wenn picked up the letter.

'John, I believe you to possess, at need, great strength of mind. Exercise it now, my dear sir. If it is in your power – and I am sure it is – then exercise it now.'

The morning sunlight, streaming through the narrow window of Mr Wenn's study, cut the room into two distinct spaces, one as bright as outdoors, the other closed up and shadowy. John was seated in the bright portion; and Mr Wenn stepped into it, to put the letter in his hands, and then withdrew into the shadowy half, with an effect as if he were leaving John quite alone.

My dear son,

I am not able to give you this news in any way that will not come as the profoundest shock to you. And if I could, it would not be true to the event. John, we have received a blow which there is no softening. Your poor mother is dead.

I have had to stop for a space after writing these last words, and even now I cannot think what to add to them. As I said, there is no softening the blow. And I see – at present I see no recovering from it.

O John I could not save her. I deserve – I do not know what I deserve – some punishment I cannot guess at. I am a doctor, and should save. I should do all in my power to save the meanest wretch that has life. What then should I not do for the sweetest and gentlest of women, the light and grace of my very existence. —Believe me that I would have given my life. Believe me that I tried – but that is no matter. I could not save her, John, and can only hope that she suffered as little as she seemed to at the end.

My dear boy, there was no time for you to have seen her, or even for me to have alerted you to what was coming. The progress of her affliction was so swift – what seemed merely a case of the chills and agues that are so frequent in our damp part of the world – God curse me that I ever brought her to it! – developed rapidly into a malignant quotidian fever, and almost before I apprehended the seriousness of her condition, respiratory problems set in, and the strain upon her poor heart . . . Well, she was taken from us, this very afternoon – so quickly; and I pray God, peacefully

59

at last. I hardly need tell you that she was brave and patient; for that is simply to say, she was Emma – she was all that you and I knew her to be.

I have had to stop again, and recover myself. But it is you I should be thinking of now, John – you I must try to give comfort to. But there is nothing to say, my dear boy. You need not me to tell you that you have lost the best of mothers. All I can do is send you a father's love. Be strong, my son; and be sure that your name was on her lips as she went away, and that she left the tenderest love for you behind her, as she left the sweetest memory in the hearts of all who knew her.

I send you this letter by Ethan Meacham, who has offered to take it to Norwich, and to bring you back home to Saltmarsh at once if you will. Mr Wenn will understand. O my dear son let me see you.

Your loving father.

John had laid the letter down, and had been gazing from the light half of the room into the dark half for some time; but only belatedly became aware that Mr Wenn was still there.

It occurred to John that he ought to thank Mr Wenn for his kindness. Something, however, stopped him speaking. Something demanded that he be still and silent, and submit himself to an onslaught of memories that came from nowhere, and advanced on him, and trampled across him one by one. Here came one of great age, which featured his mother bending over the couch where he was convalescing from an infant sickness, and displaying to him an array of little jointed figures which she had cut out from paper, and which danced on strings. Here came a memory of more recent date; his mother going a walk with him along the clifftops towards Shipden, and suddenly taking it into her head to throw off her bonnet and run at full tilt down a grassy slope – crying, as she neared the bottom, 'I can't stop – oh, John, I can't stop!' and hardly able to catch her breath for laughing. Here again was an older one, in which he stood beside his mother at the piano, and she showed him how to pick out the melody with one finger while she filled in the harmonies; now here came one that must have been about three years old, and which showed him his first evening party, when he had been too awkward and shy to dance with anyone, until his mother had taken the floor with him, saying how proud she was to do so. One after another they came, remorseless and crushing. Such memories had always been his friends: they had calmed and comforted him when he had first come to the Academy and had been lonely and homesick; but now they hurt him. He had never, indeed, known such hurt, or believed it possible.

The struggle with it, and the struggle with his throat, which burned him as if he had swallowed a live coal, left him quite helpless and immobile for a time he could only guess at; a time which Mr Wenn did not mark by any movement or sound, remaining in precisely the same posture, his arms behind him and his head bent, as if he were prepared to remain so for ever. It was looking at Mr Wenn, however, and coming to the slow and confused consciousness that this event was not confined in its effects to his own shattered mind, that stirred John into something resembling life, and brought before him the image of his father.

'Mr Wenn, I—'

His voice, despite all his efforts, failed him; but Mr Wenn turned and nodded, as if he had said all that was necessary.

'John, we are all very sorry.'

John said 'Thank you', or at least his lips formed the words. He frowned at the letter, and fought violently with the fire in his throat, and at last succeeded in saying, 'Mr Wenn, I feel I should go to my father.'

'Of course,' said Mr Wenn. 'The person who brought the letter is waiting in the parlour, and is ready to carry you back to Saltmarsh directly. As the person's conveyance is not large, I suggest we have packed only such luggage as you will need immediately, and I will have the rest forwarded by the carrier. I did not expect to be finally parting with you under such circumstances, John, but of course you must go home.'

Curious, now, the swift and careless breaking of sundry threads that, all unnoticed, had bound his life together! The room that he had shared with Stuffins, and that he had not expected to leave without at least a reminiscent pang, quickly denuded of his possessions; the friends he had made among the younger boys, parted from with a hasty word; the model ship that he had in spare moments been carving for one of the smallest and timidest, handed over with an apology for its unfinished state. All this, at least, occupied his mind in some sort, and the more rapidly performed it was, the better for his fragile self-command; but when he went into the parlour to speak to Ethan Meacham who was waiting there, he was very nearly undone. For the little old man seated in the Windsor chair with the toes of his boots just touching the floor was such a piece of Saltmarsh, and such a reviver of those marching memories, that John feared that at last the burning in his throat was going to get the better of him, and he would be lost.

Somehow, however, he won out: somehow the sight of Ethan Meacham tottering towards him did not undo him quite. Nor even did Mr Ethan's quavering assurance that he was going to drive John home in his spring-cart just as soon as he was ready, and that he was going to drive him so smooth and steady that he wouldn't feel a single jolt or bump the whole way. Whether Mr Ethan, in that helplessness which all feel before the bereaved, had hit upon this as one practical piece of consolation that he could undertake to offer, was beyond John's scope; but certainly the old man was at pains to repeat the assurance several times, even adding that if John was to feel a jolt or a bump as they went along, he was to let him know about it pretty sharpish; and the kind meaning in this was so plain to John, even in his numbed condition, that it brought him close to his undoing.

Still, he held out. He held out when Mrs Wenn came to bid him goodbye, and put her great octave-spanning hand in his, and pressed it kindly; he held out when the Wenns' little girl gave him her hand likewise, with a gravity that showed she deplored her earlier lapse. With great difficulty he managed to hold out when he said goodbye to Stuffins, who turned mute and red and cumbrous, and could not look at him; with even greater difficulty, when Stuffins ran out after him as he was going out to the drive where the spring-cart was waiting, and pressed into his coat-pocket a bottle of ale. It was a ceremonial bottle of ale, which the two of them had been saving for a ceremonial drinking at their final breaking-up; but now Stuffins urged it on John, saying in a shaky voice, 'Drink it down, Twopenny – you drink it down. It's strong stuff, you know, but *you'll* be able to take it. I never would have been able to – I'm not fast enough. But you're equal to anything, old chap – always said so.'

Still John held out; and presently he was in the Meachams' spring-cart, Mr Ethan at the reins, and heading out of Norwich under the bright summer sun. Mr Ethan knew the road pretty well, and he was easily able to make good his promise that they would go along smooth and steady, and never feel a bump or jolt the whole way. Still, the old man troubled himself a good deal about this; and whenever the sadness of his errand became intolerable to him, he burst into some reassuring remark about the road, such as, 'Here's an awk'ud turning coming up, Mr John – but don't yew worry, I've got the measure of him, and we shan't feel a thing,' or 'Smooth going here, my friend – smooth as glass all the way to Holt.'

Still John held out, even when the memories renewed their attack upon him, and came at him in wave after brutal wave. He had at least overcome his bewilderment at this; for he surmised that he was hearing the first notes of a refrain that is heard lifelong – the longing to call back a time that is gone.

61

And yet he was wildly angry – angry that time should play such tricks, and show itself so chaotic and indiscriminate. Death was the doom of all, but time should be their recompense: instead it had played false with Emma Twopenny, and run out when she was only forty years old. Forty, or forty-one? John found that he could not remember. Forty, forty-one? As he rode along the quiet lanes in the Meachams' cart, his mind beat at this question as the sun beat down on his head; until all at once he let it go, in the miserable realization that it was of no consequence. Forty or forty-one, his mother was never going to be any more than either. And at that the anger flared again, and the marching memories came at him again, and something like a coarse stone seemed to lodge itself in his heart. And yet, somehow, he held out.

The woods gathered about the road as they drew near to the coast, and formed canopies cruel in their beauty, and did heartless magic with the sunlight; and as they neared the sea, and the woods retreated again, more cruel mocking was done by the air, which was as insolently fresh as if it had never blown through sickrooms and across churchyards. And here was Saltmarsh, unchanged – of course, unchanged. The boy driving his father's cow back from the marsh pasture was not going to stop whistling because Mrs Twopenny was no more; the old dame shooing the birds from her garden-plot was not going to let the beans be plundered because the doctor was a widower. It was right that it was so. And thinking of this, John feared that he was not going to be able to hold out any longer.

Yet he did; and held out, too, when Mr Ethan turned the cart past the Meachams' own cottage, intending to continue straight up the steep lane to Dr Twopenny's house, only to find himself stopped by Old Meacham, who came hastening out into the road and motioned them to a halt. 'Bide a bit, Ethan,' he panted, 'bide a bit, and let me say a word to John before you go on. A hasty lad, my Ethan – always a hasty lad!' Old Meacham smiled feebly at John, and reaching up into the cart, gripped his hand, and held it tightly for several moments. The word that he had come out to speak, however, would not come to his lips; and after peering helplessly into John's face, he turned to his son and said sternly, 'Well, my boy, I hope you gave John a comfortable journey, and didn't lose your head. Nothing edn't fast enough for you – I know your giddy ways!'

'No, no, Dad,' said Mr Ethan, quite stung, 'I promised John he wouldn't feel a bump or a jolt the whole way – and you didn't, did you, John? Say, now, if that weren't as smooth as an ingin gooing along on tracks, because I'm concerned about it.'

John reassured him, and added with a last mustering of self-command, 'You've been very kind, Mr Ethan, and I won't put you to any more trouble – let me get down here, and walk up to the house.'

'Walk up?' said Mr Ethan. 'Why, John, don't yew be a-worried about that – the lane's a mite rough towards the top, but I'll take you up smooth – you won't feel a stone, I promise you—'

'Truly,' said John, trying to smile, 'it's not that, Mr Ethan. I'd just rather – rather not put you to any more trouble.'

'Thass no trouble,' said Mr Ethan, 'and besides, there's your luggage, you know—'

'Ethan,' said Old Meacham firmly, 'hold your clack, bor. John want to stretch his legs, and do you can't see that, you can't see nothen. We'll bring your bags up by and by,' he said to John. 'Yew go on. Give Dr Twopenny my – well, tell him old Meacham's a-thinking of him. And when you've the time, John – only when you've the time, mind! – if yew'd like to step down here, or send for me up at your house, there's a little job of measuren I'd wish to do, and for your father likewise. We shall fit you out handsomely, John, be sure of that.'

So John, thanking them again, got down from the cart, and set off up the slope.

The chimneys of his father's house stood out on the skyline as they had stood out for him a thousand times before, but never with such a direful meaning as this, and they very nearly undid him – but not quite. The ridiculous stone lions were at their old post on either side of the front door, and they very nearly undid him – but not quite. The door was open, and Tetty was there looking out for him, and the stricken expression on that normally imperturbable face very nearly undid him – but not quite.

Then John entered the house, and Tetty closed the door behind him; and at the sound of it a voice called out from the parlour – a voice that he recognized as his father's, and yet which seemed curiously shrunken, as though it issued not from so large and robust a man as the doctor, but from some such tiny, worn, and diminished a creature as Old Meacham.

'John . . .? Is that John . . .?'

'Yes, Father, it's me,' said John; and he went forward to the parlour, where a great grey head turned so eagerly at his coming, that he might have represented the last hope that remained on a blasted earth; and knowing himself to be no such thing, but only such another sufferer as this broken man starting up from his chair to greet him, John could hold out no longer, and was lost.

CHAPTER SEVEN

Blood Is Thicker Than Water, Just

She was upstairs. John faced it at last, and went up, alone: his father could not go there.

She was ghastly. John knew death, from working alongside his father and from his hospital visits: still, he was not prepared for this. The village first-and-laster had done her best, but mortality was having none of it, and insisted on its hideous rights. Randomly, John recalled the Soldier finding a body on the beach, and how he had shuddered at the thought of it; but here was no difference. His mother had been washed up on a bleak shore by a tide of unimaginable pain, and scarcely anything recognizable remained of her.

Was his father any more recognizable? John's own senses were dulled by shock and grief, and everything about him wore a strange and distorted aspect; even so, the fearful alteration in his father was obvious. Plainly, Dr Twopenny had not washed, shaved, changed his clothes or eaten in the last two days; but the most alarming change in him was what John could only identify as a sort of shrinking. His coat seemed to hang in folds about his body, and there was an odd timidity about him. In the mutual burst of grief that had broken out at their first meeting, it had been John who had supported his father, and tried to murmur words of consolation to him, and at last besought him to be calm and drink a little brandy.

This the doctor did also with a childlike obedience; but when he was recovered enough to talk, there was a wildness about him, and a feverish urgency in his speech, so that at times John could not follow him and had to ask him to slow down. 'Too much, John, too much for her. Could I not have taken better care? Care of her. Yet there seemed no harm. The carriage – the new carriage was meant for her. So she wouldn't take cold, going about so much as we did . . . Yet she enjoyed it! You see that, John? Better care . . . A better man than I, should have – should have had a better man than I.'

'Nonsense, Father,' John said. 'There is none better. I know that.'

'You know . . . What does any of us know? We grope in the dark, thinking that we see, and we see and know nothing! If I could go back . . . Oh, John, if I could go back . . .'

'Hush, hush,' John said, as his father hid his face in his hands. 'Father, I know you did all you could. I know there was nothing that could be done that was not done by you. You cannot reproach yourself, truly. It was just . . .' He hesitated, confronted by platitudes that appalled him even as he considered them. 'It was a thing – beyond us,' John said at last.

'She didn't deserve that,' Dr Twopenny said, raising his head. 'To be taken so – to be snatched away so young – so lovely – was that justice, I ask you? Was there any semblance of justice in that?'

'No, Father,' John said, for the doctor, much excited again, seemed to expect an answer. 'No justice.'

'The Meachams,' his father said, suddenly subdued again, and slumping down in his seat, 'the Meachams have been very good. Ethan came calling for his father's pills, and as soon as he heard that – as soon as he heard what had happened, he offered to go fetch you. I – I could not bear to leave her alone in the house. Not alone, of course. Tetty – she has been very good too. True as steel. But you know what I mean. I could not bear to leave her there, as if I no longer cared . . . You understand, John? But of course you do. I ramble and fret, and forget that you suffer as I. My poor boy, this is not the homecoming from school that I had hoped for you. And it is crueller for you, perhaps, so young, to suffer such a loss . . . And yet – and yet – I could not save her, John! God forbid that such a thing should ever come to you, my boy, to stand by and see . . . But no, it will not. Not like that.' His father fell silent, and appeared dazed for some moments. 'I have done nothing,' he said at length. 'Tetty has taken much on herself. There are letters to be written – and there is the funeral.' His mouth trembled. 'The funeral . . .'

'Drink some more of this, Father,' said John, mixing brandy and water. He mixed it strong, for he could tell that his father needed sleep, and in his condition only drink would summon it. His father took the glass in his hand, unseeingly; and had only raised it halfway to his lips when he paused again, and seeking John's eyes said in a tone of submissive appeal which John did not understand: 'She loved the garden-room, you know.'

'I'm sure,' said John; and remembered his last visit here, and his mother's face reflected like a beautiful mask in the garden-room windows; and felt himself to be floating away on a sea of anguish, quite beyond sight of land.

'The new carpets, and such,' went on the doctor. 'All the new things – they were for her. All for her. I would have given – given everything. And the new carriage. It stands there in the new coach-house. Came last week. We hadn't yet been out in it when she . . . That's why I ordered it – the old trap was draughty, and I feared she would take a chill. And so . . . so she must have. Mustn't she? That must have been it, mustn't it?'

'There are any number of things it might have been, Father,' John said. 'All I know is that you mustn't torture yourself in this way. No one could have been more careful of my welfare than you have been, all my life; and no one could have been more careful of Mother likewise.'

Doctor Twopenny rocked himself back and forth in his chair. 'I wonder,' he said, 'I wonder . . .'

Presently John's prescription took effect, and Dr Twopenny slept an exhausted sleep where he sat. John had a few words alone with Tetty.

'He've been distracted ever since it happened,' Tetty said. 'I never saw a man so.' Tetty's eyes were red; but she scrubbed at them viciously, as if to wipe away the fact rather than the tears. She had done her grieving privately, she seemed to say, and it was her own business. 'Well, I've got your room ready, Mr John. You're back permanent-like, I suppose?'

'I suppose,' said John. 'My time was nearly up at Mr Wenn's anyway.' It all seemed an inexpressibly long time ago.

The curate of the parish came calling later, and Dr Twopenny having woken by then, the arrangements for the funeral were made, and a date set for it two days hence. In the evening John persuaded his father to swallow a little food, and mixed him more brandy. The Doctor was vague and random in his talk, but without that alarming wildness, and soon, as John had hoped, exhaustion overcame him again. John helped him to bed, and stayed by him until he was sleeping. Then he retired to his own room. Tib the cat was there, and he scratched her cheek for a while as his mother used to do; but his touch was not the same, and presently Tib left him.

There was thunder out at sea that night. John lay in bed listening to it for some time, with the covers thrown back in the oppressive warmth; and at last got up and stood in his shirt at the window, seeking a breeze, and watching the lightning that haunted the horizon with curious half-hidden flickerings, as if there were great mountains and ridges in the sky, and a battle raging on the other side of them.

In the morning his father was more himself, if subdued, and declared his intention of writing the necessary letters to relatives and friends. The weather continued hot and airless. Outdoors no gulls were a-wing, and the sea beyond the marsh was like a sultry lake. Within the house there was a papery quietness that was quite as conspicuous as a hubbub of noise. There were many things to be said between John and his father, but they did not extend beyond the immediate concerns of the funeral. The harsh recognition that life must go on was postponed; just as nature outside the windows seemed to be breathlessly suspended, so all was suspended within the Twopenny household, and awaited some cathartic clearing of the air.

One practical matter, however, did assert itself: a small matter, as it seemed. Tetty came to speak to John about it, when his father was resting.

'It's the jobsman,' she said. 'Wittling about his wages again. The old monkey tricks. I'd say wait a day or two, but he say he've waited already.'

The house had never had a live-in male servant; instead over the years a succession of day-labourers had done the stable and garden work. Tetty, in her prickly way, had always refused to use their names, or refer to them as anything but 'the jobsman', viewing them all as one composite creature incorrigibly inclined to Monkey Tricks.

'I suppose Father forgot,' John said. 'Well, best not to disturb him now. I'll get the key to the bureau and pay the man myself. How much is owing?'

'One pound fifteen shillen,' said Tetty, and added at John's look of surprise, 'It's right enough, I'm afraid. I know what he's like for monkey tricks, so I reckoned it up myself. I don't know . . . if it's not one thing . . .' Tetty's eyes moistened, and it seemed for a moment as if she had something more to tell; but she quickly retreated into correctness, and merely said, 'I'll tell the jobsman you'll see to him, then, Mr John.'

Dr Twopenny's business habits were not of the most orderly: still, John was surprised at the confusion in the bureau. He replaced the avalanche of crumpled papers as best he could, and then opened the box wherein his father kept his ready cash. There was some there, but not enough; and by adding to it such coins as he had in his pockets he could only muster twenty-one shillings and sixpence. He apologized to the jobsman who was waiting in the yard, and promised to make up the difference as soon as he could; but the jobsman only raised an eyebrow, and went away without a word – leaving John with a curious impression that he would have said a good deal, if consideration of their bereavement had not inhibited him.

The two days before the funeral were filled, but only by such activities as made it seem a more dreary blank than if John had spent them staring into space. There was the measuring for mourning. There was the despatch of a letter to Catherine – such a melancholy contrast to the usual outpourings – and the receipt of a melancholy letter in return, in which Catherine floundered between the wish to console and the acknowledgement that consolation was beyond her. There were callers. There was grief; and while John mourned, he had also to make room in his overburdened heart for a deep apprehension about his father, who swung between that wild distraction and a sort of sunken apathy even more alarming, so foreign was it to the expansiveness of the doctor's temperament.

It might have been better if John had had someone in whom to confide his disquiet. But the family of three in the house on the clifftop had always been so self-contained. Emma Twopenny had had no near relations living: on the doctor's side there was only Uncle Saul and his downtrodden offspring in their pious seclusion at Hales-next-the-sea, and though they were coming to the funeral, and Saul had announced his intention of staying for a couple of days, nothing more was to be expected from that quarter than some stiff moralising drawn from the dourest portions of the Old Testament. No, John was quite alone; for it was not the least disturbing aspect of his father's sufferings that they seemed to take place in a private and nightmarish world of his own, which John could not penetrate.

So the sun burned sulkily through the long humid days, and at night the thunder-battles raged far out at sea. And then came the morning of the funeral, bringing with it at last a freshening of the air, and bringing with it also – though with quite the opposite effect on the spirit – John's uncle Saul, and his cousins William and Sar'ann.

Saul Twopenny owned wheeled vehicles aplenty for his business purposes, but he kept no private conveyance of any kind, despite having ample means, and despite being stiff on his legs nowadays, as he entered his sixty-eighth year. He cared nothing for show, or for public opinion. Accordingly, he travelled to Saltmarsh for his sister-in-law's funeral by dray – one of the broad, big-wheeled drays, drawn by two elephantine horses, that served his maltings. The vehicle had been converted into an outlandish carriage by the simple expedient of placing three bentwood chairs in the rear of it, and securing them to the sides with ropes; and here, with his feet among the chaff and straw, his hands clasping the head of his stick, and his eyes fixed sternly ahead, sat Uncle Saul, with his two children on either side, as the ungainly vehicle made its way up the cliff road to Dr Twopenny's house.

A carter from the maltings was driving; but when the dray pulled up outside the house, it was not he who got down to help old Saul to alight. That fell to Saul's own manservant, who had been clinging on to the back of the vehicle as best he could, and who now jumped down and held out his arm to Saul with such submissiveness that the whole scene, hatbands and umbrellas notwithstanding, fantastically resembled the arrival of some ancient Eastern potentate on his palanquin. As for the manservant, he was a curiosity in himself. Caleb Porter was the servant's name; he might have been any age, though thirty was probably near the mark; and he was a giant in everything but his brain, which had been permanently impaired by a childhood illness, and which was as feeble and undeveloped as his body was brawny and resilient. Take all this together with his colouring, which was so very fair as to render his eyebrows and eyelashes invisible, and his suit of velveteen which fitted him so tightly and scantily that it looked to have shrunk in the wash with him in it, and Caleb Porter presented a very singular appearance as a manservant. Even more singular was old Saul's attachment to him; which, though it did not show itself in any outward show of affection or even consideration, was sufficiently demonstrated by Saul's keeping him by him in spite of his incapacities. He was the son of a late employee of Saul's, who had died of the same illness that had maimed his child; and ever since then Saul had maintained Caleb in his own house, as a dogsbody certainly, but a dogsbody who need not fear the pauper asylum that would otherwise have been his lot. From this evidence, if no other, a charitable observer might have speculated that the old curmudgeon had a human heart after all; but there was little encouragement for such a conclusion in Saul's first words to his bereaved brother.

'Well, Robert, this is a bad business. But we must all die, you know: if you were a little more godly, you would have that always in mind. And you'd likewise know that this world is of no account compared with the next; and attachment to the things of this world, whether it be costly goods or wives, is vain and prideful, and hateful in the sight of the Lord. So I say to you, bear up: your wife has gone, let us hope, to a better place than this, so bear up.'

With these honeyed words Saul, who had buried his own wife fifteen years ago, and who had certainly borne up wonderfully on his own account, greeted his brother. In Dr Twopenny's look, and in the eager way he grasped the cold hand that was offered him, might have been discerned a half-smothered hope that here, in his nearest kin, some consolation might be found, and the old estrangement be repaired by a natural brotherly sympathy. It saddened John more than ever to see his father looking for warmth from that flinty old breast; and it was with no very friendly feeling that he greeted his uncle, who passed on to him like a general reviewing troops, and eyed him up and down with the words, 'So, nephew: you've finished growing at last, I suppose?'

'How are you, Uncle Saul?' John said, as cordially as he could manage.

'The Lord God made my body, and so I take care of it,' returned Saul, 'but it's the condition of our souls that we shall have to answer to him for, come the day.' Saul Twopenny's body, indeed, was in fair condition for his age, give or take a little stiffness; and he could at least be acquitted of hypocrisy, for he certainly did not pamper himself. Though not so tall as his brother, he was a large, sturdy man, tree-like in the stockiness of his limbs, in the toughness of his hide, and in his general imperviousness to wind and weather; not dissimilar, as a physical specimen, to the great dray-horses patiently waiting in the traces, but with none of their softness of eye or gentleness of temper. He was a hard-staring, hard-breathing, square-jawed, cross-grained old tyrant, grizzled and whiskered like a patriarch; though even those frightful biblical monsters could hardly have excelled Saul in leaden grimness of feature. The suit of mourning he had on differed little from his habitual costume, which was plain, dark and fusty; and it was with his customary lack of ceremony that he stumped past John towards the house, pausing only to cast his baleful eye over Dr Twopenny's recent improvements, and to declare in a voice of brass, 'A man who didn't know you might wonder at all this, Robert, and suppose you might have better things to think of!'

So saying, he passed into the house without a backward glance. That he did not wait for anyone was unsurprising: that he did not wait for his children was least surprising of all. For if there were any dispensations of the Almighty with which Saul might be inclined to quarrel, it was the matter of his children. For they were not satisfactory. They were not impressive. They were not such children as a prophet could lead out into the wilderness, confident that they would not disgrace him by declining a locust luncheon. They were not the children that a man such as Saul Twopenny should have. And even the most rigorous upbringing that Saul could devise, with liberal applications of the stick and of an equally scourging rod of religion, had largely failed to improve them. Curious result! Well, here they were, at any rate, in all their unsatisfactoriness: mutely standing by while their father handed out his dry bread of consolation, and continuing to do so when he had gone into the house – as if the background was so naturally their place that they would go all out of perspective if they stepped out of it.

'Well, my young friends, I am glad to see you,' said Dr Twopenny, whose cordiality had not deserted him even in his sorrow. 'Sar'ann, my dear, how do you do? And William, my boy, give me your hand.'

Thus beckoned, the son and daughter of Saul Twopenny stepped forward. They were as awkward in their greetings as in everything else: Sar'ann receiving her uncle's kindly kiss on the cheek as if he were applying a leech, whilst William tackled the business of shaking hands about as readily as if he had been required to turn somersaults. It was William, indeed, who laboured most under his father's disapproval, and carried the consciousness of it about with him to such obvious effect; for Sar'ann was a woman, and for that very reason there was less, in Saul's eyes, to be expected of her. She had at least absorbed her father's religion, and viewed the world through as narrow a peephole of piety as even he could wish; but otherwise she was something of a weak vessel. She was a lean, high-shouldered woman pushing thirty, and pushing it so hard that in terms of looks and complexion she had almost got to forty, and in dress fifty or more. She possessed markedly thin lips, and had carried that feature over, as it were, to the sum of her anatomy, so that her nose, her fingers, her elbows, and (probably) her very ankles had a thin-lipped look about them; and the only thing about her that was not spare, pinched and uncommunicative was her eyes, which certainly made up for the deficiency, being very large, very round, and so painfully wide-awake that it as possible to fancy that, like a doll's, they could only be closed by laying her flat on her back.

As for William, he was more prepossessing in appearance, and even handsome in a way; but what might have been a thoroughly presentable specimen of curly-headed, fresh-coloured, twenty-five-year-old manhood was dreadfully compromised by such a mixture of sullenness, flippancy, self-regard, self-doubt and sheer smouldering resentment as would have equipped a dozen sulky boys. The mutter which he offered to John by way of greeting was about as much as he ever had to say to his cousin upon any occasion; but it was at least preferable to the remark of Sar'ann who, on his escorting her into the house, gave John's whole figure a thoroughgoing stare and cried, 'Oh my stars, cousin, however did your legs get so long?'

John, whose grief had wrought itself up into a sort of savage anger, was almost ready to retort to the effect that he had grown them up to meet his backside; but the anger turned ashy almost as soon as it flared, and he merely sighed, 'I'm glad to know you're as charming as ever, cousin.'

'Oh, my stars, I only asked!' said Sar'ann; but he was spared further conversation by their passing into the house, the interior of which engaged her goggling curiosity so much that all she could do was twist her head about and stare as if she had never seen anything like it. Which was not far from the truth; for no one in Saul's household went about much, Sar'ann least of all, and everything that was not contained within that barren jail of a house at Hales-next-the-sea had a sort of prurient fascination for her.

The hulking Caleb, meanwhile, followed with their luggage, which was all musty leathery black as if made out of old bibles; and the dray drove away, to return in two days' time. Under any circumstances John would not have relished this enforced proximity with his grim relations; but the presence of it in a house that till now had known such sweetness and grace scarcely bore thinking of. The tone of what was to come was set at once by Saul, who had scarcely delivered up his hat to Tetty before summoning from memory a chilly slab of Leviticus, and hurling it at his brother across the parlour. 'Just a peg to hang your thoughts on, Robert, before the service, for I fear we shan't hear much good matter from this curate you have at Saltmarsh – a weak-voiced little simperer, I hear, with milk and water in his veins.' Thus Saul, standing in the middle of the parlour and, as was his habit, rhythmically beating his stick against the side of his leg as if he were chastising it; whilst Sar'ann boggled at the tablecloth as if she could only just restrain herself from peeping under it, and William slouched about the perimeter of the room like a bear in a small cage.

Grim, indeed; and yet of small account, after all, compared with the terrible account that was to be settled today. And John, well acquainted with hospitals, with sickbeds, with all the sorry perishability of the flesh, was still appalled, as the casket was borne to Saltmarsh church, at this dreadful assertion of the doom placed upon mankind, and the more dreadful assertion that all that was most precious and beloved was only lent, not given.

He took little note of his fellow-mourners; he saw only that his poor father was pale to the lips, and huddled his great body together, as if it were chill midwinter instead of summer's height. The church was well filled, for Emma Twopenny had been much loved; and John would not have noticed the latecomer slipping into one of the rear pews, if his father had not abruptly turned his head and given a sort of gasp, as if he had been struck a blow.

'He was not asked here,' Dr Twopenny murmured, flushing; and then, louder: 'That man was not asked here!'

John turned his head, and saw Mr Marcus Goodway seating himself quietly at the rear of the church.

'He is not welcome,' Dr Twopenny hissed, turning himself cumbrously about, his whole face suffused with blood. 'He – he was not asked here . . .!'

'Hush, hush, Father,' said John, and gently persuaded his father to turn round. That the friendship with Mr Goodway had lapsed might have occurred to John before, for there had been no mention of him these past days, and no message of sympathy as there had been from other acquaintances; but he had not given it a thought, and would hardly have done so now if it had not been for his father's excessive agitation, which manifested itself throughout the service in wild glances over his shoulder – and had it not been for his own instinctive feeling against Mr Goodway. The feeling leapt up again at the sight of him, a feeling scarcely identifiable except in its intensity; and without even knowing what was the cause of the estrangement between Dr Twopenny and his erstwhile friend, John was confirmed in a belief, vaguely formed before now, that Mr Marcus Goodway had come into his parents' lives, whether by design or accident, as a blight and a shadow. And even as he tried to calm his father and keep his thoughts on the service, John was conscious of an impulse in his own breast to start up and shoo that urbane gentleman in the rear pew out of the church, as if he were a bird of ill-omen.

Very soon the curate had run out of bespoke commonplaces, and was visibly relieved to adjourn to the graveside in the churchyard, where he could fall back on items from stock. The sun blazed on the weathered headstones, and on the white vestments of the curate, and on the vivid green turf, and on the brass of the coffin-lid. But its rays could strike no answering light or colour from that square pit of darkest earth, and they seemed to fail and die at its dark lip, as if the sun itself knew its master.

It was done at last; only the sexton's spade remained to have its say, and life summoned the mourners back. Dr Twopenny had rallied, and had been as stout-hearted as John knew him to be; but as he turned to leave the graveside, leaning on John's arm, he caught sight again of Mr Goodway – standing with folded arms and bowed head, a little way off from the main group of mourners.

Again it was as if the doctor had been struck a blow, but this time John could not soothe him, and, wrenching himself from John's grip, his father made a shambling run across the churchyard at Mr Goodway, as if he would knock him to the ground.

John caught up with his father and held him: Mr Goodway drew back; but all at once the strength seemed to go out of the doctor. He could only point a trembling finger at Mr Goodway, and say in a breaking voice, 'You were not asked here – you intrude – you intrude where you have no right – no right . . .'

Mr Goodway, a little pale, but quite composed, regarded Dr Twopenny steadily; then with an acquiescent motion he said, 'I wished only to pay my respects. That can hardly be a question of rights, surely? You will at least, I hope, accept my condolences.'

'I will accept nothing from you,' gasped Dr Twopenny, his breast heaving.

Mr Goodway looked hard at him. 'That has hardly been the case in the past,' he said crisply. 'However, this is not the time to argue the point. I simply wished to pay my respects, and that I have done, and so I will go.'

John did not understand, but he understood that his father was dangerously overwrought and must be got home directly. He was thankful that no reception of mourners had been planned at the house, for Dr Twopenny was now plainly unequal to it; but there was still the gloomy presence of Saul and his family to

70

prevent him talking with his father in confidence, and finding out what lay behind the strange outburst. However, it fell out that the doctor, on returning to the house, withdrew into a haggard introspection that John felt was beyond his reach in any event. Old Saul, moreover, claimed the occasion as his own. He first fortified himself with half a glass of port and a frugal slice of ham, served to him by a very stiff-backed Tetty; and then, having disposed of the wants of the flesh, Saul took up his Bible, and began to lay out a spiritual collation, reading out a generous selection of passages in his hard, colourless voice. John did not trouble to attend closely, and hardly noticed which books of the Old Testament Saul drew his texts from; remarking only that they were full of washpots, adders, tents, chariots, pelicans, cymbals, ointment, leopards, and grasshoppers, and other such inspiring items, wonderfully appropriate to the occasion.

There was an end to this at last, just when John was thinking he would be trapped in this parlour, hearing this vengeful drone, for ever more. Saul laid down his Bible and, fixing Dr Twopenny with his most piercing glare, said, 'Well, Robert, you were never one to take godly instruction; and I think even now, when you have sorest need of it, you let it pass you by.'

'Saul, I'm grateful to you,' said Dr Twopenny, drawing a great laboured breath, and seeming to muster up the semblance of his old courteous self with equal effort. 'You mean well, I know; and believe me, it's not for want of trying that I cannot – cannot command myself as I would wish . . . But I thank you for your concern, and I would certainly wish to have some serious talk with you; but not just now. I am better by myself a little while, I think.'

So saying, Dr Twopenny went out into the garden, where his wife's beloved flowers were just closing their petals in the soft dusk, and looking altogether too delicate to have outlived the woman who had planted them. He remained there long; and whatever he found there, among the long shadows and late-homing bees, seemed to benefit him, for he was more himself over supper. But plainly the day had exhausted him; and as Saul did not keep late hours, presumably having received confidential information that the Almighty disapproved of them, there was a general move to bed before ten.

John, however, had scarcely trimmed his bedroom candle and begun to undress, before the conviction came upon him that he would not be able to sleep for some time yet; and so he went out to the passage again with the intention of going downstairs for a book. Seeing the door of William's room ajar and a light burning within, he stopped to ask if there were anything his cousin wanted. William was at the window, training a telescope on the distant sea; and when John spoke he turned hastily, like a guilty boy.

'Sorry,' John said, 'I didn't mean to startle you. I just wondered whether—'

'I got it from downstairs,' William said in his graceless way, indicating the telescope. 'It is all right, isn't it? Is it yours?'

'No, it's Father's. But it's quite all right—'

'I won't break it, you know. I know how to handle a telescope.'

'Of course.' What William's home life must be like, to make him so habitually furtive and quickly defensive, could only be imagined, and pitied; but consideration of this did not make him any easier to talk to. 'I'm afraid there's not much to be seen from here. We get mist on the marshes all the year round—'

'Why, you needn't brag of that,' William said. 'We get mist at Hales too. Sometimes—' William started and broke off, hearing a creak; and it was not difficult to guess who it was that caused that lurking fear in his eyes.

'That's just the timbers stirring,' John said. 'They always do at night.'

William visibly relaxed. 'Your father's made quite a little palace of this place, hasn't he? I reckon it looks a treat,' he said; and from being sullenly resentful, his tone suddenly became appreciative, and confidential. This was the way with

71

William: nothing was fixed about him. Even his dress was undecided: through the austerity imposed by Saul could be seen the lineaments of a dandy. 'I say, John, have you ever been to sea?'

'I've been out to the Point in small boats,' John said. 'And out in a lugger from Yarmouth Roads, once.'

'Ah, there's no life like the sea,' William said. 'I've sailed out with the fishermen at Hales odd times, when I – when I feel like it, you know; and once you get out of sight of the coast, and you ride the swell, and feel the breeze in your face like you never feel it on land – oh, you feel like a king. Like—' William pushed his curls back from his brow impatiently – 'well, like Neptune, I suppose. King Neptune. All that's missing is a few mermaids.'

'I saw a mermaid once,' John said; and all the sadness of the day seemed to surge up and beat against him like an irresistible wave, and overwhelm him, and then to withdraw with the tide, leaving him bleak and chilled and forlornly stranded.

'A mermaid?' The suspicious look was back, as if William feared he was being made fun of. 'Where?'

'It was where you live – at Hales,' said John. 'It was in a raree-show. The mermaid wasn't quite what I expected, but . . . it was worth the walk.'

'A raree-show! I wish I'd seen it . . .' William had closed the telescope, and now he began beating it absently against his leg, in an unconscious echo of Saul's habit with his stick. 'I never – I never see anything like that. I miss things. It isn't fair. I dare say it was quite commonplace to you, cousin, but you needn't suppose that everybody's in the same circumstances as you. It's not so at all—'

'What are you two talking of, at this hour?'

It was Sar'ann, who had come creeping from her room with her candle in her hand, and who now peered in at the two of them with her most voracious curiosity. Over her nightdress she wore a floor-length wrapper of some coarse and wiry material, like a horse-blanket, and her sallow hair, innocent of such vain and prideful things as curl-papers, was done up in a huge white cap, which gave her the appearance, as she loomed out of the dark, of some tall stalky mushroom, of the sort it would be inadvisable to eat.

'Oh, go back to bed, Sar'ann,' grumbled William.

'Indeed I shan't! A cat may look at a king!' piped Sar'ann, seeming to consider this doubtfully relevant remark as quite a clincher; and holding her candle aloft, inspected John, who was in trousers and shirt, the latter open at the throat. 'Oh, my stars, there's not much meat on you, is there?'

John felt that he might with some justice have returned the compliment; but he held his peace.

'And so that's where you sleep, is it?' Sar'ann pursued, stealing forward to the door of John's room, and submitting it to a similar scrutiny. 'How do you manage when you go to bed? Don't your feet hang over the end?'

'Don't be an idiot, Sar'ann,' said William. 'It fairly makes me seethe to hear you talk sometimes.'

'I only asked!' said his sister, not at all put out; and returning her attention to John, and seeming to resist an impulse to complete her inspection by walking all round him as if he were a statue, she said, 'So *you're* to be a doctor, too, so I hear?'

'Yes, I hope to be a physician like Father,' said John; and the beacon of that ambition, though burning low in his current wretchedness, gave a gleam through the darkness at these words, and lightened his heart just a little.

'Physician heal thyself, is what scripture says,' retorted Sar'ann. 'After all, cousin, and don't take this amiss, but physic couldn't save your ma, could it?'

'I declare, Sar'ann, I'd rather hear a parrot talk than you,' snorted William.

'No, Sar'ann, you're right,' said John, 'physic couldn't save my mother. But then God didn't exactly fall over himself to save her either, did he?'

Sar'ann gave a little squeal, and her eyes widened further until she had no more face, comparatively speaking, than a housefly. 'Oh, you'll burn! You'll suffer torments of fire and water, you will!'

'Wouldn't the water put the fire out?' said John.

'Oh, you won't mock when it comes to you!' said Sar'ann. 'When you're roasting over a spit, and having your innards winched out, and red-hot pokers laid to the soles of your feet, and boiling oil poured down your throat, you won't laugh *then!*'

As this seemed a logical enough supposition, John did not contest it. Sar'ann besides seemed rather to relish this exposition of some of the articles of her beautiful faith, and was about to relate some more, when she caught sight of a crack in the wainscoting of the passage. At once she sprang forward, holding up the candle to examine it. 'Look! Just big enough for a mouse! Do you have mice here?'

'I've seen the odd one,' John said. 'Are you afraid of them?'

'No, not I,' said the fair one, with a curious cunning look. 'If anything, it's they who should be pretty afraid of me. Ain't it, William?'

'Upon my soul, Sar'ann, you're enough to make a pig sick sometimes,' was all William would say; but Sar'ann, beginning to laugh, only repeated her mysterious assertion, hugging her wrapper to her bony figure. 'Oh, my stars, it's they who should be pretty afraid of me! A-ha-ha-ha-ha! It's *they* who should be – pretty afraid of *me!*' she chanted, almost making a song out of it, until laughter overcome her completely. Extraordinary, shrieking, high-pitched laughter, rather alarming in its resemblance to a fit; and John was just wondering whether something should be done with water or smelling-salts to bring her out of it, when Sar'ann took remedial action herself, by rapidly slapping her own cheeks with both hands until their normally waxen colour had turned bright red, a proceeding which seemed greatly to refresh her.

'You'll slap your brains out of your head one of these days, Sar'ann,' said William with distaste. 'Either that, or laugh them out.'

'Good wine needs no bush!' retorted Sar'ann, with her former irrelevance, and her former air of saying something brilliantly pointed; then held up her hand at a faint sound from the end of the passage. 'Hark! That's Father's room!'

'We must have woken him,' said William, dropping his voice; and though the noise, John thought, was probably only the bed-springs creaking as Saul turned over, it was enough for Sar'ann and William, who both blew out their candles and whisked themselves off to bed – much as the mice who caused Sar'ann such amusement might scamper away at the opening of the pantry door.

No more sleepy than before, John went downstairs and found a book. He had been sitting in his bedside chair long enough for the candle to have burnt low when there was a soft tap at his door, and his father slipped inside.

'You couldn't sleep either, eh, John?' said Dr Twopenny, who was still dressed. 'Well, I dare say we are neither of us used to these early hours. Just lately, especially, I have . . .' The doctor's voice faded, and for some moments his face was curiously drained of expression, as if his soul had flitted from his body. Then, recovering himself, he offered John a pale smile, and sat down on the bed. 'Well, my son, how do you go along? We have scarce had a chance for a word today, you and I. Brother Saul is rather an emphatic character.'

'I must confess I shan't be *very* sorry when they're gone.'

'Well, well, they're kin, you know. And there are certain occasions when the claims of kin . . . well, they cannot be denied.' The empty look was there again, just for a moment; and then indicating John's book the doctor went on, 'Is it worthy, or is it interesting? I have some very worthy books by my bedside – sermons and such, that I find an infallible cure for insomnia.'

John smiled at this little spark of the old Dr Twopenny that he knew. 'Mr Wenn would not call it worthy. Just a novel – Scott.'

'Scott, eh?' Dr Twopenny took the volume in his big hands. 'All the rage in my younger years, you know, Scott, and Byron; but Scott was the more decent one. Also the duller one, some might say. But he certainly knows how to tell a story.' Leafing slowly through the pages, Dr Twopenny drew a deep breath and said, 'John, it appears to me that the stories going on around us, in our everyday lives, beat anything that a professional teller of tales can conjure up. See, for instance, what you think of this one. Suppose . . . suppose a man, most happily married and fortunate in every respect; but living in a somewhat retired spot, and naturally inclined to conviviality, and feeling the want, sometimes, of a little society, and a higher way of living than such a spot normally affords. Suppose, too, the wife of this man . . .' There was the sudden emptiness again, and the sudden coming back to life. 'The wife of this man, a lovely and accomplished woman, who – though she would never say so – rather buried herself away when she did him the honour of marrying him, and closed off many avenues that might have been open to her. I repeat, she would never say as much: no, no, her nature was too kind and – and loyal, for that; but still, the man was aware that her life was limited – perhaps dull. Now suppose there comes, into their sequestered spot, a stranger from London: a man fond of society, like them; a man, like them, with civilized tastes, a neighbourly, clubbable and hospitable man; and a wealthy man. Imagine his effect upon them, and how they begin to feel they have entered on a new lease of life, and even – even let themselves get a little carried away in the enjoyment of it.' Dr Twopenny turned another page, slowly. 'Can you – can you suppose such a thing?'

'Yes, Father,' said John, 'I can suppose it very easily.'

'Suppose, then,' his father went on, after a strangely timid glance at John's face, 'that this couple . . . No. No, I speak only of the husband. Not the wife, no, not the wife.' Again the terrible vacancy, for several seconds. 'The husband. Suppose that he, never having been as prudent as he should have been when it came to money – careless and improvident even—'

'Father—' John said; but Dr Twopenny held up his hand.

'No, no, John. Please, hear the story out. Suppose that this imprudence has always been his habit; but, living a retired country life as he had, it has never brought him to grief, simply because the opportunity has been lacking. But now he quite loses his head. The wealthy neighbour feels no need for economies – so why should he? The wealthy neighbour lays down large stakes at the card-tables and at races – so why shouldn't he likewise? The wealthy neighbour lives in high style, and undertakes great improvements to his house along the coast – so why shouldn't he too? Well, there is a very good reason why not. Because he is a country physician of modest means, and should not forget it. But he does forget it. He is enjoying himself, and he does forget it. And it is made easier for him by the wealthy neighbour . . . because the wealthy neighbour lends him money.'

The candle had a thief in it, and John stirred as if to get up and trim it. But he could not move.

'The wealthy neighbour,' went on Dr Twopenny, after another timid glance at his son, 'encourages him in his extravagance, and to facilitate it he lends him money, freely. Oh so freely! And the country physician is glad to borrow it, for it is simply a loan between friends, and he cannot see a time when they will not be friends. He cannot see a time when their friendship will turn sour; he cannot see a time when he will awaken to his wealthy neighbour's true character, and know its smooth, hard, impenetrable coldness, and see that the mask of good fellowship covers a monstrous self-seeking, an utter indifference to the other human lives with which he plays . . .'

Dr Twopenny's voice had grown thick and guttural, as if he could barely keep it under control; but still his hands slowly turned the leaves of the book, and still he kept his unseeing eyes fixed on them.

'And so the country physician borrows, and borrows more. And because it is a matter between friends, he borrows upon terms that would appal his banker, if his banker had not already washed his hands of him; and which do appal his lawyer, when he comes to know of it. By which time it is too late . . . A story should always have a happy ending, should it not? But suppose that the country physician and the wealthy neighbour fall out; suppose that the country physician sees how coolly and carelessly he has been used and led into disaster by the wealthy neighbour. Suppose that in the midst of his trouble and anxiety over the quicksand of debt into which he has been inveigled, he suffers . . . suffers . . .' Dr Twopenny's hands faltered, and it was just as if the story were really written on those pages, and he could not go on until he had turned the next. 'He suffers a terrible bereavement,' he got out at last, turning the leaf as he spoke. 'Not the first person in the world to do so, of course; but this occurs under such circumstances as – as quite break him. Now suppose that the only communication he receives from the wealthy neighbour is a letter reminding him of the loan: suppose that in the midst of his torment, this – this creature without a soul duns him for payment, and then has the insolence to appear at the funeral, where he knew his presence could only be like the coarsest of salt rubbed into the freshest of wounds . . . this man whose influence has been so corrupting, and who knows that the Devil himself could not be more unwelcome at that sacred occasion than he . . .'

Dr Twopenny closed his eyes for a moment; whilst John, staring into the candle-flame, saw himself on the foggy marshes, reaching down into a creek to grasp a pair of strong white hands.

'Now you know – or you have some inkling,' said his father, 'of why I could not bear to see – that man at the funeral today.'

'Goodway,' said John.

Dr Twopenny nodded, and bit his lip. 'I have been a fool,' he said. 'An unforgivable fool. I am deep in debt to him, John, and under such terms as – well, as give him a fearful advantage over me, if he should choose to exercise his power. As, I perceive, he has never had any qualms about doing. So . . . the mess is of my own making. Yet if you only knew how subtly he manipulates – if you only knew . . .'

John said nothing; for though his own uneasy feeling about Mr Marcus Goodway was now confirmed, there was no satisfaction in being proved right. He would far, far rather have been proved wrong.

'Led astray, at my age, and with these white hairs!' said his father, with a mirthless chuckle. 'Do you despise me, John?'

'Father!' said John hotly; for taken aback as he was, that was the furthest thing from his mind.

'No,' said his father, smiling a little, 'the question is unfair on you. You cannot know . . .' Dr Twopenny threw down the book, and brushed his hands across his eyes. 'John, you had a right to know this, because – well, because I am in deep trouble, and it is not going to go away. If I could take the trouble solely upon myself, I would; but by its nature, it concerns you too. I never thought that when you finished schooling and were ready to embark upon life on your own account, it would be under such shadows as these.'

It was, indeed, a shock; and all the more painful because a glance of retrospect showed John many small hints and signs of things going amiss, that he might have taken up if his head had not been so firmly fixed in the clouds. Yet there was relief also. This revelation, at least, was concrete. Something could be done about it, or attempted; and as a beginning he could assure his father that they would weather this storm together.

This he proceeded to do; but though Dr Twopenny smiled gently on him, and thanked him, and murmured agreement that things were not so bad as all that, he was, John felt, only half listening to him. 'You may be right, John,' he said at last. 'Indeed, I'm sure you are, for I think it is the young, after all, who see the world aright – or at least, they see it in the only way it *can* be seen, if we are to live in it at all without turning quite mad. But I am old . . . and I wish, I wish I were not!'

However, John persisted, and counselled his father to get some sleep and put this trouble entirely from his mind until tomorrow; and he convinced himself that Dr Twopenny's face, when he said goodnight, seemed less burdened in its expression.

John's advice might have been sound, but he found he could not so easily follow it himself that night. Confused images of his mother, and Mr Goodway, and his father, whirled about his mind and kept him awake; and when he did settle himself, and draw near the brink of sleep, he was jerked back from the edge, either by a burst of grief for his mother, or a burst of pity for his father, or a burst of fury at Mr Marcus Goodway. And even when he drifted at last, the same visions shimmered back and forth through his dreams, like fish in a murky pool, and turned sleep into something as fatiguing as exertion.

It was John's intention that they should begin to address this question of the debt in earnest tomorrow; but he was forgetting the presence of his relatives. There they still were, alas, when he came down to breakfast next morning – Uncle Saul presiding over the saying of a most tremendous Grace, which seemed to make a sin out of eating; and after breakfast, the domineering old man took charge of the day, declaring that he and his brother needed to have some serious talk, and proposing therefore that John take his cousins out on a long walk. John might have protested; but there was a sort of meek resignation about Dr Twopenny, as if he felt he might as well get it over with, and it was after all only one day. The dray would be coming to take them back to Hales tomorrow, and then John and his father would be free to talk by themselves.

'I've no need of you today, Caleb,' Saul told his servant, 'so you may as well go along too. No foolishness, mind – come back up to the ears in mud, and I shall make you sorry for it.'

The simple Caleb was inexpressibly delighted with this meagre ration of holiday. It was plainly all he could do, as they set out along the cliff-path, to prevent himself breaking into a skip; and John could not help reflecting on what a curious foursome they must make. The big fair man, swinging his arms, hurrying ahead and then walking backwards, scrambling up on to walls and balancing along them, exactly like a child let out of school; Sar'ann stalking along with a sunshade held vertically above her head, and surveying the summer countryside like a big-game hunter with a tiger-skin in mind; William slouching along with his hands in his pockets, giving an occasional doglike jerk of his curly head as if he felt the chafing of an invisible collar and leash; and John, preoccupied and weary, and at ease with none of them.

John took them by the cliff road east, towards Shipden, as William expressed a strong aversion to going in the other direction towards Hales-next-the-sea – 'Where home is,' he grunted, as if this were sufficient explanation. But the walk was rewarding in itself, especially when the marshland gave way to the true North Norfolk cliffs; the change being marked at Weybourne Gap, where the longshore fishermen's boats were drawn up on the beach, and where the road skirted a startling cliff-face, like a bite taken out of the world. Side by side with the huge lumps of flint that scarred the cliff-face grew a field of barley, extending in its neat smoothness to the very edge, and presenting a forcible contrast of nature and cultivation – man, as it were, hanging on to this craggy cusp of land by his fingertips; and with what precariousness was shown by the upper slopes, where great sandy wounds had been opened up by landslides, and where nesting sea-birds made wild swoops and shrieks, witch-like, as if they gloried in the chaos of their dominion.

The road, which ran the whole length of the changeful coast, was well-used, and several times they had to move to the side to let a farm-wagon go rumbling by, so that it became an automatic habit, whenever the sound of hoofs and wheels was heard, to fall into Indian file. But there came a time when the hoofs and wheels did not pass them by, but stopped alongside; and John, dreaming along at the front of the file, looked round out of his reverie into the eyes of Catherine Fernhill.

She was in the Fernhills' carriage, an open barouche with red wheels and the admiral's coat-of-arms, or what would have been his coat-of-arms if he had had any, painted very large on the side. Verity Deene was with her.

'John!' Catherine said; and that was all she could say for some time, or needed to say – the look that she fixed on him, from eyes made even more beautiful by their film of tears, turning silence into profoundest eloquence. She leaned out to give him her hand, and he took it; and that look and that touch, breaking suddenly upon him after all the sadness and trouble of the past week, seemed to unravel great tortured knots of feeling within his breast, such that he wanted to say everything at once, and could say nothing at all.

It was Verity Deene who spoke. 'We were all very sorry to hear of your loss,' she said in her cool voice. 'It must have been a great shock to you and your father.'

'Yes, your poor father, John,' said Catherine. 'How is he? Is he bearing up? Oh, but that's such a detestable phrase, as if all one had to do was bear up and everything would be all right . . . I'm more sorry than I can say.'

'Thank you,' said John, relinquishing her hand at last. All communication between them, in these circumstances, must be of the unspoken sort; for as he found his voice, he awakened to the presence of his cousins, and Caleb, who was nuzzling the carriage-horses' heads, and blowing into their nostrils, to the seeming pleasure of the horses themselves, but to the astonished indignation of the coachman. There must be introductions, and so he made them, whilst something like a long, inaudible, disembodied sigh passed between him and Catherine.

'Oh, we are nearly neighbours, you know,' Catherine said in her friendly way to John's cousins. 'We live just inland from Hales, at Buttings Court, on the Fakenham road.'

'Oh, my stars, I don't think so, I don't think you could call us neighbours at all,' said Sar'ann. 'We live quite in the middle of the town. I don't think we could live any more in the middle of it if we tried!'

'Don't talk nonsense, Sar'ann,' muttered William, who in the presence of these young ladies assumed a manner half-sheepish and half-preening; and inclining to the latter, went on, 'They say – they say Buttings Court is very handsome, Miss Fernhill.'

'Handsome is as handsome does!' shrilled Sar'ann.

'Oh, I'm sure you're right,' said Catherine agreeably. 'Though Buttings doesn't really do anything, you know. It just sits there. I suppose there's not much a house can do – unless it subsides, or falls down . . .' She telegraphed John a look of helpless contrition, as if aware that it was she who was talking nonsense now; and went on hurriedly, 'We're just on our way to Shipden. We have some shopping to do there for Mama, and . . .' Poor Catherine bit her lip, and her eyes filled with tears again, at this mention of her mother; and John could tell that at that moment she genuinely felt dreadful for having one at all. It made his love for her soar higher still; but that love was not for here and now, and they both knew it.

'Shipden's a fine spot,' said William, making another awkward excursion into gallantry, 'and very healthy, they say.'

'Not for the crabs, it ain't,' declared Sar'ann. 'They get caught in nets and boiled up for dinner. I wonder how much it hurts them? Quite a bit, I'd say – ' with a very eager look – 'quite a bit!'

'I wish you'd try it, and find out,' said William under his breath; whilst the phantom sigh passed between John and Catherine again, and with it the recognition that they must say goodbye, without having really said anything to each other at all. The coachman was, besides, becoming restive at Caleb's attentions to the horses – the big man was now whispering in their ears, and they were shaking their heads as if they found him irresistibly amusing – and so Catherine reluctantly said they had better go.

A last word: not from Catherine, but from Verity Deene, who, leaning over the side of the carriage as it passed, said distinctly to John, 'It will get better. Not soon, not easily, but it will get better.' And then they were gone.

He was so used to the teasing antagonism between the two of them, that John supposed for a moment that Miss Deene meant to reproach him with his grief. But she had seemed in earnest; and he recalled then that she was an orphan, and must know whereof she spoke. 'Not soon – not easily': he found to his surprise that there was comfort in those words, which seemed to come from a clearer, saner world than he had inhabited just lately. Strange source of comfort! – a young woman who seemed no more capable of compassion or fellow-feeling than an iron poker; but then so much of his world had been turned upside-down, that this minor revolution was scarcely remarkable.

For the rest of the excursion Sar'ann plied him with so many questions about Catherine and Verity, and William was so offish with him, throwing out hints that John 'would rather be with his Ladies,' he was sure, 'than with his own flesh and blood', that by the time they reached Saltmarsh again, John was heartily sick of them, and looked forward to being free of them for a space. It was not to be. Uncle Saul was still closeted with his father in the study, and was plainly still administering some stiff spiritual treatment to his hapless patient; and so the entertainment of his cousins fell to John again, for the evening. Fortunately Sar'ann had brought her basket of needlework, and this furnished her with occupation enough. It was noticeable that she used no needle-case or pincushion. Instead, whenever a needle or pin was not wanted, she popped it into her mouth – not just between her lips, but right into her mouth; and then made contented munching motions with her jaws, as if the mouthful of sharp metal were delicious comfits, until John's teeth were quite set on edge. As for William, after a few more sour sallies about Ladies, he went into a moody abstraction over a book; and so John took refuge in his own thoughts.

'How different from the pleasant evenings we used to spend in this parlour – Mother, Father, and I!' he mused. 'Father with his anecdotes that you knew were exaggerated, but it didn't matter because they were so entertaining; and mother crowning them with the slightest and driest of remarks, that would set us all laughing. And then Mother would go to the piano, and play something wonderfully sweet and melting – and then, subtly and devilishly, she would turn the music into the most familiar and ridiculous of tunes, so that Mozart would become 'Pop Goes the Weasel', and we would laugh again . . .'

His father and uncle were still in conclave when he went to bed, taking this mood of gentle melancholy with him; and, finding his grief purged of its former bitterness, John slept well for the first time since his return. Even the horrible waking to the knowledge that his mother was not there was mitigated by the knowledge that his relatives were to leave that morning; and indeed, when he came downstairs, the dray was already waiting in front of the house, with the three chairs lashed to it as before, and Caleb was loading the dingy luggage on to the back.

'Well, boy,' said Uncle Saul as John went out with them to say goodbye, 'I could have wished to have had a few words with you too, man to man. I fancy you're in need of it. I've half a mind to stay another day – ' John tried to conceal his alarm here – 'but I'm needed at Hales. The best of workmen turn slackers without the master's eye on them.' The long session with his brother seemed, in fact, to have exhausted Saul quite as much as Dr Twopenny; the truculent fire had left the old man's eyes, so that he looked his age and more, and his manner was almost subdued as he briefly shook his brother's hand and grunted, 'Farewell then, Robert. Bear in mind what I said: lay it to your heart. It's never too late to put yourself in the hands of the Lord.' Saul paused to bestow another lowering glance of disapproval on the house, as if it were a Babylonian temple full of graven images; then gave his leg a refreshing whack with his stick and stumped to the backboard of the dray, where Caleb was waiting to lift him up. William and Sar'ann, disregarded as ever, followed; and soon the whole retinue moved off, under a sky beginning to spit rain – Caleb clinging to the backboard and holding an umbrella over Saul, so that he resembled a funereal sort of Rajah.

'Just you and I now, eh, Father?' John said.

'Just you and I. Well, well, we are different people, Saul and I – very different: but still kin, you know. Still kin.'

Dr Twopenny was drawn and weary; but he seemed coherent enough in his mind for John to raise the matter, as they breakfasted together, of the debt owed to Mr Goodway.

'It's not my only debt, John,' Dr Twopenny said, toying with his teaspoon. 'I've always been a little inclined to run up bills, and stretch my credit to the limit. But these other claims would be of no great account, if it were not for this infernal loan. I wish to God I had never taken it . . . But perhaps the mischief lies much further back. If I would indulge these extravagant notions, then at least I should have set out my life accordingly. If I were going to spend a gentleman's income, I should never have taken a small country practice like this: I should have gone to London, and made my mark there. Like Frank Spruce – remember him?'

John remembered well. In fact, the seed of ambition planted when he had watched his father set the carter's broken bone had been watered by Dr Frank Spruce, who had been a frequent visitor at Saltmarsh in John's childhood. Frank Spruce was a man some twenty years his father's junior, who had practised at Norwich for a time but had always cherished ambitions to work in London amongst the poor. It was he who had first drawn John's attention to Chadwick's *Report on the Sanitary Condition of the Labouring Population of Great Britain*: a fresh-faced and enthusiastic man, genial like his friend Dr Twopenny, but with a strong streak of idealism, his example had been a profound influence on John – not least because Frank Spruce had achieved his aim, moving to the capital with high hopes some half-dozen years ago.

'Do you ever hear from him now?' John asked.

'Seldom. A busy man, no doubt: he seems to have moved around a lot. Ah, but that wouldn't have been the answer either. Whatever Frank Spruce is doing, he's certainly making no fortune. No, I should have cultivated a grand manner, and set up as a society physician. Harvested guineas from the ripe fields of the West End. But my conscience would not let me do that. Rather skittish in my conscience, don't you think? – for God knows it has let me do other things quite as reprehensible in their way . . .'

Dr Twopenny fell to playing listlessly with his teaspoon again: his breakfast was untouched. John, seeing that vacancy returning, felt the want of an ally in rousing his father to a consideration of what must be done. And an ally came to call that morning, if not a forceful one: Mr Flowers, Dr Twopenny's solicitor.

He had driven over to Saltmarsh in his little gig. The day being warm, they received the lawyer in the garden-room, with the french windows open to the balmy air; and though they were accosted by bees, which seemed to concentrate their attentions on Mr Flowers as if mistaking his name for his substance, he was as phlegmatic as ever.

'Oh, it doesn't trouble me,' Mr Flowers said, as a particularly insistent bee made an amorous circuit of his neat brown hair. 'We can get along together, I'm sure. Deedle-deedle-dum. So, Doctor, how do you get on? Foolish question, I know. Impudent even. But still.'

'Well, we bear up, you know,' said John's father. 'We bear up.'

It was so plain from his demeanour that Dr Twopenny was not bearing up, that Mr Flowers could hardly have failed to observe it. But the lawyer made no remark – that was not his way – merely nodding, with a sympathetic wag of his jowls, and murmuring, 'Just so. Just so.'

'You come here, of course,' said Dr Twopenny, with an odd knowing look, 'to impress me with the seriousness of my financial predicament.'

'Impressing,' said Mr Flowers, 'has a hard, domineering sound. Like the press-gang, you know. I prefer to think of myself as a friendly recruiting officer, simply setting out the advantages of joining up. Or the advantages, in this case, of looking the facts in the face. Just a . . .' He consulted the bee that was weaving drunkenly a few inches from his nose. 'Just a brief buzz around the facts of the case, and then back to the hive. Dear me, what a feeble figure. Rum-ti-tum-ti-tum.'

'The facts of the case,' said Dr Twopenny in a stormy voice, rising to his feet and roaming about, 'are plain. That man is a designing rogue, and he wants his pound of flesh, for no other reason than – than sheer malice and cold-hearted calculation—'

'Well, now, maybe not so,' said Mr Flowers temperately. 'The fact is, though Mr Goodway is a man of large fortune, and makes a habit of loaning out short-term capital, he also has been living rather high; and Beacon House, I fancy, has swallowed up a good deal. Quite understandable, in a way, that he chooses to call in some of the debts owing to him. The pity is, when these advances are made in friendship, and recalled—'

'In friendship?' Dr Twopenny turned a livid face to them. 'Under cover of friendship – in the *disguise* of friendship – when all the time his intent is—'

'Well, well, as you say, Doctor, as you say,' said Mr Flowers soothingly. 'As a lawyer, I must say that these informal arrangements between friends – acquaintances, then – are dubious at the best of times. I would never advise them – if I felt it my business to advise, which I don't. However, that's beside the point, which is—'

'Which is that if the man chooses, he may ruin me,' said Dr Twopenny, who had his back to them, and was touching the petals of a hibiscus that had been a favourite of his wife's with a gentleness quite at odds with the curtness of his words.

'Not so bad as that, my dear sir,' said Mr Flowers. 'At least, I hope to determine so, when I communicate with Mr Goodway's solicitor. Have I – excuse the legalistic formality, force of habit – have I your permission, Doctor, to do so?'

There was a long pause, while the doctor kept his back to them. 'Of course,' he said at last, turning, 'of course, my good friend: whatever is necessary. You legal fellows understand each other's language, which is a mercy, as I fancy no one else does. Please, do whatever is necessary, and many thanks.' He was himself again – or, at least, a brave imitation of himself, which John saw through even as he admired it. How much Mr Flowers saw likewise John did not know – probably much; but the lawyer was not a man to give anything away.

'Very well,' Mr Flowers said, rising, 'I shall leave you to the bees, and go home and see what those dreadful encumbrances of mine, commonly called children, have been up to in my absence.'

'How are the little girls?' said Dr Twopenny, authentically himself now, in the kindliness of his inquiry. 'They've run the gauntlet of the childhood ailments now, I hope?'

'I hope so too. If they haven't, I have no doubts about who I shall come to, at the first cough or speckle,' said Mr Flowers. 'They will ask for nice Dr Tup'ny, as before; and very good judgement in them too.' Mr Flowers spoke with unusual warmth; and as if that warmth had carried him away, he added unexpectedly, 'They need a mother. Conventional idea, I know. But still. I feel it would be good for them. Not any old mother, but a person of – attainments, and character, and with her wits about her . . . Biddi-bom, ra-ta-ta.' The lawyer corrected himself with an abrupt snatch of onomatopoeia, and went on casually, 'Well, you must come and see them, and me, any time.' These words were addressed to both of them; but Mr Flowers caught John's eye in passing him, and John interpreted this as, *Come and see me if you need someone to talk to*.

He fully intended to; but first of all it was his resolve to make another visit along the coast, a resolve that had been quietly forming within him since he had first opened his eyes that morning. He was going to call on Mr Marcus Goodway at Beacon House.

CHAPTER EIGHT

The Doctor Makes a Decision; the Soldier Makes a Discovery

John had examined himself thoroughly on this question of going to Beacon House, and acquitted himself of any suppressed adolescent desire to cause a vengeful rumpus. His intention was, rather, to discuss the matter of the debt coolly, and plead his father's cause.

He knew that there would be objections even to this, in the legalistic view of Mr Flowers, for example. The matter was after all between Dr Twopenny and Mr Goodway: a personal intervention by Dr Twopenny's stripling of a son – so the argument might run – was a mere muddying of an already murky business. But Mr Flowers did not know the peculiar link between John and Mr Goodway that had been forged on the misty night when John had rescued him from the marshes. Whatever else they might be, John felt, he and Marcus Goodway could never be indifferent to one another; and in that alone he saw grounds for hoping that a personal approach was worthwhile. As for the fact of having once saved his life, John surmised already, from his ruthless behaviour towards Dr Twopenny, that Mr Goodway did not feel that that laid him under any special obligations to the family; but perhaps seeing John face to face might revive the memory which Mr Goodway seemed so readily able to forget. Certainly it was a weapon worth holding in reserve, and not one that John felt it would be ignoble to use under the circumstances.

So he did not suppose he was acting rashly or unwisely when he went over to Beacon House that afternoon, making an excuse of going for a walk on the marshes. Yet the faintest of misgivings touched him as he came upon Beacon House, and was once again dismayed by its look. More clearing work had been done on the grounds, and along the drive several pollarded trees still bled sap where their limbs had been cut off, and looked like ghastly amputees; whilst the house itself, cleaned of soot and stripped of ivy, appeared more baldly unwelcoming than ever, like the cropped head of a convict or a fanatic.

Mr Goodway was at home: she would tell Mr Goodway he was here. Thus the maid, who left him alone in the hall that he remembered as icy on his first visit, and even now at the height of summer seemed improbably cold, as if the rows of marble busts and pilasters acted like fires in reverse, and communicated their chill to the air. Wealth, written everywhere; but written with a subtle hand. John could see why his father had emulated it: somehow Mr Goodway made his way of life seem natural.

'Well, John, what can I do for you?'

Marcus Goodway had noiselessly appeared at a door to his left, and was regarding him with that penetrating, we-understand-each-other look – the look that, in spite of all his resolutions, threw John into tongue-tied confusion, like a child strayed into a gathering of adults.

'I wondered – I wished to speak a few words with you.'

'As many as you like. As long as they're not too loud – Mrs Goodway is in poor health again, and has only just this moment got off to sleep.'

82

'I'm very sorry to hear it,' said John, determined not to be the graceless youth to which Mr Goodway's presence usually reduced him. 'I hope her complaint isn't serious?'

'Grace's constitution is not strong, and susceptible to the mildest of infections; and the low standard of medical attendance in this district does not help matters. But she improves a little, thank you. Come.'

John had followed Mr Goodway into his study, and taken a chair, before the unfriendliness of that reference to medical attendance had quite sunk in. Not an encouraging beginning; but there was nothing for it but to plunge on. 'It's about my father's debt to you, Mr Goodway. I wished to—'

'To pay it?' Mr Goodway cut him off, as much with the sudden sharpness of his glance as with his words. 'Well, no, of course: wishful thinking on my part, for I see no money-belt about your waist, my friend, and I don't imagine you're carrying a strongbox about you.' He smiled, but with an effect that was like the slight loosening of a tight grip. 'Your father sent you here, I suppose?'

'Why should you suppose that?'

'Come, John, don't pretend to be a fool. You once did me a service, and no doubt your father would like to remind me of the fact, in the present circumstances. But it doesn't alter the present circumstances, John. It doesn't entitle him to cheat a man out of money that was advanced in good faith. This is the crux of the matter, is it not? Your father can't pay, or won't pay, the debts he has incurred: I suffer as a result; and you are here to convince me that I should go on suffering. This seems rather like persuading a man who has just been burgled not to pursue the thief, even though he can see him trotting away down the garden path with his silver in a bag over his shoulder. But, I am open to persuasion, if you can do it.' Mr Goodway smiled again, and this time it was as if the grip tightened unmercifully. 'Give me a good reason why I should not have what is mine.'

John hesitated. The scenarios that he had rehearsed in his mind on the way here had all featured him taking the initiative: he had reckoned without the seamless way Mr Goodway made himself master of every situation.

'My father is not well,' he began. 'He is not himself—'

'My wife is not well,' said Mr Goodway. 'She has not been well for a long time. That does not absolve either her or me from our responsibilities.' Still smiling, Mr Goodway leaned against his desk, arms folded and chin up. It was as if he were a tutor supervising a debate. 'You will have to give me a better reason than that.'

'His – his state of health,' faltered John, 'is attributable, I think, to the grief of bereavement, which was and is so profound that—'

'No, no. That won't do. I'm glad in a way that this is you, John, coming to me with this excuse, and not your father; because I think a man who would so cravenly make use of a tragic circumstance, and seek to profit by it, is beneath contempt.' There was no heat in Mr Goodway's tone: he seemed merely to be becoming more and more interested in the debate. 'You must give me a better reason, my friend – or any reason, for that is no reason at all.'

'Common humanity, then.' There was plenty of heat in John's tone – in his stinging cheeks too; for the very thing that he had tried to guard against happening to him had happened, swiftly and uncontrollably. All at once the coldness emanating from this blandly smiling man smote him like a blow, rousing everything that was quick, violent and passionate in him, and it would have been a lie to his own nature to smother it. 'In the name of common humanity, I ask you to think again about my father's debt. Isn't that a good reason?'

'Common humanity . . .' Mr Goodway picked up a silver paper-knife from his desk, balancing it on the tip of his finger, and seeming to weigh the words likewise. 'But John, that phrase has rather a doleful sound. Do you wish to be numbered amongst "common humanity"? I certainly don't. I would rather distinguish myself from it. I had thought you were the same. You have ambition, do you not, and wish to do great things, and live your life to the full? Then don't, I beg you, prate of "common humanity" to me, like some cheap demagogue at a country preaching. If obtaining money under a gentleman's agreement, and then declining to honour the terms of that agreement, and trying to escape it by the most mean and shuffling excuses, presented at second-hand as if in very shame of them – if *that* is being part of common humanity, then really I would rather decline membership of that body altogether. Sloppy thinking, John – always beware of sloppy thinking.' There was a sort of playfulness in his conclusion, which he pointed by tossing the knife in the air, and catching it by the blunt end; but it was the intent, merciless playfulness of the hunting cat.

'You're a wealthy man,' said John. Without being aware of it he had risen to his feet: the chair to which Mr Goodway had motioned him placed him at a disadvantage. 'You cannot stand in need of immediate repayment.'

'It was a short-term loan,' said Mr Goodway, looking politely bored. 'It was advanced under those terms, and under those terms I seek recovery of it. Let me just add, my friend, that I find it just a little impudent of you to speak so familiarly of my affairs, as if you knew all about them. You do not know: in fact I can say with confidence that you really do not know what you are talking about. Forgivable: you are not yet a man, after all. But your father is, and should take the consequences of a man's actions, like a man. Don't you see that the more he tries to evade the responsibility he has incurred, the more concerned I am to pin him down to it? Natural, surely. If my dog does not answer to my whistle, I don't assume that all's well, I assume he's up to mischief.'

'My father,' said John, speaking with difficulty through a swimming haze, 'is one of the most respected men in the county, and his professional reputation—'

'Oh, John, John. Filial in you – but to be truthful, now, is he really *so* respected? Is there not a little something of the buffoon about him? A jolly companion, in small doses, certainly, but relentless joviality can pall, you know. As for his professional reputation—'

'You had better be careful,' said John, the haze thickening about him. 'You had better be careful what you say.'

Mr Goodway spread his white hands. 'I was merely going to observe that his professional reputation is not at issue. But an unprejudiced observer would surely feel that Dr Robert Twopenny's professional reputation is not enhanced by his being a bad debtor.' He looked bright and amused, as if the debate had come to a thoroughly interesting climax. 'The same observer, indeed, might wonder whether Dr Robert Twopenny's professional reputation is not a little undeserved, as he failed to save even his own wife.'

It all happened so quickly, and with so little conscious volition on John's part, that as soon as it was done he had a strange sensation of its being done a long time ago. What happened was, that he stepped forward and hit Mr Goodway in the face, hard enough to send that gentleman sprawling backward, striking his shoulder against his desk-chair as he fell. The haze lifted, and John found himself looking down at Marcus Goodway picking himself up off the floor; and madly enough, some other John Twopenny who also occupied his body was momentarily shocked, and instinctively moved as if to offer Mr Goodway his hand and help him up.

'Well, well, my friend,' said Mr Goodway, standing straight, and dusting himself down with as little perturbation as he had shown when John had pulled him from the creek. But his face was flushed, giving his blue eyes a pale glitter, and John knew that the blow he had struck against this man's invulnerable self-possession was hated and resented far more than the physical blow. 'Well, well. This ruffianism, now – is this on the good doctor's orders also, or is it simply his son's true nature coming out? I merely ask for information's sake.'

'It was from me, and you deserved it,' said John, whose fury still leapt up like an unsteady fire. 'And anyone would have done the same. All this talk of gentleman's agreements! Why, you're nothing but a vulgar, smirking, money-grabbing brute—'

'That – ' Mr Goodway held up one finger sharply, and for a moment John thought he was going to hit him back – 'that, my friend, is quite enough.' His jaws worked for a moment; then he was faintly smiling. 'Well, John, I am not such a brute as to break your back for you, as I might easily do if I chose. You are a boy, John: you talk like a boy, and you act like a boy. Come back when you are a man, if you like, and we'll try our strength. As for your father, I have strong doubts whether he has ever played a man's part in his life; but it's of no consequence. The law will take its course, and the law is on my side. As for that blow . . .' Mr Goodway touched his cheekbone, where a livid mark was beginning to appear. 'Well, I shall not forget it, John. Trust me for that. And now I think you had better leave, had you not?'

Even now, that twinkle of fellowship was in his eye – as if he saw quite plainly the realization awakening inside John, that he had not only failed in his endeavour but made matters worse. No answering blow could have diminished and defeated John as that merry look of understanding did; and it pursued him like a dismissive laugh as he made his way blindly out of the study, and out of that house to which he had journeyed so hopefully.

Pursuing him, too, through his walk home, was horror at what he had done: not only the act, but the betrayal of himself that it entailed. He had gone to Beacon House in the certainty that reason and sanity would prevail: this certainty sprang from his deepest beliefs. And yet here he was groping in the darkness of violent animosities and primitive instincts. The whole encounter had left a bitter aftertaste in his soul, all the more bitter because the consequences of his failure did not only touch himself.

He said nothing of what had happened to his father. Shame inhibited him, of course, but there was also Dr Twopenny's fragile state of mind to consider. Haunted was the nearest word to describe Dr Twopenny's condition; but whether it was simply that lingering presence of his dead mother which permeated the house, or whether the ghost that haunted his father was a more complex entity, John could not tell.

Another day elapsed in this way, with no further action of John's part. His failure at Beacon House had discouraged him, and he was occupied besides with going over the household accounts with Tetty. A simple if dispiriting conclusion was reached: no one's bills had been paid for some time. And John suspected that Tetty's wages had not been paid either, though her bristling loyalty would never admit the fact.

A new idea was, however, glimmering in his mind. On the third day after his disastrous appeal to Mr Goodway, he again made an excuse of a walk on the marshes, and set out for the little fishing-town of Sheringham, along the clay cliffs, where Mr Flowers had his office and his home. He had learnt his lesson, and this time he would consult with the solicitor first.

Mr Flowers' office was part of an ancient flint house, tucked up a cobbled side-alley of the little town. On either side of the door were two bleary bull's-eye windows, set so low in the bulbous wall that the clerks within saw nothing but headless people walking by: the door itself, warped with age, would open only after some hearty pushing, with the result that you tumbled down the unexpected three steps on the other side from your own momentum. But the two clerks were so accustomed to this that it had long ceased to furnish them with any amusement, and when John made the usual precipitous entry into the outer office they merely waited politely for him to pick himself up before the senior asked what he could do for him.

Mr Flowers was with a client, but John did not have to wait long amongst the faded auctioneer's bills and yellow estate maps, and was soon being shown into Mr Flowers' own office. A cosy room, as befitted a comfortable sort of man like Mr Flowers, with two well-stuffed armchairs by the hearth, and a decanter and glasses on a side-table: even the desk at which the lawyer sat was so well padded with leather that you could have curled up for a doze on top of it.

'Ah, John. Hoping I would see you. Just written to your father this morning. Tirra-lirra, ta-ta-tee. Have a chair, won't you?'

'I suppose you know what I wished to speak to you about.'

'Trustees of the estate of Thomas Rawlins,' Mr Flowers mused, placing the lid on a japanned deed-box. 'I wouldn't trust them with a spent match myself, but there's no telling who folk will appoint. Hey-ho . . . It looks bad, John.'

'Mr Goodway?'

'Mr Goodway's solicitors, to be exact. They're going to commence action for the recovery of your father's debt. Which is what I've just written to him about.' Mr Flowers rested his jowls on his hand, watching John with kindly, resigned eyes.

'How . . .' John cleared his throat. 'How long?'

'Oh, well, the law's not a vehicle built for speed, but it always gets to its destination in the end. The question in this case is . . .' The solicitor frowned. 'Now look here, John, how is your father? Really?'

'Not well,' said John reluctantly. 'Not himself.'

'Thought so. Rum-ti-tum. Well, I'll be frank with you, John, as the doctor's still too beaten down to take much notice, and as it will concern you as much as he. Your father's finances are in a pretty pickle. His debts are so large and so pressing that his professional income – supposing it ever revives – would be insufficient to clear them in his lifetime. That's not so very uncommon in this world of ours, alas; but this loan from Goodway is the majority difficulty. Rather than renegotiating it at higher interest, or disposing of the bill to one of the brokers who deal in such things, Goodway is sticking by his rights. And as your father has already exhausted his credit, on security of part of his property, and put up the rest as security for this infernal loan, then . . . I'm afraid he really has nowhere to turn.'

'But even the law,' said John, as Mr Flowers looked grim, 'even the law must recognize the impossibility of getting blood from a stone.'

'Not so in this case, I'm afraid. Your father has property – the house and grounds, and effects. A little grazing land in the parish of Saltmarsh; a few stocks, which I persuaded him to buy, and which he has clung on to. Oh, yes, John, there is blood to be got from this particular stone. Now, if there has to be a forced sale of your father's property—'

'There will not be,' blurted John. Whether or not the moment had come to put forward his idea, he simply could not bear the implications of Mr Flowers' words, and had to cut them off sharp. 'Mr Flowers, that will not – that must not happen. It *need* not happen. It isn't true that Father has nowhere to turn.'

Mr Flowers raised a wrinkled eyebrow.

'There is my uncle Saul,' said John.

Mr Flowers raised the other eyebrow.

'He is a wealthy man,' John pursued, 'and my father's only near relation. If Father will not or cannot appeal to him for help, then I shall certainly do so.'

'Dear me, dear me,' said Mr Flowers, pulling at his jowls, 'Mr Saul Two-penny . . . Unfortunately, as with this debt to Goodway, the wretched personal element obtrudes. Mr Saul Twopenny is not a client of mine, but I know well that there is not the friendliest of feeling between him and your father. I also know that Mr Saul obeys the Shakespearean injunction – neither a borrower nor a lender be. I would not care to be the man to suggest that he toss a couple of thousand pounds of his own money down the well of your father's debts.'

'You will not have to be the man, Mr Flowers,' John said. 'I will do the asking. Why – ' he laughed nervously – 'I would walk into a lion's cage if it would help my poor father; and even approaching Uncle Saul for money cannot be as bad as that.'

'Commendable in you – commendable, John.' There seemed to be a genuine sadness mixed up with the natural sadness of the lawyer's drooping features, and he hesitated before saying, 'John, I hate to keep dashing down your hopes like this. But really, you must bear in mind that though your uncle is a wealthy man, certainly the wealthiest man in Hales-next-the-sea, his wealth is all in assets. The maltings, the warehouses – I believe he owns coastal vessels too. I doubt whether he keeps large capital sums by him—'

'But he could realize them,' said John, 'very easily. Could he not? If even my father's property, in the last resort, will meet the debt, think how more than equal to it my uncle's resources would be!'

'You argue like a lawyer, John,' sighed Mr Flowers. 'But what, I ask you, would be your uncle's motive? Why should he help to save your father from – forgive me – from possible bankruptcy?'

John flinched inwardly at the word; but he recalled another word, one that his father himself had used with emphasis during Saul's visit. 'Kin,' he said. 'My father and he are kin.'

'A little more than kin, and less than kind,' murmured Mr Flowers. 'Shakespeare again. *Hamlet* again, in fact. Funny how these things crop up. Fol-de-rol. Well, John, you've obviously thought it out, as far as it goes. I cannot of course prevent you from applying to your uncle, but what I can do is warn you that not a man in the county would lay odds on Saul Twopenny agreeing to act like the genie of the lamp for anyone, kin or no kin. And warn you too – as a friend – not to allow this hope, if it is a hope, to blind your eyes to the very serious consequences of your father's insolvency.'

John assured him that he would not; and thanking him for his confidence, made ready to leave.

'I shall probably be over at Saltmarsh to see you soon,' Mr Flowers said, accompanying him to the outer office. 'I often go that way – calling, you know . . . Give my regards to your father. You wouldn't care to give me a little something before you go, would you?'

'Surely – what?'

'A little of your hope. Commodity I have rather undervalued. Goodbye, John.'

Certainly John had hope to spare, now that his idea of Saul as saviour had taken hold of him. And yet, though that hope lightened his steps on the long tramp back to Saltmarsh, something acted on him in quite a contrary manner, as if a heavy pack were strapped to his shoulders, and growing heavier with every stride. It was Mr Flowers' warning. For John had heeded it; and, as he walked, he opened his eyes to those very serious consequences Mr Flowers had hinted at, and looked them in the face.

And though it was the ruin of his poor father that he first saw, self would not be kept out of the picture. Self shouldered its way in, and cried 'Me too!' Self summoned up a memory of a year or two ago, when it had been definitely decided that John was to study medicine, and Dr Twopenny, with much cheerful reminiscence of his own student days, had set out a plan of expenses. Registration fees; lecture fees, for all the individual disciplines – surgery, anatomy, midwifery, pharmacology, chemistry, osteology, pathology, materia medica; cost of medical instruments; cost of textbooks; cost of board and lodging; cost of premium for a hospital dressership – all extending over five years or more, and representing an expenditure of hundreds of pounds. 'It will not be wasted, Father, I promise you!' John had said, chastened even then by the total, but excited beyond measure by the prospect . . .

87

And now, the whole prospect might be destroyed! The pack of foreboding dragged at John's shoulders, and he could not shake it off. Was there no other way? Supposing the worst should happen, was there no other way of reaching his goal? He could not see one. Poor men did not become doctors. Even the old apothecary's apprentice required a hefty premium. The future that had been planned for John, and that he had set his heart on from childhood, depended on foundations of financial security, and the foundations were gone.

The pack grew heavier still as John thought of Catherine, and how blithely he had looked to that same future to furnish the means of uniting them. Self, in fact, would not be silent, and cried its woes until the church-tower at Saltmarsh came in sight.

And then, somehow – perhaps on seeing the gabled roof of his father's house, and thinking of the generous, flawed, suffering man within it – John got hold of self, and choked it into silence. And when it made a last feeble groan, he shouted it down with the assertion that he was young, and strong, and taught, and had a great expanse of years at his disposal, and that all other considerations were mere querulous complaining. So he fortified himself for whatever lay ahead; although as he opened the door and prepared to show a cheerful face to his father, self exacted a sign from him before he could stop it.

Dr Twopenny was in his study, and from the mass of papers spread out on the desk, John at first supposed that he was trying to turn his mind to the outstanding bills. But then his father gave him an aching, beatific smile, and held up one of the papers, and John saw that it was covered in his mother's elegant handwriting.

'Her very first letter to me!' Dr Twopenny said with childlike wonder. 'More than twenty years old, and the ink has hardly faded! I have them all, you know – I kept them all carefully. See? She was a wonderful writer of letters. She would make the most acute observations in the slyest way – she could picture people in just a few words, so amusingly – oh, but not with malice, never with malice . . .!'

'She always wrote me delightful letters when I was first at school, and homesick,' said John with a smile. He studied his father a moment. 'Father, I – I have been to see Mr Flowers.'

'Aye, aye, have you, my boy?' Dr Twopenny said, hunting through the heap of letters. 'And how is he?'

'Oh . . . very well, I think. Father, he told me what desperate straits we are in.' John went on to recount his conversation with the lawyer, omitting his idea of appealing to Uncle Saul. However little hope there was in that plan, he still meant to carry it out – but alone, and without his father's knowledge. While he spoke, his father continued to sort through his mother's letters, stopping to read a line or two here and there with that lost smile on his face; and John began to wonder whether he had heard a single word.

'Well, anyhow, Mr Flowers has written you,' John concluded, 'and can probably explain it better than I.'

Dr Twopenny met his eyes. 'Oh, I know it all, well enough, John. I have dug myself into a dreadful hole, and you with me. The first does not matter; the second matters more . . . more than I can say. You have lost your prospects, my boy, and the knowledge of it is written on your face, though you are trying so hard to disguise it.'

'Nonsense – nonsense, Father, I have lost nothing—'

'No, no, John. Hush. It's said now. All's said and done, now . . .' Dr Twopenny lifted another letter reverently, and his voice trembled as he went on, 'She was my mascot, John – my luck, if you like. It was a great deal of luck for a man to have, and it ran out . . . Will you leave me a little while, John? We will – we must, of course, talk of this tomorrow. But for the moment I am a little unmanned, and need to be alone. You are not offended?'

'No, Father. Of course not.'

Dr Twopenny gazed at him, and something seemed to kindle at last in the eyes that had been so empty and helpless. 'Your mother's son!' he said. 'God bless you.'

John went to his room. The afternoon was too far advanced, and he was too tired from his earlier journey, to contemplate going to Hales today; but he was determined to make the approach to Uncle Saul the very next morning, and he spent the rest of the day carefully plotting how it was to be done. A bleak voice murmured that all his arguments – family feeling, Christian charity, regard for the reputation of S. Twopenny & Son – would simply rebound off the granite obduracy of Saul; but he chose to ignore it, and rehearsed his persuasions until he was word-perfect.

He came down to find Tetty laying supper. 'I hope the doctor will eat a bit tonight,' she said. 'He've hardly touched a bite lately. I wish you'd persuade him.'

'I'll try,' said John, going to the study door; but Tetty called after him, 'He's not in there, Mr John – I saw him go out to the garden a while since.'

The light was dimming, and in the garden Emma Twopenny's flowers were trading their colours for scents, which hung so rich and heavy in the air they seemed on the point of distillation into oozy essences. A shape lay athwart the garden-seat which John thought from a distance was his father, resting, but on drawing nearer he saw it was only the shadow from the cherry-tree, falling long and dark in the westering sun. He went on to the foot of the garden, where the inland cliff climbed away to dissolve in dusk; the garden gate was unlatched, but there was no sign of his father along the public path beyond.

'The gate's open,' John said to Tetty on his return to the house. 'He must have gone for a walk.'

'Ah. Well, that'll do him good, I reckon. He've hardly stirred from the house this past week.'

'Yes,' said John, 'yes, it's a fine evening.'

If both were a little uneasy, neither would admit to it. John asked Tetty to postpone supper until his father's return, and sat down with a book; and could make nothing of it, though he read the same page over and over until at last darkness obscured it altogether. He did not know how long he continued sitting thus; but he gave a start like a sleeper when a bloom of light appeared before his eyes, and Tetty stood before him, bearing candles.

'Is Father back yet, Tetty?'

'No sign of him.' The candle-flames wavered slightly, though there was no draught.

'Perhaps he walked further than he meant to,' John said, 'absent-mindedly – you know.'

'Just what I thought,' Tetty said.

'Perhaps I should take a turn outside myself, and – and see if I can meet him on the way home.'

Tetty nodded. 'Perhaps that'd be best.'

They were both striving with all their might to maintain the fiction of there being nothing wrong, and both knew it, and neither knew why. But somehow it seemed dreadfully necessary that neither of them betray the slightest anxiety. Even when Tetty suggested that he take a storm-lantern, and neither of them could get a steady enough hand to light it for several minutes, they still behaved as if they did this every night of their lives. And when John set out with the lantern, calling, 'I shouldn't be long,' to Tetty waiting in the doorway, the same fiction inhibited him from hurrying, or giving any sign that he was doing anything more than taking a stroll, until he was out of sight.

Then he did hurry, but with such panicked aimlessness that at last he forced himself to stop, and get his breath, and think.

His father could not have gone far; he was no great walker since putting on weight, and he had been in lowered condition lately. The conclusion first reassured, then alarmed John. Supposing, in his distracted state, he had outwalked his strength – somewhere along the cliff-paths, or the marshes, with darkness coming down, and the going treacherous even to the alert and sure-footed?

The thought filled John with such dread that his mind instantly cast about for another. The village: perhaps his father had wandered down to the village, and been waylaid there. The Dun Cow? He had rather shunned human company than sought it of late, but it was worth a try. Or someone might be ill, and he had been detained because of that – or someone, at least, might have seen him . . .

Try it, try it: be quick. John ran. The village of Saltmarsh after dark was quiet. John met no one but a boy bringing back a recalcitrant heifer from late grazing. The doctor? Hadn't seen hide nor hair. Hadn't seen nothen but this blamed old beast what had made him miss his supper.

John ran. The conversation died a little in the bar-parlour of the Dun Cow when he burst in: everyone was merry, and it was embarrassing to find someone touched with tragedy in their midst. The doctor? Not been here. Anybody see him? Tom? No from Tom. Nat? No from Nat. Benjamin? Some hesitation from Benjamin the feed-dealer, not because he had seen the doctor, but because he was a pontificating old blockhead who liked to think he knew everything, and wished to differ from his fellows even in this. But at last, regretfully, no likewise.

No, too, from little Ethan Meacham, bashfully seated in a shady corner with his half-pint mug; but just as John, after thanking them all, is about to leave, Mr Ethan arrests him on the threshold with a tug at his sleeve.

'John, you'll not breathe a word, I hope, to Dad? About me being in here? Only he don't know, you see – he think I've just stepped out to bait the horse – hee, hee!'

'Of course not, Mr Ethan,' says John; and the trouble in his face must be plain even to Mr Ethan's dim sight, for the little old man touches his sleeve again, and quavers, 'You're a mite worried about the doctor, John? Afraid he's little upset in his mind, as you might say?'

It is what John wishes above all not to admit, even to himself, but he admits it. Yes.

'Then say no more. I've got my jag here, so I'll soodle along now, and get out our horse and buggy. No, thass no trouble, John. I'll trot her down to the Gap, and come round by Holt, and we'll see if we can't find out where the doctor's gone to; and do I come across him, I'll bring him home as smooth and steady as a railway-ingin – he won't feel a bump!'

With heartfelt thanks, John parts with Mr Ethan outside the Meachams' cottage; and, after a moment's indecision, makes his way down to the marshes.

Mist here, off the sea, but not so thick as in winter: an evanescent mist, rather, which rolls of a sudden towards you, so that you expect to feel the impact like a curtain, but which then seems to disappear as it reaches you. Brackish water throwing off sullen gleams from John's lantern, as if it would rather he didn't see it, but be sucked down into it instead. Thorn bushes, catching the same light strangely, and rearing up in the shapes of horned creatures and giant faces. Noises, all subdued and murmurous – the sea beyond the shingle bank, roosting birds, breeze in the dune-grass – so that even John's own footsteps sound furtive, and give him an odd sensation of being up to no good. Mist, and water, and thorns, and noises; but no sign of anyone.

'Father!' Again. 'Father!'

Somehow the sound does not seem to carry in the damp salt air, and John's voice comes back to him flatly – as if the marshes, in their enduring emptiness, know nothing of fathers and sons, of love and grief and death and all the little human story. Father? He is not here. Why should he be?

'Father!'

John tries to shout the ancient indifference down; hears only a sigh from the retreating sea. Wheels about, to call again, and finds a figure facing him in the lantern light.

The Soldier: with his bait-sack and spade over his shoulder, and in his eyes a startled expression that brings home to John how wild and agitated he must look. Brings home, too, how wild and agitated he feels.

'Soldier – you haven't seen my father, have you?'

'Well, we saw him about an hour ago, didn't we, mice?' says the Soldier; and then something crosses his face, as if he were impatiently recalling the man he once was, and the Soldier addresses John directly. 'Yes, John, I saw him – about an hour ago, perhaps more. Just as the light was dying. I was digging on the flats, and I saw him go by, up on the cliff-path. Heading west, Hales way. His head was down, and he took no heed of me. You're troubled about him, John?'

'Yes, I – I don't know why. He went out without leaving word, and he's been gone some time, and so I . . .' John's agitation is no less, but something of that cold dread leaves him, now that he has definite word of his father; and in a moment a leaping idea possesses him. Hales-next-the-sea – he was heading in that direction . . . Could Dr Twopenny have hit on the same scheme as John, and gone to appeal to his brother Saul?

But why after dark? And why not in the new gig? Secrecy, of course: his father must have felt shamefaced; and, after all, John had been intending to apply to Saul secretly too. How prompt John's mind is with comforting answers!

'Where do you suppose he's gone to, John?' says the Soldier, looking most searchingly into John's face.

'I think perhaps he may have set out for Hales,' says John; and a little of the dread brushes him again. For it is more than five miles to Hales-next-the-sea, along a dark coast road. Dr Twopenny is simply not up to such a journey – though in his current state of mind he may not know it.

'A long way,' says the Soldier, echoing John's thoughts. 'Not advisable, I'd have thought, for a man past middle age, at night. A sorrowing man, too . . . I think we ought to walk that way ourselves, John, and see if we can't find him – if you've no objection to company, that is. Whatever business he has at Hales can wait till tomorrow, I'm sure.'

John nods tightly, and thanks him; and they set out together, leaving the marshes, and striking the coast road beyond the dyke. He is glad of the company, indeed; for that surge of relief he felt is receding, and misgivings are stealing on him again like waves on a cold shore.

Onward then, swiftly, with the inland hills on their left, dark with whispering woods; onward with the light of the storm-lantern sweeping the shadows like cobwebs from their path; onward, with vagrant memories flitting through John's brain, of the many times he has tramped this same road, and one in particular returning ever and anon to torment him with its vanished brightness – a memory involving Philip, and a mermaid in a glass bottle. And here – here is a part of that memory: the Hanged Man's House, brooding in its blighted cliff-nest above them.

Stop: the Soldier's hand is on his shoulder. The Soldier screws up his eyes. He has seen a slight movement in one of the gaping windows of the Hanged Man's House.

There: John sees it too. Definitely a movement within! A grim place for the doctor to stop and shelter and rest himself – but no matter, let it be so, let it be so!

John starts up the overgrown path towards the house, but the Soldier starts up too, and overtakes him; and with a firm but gentle hand, holds John back on the threshold. For the Soldier's eyes have seen that movement inside the ruined house more keenly, and the Soldier is afraid he understands what it signifies.

'Wait a moment, John,' the Soldier says. 'I'll look. It – it may not be anything.'

He takes the lantern, and with another firm injunction to John to stay where he is, the Soldier steps inside the house. The uplifted light shows him, in an instant, what he feared to see; and even the Soldier, hardy creature that he is, almost drops the lantern at the sight.

He recovers himself, however, in time to dart back outside, and wrestle John backwards, to prevent him from seeing what it is that is in there, moving back and forth like a slow pendulum. John struggles, but the Soldier's grip is tight; and he holds him there like a stern brother, until John sags in his arms, knowing, knowing all, and beaten down by the knowledge as if by a brutal club.

The Hanged Man's House has earned its name now, if it did not earn it before. If it is the abode of ghosts, as superstitious folk hereabouts say, there will surely be another haunting its gaunt spaces after tonight – the ghost of the big, generous, stricken man who has thrown a rope over the stoutest of the bare beams, and extinguished his own life at the rope's end. Scrawled on the wall with a piece of chalk beside his dangling feet are two words, in which the boldness of Dr Robert Twopenny's handwriting may yet be discerned. The words are NO HOPE; and with those words, and that ignoble death, the disaster that has descended upon John Twopenny seems complete, and he is in darkness.

Book Two

CHAPTER ONE

The Facts of the Case

The carriage bearing Admiral Fernhill's putative arms was in service again, and again carrying the two young ladies, Catherine Fernhill and Verity Deene, along the coast road of North Norfolk. The season now, however, was autumn, as the dun colours of the hedgerows showed; and if not yet cold enough for the top of the barouche to be raised, cool enough for wraps to be superadded to the ladies' voluminous profusion of skirts – which gave them the appearance of a pair of hot-air balloonists who had fortuitously fallen, balloon and all, into a moving vehicle.

'Catherine,' Verity said, noticing her companion's wistful expression, 'I'm afraid I know what you're thinking of.'

'Do you?' Catherine said with a start. 'Well, I don't wonder at it. I declare you're quite a reader of minds sometimes.'

Verity refrained from commenting that Catherine was, on the whole, no more difficult to read than an ABC; and she was, besides, thinking of the same thing herself.

'It was just along this stretch of road,' Catherine sighed, 'that we came across John, back in the summer when he lost his poor mother. How pale and drawn he looked then! And yet worse was coming to him, though none of us knew it. There was another terrible blow waiting to fall on him – and yet we didn't know . . .'

'No one could have known,' Verity said. 'Perhaps it's as well we don't have foreknowledge of what's going to happen to us – or we should be afraid to live at all . . . Was there a letter from him today?'

'Not today,' Catherine said sadly. 'He tries to keep it up, but in truth I think the poor fellow still hardly knows where he is. Oh, but I don't want to talk about that,' she added, though Verity knew perfectly well that she did, and would do again presently. 'This isn't a day to be thinking about such things. It would be most unkind to arrive at Mr Flowers' house with long faces. He's been so looking forward to this day. *Your* day, Verity.'

'*My* day? Oh, dear – I would just as soon disclaim the ownership, you know, and let someone else have it,' said Verity, laughing a little constrainedly.

'Now, you can't mean that, I'm sure. I don't have your way of seeing right into things, but I can see quite plainly what Mr Flowers means by inviting us to luncheon today. If the subject of marriage doesn't come up sooner or later, then I'll be – well, I'll be *very* surprised.'

'Marriage, eh? You think Mr Flowers means to take us both – wives by the brace, like a sultan?'

'Verity, of course not. Would that, by the way, make us both sultanas? —What a curious idea. No, the proposal of marriage is going to come *your* way, of course; but as it doesn't do, apparently, to ask a young lady to your home unchaperoned, even a young lady you want to be your wife – well, then poor Mr Flowers has to be at the expense of feeding me into the bargain. But I shall look sharp, my dear, and make myself scarce whenever you want me to. You were always very discreet when you had to play chaperone to me, and I hope I shall be the same.'

Catherine spoke brightly, but this reference, and its inevitably associated thoughts of John, cast a visible cloud over her expression; so Verity, though haunted by phantoms of her own, said gently, 'I was very glad to do it, Catherine, though I dare say I never showed it – and I hope to play that role for you again, whatever happens.'

'Thank you,' murmured Catherine, with the perplexed, myopic look that Verity knew meant she was close to tears. 'But I – just now I really don't see how that will ever be, you know. Poor John will, I suppose, recover his spirits eventually, though having to live with that fearful uncle of his can't be hastening the process; but even when he is himself again, nothing can be quite as it was before. There was absolutely nothing left for him, Verity, when his father's property was sold – everything was swallowed up by Dr Twopenny's debts. He has no means of support except such as that monstrous uncle may offer: all his plans and his prospects have come to nothing. I simply don't know what he's going to do.'

'I know what you mean. In fairy-tales, lovers can ignore practical considerations, but life, alas, is not so accommodating.'

'And then there's his poor father's . . . well, disgrace. Considering how many lives Dr Twopenny may have saved with his skills, I don't see that the taking of his own life, in terrible distress of mind, is so very unconscionable; but I know other people don't see it that way. And considering how many fine gentlemen live in debt, I don't see that dying in debt is so very much more reprehensible; but I know that other people think otherwise . . .'

'You are too loyal to say "Mama and Papa", instead of "other people",' said Verity, 'so I will say it for you.'

Catherine looked deeply unhappy. 'I'm sure – I'm sure they have my best interests at heart,' she said, 'but wishing me to end the association altogether – even to the extent of forbidding John to come to Buttings – it seems hard. It's not as if the fault was John's . . .'

'I know,' Verity said. 'But mud, as they say, sticks. And when it comes to bankruptcy and suicide, that sort of mud takes a lot of washing off, as far as – as far as other people are concerned.' As so often, there were things in Verity's mind that she could not say. She could not say, for example, that far from condemning the late Dr Twopenny and all his works as vociferously as the admiral and Mrs Fernhill and all their cronies had been doing, they ought to be thanking his departed shade for furnishing them with such a fund of gossip, for their dreary dinner-tables had never been so lively before they had had this choice morsel to chew over. And she could not say, either, that Catherine's meek acceptance of her parents' prohibitions did no honour to her love for John, or John's love for her, or the unfortunate position in which he had been placed. For very love of Catherine, she could not say it; for she knew Catherine to be true, and good-hearted, and very loyal. Little as her parents had done to merit Catherine's devotion, they had it in full measure; and her tender heart recoiled at the thought of going against their wishes. So, she could understand this acquiescence of Catherine's, if not condone it; and it was, besides, none of her business.

Ah, but it was; at least, her own heart meddled in the business, though it had no place there. And that was something she could not say either. She could not speak of Catherine's love for John, or John's love for Catherine, with objectivity: she could not put the hypothetical case, that if *she* were in Catherine's shoes she would snap her fingers in the admiral's face, run to John, and be with him come hell or high water – because it was not, really, a hypothetical case at all.

Quick, the trapdoor: push it down, nail it down. There. Keep it so.

'I hope Mr Flowers has not put himself to a lot of trouble on our – all right, on my account,' Verity burst out, in a cross-grained way that she had not meant but could not help.

'Why, you are a curious creature!' Catherine said, laughing, 'I would think it odd if he had *not* put himself to a good deal of trouble for such an occasion.'

Verity silently acknowledged the truth of this; and said, watching the glimpses of the sea winking between the trees, 'You would very much like to see me married to Mr Flowers, wouldn't you, Catherine?'

'I would like to see you happy,' Catherine said after a hesitating moment. 'And if – if Mr Flowers can . . .'

'Happiness,' said Verity reflectively. 'There isn't so very much of it in the world; and I think I can unreservedly say that the wife of Mr Flowers can expect to find, in any event, a reasonable amount of it. Oh, but Catherine, should it *be* like this? So *very* civilized? Lord knows, I have never felt the least inclination to run away in a gypsy caravan in a thunderstorm, with a swarthy adventurer who will be bewitchingly beastly to me. But this . . . I almost feel as if I were going to Mr Flowers' house like a prospective tenant, and were expected to haggle with him over the carpets and cutlery. And there – I have called him Mr Flowers again. I should be calling him Arthur, shouldn't I?'

Catherine was unable to forbear smiling at her expression, but said, 'Arthur's a very nice name, I think. Very knightly and sturdy. I always felt sorry for poor King Arthur, you know, the way Guinevere carried on . . . Oh, but Verity, it's only natural you should see Mr Flowers' house, and meet his little daughters; and I think he's rather proud of both, in his way.'

'Yes . . . I think he is. Oh, I don't know what to think. Talk of something else until we get there. When does Augustus go up to Cambridge again?'

'Next week. He's bought himself a new gun, to go wildfowling on the Fens. I do hope he doesn't shoot himself again. I suppose . . . I suppose we shall be hearing from his friend quite soon, shan't we?'

'I suppose so.' Augustus had had a friend from the university to stay at Buttings recently. The friend, on learning that Verity was to be a governess – unless something else intervened – had mentioned some connections of his in London who were looking out for a governess, and were despairing of finding one to suit. 'Sterling people,' said Augustus's friend, whose name was Crisp, but who was the very opposite of his name in manner and appearance. 'Sterling people, tip-top establishment. He's a partner in the City: rock-solid. She's a splendid woman: take her for twenty-one. Four children. Apples of parents' what's-name. Position of governess vacant, generous remuneration, extremely respectable situation. Like me to inquire?'

Verity had said yes; and the admiral had said yes, very emphatically. Here, it seemed, was the perfect opportunity. Young Crisp had been as good as his word, forwarding Verity's references to the family in London himself, and a reply was expected with every post. It was expected too that if the reply was favourable, Verity would take the situation. The admiral had made that quite plain. Verity fancied him ready to pack her trunk with his own hands, if it meant he was rid of her more quickly.

And yet all was not so clear-cut as the admiral and Mrs Fernhill supposed. Self-absorbed as they were, they had taken little heed of Mr Flowers' decorous courtship of their poor relation, and did not suspect what the issue of today's visit to Sheringham might be. Almost a reason in itself to accept Mr Flowers' proposal – just to see their faces . . .! But this flippancy would not do. Her thoughts kept taking refuge in it, more and more as the carriage drew nearer to Sheringham, but it would not do. Mr Flowers might be an easy-going sort of man, but he was serious, and this was serious.

'Oh, it's charming!' cried Catherine, as the carriage drew up outside their destination.

No other word would have sufficed for Mr Flowers' house. Everything about it carried an invitation. The little front garden, fenced about with neat wooden palings, and still colourful in September, invited you to take a look at the back garden, and see if that wasn't even prettier. The latticed windows on the lower floor promised window-seats and snug corners; the dormer windows in the roof promised airiness, and views out to sea. The whole house suggested that, whatever you wanted, it would have; and it promised privacy too. 'Are there people you would not have here?' it said. 'Are there things in the world you wish to escape – circumstances, influences, sensations, against which you wish me to close my door, and put up my green-painted shutters, and exclude for ever? Consider it done.'

Tempting, tempting indeed! Verity was certainly not proof against such blandishments. 'Am I a very bad person?' she asked herself. 'I have never thought so. But whatever the outcome of this day, I fear I shall think myself a very bad person – or a foolish one, which is the same thing, and deserving of the worst punishment that even I can devise – I know I shall!'

And here was Mr Flowers to greet them. Amiably formal as ever, but adorned, in honour of the occasion, with a new white waistcoat. And pleased though Verity was to see him, she knew that she should have been more than pleased, and that the sight of him, not of his house, should have lifted her heart.

'Quite a red-letter day for a dull old dog of a lawyer,' Mr Flowers said, handing them out of the carriage. 'Quite a red-letter day indeed.' And Verity's heart, instead of lifting, sank: because the terrible certainty that she had been trying to fend off would no longer be denied, and had made a pounce, and had her fast.

But it was too late now; she was here, and the visit must be got through, somehow. She shook Mr Flowers' hand, and noticed that he retained it longer than he did Catherine's – just a little longer. Still tactful – still discreet and unpressing! It ought to have made it easier for her, but it made it harder.

The same applied to Mr Flowers' two little girls, who were waiting, in a parlour as neat and trim as the exterior of the house, to be introduced. Nothing of their father's sleepiness of feature about them; they were, as their mother must have been, blue-eyed, fair-headed little creatures, bright as two new sixpences. Caroline, aged nine, asserted the dignity of seniority by shaking hands with the visitors, very gravely: Jane was seven and settled for a kiss. Their presence covered over the initial awkwardness – for Verity, not usually at a loss for a word, found herself tongue-tied, while Mr Flowers betrayed his nervousness by falling back on hums and tiddly-poms more than was his wont. And yet while she was thankful for the distraction provided by the two girls, at the same time Verity almost wished they were intolerable little monsters; that, at least, might have set an obstacle in the path that Catherine was expecting her to take, and that Mr Flowers was hoping she would take, and that all practical and rational considerations suggested she ought to take – and which she knew she could not take.

Their meal was set out on the snowiest of white cloths in the cosiest of dining-rooms, with windows opening on to the rear garden. 'Quite an attractive prospect, is it not?' said the shining silverware, and the honeysuckle outside the window, and the long-case clock comfortably ticking, and the engaging faces of the girls, in persuasive chorus: 'You could be happy, seeing us every day, could you not? Surely!'

So easy: so hard.

After luncheon the little girls, who attended a day-school, showed the visitors their exercises, and Jane read aloud from a story-book of firmly moral character, in which Georgy Gentle received, as a reward for his virtue, an unwarrantably large apple tart, whilst Nicholas Ne'er-do-well concluded his nefarious career by falling down an abandoned mine-shaft, with snakes in it. Mr Flowers looked on with perplexed fondness, and said to Verity: 'Prodigies, or merely infants of average abilities? I pride myself on impartial judgement, but fatherhood throws it.'

Panic: Mr Flowers was asking whether they would like to look over his little library, and Catherine was laughingly declaring that she would only show her ignorance there, and proposing that she take the little girls out into the garden. The proposition was accepted, as Verity knew it must be: the moment had arrived, as she knew it must arrive. Her heart sank lower, and she was sore with the unfairness of life. Mr Flowers did not deserve a refusal: he was a well-set-up man whose life did not entail a great deal of suffering, but it still seemed a crying pity that, having conceived (for whatever reason) a great liking and respect for her, and being able to offer her a thoroughly pleasant life, he should not have her as his wife.

Why not? Because, certainly, she did not love him; and a loveless marriage was not a good thing; and a loveless marriage into which the woman had been tempted merely by the prospect of material comfort was not at all a good thing. Yes. But there was more to it than that.

And the further pity of it was that, even now, when they were less at ease with each other than they had ever been, simply because each knew that their relation was coming to a crisis – even now, they got on well; and as Mr Flowers showed her over his library, they kept forgetting, as it were, what they were there for, and the old ease kept breaking through the new unease.

'Nothing compared with the library at Buttings, of course – more of a study, really,' Mr Flowers commented, 'but still, I enjoy it.'

The room was indeed the room of someone who loved books. Three walls were covered by them; the fourth was chiefly taken up by a broad bay-window, with a brocade window-seat. Nervous as she was, Verity's hunger for books was stirred, and she could not help roving about the shelves; though she knew they had not come here solely to talk of books.

'If anything catches your eye, do take it down,' Mr Flowers said. 'I'm a parsimonious lender of books as a rule, but not when it comes to – to special friends. Dum-de-dum, diddly dee.'

I must be a very bad person, thought Verity, whose back was to him as she scanned the bookshelves. I must be a very bad person indeed, because I am simply letting him go on, I am hiding, and what I should do is speak out and put an end to his torments.

His hopes too?

His hopes too. It must be so. But at least the suspense and indecision would be ended.

'Mr Flowers . . .' she said; and did not know how to go on.

'Miss Deene?'

She turned to him. He was looking at her expectantly, one hand resting on a fine terrestrial globe that stood in the corner of the room on a mahogany base. When she still did not speak – could not – he gave his sad smile and said, 'What do you think of this? Rather an extravagant purchase, but I couldn't resist it. Had a fascination for these things since I was a boy. Thought I wanted to go to sea, in those days. Nonsense really.'

'Why nonsense?'

'Oh! It was one of those things that one knows, deep down, one will never do. Or *I* knew, at any rate . . . Here's another confession. Every Sunday morning, when I have time on my hands, I come in here, and I spin this globe – so; and stop it at random – so; and wherever on its surface my finger falls, I say "Very well – that's where I'll go today," whether it be Berlin, or Boston, or Katmandu. Isn't that the absurdest thing? I do it every week without fail; and yet I know that I shall never go to any of these places.' His jowls waggled in what might have been a smile, and might have been a wince. 'I don't even like going to Norwich.'

'Mr Flowers . . .' Again she could not go on. Oh, a very bad person.

'Why am I telling you this? Oh, as a preamble, I suppose. Habit of the law – never use one word where ten will do. Rat-ta-ta. And also it's a sort of circumstantial evidence. About myself. So that you will know all the facts of the case, before . . .'

'Oh, Mr Flowers,' she said hurriedly, 'I'm sure I know all the facts of the case, indeed I do, because you have never shown me anything but – but perfect frankness and confidence, and I don't believe you capable of being anything but honest and straightforward even if you tried.'

'Well, thank you. Not often a lawyer receives such a compliment.' Mr Flowers frowned at the globe, and placing two fingers on India, walked them up to the Himalayas. 'I detect, however, a sentence beginning with "But".' He looked at her, and then at India. 'Am I right?'

Verity lowered her eyes. 'I fear I have not been as frank with you as you have been with me. I fear I have led you to suppose—'

'You have led me to suppose that we enjoy an excellent friendship. Nothing more,' said Mr Flowers punctiliously. 'If I choose to make a leap from that steady ground, to a more – speculative region, then the responsibility is mine, and I should take the consequences. Please, Miss Deene, don't give yourself a moment's uneasiness on that score – your conduct has been—'

'My conduct has been less than frank,' Verity persisted, 'because I have not given you any indication that – that our friendship may not lead to something more.'

Mr Flowers took a walk across Russia, and came to a halt at St Petersburg.

'And because I have not given you any such indication, you have very naturally supposed that it – it *may* lead to something more. And so I think you have it in mind to ask me—'

'I do have it in mind to ask you,' Mr Flowers said gently, 'but only if the asking is welcome.'

Oh, a very bad person! 'To any woman with a heart to feel, and a mind to understand,' she said, 'the asking would be very welcome. And from any such woman, including myself, if differently circumstanced, the answer would be yes—'

'Ah,' said Mr Flowers; and waded into the Baltic Sea.

'I am very sorry . . . You have a right to ask, of course, what those different circumstances are that prevent me—'

'I have no right whatsoever,' said Mr Flowers firmly. 'They exist: you have told me so, and that should be enough for me, and it is.'

'The only excuse I can make for myself,' said Verity, 'is that those – different circumstances are difficult to put into cogent terms.'

'All these things are, aren't they?' Mr Flowers sighed, and made a brief tour of Scandinavia. 'You have been frank with me,' he went on, 'and I thank you. I have only one misgiving. I would regret having ever spoken, if I felt that I had been so clumsy as to – as to press my attentions on a heart that is already . . . a heart on which there is a prior claim.'

He was a lawyer, of course: he missed nothing. And though she knew that silence would speak volumes, Verity found she could not utter a word; and so the volumes multiplied, and became enough to fill a library twice the size of this.

'An unfair question. Believe me, I would withdraw it if I could,' said Mr Flowers, looking from her to the globe; and descending through Germany, he crossed the Alps into Italy, with a melancholy indifference to the scenery.

'No, not an unfair question,' Verity said. 'A very natural one. But you shouldn't regret ever having spoken, because of that. You could hardly be expected to know, or even guess. You could hardly be expected to understand what I . . . hardly understand myself.'

'Well. I understand now. Diddle-de-dee. And I do not regret having spoken, Miss Deene. Not as long as our friendship is . . . still intact. And I think it is, you know.'

'Yes,' she said, 'I think so too.'

Mr Flowers took a plunge into the Mediterranean, and came up with a deep breath, as if refreshed. 'And I'd even go so far as to say it's been strengthened, in a curious way. Because – again in a curious way – we are both in the same boat, are we not?'

A sad, worldly amusement kindled the bloodhound eyes for a moment, and then Mr Flowers gave the globe a spin, as if in rueful acknowledgement that the world represented therein would keep on turning for all their heart-searchings. 'Well, let us go and see what those offspring of mine are up to. Are you composed?'

'Yes.'

'Good. I am composed too.'

And Mr Flowers gave her his arm, and they went out to the garden. And he was indeed composed, and remained so until it was time for Verity and Catherine to go, and stood outside the house waving them off, with his little girls by his side. Whether he was composed after that, Verity did not know, and never would; but she was not composed herself, not only because of the interview in the library, but because of the insight into herself that it had forced upon her.

But there was no time yet for reflection on that insight, because of Catherine – who was dying of curiosity, even though she tried with all her might to conceal it. So, Verity satisfied it as best she could, by saying that she and Mr Flowers had come to an amicable agreement, but the agreement did not include marriage, and there was an end of the matter. Her face must have been a discouragement to further questions, because Catherine kept looking at it whenever one rose to her lips, and then falling silent; and soon she accepted, in her good-natured way, that she would learn no more, and simply patted Verity's hand, gently, until they were home.

Reflection came with solitude, that night in her bedroom; and there was even more matter for reflection now, for during their absence the expected letter had arrived from London. Mr and Mrs Alfred Spikings, of Montagu Place, having the favour of a communication from their kinsman Mr Crisp, asked Miss Deene to wait upon them at her earliest convenience, with a view to her filling the place of governess to the Masters and Misses Spikings.

Here lay her way, then. The trunk that Admiral Fernhill could hardly wait to have packed was to be directed to Montagu Place, London, not to Mr Flowers' delightful house in Sheringham. It was for the best. Though her heart still ached for having to give Mr Flowers the pain of refusal, and reproached her for having allowed the matter to go so far, still she knew it was for the best.

'I must be quite away from him,' Verity said to herself; and it was not of Mr Flowers she was speaking. 'I must be far away – especially now, when my heart goes out to him so much that I can't answer for myself if we should meet. Of course, it may be that his present unhappy circumstances have softened me further, and brought me to the point of admitting to myself that I could love him – all right, that I *do* love him, in the most curious way – and that under normal circumstances, we would soon fall to arguing again. But no, that isn't honest: for why *do* I always try to provoke him so, as he once accused me of doing? Isn't it because I'm striking out at what can never be mine? I don't know. Anyhow, that's the one point I must bear in mind – *what can never be mine*. It's no use even thinking of him, for that reason; and here, I always will be thinking of him.

'So, it is for the best. Marrying without love isn't such a very bad thing as they say – but still, it is a bad thing. And how much worse, if your secret thoughts are treacherous; worse still, if the object of those thoughts lives just along the coast, and you can never be sure of not bumping into him!

'All for the best, then. Montagu Place, whatever it be like, is far away from him; there can be no sweetly tormenting associations there; and if I should take thoughts of him there, they will soon fade, in that alien atmosphere, I'm sure. For the best, then. All for the best.

'I just wish it felt like the best – instead of the worst!'

CHAPTER TWO

A Family Portrait

'It was no dream; I lay broad waking.'

The poem of which these words were a part had never been a favourite of John's, and he could not say he was greatly fond of it now. But he kept reading it and re-reading it, because something about that line haunted him.

Quietly, he spoke it aloud. ' "It was no dream; I lay broad waking".' And having read it again, he turned his eyes from the book to the dismal room in which he sat. He marked the gloomy wainscoting, dark as a coffin and just as wormy; he marked the iron bedstead, like a cage to keep a sleeper in; he marked the marble washstand and the earthenware ewer in which came the cold morning water; he marked the little high window with a lot of frame in it, and hardly any glass; he marked the engraved print hanging on the wall, in which a Teutonic and muscular Abraham offered his son for sacrifice, in what appeared to be highly inclement weather; he marked the single candle in its old pewter holder, rapidly burning down and bringing nearer the time when he would have no choice but to stop reading and go to bed. He looked at all these things, and tried to convince himself of their reality.

It *was* no dream: he *was* waking. This, now, was John Twopenny's world. Yet every day he had to reconcile himself to the fact afresh; and every day some part of him that was not absolutely dazed, bewildered and crushed to the point of indifference, protested that this could not be true.

'It did not happen,' cried out that intransigent part of his self now. 'My poor mother and father did not die; the house was not sold; I was not left penniless; I am not immured in Uncle Saul's grim house, and under Uncle Saul's grim guardianship, with no other prospect in sight: these are the phantasms of a dream!'

But the candle guttering at that moment, threw into stronger and more ghastly relief the features of the room, as if to remind him of their invincible reality; and a moment after that, there was a tap on the door, and another harsh reminder appeared in the shape of his cousin Sar'ann, who came creeping in dressed in her fearsome night attire, with her Bible under her arm.

'Not in bed yet?' she hissed. 'You owl! You'll suffer for it in the morning!'

'Why, you're not in bed yet either,' said John.

'Fine words butter no parsnips!' shrilled his cousin. 'What's that book you're reading? Is it devotional? I'll bet it isn't. Is it indecent? The circulating-library in Ship Lane has all manner of indecent books, Pa says, and the women who take them out are no better than harlots.'

'The candle's nearly spent. I'm going to bed, Sar'ann.'

'You'll miss the fun if you do!' Sar'ann's neck seemed to grow another inch in her pop-eyed excitement. 'What do you suppose? William's only gone and slipped out, and ain't back yet! Oh, my stars, won't he catch it! Oh, *won't* he come to grief! Ah, ha ha ha! *Won't* he just! Ah, ha ha ha ha . . .!' Sar'ann nipped the laughing fit in the bud with an adroit slap across her own cheek, and went on, 'Pa's sitting up, waiting for him. He's put Caleb at the kitchen door, in case William thinks to steal in that way; and he says he'll wait all night if he has to. He will, too: that's Pa – I know him!'

'What on earth makes William do it?' said John, more to himself than Sar'ann. It was not that he could not comprehend William's impulse to rebellion – three months' residence in his uncle's house was quite enough to furnish an understanding of that – but it was the way William went about it that perplexed him. He would come back from his occasional expeditions cringingly apologetic, as if the trifling trips to the waterside or the tavern were as dreadful a sin as Saul made them out to be.

'It's the devil, no more nor less,' said Sar'ann. 'The devil gets in William, and tempts him to run wild. And that's why Pa has to chastise with the rod. The only way to get the devil out of you is to *beat* him out. Why, I should know. I've had to have the devil beaten out of me in my time; and though I'm godly now, I still feel the devil moving inside me now and then – I feel him inside me, oh, yes, like a great nasty wriggly worm!'

'Well, I wish William could be a little more clever about these things, and not get caught,' said John.

' "Be sure your sin will find you out" – that's what scripture says.'

'There can't be any sin in having a little freedom once in a while.'

'Oh, my stars, I know *your* game! You reckon to slip out yourself one of these nights, and meet up with Miss! Well, I'd like to see you try. You ain't welcome at her Pa's, so I hear, now you're ruined – he wants bigger fish than *you* in his net – but I'll bet that won't stop you and Miss trysting, if you can manage it—!' Sar'ann broke off abruptly, and held up one bony finger in an attitude of listening suspense. 'Hark! There's one! Hear it snap?'

'I didn't hear anything.'

'Your ears ain't keen like mine. I can always hear the mousetraps go: even if I'm sound asleep, that noise wakes me. I can even hear 'em go in the kitchen down below. What do you think of that?'

John did not think much of it, and said so; but Sar'ann, for whom the setting of the mousetraps about the big old house was something in the nature of an absorbing hobby, only went off into a squeal of laughter. 'Now that one,' she said, 'sounded like the one I laid just outside the broom cupboard. They all have their own sound, you see, just like musical instruments. I'll bet I'm right – I'll go and see!'

So saying, the fair one darted off down the passage, presently returning with an expression of gleeful triumph. 'I was right! Caught, as smart as you like! There's a bit of life left in him, but there won't be by morning. Oh my stars – ' hugging herself with her rangy arms, and dancing on the spot – 'there won't be by morning!'

John, between weariness and disgust, was about to go and put the poor creature out of its misery when he was startled by the bang of the front door. Sar'ann was instantly all alertness again and, tiptoeing to the landing, leaned out over the banister, thrusting out her neck so far that she looked like some outlandish species of vulture sighting a kill. There were clumsy noises, a snatch of singing, and then two voices raised in disputation – one of them immediately recognizable, even at this distance, as the bass growl of Saul Twopenny.

'William's drunk! Oh my stars, William's as drunk as a bee!' pronounced Sar'ann in a penetrating whisper. 'Come and listen!'

Loath to share Sar'ann's morbid curiosity, but concerned in spite of himself, John went out to the landing and joined her at the banister. The hall below was in darkness, but a light was showing from Saul's private office off to the left, and from there came the voices. John now recognized the other as William's – but this was a new William, to John at least. He had smelt whiffs of drink on his cousin's breath once or twice before, but William was now plainly, as Sar'ann said, drunk as a bee, and was loudly denying the fact in the intervals of confessing the fact, all with a great deal of maudlin bluster and self-justification.

'. . . A man may take a drink! Pa, there's nothing against a man taking a drink, though I'm sorry I did, and I promise I won't do it again. But all the same, a man – a man—'

'Where is this man?' Saul's voice, measured and powerful, supremely self-assured even in his anger. 'Show me this man. I see no man here – only a boy, a mewling, whining boy in need of correction. Look at me, sir: don't hide your face from me, sir, else I shall cut you deeper!'

'Noah was drunk in his tent! It's in scripture – Noah was drunk in his tent!'

Sar'ann gasped. 'He'll catch it now,' she breathed. 'Oh, *won't* he just catch it!'

'You dare to cite scripture to me, do you?' rumbled Saul with ominous calm. 'You cite scripture to me, sir, do you, sir, to justify your depravity, do you, sir? You come home in the dead of night when godly folk are abed, reeking of the beer-shop and worse, and you cite holy scripture to me? Do I hear you aright, *sir?*'

The last 'sir' came out like a gunshot, and at the same moment there was a swift movement of shadows across the square of light in the hall below.

'Pa . . .!'

'Be silent, sir, or I'll flay you!'

Sar'ann sucked in a sharp breath as the first crack of the stick echoed about the hall.

'Pa . . .!'

'Still mutinous, sir?'

Crack went the stick again, and this time William yelped – a curiously sickening sound from a man of twenty-five. Sar'ann, at some hazard of overbalancing, lifted one hand from the banisters, and John saw it convulsively tightening in the air, as if she grasped an imaginary stick.

Crack. 'Now, sir, let me hear you cite scripture to me!' The old man breathed hard from exertion, but his voice was fierce and righteous and exulting. *Crack.* 'Let me hear it!'

'No . . . No . . .' It was impossible to tell whether the word groaning out between William's clenched teeth was No, or Noah; whichever it was, John had heard enough. 'I'm going to bed,' he said, turning away.

'Oh, Pa ain't finished with him yet!' Sar'ann said.

'Well, I'll leave you to enjoy the rest of the performance.'

His book was still open where he had left it; but as he entered the room the candle gave out, and there was nothing for it but to undress as best he could in the dark, and get into the bed. The sounds of 'correction' from below were indistinct now, but he pressed the hard bolster against his ears to shut them out completely, and stared into the blackness.

' "It was no dream; I lay broad waking".'

Something like a hard weight pressed itself down on John's chest as he whispered the words, the truth of which had just been so wretchedly confirmed; but the weight was nothing so concrete as grief, or despair, or rage. Rather it was a kind of heavy emptiness; and it was that heavy emptiness that had been with John for the past three months, and seemed to have taken the place of every active emotion.

The grisly exhibition downstairs, for instance, which would formerly have roused the most impetuous feeling in John's breast, affected him only insofar as the emptiness intensified, and bore down on him more suffocatingly. It was no dream, indeed, this new life of his, but the self that drifted about in it had no more substance than the self of dreams, and the wildest dream could not have supplied a more violent and drastic overturning of every familiar circumstance.

It had begun on the night when the Soldier had pushed him back from the

105

threshold of the Hanged Man's House, and had pursued its own remorseless logic ever since. In memory the whole business appeared swift, vague and – well, dreamlike; but John could not console himself that it had felt so at the time. In reviewing the events of the past three months he saw no kindly oblivion enwrapping the figure of self that moved among them. Every successive blow had been felt, agonizingly. His father's dreadful death; the funeral that had followed so swiftly upon that of his mother; the long bewildering meetings with Mr Flowers, in which the solicitor had gently tried to explain to John what must happen to his father's debt-encumbered estate; the assessors methodically going over the house, and making an inventory of its contents, whilst John and Tetty stood by like helpless children; the auctioneers' bills announcing the sale of the property; the parting with Tetty, who was going to stay with her sister-in-law until she could find another place, and who astonished him by bursting into tears for the first time in his knowledge; the carrying of Tib the cat over to an accommodating neighbour in Saltmarsh; and the intercession of Uncle Saul, who sat like a lowering prophet through several sessions in Mr Flowers' office, grunting righteously at each new revelation of his brother's financial delinquency.

'Robert was a fool,' was Saul's verdict. 'A man must speak the truth in the sight of the Lord, and so I say Robert was a fool. He reaped what he sowed – no more nor less; and so do we all.'

In the light of this stern philosophy, John had soon seen how vain had been his hope of applying to Saul for help, before his father's death had overturned everything; and now that the doctor was in his disgraced grave, Saul showed no more sign of seeking to mend matters. 'A man's debts must be paid, whether the man be living or dead,' was all he had to say; and the disposal of Dr Twopenny's property had continued apace. John inherited no debts: the creditors, including the ill-omened Mr Goodway, were all satisfied at last; but nothing reverted to John but a few books, clothes, and other personal possessions, and a box of his father's papers, together with some twenty pounds sterling, which John divided with Tetty. His mother's piano, her jewellery, her very dresses became lots at auction; and the life the three of them had had together in the house on the cliff at Saltmarsh was destroyed, rooted up, ploughed under and obliterated as completely as the ruins of Carthage.

All that remained was John, himself an undisposable piece of goods, though the tragic strokes that had fallen upon him had rendered him so spiritless and incapable that he might well have submitted to being put up at auction, and sold off to the highest bidder. Instead, a prospect hardly less forbidding was the only one open to him: the guardianship of his uncle Saul. He had no means, and nowhere to live once the new owners – a partnership of Norwich bankers – had taken possession of the house and land at Saltmarsh; and he was still a year short of his twenty-first birthday. The claims of kin operated at last merely in guaranteeing him a roof over his head. 'Well, you had better come to Hales, and shake down with us, boy' – it was thus that Saul took his orphaned nephew to his stony bosom. 'I see no help for it, unless you care to go on the tramp; and the condition you're in, I don't think you'd last a day. This is what comes of your upbringing: if you'd been brought up godly, you'd be prepared for death, instead of being broken up by it, and fit for nothing. But, as I say, there's no help for it. You may do as you please when you're of age, of course; but in the meantime you'll make yourself useful, I hope, and never forget that you dwell in my house, and that I am master in it.'

And that settled the matter: for 'broken up' and 'fit for nothing' very accurately described John's state of mind when he was taken in to his uncle's house at Hales-next-the-sea, and a blank indifference to his surroundings was a consequence of it. All the things he cared for were gone, and it was only an unheeding shell of John Twopenny that climbed down from the dray and entered the sombre quayside house that was to be his home for the foreseeable future. He was here because there was nowhere else for him to go, and because in his first wounded sorrow one place was much like another – not in what it had, but in what it lacked.

And never was there a place more lacking in every humanizing and encouraging influence than Saul Twopenny's house. The dwelling-house was only part – the most cheerless part, as it happened – of an extensive collection of buildings, including the maltings, the grain and coal-stores, and the counting-house; but it was large in itself. Not grandiosely large – more like the diggings of a badger, in the way its numerous cell-like rooms ramified from its cold corridors, and in its dank, earthy, lightless smell. The furniture was either massive and oaken, or bare and steely, as if it were all meant to survive a second Flood or some such apocalyptic overthrow, whilst of decoration there was none except some prints like the one in John's room, all illustrative of episodes from that most beautiful of books, such as the plagues of Egypt, Cain killing Abel, and the slaying of the first-born. The chief ornamentation the place boasted, indeed, was such as had been provided by the locksmiths, in fitting the numerous locks and bolts and bars with which every door and window was equipped, so that morning and night the house resounded with their grating and rattling like an almighty jail.

As if Saul had not already sufficiently impressed the whole house with his overbearing personality, he had his own private room on the ground floor, opening on to the hall so that he might see anyone coming in or going out. In this room he pursued his private devotions; in this room he received visitors; to this room he summoned his children for correction; and it was this room too that served as an annexe to his business premises, being filled with ledgers, files, account-books, cashboxes, and bundles of bills and invoices hung up by pegs like dismal laundry. For religion did not dominate Saul's every thought and impulse – or rather, it did, but it was a dual religion. There was the religion of Jehovah, and the religion of S. Twopenny & Son; and Saul brought to both aspects of his monomania the same fierce reverence.

His pride in the firm was a jealous, possessive pride – an emotion of an intensity normally associated with human objects, rather than abstractions. The firm of S. Twopenny & Son was, of course, more than an abstraction – it also represented so many thousand pounds worth of buildings, coastal vessels, industrial equipment, horseflesh, employees, and capital, and it was a thriving concern; but Saul's passionate attachment, John soon recognized, was to the idea as much as to the physical reality. The father of Saul and Robert Twopenny – John's grandfather, long dead before he was born – had been an indolent piece of small gentry who had married into trade, spent much of the money, and left his elder son scarcely more advantaged, in his scanty inheritance, than the younger who had no expectations and so went into the medical profession. But that elder son, Saul, had not been content to eke out the inheritance and console himself with the gentlemanly pretensions that went with it. Instead he had bought a dilapidated warehouse on the quayside at Hales-next-the-sea, and begun dealing in corn when the prices were still high; through fanatical industry, shrewdness and sheer hard-nosed cussedness, he had risen to be the wealthiest man in the town and, like some ancient Mesopotamian potentate, to write his name in giant letters all over it.

The embracing of trade bothered him not a whit. He might have been a country nobody: instead he was a merchant prince. Saul Twopenny, Esquire, might have lived and died unnoticed: Saul Twopenny the only begetter of S. Twopenny & Son was a man of power, and if the power was not of the sort that brought Society to his door, Society was a thing which his bleak ruggedness of temperament disdained anyway. The outer world was a matter of indifference to him; when he crossed the yard from his house to the maltings, he could truly say that he was monarch of all he surveyed. For while much about his appearance and demeanour suggested the prophet, to see Saul stumping indomitably about his rambling premises was to draw another irresistible comparison. He was a king, and this was his kingdom.

Alas for Saul, the kingdom was a hereditary monarchy. This wondrous creation of his could not in the nature of things remain his for ever: the God with whom he was on such intimate terms would call the old man to his gloomy heaven sooner or later. The eventuality had indeed been part of Saul's plans from the beginning; the words '& Son' had been added to the whitewashed signs on the day William was christened. If Saul's own hands must relinquish the orb and sceptre at last, they should at least be passed on to someone who was as nearly as possible a replica of Saul himself. Who else but his son?

And the son, the only son, was William. William the awkward, William the sullen, William the ineffectual, who displayed no interest in the business, no aptitude for it, and no consciousness that it was the supreme life-work to which the Almighty had been pleased to appoint him. Strange, unthinkable even, as it must have seemed to Saul, William gave strong indications that only lack of courage prevented him from affirming that he hated it.

The three months that John had passed in Saul's house, as he lay in bed that night reviewing them, seemed to blend into one joyless prayer-filled monotone, with one day much like another; and yet the salient points of that dull terrain were plain to see, and plainer still after what had occurred tonight. They were the clashes between father and son. Stubbornly Saul tried to mould his unsatisfactory son to his will; and with a stubbornness more fitful, yet with something underhand and slippery about it that infuriated the old man to frenzy, William waved his little flags of defiance, either with boyish truancies and dissipations, or with a lackadaisical negligence towards the business which was, in its way, the most thorough-going flouting of his father that could have been devised.

Three months was not long to form a judgement, but it did seem that the antagonism between Saul and William was growing worse. Did the presence of the newcomer in the house have something to do with the increasingly poisonous atmosphere? His welcome from his cousins had not been fulsome, and William in particular had seemed to resent even such sparing attentions as John received. Could it be that Saul now had a new stick wherewith to beat William, and that the stick was John – not John as he was, but John as he might be? For John was a Twopenny: he was young, able, and needy; might his presence not be the spur that was required to goad William into an appreciation of his position, simply by illustrating that, if he did not want it, there were others who might take it from him?

Whether this factor had entered into Saul's calculations in taking in his orphaned nephew, John could not tell; certainly his uncle was hard-headed enough to be capable of it. But he found no firm evidence to support a suspicion of his being groomed as an alternative successor to the throne – or at least as a Pretender, to make the Crown Prince change his ways. No firm evidence, that is, until the morning after the night of William's drunkenness and impiety.

Things proceeded as normal until after breakfast – which was a grey affair of porridge and weak tea, preceded by prayers for the whole household; the only thing at all out of the ordinary was William's silence, which was more constrained and brooding than ever. But when breakfast was over Saul, instead of leaving John to his own devices as usual, commanded him to follow him to his private office.

'As for you,' he added curtly to William, 'cut along to the quay, and tell the skipper of the *Henrietta* I wish to see him before noon. Now look alive.'

It was November, damp and raw, but no fire burnt in Saul's office. He sat at his desk, which was big and forbidding enough for a human sacrifice, and studied John for some moments, knitting his wiry brows.

'You are in mourning, nephew,' he said.

True enough: it had begun to feel like a second skin to John.

'You have lost your parents, as we all must, and it is natural you should grieve. The Almighty's will must be done, and is not to be questioned; but still, it is natural you should grieve. Right, too, that you should spend some time in reflection and, I trust, prayer; for your father committed the sin of self-murder, and I fear his soul is sadly in need of all our prayers, after such a death.'

John said nothing, and he was sure his face betrayed nothing; but the mention of his father was like the thrusting of a cruel blade. The thought of his father, indeed, was the one thing that turned his dazed apathy to nerve-tearing pain, and it was for that reason that he tried to keep it at bay every waking moment. It was impossible, of course. Try as he might to evade Dr Twopenny, Dr Twopenny would not be evaded: he hung from the great gantry that straddled the road in front of Saul's house, he swung from the masts of the ships that moored by the quay, and he dangled every night, most horribly, down from the rafters of John's bedroom, and into his tortured dreams.

'All this is right and dutiful; but a man must live in the world, nephew. I would not have you fall into the devil's hands through indulging in a fruitless repining; nor must you suppose that your keep costs nothing. There is plenty of work to be done here, and I propose that we put you in a way to take a share in it; which means, first, showing you over the whole establishment, so that you may see how it goes on. So: come.'

Saul grasped his stick, and stood; then, throwing John his most piercing glare, added, 'You're not too proud to work, I hope?'

'I'm willing to do anything you require of me, Uncle,' said John flatly. And with truth; for little as the business of S. Twopenny & Son interested him – little as anything interested him – he wished to earn his keep, and occupation might at least tire him bodily.

So Saul took his nephew on a tour of his kingdom. The oldest part, which directly adjoined the house and was reached by a little grim spiked gate set in a fragment of flint wall, was the warehouses. Here Saul dealt, in the old Anglian way, in corn and coal; the one going out from the rich Norfolk hinterland behind the town, the other coming in from the sea by coastal vessels. The warehouse-men, like the house servants, blanched and trembled at the king's passing; and when Saul made a sudden dart at a sack, plunging his hand in as if he suspected short measure, John saw one of the men actually buckle at the knees, as if he were about to flop down in an Oriental kowtow and beg for mercy.

Out at the little iron gate again, and they crossed the cobbled yard behind the house, with an array of stables and coach-houses on either side, and horsekeepers grooming brawny horseflesh. Ahead of them, and dominating the whole establishment, was the maltings; a giant building of dingy brick, three storeys high, and half as high again from its tall hooded chimneys, which seeped steam and a peculiarly rich odour, halfway between bread and beer. This was an operation very different in scale from the old backyard malt-house, and Saul paused before it with justifiable pride, gesturing with his stick.

'There was nothing here, nephew, but a few old timber outhouses, when I took it up,' he growled. 'Now every barley-grower in Anglia, and every brewer in Mercia, knows it. Here is what a man may do, if he fears the Lord, rises early, fills each day with industry, and keeps his feet from the paths of vanity and luxuriousness. You know, I hope, the parable of the talents?'

'Matthew, chapter twenty-five,' murmured John.

Saul looked a little discomfited at this, tending to consider the Bible as a confidential communication from the Almighty to him; but he let it go, grunting, 'Well, then, I hope you'll always bear it in mind. Would that your father had! But it's no use talking of that now.'

109

By the time John had recovered from the stabbing pain of this, they had entered the maltings, and Saul was introducing him to a man whom he identified as Addy, the foreman. It was John's initial impression that Mr Addy, for whatever reason, was standing in a hole, but when his eyes grew used to the dimness within the building he saw that the foreman was simply of very short and squat figure, with so little length of leg that John felt like a very giraffe beside him.

'Addy, my nephew,' said Saul. 'Rather than have him idling about the place, I propose to have him learn a little of the business, so that he may make himself useful.'

Mr Addy looked at John, and gave him a little nod which seemed to include acknowledgement of his acquaintance, commiseration with his mourning, and a readiness to instruct him in the mysteries of malting. He was an elderly man of tight, brisk, braced, choking appearance, with close-cropped white hair and a florid complexion, not improved by his neckcloth, which was wound about his neck like a tourniquet.

'Addy's been in my employ for thirty-odd years now,' said Saul, 'so he knows the business pretty thoroughly – as thoroughly as any man here, excepting me.' Saul scowled as his eye fell on a paper that lay on top of an upturned crate, weighted down by a lump of coal. 'Though you'd never suppose he knows it, on this evidence. What's this, man? A receipt?'

'Receipt,' said Mr Addy, perspiring, 'Mr Holmes of Fakenham, twelve bushels.'

'And you were just going to leave it there, I suppose, till you thought fit to send it over to me? Or until it blew away in a draught, and you could forget about it? I dare say you'd like me to forget about the twelve bushels, as well? And as for this –' picking up the lump of coal – 'I suppose you think coal comes so cheap you can use it for paperweights, eh? Perhaps if it was you who had to stump up for the coal, you'd think different. But it isn't you, Addy. It's my pocket you're picking, on top of your wages, and the Lord knows they're enough.'

Mr Addy stood quite still, reddening and perspiring, throughout this diatribe; and when Saul had done, he merely said, in his clipped way that was something like an oral equivalent of jotting with a stub of pencil, 'Busy morning – didn't seem to find time.'

'You'll find time for loafing, though, when I'm not around,' Saul grumbled. 'You all seem to find the time for that. Well, what now?'

There was an apologetic cough behind them: it was William. 'Skipper of the *Henrietta*, Pa,' he said, with a dark glance at John. 'He wants to catch the tide, so he says can he see you now?'

'Very well, if there's no help for it. Addy, you can show my nephew over the workings. I suppose you're capable of *that*, at least.' Saul turned to go, then addressed his son fiercely. 'Well? Are you putting down roots there, boy? There's a hand wanted in the warehouse – go and lend it.'

William went, though not without another mistrustful glance at John; and Saul went too. Mr Addy, however, did not move or speak until the king had departed; then he turned to John, said in his rapid jotting way, 'One minute – something to do,' and going over to an iron hand-pump in the corner, worked it until the water was as cold as could be. Then he filled a tub to the brim and, bending right over, doused his whole head in it. John could not forbear sucking in a sympathetic breath at this proceeding, but it seemed to refresh Mr Addy, who came up blowing and gasping and – so John fancied – visibly steaming, as if his lobster-coloured head were as hot as a blacksmith's iron.

'Better,' he said, breathing stertorously, 'but he've got me so hot today, that I shall have to take another.' So saying, he quenched his head a second time, and though he snorted and bristled tremendously, seemed to feel an appreciable benefit.

110

'Well, that's cooled me a little. I didn't shake your hand before, with him here, because I didn't know whether it would be right. Not that anything ever *is* right, with that one . . .' Mr Addy reddened again, and looked at the tub as if contemplating a third plunge, but recovered himself. 'So I'll shake hands now. Ever been in a maltings before?'

'Never in my life,' said John.

'We make the best malt in the county here, if not in all Anglia. Not that *he'll* give us any credit for it. —OH!' Mr Addy burst out explosively, dragging a handkerchief from his pocket, and dabbing his face gingerly as if it were an overheating boiler. 'He get me so hot, that one! Says I to myself, I won't let him stoke me up so, but he always does. He's like mustard, and pepper, and ginger, and devilled kidneys, all in one, to me!'

Having fumed himself into a tolerable coolness, however, Mr Addy shook hands with John again, and led him on a tour of the maltings. The building was certainly typical of Saul in its darkness and massiveness, but these, John learned, were also necessary to the malting process. The thick walls were required to support the malt floors, where the wet grain was spread out and turned with wooden shovels during the germinating period; the small windows and low beams ensured a close dark atmosphere, to regulate the growth of the grains. Though the malt floors took up most of the space, and gave the building its peculiar character, there was much more to be seen and understood: the chain hoist by means of which deliveries of grain were brought up to the top storey, the steeping tanks where the barley was soaked before being spread on the floors, and the kiln where it was finally dried over heated tiles to become malt and to send its tantalizing aroma up the chimneys and over the rooftops of Hales-next-the-sea.

The workforce required for this operation, which proceeded for nine months out of the year, was not small; and it soon became clear to John that, in this kingdom of Saul's, Mr Addy, in knowledge, experience and authority, was very much the first minister, and filled his office loyally and well. Interest was getting the better of John's listlessness, and he tentatively asked Mr Addy if Saul was usually such a hard taskmaster as he had shown himself that morning.

Mr Addy seemed on the verge of another explosion; then looked embarrassed, and muttered in his jerking way, 'Said too much already. Shouldn't. Specially to his nephew.'

'I'm his nephew,' John said, 'but I may as well say, right from the start, that I'm not like him at all.'

Mr Addy shook John's hand again, seeming to find this a better way of expressing his feelings than words; then, giving the ends of his neckcloth a yank, as if to tie himself in tighter, burst out, 'Usual? If it ain't usual, thass only because he's usually even harder than that. Usual? Why, he've been getting me so hot that I can't even sleep with bedclothes, and Mrs Addy say thass like lying down alongside a stove – he've been doing that to me, I say, every day since I first come here. Thirty-two years, two months, and some-odd days. He do that so bad sometimes, I swear I'm going to go up into the sky like a firework!'

Mr Addy, whose very perspiration seemed to sizzle on his brow, looked around him in a wild throttled way; but finding no water at hand, he had to content himself with getting out his handkerchief again, and wrapping up his head in it like a hot brick.

'I see,' said John. 'What I mean is, I suppose there are a lot of maltings in this part of the world . . .?'

'Scores,' answered Mr Addy, from behind the handkerchief.

'And a good foreman, I would have thought, is always wanted. What I mean is—'

'What you mean is, why stay with him, when he gets me choked up so?' Mr

111

Addy whisked off the handkerchief with a snort. '*I* don't know. I *can't* go elsewhere, somehow. I'd as soon think of skipping off and leaving Mrs Addy, I reckon. I shall end up as a Roman candle, or a catherine-wheel, no doubt, but I shan't leave him . . . Not that there's others as mightn't up and go one of these days, do he's not careful!'

Mr Addy seemed immediately to regret this cryptic confidence; but the reference was not lost on John. As for his own feelings about the work and the possible role to which he was being introduced, he could not with honesty say that he had any. He did not relish being made an instrument to fasten the errant William down to his duties; but as the days and weeks went by, and he obediently busied himself about the maltings and the warehouses, now supervising a delivery, now taking a turn with the malt-shovel, now working the pumps that fed the steeping-tanks, it became clear that he was such an instrument, and that William knew it. His manner became even more smothered, doubtful, and defensive; and one evening when his father casually asked him about some minor detail of the day's business, William blurted, 'Oh, why ask me, Pa? I've only lived here all my life, what would I know about it?' But the stern chastisement that such insubordination would usually have elicited was not forthcoming. Saul merely remarked that sarcasm was low and unmanly, and repeated his question, carefully observing his son with hooded and complacent eyes.

Some seeds of jealousy were thus planted: even such tyrannical attention as William had been used to receiving, was better than no attention at all, and so far Saul's experiment was succeeding. As for John, he did the work because it was occupation, and he had nothing else. He certainly had no ambitions about his uncle's business, least of all at the expense of his cousin. Ambition he had had in great measure from an early age, but only where the medical profession was concerned; and that had been buried with his parents, and just as irrevocably. He was penniless, and the years of expensive training necessary to be a physician were simply beyond his scope. The loss of that prospect, along with almost everything else that he held dear, contributed to something that he could only call a loss of identity. He was not himself any more, and so he might as well drudge at the maltings as do anything else.

His individual soul remained, of course, and that was all that mattered: so Mr Bream the minister assured him, one bitter winter's morning when he called at Saul's house. He was making a collection for a missionary settlement in Africa, and knowing Mr Saul Twopenny to be the warmest friend to the propagation of the Christian faith, was confident that he would be happy to subscribe to such an enterprise.

'The salvation of souls for God's kingdom,' Mr Bream enthused, with his young hair all wild from the wintry wind, and his old face dreadfully beaming. 'Is that not an inspiring thought? Only the responsibilities of my family – to which we are joyfully expecting, by the way, another addition – prevent me from taking ship, and going to convert them myself!'

'I'm sure I should be happy to go too,' said Mrs Bream, who had accompanied her husband, and sat bovinely beside him with her hands folded across her fecund belly, 'if it were not for the circumstance Mr Bream mentions. And the idea that they have little black babies, you know, practically like our own, is perfectly charming!'

'Oh, but ain't they cannibals there?' cried Sar'ann. 'No good sending a missioner, if he's only going to get eaten. I wonder why they do it? They say human flesh is nasty, but perhaps it isn't. Perhaps it tastes just like pork, or mutton. I wonder if it comes out bloody, like beef? I'd dearly like to know!'

'Now that is a curious instance, Miss Twopenny, of how things fall out,' said Mr Bream, 'for Mrs Bream and I were improving the shining hour just the other day by looking over a book which related stories of missionary endeavour, and of those who had suffered for the faith. A melancholy catalogue! And yet, do you know the chief feeling with which Mrs Bream and I laid down the volume? It was joy! Because we knew that not one of those glorious men and women would have changed places with anybody, even at the moment of extremest agony, and I would even go so far as to say they were happy! How could they not be? They were assured of the salvation of their immortal souls, and they simply couldn't help it!' Mr Bream's exulting eye fell on John, who had been summoned to greet the visitors with the rest of the family; he performed a little bounce in his seat, and cried: 'Mr John – you will forgive my singling you out, because really you furnish such an excellent opportunity of illustration that I am astonished again at how providentially things turn out. Mr John, you have been orphaned. The shadow of death has fallen across your green path, and I fancy that bitter and angry questions may have raised themselves in your mind. But let me tell you this, Mr John. I do not pity you in your apparent misfortune – not a jot. Why do I not pity you? Shall I tell you? Because I envy you! And why do I envy you? To answer that question, let me draw, in imitation of our Founder, a similitude. Our second youngest boy, Georgy, recently celebrated his sixth birthday. Though offering him heartiest congratulations on the morning of the occasion, and allowing him as a tribute to it to have two eggs for breakfast instead of one, I did not mark Georgy's birthday morning otherwise than this; and having been brought up from the cradle to appreciate the many blessings with which we are surrounded, Georgy made no repining remark, and applied himself to his studies as usual. But later in the day, I sprang a surprise on Georgy. The two eggs were not the whole extent of his birthday celebrations – far from it. I had long decided that the occasion merited a special treat, and accordingly he was to go with me to the Octagonal Chapel at Norwich to hear a preacher who is renowned for the fervency of his addresses, and who has even been known to continue for three hours at a stretch when the spirit moves him! I will not trouble to describe Georgy's transports at the prospect of this expedition – suffice it to say that he was for some time without the power of speech, unusual in an infant of his years; for you will already have discerned the purpose of this illustration, Mr John. No gift can be more delightful, sir, than that which comes as a *surprise*; and that is why I tell you, that I envy you. For the superficial troubles that have lately come upon you, my dear sir, are the plainest tokens that Providence has in store for you the most delightful *surprise*. And I wonder what it will be? A wonderful realization, perhaps, that the deaths of your parents are to be rejoiced in, as evidence that their souls have joined the Infinite? Perhaps it may be that – perhaps something else! But whatever it is, I . . . What is it, my dear friend? Do you have something to communicate?'

These last words were addressed to simple Caleb, Saul's manservant, who as usual when he was not immediately required had taken up his station in the corner of the room, squeezing his great body on to the humblest of stools, with one foot beneath him, and going into a child's contented abstraction. Now, however, he was shifting about agitatedly, and seemed to wish to say something that burdened his mind.

'What ails you, Caleb?' said Saul, who gave a grudging attention to Mr Bream, but did not like to snub any minister of God short of a Papist. 'Speak out, boy.'

'I don't like it,' Caleb got out at last, with his great fair cheeks all flushed, 'what you were saying. I feel sad for Cousin – ' this was his name for John – 'on account of his ma and pa. And on account of my ma and pa, because *they* got took away. And they say it was the angels took 'em away but I say what did the angels want with 'em? They don't need any mas and pas. Why can't they let 'em alone!'

'Oh, hold your tongue, boy,' said Saul, 'you're talking nonsense.'

Strange, for John to find himself defended by Caleb Porter; yet not so strange, perhaps, for John liked Caleb better than anyone in Saul's house. He ought, of course, to have pricked Mr Bream's balloon of idiot optimism himself, but he was still too low and apathetic; just as he looked on at his uncle's brutal punishments unmoved. Suffering and injustice, it seemed now, were so woven into the world's web that there was nothing to be gained by striking out at them.

This, then, was the extent of the change wrought upon John. But something at least did remain from his old self. It was his love for Catherine.

It remained: though not unaffected. The language of love had been learned in his old life; now he lacked the means of expression, and even wondered if he had a whole heart to express. There were, besides, practical impediments. Not only was his freedom severely curtailed under his uncle's regimen: he found that he was no longer welcome in the Fernhills' circle. *Not at home*, was the maid's reply on the one occasion he was able to slip away and call at Buttings; and at last Catherine reluctantly confirmed to him by letter what he had already guessed – that her parents did not want her mixed up in such a story of disgrace and ruin, and had ordered her to end the association with John immediately.

Poor Catherine was torn. Impossible directly to defy her parents – impossible, that is, to someone of her nature; impossible likewise to give John up. A touching, if rather vague hope shone fitfully through her letters, the only communication left to them – a hope that things would somehow right themselves, without the necessity of anyone being hurt.

Not that John was in any better case, or could construct any more realistic model of their future. The future, indeed, which had once been the constant and stimulating companion of his thoughts, had become a nullity for him; and as much of the past was unbearable to think of, he found himself existing in a perpetual present, as if his life were a dark staircase of which only one laborious step was visible at a time. And the present was, simply, Saul's house, and the warehouses, and the maltings. It was learning, day by day, to make himself useful about them; it was the husky, musty shushing of germinating barley turned and turned again on the malt floors; it was the stoking of the kiln and the priming of the pumps; it was the rumble of dray-wheels and the jingle of harness and the rattle of chain and pulley; it was Mr Addy, taking John under his stubby wing in the intervals of relieving his feelings by plunging his head in a tub and once, under extremest provocation from Saul, placing it under the hand-pump and sousing himself until he streamed and steamed like a miniature Niagara.

And the present was, when work was over, returning to the house through the little gate that was like a handful of grim spears soldered together; and cold ablutions before the evening meal, and stony prayers before the meal, and stony silence throughout the meal. And it was long cheerless evenings after supper, with Saul devoting his scant leisure to accounts, or to some pious volume, his face as he read resembling one of the more thunderous visions of Michelangelo; with Sar'ann sewing by the dim candlelight, occasionally lifting her head with an expression of rapt alertness at the sound of one of her mousetraps; with William lounging and brooding, and seeming quite unable to prevent himself irritating his father, like someone picking at his own wound; with John wishing away the hours until he could retire, and counting the ticks of the Dutch clock, and picturing goblin faces in the gloomy wainscoting, and doing anything to stop himself thinking of what he had lost, and the manner of its going.

And then, one day out of this featureless procession of days – when John had been some six months in his uncle's house, and Christmas had come and gone, and a cold starveling new year had followed it – one day, something happened to John. It was not much in itself; but it began something, something which was rather like the slow return of appetite after debilitating sickness.

He was making a rare foray out of Saul's kingdom, and into the mazy little town of Hales, being entrusted with an errand to the ironmonger's there; and was finding it curious to be among so many busy strangers, endlessly varied in form, feature and dress, in contrast to the bleak uniformity of Saul's establishment. He stopped to let a waggon emerge from a narrow side-turning, and when the vehicle had at last squeezed its way past, he looked up to find himself face to face with Catherine Fernhill, who was waiting likewise on the other side of the lane.

They might have stood there gazing at each other for any length of time, if a shell-fisher with laden baskets had not nudged John in the ribs, remarking, 'Now then, now then, are yew a man or the parish-pump?' So John hastily moved, and Catherine hastily moved, and he had her hand in his before he knew anything about it.

She had on a sea-green walking-dress – the self-same walking-dress she had worn on the occasion of their first meeting; and this, together with all the powerful and poignant associations it brought with it, left him stricken and wordless. He could only look into her face – so different in its beauty and tenderness of expression from everything that had surrounded him for half a year and more, that after a few moments he could not look any more. He closed his eyes, and pressed her hand to his lips.

'Oh, John,' said she, 'how pale and drawn you look!'

He knew that he did, indeed; but before he could say anything she caught herself up and said anxiously, 'Oh, dear, what must you think of me – we haven't seen each other for I don't know how long and then all I can do is make a personal remark as if I hadn't any manners at all, and you might very well ask what you are expected to look like after all you've been through and now living with a man who's, well, more like a bear than a man, at least, I don't mean to be rude about your uncle but they do say . . . Oh, John, I don't know *what* to say!'

'Well,' he said, mustering a smile, 'you might tell me how you've been.'

'Oh, I've been very well – except I don't feel I should say that because it seems wrong to be well when you – when your poor father . . .' She bit her lip, and squeezing his hand went on hurriedly, 'It was a little lonely at first without Verity at Buttings – she went away to London, you know, to be a governess – well, of course you know, because I wrote you all about it . . . I hope that stern old uncle doesn't open your letters, or forbid them or anything like that?'

'Not so bad as that,' said John. 'Though I'm half afraid of something similar happening at Buttings.'

She looked pained. 'Not so bad as that, either,' she said faintly. 'John, I wish they did not feel as they do; and if I thought for a second you suspected me of any such feeling, I would—'

'Hush,' he said, 'I know you better than that, my dear. As for your parents' feelings towards me, it is . . . not to be wondered at, I suppose.' He could find no kinder words for it.

'It is really no malicious feeling,' she said, 'though I know it seems so. They are so careful of my welfare, and so they think it would be better for me if – if I ended the connection. Oh, which I will not do, John, not on any account!'

'Which leaves us in a difficult, not to say impossible position.'

'Oh, not impossible – don't say impossible. Things – things can always change.'

He had certainly learnt the truth of that, in the hardest way, of late; and he had no wish to dispel the glow of hopefulness about her face. However, his love for her was not a blind love, and had always included an awareness that reality and Catherine, unless gently pushed together, had a tendency to drift apart; and so he said carefully, 'Things can change, certainly, but I can't see them doing so at present. My uncle is merely my guardian until I'm of age, and I have no claim on him; and whatever he intends for me, if anything, will be nothing like I had hoped to make of myself. And I know your father is – ' he could not say *as stubborn and pig-headed as they come* – 'is tenacious in his opinions. And so the look-out is not encouraging, taken all in all.'

And then, looking at her face with its grave, troubled, attentive look, he felt something of the old radiance that that face always occasioned in him spark and kindle, and he wished to throw such carping words away and tread on them. For it faintly dawned on him that he had become fixed in an unconscious habit of regarding the world as his enemy, with nothing in store for him but cruel misfortune and disappointment; and yet here, in these blue eyes and the tender look they bent upon him, was firm evidence to the contrary. Their road as lovers was beset by obstacles, obstacles so formidable and perplexing he could see no way around them; but he loved, and was loved. Green shoots amidst the waste, blighted though they might yet be.

'I wish I could say something cheering about clouds and silver linings, and the darkest hour being just before the dawn,' she said with a tremulous laugh, 'but I fear I shall only end up sounding like Mr Bream. All I can say is I have the greatest faith in you, John; and I am always thinking of you, and with – with the same feeling I have always had. And – oh, John, I have to meet Mama, she's waiting for me at Langley's the dressmaker's.'

'It was too much to hope that you were alone,' said John.

'I know, isn't it nonsense the way young ladies can't go about without being eternally accompanied, as if I were going to be whisked off by white slavers in the middle of Hales-next-the-sea . . . But I do manage to escape on my own sometimes – and if I could let you know when . . .?'

'I shall scale my uncle's castle walls,' he said, 'if the guards don't pick me off.'

It was a curious sensation to be smiling again: curious, too, to feel the press of a loving hand, and know it to be no part of a dream which would leave him broken and aching when he woke, but real, and only to be snatched from him by a combination of unlucky circumstances, not by implacable death.

Of course those circumstances were as difficult to evade or overcome, in their way, as death, were they not? So he had thought; and after he had parted with Catherine, and the baleful shadow of his uncle's house had once more enveloped him, he thought so again. And yet a candle had been lit in that shadow, and it did not go out; even if John could not yet see, in its feeble glimmerings, the beginnings of a hope of something better than this.

CHAPTER THREE

Saints and Angels

Verity had never, in her four months' residence there, known such excitement in the Spikings household as filled it one memorable Saturday in February; and this was saying something, for the Spikings were, in general, an excitable family.

It had begun the previous day at five o'clock, when Mr Alfred Spikings had come home to Montagu Place from the City as was his wont; and, as was not at all his wont, had hurtled into the drawing-room without even giving himself a glance in the great pier-glass above the festooned mantelpiece.

Mr Spikings darted over to the sofa where his wife was having a headache – Verity was present to report on the children's lessons, and had stayed to be complained at – and with a disregard for the presence of the governess which was also unlike him, seized Mrs Spikings' languid hand in both his own.

'My dear,' he cried, 'you will never guess who I ran into today.'

'Very probably,' said Mrs Spikings peevishly, withdrawing her hand, 'and I have no intention of making the attempt. However, I congratulate you, Mr Spikings. If, as I assume, you came home thinking "I know what I'll do – I'll make Felicia's headache twice as bad by bursting in on her like a jumping-jack," you have been entirely successful.'

'The person I met,' went on Mr Spikings, taking no notice of this, 'was Uncle Pomeroy.'

The change in Mrs Spikings' expression was startling to see. 'Uncle Pomeroy! Dear Uncle Pomeroy! How did he look?'

'Remarkably well,' said her husband. 'Fit as a man of forty, in fact.'

'Oh,' said Mrs Spikings, not seeming to receive this information with the pleasure that might be expected; and then, as if suddenly becoming aware of this, 'Good! That is splendid news! And yet, you know, he must be over seventy.'

'Seventy-five, if a day.'

'Seventy-five, if a day!' repeated Mrs Spikings, with a laugh like silver bells – or, at least, some item of ironmongery. 'How time flies! Dear Uncle Pomeroy! I hope, my dear, that you gave him our very best regards, and mentioned how often and how fondly we think of him.'

'More than that,' said Mr Spikings, with something very like a smirk. 'I asked him to dine, and he's coming tomorrow.'

Mrs Spikings leapt off the sofa, very smartly for a woman with a paralysing headache. 'Tomorrow! Alfred, we must prepare!'

'Felicia, we *shall* prepare. Indeed, I have already begun. I have ordered a half-dozen of the best port from Day and Martin's, and—'

'Silver,' muttered Mrs Spikings. 'That girl has been very lax with the polishing lately, but I've let it go because of my good nature, and because her mother is Irish, but no more. No more! I tell you, Alfred, no more! Don't ask me to put up with it, because I cannot and will not!' Mrs Spikings became as heated as if her husband were quarrelling with her – a notable talent of hers. 'No woman should have to tolerate what I have to tolerate from servants, and yet what thanks do I get? None!'

'My dear—'

'It's all very well for you to say "my dear", Alfred. It's all right for you. You just carry on saying "my dear", and generally enjoying yourself; but you wouldn't say "my dear" if you came home and found your soup served in a coal-scuttle, would you? Now would you?' Mrs Spikings, having with great ingenuity found herself a grievance, made shrill play with it. 'Would you? Can you say, on your honour, that on finding your soup served in a coal-scuttle, you would say "my dear"? Can you?'

'No, Felicia,' said Mr Spikings, with absurd dignity and deliberation, 'I cannot.'

'And yet it is,' Mrs Spikings pursued, 'every night! And as for the knives, they are like garden trowels!'

'You're too soft with the servants, my dear,' said Mr Spikings. 'You're tender-hearted, and so they take advantage. In fact, where servants are concerned, Felicia, you're a saint – nothing less.'

'I suppose it must be that. I simply can't find it in my nature to be hard.' Mrs Spikings sank dramatically on to the sofa, and then sprang up again so suddenly that her husband, who was silently congratulating himself on an adroit move, visibly jumped. 'But I shall have to make the effort,' she cried. 'The girl must learn. She is only half-Irish after all. The table-linen too – disgraceful. I shall have to do violence to my nature, and be severe. Nothing, absolutely nothing, shall be forgotten or omitted.'

'We are forgetting one thing, I think,' said Mr Spikings, caressing his whiskers, and casting a glance in Verity's direction.

'Good heavens! Miss Deene, how you do loiter about!' said Mrs Spikings, drawing herself up, and checking her reflection in the pier-glass, to make sure that she had the right face on – in this case, aloof and serene. 'Have the goodness to leave us, if you please. If it were not that I am cursed with an almost inhuman amount of patience, I should say that it is very tiresome having continually to remind you of the necessity of withdrawing when you are not actively required.'

Verity did as she was told, with a curtsey, and was not actively required again for the rest of the evening, for she took her meals upstairs with the children; but on going to her own room, she overheard one or two snatches of animated conversation between the parents downstairs, in which 'Dear Uncle Pomeroy!' and 'Five thousand each for the girls, perhaps', were distinguishable.

And now here was the great day on which Uncle Pomeroy, whoever he might be, was appointed to dine at Montagu Place; and lest there be any doubt of it, Mrs Spikings came up to the schoolroom during morning lessons, specifically to apprise Verity of the fact. For though Verity had heard all about it, it was a genteel fiction maintained by both Mr and Mrs Spikings that the governess, like the magic mirror in the fairy-tale, was something quite blank and inanimate, and capable of intelligence only when directly spoken to.

'Miss Deene,' Mrs Spikings said, sweeping into the room where Verity was attempting to squeeze a little basic French into the unyielding minds of her offspring, 'you'll forgive me, I hope, for intruding in your domain – curious indeed to find oneself a trespasser in one's own house; believe me, I would not normally be so impertinent, but the circumstances are exceptional.' For it was another fiction of Mrs Spikings' to pretend that the governess was a sort of tyrannical cuckoo who had all but taken over the house, and on this matter of entering the schoolroom she was accustomed to make all sorts of pleasantries, such as 'A very airy situation – I had almost forgot!' or 'Dear me, almost half a house here, that one never has the use of!', very arch and acid in character.

Now, however, she dispensed with any further asperities and, blowing a kiss at her assembled infants seated in a row like four little gargoyles, drew Verity aside.

'Miss Deene, Mr Spikings and I are expecting a gentleman to dinner tonight: a near relation of Mr Spikings, by name of Mr Pomeroy. When I say that Mr

Pomeroy is a very distinguished gentleman, I do not even begin to do justice to his stature. I am not even sure that it lies within the power of woman to pay appropriate tribute to one of his attainments, experience, knowledge, and strength of character. I will only remark that, in the matter of generosity, delicacy, fidelity, charity and all the other virtues enjoined to us by scripture, Mr Pomeroy is, and I say this advisedly, a saint. As for social eminence, I will not enumerate Mr Pomeroy's circle of acquaintance, for fear of seeming to exaggerate. Let us just say that it goes *very* high – *very* high indeed.' Mrs Spikings raised her eyebrows and pointed at the ceiling, producing in Verity the momentary impression that Uncle Pomeroy was on nodding terms with the Almighty; but concluding on reflection that only royalty was indicated, Verity looked suitably humbled. 'Is there a Mrs Pomeroy, ma'am?' she asked, well knowing the answer.

'There is no Mrs Pomeroy. I may say with confidence, that it was no lack of opportunity that prevented Mr Pomeroy from entering that most blissful of earthly states. Mr Pomeroy might have married – I will not say whom: suffice it to say that only the Abbey would have been an appropriate place for the wedding ceremony; but he chose to remain a bachelor, to posterity's loss. Yet I hope I can say that Mr Pomeroy knows what it is to have a loving family, in his declining years; that a dutiful nephew tenders the esteem and affection that a son might have supplied, and that he does not feel the want of grandchildren, when his great-nephews and great-nieces gather round his knee, and cheer him with their merry innocent prattle.'

Mrs Spikings went into a sort of rapturous trance at this charming vision, and was only jolted out of it by a squeal from Seraphina, the youngest of the girls, who had just been stuck in the leg with a pen by Tancred, the eldest boy; but coming to herself, she was at once businesslike. 'So, Miss Deene,' she continued, 'I require you, when Mr Pomeroy arrives, to bring the children down – not that they will need any urging, they dote on him so! – and to ensure that they are most immaculately turned out, and that they know their lessons to perfection, in case Mr Pomeroy should condescend to quiz them. Their presence, and yours of course, will not be required at dinner; but after dinner, and when the gentlemen have returned to the drawing-room – which will not be long, Mr Pomeroy being, as you would expect, admirably abstemious – bring the children down again, that they may bid their great-uncle good night; and that might be the moment, perhaps, for Honoria to go to the piano, and demonstrate her accomplishment.'

Unable to tell Mrs Spikings that Honoria, the eldest girl, was a tone-deaf little goose whose habitual conduct during music-lessons was alternately to sulk and kick holes in the rosewood legs of the piano, Verity said, 'I'm afraid Honoria's execution is – not yet of the standard that would please the ears of so able a judge as Mr Pomeroy.'

'Dear, dear, what is this? Really, Miss Deene, one expects better results from you after four months of schooling. There cannot be any lack of application on Honoria's part, that I do know – unless, Miss Deene, you are about to dispute with me on that score as well, and deny that a mother knows her own children?'

'No, ma'am,' said Verity; unable to say, likewise, that a mother such as Mrs Spikings was perhaps the last person to know her own children, and that if she did have that dubious honour, she would have had the little beasts locked up in a cage long ago.

'And you must not suppose, moreover, that Mr Pomeroy is one of those superior people who make a brag of their education,' said Mrs Spikings. 'I can assure you, I am well able to spot *that* class of person a mile off. They generally don't have a shilling to bless themselves with, adopt a sneering attitude to the domestic virtues, and are remiss in their attendance at church. Mr Pomeroy, I believe, is the very last person on earth who could be placed in that category; and you will forgive me,

Miss Deene, if I defend him from your charge most vigorously.'

'I beg your pardon,' said Verity. 'I didn't mean to suggest—'

'Oh, Miss Deene, always talking and never doing! If you will allow me to speak for *one* moment, I was going to suggest that we omit Honoria's performing on the piano, as you have made such a great fuss about it, and that she might instead offer a recitation. Your teaching, I hope, has not failed in that regard also?'

'Miss Spikings knows several verses of Dr Watts', if that will suit,' said Verity.

'Oh, Miss Deene, whatever you think best – I would not presume to dictate in your own domain, you know!' said Mrs Spikings airily; and then, turning to her brood with her maternal face on, 'Well, my dears, you will be delighted to know that your great-uncle Pomeroy is coming to dine tonight, and so you must be perfect little angels – not that you are not always perfect little angels, but you must be even more so!'

'Uncle Pomeroy's old – ain't he, Ma?' enquired Knight, at five the youngest of the litter, but with a face like a little fat, sly man.

'Uncle Pomeroy is indeed an elderly gentleman,' agreed Mrs Spikings.

'And he's monstrous rich – ain't he, Ma?' said Tancred, who was even fatter, slyer, and more knowing than his brother.

'Rich, a-ha-ha, what comical things you little babes and sucklings come out with, to be sure,' trilled Mrs Spikings cheerfully. 'Yes, Uncle Pomeroy is rich, though I have never really given the matter a thought before now; but you must not love and honour and respect him any more for that, my dears. And always remember that you must love the poor too, in a different way, and as long as they are deserving, and don't swear or drink gin. Well, as lesson-time is nearly over, I suggest you run off now, like the little fairies you are, and find Nurse, because I want you all to be bathed and as clean as new pins for your great-uncle.'

The children departed in their usual manner, which more nearly resembled stampeding cattle than fairies, and Mrs Spikings smiled fondly after them. 'Mr Pomeroy dotes on them,' she remarked, 'and even leaving aside a mother's natural partiality, is it any wonder . . .! Well, Miss Deene, I suppose you may occupy yourself as you see fit, until the children are dressed. On the subject of your own dress this evening, it must of course be suitable for social presentation, but not such as to give a misleading impression of your position in the household. However, I have no worries on that score. One thing I will say for you, Miss Deene, and that is that you never betray yourself by an ill-advised attempt to shine in company.'

All Verity could do was offer a smile of humility in return; and for some time after Mrs Spikings had left her, it remained fixed on her face. At last, however, it fell; and while she tidied up the schoolroom, Verity invented some new punishments for Mrs Spikings.

'She shall be the centrepiece of a second Great Exhibition, hung up on a pole in her petticoats, for everyone to look at,' she thought.

'Or served up at the Lord Mayor's Banquet, with an apple in her mouth and parsley in her hair,' she thought again.

'Or made to sell lavender at house-doors, and be continually turned away, and end up sleeping under the arches of Waterloo Bridge.' This was the most pleasing image of all and, added to the prospect of being free of the little Spikings for a space, lifted her spirits considerably.

There was little rest to be had in the house that day, however, for the imminent arrival of Uncle Pomeroy had set it all tail-on-end, and the servants had been urged on to a wild rampage of cleaning, everyone down to the scullery-maid coming into the orbit of Mrs Spikings' wrath; for it was that lady's idiosyncrasy to be moping and discontented when she had nothing to do, and violently ill-tempered when she had something to do. Mr Spikings meanwhile expressed his own ill-humour, in the intervals of dodging his wife's, by doing a good deal of red-faced striding about, and declaring his intention of giving everybody notice. All of which did not prevent them from periodically returning to the theme of Uncle Pomeroy, and sounding it in the most glowing terms. Dear Uncle Pomeroy was the refrain that recurred even through the hullabaloo; though Verity felt it might more appropriately have been Cheap Uncle Pomeroy, they made so free with his name, and speculated in him in such a wholesale manner.

She managed, however, an undisturbed half-hour in her room: a combination of bedroom and sitting-room, which had an uninterrupted view of a large chimney, and which might as well have been in one, in point of size and general dinginess; and used the time to write a letter to Catherine in Norfolk. To give an accurate idea of the Spikings, and her life with them, was beyond her pen – at least when writing to a girl so innocently well-disposed towards people in general as Catherine – and Verity usually contented herself with a few commonplaces, and inquiries after her family. Also, after John Twopenny. It would have looked strange if she had not.

If, however, she had had a correspondent with whom she could have been mercilessly frank, she would have described the Spikings as people who possessed only one idea, and that a wrong one. They proceeded on the principle that there was nothing in life that would not be improved by being made larger – whether their house, their income, their consequence, or their looking-glasses. The latter particularly; for while neither of them was excessively handsome, they did a good deal of looking at themselves.

Mr Spikings was, perhaps, the vainer of the two, on account of his undeniably glossy and luxuriant whiskers, though he was otherwise no more than a balding, dyspeptic, gingery swaggerer, with a thrustful lower lip like a sulky boy's. As for Mrs Spikings, it was difficult to say precisely what she looked like, she changed her face so often according to the occasion; but if you could catch her when she thought she was not being observed, you saw a dumpy light-haired lady with a nose on the generous side and a mouth on the mean side, who had resolved to be no more than thirty, and who after five years of the resolution was looking a little worn and strained by it. The four children whom it was Verity's task to teach, Honoria, Tancred, Seraphina, and Knight, were recognizably true branches of the Spikings tree; for the boys already had loud hard laughs suitable to smoking-room stories, and the girls were little frosty snobs who could sum up a person's social position with one glance of their button eyes.

They were wealthy, of course, these Spikings; their house was 'out west, among the squares' – if not among the aristocratic mansions of old Whig London, then certainly in a neighbourhood of unimpeachable respectability. It was staffed by a platoon of servants, who perpetually ran up and down their own separate staircase like so many caged mice in a revolving wheel; and it contained a quantity of heavy furniture and plate, the vulnerability of which to housebreakers continually interrupted Mrs Spikings' rest, though they would have had to have been as mighty as Hercules to have shifted any of it. And yet, far from being contented, Mr and Mrs Alfred Spikings spent their lives in a permanent state of wanting more, and could hardly have been more naggingly concerned about their material lot if they had lived in a hovel on turnips.

They were, for example, compulsively sociable, and often gave those dinners revealingly known as fourteeners, with a great deal of ceremony and expense. Facsimiles and resemblances of Spikings, tall and short, ugly and fair, young and old, came two by two to admire themselves in the Montagu Place mirrors, and graze in an acre of dining-room; but the interest felt in them by their hosts was much of a piece with the interest they might feel in a costly item displayed in a shop-window. Thus, if Mr Bullion had successfully disposed of his daughter in marriage, the congratulations and good wishes for the happy pair were the merest froth on the surface of the conversation; and what really exercised the minds of the Spikings, and formed the chief topic after the fourteen had gone away, was how much old Bullion had been able to give her, and how much Bullion's new son-in-law was worth, and how much it came to altogether; so that all in all, any guest who set foot over the Spikings' threshold was effectively stepping into a giant pair of scales, and being weighed to the last ounce.

This matter of bestowing wealth upon offspring was of particular fascination for Mr and Mrs Alfred Spikings. For while they were firm advocates of self-help for the lower classes, they certainly did not apply this bracing philosophy to their own children. An observer might have wondered why, if this was the freest country in the world, where there were no obstacles to a man's making his way from the gutter to a mansion, as Mr Spikings often asserted – why, in that case, he should be so anxious that his children should go out into the world armoured and cushioned by as much money as possible, as if there were something to fear out there. Verity wondered herself; and wondered, too, whether such a reception would have been prepared for Uncle Pomeroy if he had not been rich, old, a bachelor, and presumably in need of some names to put in the blank spaces in his will. But perhaps she was being cynical. Mrs Spikings had already reproached Verity for this, for mildly observing that all the stories for children and adults alike seemed to have happy endings, and that this did not constitute an entirely faithful reflection of reality. 'Oh! Miss Deene, I hope you are not one of these cynical people, who take a pleasure in doing everything down,' Mrs Spikings had said. 'There are altogether too many of that sort nowadays, and sometimes I think they won't be happy till they have us living in an atheistical republic.'

For the Spikings were in their way romantics. Insofar as they had any individual taste at all, they had a taste for the medieval. They got sentimental about chivalric virtues, taking the queen and her manly consort as their model; and the library at Montagu Place was decorated with Arthurian themes. Yes: there was a library, alas for Verity. Alas, because she was not free to enter it, being penned in the schoolroom with Georgy Gentle and Nicholas Ne'er-do-well; but perhaps not so much alas – for Mr Spikings chose his volumes for the bindings, not the contents, and Verity suspected that if he could have bought books that were all leather and no pages, he would have been eminently satisfied.

Was the life she lived here, then, preferable to the one she might have had with Mr Flowers, in the snug house overlooking the sea? Verity was not good at lying to herself – except in one regard – and could not deny that the question had occurred to her dismayingly often on her first arrival, and sometimes still did. The disadvantages of her position were many. From neither of her employers did she receive any more consideration than they gave to their servants, and they were not even wary of going too far with her as they were with the cook or the groom, for fear of revenge in the form of slack service; though the worst part of this powerlessness was, that though the Spikings recognized it very well, and made every ungenerous use of it, they liked to pretend to their friends that they were quite afraid of her. 'Oh, my dear, you have quite a treasure in that mousy little governess of yours, believe me – our Miss Deene quite tyrannizes us, you know, and I half feel that I'm in the schoolroom myself!'

And then there were the little Spikings. On the journey from Norfolk to London to take up her new position, when she had begun to feel lonely and troubled at what lay ahead of her, she had cheered herself with visions of the fulfilment that might at least be found in coaching her pupils, gently guiding them down the paths of knowledge and building up a friendship with them along the way. Well! She had thought herself free of illusions by now, but here was another one gone tumbling. After four months of the little Spikings, the only path Verity wished to guide them down was the path to the Zoological Gardens; for the one suitable punishment her ingenuity could devise for them was to throw the brats into the lions' cage and watch them being eaten with a good deal of smacking and slurping.

Which of the little Spikings, she wondered sometimes in a spirit of despairing inquiry, was the most repulsive? Honoria, at eleven, had added ladylike nonsenses to her innate stupidity, and made mincing criticisms of Verity's posture – which Verity, who was a very trim and upright young woman, did not at all like; and so that was pretty repulsive. Tancred, who was a nine-year-old bully, was openly resentful of petticoat government, and jeeringly informed Verity, if she tried to discipline him, that he was to go to a public school soon, and there weren't any women *there*; and so that was pretty repulsive. Seven-year-old Seraphina, slightly less robust than her siblings, had carved a niche for herself as an obsequious tattle-tale, and was an infant version of the sort of people who became informers, censors, and missionaries; and that was pretty repulsive. Knight, being only five, had chubby innocence on his side, and milked it for all it was worth, having plainly discovered that pretending not to know better granted you all sorts of immunity; and that was pretty repulsive. The question was, in fact, unanswerable, for the children were repulsive individually, and repulsive *en masse*; and on top of that, they were tremendously efficient little spies, who had turned several governesses out on the street through reporting real or imaginary misdemeanours on the part of those ladies to their parents, in a very public-spirited manner.

So, the family with whom Verity was employed were not a happy choice, insofar as she had a choice; and she had not the consolation of most employees, which was a place to go to, and people to be with, separate from the place of employment. She earned her meagre pay in the schoolroom, and lived in the governess's room, twelve feet apart: even the conviviality of the servants' hall was denied her. And she had no friends. Catherine and her circle were far off, and there was scant possibility of Verity making acquaintances on her own terms, for it was as difficult for her to go about freely as a horse in a hobble. There were governesses aplenty in and about Montagu Place, to be sure, and Verity knew several of her sister-sufferers by sight; but they were firmly discouraged from mixing, just as if the governesses of Marylebone might, if allowed to meet, throw up a female Spartacus who would lead them all on to revolt, and leaving their precocious pupils hanging from the gas-lamps, sweep on to Mayfair baying for blood.

Where, then, the compensation? What reason could Verity have, imprisoned in this fortress of gentility in the midst of London, for feeling that she had made the right choice? Only the old reason. And the cure that she had sought in coming here *was* working, inasmuch as she thought of him less often, and hoped little by little to rid herself of the habit of thinking of him altogether. There was, as she had hoped, simply nothing here to remind her of him – except Catherine's letters; and she was able to look out of the schoolroom window in the perfect confidence of not seeing him, ever. 'Whereas,' she told herself, 'if I was to see him walking down there, with his long legs, and the sun on that fair hair of his that will never lie down straight, but always sticks up a little in the most provoking way; and his fresh keen look, and that little something at the corner of his mouth which suggests that he likes the amusing and hates the dull as much as I – if I was to see him down there, then . . .' But that was a sentence better not finished; and she attributed such thoughts to a mere relapse, to which all cures were liable. For she was, after all, a good liar to herself, where her heart was concerned.

There was, besides, something that her present life offered her that she could not do without, and that was a plentiful opportunity for amusement. If she could not have inwardly laughed at the Spikings, she would have been wretched indeed; but she was not so ground down as to lose her sense of the ridiculous. And she had to suppress a smile that evening when Mrs Spikings – who had been audibly haranguing her maid throughout her dressing, and also, by the sound of it, relieving her feelings by hurling scent-bottles and hairbrushes at her – came floating out of her bedroom and into the nursery, a perfect picture of maternal serenity, and sang out: 'Well, my angels, now that you are all bathed, let me see your shining little faces!'

The shiniest face there was that of the nurse, who had had a gruelling time of it. Her surname was Tripp, and it was as Tripp that she was known to everybody there; if she had a Christian name, Verity had never got to it, and wondered if it had been simply worn away by long association with the children, like everything else. For there was not much of Tripp, physically; her voice had decayed to a cajoling whisper, and her human feelings seemed to be going the same way. Once Knight had kicked her on the shins with more than his usual violence, and Verity, quite concerned, had commiserated with her on her pain; but Tripp had merely said, 'Pain, miss? Oh, I don't feel that any more. I used to, once, I think; but if you was to ask me to name the last time I felt a pain, I couldn't do it, it's been that long. It all goes, you see.' The bathing and dressing of the children for Uncle Pomeroy's visit had taken an inordinate toll on Tripp, and she could only stand by like a dismal wraith, clinging on to the washstand for support, whilst Mrs Spikings inspected the angelic quartet.

'Well, my lambs,' sighed Mrs Spikings, 'if anyone can look at you without hearing echoes of heavenly harmonies, then that person is a brute of stark insensibility. As for Uncle Pomeroy, if he doesn't just want to eat you all up, I shall be extremely surprised!'

Lest Uncle Pomeroy, however, should prove more conservative in his appetite, a dinner of exceptional magnificence had been prepared for him, and Mrs Spikings now floated downstairs for a last berating of the cook about it. Soon there came the sound of carriage-wheels in the street, and the children rushed to the nursery window to press their flat faces flatter against the glass, and witness the arrival of Uncle Pomeroy. For her part Verity felt she could quite comfortably wait for her first sight of the great man; and the summons to bring the children down was not long in coming.

Behold Uncle Pomeroy! Enthroned in state in the Spikings' reception room, with Mr Spikings smirking at him from his station in front of the mantelpiece, and Mrs Spikings fawning at him from a stool rather low for one of her years and figure, but affording her the opportunity, if her feelings of admiration should become ungovernable, of embracing his saintly knees. The children at once ran, with carefully rehearsed spontaneity, to tender him their loving kisses and embraces; and it was only when Uncle Pomeroy was clear of little Spikings, that Verity was able to get a good look at him.

Certainly he was a well-preserved old gentleman; but the means of preservation were rather obvious to the eye. Such artful things had been done to his white hair that it resembled a confection of whipped cream placed atop his head: the bloom on his cheek was like no bloom that nature ever supplied to anyone, young or old; and there was a corseted, plumped, stuffed look about his rigid body in its tight-buttoned white waistcoat, which suggested that Uncle Pomeroy in *déshabillé* looked very different from Uncle Pomeroy in full regalia. Stuffed was, indeed, the word that occurred to Verity; for one could fancy that besides a hairdresser and a valet, Uncle Pomeroy availed himself of the services of a taxidermist in preparing to go out. Such glassy eyes, and such a dreadful display of huge yellow teeth and pink gums, Verity had never seen outside the glass cabinets that contained stuffed and mounted foxes. A great tailor's-dummy of an Uncle Pomeroy, in fact, with nothing natural about him from the crown of his pomaded head to the toes of his pointed shoes; and with such a look of pompous complacency as suggested that he entirely shared the Spikings' high opinion of him.

'Well, and here's a new face!' cried Uncle Pomeroy on beholding Verity. 'I think

I can say I've a pretty good memory for faces: at my club the other day I spotted a fellow I'd been at Eton with – hadn't seen him since he gave me a flogging for bringing a squirrel into the dormitory, and serve me right – but I knew him immediately. Wideacres was with me at the time – young Lord Wideacres, you know, sturdy fellow, knew his father well – and he said to me, "Pomeroy, I don't know how you do it. I hope *my* noggin will be in such good fig when I reach your age." And *this* young lady's face I know I have not seen before.'

Mr and Mrs Spikings expressed their admiration at Uncle Pomeroy's acuteness of mind; and Verity was introduced.

'Deene, eh? Northamptonshire name, I believe. What part of the county are you from? I think I can say I know Northamptonshire pretty well.'

'Well, I was London-born—'

'PARdon?'

'I was born in London, Mr Pomeroy,' Verity said, raising her voice, 'though it may be that my family came from Northamptonshire originally.'

'Miss Deene came to us from Norfolk, Uncle,' put in Mrs Spikings, 'where she had been residing with her kinsman, Admiral Fernhill – a very distinguished figure in the Navy.' For though the Spikings looked down on Verity, they also liked to make the most of her social extraction – rather like Imperial Romans owning a slave who had been king in his own country.

'Now, you may put me among the old school if you like,' said Uncle Pomeroy. 'I've often been put there, and I'm not ashamed of it: Mintsworth said to me just the other day – Sir Henry Mintsworth, you know, Treasury, splendid fellow, we've known each other for years – he said to me, "Pomeroy, you're one of the old school – that's what you are. And God bless you for it!" And as one of the old school, I say this: the Navy is the guardian of our freedoms. If the Navy falls, England falls, and that's all there is to it.'

Wild rapture on the part of Mr and Mrs Spikings, at this unparalleled specimen of originality and freshness.

'Now, you have no sea-coast, of course, down in Northamptonshire, Miss Deene,' went on Uncle Pomeroy, 'but if you had ever lived at a sea-port, you would know what a stirring sight our ships are. Heart of oak – you have heard of the expression, Miss Deene?'

'Yes, from the song by—'

'PARdon?'

As was plain from this, Uncle Pomeroy had a habit – partly from deafness, but chiefly from an egotistical inattention to other people – of saying 'PARdon?' as soon as anyone began to speak; and saying it, too, in a very loud, booming, arrogant, puffed-up and infuriating way – such that Verity thought, 'Oh, I shall have to think up a good punishment for *this* one!'

'I have heard the song,' she repeated, 'by Garrick.'

'Miss Deene plays, you know, Uncle,' put in Mrs Spikings, 'and Honoria and Seraphina are learning, under her tuition.'

'You are learning music, are you, my dears?' said Uncle Pomeroy, with such a frightful display of teeth that Seraphina, who was twining herself about his chair, quite flinched. 'And what else are you learning, I wonder? Come, Miss Deene: you needn't be tongue-tied in the presence of an old warhorse like me, you know – tell me what you teach these little irresistibles.'

'Well, we have French—'

'PARdon?'

'FRENCH, drawing, some arithmetic, geography . . .' Verity remembered her instructions. 'And the children have lately been learning some verses of Dr Watts – I believe Honoria would be glad to recite to you.'

If Honoria was glad, she did a good job of disguising it; but hooking one arm

125

behind her, she went ahead with her task, reciting in a deadly monotone, and apparently reading the words off the picture-rail. Having droned through 'Birds in Their Little Nests Agree', she encored with 'Against Pride in Clothes', the verse:

> 'The tulip and the butterfly
> Appear in gayer coats than I:
> Let me be dressed fine as I will
> Flies, worms and flowers exceed me still'

being warmly approved for its improving sentiments by Mrs Spikings, the cost of whose gown alone would have kept a family in coals for a year.

'Very prettily done, my dear,' said Uncle Pomeroy, who had shown some impatience at not being able to speak while the recitation was in progress. 'And a very fine lesson to be learned. It reminds me of something that happened to me just the other day, when a ragged boy accosted me in the street, begging for money. Now, you may put me amongst the Bluffs, if you like: I don't mind it; I have never pretended to be anything other than what I am, a plain-spoken Englishman who doesn't expect too much of his fellow-man, but loves him just the same. Well, I spoke to this ragged boy. Some would have passed by, I dare say: that's up to them; but I spoke to him. "You want a penny, do you, my boy?" said I. Came the reply, "Yus, if you please, guv'nor!" '

(Mr and Mrs Spikings in transports at Uncle Pomeroy's powers of comic mimicry.)

' "And what", said I, "will you do with the penny, my little man?" "Why, guv'nor," says he, "I shall buy a roll with it from the cook-shop." "And now suppose," I pursued, "that someone else was to come along later, and give you another penny?" "Why, guv'nor," says he, considering a little, "I should buy a penn'orth of milk with it." "And I suppose," said I – for I had him, you see! I had set the trap, and he had walked into it! "I suppose," said I, "that if someone gave you a penny tomorrow, you would spend *that* at the cook-shop too?" "Yus!" comes the reply.'

(From Mrs Spikings, shrieks of mirth; from Mr Spikings, an admiring murmur that no one could tell a story like Uncle.)

' "So, my little man," said I, "there is threepence gone, that might have been saved! Threepence frittered away in fleshly indulgence, that might have been added to another threepence, and another, and so on and so on! And yet you wonder, I dare say, why you are in rags, and houseless!" Yes, I had him: he knew it. I could tell he knew it, for he was lost for a reply; and so I pressed the point home, and brought him to understand that *not thinking ahead* was the source of all his distress. It came as quite a revelation to him. Some people, perhaps, would not have taken so much trouble with such an urchin; but when I see an opportunity of doing a little good in the world, I tend not to think of the trouble. I am one of the Doers, and I cannot pass by on the other side, I don't care who knows it.'

(From Mr Spikings, a further admiring murmur that there never was such a man; from Mrs Spikings, tears, and a pantomime gesture suggestive of kissing the hem of Uncle Pomeroy's garment.)

'Well, well,' said Uncle Pomeroy, leaning his stiff body back in the easy-chair like a waxwork, 'I hope the lesson was learned; for I gave the boy a penny, anyhow. He shall have the penny, I vowed, whether he spends or saves it.'

'Dear Uncle Pomeroy!' said Mrs Spikings, unable to contain herself any longer, 'you are just like staunch old Dr Johnson, who used to walk the streets at night putting coins in the hands of beggar-boys! Seraphina, give your great-uncle another kiss, for you will never kiss a better man no matter how long you live!' And then, conscious that this rather gave the impression that Seraphina was going to

126

make quite a career out of kissing men, Mrs Spikings became flustered; and ordered Verity to take the children up again, as it was nearly time for dinner.

The angels, having been on good behaviour in the presence of Uncle Pomeroy, made up for it over their meal upstairs; but Tancred took advantage of a lull in the din to inquire of Verity, with a very shrewd look, 'Miss Deene, do you suppose that Uncle Pomeroy wears corsets?'

'Oh, I shall tell Mama you said that!' squealed Seraphina. 'It's indecent, ain't it, Miss Deene?'

'Not very,' said Verity, 'but it's not good manners.'

'I suppose,' said Tancred, looking shrewder than ever, 'it wouldn't be good manners if I asked him?'

Verity fixed him with a look. 'It would be extremely ill-advised.'

Tancred gave a snigger. 'Ma and Pa want us to butter Uncle Pomeroy up,' he said. 'It would be fun to put butter on his chair, wouldn't it? *That* would be buttering him up!' And the whole grotesque foursome went off into screams of laughter, Knight in particular crowing over the joke at tedious length, until much to Verity's satisfaction he nearly choked on his gooseberry tart.

The dinner down below was long in duration, and the children grew cross and sullen at being kept from their beds in order to be presented a second time to their great-uncle. At last the summons came, and Verity steered them all down to the drawing-room; where Mrs Spikings cried, 'Ah, here they all are, you see! I simply knew they would not be able to tiptoe off to dreamland without saying good-night to you, Uncle Pomeroy – they are so excessively fond of you!'

Fond was not, perhaps, the best word to describe the four crabbed little faces that preceded Verity into the drawing-room; but Uncle Pomeroy was not in a condition to notice it. Uncle Pomeroy, if he was as abstemious as Mrs Spikings claimed, must have broken the habit of a lifetime whilst in the dining-room with Mr Spikings, and broken it good and proper; for Uncle Pomeroy was as drunk as a fiddler, and it looked to Verity as if only his starch and stuffing were holding him upright.

'Now here's a face,' said Uncle Pomeroy, whose voice had grown even more booming and overbearing, and whose face was flushed with drink as well as rouge, to very dramatic effect, 'that I do not recognize. And I think I can say I have a good memory for faces . . .'

'Miss Deene, Uncle,' said Mrs Spikings, with a fixed smile, 'of course you—'

'PARdon?'

'Great-uncle Pomeroy,' said Tancred, 'is it true that you wear—'

'Honoria,' Verity burst out loudly, taking a discreet hold of Tancred's collar, 'Honoria was – er – wondering if you would like to hear her recite again, Mr Pomeroy.'

'I was not,' said Honoria sulkily. 'I'm sick of beastly reciting, and I hate it to death!'

Uncle Pomeroy, however, was not listening. He had scooped up Knight and placed him on his knee, and in a manner which in anyone but the great Uncle Pomeroy would have been described as maundering, was saying, 'You may count me, my little man, amongst the Elephants of the world. Some people have memories like gondolas. Like calendars. Like colanders. They have memories, I say, like colanders, and nothing is retained but the newest and latest fashion. Not I. Like an elephant, I never forget. And I have never forgotten the old jigging-rhyme that my nurse used to play with me when I was your age. It goes like this.' Uncle Pomeroy looked blank for a moment. 'It goes like this. "Ride a cock horse to Banbury Cross, To see a fine lady upon a white horse . . ." '

But Knight had discovered something far more interesting than anything that was to be found at Banbury Cross. From his position on Uncle Pomeroy's knee, he could see the old gentleman's singular coiffure at close quarters; and with scientific thoroughness, he investigated the phenomenon by reaching up his hand and plunging it right into the elaborate confection that was Uncle Pomeroy's hair. Both Verity and Mrs Spikings made a dart at Knight to pluck him away; but already the damage was done, and above Uncle Pomeroy's startled face there was now something resembling a broken meringue. And Knight was not finished yet: with an appalled look at his hand, he announced the result of his researches in a voice that penetrated even to Uncle Pomeroy's ears.

'Ma, Uncle Pomeroy's got all *stuff* in his hair, and it *stinks!*'

The good-nights of the children were not protracted after that. Verity did not know which was more urgent, to get them away before they did anything worse, or to get herself away before she collapsed into laughter; however, she achieved both, and spirited the four angels upstairs while Uncle Pomeroy was still haplessly trying to repair himself aloft, an operation not dissimilar in terms of difficulty from putting Humpty Dumpty together again.

'How did they behave themselves this evening, miss?' listlessly inquired Tripp, who was waiting to put them to bed.

Verity gave her a brief outline.

'Not so bad, then,' sighed Tripp. 'I'd best put them to bed.' And she shuffled off to take her nightly punishment, like someone who had offended the gods and was resigned to it.

Verity did not go to bed yet, as she thought it likely that Mrs Spikings would like a word or two with her. She waited in the nursery, listening to the sounds, first of Uncle Pomeroy's departure, which was a lengthy business, for getting him into the fly – starched, stuffed and soused as he was – plainly was not an easy matter; and then of some candid marital discussion between Mr and Mrs Spikings, which culminated in Mrs Spikings notifying her husband that he was an ogre, a bear, an ass, a booby, and a sot, these descriptions being punctuated with small explosions suggestive of flying china. Shortly after this, Mrs Spikings came thundering upstairs and, flinging herself into the nursery, cried: 'Miss Deene, Miss Deene, I hope you can explain yourself!'

'I'm sorry, ma'am, I—'

'It's of no use being sorry!' wailed Mrs Spikings, looking about her for a mirror, in vain. 'Instead of being sorry, it would be a better thing if you taught the children properly! Their behaviour this evening does you no credit, no credit at all!' Mrs Spikings, in her extremity, seized on a silver candlestick, and tried to see her reflection in that; and apparently not liking what she saw – for her hair was coming down, and her face was as red as a beefsteak – she hurled the candlestick across the room. 'Really, Miss Deene,' she concluded before prancing out again, 'you should set them an *example!*'

CHAPTER FOUR

High Treason

Love had made a start at reawakening John to life. It was a very different emotion that completed the process.

Superficially his existence under the aegis of S. Twopenny & Son continued in the same monotonous, unreflecting way. Through slow spring and into sudden summer, John applied himself to his uncle's business, doing what he was told, doing it with no real interest or enjoyment but with an uncomplaining doggedness, and steadily amassing knowledge of the malting trade under the supervision of Mr Addy. Through spring and into summer, John remained a part of Saul's morose and spartan household; and he gave no outward sign of passing through his own spring, and was hardly aware himself of the slow freshening and renewal going on within him.

But so it was. The lessening of the agony of memory, and its gradual replacement by proud and loving thoughts of the parents he had lost, was like the thawing of the winter. And his meetings with Catherine, though they were few, and short, and difficult to arrange, and without the rapt spontaneity of their first times together, had their effect likewise; and in their gentle influence upon him, were like the lengthening of the vernal days, and the receding of the defeated darkness.

Small changes and developments, which were no more capable, it would seem, of making a whole man again out of the shattered remnants of John Twopenny, than the tender shoots of thrusting their ways through the hard earth and becoming flowers; yet flowers did bloom in the little town gardens of Hales-next-the-sea, even if none were to be seen in the bleak vicinity of Saul Twopenny's house. And as the loving and responsive side of John reasserted itself by slow degrees, so the part of him that passionately believed in justice, and waxed wrathful when it was not done, stirred and quickened too.

He had never, from the beginning, liked being a pawn in Saul's game; now he began actively to dislike it. The fierce old man, unable to conceive of a human object neither bending nor breaking to his will, persisted in his harassing of William. When the young man was remiss, Saul flogged him harder than ever; and when there was no flogging to be done, Saul kept before his son's eyes the admonishing spectacle of John, rapidly becoming at home with the ways of the business. Whether Saul meant to go the whole way, and make his orphaned nephew his heir instead of his son if William remained recalcitrant, or whether he only intended to keep on with this sly stratagem until he wore William down with the uncertainty of it and brought him to heel, John could not tell. All he knew was that the consciousness of being his uncle's puppet was increasingly irksome to him.

It was not that William was very easy to like. Saul's manipulations had been so far successful, that William was more than ever mistrustful in his relations with John; and one or two faltering attempts on John's part, to convey to his cousin that he had no wish to supplant him, met only with black looks and curt replies. But John could understand how William felt, very easily. Why, indeed, should he believe that John was an innocent party? And could John believe himself to be an innocent party, when he stood by and watched yet another quarrel between father and son proceed to its violent conclusion, in the knowledge that his presence had made this combustible situation even more explosive?

The worst thing was, there was no way of showing his sympathy and indignation to William – not without seeming the veriest hypocrite. Often he hesitated outside his cousin's room, when William had retired thither smarting after a chastisement, wondering what he could say; and once William flung open the door and caught him hovering there.

'Why are you spying on me?' William's eyes were red: he brushed his arm across them like a whipped schoolboy. 'Did *he* set you to it?'

'I – I'm not spying,' John said. 'I wanted . . .'

'Wanted what? To crow? Well, go on with it. I don't care. But *he* won't break me, and I'm damn sure *you* won't either!'

Again, failure. But William's stormy question found an echo in John's own mind. What, indeed, did he want when he hung about William's room, troubled and perplexed? To right the wrongs he saw in this house? A tall order; and though John was recovering his old spirits, the doubt that human action could ever avail in a universe governed by a cruel and arbitrary Fate still lurked in him. But the question echoed in his mind still, not fading; and it seemed to him that he could not begin to answer it until he addressed the larger question of which it was a part. What did John Twopenny want out of life? He was nearly twenty-one: there were years ahead of him; what did he want to do with them?

The question itself was evidence that he was healing; for six months ago it would have seemed irrelevant, and the years ahead intolerable to contemplate. But that did not mean he was any nearer to an answer; and he was still revolving it in his mind when he received the most obvious indication yet that Saul meant to play him off against William, and play him till he forced a crisis.

William had slipped out at night to go to a waterside tavern. Sar'ann whispered that there were Girls there, though John had a notion that the proceedings were innocent enough, and that all William was satisfying was his desire to be a little rakish. However, this night was different. Saul did not wait up, rod in hand. He went to bed, ordered the servants to do likewise, and told them not to bother to rouse his son at his usual early hour in the morning, in spite of the fact that William was supposed to be going on an errand to Norwich tomorrow.

Came the morning, and William, who had crept in after midnight and must have been surprised to find no patriarchal fury awaiting him, slumbered on. Saul, with his severest composure, breakfasted as usual with John and Sar'ann, and then when the cloth was taken away beckoned John into his private room.

'You are to go to Norwich today – to the Corn Exchange,' he said without preamble. 'There's some imported grain come upon the market, I hear – too much; and going at a low price. You've learnt to be a judge of it, under Addy. Now you can put your knowledge to use. I'll give you my note of hand – that's good enough the length and breadth of Anglia for any sum you care to name; and if you can get decent grain at a shilling a quarter less than we've been paying at Hales lately, then settle the bargain.'

John was greatly surprised, not only at the trust being placed in him, but in his being so deliberately given what would have been William's job; and his surprise must have shown, for Saul growled out, 'Well, nephew? What is it? I hope you are not unwilling to go. While you are under my roof, I consider you owe me obedience.'

'No, Uncle, it's not that,' John said. 'It's just that – I thought William was to go.'

'You are to go, not he,' said Saul evenly, though with a wilful hitch of his chin

130

which indicated that this was no casual decision. 'The cart and the driver are ready. I will give you a little money so that you can buy a meal in Norwich. Be sure to be back before dusk.'

So saying, Saul opened a cashbox, gave John two shillings from it, locked the cashbox up again, and stumped out, as if he considered the matter settled.

Which indeed it was, as was any matter in that absolute monarchy of his, when King Saul had pronounced on it. The cart was waiting in the yard, as he had said; and having paused only to collect his hat, John was soon climbing up beside the driver. Saul stood by to see him off, his granite expression betraying no hint that he was doing anything out of the ordinary; and the driver had just gathered up the reins, when there was a shout for him to stop, and William came running out to the yard.

'What's the game? Nobody woke me. What's the game?' He looked seedy from the night before, and had run out in only his shirt and trousers, a fact sternly noted by Saul, who snapped, 'You're not half dressed, boy. Turn yourself out properly before you face me!'

William took no notice; for he was staring at John, much to John's discomfiture. 'Why,' he cried, 'where's *he* going?'

'To the Corn Exchange at Norwich,' said Saul, 'and you're delaying him. Go and get dressed, boy.'

William's pallor became scarlet. 'But I was to go – I always go! How comes *he* to be going—'

'Because I ordered him to,' said Saul. 'Because it is my will that he should go.' He slapped the stick against his own leg, as if admonishing himself to keep his composure. 'An early start is needed, else the best bargains will have been snapped up. Do you pretend that you are in a fit condition, boy, for an early start?'

'But it's my job! I always go!' In his fuddled bewilderment William could only repeat himself. 'It's my job . . . it's my job . . .'

'So you say,' said Saul. 'But if a man would keep his job, he should show willing. He should do it properly. He should shoulder his responsibilities, if he would not have them taken from him. Can you say you do those things, boy? The last time you went on this errand, you bought corn that had grown in the ear and was fit for nothing; and this time, it is you that are fit for nothing. You neglect even to rise – you pursue your dissipations till the most ungodly hours – and you expect me to wait upon your pleasure! Get gone, boy. Dress yourself, and don't be even more of a fool than you already are. And you, nephew, go about the business I have charged you with; we're wasting half the day here.'

The very horse in the shafts of the cart seemed to start nervously forward in obedience to Saul, and before John could speak a word they were on their way, rattling out of the yard, beneath the giant gantry, and on to the waterside road. His last backward glance showed him Saul giving his son a curt shove in the direction of the house.

John disliked the fact that he had been silent. It made him appear to be in smug complicity with the humiliation of William, whereas he was deeply disturbed by the whole thing. A trip to Norwich, especially on such a bright day, was certainly a welcome diversion, but he could not be wholly glad of it under such circumstances. He should have known that Saul would give with one hand whilst taking away with the other.

There was little to distract his perturbed thoughts about this as they went along; for the cart was driven by one of the most taciturn of Saul's generally uncommunicative employees, a stubby little man whom John knew only as Bobbs, and who seemed to have put all his growing into his whiskers. Bobbs, though John was sitting right beside him, kept his eyes on the road, betraying no consciousness that anyone was making the journey but himself and the horse, and John, besides being

131

deep in reflection, respected his right to keep his thoughts to himself. It was not until they were past Fakenham that Bobbs gave John a shy glance, and said with great volume and emphasis, 'All right?'

John thanked him and said that he was, and hoped Bobbs was the same; but the driver seemed to feel that he had said quite enough for the time being, and omitted to reply, merely turning his attention back to the road, though with a pleased and freshened look.

The day was very fine, perfect harvest weather, and bronzy colours were everywhere in evidence, so that it was impossible to look at the reaped fields without thinking of the new-made bread and golden ale that would come from them; impossible, too, for John not to contrast this air and freedom with the narrow life he led at Saul's. Memories of a time when beauty, hopefulness, variety and imagination had played a part in his existence returned upon him insistently, and returned upon him, moreover, not as tortures but as inspirations. Surely, they seemed to say, we are not the last of our kind – surely our like are to be found again, in that dim vista called the future?

He could not see how; but he could not leave the question alone. And he became so absorbed in consideration of what he was doing and where he was going, that he jumped when his companion abruptly spoke again.

'Been down the Hole lately?'

It took John a moment to work out that this enigmatic utterance referred to the Hole in the Wall, a public-house in Hales-next-the-sea. He replied that he had not; and as the moment for talk seemed to have arrived, said that he had heard they served a very good drop of beer there. This opening up of new conversational avenues, however, seemed rather to alarm Bobbs, who after a startled look fixed his eyes on the road as before, and drove on another half-mile before suddenly declaring, 'Dropsy.'

John could not work this one out, and his look said so.

'Landlord of the Hole,' said Bobbs. 'Got dropsy.' And seeming to feel that they had had quite a long and stimulating discussion, Bobbs returned his attention to the road with that refreshed look once more.

John had not been to Norwich since his hasty departure from Mr Wenn's Academy – a year ago now; and as the many church towers of the city came into view, more memories chivvied him. Young Stuffins – where was he now? Was he studying to be a lawyer in London, and living in a fast set as he had always declared was his intention? John hoped so. Were there other parlour-boarders now at Mr Wenn's, suffering the daily ordeal of the post at breakfast, and being lightly basted in Mr Wenn's sizzling sarcasm? And were they as innocently eager and hopeful for life to begin as he and Stuffins had been?

It must be so. But John found that these thoughts did not depress him as they would have done a few months ago. Nor did the other associations that the city had for him. Chapel Field, for example, where he had walked with Catherine in the pouring rain, pretending not to mind it, and Verity Deene – he now realized – had been in paroxysms of laughter; he found himself smiling at the recollection. And now Miss Deene had gone to London too. Change and growth, all around him: all around him, life and movement, especially as the cart came into the old city, and became one of a myriad wheeled vehicles trying to get around it, and jostling for space with a myriad people, all going somewhere, all doing something, and all marked with such vivid individuality that John found himself studying them wonderingly as if, Miranda-like, he had never seen people before.

His conveyance put up at the Back of the Inns, amongst the carriers' carts, where Bobbs was to wait for him. It was a short distance to the Corn Exchange, but John made it longer by wandering a little, drinking in the bustle of the streets, and reflecting on the fact that all this intense life had been going on without him. He could not say what emotions were stirring in his breast, except that a curious, not unpleasant impatience was among them.

And then, out of all the fascinatingly unknown faces that passed him, there arose two that he recognized. Admiral and Mrs Fernhill emerged from one of the lawyers' houses in Tombland, and crossed the road with a lofty disregard for the traffic, the admiral's head shining lustrously in the sunlight as if half a crew had been polishing and buffing it since the first pipe. They were coming straight towards John; and John saw no reason why he should not stop and greet them.

They did not quite cut him dead. Rather, the admiral looked him up and down as if he were about to mutiny over the grog ration; whilst Mrs Fernhill responded to his determined greeting with a vague murmur of, 'Oh, yes, Mr Fourpenny, hm,' without looking at him at all.

'Twopenny, ma'am,' John said.

'Yes, we know who you are, young man,' said the admiral, 'we know quite well who you are, and now I suggest you go about your business.'

They were moving past him; and in his reaction to this, John crossed a border. A month ago, even a week ago, he might have meekly accepted it. Today he did not. He would not.

'Will you not allow me to ask how you are?' he said, stepping in front of them.

'That,' said the admiral, 'is none of your concern, sir.'

John persisted. 'In what way have I offended?'

The admiral, stuck for a reply, reddened and swelled like a great bullfrog; whilst Mrs Fernhill looked supremely vacant, as if surprise had robbed her of the last vestiges of intellect.

'I assume the offence,' John said, 'because I was formerly welcome in your society, and am not now. That's the impression I've received, and still receive. So please tell me, where the offence lies.'

'Really, Mr Sixpenny, we must not be bothered in this way, in the common street with I don't know who looking on – we must not, indeed, or I don't know what will happen!' cried Mrs Fernhill, with the flowers on her bonnet nodding in her agitation.

'You are not welcome in our society, no, sir,' said the admiral. 'You made your intentions plain in a certain direction, and those intentions are not welcome. They are not to be entertained. I have told my daughter so, and I tell you so now.'

'Well.' He knew it well enough already, but still it stung to hear it. 'At least you have had the courage to say it to my face at last. The accidents of my history and my reduced circumstances, I suppose, are responsible for your disapproval. I cannot change that; but I can tell you that you are hard, sir, and unfair. And I hope you will remember it, if *you* should ever come to misfortune. Good day to you sir, ma'am.'

He turned and left them. It had been on his lips to say that he and Catherine still loved each other, and that they could not direct their daughter's feelings as they directed her movements; but that might involve repercussions on Catherine herself, and he did not want that.

Still, he felt a sort of bitter relief at having spoken out, which was all mixed up with that curious sensation of impatience. For he had after all only given them words, not deeds: confessed his helplessness, but done nothing to change it. And as he went on to the Corn Exchange, he felt a renewal of pride and indignation; and for some reason it was Mrs Fernhill's habit of getting his name wrong that chiefly caused it.

'I am John Twopenny,' he said to himself, and had a wish to proclaim it aloud. 'Yes, I am John Twopenny, and my late father was Dr Robert Twopenny, and I am proud of it. I have nothing to be ashamed of, nothing whatsoever. And I have

133

no reason to feel that my life is over, and that I am a nothing, a nonentity, and must accept my lot accordingly. No!'

His defiant mood continued through his dealings at the Corn Exchange, where any farmers inclined to treat him as a naïve stripling who could be easily hoodwinked got a spirited response; and he made his purchase of barley at last at a price that even Saul's thriftiness must approve. There was satisfaction in this, at any rate; and he made his way back to the Inns still doggedly asserting his identity in his own mind, and still finding that odd mixture of relief and impatience in it.

He found Bobbs having a phlegmatic parley with an ostler over a tankard of beer; and the sight reminded him that he was hungry, and that Saul had made provision for his dinner. So, he went into the dining-room of the inn where the cart was drawn up, and bespoke a meat pudding with potatoes and greens, and half a pint of wine. The dining-room was divided into curtained boxes, and John had one of these to himself, and possessed himself of one of the newspapers that were circulating; and he smiled as he thought about Stuffins again, for this, compared to the regimen of Saul's house, was pretty fast living, and he felt it so.

He had glanced through the paper by the time his dinner came, and put it aside while he ate. His stomach was just refusing to consider the last potato, when a gentleman sat down in the next box, and drew aside the curtain.

'Pardon me, might I look over that paper?'

'Surely,' said John, holding it out. 'Oh—!'

Recognition dawned on them both at the same moment. The gentleman in the next box was Mr Marcus Goodway; and though he took the paper calmly enough, John snatched back his hand as if he had touched poison.

'So, John,' said Mr Goodway, glancing over the front page. 'You're looking well.'

John could with truth have said the same, for Mr Goodway was as sturdily handsome and hale-looking a gentleman as ever. But civilities, to this man, were out of the question. John had an impulse to get up and leave at once; and yet, why should he? His wine was not yet finished; and Mr Goodway, settling back in his seat and looking comfortably at home here as everywhere, obviously had no intention of letting this encounter disturb his equanimity. 'I shall stay,' John thought, with the same defiance with which he had mentally pronounced his name. 'I shall not give him the satisfaction of slinking away.'

Yet it was one thing to stay, and another to maintain his composure when he was just a few feet from the man who had played so prominent a part in his father's downfall. Goodway's very ease, he felt, was an affront; and he could not help glaring at that leonine head bent over the newspaper, and burning with a sense of the injustice which allowed this man to walk the earth yet while his father lay in a shamed grave.

Mr Goodway presently became aware of John's look, and lifted his head. 'Was there something you wished to say to me, John? I suppose we can hardly expect to be on cordial terms after what happened at our last meeting; but I'm prepared to overlook that for now. Shall we be civil with one another, John? What do you think?'

'It is impossible,' John said, surprised and vexed to hear a quiver in his voice, 'that we could ever be on cordial terms, and you know very well why.'

Mr Goodway heard the quiver too, and smiled. 'Still passionate, John? It won't do you any good in the world, you know. Oh, well, it doesn't matter. I am leaving these parts soon, so you and I need not trouble to get along.'

'Are you going for good?'

'Not necessarily. But Mrs Goodway's health has been to some degree restored, and she lacks the stimulation of society that is to be found in London. We shall close up Beacon House for the time being – perhaps let it – and return to town.'

'In other words,' said John, 'you have turned a nice penny by fleecing the country yokels, and now you are scuttling back home with the proceeds.'

Mr Goodway raised an eyebrow. 'John, I don't *think* you're a fool,' he said, 'so I wonder, really, why you talk like one.'

'Not such a fool that I can't spot a trickster when I see one.'

'I am not aware of having committed any crime. If I'm wrong, please enlighten me.'

'Perhaps no crime in law,' John said, 'but a crime against your fellow-man. You are not an innocent – that you must admit; you are a worldly man, a man of wealth and experience and power; and when you let my father have his head, and fostered his extravagance, and fed it in the certain knowledge that you would have your pound of flesh from the result – well, you committed a crime as surely as if you had done murder with your bare hands.'

'Strong stuff,' said Mr Goodway, clasping his hands behind his head, and regarding John with an expression of mild interest. 'But really, John, if a man can't handle his own affairs, that's no business of mine. I can't live another man's life for him. Now can I?'

'You can respect and honour the lives of your fellow-mortals,' said John. 'As my father did all his life.'

'Oh, believe me, John, I'm sorry, sorry indeed that your father came to the end he did; but I'm afraid that end in itself is significant. Failure to face up to one's responsibilities – failure right to the last – may be pitiable, but don't ask me to admire it. And I must protest, really, at this canonization of Dr Twopenny. Incurring debts with no intention of honouring them, and then taking the coward's way out – if that is evidence of shining virtue, then all I can say is the world is in a sorry state. Don't you think? Honesty, John, honesty above everything. As Johnson said, clear your *mind* of cant.'

'You exploited my father when he lived,' John said, jumping to his feet, 'and you insult him now that he's dead. You deserve—'

'What? Another blow? Don't think I have forgotten the last one, John. Such melodrama! God preserve us from melodramatic boys. Sit down, or go, but don't weary me with any more of this cant, please.'

John stood looking down at Mr Goodway, in a perfect transport of hatred; and yet the striking of a blow did not really occur to him as a worthwhile possibility. The irresistible comparison would be with a furious child beating its fists against an adult, and a child was what he hated to feel and always felt next to Mr Marcus Goodway. And in the amused look with which he returned John's glare, it was plain that Mr Goodway knew this. Always that curious penetration; it was as if strong enmity shared something of the clairvoyant quality of strong friendship.

'I suppose a blow would hurt you, wouldn't it?' John said.

'I suppose it would,' said Mr Goodway readily.

'But not greatly, and not for long. The pain would pass.'

'The pain would pass, as you say.'

John took money from his pocket, signalling the waiter. 'Well,' he said. 'If it is ever in my power to really hurt you – to hurt you more profoundly, more lastingly, and more according to what you deserve, I will do it.'

So saying, he paid his bill, and left Mr Goodway sitting there.

No telling what he was feeling as he went out to the innyard; all he knew was that he was subject to powerful emotions once more, after a seemingly endless period of blank and vegetable existence. He was alive again, with all the vulnerability to pleasure and pain that that implies; and he was grateful that he had so unassuming a companion as Bobbs on the drive back to Hales, for he felt for some time unequal to talking. Images of Mr Goodway, of Admiral Fernhill, of Catherine, of Miss Deene, of Mr Wenn, of Stuffins, of Uncle Saul, of William, of his mother, of his

135

father, all whirled and danced giddily about his mind as if to some inscrutable purpose, and he could only let them do so, while that sensation of something that could only be called impatience clung about his heart and made it beat faster.

Though it was early evening when they entered Hales-next-the-sea, the light was still warm and golden, and had brought strollers out on the quayside, where the sound of a fiddle could be faintly and sweetly heard from the deck of a sloop that was moored there. But once they had passed the iron gates of S. Twopenny & Son, the light seemed to die; the yard was all in shadow, and it was impossible to imagine that the sun had touched it all the glorious day.

Mr Addy was there to greet John as he got down from he cart. It was clear from his bristling look that he had had a hard day of it, an impression which was confirmed by his at once declaring: 'Never – never *never* have he got me so hot as he've got me this day. I've had to douse myself so many times, I'm all crinkled like a babby from a bath; and yet it didn't cool me even then. The way that one have carried on today – the way he've come down on me, and picked and pressed and prodded – well, he've got me Broiled, and I can't say fairer than that!'

'What has he found fault with today, in particular?' asked John.

'What haven't he? Ask rather, what haven't he? And I'll tell you: nothing. Oh, but it've been a day I'd rather forget, all round. The young one –' meaning William – '*he've* been playing up. That's what's at the root of it.'

'Ah,' said John, remembering how William had acted that morning. 'Well, that's to be expected, I suppose. In fact I think my uncle knew quite well what he was doing when he sent me to Norwich today.'

A glance of understanding passed between him and Mr Addy, who nodded and said, 'Well, I'm not so sure as it's turned out the way he wanted . . . But I shouldn't be saying these things. I just thought I'd warn you there's pepper in the air – I've never known it so thick; and I don't reckon it can carry on like this much longer. I'm sure *somebody's* going to explode, if I don't do it first!'

Mr Addy had not exaggerated. John found the atmosphere in the house more oppressive than he had ever known it. Supper was preparing, and there was that unrestful pause that prevailed in Saul's house whenever there was neither work to be done nor prayers to be said. These were the times, in kindlier households, when the air was filled with pleasant chat about what had happened during the day; but there was none of that here. The parlour was more like an ante-room to some place of execution, where the victims waited in strained silence.

Something new today, however: Saul did not call John into his private office to give an account of his doings in Norwich, as would usually be the habit. Instead he made the inquiry as they sat in the parlour.

He made the inquiry in the parlour, with William present: William, whose stormy expression sufficiently indicated the confusion of resentful, jealous and mutinous emotions that he was suffering; and John hated the part he was having to play in this deadly charade more than ever. He could not help noticing, too, with a sort of bitter admiration for his cunning, that Saul did not overplay his own part: he commended John's bargain, but not fulsomely; and he did not belabour William with comparisons. In fact, he took no notice of William at all. And meanwhile Sar'ann sat with her bony hands in her lap, and looked from Saul to William, and from William to John, and back again, with the most fervent attention; pausing now and then only to fan herself with a fly-paper, and murmur, 'Oh my stars, there's no air . . . oh, my word and bond, there's no air at all tonight!'

The same mood persisted through supper. But Saul was quite calm. If he was relishing the discomfort of this situation that he had created, he gave no sign of it.

No sign of it, either, in the parlour after supper, even though William would not sit down, but drew back the curtain at the window and stood brooding there. A book of the driest devotional matter lay on the table, and Saul, saying that his eyes were a little tired, instructed Sar'ann to read aloud from it.

She had barely commenced when her father stopped her with an abrupt motion of his hand. William was still at the window; and directing at him a stare in which John saw all the old truculence grimly kindling, Saul snapped: 'William, you will attend to this good matter. Sit down.'

William did not answer. He remained where he was, with his back to them, chewing on his thumbnail.

'Do you hear me, boy?'

'I hear you,' muttered William, still not moving.

'Then do as I tell you,' said Saul quietly.

For a moment John thought William was simply going to say 'No.' But even at this pitch of his resentment the young man could not offer a downright negative to his domineering father. He stirred, and shrugged, and said awkwardly, 'I've heard that book before, Pa. I know all about it. I'd rather – I'd rather go out.'

The movement he made towards the door was irresolute enough, in all conscience; but Saul forestalled it promptly – as if it were what he had been waiting for. He got swiftly to his feet, and thrust out his stick horizontally at the level of William's chest, like a barrier.

'You may go out when I permit you, boy. I do not permit you. Sit down.'

'I won't! Pa, a man of twenty-five may come and go as he pleases!'

'Not in my house. As long as you are in my house, boy, you owe me duty.'

'Why? Why do I owe you duty?' William's voice became shrill. 'If I am to give you duty, surely I should have rights in return! But where are my rights?' He pointed at John, with a burning look. 'What about today? By rights *I* should have gone to Norwich. That should have been *my* job. By rights—'

'If you would have your rights,' said Saul, 'then earn them. If you would have your rights, boy, mend: mend, or they will be taken from you as surely as my God is in heaven. You will obey me as my son should, boy, or you will be no son at all. If you value your place here—'

'My place here? Why, what is that worth? My place here – why, it's more a curse than a blessing! I'd rather – I'd rather be a common sailor on the quay! I'd rather be the meanest drudge in your kitchen, than be your son—'

William was cut off by his father's swinging the stick at him. It fetched him a terrific crack on the elbow, and William yelped and jumped back; but the fierce old man was on him in a moment. Grabbing William by his collar, Saul pushed him against the table, upsetting the lamp, and began beating him with the stick, violently, all across the shoulders and back.

'No! Pa, no! I'm sorry for what I said!' squealed William, covering his head with his hands, and squirming in his father's strong grasp. 'Don't, Pa, don't! I'm truly sorry – please, Pa . . .!'

'I shall *make* you sorry,' said Saul between his teeth. 'I shall beat respect into you, boy, if it's the last thing I do. "A worm, and no man; a reproach of men, and despised of the people" – think on that text, boy. "The way of transgressors is hard" – there's another for you. "He that spareth his rod hateth his son" – another. "A whip for the horse, a bridle for the ass, and a rod for the fool's back" – another.' And between each harsh mouthful of scripture, Saul brought down the stick with fearful force upon his son's writhing back. ' "My father hath chastized you with whips, but I will chastize you with scorpions" – there's another. "They have sown the wind, and they shall reap the whirlwind" – there's . . .' But though Saul had lifted his stick to strike home this last amiable lesson, he found he could not bring it down; for John had sprung forward and seized it in his hand, and though the old man tugged and twisted at it, John had it fast, and would not let go.

'Stand away! Stand away, sir, or I shall make you bleed in your turn!' said Saul, his eyes blazing. 'Do as I say, nephew, or it will be the worse for you!' He gave

137

another mulish tug at the stick, twisting it as he did so, and the lacerating pain in John's hand made him let go.

But only for a moment; for as Saul raised the stick towards him, John flew at his uncle and, gripping him by the lapels of his coat, thrust him steadily backwards.

'You will not strike one more blow with that infernal stick whilst I am in this house!' John cried in a passion. 'I will not stand by and see it, by God I will not!'

Sar'ann had leapt to her feet, and in a tone that sounded uncommonly like excitement was shrieking: 'Oh, my stars, John's gone mad! Oh my stars, it's murder! Look at it, just look at it! Oh my word and bond, it's horrible murder, just like in the prints!'

The old man, in his pride and stubbornness, grappled still with his adversary, and got in a glancing cut with his stick; but John had the advantage of him, and at last shoved him down into the chair from which he had risen; and before Saul could recover himself, John snatched the stick from his hand, and lifted it high. Sar'ann gave a shriek like a train whistle, in the expectation that John was about to use it in Saul's own manner; but John, after looking down at the grim old face glaring back at him, did not. Instead he broke the stick over his knee, and threw the two splintered fragments into the grate.

'Nephew, you shall be punished for this,' said Saul, who was breathing heavily, and more exhausted than he would admit.

'No, Uncle, I will not,' said John. A sort of black disgust had succeeded his wild fury. 'No, I will not. Come at me with a stick, and I shall simply break it again. I am quite in earnest.'

Caleb had come running from upstairs, where he made a nightly ritual of preparing his master's hard bed, at the sound of Sar'ann's screams; and now Saul beckoned to his bewildered servant.

'Help me up, Caleb. Good lad. That's it. Now fetch me another stick from the stand in the hall.' Saul advanced slowly towards John, ignoring William who was gazing at them through a mask of astonishment and humiliated tears. 'Nephew, I took you in on condition that you obeyed me in my own house. You owe me obedience, just the same as that blubbering boy there; but I owe you nothing. Think on that, boy, before you decline to take your punishment. I can turn you out of this house tomorrow – tonight – at any moment: you will have nothing; you will have to fend for yourself. I am ready to do it, nephew.'

'Do it, then,' said John.

Saul's eyes hardened; but was there surprise in them too – bafflement even?

'Do it, Uncle,' said John. 'But no, wait. I'll do it for you, if you like. You say the price of my staying here is obedience? You say the price of my staying here is total subservience to your will, so that you may mould and shape me in your own image – or break me, if I prove unsatisfactory? And otherwise, you turn me out? Have I understood you aright? Well, there's no need for you to turn me out, Uncle. I am almost of age, and the responsibilities of your guardianship are nearly over, and I'm not going to quibble over a few weeks. I shall go tonight.'

Saul gave him a close look, as if he suspected for a moment only the empty bravado with which William challenged him; but seeing from John's expression that he meant what he said, the old man flushed, and grasping at the air as if even now he felt the lack of his stick he bellowed, 'You'll get nothing, boy! You'll take nothing away from here but what you brought with you; and once you've gone, there's no coming back! Whatever becomes of you, I will not stir a finger on your behalf. I will have no communication with you. I will not acknowledge you as my kin. This is my solemn promise, nephew, and I have never broken a promise.'

'Well, you will not have to break this one, Uncle,' said John. 'I shall never apply to you, have no fear. As for not acknowledging me as kin, there you do me a favour and not a disservice. My pride in my name attaches to my poor father, not to you.'

The passionate indignation that had spurred him into action swelled up again as he thought of his father, dead and dishonoured while Saul still tyrannically strutted the earth; but he had done all that needed to be done when he had broken the stick over his knee, and so he swallowed it down, and left the room, and went upstairs to pack.

Well, he had crossed the Rubicon now; but it seemed to him, as he set about his packing and was able to reflect a little more coolly, that what had just happened had been the inevitable culmination of a long process. He had defied his uncle in a moment of unthinking, ungovernable rage at his cruelty; but the moment had been long preparing. If it had not happened today, he thought, it would have happened next week, or next month. The rebirth of his identity from the ashes of his blank despair made it certain that life as it was lived in his uncle's house would sooner or later become intolerable to him; and as that identity included impulsiveness, a hot temper, and a readiness to take a leap into the unknown, his action became more natural than surprising.

All very well, of course, to view it in those terms, as if it had happened to someone else; but it had happened to him, and his body soon acknowledged the fact, for he had scarcely begun his packing when he was taken with a violent fit of shaking, and had to sit down on the bed with his head in his hands.

He did not regret what he had done: he would do it again; but he knew that the consequences must be faced in quite a different frame of mind from the impetuous deed itself. And as he reviewed the events of the day, it occurred to him that he had burnt more than one bridge in the course of his reawakening.

'Ah, well, John,' he found himself saying, 'today you have got at cross with Admiral and Mrs Fernhill, with Goodway, and with Uncle Saul. Not bad, in the space of twenty-four hours.' He seemed to hear his father's accents in the words; and that in itself freshened his spirits, and he returned to his packing with a will.

It did not take long, for his possessions were few. Though he was dog-tired, and had not yet given a thought as to where he was to go, he was adamant that he would leave this very night; and he was just wondering whether he could manage to get his box down the stairs by himself, when there was a tap at the door.

It was William, who even now would not look him in the eye, or speak above a mutter, or behave as if anything out of the ordinary had occurred. But he had come of his own volition to offer his help with the box, and that, perhaps, was significant.

In silence they carried the box down to the hall; and there Saul was waiting, with a new stick in his hand, and with Sar'ann and Caleb looking on.

'Where do you intend going, nephew?' said Saul, who seemed to have undergone some further process of petrifaction, and was more stony and unyielding than ever before. 'I ask, not because I am concerned for your welfare – you have forfeited any right to that – but because I have had the cart made ready to take you and your box, and the driver is waiting for his instructions. This is the last thing I will do for you, nephew: I hope you know it.'

'I know it, Uncle,' said John, returning his look steadily. 'I shall go to the White Hart.'

The White Hart was the chief inn of the town, and merely suggested itself to John for want of anything else; though the few pounds of his own that he retained would not secure him accommodation for long. However, all that mattered to him now was that he be out of this house, and away from its baleful influence. The departure was soon accomplished. The self-same cart in which he had travelled to Norwich was in the yard, and the self-same Bobbs was at the reins, and looking, as far as his whiskers allowed, thoroughly puzzled at this transformation in John's fortunes; and the box was put on it, and then John put himself on it; and then the wheels were turning, and taking him away from S. Twopenny & Son for the last time. Saul turned and went back into the house before the vehicle had even passed the gates; but Sar'ann remained, staring as if she were committing this exciting scene to memory. William hung about, too – though he still would not look at John, and stood drooping and chewing his thumb. And then there was Caleb Porter; and he was the only one who showed any emotion. Caleb, in fact, was crying bitterly; for faithful though he was to his master, and no more capable of believing ill of him than of flying, the big man had a child's attachment to familiar faces, and a child's fearful dislike of change; and so it was not quite unwept that John was exiled from Saul's kingdom, and turned out into the world alone.

As for John, he did not look back – not, at least, at the house itself; for there was nothing within its massive walls that could move him with any grateful or friendly association. With the men who had worked alongside him in the maltings, it was a different matter, and poor Bobbs was so discomfited by this errand that he was quite lost for words, and would have had to have driven John twenty miles, rather than the short distance to the White Hart, before he would have been equal to speaking. However, John thanked him warmly as he was set down with his box outside the inn, and bade him goodbye; and then the cart rattled away, with the words S. TWOPENNY & SON, painted on the backboard, departing with it, and disappearing at last.

'I wish, by the way,' he thought, 'that I had been able to say goodbye to Mr Addy . . . But perhaps it's just as well.' For such a demonstration might, in Saul's suspicious eyes, have tainted Mr Addy with John's own rebellion, and made the old man even harder on his foreman than ever.

His first wish was, however, to be granted; for at that moment there was a shout, and there, coming at a perspiring trot up the narrow funnel of a street towards him, was Mr Addy himself. He was too heated and breathless to speak at first; but he shook John's hand, and then shook it again, and then shook it a third time, as if only such a repetition could convey his feelings on this occasion.

'I knew somebody would go bang,' Mr Addy said, when he had recovered his breath. 'I knew somebody would blow up in that one's face, one of these days; if you turn people into gunpowder, it's bound to happen sooner or later. I shouldn't say this what I'm a-going to say now – I shouldn't say it at all, and if that one was to hear me saying it I don't know what my life'd be worth. But I'm a-going to say it anyhow. Here it comes – John, I wish I'd been there to see you do it, and if I had, I would have *clapped*!' Mr Addy pronounced the words rapidly, but with great emphasis; and as soon as they were out, glanced nervously over his shoulder, as if he feared that Saul, like his name, was all over the town, and listening at every doorpost. 'There – it's out. Anyhow, I didn't see it; I only happened to hear because I was working late at the maltings, and the maid came a-running over to the house, to tell us what was afoot. And so I thought I'd come after you, and see how you were, and what you were going to do . . . And what *are* you going to do?' said Mr Addy with sudden sorrowfulness. 'I suppose there's no going back? You've blown up good and proper?'

'There's no going back,' said John. 'Not to my uncle.'

'Well, I've been close enough to going bang myself, many a time, and I can understand it . . . And yet it's a pity, for you were learning the malting business like a good 'un, and I was hoping to learn you more!'

'Believe me, Mr Addy, it was nothing about the malting business that made me – go bang; and the happiest times I have had here have been connected with it, and with you. But I can't stay – not for all the money in the world would I stay. As for what I'm going to do . . . I really don't know.' He confronted the enormity of the question for the first time, having spoken it aloud. 'I must . . . do some thinking. But I shall stay here the night, anyhow.'

Mr Addy hesitated. 'Well now – look here. I don't suppose you've much money, and what you've got you can't afford to throw at innkeepers and waiters; and it won't be homely for you, staying there all alone. So we'll find a lad to carry your box, and you can come along of me, and stay at my house tonight.' Mr Addy glanced over his shoulder again. 'Only it mustn't get back to that one, for if he heard about me sheltering you, he'd come down on me that hard, I daren't even think about it!'

John, though extremely grateful, was reluctant to jeopardize Mr Addy's position, and he said so; but Mr Addy was insistent. So John, glad enough at the prospect of spending the night under a friendly roof, agreed with more thanks, and followed the little trotting man through the streets of Hales, until they stopped short in front of a neat, bow-windowed house with its doorstep giving directly on to the cobbles.

'Mrs Addy knows all about that one, and the way he carry on,' said Mr Addy, lifting the latch, 'so I'll hardly need to explain. She get a little fiery herself, when she talk of him; and she ain't a fiery woman by nature.'

Mrs Addy, indeed, was a pleasant round rosy lady, for whom the affectionate epithet of My Little Biffin, which her husband bestowed on her along with a kiss of greeting, was entirely appropriate. But she did look a little inflammable when Saul's name was mentioned; and having heard John's story, gave it as her opinion that the old man was made of something, but it wasn't flesh and blood. Though John had already supped, after a fashion, they pressed him to take a share of their meal, which was set out with the utmost neatness in a nook of the parlour, just large enough for a little table and three chairs.

The question of what John was to do was raised again after supper, when Mr Addy filled a pipe and took his ease; and he mulled over such openings as he knew of for young men in the vicinity, becoming quite enthusiastic over the idea of a fishing-smack. But then, seeing John's drawn and absent look, he said that the best thing to do was sleep on it; and, taking a candle, conducted John to a guest bedroom of such small dimensions that, when both John and his box were in it, there was no possibility of opening the door. But it was neat and clean, and John was far from unthankful for his hosts' kindness.

It was his very sense of respect and obligation to them, indeed, that made him conclude that this was the last and only night he would spend beneath the Addys' roof. There was little hope of keeping a secret in a small town like Hales-next-the-sea, and if his stay here were prolonged, news of it was sure to reach the ears of his uncle Saul. John would not have Mr Addy lose his job, burdensome though it might be; and so he determined that he would go in the morning.

As to where he would go, he did not know – or at least, his conscious mind did not; but something had been tugging at him all evening, and perhaps for longer. The sight of the bundle of his father's papers, when he had packed his box, had set it tugging harder; and now John knelt down and drew the papers out and began riffling through them, still only half knowing what he was looking for. It was melancholy to find a man's whole self reduced to these few perishable effects, but John resisted the melancholy. It was not his father's death, but his father's life, and the example it had set him, that concerned John now, as the buried notion began to claw its way to the surface; and when he at last came across a letter bearing the signature 'Frank Spruce', the notion came out into the light, and he knew it for what it was.

He only glanced over the contents of the letter; it was an address he sought, and an address there was, in Southwark, London. Having found it, he sat back on the bed and thought.

He remembered that his father had mentioned his old friend Frank Spruce shortly before his death, when in his distress of debt he had lamented that he had not gone to London to practise, as Dr Spruce had done. For London, of course, was the place to go to make your fortune, whether in medicine or anything else; in London above all other places lay opportunity. And though the ambition to be a doctor had sickened and wasted through the long twilight of John's grief and despair, it had not died. It had shared in the general revival of his selfhood that had taken place over the past weeks, and now it was as strong as it had ever been, and invigorated by a new resolve.

'The Royal Road to medicine is closed to me,' John said to himself. 'A medical student, such as I used to dream of being, must be supported through years of training; he must have means, whether of his own or furnished by his family; those means I do not have. But I have the will. If I cannot enter the profession in the grand manner, I will approach it some other way, if it can be done; if sweeping away the bloody bandages in the wards will bring me nearer to my goal, then I will do that. Or I will gain the means, somehow, to study. And it must be London; there are all the great teaching hospitals and foundations and dispensaries; there is where medical knowledge is most to be had, and most needed. I know that young men in tales are always going to London to make their fortunes, but it must happen in real life too – surely! If I had no one there to consult with, and on whose judgement of my best course I could rely, it would be a rash idea indeed; but Dr Spruce was always kind to me, and encouraged my ambitions, when he lived in these parts. He has been practising in London for some years now, and can surely point me in the right direction.'

It was proof indeed that John had entirely recovered his old spirits, that he could contemplate this undertaking – contemplate it, moreover, with such a flush of enthusiasm that even his tiredness fell away from him, and he jumped to his feet, feeling ready to start for London at once. In fact he was not blind to the signs of his old hastiness; and he made himself sit down, half-laughing and half-angry with himself. 'Quarrelling with half of Norfolk is quite enough for one day, I think,' he said; but that in itself, when he reflected on it, furnished a further motive for his going. For what was there for him here? The corner of Anglia that was the place of his birth and bringing-up had become a place of enmity. Even if he were to reconcile himself to some other pursuit than medicine, there was precious little here to help him, and much to hinder him. The breaking of Saul's stick had been more apt than he knew, for a clean break was what was demanded, if he was fully to live again.

No, there was nothing to keep him here – one vital thing excepted. And that one vital thing, by a sad paradox, was also a powerful reason for him to go. Catherine – ah, Catherine! Thinking of her, and thinking of going away from her, John was almost ready to embrace Mr Addy's idea, and ask the herring-fishers if they would have him; for to part with that one bright jewel that remained amidst all the ruin of his old life in Norfolk would be bitter beyond words. And yet separation by some hundred-odd miles could not exceed their separation here. The complete control over her that the law allowed to her parents until she was of age was reinforced by her affectionately dutiful nature, and that was not going to change when she turned twenty-one. He would have to transform his fortunes if he were going to transform their opinion of him; and if finally it proved necessary to do without their approval, he would likewise have to be pretty firmly established in life, for he had no illusions that the break would be easy for Catherine, and it would be potentially disastrous for both of them if he severed her from the family she loved only to make her live in a garret room on black bread and cheese. Out of very love for her, he must offer her security: he could permit himself no less.

But he had no illusions, either, about the burden this course of action would place on her. He would have to ask her, in effect, to wait for him. The phrase had quite a romantic sound; but it also, to his ears, had an arrogant and conceited sound. He felt he had no right to place her under any sort of oath or promise of faith, especially when the issue was so doubtful as even John's optimism perceived it to be. Any engagement, whether formal or tacitly understood, must have a definite limit set to it, or it became merely a shackle, it seemed to him. Yet he was in no position to name a date when everything would be all right – not a year, not two years, not five years hence. A man who could parade that sort of assurance must be either a liar or a fool.

'Well,' he said to himself, 'I shall simply promise her my fidelity – that's easy enough, for I love her and always will; and if she wishes to do the same, freely and spontaneously, then very well; if not, I shall rest content without it. I shall bind her to nothing . . . But by God, I swear I shall do it – I *shall* make something of myself, and we will have our life together, no matter what obstacles I find in my way. And if the shades of my poor mother and father are looking on, I shall make them as proud of me as I am proud of their memory. I swear it!'

So his decision was made; but there remained the immediately practical aspects to consider. A few pounds and shillings was all the money he had in the world. With that he would have to get to London, and find a lodging: it would have to be husbanded carefully. The carrier would be the cheapest method of getting to Norwich, and from there he could proceed to London by rail; for the old city was now fully served by the railways that were still something of a novelty in Anglia, and had two boastfully turreted new stations to prove it. Once in London, he would seek out his father's old friend Dr Spruce, and follow his guidance. If Dr Spruce could not point him in any medical direction, he would have to find some other means of earning his bread at first; and he was confident, again, that in the immensity of London, some opportunity would present itself for a willing young man.

But before he left, he must see Catherine, somehow; that must come before everything. He did not know how he would contrive it, and was by now too weary to set his mind to the problem; so he postponed it till the morning, and insinuated himself into the bed, which was so unaccommodating for one of his height, that when he lay at full length his feet were in the fireplace.

His thanks to the Addys for their kindness were nonetheless heartfelt, when he told them of his intention next morning; and though Mr Addy pressed him to stay longer, John could tell that the little foreman was secretly relieved at being free of his dangerous guest. 'And if that one should ask me whether I know what's become of you,' he said, 'I'll make out I don't know nothing about it, shall I?'

'That would be best,' John said. 'But I somehow don't think Uncle Saul will ask. As far as he's concerned, we are strangers to one another for ever more.'

'Ah! He's a stubborn one, all right. I wonder how things will turn out betwixt him and his son now?'

John had wondered too, but felt that it was no longer any business of his. The strange interlude that had been his life under Saul Twopenny's guardianship was over, and he was about to begin afresh. One last favour he had to ask of Mr Addy – to store his box until ten, when the carrier departed from Hales for Norwich. In the meantime, he had a couple of hours in which to contrive, somehow, a meeting with Catherine.

It was only a short walk to Buttings Court, just inland from the town; but it might as well have been in China, for all the chance of his being admitted there like any other caller. John hoped that an idea would come to him on the way, but when he arrived outside the gates of Buttings, the only possibility that suggested itself was to slip into the extensive gardens at the rear, and hope that Catherine might walk there, as he knew she often did in the mornings. Getting round to the gardens proved more difficult than he thought, for Buttings was surrounded by dense woodland; but at last he came to the flint wall that surrounded the oldest part of the gardens, and choosing a spot that was leafy and well covered, he climbed over it and dropped on to the soft turf beyond.

'Damn me! You jolly well gave me the fright of my life! What d'you mean by it, anyhow, dropping over walls at a fellow like a – like a jolly great apple or pear, you know?'

The speaker was Catherine's brother Augustus, who was taking the air in a casual costume of bright-check trousers, a surtout with buttons the size of sovereigns, and a tall silk hat, and who was startled into unusual animation by John's sudden appearance. It was over a year since John had seen him, and it was plain from his look that Augustus's less than powerful mind would have to be prompted into recognition.

'I'm sorry, Augustus – this must seem a very odd manner of proceeding. I didn't mean to startle you.'

Augustus appeared rather staggered at this apparition's knowing his name, and gave a nervous glance all round him, as if suspecting magic.

'Do you recall? John Twopenny. From Saltmarsh. You invited me to Buttings once, and . . .' Augustus continuing to look blank, or more blank than usual, John cast about for something that would jog his memory. 'We first met on the quayside at Hales, when we saw a mermaid.'

'By Jove, the mermaid. D'you know, I *do* remember you. Of course, you're the fellow that Kitty used to be mixed up with. Damn me!'

John winced inwardly at that *used to be*, whilst Augustus pumped his hand and, apparently quite forgetful now of John's unorthodox method of entry, welcomed him to Buttings. 'Haven't seen you in an age, my dear fellow. Let's see, it's Twopenny, isn't it? I'm pretty fair with names. Well, what have you been up to all this time? Needn't tell you what I've been up to. Beastly Cambridge and beastly studies. All those ancient Greek chaps. Plato, you know, and – what's the other fellow? – Aristotle. Beats me how all these ancient coves only had one name. Suppose there were two chaps named Plato? Confusing, surely. Whereas if you had Jack Plato and Tom Plato, as you would in jolly old England, you'd know where you were—'

'Augustus,' said John, 'I wonder if I might ask you a great favour.'

'Certainly, my dear fellow, ask away. If it's money, I may as well tell you I'm pretty strapped myself – tailor's bills, you know – Father's getting a mite waxy about 'em—'

'No, no, nothing like that. It's . . . well, I am very anxious to speak to Catherine.'

'Is that all? Nothing easier, my dear fellow. Come on up to the house, and we'll all breakfast together.'

'I'm afraid I can't do that. I'm not welcome at Buttings any more; your parents disapprove of my connection with Catherine. That's why I've had to act in this rather sneaking fashion. I'm sorry – I know I shouldn't make you an accomplice in this way, and if you should share their disapproval—'

'Good heavens, I've never disapproved of anyone. Wouldn't dream of it. Why, what's the old man got against you? No – don't tell me – it's money. Understand perfectly, my dear fellow. As it happens, I'm in a similar pickle myself – but don't breathe a word of it! Young lady at Cambridge – fascinating creature – face like an angel. Well, no, she has rather an acid face as it happens, but still a captivator, Twopenny, a captivator. Now *her* people don't think much of me. The father told me to my face that I lack bottom. Pretty stiff I call it—'

'You'll understand perfectly then,' said John hastily, conscious of time running out, 'that we have to be very discreet, and that I have to meet Catherine secretly. So I wondered whether you might tell her that I'm out here, and that I need to speak with her rather urgently, if she could slip out alone . . .'

'Say no more, Twopenny; I'm there,' said Augustus, tapping the side of his nose. 'I'm wise to the game, my dear fellow. You stay out of sight here, and I'll go send her to you directly. There's one thing I know how to be, and that's discreet.'

Augustus tapped his nose again, and set off towards the house whistling, sauntering, tipping his hat at a jaunty angle, glancing up at the sky, and generally presenting the most conspicuous appearance of something being up that could be imagined. However, his enterprise must have been successful, for presently John – lurking behind a lime-tree, and not unconscious of an element of absurdity in his situation – perceived Catherine making her way across the lawns towards him. She was no better an actor than Augustus, and when she saw John she burst into nervous laughter and cried: 'Oh, John, what curious things we have to do, I thought I would take Gelert out with me as an excuse, but the little beast wouldn't come and kept hiding under his pillow, and I was already in a fluster because Augustus came up to me in the most mysterious manner and whispered in my ear "He's waiting for you at the bottom of the garden" and made it sound quite sinister, as if you were a goblin or the Grim Reaper or something, instead of who you are which is my dearest, dearest John and I've gone shy for no reason at all . . .'

So had he; but they mutually conquered it, in the shade of the tree, and then John told her what had happened at his uncle's house, while she leaned her hands against his chest, tying and retying his cravat, and from time to time raising her eyes solemnly to his.

'. . . And so I am quite without the means of support, and houseless, and I must begin life anew. And as I have no prospects here, I must go to a place where prospects are to be found. My love, I must go to London. I have found the address of an old friend of my father's, a doctor of great energy and experience, and I hope he may set me on my way to earning my bread in his profession. And if not, London must surely offer other opportunities for a man to make his way in life.'

'I was afraid you were going to say something like that,' Catherine said in a small voice. 'Oh, John, is there no other way . . .?'

'I wish there were. But at present, Catherine, I have nothing. Your parents' opinion of me is entirely justified, as far as that goes. And I don't imagine that opinion has improved, after yesterday.'

'No . . . John, I'm afraid they're not even going to let you write to me now. Papa says he will have all the letters brought to him first, and any from you will be thrown away.'

'What? Not even to be able to write . . .!'

'They say it's for my own good,' Catherine said miserably. 'Oh, don't think ill of them, John – they believe what they're doing is right. I know it's hard to see it that way and I know it's hard for you to hear me defending them, but you see I can't bear to turn against them . . . But there may be a way for us to write, after all. Verity. She writes often to me, and Papa would never suspect any letter in her handwriting. I'm sure she would act as a go-between for us, and forward your letters inside hers, if I asked her, because she's the kindest creature even though she pretends to be severe.'

John could have wished for a go-between with whom he was on easier terms than the satirical Verity Deene; but that was an ungrateful thought, and he quashed it. 'That would be a great help, if it could be arranged.'

'I'll write to her today. At least then I would be able to have news of you . . . Oh, John, I've tied your cravat into the most fearful knot and I can't undo it and I wish you were not going.'

He took her hand, and touched it to his lips. 'You do understand why it must be, though, don't you? It's a curious piece of logic to say I'm going away so that we can be together, but I must make something of myself, if we are to have any chance. That is . . . I have not formally asked you if that chance is what you wish for, but—'

'Oh, John, it is. There's nothing I want more. And I'm sure you will make your fortune, I have the greatest faith in you. But you won't – you won't forget me, will you . . .?'

Words were inadequate to answer this question, and so he answered it in the directest manner possible. They clung together for some minutes, with his lips against her soft hair; and at last she said, her voice muffled against his shoulder, 'Well, I'm glad you did that to your monstrous old uncle, anyhow. Though I've been thinking, John – didn't it hurt when you broke his stick over your knee?'

'It hurt like the devil,' said John, 'and I had to pretend I didn't feel a thing.'

So they managed to laugh together, even though the laughter was of the sort that skirts the very edge of tears. And as for promises and engagements and solemn undertakings . . . well, they seemed of no great account beside the parting look she gave him, and the parting embrace that turned into another embrace and then another. The compact that was sealed in the shade of the lime-tree could not, he felt, have been made more binding by any words; and when at last he slipped away again through the woods, with her gentle admonitions to take the greatest care of himself for her sake still echoing like a sweet tune in his ears, he felt as if a silken thread bound him together with that willowy figure standing crowned with sunlight in the garden, and that it would stretch a lot further than mere London before it would break.

CHAPTER FIVE

More Surprises Than One

It was market day in Norwich, and when John got down from the carrier's van it was as if all the whirling confusion that had filled his mind as he rode here from Hales had somehow got outside his head and spread itself about the city. 'Well, it will be worse than this when I get to London,' he thought; and having stowed his box at the inn where the carrier put up, he set off with something of exultation and something of fear to book his railway ticket for that momentous destination.

Thorpe Station had been built outside the city walls, on open land beyond the river; but to get to it John had to pass through the older streets, some of which were not wearing at all well, and which presented a grim contrast to the prosperous bustle of the market. The big houses of long-dead merchants had been turned into tenements, with dingy courts and yards where once the merchants had strolled in their gardens. Here, John knew, was where cholera and typhoid had their fetid breeding-ground; and he had paused to glance up at a particularly frowsy corner house that leaned crazily on timber supports, when his eye fell on a figure sitting crouched on the grimy doorstep.

It was a young woman. She was poorly dressed, and there was a patched bundle beside her on the step which had the look of being all her worldly goods. She was leaning her head on her hand, which screened her face, and the prominence of her wrist-bones confirmed that she was in extreme want. Moved to pity, John stepped forward; and as his shadow fell across her, the woman looked up, and he recognized her.

It was their old servant Tetty. Not the brisk, smart, unassailable Tetty that he had known, but a wretched shadow, who hastened to cover her face with her hand again as if she did not want him to see her.

'Tetty!' cried John, kneeling down beside her. 'Tetty, don't you know me?'

'I know you, Mr John,' she said, her voice muffled. 'I know you.'

He found her other hand, and clasped it. 'My God, this is a dreadful sight to see. What's happened? Have you no home – no place?'

'I had a place, but I was turned out of it.'

'You, turned out? Why?'

Tetty looked at him at last, and said with a sad echo of her old sharpness, 'Gave too many smart answers, I suppose. Not every mistress is like your poor mother, I'm afraid . . .' She drew a deep breath. 'And my sister-in-law died this spring, so I couldn't go back there. I've been scratching a living as best I can, and lodging . . .' Her voice faded.

'Here?' John looked up at the peeling house.

Tetty nodded. 'There are – there are worse places. But now I . . . I haven't got the rent. I've pledged everything I can at the pop-shop. I begged the landlord to give me another week, just till I can find some work, but this morning he wouldn't hear no more and . . .'

John held her hand while she wept. He knew that Tetty, so proud and upright, felt her shame as keenly as her distress.

'How much is the rent owing?' he said, when she had recovered a little.

'I'm seven shillings behind . . . Oh, but no . . .'

'Oh, but yes,' John said. 'Why, I have the money – look, here it is. You are in need of the money, and I have it, so what could be simpler?'

'Mr John, I can't . . .'

'Yes, you can. For the simple reason that I know you'd do the same for me. And look here – take this too, so that you can pay this brute of a landlord a month in advance. That should make him hold his peace. And redeem your goods from the pawnbroker too . . . and then there's food – you must get yourself strong if you're to work, and new clothes, so you can be turned out well . . .'

He spoke rapidly, pressing the money on her, so that she should not have time to refuse; and the sight of it seemed to daze her, until at last she frowned and shook her head. 'If I – if I take this, I must pay it back – I must . . .'

'Well, if you like. But only when you're on your feet again.'

'I shall . . . I shall indeed.' Tetty looked up from the money to John, and suddenly the lineaments of her old determination were to be seen in her haggard face. 'I'll take it only on that promise. As soon as I can pay it back, I shall send it to you at your uncle's.'

'Not there. I've left my uncle's. We couldn't agree, and . . . well, you know well what he's like, Tetty. No, I'm bound for London, and if I don't make my fortune there, I'll eat my wig, as Father used to say.'

Tetty faintly smiled at these words, and said, 'Well, I'm glad to see you haven't changed, anyhow . . . But I must pay this money back to you somehow, and I've got to know where you are.'

'I still say it isn't necessary, but if you insist. I'll write you here, as soon as I've a lodging, and then you'll know where I am.'

Tetty, still caught between reluctance and wondering relief at the money in her hand, agreed; and it was only after he had parted with her, after extracting a promise that the first thing she would do would be to eat a good meal, that John came to a full consciousness of what he had done.

Not that he regretted that; for he well knew that Tetty's only resort otherwise would have been the workhouse, and he only wished that he could have offered her a more permanent relief from her distress. But the fact remained that he had given Tetty nearly all the money he had in the world, having retained a few coins only to give the impression that he had more; and now he could not afford his fare to London.

He did not know what to do. For some reason he carried on walking towards the station, and stood before its proud new arches, and smelt the steam and smuts on the air; but without money, he might as well have proposed to fly to London as enter those brick portals. With a sigh of vexation, John faced the fact that he had in truth thought none of this through properly. The passion of indignation that had carried him from his uncle's house had disdained practical considerations, and now he saw how very precarious his position was.

For a moment he considered abandoning the idea of London altogether; but then, where would that leave him? He could not return to his uncle's house, or apply to him for aid, even if he wanted to, and he had no other family. No, there was nothing for him here; but neither, it seemed, could he lay hold of the means of escape. His best friend, whom he knew would have helped him to his last farthing, was in India. There was, of course, Catherine, who would surely have money at her disposal; but his pride revolted at the thought of begging from her. His pride, indeed, revolted at the thought of accepting help from anyone, when the whole point of this undertaking was to assert his independence.

He wandered disconsolately back into the heart of the city. In the market-place he glanced over some posted bills advertising the journeys of carriers and coaches;

but they were only local, for the railway had swiftly done away with most long-distance coaching, even supposing he could afford it.

Two ideas only suggested themselves. The first, which even John had to admit was a little wild, was to make his way somehow back to the coast, and see if one of the coastal vessels that carried goods round to the Port of London would take him on as a temporary hand, and let him work his way to his destination thus. 'And a fine seasoned seaman I must look,' he thought ruefully. 'I should think the skipper would laugh till he cried.' The other, which was slightly more rational, was to reclaim his box from the inn, and try to sell his few possessions for whatever they would fetch from the second-hand dealers of the city. 'Which might get me to London,' he thought, 'but would leave me with no more than the clothes I stand up in. Turn again, Dick Whittington!'

No nearer reaching a decision, he found himself moving aimlessly with a flow of people towards the south side of the market-place, beneath St Peter Mancroft, where there seemed to be something of an attraction. Looking up out of his abstraction, he saw that the covered cart of a cheap-jack had set up there. The cheap-jack was standing on the footboard, and giving the crowd the usual patter; but though he was getting plenty of laughs out of them, he was not apparently succeeding in parting any of them from their money, no matter how many times he knocked down the crate of crockery of which he was trying to dispose, and no matter how impressively he spun the plates and saucers on his upraised finger. And one wag in a spotted neckerchief, who seemed to have taken a drop or two in honour of market-day, persisted in harassing the cheap-jack with sarcastic retorts, much to the delight of the crowd.

'. . . Now look here, my good friends, this is my very last offer, and I'm already operating at such a crying loss that there'll be an excess of dew on the roses tomorrow morning, as a result of my sainted mother dropping tears from her heavenly vantage to see her son so reduced. But it was ever so, my good people: in the humble rustic nook that saw my nativity, I was known as the tenderest-hearted infant that ever gladdened his mother's soft black eye, and it was a matter of common remark that on being presented with an apple tart at the age of three I spontaneously divided the confection amongst my peers, and contented myself with licking the dish.'

'I hope it weren't cracked then,' cried the man in the spotted neckerchief, 'like that there ole rubbish you're a-trying to sell!'

'I'm sure, my friend, that your ready wit makes you a great favourite with the duller sort of schoolboy,' said the cheap-jack loftily, 'but as it's good bargains we're concerned with here, and not bad jokes, you'll forgive me if I proceed. Now, good people of Ipswich, I mean Norwich of course, this is positively the last opportunity for you to purchase Staffordshire ware of this quality. Now, having already named the derisory sum of five shillings, I shall further astonish the listening earth, shake the stars in their courses, insult the honest craftsmen who laboured to fashion these masterpieces of ceramic art from the sullen clay, and generally do myself down something shocking, by declaring that the first person to say four-and-sixpence will be eating off these same plates tonight. Yes! Four and sixpence I say, and four and sixpence it shall be, though my sainted mother up aloft will be chewing her harp in vexation to see her only son so cruelly abused.'

'If your mother's up there, where's your father? In the other place?' called the spotted neckerchief. 'Or couldn't your ma remember who he was?'

'My good friend,' said the cheap-jack, struggling to be heard over the laughter, and becoming rather heated, 'if I were tempted to bandy pleasantries with you about *your* parentage, I might be inclined to echo the great Dr Johnson, and remark that your mother, under pretence of keeping a bawdy-house, is a receiver of stolen goods; but as it is, I will merely remark that both your appearance and your conversation suggest that you are standing on your head, and vocalizing from your fundament. Now, who's going to earn the gratitude of their grandchildren, and say four-and-six . . .?'

At that moment, however, things turned rather ugly, for someone explained to Spotted Neckerchief, in plain terms, what the cheap-jack's last remark meant; and Spotted, with the drunkard's touchiness, and seeing that the laughter was now at his expense, made a lunge through the crowd, plucked the cheap-jack off the footboard of his cart with a great hairy fist and, using the same instrument, punched him in the jaw. Not surprisingly, the cheap-jack went down as if pole-axed and the mood of the crowd having turned against Spotted, he was hustled muttering away by some of the same fellows who had been cheering him, while others gathered around the prone form of the cheap-jack.

Not the last among these was John, for he feared that the blow might have done real damage. 'Saints alive, he's bleeding!' cried a woman; and as nothing more effective for the injured man's relief was suggested by the onlookers than that he should have a door-key put down his shirt, John pushed his way through, and kneeling down lifted up the cheap-jack himself, and sat him on the footboard of his cart.

The man was conscious, and not so badly hurt as John had supposed. A rapid exploration with his fingers confirmed that there was no fracture, though he suspected that a tooth was broken, and the cheap-jack's nose was bleeding profusely; a fact that, once he had recovered his senses, alarmed the man considerably.

'Blood!' he cried with an appalled glance down at himself. 'I'm fountaining blood! Calamity!'

'It's all right,' John assured him. 'Just a nosebleed – you're not seriously hurt.'

'It's not that,' said the cheap-jack, looking all about him. 'I'm afraid of bleeding on the stock. I've two dozen huckaback towels here, and I should like to see the man who could shift towels that had been bled on, even at the price I'm asking for 'em . . . Ow!' He put a hand gingerly to his face. 'Either I've gone back thirty year, and started teething all over again, or else that uncompromising gentleman who just invited me to smell his fist has knocked a tooth loose.'

'I fear it's so – your mouth's bleeding too. Will you let me look?' said John.

'Are you a medical man, sir?'

'I'm not,' said John, 'but my father was a physician, and I've helped him bind many a broken head. Will you trust me?'

'My dear sir, when a man cannot trust his fellow-man, what remains? Lay on, Macduff. Be of good comfort, Waldo Tuttle, and play the man, we shall this day light such a candle as something something – I'm sure you can supply the rest of the quotation yourself, sir, and will allow me an interval of silent agony . . .'

John gently opened the man's mouth, and saw that a molar was loosened in its socket, though not sufficiently to come out by itself. There might be putrescence, he thought, if it was not removed quickly; and so, using a technique that he had learned from his father, he said to the cheap-jack, 'Yes, I am afraid there is a tooth there that might have to come out. Allow me just to touch the tooth next to it, and make sure there is no damage to that one, and then we can address ourselves to the main problem . . .' And while he was speaking, he grasped the damaged tooth between forefinger and thumb, gave it a gentle twist, and swiftly yanked it out. The cheap-jack gave a gasp more of surprise than pain, and in the meantime John had delved into one of the crates on the footboard of the cart and, finding some scraps of gauze wrapping, rolled them into a pellet between the fingers and thumb of his other hand to make a styptic for the bleeding. 'Now, if you will just hold that against the tooth-socket . . . so. I'm afraid it will ache for a time: oil of cloves will relieve it, if you have any.'

The cheap-jack, slowly sitting upright on the footboard, working his jaw, and staring at the bloody molar in John's hand, declared, 'Sir, you are a worker of miracles.'

'Nonsense,' said John laughing.

'No, no, sir. Though it would be base flattery to tell you that I never felt a thing, I can certainly vouch that if you were to set up a booth, and draw teeth for a living, your fame would go like a girdle round the earth in forty minutes – I quote from memory.'

'Not such a bad idea,' said John smiling, 'if it would help me to a living.'

The cheap-jack shot him a keen glance; and then, noticing that a number of spectators were still gathered round him, and were manifesting some disappointment that he was not mortally wounded, he drew himself up and cried, 'Holla, you pampered jades of Asia! Did you never see a man bleed before? Well, you've missed your opportunity to make the bargain of a lifetime. I happen to know that the good people of Attleborough were so clamouring for Waldo Tuttle to visit 'em, that they had to call out the dragoons to keep 'em down; and *won't* they just laugh tomorrow, when they contemplate their teacups, and brand-new copper kettles, and fine linen bedsheets from Erin's lonely shore, all bought for a song, and think what the silly folk of Norwich missed out on! So boo to you!' Turning back to John, and touching his own face again with a look of misgiving, he went on, 'Will there be disfigurement, do you suppose?'

'I don't think so. Some painful swelling, but that will soon go down.'

'Not that my looks, fair or foul, are of any account whatsoever, since my Arabella and I were torn apart by cruel circumstance, and in consequence of her going into service with a flying master. Nurslings of the same humble hamlet, sir – Sweet Auburn, loveliest village of the plain! – except the name of the place is in fact Muckleford, but the poetry still applies; yes, we lisped our vows there, my Arabella and I, beneath the Spanish chestnuts, when we stood no higher than the gravestones in the churchyard, and I have been faithful to them ever since. But where's the point in talking of it? She's gone, gone who knows whither, and it must be borne. Oil of cloves, did you say, sir? I have a box of medicinal apparatus which my supplier bought of a distressed apothecary, and I was hoping to knock down as one lot – there, above the bunk – would you be so good as to step up and reach it down, and see if you can lay your hand on the article you mentioned . . .? And while you are there, sir – if I might impose upon your goodness just a little more, and ask you to pass down the bottle which you will find beneath the pillow, and the two glasses which you will find in the heel of the top-boot underneath the bird-cage . . .'

John climbed up into the cheap-jack's cart, which was constructed on the gipsy-caravan principle, and which in its interior was a wonderful medley of dwelling-house and stockroom, with every conceivable item of ironmongery, crockery, cutlery, drapery, haberdashery, and, it must be admitted, trumpery, crammed into its confines and hanging from its painted walls and roof. The apothecary's box contained a serviceable pharmacy, as well as bandages with which John bound up the cheap-jack's jaw; and when his ministrations were complete, the cheap-jack uncorked the bottle, and inviting John to sit with him on the footboard, poured him a glass.

'I don't know what your medical opinion may be of alcohol as a painkiller,' said the cheap-jack, 'but my retailing, wholesaling, and independent trading opinion is, there's nothing to beat it. Which is not, I hasten to add, to undervalue the efficacy of your own treatments, my dear sir. Waldo Tuttle salutes you, as a true Samaritan; and the more so, as I never saw such a set of Philistines in my life, as in this fair city. I dare say you're wondering, my friend, why I didn't have the law on that ruffian; but the fact is, I ain't a vengeful man. The quality of mercy, says the poet, is not strained, and becomes the throned monarch better than his crown, et cetera, and if it's good enough for the Swan of Avon, it's good enough for Waldo Tuttle, I should hope. And besides that, I'm a little chary of applying to the law – not on account of my hawker's licence, no, sir, that's as tight as a drum – but these old cities tend to stand on their dignity when it comes to market-places, and make a to-do about ancient rights and privileges, and how nobody's allowed a pitch unless they've got a chitty from William the Conqueror saying so. Well, I tell you frankly – ' apostrophizing the crowd, who had drifted away to other diversions now that there was no more blood to be seen – 'you're welcome to your ancient rights and privileges, and I cordially hope you choke on them. They're spoilt, you see,' he said, turning back to John. 'What with market-day and all, they're spoilt for choice. It's choice as turns the custom into saucy ingrates; and besides that, they want a sweetener. I was a fool to try and work a sticky crowd like this without a sweetener, and I should have known it.'

'Why, what's a sweetener?' said John, whose voice was rendered a little husky by the potency of Waldo Tuttle's liquor.

'A sweetener, sir? Well, by rights that's a mystery of the trade as I shouldn't divulge; but as we're talking confidentially, I'll tell you. A sweetener is a sort of 'prentice, who besides minding the horse, and generally making himself useful, starts the crowd buying. He mingles with 'em while I give them the patter, just as if he's one of them, and never set eyes on me before; and when I toss up the plates and tea-cups, and makes the knives and fork glitter in the sun, he throws in an admiring gasp or two, and remarks on their quality; and if the crowd are still slow to bid, he comes forward and makes a purchase himself, with money I've supplied him for the purpose, and congratulates himself on what a bargain he's made. That starts them off, nine times out of ten; for the custom, sir, if the comparison's not disrespectful, are like sheep, and it only needs one to go through the gap in the fence, and before you know it the whole flock's in the clover. Yes, a sweetener's what's wanted, for a place like this; and I had a capital sweetener travelling with me till just last week. To see that lad shoulder his way to the front, and press the money into my hands as if he wished I could be persuaded to take more, and receive the boot-jack or the teapot into his arms with a catch in his voice and a tear in his eye – he would pull the hairs out of his nose with a pair of sugar-tongs beforehand, to get that effect – well, it was better than a play. I often told him so. I wish I hadn't told him so quite so often, in fact, and put the idea into his head, because he was enticed away from me at Clenchwarton by a company of strolling players, and is now to be seen, I believe, as the Sicilian Rover in yellow tights, dying twice nightly from a poisoned handkerchief. Another drop, sir? I'll take some more myself, because I can feel it doing me good.'

'You don't, I suppose,' said John, after another fiery sip, 'buy as well as sell? Second-hand goods, I mean?'

'I don't as a rule,' said Mr Tuttle, 'for I stock up at the swag-shops in Cheapside, which is where I start from, and that generally sees me through the circuit. However, I've been known to snap up a bargain here and there, if it *is* a bargain.' The cheap-jack gave John another appraising, penetrating look, and said, 'You'll pardon the liberty of saying so, my friend, but you don't look like the sort of man I'd expect to be offering personal effects at a discount – if such is your meaning, and pardon me again if I've took you wrong.'

'Not really,' said John. 'The long and the short of it is, I'm bound for London, and I need money to get me there.' As Mr Tuttle looked curious, John gave him the barest account of his history; the cheap-jack listening with great attention, and performing the considerable feat of replenishing his own and John's glasses several times throughout it, without once removing his eyes from John's face.

'Now look here, my friend,' Mr Tuttle said when he had done. 'You're a man of science, and as such you've no time, I dare say, for unscientific notions like fate and destiny. Now, you may be in the right of it; but I don't reckon so. I reckon there's a divinity that shapes our ends, to quote the Swan again, and that when blind chance threw us together, my friend, he peeped under the blindfold, and knew quite well what he was about. Sir – and now that I come to think of it, I haven't been favoured with your name . . .?'

John favoured him.

'. . . Well, Mr John Twopenny, our meeting was Meant to Be. Where do you want to go? London. Where am I going to? London; for that's where I take my stand when I'm not on the circuit, and it's there that I set out from with a full cargo, and there I return with the stock all sold and the horse looking happier about life. Why, I'm heading southward now, and allowing for the odd stop in my native Essex, to ask for word of my lost Arabella, I expect to be entering London this time next week. And you, my friend, could be with me!'

John was somewhat at a loss for words; but Waldo Tuttle took no notice of that, and clapping him on the shoulder went on, 'Now I know what you're going to say. You're about to remark that a week's journey in a cart is a very different proposition from a swift afternoon bowling along in a railway-carriage. True! But look here. I'll tell you what I'll do, and this is my last offer – whoops, pardon me, my friend, it's force of habit. What I was going to suggest, is that you travel with me, and act as my sweetener. Now I've told you what the job entails, and I reckon you can come up to it; and you're a positive advantage to start with, just being so tall, for everybody in the crowd'll be able to see you making a bid; and being a man of education, and so not likely, they'll think, to be imposed upon, it comes out even better! You'll have your meals – rough and ready upon the road, sir, but wholesome – and turn to in the other bunk; and when we get to London, you'll take your share of the week's profits, and you can embark upon your new life in the metropolis with money jingling in your pockets, and your goods and chattels intact. Now, my friend, if there's a single reasonable objection to this plan, let's hear it!'

And John, though he could hardly believe that he was about to begin the adventure of his new life in such an unorthodox fashion, could not think of one. 'After all,' he thought, 'there can be no appreciable difference between arriving in London tonight, and arriving there next week. And if I can earn a little money along the way – and God knows I am in sore need of it – then all the better.' And so, almost before he knew it, he had agreed, and shaken hands with Mr Waldo Tuttle, as a form of contract, and sealed it in another eye-watering glass.

It only remained for John to fetch his box from the inn, and stow it in Mr Tuttle's cart, which was soon done; and before the afternoon sun had dipped behind the castle on the hill, they were on their way out of Norwich. John sat up front beside Mr Tuttle, who modified his costume for travelling by clapping a wideawake hat on his head, and pinning a shawl round his shoulders. The shawl was a little fancy, as befitted Mr Tuttle's taste in clothes; for though not richly dressed, he had stripes to his waistcoat, and a tremendous watch-chain stretched across it, and a tremendous coloured handkerchief dangling down from his breast pocket, which he occasionally drew out, in the course of his conversation, with a very dashing and flamboyant gesture, to illustrate a point. He was a gangling man of, John guessed, thirty-five or six, with a long chin, and a long forehead from which the light hair was much receded, and large ears, and large eyes like peeled eggs, and a general appearance of having seen himself for so long in so many sets of cheap tablespoons, that he had come to resemble his reflection therein; and he had, as befitted his trade, a fruity and mellifluous voice, in which his native Essex contended with his love of the grandiloquent to very singular effect.

With this colourful personage as his coachman, John put the first miles between

153

him and the home of his youth; and as the brightly painted cart made its slow way down the Norfolk lanes, with its inside cargo rattling and jangling, and its miscellaneous conglomeration of effects, from bedrolls to strings of onions, strapped to the roof and dangling in nets from the eaves, he could not help contrasting its fantastical aspect with the dreary severities of his uncle's house, which he had left but a day ago, but which already seemed a world away. Waldo Tuttle expatiated much, as they went along, on the delights of the cheap-jack's life, and John from his comfortable vantage point could well believe in them; but then, the weather at present was gloriously fine, and the roads in good condition. 'Ah, it's a different matter in the winter,' Mr Tuttle admitted. 'I'd cut out the winter circuits altogether, if I could afford it, and lay up somewhere salubrious – say, Walworth – until the spring time; but the cheap-jack line doesn't pay like it used to, and a man has to be on the circuit all the year round if he wants to keep the wolf from the door – and I've heard him snarling and scratching there, Mr T., many a time. Ah, well, you don't miss the shade till the tree blows down, as my father used to say. Mind you, that's all he ever *did* say.'

'Your father was not in the cheap-jack line, then?'

'My father,' said Mr Tuttle with a heavy sigh, 'was never much in any line, I'm afraid to say – unless you count the beery line, and the lounging line, and the black-eye-giving line, especially where my mother was the customer, and he certainly never gave her short measure there. Well, when poor mother was no more, I left him, and lit out for London, and found a berth as an errand-boy for an old bookseller in Paternoster Row, and a very good berth it was too; for the old party wouldn't have me handling the volumes unless I knew something about them, and it is from that time that I date my acquaintance with the English poets, which has made me the only cheap-jack in the country, I believe, who can patter in deathless verse when the fancy takes him. Well, I served the old party faithfully until I began to hanker for a little freedom, and for going into the selling line on my own account; and the old party, who was the kindest old party going, gave me a gross of books that he couldn't shift on account of their bindings coming off and pages missing just where you come to the villain about to steal into the heroine's bedchamber with a moustache and a dark lantern; and I hawked 'em about Covent Garden on a handcart. That was what set me off in the itinerant trading line; and I've never looked back, as the saying is. Though in this case the saying is a trifle inaccurate, as I *have* looked back, and with a moistened eye, to the village of my birth, and the palmy days I spent there with my childhood sweetheart.' Mr Tuttle seemed to gaze into misty distances. 'Arabella!'

'She . . . remained in Muckleford?'

'Would that she had! There's the bitter irony of it, Mr T. Everything seemed set fair for us, for Arabella moved to London too, and secured herself a very good position housekeeping for a gentleman of means who had been in the Turkey-merchant line. And we were close enough to meet regular, and renew the vows we first made under the Spanish chestnuts, and take an outing to Sadler's Wells together, with an oyster supper to follow; and to plan our future bliss right down to the orange blossom. Ah! It was not in the winter our loving lot was cast; it was the time of roses – we plucked them as we passed! I quote from memory. There was one drawback to Arabella's situation, Mr T. Her retired Turkey-merchant, who was the best of employers in most ways, had one peculiarity. He couldn't settle in one place for five minutes together. He moved out of Holborn – too crowded. Moved to Pentonville – too dull. Marylebone – too expensive. Norwood – too rural. It went on in this way, I believe, till he had tried every district in London short of Seven Dials; and when he had done that, he moved out to Kent. And then to Sussex. And then to Berkshire . . . You can guess, sir, the unhappy end to this tale. Arabella and I kept our mutual flame a-burning by means of letters; but me being of necessity a rather perambulating individual myself, and lacking a permanent address, it wasn't easy, and at last the time came when the fragile thread was broken. Arabella's flying master flew on again – I know not where; my final communication was returned as not known at this address. I didn't know where to find Arabella: she didn't know where to find me. It's nearly two years since I last set eyes on her, Mr T.; and whether I ever shall again, who knows?'

'But this is terrible,' said John, who could not help picturing himself and Catherine in such a case, and was appalled at the picture. 'There must be a way, surely . . .?'

'If there is, I haven't thought of it,' sighed Mr Tuttle. 'The best I can do is ask, at every pitch I come to, Mr T.; and if you would do the same, in the intervals of sweetening – Arabella Peck's the name – I'd be very much obliged.'

Southward, thus, they pursued their way through Anglia; crossing from Norfolk to Suffolk through a country of watermills that came into view at sudden turnings and then disappeared again, leaving a memory of freshness and plashy music on the air; past harvest-fields where great waggons stood in the midst of the stubble, so massy and substantial they looked more like something enduringly built there, than vehicles that would presently move away on wheels; through tiny villages where traffic was so infrequent that people came out of their houses to stolidly watch the cart go by, and children ran shouting after it, and dogs barked themselves into a frenzy.

John enjoyed this; and he also enjoyed fulfilling his part of the bargain, and acting as sweetener when Mr Tuttle drew up for business in the towns and larger villages. He was conscious, at first, of a certain ludicrousness in the proceeding; but he soon got into his role, and commended tea-trays, gasped at pepper-mills, and went into raptures at rolling-pins. He even threw in some interjections on his own initiative, loudly remarking to his neighbours in the audience, for example, that he had seen the self-same milk-jugs selling for ninepence more than Mr Tuttle was asking; and when he was forced, in consequence of a very slow crowd, to buy a butter-dish with large purple roses on it, he put on a very covetous look, and hurried away with his purchase as if he were going to take it home and gloat over it. He bought that same butter-dish at Long Stratton, at Bury St Edmunds, at Sudbury, and at Braintree; and Mr Tuttle was so pleased with the results that he declared he would give it to John as a present when they reached the end of their journey. For it was a likeable point in Waldo Tuttle's character that he did not at all despise the goods he sold, and often when rearranging his stock would admiringly hold up some article, such as a Toby-jug in the likeness of Palmerston, and murmur, 'That's a fine thing! Upon my soul, that's a fine thing!'

Come the evening, and when a stopping-place for the cart was found, Mr Tuttle would mark the transition from work to leisure by replacing the wideawake hat with a smoking-cap; and while John went to find a bait for the horse, the cheap-jack made himself busy with their evening meal, which was always cooked over an open fire, and as greasy as it was savoury. After supper Mr Tuttle would often lie flat on his back on the grass, contemplate the stars, and – if he had taken a little liquor as a restorative – rhapsodize over his lost Arabella. 'I don't know whether it comforts me, or tortures me, Mr T.,' he said, 'but whenever I look at the stars, I cannot help reflecting that my Arabella may be looking at those very same stars (if fine) at the very same moment; and if you could see her eyes, Mr T., you'd be hard put to it to choose between the heavenly orbs, and judge which was the brighter!' And so Mr Tuttle would turn in to bed in sentimental mood, and snore like a lion.

Then, on the sixth night of their journey, they stopped in a jumbled, sooty, half-finished country of straggling villages and brick kilns and scrubby market-gardens where the cauliflowers came up more black than white, all of which signalled that London was close at hand. They were in the district of Mr Tuttle's birth, and after supper he announced his intention of walking down to the public-house in the village outside which they were camped, and seeing if he could hear any news of old acquaintances there. 'Who knows,' he remarked, 'I might even run into someone who knows something of Arabella – stranger things have happened!' And half-mournful and half-jaunty, he went off wearing his favourite hat, which was a tall white beaver that could be seen half a mile off. John, who found the unaccustomed fresh air a great encourager of sleep, yawned over the fire a while, conjuring visions of London in its dying flames, until at last he scattered the ashes, hobbled the horse for the night, and turned in. He was tired enough to fall asleep at once even in the spare bunk inside the cart, which was so diminutive that in order to go to bed he had to hug his knees, tuck his head down, and roll into it like a circus tumbler; and he had drifted far out on the sea of oblivion, and was quite out of sight of land, when he was jerked awake by a thunderous hammering at the sides of the cart.

His first thought was that he was under attack from thieves, and he was still bemusedly debating between a roasting-spit and a paper-knife as his best weapon of defence when he recognized the voice of Waldo Tuttle without. There was another voice, unmistakably feminine; so he paused to pull on his trousers before unlatching the door between the shafts, and stepping out to see what was the matter.

'My friend! My dear friend John Twopenny, the prince of sweeteners, give me your hand! His name is John, my dear – John Twopenny – did I tell you that? – and he's the best sweetener I ever had, and he's going to leave me when we get to London tomorrow, and I wish with all my heart he wasn't, now isn't that a shame? It's a shame, that's what it is!'

Mr Tuttle, very unsteady on his feet, and with his white hat askew on his head, extended his right hand to John. His other hand was round the waist of a dishevelled young woman in a print frock and pattens, who was laughing good-humouredly as she tried to prop him up to the perpendicular. John immediately supposed that this was Mr Tuttle's lost sweetheart, and had said, 'Arabella?' before realizing that he was perhaps making a great mistake.

'Arabella?' echoed the young woman sharply. 'Why, who's she? Here, you've never got a wife in that there cart, I hope?' – giving Mr Tuttle such a poke in the ribs that he fell sideways. 'And after all them pretty things you said! Why, what are you like, you wicious article!' But she soon fell to laughing again, and Mr Tuttle pulling himself up by means of her waist, they made a staggering circuit of the cart, and came back to where they had started. 'The Minstrel Boy to the war is gone, in the ranks of death you'll find him, his something something girded on, et cetera behind him. I quote from memory,' mumbled Mr Tuttle, trying to kiss the young woman's lips, and getting her ear instead; and then, with a roar of delight, 'Here he is! Here's my friend and companion, John Twopenny! My dear, allow me to introduce. What do you think of that, for a figure of a young man? Tall as a paladin, fair as a young Apollo, profile like something off a coin. Why, he could get a crowd buying just by taking his hat off. But he's going to leave me. It was ever thus. I never nursed a dear gazelle, et cetera et cetera. God bless you!'

It was impossible to tell whether this last remark was addressed to the young woman or to John, for Mr Tuttle fell over backwards as he delivered it. This time John's assistance was required to get him to his feet, though Mr Tuttle appeared to be under the impression that he was still upright, and could not understand why his hat was not on his head. 'Where's my hat? I had a hat when I came in. Where's my hat?'

'There it is,' said the young woman, clapping it on his head, 'and now I reckon you'd better get to bed, and start preparing yourself for the head you'll have tomorrow.'

'Ah, sleep – sleep that knits up the ravell'd sleeve of care. So it shall be. But before I go, a nightcap . . .'

'The only nightcap you want is the one you put on your head,' said the young woman; and John, agreeing through his laughter, helped her to heave Mr Tuttle up the step into the cart, and snatched off the beaver hat just in time to stop it being crushed as he toppled into his bunk. The young woman then left, after evading a few last blind embraces; and Mr Tuttle dozed for a few minutes before stirring with a great groan and crying, 'Arabella! I could not love thee, dear, so much, loved I not honour more . . . John, I am a wretch!'

'I should go to sleep, if I were you,' said John. 'You'll feel better in the morning.' Though this, he felt, was highly unlikely.

'I am a wretch. John, deny it if you can! Look me in the eye, and tell me I ain't. See? You can't do it. John, will you do something else for me? Hit me.'

'I'll do nothing of the sort. Why on earth should I hit you?'

'Because I deserve it,' said Mr Tuttle woefully.

'Well, I don't know about that,' said John, doing his circus tumble again, 'but you've been hit once this week, anyway.'

'Not hard enough,' came the reply, half in sleep. The other half was not long in overcoming Mr Tuttle, and presently the lion's roar of his snores filled the cart, so that John dreamt of being lost in the jungle, and trying to sell butter-dishes to a native chief who had Mr Bream's head on his doorpost.

Very seedy was Mr Tuttle when they set off the next morning, and very subdued, and disinclined to conversation. But he recovered his spirits by degrees – seeming to freshen, indeed, as the air grew less fresh, and to brighten as the sky darkened with coal-smoke; and at last he drew out the tremendous handkerchief, and waving it at the dark horizon ahead, cried with his usual animation, 'London! Be it ever so dirty, and coaly, and unseemly, and inconvenient in point of the drinking-water looking like coffee, there's no place like it!'

But Mr Tuttle had little time to talk from then on, for he was fully occupied by the business of manoeuvring the unwieldy cart in the busy narrow streets that pressed in on them. John had never been more conscious of being a countryman in his bewilderment at the endless streets, the noise, the smoke, the confusion and the jostle; and it was natural in him to experience a moment or two of dread, and briefly to wish he was walking on the broad flats of Saltmarsh with the Soldier, and not another human being in sight.

Mr Tuttle's destination, he explained to John, was an open area near old Spa Fields, which was used as a winter quarters for travelling showmen, and where, he said, there was always room for another cart. Their route thither took them through a flourishing wilderness of new brick, where the new railway station of King's Cross had been built; and proceeding from this to the grassy space where the vehicles of Waldo Tuttle's fellow-travellers were drawn up was like going back a couple of centuries. Mr Tuttle's cart was drab compared with many to be seen here; Mr Tuttle himself was as sober as a curate compared with many of the figures sitting smoking on the steps of their brilliantly painted caravans, or hanging out their laundry on strings between the caravan-roofs, or practising juggling, fire-swallowing, sword-dancing, and other such occupations in the open air; and John was tempted to rub his eyes when he caught a glimpse of a man eight feet tall playing dominoes with a man four feet tall on an upturned dolly-tub.

'An interesting set of people,' Mr Tuttle agreed, guiding the cart into a space between a travelling-waxwork and an educated pig. 'Not half full at the moment, but most of them are out on the circuit. There's some cheap-jacks, Mr T., who wouldn't care to be associated with show-folk like this, but I don't mind it; bless you, it's the theatrical side of the cheap-jack trade that I like, and I'd omit the selling altogether if I could.' And as if to prove that he was quite recovered from the previous night, Mr Tuttle proposed, as soon as they were settled, to toast the successful completion of their journey in a glass.

'And now, my friend,' said Mr Tuttle, setting down his empty glass on the footboard with a smack of his lips, 'we come to the division of the spoils. Five pound seven shillings and sixpence is the week's proceeds: say three pound cost, and the rest profit; what do you say to a guinea?'

'I call it handsome, Mr Tuttle,' said John, 'and I can't think of a pleasanter way of earning a guinea.'

'Well, now, I was hoping you might say that,' said Mr Tuttle, stroking his chin. 'Because I'll tell you what I'm going to do. After I've rested up here a while, and stocked up at the swag-shop, I mean to go out on the western circuit; and as getting money out of those Dorsets and Somersets is like getting a wink out of a Methodist, I shall be in need of a good sweetener. So, say the word, Mr T., and you and I shall not part here, but set out together across the chalky downs – and we'll take many a cup of kindness yet, for the sake of auld lang syne!'

John was touched, the more so because at his uncle's he had become accustomed to such a harsh, mean, grudging attitude to life; and he almost wished that he were another person, and could take up Mr Tuttle's offer. But he could not relinquish his old dreams and desires so easily. Lacking the words to explain, he grasped Mr Tuttle's hand.

'Ah!' Mr Tuttle said. 'Not the handshake, I fear, that says "Done", but the handshake that says "No sale", in the nicest way. Oh! well – if the world was all cheap-jacks and sweeteners, there'd be no custom; and you've got your own shining vision before your eyes, Mr T., medical as you've told me, and Waldo Tuttle's the last man to turn you from your shining vision, for I haven't I got one of my own, and isn't her name Arabella?'

'I'm glad you take it so,' said John, 'for I am deeply grateful to you, and wish I could show it better. But the fact is, I have set my heart on London, as the place that will be the making of me.'

Mr Tuttle was silent for a moment, and might perhaps have been thinking of a rhyme for those last words of John's, less hopeful in its import; but then he brightened, and said, 'Well, my friend, when a man's wanted who'll mock at ambition, and throw dust in the eye of hope, don't come to Waldo Tuttle, for he's not in that line and never has been. Why, I don't intend to be a cheap-jack all my life, especially if I should find my Arabella, for she deserves nothing less than a high-class shop in New Bond Street, with two parlours above it. So, consider my sympathies entirely with you, Mr T., and now don't be offended when I ask you, do you know London?'

'Scarcely at all,' said John frankly.

'So. You will need a lodging, sharpish, and not dear. Am I still right?'

'Very much so.'

'Then we shall find you one. My brother itinerants here, none of 'em being of fixed abode, are well up on the cheap-lodgings intelligence, and if you'll have the goodness to mind the cart, I'll ask around.'

So Mr Tuttle made a tour of the other carts, and John felt a little shy as one after another of his colourful neighbours turned to regard him, and nodded or shook their heads. Presently Mr Tuttle returned – having plainly, from his heightened colour, been pressed to a glass or two in the course of renewing acquaintances – and announced, 'Mr T., I have found you the very place. It's only two rooms, but furnished; and it's a very select berth. Signor Gemmiani over there, who sings at the Italian Opera sometimes, speaks highly of it; only it's a strict landlady, and she won't tolerate racketing.'

158

John assuring him that it was not his intention to do any racketing whatsoever, Mr Tuttle engaged to go over there with him now, and look over the place; and though John protested that he didn't want to put him to any trouble, he was thankful to have a guide. So Mr Tuttle engaged a boy of his acquaintance, from a family of stilt-dancers, to watch over the cart while he was away, and, taking John's arm, plunged him into the London streets.

'I wonder if I shall ever come to know this place as you do!' John cried, half in admiration, half in despair, as he was conducted through a bewildering maze, and plucked by his guide out of the path of half a dozen hackneys, and prevented a score of times from treading in great gluey puddles of filth.

'Oh, I was the same when I first came to London,' said Mr Tuttle, pulling John out of the way of a coster's barrow. 'I was afraid to step beyond St Paul's Churchyard, in case I should get lost and never find my way back; but you get used to it.'

Their destination was off Fetter Lane, in High Holborn. Thimblebee was the name they were after, Mr Tuttle said; and Thimblebee – Miss Thimblebee, and just that – was the name they found at last, modestly inscribed on a wooden plaque on a modest green door, which was squeezed in between the front windows of a gunsmith's and a music-shop – like a mediator between discord and harmony. Mr Tuttle spotting a public-house across the way, said he would step over there, just to see what o'clock it was, and leave John to transact his business in private; and with an admonition to him not to pay more than five shillings, and a promise to meet up again in a quarter of an hour, Mr Tuttle left him.

John's knock was answered by a little serving-girl, who on his stating his business admitted him into a dark vestibule, and was about to start up the stairs when a lady's voice called over the banister: 'Minnie, is that Mrs R.?'

'No, mum; it's a gentleman come about the lodgings.'

After a short interval of noises suggestive of things being briskly put away, the voice, in a stately manner, invited the gentleman to walk up; and John presently found himself in an apartment very neat, very gilded, and very discreet and tactful in its illumination. A number of portrait miniatures on the walls, in which the features of the sitters were less apparent than their profuse heads of hair, gave a clue to the occupation of Miss Thimblebee; as did some little bottles of oils and lotions, and some dainty scissors and tongs set out upon a side-table; as did the large gilt mirror, and the gilt chair set like a throne before it. As did, too, the lock of unreal-looking hair just peeping out from the lid of a japanned box which had been pushed under the table – but John had a feeling he was not supposed to see that.

Miss Thimblebee herself was a sharp-featured, though not ill-favoured lady, tall and thin, and very straight and precise, with intensely black hair parted in the middle with mathematical exactitude and combed down smooth on either side of her head, giving her quite a varnished look; her whole appearance was suggestive, indeed, of the species of dolls that live in dolls' houses, right down to the two round spots of colour on her cheeks. She inspected John very thoroughly on his introducing himself, and it occurred to him that, all unprovided as he was, she might not consider him an eligible lodger; but his producing the money for two weeks' rent seemed to settle any doubts on that score, and his being a newcomer to London seemed to be a point in his favour.

'For the one thing I do insist on in my single gentlemen,' Miss Thimblebee said, leading him up a further flight of stairs, 'is discretion. Some young gentlemen have a large circle of acquaintance, who are forever calling for them, and going up and down the stairs, and taking an interest; and I simply can't allow it. I am by profession and calling, Mr Twopenny, a friseuse – that is, I personally attend to the coiffure of a select number of clients, on terms of the strictest confidence. My

159

clients and I must be undisturbed. It may chance that you may pass one of my clients at the door, or on the stairs; but if so, I beg you to be as unobtrusive as possible, and even to consider it quite admissible, under the circumstances, not to acknowledge them at all. Now, here we are, sir.'

The lodging consisted of a reasonably sized room, in which various ill-assorted pieces of furniture languished like poor relations, and a sort of walk-in cupboard with a bricked-up window which Miss Thimblebee loftily described as a dressing-room. 'My single gentlemen understand,' said Miss Thimblebee, 'that laundry is not considered in the rent, and that any cooking productive of odour is quite unwarrantable. Single gentlemen sometimes take it into their heads to entertain, even in so compact an apartment as this; but I will say to you now, Mr Twopenny, that I simply couldn't hear of it.'

John was thankful to have found a lodging which, if a little pinched and shabby, was clean, and he was eager to begin his new life in the city; and so he swiftly settled the business, and having shaken Miss Thimblebee's hand, and engaged to move in that afternoon, he went out again by the little green door to rejoin Mr Tuttle.

The cheap-jack was outside the public-house, engaged in a lively controversy with some small boys who were drawing attention to his white hat, and asking him in a disrespectful manner why he had got a cheese on his head. 'That's something to be said for going on the circuit,' Mr Tuttle said, greeting John with relief, and walking him rapidly on. 'The country youth don't sauce you so, for they aren't so knowing. Well, Mr T., you're all fixed up, I hope? And what do you think of your landlady?'

'Very ladylike, at any rate.'

'And what do you suppose, now,' said Mr Tuttle with a sly look, 'that she does for a living?'

John answered, with a smile, that he believed Miss Thimblebee made wigs and hairpieces.

'So she does: that's what Signor Gemmiani found out – his real name's Jemmy Croker, by the way, but it comes out better in the Italian style – yes, he found it out when he lodged there, on account of seeing Miss Thimblebee creeping in one night with a bag of horsehair. Only, you mustn't let on that you know. She maintains that she's a hairdresser out of deference to her custom, though most of them haven't got any hair to dress, and you have to go along with it. Jemmy says he quite got used to seeing ladies going into Miss Thimblebee's with blonde locks, and coming out with brown curls, and he knew better than to remark on it.'

John accompanied Mr Tuttle back to his camping-ground, and there engaged the stilt-dancing boy to carry his box to Fetter Lane; and now came the time for them to part. Mr Tuttle wished him luck with great heartiness; and, as he had promised, made him a present of the flowery butter-dish. 'The quotation that springs to mind on this occasion, Mr T.,' said the cheap-jack, 'is thus: "She brought forth butter in a lordly dish". Scripture, sir; it may not be reverent, but it's apt!'

And so John, with many thanks and good wishes, left him; and was highly pleased with himself for finding his own way back to Fetter Lane without getting lost more than twice. The evening saw him comfortably established in Miss Thimblebee's third-floor back, and dining off a pudding bought at a cook-shop across the way, with the window wide open in case any culinary odour should penetrate to Miss Thimblebee's gilded apartments; and as the great city without turned itself into a vast jewel-box with gaslight, John addressed it thus: 'I shall tackle you tomorrow, old London. You're a tough customer, and quite frightening at first sight, but I shall have a go; you may throw me, or wrestle me down, but I shall keep coming at you, until one of us throws up the sponge – that I promise you!'

160

CHAPTER SIX

More Kicks Than Halfpence

With Dr Frank Spruce's last letter to his father in his pocket, John set out early next morning to seek him out.

Whence came all these people, so early? John had supposed he might have the streets pretty much to himself, but Fleet Street was already like noonday. The coats of the horses were already steaming, the flowers in the street-sellers' baskets were already wilting, and already the bright summer's day had had a dingy foggy one superimposed on it by the chimneys that were smoking as if the fires had been stoked for hours: and how many chimneys! Chimney upon chimney, housetop upon housetop, as if in the dearth of unoccupied land men had started to build dwellings on the roofs of other dwellings; and how many vehicles of every description too! Lumbering drays, hackneys, horse-omnibuses, gigs, chaises, vans, private carriages; all fighting for space, and fighting to get along, and getting along only with the greatest difficulty, and up at Temple Bar not getting along at all, for a whole boiling of such vehicles were simply crammed in there, and apparently not moving an inch – just as if they had decided to play a sort of four-wheeled parlour-game, and all tried to crush into the smallest space possible. Scarcely more room on the pavement, either, where tall hats, like more chimneys got down from the sky, performed a weaving dance with bonnets, interrupted now and then by baskets of cabbages, and great milk-churns, and strings of fish and carcasses on poles, as if somewhere near at hand a giant were waiting to have his giant appetite fed.

A little less traffic at Blackfriars Bridge, but a good deal below: a steamer ploughing its way through the water of the Thames – which wanted ploughing indeed, so thick and brown did it appear – whilst a multitude of smaller vessels gave place to the coaly tyrant and its foaming wake, and made the best way they could. Such a smell from the river as made John reluctant to draw breath, for fear it should catch in his lungs and never leave them: such a jangle of contrasts – between St Paul's nobly hovering above the coal-smoke and the sooty pates of tenements gathered round it, between the look in the eyes of a buttoned-up gentleman bustling on his way to the City and the look in the eyes of a drunken wretch tottering on his way to the grave – that John felt as if he had been thrust into a world to which his senses were unequal, like a tame bird turned out into the wild.

He crossed the river, and by diligent asking-around, was directed at last to the address at the top of Dr Spruce's letter. But when he found the place, he could not help wondering if there had been some mistake. He remembered Frank Spruce as a bright, smart, pugnacious man, of whom it was generally prophesied that he would go far; and he could not quite reconcile that memory with this address in the Borough, which was a drab street near the shell of the old Marshalsea debtors' prison. The house itself was not small, but it was dilapidated; and when John, after some hesitation, mounted the steps and rang the bell, he elicited no sound but a cracked clanking, and had to apply himself to the knocker.

The door was answered at last by an old red-faced woman in down-at-heel slippers, who on John's inquiring whether Dr Spruce lived here, croaked out, 'Who wants him?'

'I – I am an old friend of his. My name is Twopenny.'

'Oh!' said the old woman dismissively. 'I thought it might be the Irish childbed again. Well, he ain't home. You can wait, if you like. *I* don't care.'

'Do you expect he'll be long?' John asked, following her in.

'I don't expect nothing,' said the old woman, 'why should I?' And she opened a door and gestured him inside.

The room was a grubby parlour, with a few books heaped about on chairs, a number of dead spiders curled up in dusty corners, and a smell of stale tobacco. John did not know how long he waited in it, for he had no watch, and the clock on the mantelshelf was unwound; but it was long enough for him to ask himself the question 'Can this be the same Dr Spruce?' a hundred times, and still come to no conclusion.

At last there was the sound of the front door, and John jumped up expectantly. The voice of the old woman was heard, very argumentative, in the hall; another voice, weary in tone, replied to it, and seemed to escape it at last with impatience. The door of the spidery parlour opened, and Dr Frank Spruce entered.

Yes: it was he. John recognized him, at least; but only as one recognizes a childhood landmark, decayed and diminished. Their eyes met, and John did not know what to say.

'Yes? Did you want me?'

Without waiting for a reply, Dr Spruce went over to a battered old cabinet, and drew out a bottle and a glass. He was pouring a drink when John spoke.

'Dr Spruce, I – perhaps you don't remember me. My name is John Twopenny.'

'Good God.' The glass and bottle rattled, and Dr Spruce set them both down with an unsteady hand. 'John . . . How did you come here?' He turned to look at John, and then his eyes flicked nervously round the room. 'Is your father with you?'

'No . . . My father . . . I'm afraid my father died last year.'

'Robert Twopenny . . .? No – no, not Robert Twopenny . . .' Dr Spruce looked his sorrow; then, frowning, turned away, and picked up the bottle and glass again. 'That is melancholy news . . . Forgive me, John – if I may call you that – I didn't recognize you at first. It's been a long time. Will you take a drink with me?'

John consented, hardly knowing what he said; and there was silence for a while as Dr Spruce emptied his own glass, refilled it, and drank it down again. He had been handsome; and he was still not an ill-looking man. But he was shabby, his coat shiny and his linen soiled; his hair, which had been lustrous, was unkempt and sprinkled with grey; his once merry eyes were sunken, and his once fresh complexion sallow; and his mouth and jaw, which John remembered to have typified him in their humorous arrogance, had undergone the saddest and most premature change. The way the flesh had sagged and wasted reminded John horribly of the wax pooling at the sides of a spent candle.

'So, John,' said Dr Spruce, who since the first look had avoided John's eyes, 'you have tracked me down from dear old Saltmarsh. I'm glad to see you, though I'm sorry you bear such news, more sorry than I can express. Your father was a good friend to me, and I often think of the times we had together in Norfolk. Your mother, I hope, has borne up as well as can be expected?'

'No, I . . . I am afraid . . .' The telling of the second cruel fact affected John deeply, for he had become accustomed to keeping this pain within himself, and dealing with it in private; but Frank Spruce, having heard him out, did not embarrass him with condolences. He remained silent and thoughtful, pouring himself more drink with an absent and too-practised hand, and at last said with a sigh, 'I was about to say I wish I had known – but on reflection, I see what a foolish remark that is. What difference could my knowing have made to anything? What difference, indeed, can any one man make to anything in this botched world of ours? But no matter. I'm glad to see you, anyhow, John; and I appreciate your thinking of me, and coming to tell me the news. So. What brings you to London, my friend?'

John, after seeing what he had seen, hesitated over his answer; but finally said, simply, 'I came to find you.'

'Good heavens, hardly worth the journey,' said Dr Spruce, laughing and returning to the bottle; but on looking up, and seeing that John was in earnest, he frowned. 'Why – and I wish you'd drink up, John, if only for my sake – why should you do that?'

'Because I always admired you, and wished to follow in your footsteps,' said John readily. 'My ambition, my one dream, is to be a doctor, just as it was when you knew me as a boy. But my father – my father died a bankrupt, and all the plans that we had formed to that end came to nothing as a result. But I am still determined; and having no family ties in Norfolk, and no other prospects, I have come to London – I must confess it – in the hope that you will point me the way to realizing my old dream. Oh! not fully, perhaps; but if there is a living to be earned in medicine, without independent means, I want to earn it, no matter what it entails; and remembering how you told me that the will is always greater than the circumstances, I thought . . .' John stopped; for Dr Spruce, having sat heavily down, was laughing. Silently, not merrily, and with his hand covering his eyes, Dr Spruce was laughing.

'Please, forgive me, John,' he said at last, shaking his head. 'My laughter is not at your expense, believe me. Hard to say who or what I am laughing at, really. It's just that I have spent much of the night at the workhouse infirmary at Lambeth. There I observed the death of an undernourished child from enteric fever; the child was eight years of age, looked four, and screamed continually until life was extinct. And so the . . . glowing words you have just spoken fall rather oddly on my ear just now . . .'

'I'm sorry,' said John, 'I've intruded on you quite unthinkingly – you must want to get to bed—'

'No, no. Not I, not yet. This – ' Dr Spruce held up the bottle – 'is all I require at the moment. As a doctor I am old-fashioned enough to believe that if it makes the patient feel better, the patient should have it. Your father would agree with me on that score . . . Dear God. Robert Twopenny. Even at the worst, one hopes that something of decency survives in this world, and then one hears something like this . . .' Dr Spruce drank deep, and shuddered. 'How do you live here in London, John? What are your circumstances?'

John told him; speaking cheerfully and boldly at first, but faltering as he saw Dr Spruce's expression. A silence ensued, Dr Spruce staring at him with pale eyes.

'You have no means at all? No income, no capital, no paid employment, no support or hope of support from any quarter?'

'No,' said John. 'Only my own determination.'

'Which will get you precisely nowhere,' snapped Dr Spruce, as if unable to prevent himself. Then he sighed, and ran a hand through his lank hair. 'John, John. I'm flattered that you should think of me when you came to London, indeed I am. I remember, I remember well your eagerness as a boy, when I lived in Norfolk; and God forgive me, I believe I fostered it . . . And you have been educated, I suppose, with a view to this? But you have begun no medical training?'

'I was about to begin when my parents died . . . Dr Spruce, why regret your encouragement of me? I have never regretted setting my heart on this course; and even though my circumstances are not of the easiest—'

'I regret it,' said Dr Spruce harshly, 'because whatever happens, you are in for

163

wretchedness and disappointment.' He looked at his empty glass, then set it down. 'John, how do you suppose I was enabled to study medicine? Because I had money in trust from my family. Gone long ago, I regret to say. But I did it, and I qualified. And I had great hopes. I came to London with some idea of medicine as not far removed from chivalry . . . Well, you've seen my commodious and luxurious accommodation – I rent only this floor, by the way, and am in arrears for that. You've seen, likewise, what it is that comforts me in my affliction – ' gesturing to the bottle – 'and I may as well add that the money that should supply the rent goes instead on this most reliable of tonics. If I add that I am no stranger to opium, and not merely in the course of my professional duties, you will have a fair idea of my manner of life. And as for those professional duties, John, I am no more nor less than a Poor Law surgeon. I receive a – what is the polite term? – a modest stipend from the Poor Law Guardians, for enabling wretches to continue to live in the workhouse instead of dying – or, if they choose that far more sensible course, for certifying them dead.'

The bottle was empty. Dr Spruce searched the cabinet for another. John watched him, wishing to say something, something that would push back the darkness that seemed to surround the doctor like a tainted fog, but he could think of nothing.

'I am not rambling, John, though it may seem so. I am setting out for you some very cogent facts, because you have come to me to – to ask for advice, and guidance – am I right?'

'It was . . . it was with that idea that I came to London.'

Dr Spruce winced. 'Very well. I have just given you a notion of where *my* grand ambitions led. Indeed, the evidence of that is before your eyes, and that you have found it sufficiently appalling is written in your face, John, though you try to hide it. Another thing that is clear to me from your face is that you are thinking, "Well, Frank Spruce may have come to nothing but ruin and disillusionment, but that is probably due to his character." ' Dr Spruce looked at John with saturnine shrewdness. 'Am I right, again?'

John wished to, but could not speak.

'Well, there may be truth in what you are thinking, John. Perhaps it *is* my fault. But the point I am trying to make to you, my friend, is that I had every advantage. I was comfortably supported through my medical training—'

'But I know,' cried John, unable to bear this systematic dissection of his hopes, 'I know I lack the means for that. But the great hospitals here – there must be a place I can fill within them, and earn my bread at the same time.'

'My dear John, I wish I could offer you some hope in that direction. But consider. Would you be a nurse? Old hard-handed women, recruited as cheap as they can be got. You think to be the man who unloads the cadavers on to the dissecting-table at Guy's? You must fight the old drunkard who currently does it for the position. And in the unlikely event of your getting it, you will do nothing but wheel corpses about for the rest of your life. There is the medical profession, John, and there are the domestics who serve it in its institutions; and they don't meet. Doctors don't recruit from the ranks, not these days. You must be licensed, you must be qualified. The Society of Apothecaries are as strict as the Royal College of Physicians. Certainly, there are different routes. A dressership at one of the teaching hospitals always used to be helpful for the needy student; learning and practising at the same time. But even a dressership requires a premium, John, let alone the lecture fees to prepare you for it. Got the money for those, have you?'

'But when I decided to come to London,' said John, with a feeling as if he were trying to hold up a collapsing building with his bare hands, 'it was because I thought this was the place where circumstances such as mine could be overcome . . .'

'Circumstances,' said Dr Spruce with a sort of weary violence, drinking again, 'are not overcome. They are adapted to, or accommodated, but they are not overcome. And from what you tell me of your circumstances, I can only tell you that you are on a fool's errand, as far as medicine goes.' Dr Spruce got up and pulled the moth-eaten curtains across the window, as if the light distressed him. 'This is not what you wanted to hear. I am sorry for it. I shall try to say something more hopeful. John, you have had a gentleman's education. Use it. You have made the right choice in London, inasmuch as an educated young man can get a living here. Clerks are always wanted: clerks earn a salary. How old are you, John? Twenty-one? Well, you are a young man. You might, I suppose, walk the wards in a few years' time; in the meantime, earn and save, if you can. That's all the advice I can give you. Get a secure position, and reap a salary. Very dull and unromantic, no doubt. But preferable to starving.'

John was silent for some moments, his eyes fixed on the threadbare rug at his feet; this was one of those occasions in which we say nothing, look at something entirely irrelevant, betray no expression, and yet undergo an internal revolution. When he spoke at last, it was in a tone which seemed to have taken some infection from Dr Spruce's bleak practicality. 'I cannot hope, then, to enter the medical profession in the near future. I have been foolish.'

'Not foolish,' said Dr Spruce, 'but not realistic. The only realistic course for a young man in your position is to take a post with a salary, in the City perhaps. At least then you are earning; and in a few years' time, if you are still set on medicine, you will be a little nearer your goal, insofar as you have a little money. Not enough, certainly; but then I am rather inclined to say you should stick with the clerk's job anyway, and forget medicine. Much safer. I wish *I* had done something like that.'

'You don't mean it,' said John, mechanically.

Dr Spruce merely chuckled again; then became abruptly serious, in the manner of intoxication, and went over to the table where there was ink and paper. 'Listen here, John, there is something I'm going to do for you. It isn't at all the sort of thing you expected when you came here, but that's the way it goes. I am going to write you a letter of introduction and recommendation to Bowerman and Dillen. They are shipping insurers in the City. How do I know such people? Because I was at school with Charles Dillen. I was the bright young spark who was going to be a doctor, and he was the dull plodding fellow who could see no further than a City counting-house. And now I am – what you see I am; and Charles Dillen is the junior partner in a thriving firm. I think that amply illustrates what I've been saying to you. Clerks, as I say, are always wanted; and if you take my letter of introduction to Bowerman and Dillen's, in Fenchurch Street, I think Charles Dillen will look kindly on you for my sake. Now don't protest, John. This is, God knows, all the influence I wield. Unless you object. Do you object, John?'

'Dr Spruce, I am in no position to be anything but grateful for any influence exerted on my behalf. It's just that . . . I had so set my hopes on medicine. I see, I do see the force of your arguments—'

'You will see them a good deal more clearly when your money runs out,' said Dr Spruce with sudden harshness; then waved a hand, as if he repented of it. 'John, you came here to seek my advice and I have given it to you. Whether you take it or not is up to you. I mean you to have this letter anyway, because your father was kind to me, and I wish to be kind to you. So. A moment, while I write.'

The letter was soon written, and having sanded and sealed it, Dr Spruce thrust it at John. 'There – take it,' he said, pouring himself another glass. 'What you do with it is up to you. Think on what I have said, John: think on it well. And now we shall say goodbye. I am a three-bottle man these days – ' he lifted his glass with a grim and sardonic smile – 'and the third bottle is when I cease to be fit for

165

company. Good luck, John. Accept my condolences, for what they are worth, for your parents.'

John hesitated, about to shake his hand; but Dr Spruce seemed to shy away from that. And so he tucked the letter in his breast pocket, thanked him, and left him.

Long and bitter, the slow walk back to Holborn, with a thousand baffled and disappointed thoughts crowding upon John's mind: long and bitter, the sleepless night he spent turning over the same thoughts, and seeking in vain for some nugget of hope amongst them.

Long and bitter, the succeeding days, in which he paced his comfortless room, and found no answer there; in which he stared from its window at an infinite expanse of roofs and chimneys, and found no answer there; in which he roamed the streets, from Hyde Park Corner to the Tower, and found no answer there. Long and bitter, the hours he spent in cheap coffee-houses and taverns, knowing not one of the countless faces that passed before him: conscious of being alone, conscious of time passing, conscious of money running out, and conscious of the letter still tucked in his breast pocket.

Longest and bitterest of all, the evening that followed his visit to Guy's Hospital. He did not know what self-torturing impulse made him go there; but he went, and he lounged about the gates, and watched the medical students going in and out, chaffing and noisy and supremely indifferent to the young man watching them with dull, haunted eyes.

John was almost tempted to follow Frank Spruce's example that night, and seek solace in a bottle. But something stopped him. Some uncompromising voice of bleak realism spoke up in his mind, and told him that since he could not be one of those medical students, he had two other choices. One was to brood on the fact that he could not be one of those medical students, and brood himself into the grave; the other was to do something else, and continue living. Even now, his bitterness and gloom was such that he tried to shout the realistic voice down; but the voice had an ally, in a very simple and trivial thing. John saw that the heels of his boots were wearing, and would soon be worn to the uppers. He had had no new clothes since the death of his parents, and the ones he possessed were not going to last for ever.

'Shabby-genteel,' he said, addressing the little square of unframed mirror that Miss Thimblebee supplied to her single gentlemen. 'Shabby-genteel is the phrase that will soon describe you, my friend. There is some honour in being honestly shabby, and there's nothing wrong with someone being genteel if that's what they want; but a shabby-genteel young man, sullenly living on disappointed hopes, and doing nothing to rectify them, is a sorry spectacle. So come: what is it to be? Begging in the streets, because you are too spoiled and proud to do anything but what you had set your heart on? Or honest work, which you have the good fortune to be helped towards by Dr Spruce's recommendation? Think of Catherine: are you going to ask her to join you in the workhouse? You told her that you were going to London to make your living somehow – whether medicine or not. If you didn't mean that, what else didn't you mean out of all the fine things you said to her? No, John Twopenny, this won't do. That letter in your pocket – it's doing no good in there. Take it out – use it!'

Yes: it was settled. But there was more of acquiescence in it than decision. John's encounter with Frank Spruce had administered a blow to all the vivacity and self-belief that he had struggled to recover over the past months. Disillusion had struck deep, deeper than even he could yet gauge.

But he was still sufficiently himself to dress carefully for presenting himself at the offices of Bowerman & Dillen, and to make his way thither with a determined step and a hopeful heart. 'Marine insurance,' he said to himself, as he paused outside Bowerman & Dillen's, which presented an old, bottle-glassed, low-doored, inconvenient, and uncommunicative face to the world. 'Well, I know nothing about marine insurance, but I suppose I can learn.'

He entered, and found himself in a counting-house of a dark and old-fashioned kind, with a row of copying-clerks up on high stools like so many circus lions, who all immediately turned to stare at him. There was a head clerk at a desk of his own, so high that he seemed to take his life in his hands, being short-sighted and stiff-jointed when he got down from it; and John was almost moved to apologize for putting him to the trouble, so self-conscious did he feel.

The clerk listened to his preamble without comment, took the letter without comment, and without comment disappeared into an inner office with it. John supposed that he was to wait; and feeling curiously shy of sitting down, even though there were chairs, he stood awkwardly about pretending to read some shipping-notices on the wall, and dreadfully aware of the gaze of the copying-clerks fixed on him. He thought he heard one of them say to his neighbour: 'Perhaps it's wooden legs – two of 'em,' and he thought he heard the neighbour reply, 'Or the teacher caned him, maybe, and he can't,' but when he looked round, the clerks were deedily occupied with their work, and seemed unaware of his existence.

The head clerk returned, and said Mr Dillen would see him. This turned out to be slightly misleading, for though John saw Mr Dillen, Mr Dillen scarcely looked at him, and John felt that he might as well have worn a cap and bells for all Mr Dillen would have known about it. Mr Dillen, it seemed, was rather a harassed man. How much of the firm's work passed across the desk of Mr Bowerman, John did not know – he was given to understand that Mr Bowerman was in his office upstairs, with an important client – but he rather suspected that it was not a tenth of what encumbered the desk of Mr Dillen, which in its heaped-up, ticketed, sealed, paperweighted and inky confusion almost buried that gentleman completely. Dr Spruce's letter, however, lay on the top of it all, and Mr Dillen assured John that he had read it.

'Frank Spruce,' Mr Dillen murmured, shuffling papers. He was a pale, washed-out, soft-faced man, who somehow reminded John of a mother cat with too many kittens. 'I wonder how he's getting on. Doing pretty well, I should think? – we always said, at school, that he'd go far.'

John, remembering the bottles and the dead spiders and the haggard eyes, said he was doing very well.

'Thought as much. Old Frank Spruce. Nice fellow. Well, Mr Twopenny, here is a high recommendation for you. I hope you may live up to it, if you join the firm. You are a single man, I hope?'

'Yes, I am,' said John in surprise.

'Good, good. No premium on bachelors, of course; but if a man will marry as a clerk, he can expect to live pretty miserably as a clerk, and it's as well to state it straight off. Of course there are expectations in a firm such as this, Mr Twopenny. Your salary will progress from the initial increment, which is eighty pounds a year. For that we require a good manner, a fair neat hand, correctness in dress, the utmost punctuality, and no loose habits.' Mr Dillen, with his pale hand supporting his pale head, seemed to be on the point of adding that they did not always get them; but he shrugged that off, and hunting about among his papers again went on, 'Now, we keep a large staff of copying-clerks, and could well use the services of another, for we are busy – very busy . . .' Here Mr Dillen briefly put his hand to his head again. 'And as you bear a good recommendation, and have been educated to the requisite standard, I see no reason why we should not give you a try. This firm has a high name, Mr Twopenny, that is not to be disgraced: you may count yourself pretty fortunate to join us . . .' Here Mr Dillen applied head to hand again, and seemed for some moments to be reflecting on his own good fortune, and finding it not unmixed. 'Well!' he said, making such a sudden stir amongst the heap of papers that they toppled in all directions. 'Come tomorrow morning at eight, and we shall set you to work.'

It was done; the mysteries of marine-insurance had not even been mentioned, and John realized, as he passed through the counting-house on his way out, that it would hardly be required for such a mechanical task as his would be. He felt, anyway, that he ought to celebrate, and did so at an alamode beef-house, where he found the realistic voice still strong enough within him to point out that eating was a good thing, and that having just secured himself the means to carry on eating, regularly if not grandly, he should be grateful.

And he was: which is a different thing from satisfied, or content. But he tried to reconcile himself to that essential difference, and when he returned to Miss Thimblebee's – where he passed a gentleman on the stairs who appeared to be wearing a small mammal on his head, but remembered himself sufficiently to look unsurprised – he set himself at once to write to Catherine. He had baulked at this, in his first stunned disappointment; but now he had something worth communicating.

He directed the letter, as Catherine had suggested, to Verity Deene at Montagu Place, so that she might pass it on; and added a covering note thanking Miss Deene for her trouble, and politely inquiring after her health. He could just imagine her dry smile at that – could imagine her, indeed, dryly smiling over this whole subterfuge that he and Catherine were forced to adopt – but there was no help for it.

In the meantime, he commenced his employment as a copying-clerk at Bowerman & Dillen's. The title of his job gave a fair idea of his duties. Bowerman & Dillen's, considered as an establishment, consisted of that dusty set of offices in Fenchurch Street, so many thousand pounds of capital, and an enormous quantity of documents, like a mountain which John and his half-dozen fellows were continually engaged in digging with little spades, in order to create another mountain beside it. There were senior clerks with a degree of administrative responsibility, and it was their exalted position that was held up as a goal which the diggers might in time reach, if they dug well; but for now, and for the foreseeable future, John was simply to keep his head bent over his work, keep his pen continually moving, and hope that the documents did not send him completely blind before his retirement.

One other thing was required of him: servility. The personal tyranny that his uncle Saul exercised over his employees seemed almost intimate compared with the frigid rules under which the clerks existed at Bowerman & Dillen's. There was not so much to fear from Mr Dillen, who was generally too harassed to take much notice of them; but the senior partner, Mr Bowerman, was a different matter – a sharp, hawk-like little man with a piercing eye, and a nose that struck terror into the hearts of timid juniors. 'When his nostrils start to flare,' John was told on his first day, 'look out.' It was Mr Bowerman's boast that he ran a tight ship, and the clerks certainly ran to do his bidding as if the cat-o'-nine-tails awaited offenders. The necessity of servility irked John far more than the monotony of the copying. When important clients came to the offices, the clerks were required to wait on them; there was a plush private room for the reception of such, and here the client was to be ushered in, helped off with overshoes, his hat and gloves taken, refreshments served to him, and his every wish and whim attended to, all with the humblest submissiveness. To look him in the face, for example, would have been impertinence; and if Mr Bowerman suspected a clerk of impertinence, the clerk would receive an icy invitation to step into his private office – an experience which, John was assured by his fellows, no one had ever been through and lived to tell the tale.

However, it was work. John had already seen enough indigence and distress in

London to appreciate how small was the distance between security and destitution, and to realize that he was lucky.

Which was not to say that eighty pounds a year, and a room and a half above a wig-maker's offered a very good lookout for him and Catherine; though the letter he sent care of Verity Deene carefully avoided such gloomy conclusions. Soon came a note from Miss Deene herself, saying that she had forwarded his letter to Buttings under a cover of her own handwriting, and saying that she was quite happy to be their go-between. She also asked him to meet her, as Catherine required assurance that all was well with him, and would feel happier if Verity had seen him with her own eyes; and she named Sunday morning in St James's Park as the rendezvous.

John agreed, not without a certain misgiving at the thought of facing Verity Deene all alone. But he was glad, at any rate, to be brought closer to Catherine, even by proxy.

He met Verity by Horse Guards Parade. The early morning was dewy and hazy, and when he saw Verity Deene coming towards him, her skirts brushing the damp grass and her head haloed by the soft light, he was struck with a sort of shy surprise. The mental image he associated with the name Verity Deene was of something angular, precise and urbane; but the young woman before him seemed very much in harmony with the mellow scene, as well as rather a striking person in her own right.

She gave him her hand, in her forthright way, and he shook it.

'How are you?' she said.

'I'm very well. Thank you,' he said – in such a strange state of embarrassment, that he omitted to ask her the same question.

'You look well,' she said, studying him; and then, with a little twist of her lips, 'You look well for a woman of eighty, anyway.'

'I beg your pardon?'

'You are my elderly and infirm great-aunt, Mr Twopenny. That's the excuse I gave to my employers, who wish to know where I go even on my half-days: visits to ancient female relatives being about the only thing that's acceptable.'

'I see,' said John. 'And where do I live, in my elderly infirmity?'

'Chelsea,' said Verity promptly. 'You have a parrot in a cage for company, and you like to have the sermons of Bishop Jeremy Taylor read out to you, in a good strong voice. And you're partial to tea, to a rather inconvenient degree.'

'Well,' John said, amused, 'I don't mind playing the part, as long as I don't have to do it in costume . . . Shall we walk?'

'I think it would be as well. A stationary young woman with a stationary young man is always assumed to be up to something discreditable. Why ambulant motion should be considered more decent I don't know, but there it is. Not that my employers would approve even of that, if they could see it.'

John, after a fractional hesitation, gave her his arm: Verity, after a fractional hesitation, took it.

'Are they so very severe?' he asked.

'Mr and Mrs Spikings are . . . very careful of their property. Amongst which the governess is naturally included. Just like the plate and the china, and supposedly as little liable to human feeling.' Verity's tart tone seemed to conceal, imperfectly, some strong emotion, and John was curious; but she changed the subject quickly. 'So: Mr Twopenny. It's been a long time. Catherine told me in her letter that you'd left your uncle's, with London in mind. A sudden decision?'

'It was decided for me, really. When a situation truly becomes intolerable, the body seems to take over from the mind, and act for you.'

'Yes . . . I understand that . . . Strange that you and I have both ended up in London. You have a position, now?'

169

'A clerk's post,' said John. He intended simply to state the fact; he was surprised at the bitter emphasis with which the words came out. He hoped for a moment that Verity had not noticed it – but of course, she had.

'Is it not to your liking?'

'Oh well! Beggars can't be choosers. But . . .'

'But it is not what you had hoped for yourself in life.'

'No.' Suspecting her of teasing, he said, 'I sound very spoiled and ungrateful, no doubt.'

'I don't think so. It isn't wrong to expect the best out of life, surely. Where's the point in living if we are just to be like cattle in a meadow, never reflecting, never questioning, never thinking of what might be instead of what is?'

The sympathy implicit in her words had the effect of releasing the disappointed feelings that John had been hiding even from himself; and he burst out: 'Miss Deene, I am most damnably trapped!'

She gave him a quick look; was silent for some moments, and then said, 'For ever?'

John shrugged. 'I don't know. It seems so . . .'

'There is no possibility whatsoever of advancement for you?'

Her voice was cool; and a little nettled by it, and conscious of having rather given himself away, he said, 'Oh, there is that possibility, of course. But I can see nothing but a long, long road ahead of me.'

'Which at least is there.'

He frowned at her, not understanding.

'Well,' she said, 'if it is not too egotistical of me to use this example, consider my own case. Even if you suppose that being a governess is a thing I love consumedly, you can hardly suppose I would be equally happy at the prospect of being one for ever, or rather until I am too old and shaky and disagreeable to be employed any more; and the lookout after that is exceedingly un-rosy. But those are all the prospects for women like me. There is no long, long road; or, to change the metaphor, there are no steps ascending to even a modicum of independence. But this is taken for granted; and when a man chafes at his degradation, he is called high-minded, whereas a woman who does the same is called discontented. And by the way, having admitted myself discontented with my lot, I may as well add that the worst part of being a governess is being continually Miss-Deened, so I'd be obliged if you'd call me Verity.'

This abruptly friendly tailpiece to what had seemed a typical exercise in cutting him down to size left John quite baffled. Part resentful of being accused of self-pity, part acknowledging the truth of her accusation, part intrigued by Verity's uncharacteristic piece of self-revelation, he could only look at her in perplexity, and say at last, 'I don't know what to make of you – I never have!'

'Well, I know what you'll make of me now. Acid old-maid-in-the-making, venting her frustrations on the male of the species.'

'No,' said John. 'There you do me an injustice. It's true I hadn't thought of how much worse the position of a woman without means is; but I see it now, and I won't forget it.'

Verity smiled: the wry smile that he knew, but he saw tiredness there too, and was surprised – he had not thought of the trim, self-possessed, unflappable Miss Deene as liable to fatigue. He was seeing her in several new lights today. 'I'm sorry,' she said. 'A little hard on you, that. I shouldn't be so sharp . . . Oh, but it's those *damned* children, insufferable, monstrous little brats . . .! There. I feel better for that. Sorry again – you don't like to hear a woman swear, perhaps?'

'I like it very much,' said John, amused. 'How many of them are there?'

'Four,' said Verity grimly. 'Their names are Honoria, Tancred, Seraphina, and Knight.'

'Good God. What do you teach them, tilting and jousting?'

'I teach them nothing,' Verity said, laughing at last. 'They're unteachable. Their stupidity is surpassed only by their rudeness and unpleasantness. John, do you recollect what your heart's desire was at the age of nine?'

'I think it was to have a whole plum-duff to eat all by myself.'

'Sensible enough. Well, Master Tancred's heart's desire is to have a bow and arrow so that he may shoot the blackbirds in the garden. When I tell you also that Mr Spikings often speaks of Master Tancred's future as one of the legislators of the country, you will understand why I sometimes contemplate infanticide . . . Well, enough of that. It's been a relief to speak the truth about them out loud, at any rate. So. I may tell Catherine, then, that I have seen you with my own eyes, and that you are as well as can be, and happy, and thinking of her all the time, and so on. May I?'

The sudden descent into the old tart briskness left John surprised again, and at a loss to explain it. 'Whatever you say,' he said. 'I'm afraid I – I *was* rather betrayed into self-pity just now. Don't think I feel like that all the time.'

'And don't tell Catherine so, eh? No, no, John, I'm not being satirical this time. I know how it is. I don't let her know quite how ghastly life with the Spikings can be, either, because she takes other people's troubles too much to heart. Well, we have both vented a little spleen this morning, and perhaps it has done us both good.'

'Yes . . . Verity, I haven't thanked you, by the way, for acting as our go-between.'

She looked away from him; then said, brisk again, 'Oh, yes, you have. In your covering letter. You made a very precise and formal acknowledgement – rather like a letter from Dr Johnson.'

'You have not been cured of your habit of making fun of me, I see.'

'And you have not been cured of your habit of taking yourself too seriously.'

'I shall think of an answer to that,' John said, half laughing, half angry. 'I shall think of an answer to that, if it takes me all day. And I *am* grateful to you, Verity, no matter what you say.'

'Ah, the soft answer,' Verity said, her dark eyes glinting. 'Very good, John, very cunning – I wouldn't have thought of that one.'

'Obviously not,' he said, 'because when it comes to softness, I think an iron lamppost has the advantage of you.'

'Oh, a hit, a very palpable hit! Well, now I definitely know you are quite yourself, and can reassure Catherine so, because you are getting cross with me, and your ears are turning red just as they used to. And no, I won't allow you to have the last word, because I must be going.'

'A fine way to treat a bedridden old woman!' said John. 'Lucky I've got me parrot!'

He had made her laugh, and she was still laughing as she said goodbye and left him; why he should feel so pleased about this he could not tell, but he did.

'A very aggravating person nonetheless,' he said to himself, as he took his own way home. 'One must be continually on one's mettle with her!' And yet his step was lighter, and he felt more intensely alive than he had felt in an age.

CHAPTER SEVEN

The King's Diplomacy

Mr Edwin Chipchase was a prosperous tradesman who lived and worked in Hales-next-the-sea. He had come to the town from Yarmouth a few years ago with a small nest-egg, and from it had hatched a flourishing trade in corn and coal and timber; not on the grand scale, not on a scale to compare with S. Twopenny & Son, but enough for the native businessmen of the port to speak of him with respect.

Mr Chipchase's business premises were at the west end of the quayside; and he had converted part of them to an unpretentious dwelling-house, where he lived a frugal bachelor existence, rising early, working till late, keeping a modest table, and abstaining entirely from liquor. He was strict in his religious observance, and notably sober in his dress, and he objected to swearing amongst his handful of employees; and he was a little over thirty years old.

All this was known, and approved, by Saul Twopenny. The old man had taken a good deal of notice of Mr Chipchase just lately; and Saul Twopenny never did anything without a reason. And the reason for his interest in Mr Edwin Chipchase, was that he had decided Mr Edwin Chipchase was going to be his son.

If anyone had been in Saul's confidence in this matter – which no one was – and if anyone had had the temerity to question him – which no one did – they might reasonably have objected that Saul already had a son, and that his name was William. But as far as Saul was concerned, he had no son, and would have asserted as much, with all the intractable certainty of his nature. For William had left him. William had finally risen in rebellion, and quitted his father's house; and to Saul, a son who defied him thus was no son at all, and he had washed his hands of him.

It was a month since John had turned against his uncle, and taken his chance with fortune. For a week or so after that event, an uneasy peace had reigned between Saul and William. All was far from well, for John's action had slightly shaken the foundations of even so massive an assurance as Saul's; but the old man had not suspected, even for a moment, that John's example might be working a change within William's sullen and secretive nature. Saul had not suspected that William, with the slowness and hesitancy that was a natural result of twenty-five years of fear, was groping towards a realization that what John could do, he could also do. Saul had not suspected that the sight of the stick being broken had had an effect on William that was like an awakening from a long, oppressive dream; he had not suspected, in other words, that the stick once broken could not be put together again.

And so it was a complete surprise to Saul when William ran away. On the tenth night after John's departure, when all the household was asleep, William had packed a bag and slipped out of the house never to return. He had chosen a voluntary exile from Saul's kingdom, and utterly abandoned his claim to the throne. The note he left informed his father that he was going, as he had always wished, to sea. The friends he had made on his illicit nocturnal expeditions to the waterside had fitted out a cutter to trade between Holland the Port of London, and they had agreed to take him as a member of the crew. The Norfolk coast would see him no more; and, as William added with juvenile defiance in his note, good riddance to it, and to his father too; *'For you are a Brute, Pa, and that's about all there is to it.'*

So William was gone: S. Twopenny & Son was only a name, unless some day William relented and chose to return. That was about as likely as an escaped prisoner choosing to go back to the treadmill; but even had it not been so, the door was now for ever closed against him. Saul had decided that within an hour of beholding William's empty room and reading his note. That it took him even that long showed what a blow had been administered to Saul's pride; and though he would as soon have walked naked through Hales-next-the-sea as reveal his innermost feelings to anyone, he involuntarily murmured to his servant Caleb: 'Dear God, my boy, be thankful that you have no children to bring you pain in your old age.' But Saul soon rallied. Saul had never shirked at grasping nettles, and within an hour he was as firmly in command of himself as he had ever been, and had made his irrevocable decision. 'Very well: he is no son of mine from this hour forth. He rejects me: I reject him. He shall be disinherited, and all the things he has left behind shall be taken away and burned; and his name is never to be mentioned in my hearing.' So he instructed a gaping Sar'ann; and he not only held to the matter of the burning, which someone who did not know him might have thought to be exaggeration, but supervised the process himself, and watched till the last plume of smoke had drifted away into the sky.

There was much furtive talk, of course, amongst the house-servants and the men who worked at the maltings. The old man had not only had his nephew turn against him; he had driven his own son away, the son who was to carry on the business that meant so much to him. A common opinion was that He Would Rue; but Mr Addy, for one, knowingly shook his head. Saul Twopenny was not so easily defeated as that. 'That one'll think of something that'll let him go on being masterful, and having his own way, you mark my words,' he said. 'If he weren't so old, I'd say he'd marry again, and get another son to high-hand it with; but he'll think of something. He always does – the old pepperer!'

What ferment of jealous and wrathful emotions disturbed Saul's breast in the watches of the night no one knew; and whether any tincture of regret, doubt, or remorse figured amongst them was a similarly hard question. But one thing was for sure: it did not occur to Saul that his urge to dominate and manipulate was productive of evil consequences. For within a week of William's flight, Saul had a new plan in mind, and was determined to execute it to the last detail.

His son had disappointed; his nephew had refused to play the part. Therefore, Saul would choose his own son. He would select a man after his own heart, and make him his heir: a man such as he had always wanted as a son: godly, industrious, humble, persevering, shrewd at business, ascetic in tastes, and utterly devoted to the name and the prosperity of S. Twopenny & Son.

And, of course, utterly loyal and obedient to Saul himself. There was the crux of the matter; and it was there that Saul felt himself to be on surest ground, as he considered his plan. For S. Twopenny & Son, its premises, trade, goods, chattels, capital, was no mean concern; whoever stood to inherit it was on to a pretty good thing. And anyone with any sense would be glad to do Saul's bidding, and recognize him as supreme master, for such a golden opportunity.

Perhaps it was a blessing, after all, that William had left him! Instead of having to be content with that weak vessel, Saul could fashion one from clay of his own choosing. So the old man reasoned. For he had not forgotten that he had a daughter. He had tended to disregard the female fruit of his loins, simply because it was female; and regarded Sar'ann only with as much favour as attached to her keeping house reasonably well, and being pious and dutiful. He had certainly not regarded her as a marriageable article – as long, that is, as he had a son. But now he looked at Sar'ann anew, and he saw that the kingdom might descend through her after all. With the prince in permanent exile, Saul turned his attention to the princess royal, and began to contemplate a dynastic marriage.

Sar'ann's feelings about the prospect did not enter into his calculations. He was going to marry her off, and she should be directed by his wisdom, and that was that. And he had very soon decided who the man was to be. His circle of acquaintance was not wide, and was chiefly limited to the business community of Anglia's northern shore; but then it was a man of business that he wanted. And when to the man of business were added the personal qualities that he perceived in Mr Edwin Chipchase, Saul decided he need look no further.

Mr Chipchase's reputation was already known to Saul before his plan was formed, but Saul set out to confirm it with his own eyes by frequenting the little corn exchange of Hales-next-the-sea more than was his wont, and talking with him there. He also visited the chapel where Mr Chipchase worshipped; and even went so far as to stump down to the other end of the quayside and make a neighbourly call on Mr Chipchase at his premises. All of this amply confirmed Saul's good opinion. Edwin Chipchase was the man, and it only remained to let him know it.

And Sar'ann, of course. As far as Saul was concerned, there might as well be a wedding here and now; but he grudgingly admitted to himself that the thing must be led up to, in some sort. So he took an unprecedented step. He asked Mr Chipchase to dine, and Mr Chipchase accepted. Again, Saul would have preferred to make the least fuss possible, and just have Mr Chipchase solus; but he knew there ought to be a few other guests, for form's sake. So he also invited Mr Bream, who never turned down any invitation, and Mrs Bream depending on what stage of pregnancy she was in; and made up the numbers with Mr and Mrs Addy. Whatever else he was, Saul was not a snob, and thought nothing of having his foreman dine as his guest at his table; though poor Mr Addy, envisioning a pretty hot evening of it, could have wished that Saul's sense of social niceties had been a little more exacting, and privately remarked to Mrs Addy that if this occasion didn't finally make a firework of him, he was a Dutchman.

Down in the servants' kitchen of the gaunt house, astonishment reigned at the news that there were to be guests, and the appearance of a case of bottles with corks in them caused a general sensation. But that was not the end of Saul's preparations. One evening, a few days before the great occasion, he was sitting as usual after supper with Sar'ann in the parlour. He had taken up his bible, and she her sewing; but he soon laid down the book, and contemplated Sar'ann so long and so fixedly that at last she burst nervously, 'Oh, my stars, Pa, how you do stare at a person tonight! It's enough to make a person frightened out of her wits, upon my word it is!'

'Sar'ann,' said Saul, 'how would you like to have a new frock?'

Sar'ann was no slouch at staring; but surely never had her enormous, lashless frog's eyes goggled as they goggled now.

'Lor,' she breathed. 'What for?'

Saul hesitated. 'Well,' he said, 'we are to have company, daughter. I am not the man to encourage worldly vanity, but I think the occasion demands a new frock, at least. An evening frock, I think.'

'An evening . . .! Do you mean with my arms showing, and everything?'

'To a degree,' said Saul judiciously. 'To a degree, Sar'ann.'

'Lor,' said Sar'ann again. 'Just imagine me, in an evening frock, with my arms showing! Oh, my stars, me with my arms showing! Oh, my stars and garters, think of it!' And she went off into a fit of laughter until, admonished by a stern look from her father, she slapped herself rational.

'Very well,' said Saul, 'we shall go and buy it tomorrow.' And he returned to his Bible, and Sar'ann to her sewing; though she occasionally broke off to murmur

174

under her breath about frocks, and arms, and stars, and garters, for the rest of the evening.

The day of the dinner came, and the guests came. Mr Addy, in a cravat so throttlingly tight that he looked as if he had beaten off a garrotter on the way there; Mrs Addy timidly placating, and so nervous at being in the house of a man she was accustomed to refer to as The Ogre that she jumped whenever someone spoke to her. Mrs Bream carrying her prolific womb before her, and ready to talk of parturition and forceps to anyone who would listen; Mr Bream in a state of wildly smiling sociability, with his cannons of optimism all loaded and ready to fire off a broadside at anyone ditto. And Mr Edwin Chipchase, punctual to the second, and quietly declaring himself delighted to have the opportunity.

Here, then, was the man Saul had chosen to be his son. A pale, sandy man looking older than his thirty-odd years; with small spectacles covering small eyes, and a head that had gone curiously half-bald on the crown, so that what there was of it appeared rather to have got stuck on there somehow, like carpet-fluff, than to be a remnant of more; with no jawbone, so that from the crown of his head to his shirt-collar there was no more variation of contour than there is on a broom-handle; with no lips, and little teeth all as alike as piano keys, and diminutive hands like white soft dough: with a shrewd, considering manner, for all his muted voice and blandness of utterance; and with something about him which suggested that, spectacles notwithstanding, he did not miss a thing. He certainly did not miss the emphatic manner in which Saul introduced him to Sar'ann. And nor, a little later, when Saul pressed him to the seat in the parlour right next to Sar'ann as deliberately as if he were moving a chess-piece, did he miss the opportunity of complimenting her on her dress. Which gratified Saul, as the watered-silk gown from which Sar'ann's bony shoulders were protruding had cost him a pretty penny, and he wanted a return on his investment.

Saul was not a man to keep guests hanging about in the parlour making small-talk; a dinner was a dinner, and the sooner it was got over the better. He recollected that the fal-lals of society required the ladies and gentlemen to pair off when going into dinner; so he thrust Mrs Addy, to her alarm, on Mr Bream, paired their respective spouses likewise, instructed Sar'ann to take Mr Chipchase's arm – which he was not slow, as it happened, in offering her; and having disposed of his chessmen to his satisfaction, stumped his way into the dining-room ahead of them all, bidding Caleb to follow him and wait by his chair.

It happened that this was one of the first evenings in which the chill of autumn had struck; but Saul, who was never cold himself, did not suppose anybody else would be, and so had omitted to have fires lighted. There never was such a chilly dinner. The maid who had been chosen to wait at table could not stop shivering, and made an almighty percussion with the plates and knives. Poor Caleb, standing by his master's chair, blew on his fingers and clapped his arms across his great chest like a guard on sentry-go; whilst Sar'ann, in her unaccustomed state of décolletage, was one mass of goose-pimples, and might have been a plucked fowl ready for the roasting, in case the two on the table should not be enough. As for the food, though it had come hot from the kitchen, it was a cold collation by the time it got to the diners' mouths – a circumstance which increased the general resemblance of Saul's entertainment to a funeral banquet.

It would have taken more discouragement than this, however, to depress Mr Bream's spirits. After some eulogies on the cool comestibles, and boisterous praises of the Providence that supplied them, he looked around the table and said with his most thumping obtuseness, 'But my dear Mr Twopenny, there is one I do not see at your groaning board today. Where is your estimable son Mr William?' Sar'ann sucked in a breath, and Mrs Addy looked ready to dive under the table; but Saul, motioning for his water-glass to be filled, merely replied, 'I have no son, sir. He

175

chose to leave this house, in express defiance of my authority, and I no longer acknowledge him. Have the goodness, if you please, not to mention him again in my hearing.'

This sparkling specimen of Saul's dinner-table conversation rather intensified the frost that lay upon the company, and even Mr Bream looked at a loss. But Mr Edwin Chipchase was not put out by this, or by anything. He carried on methodically eating, and mildly looking about him at the guests through his little spectacles, seeming to see nothing and seeing a great deal; and now he remarked to Sar'ann in his precise, unhurried little voice, 'Well, Miss Twopenny, I hear that the Crystal Palace has been moved to a permanent site, and will be preserved. I should greatly like to have seen the Great Exhibition, shouldn't you?'

Sar'ann, sitting bolt upright and looking at Mr Chipchase with mingled alarm and fascination, gave a strangled squeak in reply.

'A little obstruction in the throat, I think,' said Mr Chipchase in a soothing monotone. 'Take a little wine, Miss Twopenny.'

Sar'ann did so, never taking her eyes off his face as she raised the glass to her lips.

'That's it. I was talking of the Great Exhibition, you know. And whether you would like to have seen it.'

'Oh, no, not I, not at all, not a bit!' said Sar'ann. 'Pa says it ain't godly, a person wasting his precious time on vain amusements!'

'I am quite in agreement,' said Mr Chipchase, 'when it comes to vain amusements. But I believe there was instruction to be gained at the Exhibition. The newest productions of trade and manufacture; and the best of them, I believe, all from our own shores. Is it not so, Mr Twopenny?'

'Surely: you can't beat an Englishman for business,' said Saul, who had a suspicion of foreigners as likely to be Papists, and was patriotic insofar as he regarded England as an extension of S. Twopenny & Son.

'You have never been to London, Miss Twopenny?' Mr Chipchase said.

'Oh no, not I!' cried Sar'ann, who seemed to feel compelled to deny everything, as if she were on the witness-stand. 'I declare I've never been within a thousand miles of it in all my life, and I hope I never shall!'

'I cannot forbear putting in a word here,' said Mr Bream – as if he ever could. 'I cannot help remarking that Miss Twopenny seems to make that perfectly respectable theological connection between great cities and sinfulness – *Vanity Fair* – am I right, Miss Twopenny?'

'A nod's as good as a wink to a blind horse!' retorted Sar'ann.

'Indeed – indeed . . . but I was about to observe that there is an equally sound theological interpretation of the city, and that is the City of God,' said Mr Bream. 'For even London, you know, with its manifold wickednesses and iniquities, is under the benign direction of the Almighty. I was put in mind of this recently, when reading in the newspaper of the Tooting baby-farm, or "Mr Drouet's Infant Pauper Asylum", to give it its proper title, which gained a certain notoriety, and seems to have been run on lines not wholly compatible with justice and mercy. The compulsion laid upon the infants to eat their meals standing up, and the proprietor's remissness in failing to inform a pauper mother that her child had died until after it had been buried, are two details that remain in my memory. And yet do you know what my reaction was when I had finished reading this melancholy report? It was joy! Yes, joy abounding – and shall I tell you why? Because it burst upon me that here was a most remarkable evidence of Providential dispensation – namely, that this rather reprehensible institution was situated in London! London, where many responsible bodies for the furtherance of public health are situated – so that it was inevitable that the scandal would be discovered, and the abuses corrected, in a place where human scrutiny cannot for long be evaded. If the

176

baby-farm had been situated in a remote part of the Highlands, for example, the chances are it would never have been exposed; but the divine intercession that directs our affairs decreed otherwise! And now try to tell me, ma'am – ' he suddenly turned his ghastly smile on Mrs Addy, who shrank in her seat – 'just try and tell me that this is not a world framed for human happiness, and does not have the hand-prints of the benevolent Creator all over it! You can't do it, ma'am!'

'Well, for my part I think the notion of a baby-farm is perfectly charming, and I should very much like to have one myself, if it were not for my own lambs,' droned Mrs Bream. 'I always say that the smell of a new-bathed baby, when its clouts have been changed, is just about the nicest smell in all the world!'

Mr Addy, who had been about to take a bite out of a chicken wing, seemed to suffer a sudden loss of appetite, and applied himself to his wine instead; an act that did not escape the attention of Saul, who growled, 'Don't stint yourself with the wine, Addy; but I'd remind you that you've to be at work early tomorrow morning, and I don't look kindly on bad timekeeping.'

Mr Addy set down his glass with a sickly sort of smile, and cast a longing glance at the soup-tureen, which would certainly have been cold enough for his purposes.

'Well, Chipchase, what think you of these plans to bring the railway to Hales?' said Saul, with a penetrating look. 'Will it make us, or break us?'

'I don't think it will break us,' Mr Chipchase said after a considering moment, 'and it might well make us, if we are prepared to adapt to it. Speaking for myself, I would make a careful investigation of rail freight costs, and I would not, if I were in the position of shipowner as you are, sir – ' with a deferential nod at Saul – 'I would not invest in any more shipbuilding at present. Not until the railway is here, and its capabilities and disadvantages can be assessed.'

Saul rubbed his chin. 'You think it will kill the port altogether?'

'It will alter it,' said Mr Chipchase. 'Diminish it possibly. Not kill it.' He inclined his head towards Sar'ann again. 'Have you ever ridden upon a railway-train, Miss Twopenny?'

'No, not I – never in my life!' cried Sar'ann. 'It might crash, you know. Not that it mightn't be interesting to *see* a crash – I wonder what it looks like! – but I don't know as I'd like to be in one.'

'Railway travel isn't recommended for persons of a nervous disposition, I believe,' said Mr Chipchase. 'But you don't strike me as a person of nervous disposition, Miss Twopenny. Sensitive, perhaps, but not nervous – are you?'

'Oh, my stars, I really can't say,' squawked Sar'ann. 'There's one thing I can say for myself, and that's that I don't mind the sight of blood. I don't mind it a bit, and never have. That's queer – ain't it?'

'Very sensible, I would have thought,' said Mr Chipchase, becoming, if anything, even less animated as he became more insinuating. 'It's one of the commonest substances in the world, after all. I wish all young ladies felt as you do.'

'Oh! Don't talk to me of young ladies, Mr Chipchase! As far as I'm concerned, they're all Cats!' said Sar'ann with energy, and with some highly anatomical convulsions visible in her bare neck; and she seized her glass of wine and drained it off in one go, afterwards glancing at her father as if appalled at what she had done.

But Saul showed no disapproval. Indeed, he showed the reverse, and continued to do so throughout dinner, in which Mr Chipchase's attentions to Sar'ann were as persistent as they were restrained; and when dinner was over, Saul resumed his human chess-game, positioning Mr Chipchase and Sar'ann with the greatest care, engaging the Breams himself, and leaving the Addys, as mere disposable pawns, to shift for themselves.

In fact, Mr Chipchase seemed quite taken with Sar'ann. While she made the tea he plied her with his little mild questions, about whether she played, and whether she sang, and wouldn't she like to, and so on; and when she asked him how he liked his tea, he said that from her hands, he was sure it would be agreeable however it came – which occasioned a sort of astonished mirth in Sar'ann, who cried: 'Oh, my stars, you do talk! Oh, my word and bond, how you do talk!' and drummed her heels on the floor.

But Mr Chipchase did not press. He seemed to be obediently waiting for Saul to indicate what his next move should be; and when Saul, at the end of the evening, invited him to call on them again – say tomorrow – Mr Chipchase said tomorrow, very readily. He seemed, indeed, to add to his other qualities that of being eminently suggestible – and nothing could have gratified Saul more. Whether Mr Chipchase was his equal, or even his superior, in hard-headed calculation, was a question that did not occur to Saul; and he went to bed that night fatigued by the evening's entertainment – he was feeling his age just lately – but well satisfied with the way things were going.

And things continued to go well. Mr Chipchase called: Mr Chipchase called again and again. And Saul began to leave him and Sar'ann alone for short periods – a proceeding that at first produced an amazed, 'Oh, Pa, wherever are you going?' from Sar'ann, but which she soon got used to. Her feelings towards her future husband were something that even Saul could not leave entirely out of account; but things seemed well enough in that quarter also. 'Well, Sar'ann, what do you think of Mr Chipchase?' he asked her one evening when they were alone – no more subtle approach suggesting itself to Saul's mind.

'Oh, my stars, Pa, what a question,' said Sar'ann. 'I declare I don't know how to answer it, not if I was to try till I was blue in the face!' It was not blue in the face she went, however, but bright red.

'He is a solid sort of man,' said Saul, not displeased with this evidence, 'abstemious, and very firm in the matter of religion. A man who combines prudence with piety can usually be pretty well relied on, daughter. "Wine maketh merry; but money answereth all things".'

'He knows scripture,' Sar'ann said eagerly. 'He knows scripture, I think, better than anybody in the world except you, Pa. But lor! I'm afraid he don't always talk scripture, Pa, when you leave us alone . . .' This with a fearful glance at her father. 'Those times you leave us alone, it ain't scripture Mr Chipchase talks, Pa: I'd better tell you that, in case it's sinful. Oh, my!'

'Not sinful, Sar'ann,' Saul said. 'There is a time and a place for everything in this life. And if it should be that Mr Chipchase seeks to pay his attentions to you—'

'You mean woo me, Pa?' said Sar'ann. 'Because that's what I think he's doing. That's what he's doing, he's wooing! Oh, my word and bond, think of it! Wooing is what he's doing! Oh, my stars and garters!'

'It may be so, Sar'ann,' said Saul, concealing his satisfaction beneath his stoniest gravity. 'It may well be so. I shall of course expect Mr Chipchase to speak to me about it; but we shall see.'

They saw very soon, as it happened. Two days later, feeling that there was no point in wasting any more time, Saul asked Mr Chipchase, when he called, to step into his private office. And Mr Chipchase evinced no surprise, and seemed to know quite well what was afoot.

They talked plainly and frankly, as befitted two businessmen discussing a venture. There was, of course, a difference of degree between them, and Saul was majestically conscious that he was conferring a boon; but Mr Chipchase appeared to accept his subordinate status willingly. Did he aspire to the hand of Miss Sar'ann? Yes, he did, if he had Mr Twopenny's leave to ask it. He hoped Mr Twopenny was acquainted with his material circumstances and moral character, but if there were any reservations or questions in Mr Twopenny's mind, Mr Chipchase begged he would raise them. No, nothing like that – Saul was magnanimous on this point; but of course there were practical considerations, and they must be discussed before anything was done. Quite so; Mr Chipchase liked to think he was a practical man himself.

'Well, Chipchase,' said Saul, leaning back in his chair, 'you should know, first of all, that I have settled no money on Sar'ann.'

Mr Chipchase said nothing, merely taking off his spectacles to polish them whilst looking courteously attentive.

'I am a man of business, Chipchase: my money is all working for me. I don't believe in all that nonsense of settling so many thousand pounds on your daughter – it only attracts fortune-hunters.'

Mr Chipchase murmured that he was afraid that was so.

'However, you should know also that I lack an heir. I am wholly estranged from my only son . . .' Saul flushed, and his hand trembled a little, but Mr Chipchase was still polishing his spectacles, and perhaps did not see it. 'Wholly estranged. He will get nothing from me – ever. So it is likely that I shall settle my property on my daughter.'

Mr Chipchase continued to look attentive – no more than that.

'In short, Chipchase, a son-in-law of mine may expect prospects. And I needn't tell you that those prospects are far from negligible.' Saul made a sweeping gesture to indicate his kingdom; and Mr Chipchase made a little nod of his head, as if he were bowing to its greatness.

'Accordingly,' said Saul, 'any son-in-law of mine would be laid under certain obligations, while I live. I built up everything you see here, Chipchase, and I am determined that it shall continue. If you were to be that son-in-law, I should expect you to devote yourself to its affairs as zealously as I do: I should expect you to work as hard for the firm of S. Twopenny and Son as you do now on your own account. I should expect you to learn the whole business, master its every detail. If you would inherit my substance, you must also inherit my responsibility. So, it would be part of these obligations that you should reside under this roof once you are married, be directed by me, and consider the fortunes of S. Twopenny and Son to be your own.'

Mr Chipchase put on his spectacles, and with something like an open smile – for there always seemed to be a sort of suppressed smile about him – said that he considered such obligations as privileges, and that to be linked with the destiny of S. Twopenny & Son would be an honour.

'I'm glad you see it so,' said Saul, 'for those are my requirements, if you are to marry my daughter. And I may as well add, Chipchase, that I have always been master in my own house, and always will be.'

Mr Chipchase made the little nod again, as if he bowed to that fact too, unquestioningly.

'Then, sir,' said Saul, as near to brightly as his grimness could manage, 'I think we're agreed.'

And so, businesslike, they shook hands on it – Mr Chipchase's little doughy hand quite disappearing in Saul's great grizzled paw; though his grip was firm enough. And then Saul gave Mr Chipchase leave to go and seek the fair maiden out, and make his proposal; and the old man had so settled matters to his own satisfaction, that if Sar'ann had said no after all, he would have thrashed her to within an inch of her life.

Sar'ann, however, whether out of fear of just such a result, or out of tribute to the potency of Mr Chipchase's wooing, did not say no. If she did not exactly say yes, that was because she was too much occupied by going into shrieks of laughter, slapping herself, falling silent to stare open-mouthed at her placid suitor, going into shrieks of laughter again, covering her head with her pinafore, drumming her heels on the floor, and so on; but the understanding was there.

Saul saw no point in waiting, now that the marriage was agreed. It was not as if there was any need for delay on account of accommodation for the newlyweds, as

179

they were to live with him. And so he had the banns published at once, Mr Chipchase obediently complying, and Sar'ann not being consulted anyhow. As for Mr Chipchase's own property, he elected to let the dwelling-house, and place the corn-and-coal concern under a manager for now; for Saul had hinted that there might be a merger of their interests, in the fullness of time.

Some might have said that the haste was unseemly; but Saul did not care a fig for that. Some might have said also that it was the desire to spite the son who had rejected him that was driving Saul so precipitately on. No one who valued their life would have dared say it openly; but perhaps simple Caleb unwittingly came near the truth when, observing the marriage preparations, he said to his master: 'Won't Mr William be coming to the wedding?'

'Silence, boy: don't be more of a fool than you are, or I'll flog you raw!' snapped Saul with uncommon violence, and sent him away. But afterwards there was a most unholy light in the old man's eyes, and a look about his mouth as if he were tasting some pungent relish; and though he was sincere enough when he claimed that he never wished to set eyes on William again, it would have taken a lenient jury to acquit Saul of a wish to have William just look in at the wedding service, and see how swiftly he had been superseded.

But that was not all the trouble that Caleb gave in the weeks before the marriage. He was thoroughly unsettled, and as sullen and difficult as his devotion to his master allowed him to be. At last Saul took him up on it, in his short way. 'What ails you, boy? Are you in need of doctoring? A purge, or something like that? For I tell you, I'm tired of these sulky tricks. Now speak up – what is it?'

Caleb, shuffling his great feet, and rubbing his eyes with the heel of his hand, muttered something about the wedding.

'Aye – and what of the wedding? What's the wedding to you? Oh, you shall be there, if that's what's bothering you. A suit of clothes for it, is that what you're wanting? Well, you shall have them, you great looby, if we can find a tailor with enough cloth.'

It was only with Caleb that Saul ever attempted humour, even of this rough sort; but whereas Caleb was usually delighted with it, this time he was not to be bought off. Looking sidelong at his master, he muttered that he didn't want to go to the wedding.

'Contrary boy! Stay at home, or go, as you please. I've no patience.'

Saul sat down at his desk. Caleb, whose observation was not slow when it came to his master, saw that he was not as sprightly as he used to be, and put out his great hand to steady him down.

'Ach! don't fuss, boy. I'm fit enough . . . Well, what is it now?' For Caleb had not let go of Saul's arm, and was tugging at his sleeve.

'Sir,' Caleb said, his pale brow creased with anxiety and concentration, 'sir, please, I don't like Mr Chipchase.'

'What?' Saul was fierce. 'What nonsense is this?'

Caleb persisted. 'Sir, please. I don't mean any harm, don't be waxy with me. But I don't like Mr Chipchase; and I wish he wasn't going to marry Miss Sar'ann.'

Saul sat back and regarded his servant with more puzzlement than anger. 'Now what's put this in your head? You're my servant, not Mr Chipchase's. I don't know, boy; you must control these fancies of yours . . .' Saul hesitated. 'Now why don't you like him, hm? Tell me.'

Caleb, with a trembling lip, answered that he didn't know.

'You don't know.' Saul grunted and opened the ledger on his desk. 'I thought as much. Go, go about your business, boy, and stop talking your nonsense.'

Caleb went; but he did not stop talking his nonsense, if nonsense it was. He repeated it to the horses in the stables, that it was his favourite habit to visit, and that liked him as much as he liked them. 'I don't know why,' he said, feeding an apple

180

to a dray-horse, and stroking its whiskery nose. 'I don't know why: but I don't like Mr Chipchase!'

He made no more direct appeals to his master, however; and the preparations went ahead, and the day of the wedding arrived; and Caleb attended the service, along with the other servants, at the parish church of Hales-next-the-sea. Sar'ann in her bridal gown was a sight that several rather heartless young ladies of the little town declared they would not miss for the world, and insinuated themselves into the church uninvited to gape at; and one old gentleman who was passing the church as the bride arrived was reputed to have muttered about the things you saw when you hadn't got your gun. But the groom responded very gallantly to this apparition; whilst Saul gave her away in such an imposing and emphatic manner that the vicar quite trembled at him.

And Caleb sat at the back of the church, too overawed by the occasion to utter a word; but still under his breath he repeated it: 'I don't know why, but I don't like him!'

No matter: the vicar fairly galloped through the service under the scornful eye of Saul, and had the couple married in a twinkling. The wedding-feast at Saul's house was not a brilliant affair, for Saul classified such things amongst the fripperies and fal-lals he so detested; and the majority of the guests being merely business associates of Saul's and Mr Chipchase's, the conversation was so overwhelmingly dry and commercial in its flavour that the happy pair in the centre might have been supposed to be two lots at auction, who were presently to be knocked down and taken away in a waggon all wrapped up in coconut matting. The celebrations were not protracted. Soon the guests had had their fill of fruit-cake and shop-talk, and, recollecting with a start that they were at a wedding, congratulated Mr Chipchase on their way out – that imperturbable little gentleman giving each and every one of them his doughy handshake, as if committing the shape of their hands to memory – and likewise congratulated the new Mrs Chipchase, who had plainly found her veil rather inconvenient for staring, and since putting it back had made up for it in spades.

The notion of a honeymoon was alien alike to Saul and to his new son-in-law; and there was nothing to distinguish that night from any other night in Saul's jail-like house. There was the same early hour of retiring, the same rattling of bolts and keys, and the same tin candlesticks to light the household to bed. Caleb, as usual, attended his master to his bedchamber, helped him with his undressing, set out his clothes for the morning, and saw that the old man had everything as he liked it, and then retired to his own bed, which was in a little bare closet of a room adjoining Saul's. But Caleb, who usually slept as promptly as a child, could not rest tonight. The house was different to him: it had Mr Chipchase in it. Caleb did not like change; and he still did not like Mr Chipchase.

At the same time, Mr Chipchase exerted a sort of dreadful fascination on him. And once he had assured himself that his master was soundly sleeping, Caleb got up and, driven by what impulse he did not know, crept out into the passage and along to the room at the end that had been appointed as the bridal chamber. There he paused, regarding the door with a sort of fearful wonder; and though with a miserable, confused consciousness on him of doing wrong, listened.

There was no mistaking the voice of Sar'ann, which was of the sort called 'carrying'. 'Oh my stars, Mr Chipchase, I never saw anything like it in my life!' she shrilled. 'Oh, my word and bond, I never did! What a curious world we live in, to be sure! Oh, my stars and garters! Ah-ha-ha-ha-ha!' Her laughter was accompanied by a gurgling chuckle plainly emanating from Mr Chipchase, though Caleb had never heard him make such a sound before; and as he hurried back to his own room, with a burning face and whirling mind, Caleb thought he heard Mr Chipchase give the gurgling chuckle again, and say in a muffled voice, 'D'you know, I think I'm going to like it here.'

181

CHAPTER EIGHT

A Clerk There Was

John Twopenny had joined the army. Not the military army; though in numbers, he and his comrades were enough to fill several regiments, and in their poor pay, spartan quarters, low reputation, and subjection to strict discipline, their resemblance to soldiers was striking. But the army of which John was a part never did anything so exciting as go on manoeuvres, or take part in a parade; and no young ladies suffered a fluttering of the heart at the sight of their uniform. It was the army of poor young clerks, which was in permanent occupation of London.

A curious in-between life was theirs. Earning less than prosperous artisans, they had to maintain the appearance of respectability, and dress as if they had three hundred a year instead of a bare third of that sum. They were supposed to share the standards and manners of a polite society which their means entirely debarred them from mixing with: at work they breathed an air of suffocating decency, but outside work they sank of necessity into a world of furnished lodgings, cheap meals, and cheaper entertainments.

An awkward, unsettled, threadbare life then, with much surface and little substance. A life of dull toil which jaded without exhausting; and in the intervals of dull toil, much duller lounging, lolling, drifting, wandering, smoking, loitering, and wishing. Much frequenting of the cheap eating-houses with which the city abounded, and where the smell of gravy and boiled greens seemed to have permeated the frowsy upholstery, so that you took the smell home with you, and went to bed in it. Much cramming late into cheap theatres, and acting under a curious compulsion not to look at anything that was happening on stage, but only at the other clerks in the seats behind, who were looking at the other clerks behind them. Much sitting at the high windows of rented rooms, and looking out at smoky twilights, and thinking wistfully of what might have been – in John's case especially.

For John did all this; and whether he was more listless and dissatisfied than his fellow-clerks in doing it, listless and dissatisfied he certainly was. And there were times when he seemed to touch new depths of melancholy; times when, closing the curtains in his lodgings which would never quite meet in the middle, or pacing the streets of a windy, dusty Sunday evening when the church bells seemed to have rung the knell of all that was bright and noble, his life appeared to have degenerated into mere existence, a perpetual diet of dry bread for which there was no hope of gaining an appetite.

Just as in the regular army, the army of clerks found comfort in comradeship. But at first this was denied to John. He was a complete newcomer to the city, whereas his fellows in the counting-house of Bowerman & Dillen were old hands, and had already formed their own little circle, with its own customs and its own private slang. Their nickname for him was 'Norfolk', in accordance with his place of birth; and while they were not actively unfriendly, he was to them an outsider – a status which they reinforced by pleasantries about sheep, windmills, bloaters, dumplings, and other supposedly local peculiarities with which they assumed him to be on familiar terms. He took these in good part, but could not help but find them wearisome after the ninth or tenth repetition; and though he had formerly been of a sociable disposition, the pervasive sense of disappointment and defeat that overcame him meant that he became solitary and taciturn.

But then, as the weeks and months went by, and his work at Bowerman & Dillen's became dreary second nature to him, he found himself to his own surprise making a friend there. At a desk just below the senior clerk's there laboured a man named Bidmead. He was a thin, fair man with a narrow careworn face, always out at elbows, and with a way of buttoning up his shiny coat that suggested he did not always have on a whole shirt underneath it. He was not many years older than John, but was always referred to as Old Bidmead, and was generally made the butt of as many harmless jokes and impish impertinences as a feeble schoolmaster in a classroom full of lively boys. 'Look – here's Old Bidmead,' one of the young clerks would say, cutting an old pen into the likeness of a spindly figure; or, if a ragged beggar should dare to look in at the foxed windows of the counting-house, there would be a cry of, 'I say, it's Old Bidmead's tailor. Look, Bidmead, here's your tailor come dunning for his bill.'

'Yes, yes – good, that, very good,' Bidmead would say, with a faded smile; and John suspected, from the absent expression on Bidmead's face, and from his generally pinched and straitened appearance, that Old Bidmead, though young in years, was old in cares, and had a good deal more on his mind than the drolleries of a set of beardless clerks.

There was something about Bidmead, too, that made his superiors drop down on him. Mr Dillen, the junior partner, seemed to take out some of his own harassment on Bidmead, and would cluck his tongue impatiently whenever he was near to him, and mutter, 'Bidmead, Bidmead, what a creature you are!' And as for Mr Bowerman, that hawkish little gentleman could not put his beak into the counting-house without his terrifying eye alighting on Bidmead, and finding something amiss; and he would cry, 'Bidmead! What do you mean by it? What do you mean by it, sir? Answer me, sir, answer me at once!' with such fierce venom that even the younger clerks blanched, and felt sorry for him.

It was on a day when Bidmead had been more than usually dropped down upon that John made friends with him. A wealthy client had called, and John had been instructed to wait on him in the usual grovelling fashion. After showing the client at last into Mr Bowerman's office, he was about to go away when Mr Bowerman barked at him to come back.

'Twopenny! Send Bidmead to me at once!'

Mr Bowerman had a certificate in his hand, which John saw to be Bidmead's work, and guessed at once that there was a mistake in its drawing up. Bidmead was plainly in for it; and John wished it was not he who had to make the awful summons.

'Mr Bidmead,' he said softly, going to him and touching his frayed sleeve. 'I'm afraid Mr Bowerman wishes to see you in his office.'

'Not half as afraid as I am,' said Bidmead, laying down his pen with a resigned look. 'Ah, well. No one ever said life was going to be enjoyable.' He glanced at John, seemed to see and appreciate his sympathetic look, and gave a wry smile. 'I'd appreciate it, by the by, Mr Twopenny, if you'd call me Tom. I rather associate "Bidmead" with being dropped down upon, and unpleasant sensations in general.' So saying, he went drooping off to Mr Bowerman's office to take his punishment. Which was all the more severe because there was a wealthy client as witness: Mr Bowerman, as is usual with strict disciplinarians, being as much of a toady to those he saw above him as a tyrant to those he saw below him.

And that was how John's friendship with Tom Bidmead began. There had been such high words half-audible from Mr Bowerman's office, that John seriously wondered whether poor Bidmead had been given the sack; and when the time came for closing up the counting-house and going home, he hovered about for some moments wondering whether to ask him, and how he could put it. Bidmead, locking his desk and winding a woollen scarf round his neck, caught his eye, read his thought, and smiled.

'It's all right,' he said. 'I've been permitted to darken the doorstep of Bowerman and Dillen's again, though it was a close-run thing. Ah well. I never expected life to be so hard, did you? Or perhaps you don't find it so. What way do you go home?'

Much the same way as Bidmead, as it happened; so they walked together, and thus inaugurated a regular habit. Winter was drawing on; John and Tom Bidmead walked home under gaslight, and through fogs that had something indescribably raw and savage about them. It was unhealthy weather, and Tom Bidmead seemed to suffer wretchedly as a result of it; but when John commented on his cold in the head, he looked surprised. 'Oh, this?' he said, blowing his nose. 'Why, I don't know as this is a cold, my dear fellow. I've had it since – well, I can't remember when I *didn't* have it.'

Tom Bidmead seemed indeed to be permanently in arrears with his health, just as he was with his rent. For he made no secret of his impoverished circumstances. Many men in his position would have taken refuge in a prickly pride, and moved heaven and earth to keep up appearances, but Tom Bidmead had gone beyond that. 'There aren't any appearances to keep up, in truth,' he told John one evening, in his weak voice that sometimes gave out altogether, and became a sort of articulated sigh. 'If I was to start being solvent, people wouldn't believe me. They'd think it was all a show. The butcher wouldn't trust me at all, if I was to start acting like a man free of debt; whereas as it is, we have quite a good understanding. He knows I'm stony-broke, and that he's not in for any nasty surprises.'

John was able to live, just, within his income, and Tom Bidmead's was no less: why, then, his penury? There was a reason – five reasons, in fact. One of them was a wife, and the other four were children. 'Yes, I married young – too young,' said Tom, who sometimes seemed to take a sort of lugubrious satisfaction in confessing his mistakes and difficulties. 'Not that they ain't charming children, as children go. And Eliza's what you might call a domestic angel. But even domestic angels can't turn halfpence into gold sovereigns, and I'm afraid she despairs of me sometimes, *I* despair of me sometimes. But I say, look here: why don't you come and meet them? We're a patchy sort of crew, but you'll be very welcome. Say tomorrow night, for supper.'

Though John appreciated the invitation, he was rather reluctant to present himself as another mouth to feed at a table which he guessed was scantily supplied. But Tom Bidmead, in his amiable drooping way, insisted; adding, in response to John's hesitations, that if John should care to arrive with a small cabbage in his pocket, or half a loaf, or something of that kind, they would not be in the least offended.

So the next evening after work, instead of parting at the Temple as usual, John continued walking with Tom, and came at last to the Bidmead residence in Soho.

It was a pleasant supper. Tom's lodgings were what he termed 'airy, remarkably airy' – meaning they were at the very top of a tall, crazy, peeling old tenement, and when the wind blew hard the casements shrieked and whistled, and the dingy rugs lifted themselves off the floor as if they were about to imitate Aladdin's magic carpet. But someone – John suspected Mrs Bidmead, a pretty little woman with the bones of a bird – had done their best to make the three boxy rooms comfortable, and John's welcome was a kindly one. There was even a bowl of punch, served in something which John pretended not to realize was the baby's bath; and there was mutton, and very nearly enough gravy, and there was the cauliflower which John had brought himself. And there were the children who, as Tom had said, were very charming; and who in their eagerness for their supper, and wistful looks when it was all gone, and general darned, handed-down, undersized and unhopeful appearance, gave John quite a pang or two.

One of them affected him more deeply than that. This was a boy of not much more than two, who was named Matthew Bidmead, but whose infant tongue, stumbling over the tough syllables, had converted his own name to Murphy Burble, and who was affectionately known as such by the family. Murphy Burble, to John's untrained but not untaught eye, was not a child in full health. Privately John suspected incipient illness, which would require a much ampler diet, and a more sanitary environment, if it was to be nipped in the bud, and allow Murphy Burble to grow into Matthew Bidmead. He said nothing of it, not only because he had no wish to alarm Master Burble's parents, but because he had never so much as mentioned his old medical ambitions to Tom, or to anyone who featured in his new life. He didn't know why: perhaps because to speak of them in that way would be to consign them irrevocably to the past – old, dead dreams, never to be revived.

So he said nothing. But Murphy Burble was very much in his mind at the end of the evening, when he took what he believed to be a not particularly important decision. Mrs Bidmead had gone to put the children to bed; and Tom was smoking a pipe before the meagre fire, and John was pretending to smoke one. (He was very green – literally – when it came to tobacco.) Talk turned again to the Bidmeads' financial circumstances, and Tom confessed, with his usual complete absence of pride, that he had a broker's bill out, on which he paid monthly interest. 'Now,' Tom sighed, 'the broker's threatening to come down on me for the principal – which I simply can't even begin to pay – or else to dispose of the bill to someone who will do the same. If I can give him a name for security, he says he'll relent – he might even advance me some more, if the security's good enough; but otherwise . . .' Tom made an expressive gesture at the scantily furnished room, and added the expressive word: 'Poooooff!'

'But you have a salary,' John said. 'Isn't that security enough?'

'It might be,' Tom said, blinking his blue eyes at the fire, 'if there weren't other claims on my salary. Bless you, John, that ain't my only debt. I've more debts than you can shake a stick at, not that shaking sticks is likely to clear 'em. But those are what you might call continuing debts – they'll muddle along of their own accord, pretty nicely. The bill's a different matter. Without security, my broker can choose to drop down on me as hard as – well, as hard as Mr Bowerman drops down on me, if you like; and once he does that, then . . .' Again Tom could find no more appropriate expression than 'Poooooff!'

John gave up on the pipe, and set it down on the hearth. 'Well, Tom – could I not be your security?'

'Oh, my dear fellow, no. No, really – ' Tom was lackadaisical even in his quite sincere protests – 'really, John, please, I didn't say it for that—'

'I know,' said John. 'But I am saying it for that. Have my name, if a name is all these moneylenders want. It's not much of a name, but I am receiving a salary, and am a single man with no dependants – that should be security enough, shouldn't it?'

Fond as he was of Tom Bidmead, it was of the welfare of Murphy Burble and his siblings that John was thinking when he made his offer; and similarly it was on Murphy Burble's account that he insisted when Tom tried to demur. Perhaps if John's upbringing had been less kindly and more worldly, it would have included a stern injunction never to back a friend's bill; but even in that case, he would probably have ignored it. Tom Bidmead needed more credit, John could get him more credit by putting his name to his bill, and so he did not think twice. In fact he hardly thought any more about it until it was time for him to go, when Tom – who in truth had not taken a great deal of persuading – tried to thank him again. 'Oh, nonsense,' said John. 'It's only what anyone would do. Now, what's the procedure? I have to sign something, I suppose?'

Tom said yes, he had to sign something: seemed about to say something more, but in his chronic state of weariness gave it up; and so it was agreed. The signing of the something took place a few days later, during the half-hour the clerks were allotted for dinner, at the City office of a greasy man who smelt of camphor and brandy, and who looked John up and down afterwards as if he were mentally measuring him up for a suit; and John thought no more of it. Tom Bidmead tried to thank him again that afternoon, however; and again confessed, with a sort of luxurious self-accusation, that the reason for it all was that he had married too young. 'I married for love, you see, and very nice too; but I'm afraid the experience has taught me why "love" means "nothing" in sports and games. Love don't profit, John: I'm afraid it don't so much as break even. I'm the last man in the world to give anybody advice, but if I *was* going to give any, that would be it.'

As it happened, this was rather to the point. For John had become increasingly troubled in his mind about his own romantic position. Letters still passed between him and Catherine – but always and only letters! He had no difficulty in assuring himself that he loved Catherine Fernhill still – the difficulty lay in the question, who *was* this Catherine Fernhill? Some enchanting sprite of his imagination, or a flesh-and-blood person? The gruelling tracts of experience through which he had passed, for all his inward avowals of undying faith, had separated him from the girl he had met and loved in a long-lost time when life had been sunny and simple. A gulf, not exactly of misunderstanding, but of non-understanding, seemed to be opening between them.

The thing that alarmed John was not that his feelings for Catherine were changed, but that Catherine had become unreal to him. This unreality might not have been so prominent were it not for the totally opposite effect on him made by Verity Deene. They met again before Christmas. This time it was he who initiated the meeting. He could not have said why: perhaps she represented some spice or relish in that dry-bread diet that was his present life. His excuse for the rendezvous was to put in her hands a keepsake to be passed on to Catherine, but what he really wanted was talk. Talk was another amenity that was scarce in his drab new world. Tom Bidmead was a friendly fellow, but no sparkler; and sometimes John felt that he was dying of dullness.

They met as before in St James's Park. Cold weather for promenading; but John had retained his indifference to physical circumstances, where his mind was engaged, and Verity Deene was none of your fragile maidens. They kept moving, and were soon in a fine glow; and John felt that the keen fresh air, the crispness of the grass underfoot, the sharp blue shadows incised by the trees, and the crystalline luminousness all around, were peculiarly suited to a talk with Verity.

Whether she felt similarly stultified in her position, and in need of mental resuscitation, he did not know; but she was certainly full of conversation, and seemed to delight in her agility as she skipped from one subject to another, provokingly taking up the extremest positions and enjoying it greatly when he challenged her to justify them. It was her true and unshakable conviction, she said – after a more than usually grim week with the young Spikings – that modern man's whole system of education, indeed his very attitude to children as a species (which they were) was mistaken. Children were simply not fit for adult company, any more than mice were fit to live at the bottom of the sea.

'Really, they should be kept in something like barracks, until they're intelligent and rational enough to mix with us,' she asserted.

'You're talking of the children, not the mice, I take it?'

'A low blow, John: not worthy of you. Barracks, I say, situated in every centre of population; and there the brats, high and low, rich and poor, will be kept in the strictest isolation, until they're of an age to go out into the world without being an offence to human dignity.'

'I see. And are they to be educated in the barracks?'

'Oh, very strictly. They will study philosophy from the age of five. They will be taught to regard sensible adulthood as the one aim of human existence, and childhood as a temporary infirmity, so that they can hardly wait to grow up. They will attend ceremonial burnings of books in which chubby infants are eulogized, and will be invited to deface paintings in which children are coyly and sentimentally portrayed. There will be the severest penalties for saying "I want" in a monotonously insistent voice, and for throwing tantrums, and for meaninglessly kicking the legs of chairs, and for relentlessly staring at people with the forefinger jammed in the mouth.'

'I'd go along with those penalties,' John said. 'But what if some children refuse to improve? What is to be done with them?'

'They shall be shipped out to some empty part of the colonies – say, Australia. And with them we shall send those adults who, in spite of the new regime, obstinately persist in cooing over the creatures, making baby-talk, mistaking wind for smiles, and declaring that they never saw anything so cunning. There they can all be imbeciles together, and we can get on with our blissfully rational lives.'

'Ah, rational. As in fair and impartial, and not to be influenced by personal considerations. Like, for example, condemning the whole infant tribe just because the little Spikings are horrible.'

'My dear John, you must not suspect me of personal animosity to my charges. If I advocate the immediate execution of Honoria, Tancred, Seraphina and Knight, it is not from any personal motives, but because it would be for the public good. Consider, John: Master Knight Spikings, who yesterday attempted to push poor Tripp, his nurse, out of a third-floor window (Tripp hung on gamely, by the by, and resisted his attempts to prise her fingers off the window-ledge) – consider that this boy is going to grow up to be a man, if not prevented. And just think what sort of man!'

'Probably he'll be something in the City, and a great success, if he remains as dull, selfish and unscrupulous as you describe him.'

'Aha, do I detect the odour of an idealistic flame still a-burning?'

'Smouldering, perhaps. A bit damp and sulky. Oh, I don't know, Verity; I can't find any way of putting it without sounding priggish. But I just feel there should be more to life than grubbing away for a salary, with no aspiration except to see the salary go up. Which sounds priggish indeed, as God knows I do want the salary to go up – it barely supports me, let alone opening up any prospect for Catherine and me to marry. That is, if . . .'

She looked at him quickly. 'Yes?'

'Well, if the whole thing is not simply a dream and fancy of blind-eyed youth. I am here, she is there; and between us there stand such obstacles that I wonder if we – well, if we have not begun to take those obstacles for granted, if you follow me.'

Verity was silent a moment, her eyes lowered in thought. John noticed how dark her eyelashes were: the true raven-black, like her hair; you seldom saw that. 'John,' she said, 'understand first, when I say this, that I am not speaking ill of Catherine. Anyone who would seek to change her tenderness of heart, her trusting nature, and her reluctance to give pain, would be doing no service; they would be crushing a flower underfoot. All I am doing is considering the position the two of you are in hypothetically – like a problem in geometry. So. If I were in Catherine's shoes – that is to say, if I were deeply in love with someone who still had his way to make in the world, and who could offer me but an uncertain future, then I would not hesitate. I would sacrifice everything, accept everything, suffer any trials, just

187

as long as . . . that hypothetical person and I could have our life together. I would not care about anything else. I would not care about my family, I would not care about where we lived, I would not care about how we lived. I would walk a hundred miles barefoot, if it brought me to his side; and when we were together, I would labour at his side, with my brain or my hands, so that we might keep the world at bay, and claim our happiness in the midst of its harshness and indifference, and say, "We two have this – we have made this, and we shall keep it, let the world do what it will." That . . . that is what I would do.'

John studied her. 'Love in a cottage, eh?'

'Yes, if you like,' she said, her eyes on the distance. 'Love in a cottage.'

John's surprise was great, at hearing this from Verity Deene: in fact he felt within him a strange and disturbing overthrow of all sorts of fixed ideas and modes of feeling. It was this perplexity, perhaps, that made him revert to their old flippant fencing, and say, 'Well, this is a turn-up; I didn't think you very interested in love anywhere, let alone in a cottage.'

He heard at once the jarring note of this remark, which would once have been staple fare between them; but before he could apologize, Verity turned on him sharply. 'Well, you know nothing of me, anyhow,' she said, looking quietly ferocious. 'You don't know me at all, John, and don't presume that you do. All I am to you is Catherine Fernhill's former companion, who used to be inconvenient, and is now convenient. Well? Isn't it so?'

He saw that she was hurt, badly hurt; and there were more strange shiftings and overturnings in his heart as he saw it. He tried to speak, but it was as if whatever he had to say could only be expressed in a foreign language, and he could not master it.

'An eloquent silence,' said Verity, turning away from him.

'No – Verity, please. Don't – don't take it like that. It sounds strange, no doubt, for me to say how much I enjoy your company, when you and I used to argue so much—'

'As we are doing now,' said Verity curtly. 'Yes, it does sound strange.'

'But it's true – that's all I can say,' said John unhappily. 'But I can't understand . . . I mean, it's not as if I have any reason to suppose that you care for my opinion of you, one way or the other. And as for your opinion of me, I've never thought that was very high either – in fact I was sure of it.'

'There you go again,' she said, 'assuming that you know all about me, and what I think and feel.'

'Damn it, I'm not. All I can go on is the evidence of my eyes and ears, and that's pretty conclusive – why, you're looking daggers at me right now, for goodness' sake. What else am I to suppose?'

'You may suppose what you like,' said she coolly.

'There you are, you see.' He made an impatient gesture. 'If we fall to this sort of backbiting, it hardly matters what I say anyhow.'

'You're right – ' cooler still – 'of course, it hardly matters.'

He felt his shoulders slump; and then almost involuntarily he said: 'Except that it does matter. Because I would hate to think I'd hurt you. That's all.'

'Dear me, John,' she said in a brittle tone, 'you overestimate your power over my feelings, if you think that.'

'Good God, you're an impossible woman,' he said uncontrollably. 'You even turn an apology into a weapon.'

'What apology? I didn't hear one.'

'Ah, so you *are* hurt, and you *do* think an apology called for.'

She looked more daggers at him, but there was something about her lips that was almost a suppressed smile. There was a hair's-breadth moment, indeed, when they might both have burst out laughing; but something turned it the other way. They

188

both stood awkwardly looking down at different spots on the frosted grass, and then Verity said, 'I'm getting chilled. I'd better go. I'll pass on your letter to Catherine. Goodbye.' And then she was walking smartly away from him.

He didn't know what to think; he didn't know what to feel. That he should be under the necessity of thinking or feeling anything at all about Verity Deene was in itself a measure of the change and confusion within him. But nothing was clear. In place of certainties there were only questions. For several days after that curious meeting he found he was continually interrogating himself about where he stood – in relation to his past, in relation to his future, in relation to Catherine, in relation to Verity, in relation to his old hopes and dreams, in relation to his empty new life, and in relation to his own self, which seemed the most elusive of all. And it was in this abstracted and dissatisfied mood that he got down from his stool one morning in response to a summons from the senior clerk, and came face to face with Mr Marcus Goodway.

Their eyes met, and John felt the blood drain from his face and then rise again, stingingly; but in Mr Goodway's eyes, though he recognized John, there was only that sparkle of careless amusement, and then he turned away. In his recent questioning mood John had been thinking much of the past, which he had formerly shunned as too unbearable; and now it came boiling up inside him, with all its tragedy and injustice, and with this man at its cankered centre.

'Twopenny!'

'Sir?' The blood had been singing in his ears, and he had not heard what the senior clerk said to him.

'Wake up, man. Show Mr Goodway to the private parlour. Mr Bowerman will be with you directly, sir. Will you take some refreshment while you're waiting?'

'If it's not too much trouble,' Mr Goodway said, with the merest flicker of his eyes towards John.

'Well, Twopenny? Don't just stand there, man!'

John jerked his frozen limbs into movement. He managed to say, 'This way, sir,' though he feared he might choke on it; and conducted Mr Goodway to the private room upstairs. Mr Goodway sat down, very much at home, in the great leather armchair that was provided, and picked up the newspaper.

'Thank you, John,' he said, turning the pages.

Just the same! The same rich voice, and urbane manner, and strong crop of iron-grey hair; and the same subtle, knowing air, as if he hardly needed even to look at John to understand what he was thinking. Just the same – and here!

John went down again, and found Tom Bidmead bringing up a bottle of the wine that was kept in a locked cellar below the counting-house. 'All right, Bidmead, set it down there,' said the senior clerk, fussing and testy. 'And the glasses, man! Good heavens above!' The senior clerk drew the cork and set out the tray with anguished nicety. 'There . . . that should do. Now, Twopenny, look smart. Very important client, Mr Goodway. Any amount of business. Well, what are you waiting for?'

John blinked. He realized that he was being told to wait on Mr Goodway. The turbulent memories swelled again, and he saw himself being pulled back by the Soldier from the threshold of the Hanged Man's House.

'I would rather someone else did it, sir,' he said.

'What?' The senior clerk reddened. 'You must be mad, Twopenny. Take this tray up at once, or Mr Bowerman will hear of it. Good heavens above!'

John saw Tom Bidmead looking at him with hangdog apprehension; and the other clerks, though bent over their desks, had suspended their pens. John hesitated a moment longer, then picked up the tray.

Mr Goodway was still calmly reading the newspaper: he did not look up when John came in. John set down the tray on a little table next to the armchair, bowed, and retreated to the door.

'Coolish in here, John,' Mr Goodway said, turning a page. 'Put a little more coal on the fire, would you?'

John went forward, crouched down at the hearth, and made up the fire. He found that his hands were shaking, and he made a fearful clatter with the fire-irons; and though from the fire he could only see the back of Mr Goodway's head, he sensed ironical amusement radiating from that seamless gentleman.

'Good fellow,' said Mr Goodway when John had finished, and was on his way to the door again. 'Oh, pour me a glass of this, if you please.' The tray was about six inches from Mr Goodway's elbow.

John went forward again. He took great care, and succeeded in pouring out a glass of the wine without spilling a drop; and this small victory heartened him. Now if he could keep his self-command until—

'Ah, thank you.' Mr Goodway looked up at him for the first time. 'Set it down there, that's a good fellow. Well, well, strange meetings, John, strange meetings! So you've come to try your luck in London. I have signally failed to observe the Thames on fire, but I suppose it's early days yet. So how do you get on at Bowerman's?'

'Very well.'

'I should think so too. An excellent firm: I do a good deal of business with them. You should count yourself lucky, my friend, to have fallen into a berth like this. Work hard, John, and respect your superiors, and you may live down your father's bad name in time.'

'You insult me,' said John whitely, trying to keep his hands still, 'when I am at a disadvantage, and cannot answer you back.'

'Do I?' Mr Goodway was very twinkling, very avuncular. 'And if I do, what does that make me?'

'No gentleman,' said John.

Marcus Goodway did not like that; and John knew it.

'I must say, young John,' Mr Goodway said, looking down at the newspaper, 'you're very priggish, for the son of a sot and a coward.'

John picked up the wine-glass, and threw it in Mr Goodway's face.

Even as his head spun with wild rage, and even as the consequences of what he had done gathered like swift shadows on the edges of his consciousness, John knew a great exultation: for watching Goodway jump to his feet with an oath and wipe frantically at the stains on his immaculate linen he thought, *This is what he hates! This is what he hates most of all, to lose control of events, to struggle and sweat and look foolish like the rest of us! I have him! He has hated me from the moment I saved him on the marshes, because that was when he showed himself vulnerable, and needed other people instead of using them!*

And then the door opened, and Mr Bowerman came fawning in.

'Mr Goodway, a thousand apologies for keeping you. I was—' Mr Bowerman stopped in amazement. 'Good Lord, whatever has happened?'

'Your clerk,' said Goodway, who had recovered his composure, 'your clerk apparently took a dislike to my face, Mr Bowerman, and thought it would be improved by the addition of a glass of wine.'

Mr Bowerman's hawk-like eyes narrowed, and his hawk-like shoulders came up, as if he were readying himself to swoop and tear. 'Twopenny! Have you entirely taken leave of your senses?'

'I'm afraid we cannot put any such charitable construction as insanity on Mr Twopennny's behaviour,' said Mr Goodway, looking at John with a dark smile. 'It is really no more than I expected. I regret to say that I have had experience of this boy's family before, Mr Bowerman – to my cost. They are not a savoury set. His father was a bad debtor, who ended his life by his own hand rather than face up to his recklessly incurred obligations; and, speaking candidly, I should not be

190

inclined to place any more trust in his son's probity. But of course that is up to you.' Mr Goodway dabbed at his face with a handkerchief. 'You will not think it unreasonable in me to add that his presence in this office strongly disinclines me to bring my business here.'

Mr Bowerman stared from Goodway to John with his mouth open; then shut it with a snap like a cruel beak, and pounced. 'Twopenny! Leave this room at once, and empty your desk, sir! You have imposed upon this firm shamefully, and you will leave it at once! At once, d'you hear? Your employment here is terminated! Ask Mr Dillen to settle up your wages, and get out!'

CHAPTER NINE

John Is Admitted to an Exclusive Club

A storm of rain and wind was brewing up in the wintry night as John returned home by Lincoln's Inn Fields. The dried-up trees and shrubs that adorned that legalistic spot were all quite still at first; but then they were visited, one after another, by violent eddies of wind, and suffered so dreadfully from its wild tossing and scourging that the next one along seemed to tremble in anticipation of its turn. Then the wind would drop again, and in its place the rain would come coldly sluicing down, in such drenching volumes that it might have been emptied out of pails and tubs in the sky; and then the wind would snatch it away again, and work itself up into a passion, so that it seemed as if a giant something was leaning its colossal shoulder against the night, and trying to batter it down.

John pulled down his hat and pulled up his collar, and struggled on; half blind, and driven back a step for every two by the ruffian wind, so that he hardly seemed to be nearing his destination at all.

'This,' he said to himself, wiping water from his eyebrows, 'is serious. You are in trouble, my friend, serious trouble.'

He had been scouring the Inns of Court in the hope of finding a position. No go. There were clerks wanted here and there, but in many cases it was articled clerks that were required – legal apprentices, who had to pay a premium; and where the vacancy was for a mere copying-clerk, references were mandatory. John had no references.

'You might have crawled, you know,' Tom Bidmead had said, coming to see him the day after his sacking. 'Far be it from me to offer advice, because it wouldn't be worth taking anyway. But I just wondered – didn't it occur to you to try crawling?'

'No,' said John. 'It didn't.'

'Ah well. That's pride, you see. I haven't got any pride, myself; not a bit of it. Not having any pride, I would have crawled, and begged, and so on. I'd probably even have gone so far as to go on bended knee to Mr Bowerman and clasp his ankles; it wouldn't surprise me a bit if I did something like that. Ah well. I'm very sorry, old fellow, and I wish I could help you.'

Tom was right enough about John's pride, which would not have allowed him to clasp anybody's ankles. But pride, and crawling, and all the rest of it, were really beside the point. John knew that Mr Bowerman would not have had him back on any account – not at the risk of Mr Marcus Goodway's taking his business elsewhere.

That John had allowed Goodway to provoke him into his disastrous act was somehow beside the point too. If the clock could be turned back, John would do it again: that was simply the way things were between him and Marcus Goodway, such was his almost fatalistic acceptance of the baleful part played in his life by that man. Which was not to say that John would not hate, and oppose, and wish ill to him till the end of his days – no doubt of that. But that too was rather beside the point. There was only one point now, and it was a pretty sharp one. He had been without work for nearly a month, and his money, even augmented by trips to the pawnbroker, was almost completely gone; and without a reference, without family or connections, without any sort of special aptitude or recommendation, he could not find employment.

'You are in trouble,' he repeated, bending his head into the yammering wind, 'serious trouble.'

At least he had a lodging to return to, and very grateful he felt when he battered his way through the storm at last to the little green door in Fetter Lane. His gratitude was tempered by guilt, however; because he had not paid the rent for three weeks, and he went through tortures every time he came home and crept past the door to Miss Thimblebee's apartments.

Well: this time he would be spared that torture. Because Miss Thimblebee was standing outside her door on the first landing, and looking down at him with a candle in her hand, like an avenging angel fashioned by a toymaker.

'Mr Twopenny,' she said, 'I fear I must make a representation to you which is very painful to my feelings.'

John halted, and took off his hat.

'Mr Twopenny, you are in arrears with the rent.'

'Miss Thimblebee, I know it,' said John, unconsciously falling into her formal manner of speech.

'Mr Twopenny, I am obliged, as a single woman under the necessity of transacting such painful business herself, to ask you why.'

'Miss Thimblebee,' said John, dismally aware of his dripping and bedraggled appearance, in contrast with Miss Thimblebee's varnished correctness, 'I have lost my position.'

'Mr Twopenny, may I ask how so?'

John hesitated. 'I was required to wait on a man who had injured my family, and I refused,' he said, 'and so I was dismissed.'

Miss Thimblebee had surely heard any number of grand excuses from impecunious lodgers; but something about John's utter dejection as he spoke must have convinced her that here, for once, was a true one.

'Well,' she said, 'though I regret the consequences, I think the reason for your dismissal does you honour. I have always adhered to the strictest moral principles myself, even at the sacrifice of worldly advancement.' She frowned. 'Mr Twopenny, I perceive you are wet and cold. A good fire is burning in my apartments, and I suggest that you step in and warm yourself before proceeding to your abode.'

A kind heart beat beneath the steely brooch pinned to Miss Thimblebee's stiff-boned bodice; though it did not moderate her extreme correctness, which prompted her to instruct John, as he followed her into the gilded sitting-room, to leave the door standing open. 'For I couldn't consent to be behind a closed door with a single gentleman,' she said, 'and I mean no reflection on you, Mr Twopenny, who have always conducted yourself with the utmost delicacy: I simply couldn't allow it, out of regard for my reputation.'

John was glad indeed to stand before Miss Thimblebee's fire and feel the life returning to his chilled extremities, for he had not a scrap of coal upstairs. Miss Thimblebee, taking a seat at a proper distance from him, did a very good job of ignoring the clouds of steam rising from his trousers, and after saying, 'Mr Twopenny, my domestic will shortly bring my tea-tray; and though I am very far from making a habit of entertaining my single gentlemen, I would esteem it as a favour, under the special circumstances, if you would join me in a cup,' maintained a dignified silence until the arrival of the tea. This she poured with her own hands, and it too was very welcome to John, though the cups were so dainty they might have come from a doll's tea-set, and John could have drained five of them without winking an eye.

193

'Mr Twopenny,' Miss Thimblebee resumed, 'the question of the rent remains outstanding.'

'I know it, Miss Thimblebee, and believe me I am in great anxiety about it. As soon as I can secure another position, it shall be paid; but in the meantime, I am quite without means.'

'No – ahem, you must excuse the familiarity of the question – no family, Mr Twopenny?'

'No family.'

'Dear me . . . I am no stranger, Mr Twopenny, to the difficulties of being alone in the world. My surviving parent expired when I was at a tender age, and only a limited legacy enabled me to begin as a friseuse, and maintain my independence thus. I may add in confidence that offers of matrimonial alliance have not been lacking in my life, and there was one in particular, that I had to give the most serious consideration, before regretfully declining.' Perhaps it was the stimulation of the tea, but the two round red spots on Miss Thimblebee's cheeks seemed to grow a little redder at this. 'There was a dependent relative in the case, Mr Twopenny, with a wooden leg; and though a wooden leg in itself could hardly be objected to by any feeling person, there were the strongest objections to the dependent relative who was attached to it, in that he was inclined, when under the influence of spirits, to pass remarks about my profession, and my clients, very disobliging and disrespectful in tone. You know, Mr Twopenny, the value my clients place on my confidence; and this being so, I had no choice but to decline the proposal, as the dependent relative with the wooden leg came, as it were, with the matrimonial bargain. The confidence of my clients means a great deal to me, and I could not expose it to indignities.'

Miss Thimblebee looking, quite feelingly, to John for corroboration, he said, 'I quite see that, Miss Thimblebee. No other course was open to you.'

'No other course was open to me.' Miss Thimblebee folded her pink hands in her lap, and drew herself up straighter than ever. 'Mr Twopenny, it would not be agreeable to my feelings to part with any of my single gentlemen on those terms which I can only delineate by the unpleasant word "eviction". Therefore, I shall postpone consideration of the rent until such time as your affairs are on a firmer footing. Let me just add that there are several business gentlemen among my clients; and if I were to mention to them that you are looking for a position, in case of their knowing of such, I hope you would not take it amiss.'

'I would take it as a kindness, Miss Thimblebee,' said John warmly, 'and not the first you have done me.' In his relief and gratitude, he was ready to seize her neat little hand and kiss it, and had actually started forward to do so; but Miss Thimblebee's propriety rose up full-armed, and she discouraged him with a firm, 'Mr Twopenny, really, I couldn't allow it, not on any account!' And so he took his leave more formally, and went up to his room which, being denuded of such of his possessions as the pawnbroker would lend money on, was more cheerless than ever.

The gleam of hope offered by Miss Thimblebee's leniency, however, was only that – a gleam, amongst a skyful of dark clouds. He had run up bills with several tradesmen, and they were unlikely to be so understanding. There was no one in London to whom he could apply for help, and no one in Norfolk to whom he would apply – certainly not his uncle, and certainly not Catherine. Since his dismissal he had written her once, directing the letter by Montagu Place – though he had eschewed any face-to-face meeting with his go-between, not knowing how he stood with her after that last strange encounter – and had had a reply back. But he had not mentioned that he was out of a job; and this only seemed to amplify a feeling that he was living a lie in regard to Catherine. Her letter had been full of cheerful news about her doings, and of plans that the admiral was making to rent a house in

194

London, and take her up to town for the season; and the discordance between this and the desperate straits he was in threw into bold relief what John had been trying to hide from himself – that there was scarcely any common ground of understanding between him and Catherine now, and that their love was a thing of fairy-tale and gingerbread. If he would not admit to himself the beginnings of a slow, sure transformation in his feelings, he could not at least deny these thoughts.

He sat down that very night to try and pen a letter to her; but soon gave it up. If he could not tell her the truth about his situation, how much truth was there in their relation altogether? – this was the question that remained at the back of his mind when he set out the next day in search of employment once more.

Again, no good. The only thing that offered itself was a post as private tutor to a family at Hammersmith. John took the long walk out to Hammersmith, and presented himself as a candidate. He was kept waiting in a tiny ante-room for an hour and a half, but the interview lasted less than two minutes. A requirement of the post, it seemed, was a degree in Divinity; and when John indignantly protested that this was not specified in the advertisement, he was reproved for his insolence, and shown the door.

Wearily, wearily indeed did John make his long way back to Fetter Lane, cold and hungry, and with no prospect of being any less cold and hungry when he got home. Mounting the stairs, he found Miss Thimblebee in conversation on the first landing with a man whom he at first took to be one of her clients. Accordingly he prepared himself to pass by with a tactful inattention to whatever extraordinary creation the man sported on his head: but no. The man had a full head of his own hair, atop of a cadaverous face, and the man was advancing on John, and taking hold of him by the buttonhole.

'You're the one, are you?' he said. 'You're the Twopenny one?'

'Oh, Mr Twopenny, Mr Twopenny,' cried Miss Thimblebee, with more distress than indignation, 'I regret this circumstance extremely!'

Something was being flourished before John's face, and after a stunned moment he recognized it as the broker's bill he had endorsed for Tom Bidmead. Still his mind did not grasp what was happening; and when the cadaverous man informed him that he was a sheriff's officer, he looked blank.

'Why, look here,' said the man with some impatience, 'you put your name to this here bill, didn't you?'

'Yes,' said John, 'yes I did – but the loan was to Tom Bidmead . . .'

'Don't tell me *that*,' the man said with a snort. 'I don't need telling that, I should hope. We know *him* pretty well.'

'Then why don't you go to him?'

'We've been. He's crashed – that's about the size of it. Crashed, with more debts than you can count. Can't pay the interest, let alone the principal, and it's the principal that's wanted; and that's why he's in the King's Bench. Now, your name's on this here bill, as security; and what's more, there's other bills of yours on Queer Street – the court says so. Now, you've got to pay up – that's about the size of it. So, what's your answer?'

John stared at the bill in the cadaverous man's hand, and stared at the cadaverous man's face, and stared at Miss Thimblebee, who repeated in a faint voice, 'Oh, Mr Twopenny, Mr Twopenny . . .!' With a sensation which reminded him strangely of being a schoolboy facing the headmaster, he said, 'I – I can't pay. I simply can't—'

'Never mind simply,' said the man. 'Simply's nothing to do with it. Either you can pay, or you can't. Or else you give us a name as security. Come! What's it to be?'

Still John stared at the bill, and at his name on it, as if someone else had written it there. But he knew that no one had: he had written it. And he knew, with

195

dreadful certainty, that various financial chickens which he had blithely set free were coming home to roost, with a vengeance. His silence seemed to confirm the cadaverous man in a low opinion of him; for, with a snort, he tucked the bill away in his breast pocket, and drew out another paper.

'Do you know what this is? It's a writ, that's what it is. And it's got your name on it as well; and as you like things simply, I'll tell you I'm putting this here writ into execution simply, and I'm simply arresting you for debt. There. How do you like *that*?'

John could hardly, in the nature of things, be expected to like it very much at all; but he was still in such a stunned condition that he hardly registered any distinct emotion. It was only when the officer turned to Miss Thimblcbcc with quite an altered expression, as if he saw in that lady a possibility of compounding for the debt, or of obtaining another 'name' for the bill, that John roused himself. If this debt was to be his downfall, he wanted no one else pulled down with him. 'No,' he said, 'I cannot pay, and I have no security. I'll have to go with you. Miss Thimblebee, I'm more sorry than I can say. I promise you that whenever I am in a position to pay you what I owe you, I shall do it; though I can't repay you for the kindness you've shown me.'

Miss Thimblebee, however, could only press her fingers to the round spots on her cheeks, and murmur 'Mr Twopenny, Mr Twopenny . . .!' over again; which caused the cadaverous man to declare gruffly that it would be all right if it was a matter of two pennies, but it wasn't, and that was about the size of it.

The packing of such movables as John still possessed did not take long; and presently he was being put into a hackney-coach by the cadaverous man, who seemed to unbend a little, now that he saw that John was not going to give him any trouble. 'Bless you, I don't mean to be disagreeable,' he said, taking out a pocket-handkerchief with a pork-pie wrapped up in it, and civilly offering John a piece. 'Only it's my job, you see. If I was to start feeling sorry for people, in my line of work, I should soon be in trouble. Why, you wouldn't expect a chimney-sweep to be all white like a swan, I hope? Well then. No more would you expect a man in my position to be agreeable. It ain't in the nature of things.'

John nodded listlessly, scarcely attending. In fact he scarcely felt himself to be in this hackney-coach in the middle of London at all: in his mind he was back in Saltmarsh, at a Christmas party, and Mr Flowers was giving him some advice about living within his income, and he was cheerfully accepting it, in the serenest confidence that it would never be needed. What a contrast between that past and this present! How could one have ever led to the other? How had it happened? In this distracted state of mind John allowed himself to be led like a tired child into the Inns of Court, and into a dirty office with various grey-faced men of various ages, all alike in avoiding each other's eye with a certain pained fastidiousness; and then he was being taken out again, with a dim idea of having given his name, and of having heard the names of his creditors, mixed in with the knell-like words 'Hereby Committed', all in such a very hasty and bewildering manner that he was almost glad to find himself still in the charge of the cadaverous man, who had at least a certain familiarity amidst all this dreamlike confusion.

In a hackney-coach again, and John wondering, with a hysterical sort of humour, who was to pay the fare, and whether the coachman would be added to his creditors; and then they were crossing Blackfriars Bridge, and then the coach was turning in a whirlpool of traffic at the Obelisk, and affording John kaleidoscopic glimpses of drab attorneys' offices, and second-hand shops, and valuers' offices, all proclaiming 'Debt' and 'Debtors' as plainly as if the words had been writ large on their signboards; and then the coach had stopped, and they were getting out, and the bleakly ornate facade of the King's Bench debtors' prison was before them.

A turnkey opened the barred gate, and he and the cadaverous man gave each other a nod, as if they knew each other so well that words were unnecessary; and John was conducted into a lodge, where the cadaverous man went into consultation with another turnkey, and handed over some papers, while John stared blankly up at a high window, where there was a view of iron spikes and sky. Then the cadaverous man brushed his hands together, as if he were washing them of John, and left him there.

John was in such a state of childlike helplessness by now that the loss of this companion quite afflicted him, and he could only look at the head turnkey with a sort of mute wonder and appeal. But the turnkey seemed quite accustomed to such behaviour on the part of his guests in this establishment. He pointed to John's bag, asked him if that was all, nodded when John said yes, and then beckoned John to follow him, unlocking another iron gate on the inner side of the lodge.

'You'll have to share a room for tonight,' he said. 'You ain't partick'ler about that, I suppose?'

John, hardly knowing what he was saying, said no, he wasn't particular; at which the turnkey grunted, and said he should think not. So he was led through the inner gate, and past a noisy yard where some prisoners were playing at skittles, and others were watching and laying bets, and still others were smoking and lounging, and turned their heads to look at John with a dreary hope of novelty; whilst several children played their own games in the dust of the yard, with as cheerful an absorption as if no shadow of iron spikes fell across their playground.

Opening another gate, the turnkey led John along a cold, brick-floored gallery with rooms leading off at each side, some with the doors standing open to reveal frowsy interiors, where pathetic tokens of domesticity – bird-cages, looking-glasses, teapots – contended with the grimness; and then up a creaking stairway, dimly illuminated by the gas that had just been lit in the winter evening, and along another gallery where someone could be heard singing 'Away with Melancholy' to the accompaniment of a wheezy flute.

'Harmonic Evening,' the turnkey commented in reference to this, and then pushed open a door to a room containing a cold fireplace, two iron beds, a spittoon, and nothing else. 'Well, now, not so bad as I thought. I reckon you'll shake down here all right . . . Rose!' The turnkey approached one of the beds, where a huddled shape was discernible under a pile of rugs and blankets, and gave the shape a poke with his bunch of keys. 'Rose! Wake up, will you? There's a new one here needs a bed for tonight, so I'm putting him in with you.'

John experienced a moment of alarm at the thought that he was to share a room with a woman; but Rose turned out to be a surname rather than a Christian name, and the man it belonged to a sharp-nosed wrinkled little creature with his hair all greased down upon his head, who leapt out of the bed fully dressed.

'Well, Rose, this one's green,' said the turnkey, as he left them, 'but you'll show him how things go along here, I should think – you've been here long enough.'

'True, my dear sir, true!' said Mr Rose with a mincing laugh. 'Randal Rose at your service,' he added to John, shaking his hand. 'Oh dearie me, you look quite done up, my friend. Taken, as it were, by surprise?'

'Very much by surprise,' said John, sitting down on the other bed, and burying his head in his hands.

'Oh dearie me! There's something to be said, after all, for going into a slow decline as far as financial matters are concerned. It prepares one, as it were,' said Mr Rose, sitting on the other bed and crossing his legs demurely. 'You've eaten, my dear sir?'

John shook his head. 'I don't believe I could.'

'Oh, but you must eat, you know! I was just going to send out for some supper myself. The strangers' bell won't ring for another hour yet – that's when they lock the gates, sir, and when all the visitors have to be out of the prison – and there are

197

always plenty of boys going in and out, who'll purchase your viands. Forgive the familiarity, sir, on so short an acquaintance, but – do you have any money? A curious question it may seem in this place,' Mr Rose added, wriggling himself about with a tittering laugh, 'but we must have money, you know – even in the King's Bench!'

John emptied his pockets on to the bed. There was a solitary sixpence, and a few coppers. 'Not so bad,' said Mr Rose, 'not so bad at all. If I add my – let's see, here's sixpence more – quite enough for a feast. Are you partial to saveloy, my dear sir? I think you'll find saveloy, with hot roll, to be quite reviving to the appetite.'

John, so low in spirits as to care very little one way or the other, submitted to Mr Rose's direction. A boy was sent to fetch the supper, which Mr Rose set out with great delicacy on a sheet of newspaper; and then, having borrowed a glass and a tea-cup without a handle from an adjoining room, he produced a bottle from a hiding-place under his bed.

'Making do,' Mr Rose said, pouring out, 'making do, is what we're very good at here, my dear sir. Now, if you can make do without lemon-peel and sugar, I think you'll find this gin quite palatable.'

John roused himself sufficiently to thank Mr Rose for his kindness, and forced himself to eat. Little Mr Rose, meanwhile, gnawed his way with great satisfaction through his portion of the repast, and drank gin very genteelly, if liberally, from the tea-cup; and when, as often happened, some fellow-prisoners stopped at the open door to look in, he did the honours, remarking, 'Mr Twopenny – new in, you know – allow me to introduce,' with great suavity.

When the supper was gone, and the strangers' bell had rung, Mr Rose bundled himself up again in his rugs and blankets against the growing cold, and pouring himself the last of the gin, inquired, 'So, my dear sir, and when do you expect to be released?'

John, who had been staring in abstraction at the spikes outside the window, stirred and said with a sigh, 'Lord knows!'

'But you have family?' said Mr Rose.

John shook his head.

'Oh dearie me . . . You have friends who, as it were, would compound for your release . . .? Connections outside the walls, who are active on your behalf . . .? Dearie me!' – as John shook his head again. 'Dearie me, quite a perplexing difficulty indeed!'

John asked whether Mr Rose was in a similar case?

'You might say so,' said Mr Rose. 'Though I must confess, my dear sir, that I am no stranger to incarceration of various kinds, and it's quite become second nature to me. I have had what you might call a chequered career, my dear sir; and to be frank, I have had shadier passages than this. But come! I can propose a way out of your difficulty. If you can think of a court, or a public body, or a charitable organization, to whom an application might avail you, name it, and I will write a testimonial for you.'

John's face must have shown his puzzlement, for Mr Rose chuckled. 'I know what you're thinking,' he went on, 'you're thinking, what use is a testimonial from an insolvent debtor in no better case than yourself? None at all, my dear sir. You are right. But I shall let you into a secret. I am a master of disguise – epistolary disguise, my dear sir. Before an unfortunate combination of circumstances brought me here, I got my living as a screever, Mr Twopenny. What do you think of that?'

'I'm afraid I don't know what a screever is.'

'Well, you *are* a new one! A screever, my dear sir, composes, writes, and retails testimonials, credentials, certificates, letters of recommendation, and other such documents as may be required by people who can't get them.'

'Oh! You mean, like a forger?'

Mr Rose pursed his lips. 'I prefer to think of the occupation in more exalted terms than that, my dear sir. Forgery is mere base counterfeiting, whereas there is an artistic dimension to the screever's work which elevates it above the crudely fraudulent. For example: I once made acquaintance with three gentlemen who had taken to begging as a profession – many such, my dear sir! We must all live! – and who had hit upon the notion of presenting themselves as distressed sailors. Nautical slops were easily acquired from the waterside dealers in Ratcliff; but for the testimonials that would make the performance, as it were, complete and convincing, they came to me. The document I created was a letter from the captain of the supposed sailors' supposed ship – I think I named her the *Invincible* – written in a strong hearts-of-oak hand, witnessed by a Justice of the peace, and giving particulars of the shipwreck in which the three tars had been involved, with latitude, longitude and all the rest, and enjoining private citizens to subscribe to the unfortunate fellows' relief, and parish officers to grant them passage, as they made their way back to their home port. Now this was a document requiring a good deal of skill and invention, you'll agree, sir, besides mere penmanship, and well worth the three-and-sixpence I charged them for it. For a simple letter of recommendation, signed with a gammy monicker – a false name, sir – I would charge only ninepence. Ah me! It was an interesting line of work. So what do you say, my dear sir? Can I be of use to you?'

John thanked him for the thought, but could think of no one off-hand whose aid could be solicited for him by a testimonial either authentic or forged; and he was besides too weary now to address himself to the question. So he covered himself up as best he could in the grubby bed, and spent his first night in the King's Bench prison, without the faintest idea of what the morrow would bring.

It brought a merciless daylight filtered through bars, a melancholy racket of slop-pails and crying children, and a familiar face. John woke to find Tom Bidmead looking in at him.

'They said there was a new chap come in, called Twopenny,' Tom said, 'and as it isn't a common name, I thought it must be you. My dear fellow! I'm rather afraid it's me who involved you in this. All I can say is, I didn't think my affairs would come to such a resounding crash, and never dreamt it would come to this for you; and that as soon as any means come my way, I shall act to secure your release before my own.'

Kindly said, and kindly meant, no doubt; but in such a sighing, whimsical, resigned, Tom-Bidmead way that John at once realized that his hopes of aid from this quarter were slim indeed. However, it was good to see a friendly face; and as Mr Rose was still sleeping off the gin, John agreed to go and breakfast with Tom Bidmead, who had accommodation on the ground floor. 'It's much more convenient for the yard, and for visitors,' Tom said, 'and I think we're pretty nicely situated, all in all.' He said this with as much complacency as if he had taken rooms in an hotel, a circumstance which discouraged John even more; for though he soon learnt that Tom had only been in here a couple of weeks, he seemed to have become depressingly adapted to it in that space of time.

'We must see about getting you a room of your own, old fellow,' Tom said. 'Rose is all right, but he's been a felon in his time, you know; and we who've been imprisoned for debt don't generally care to mix with those who've been in other sorts of prisons. Principle of the thing, you know. Well, here we are.'

Tom had secured two rooms on the ground floor; for John found to his surprise, and then to his unsurprise, that Tom's family had come with him into the King's Bench. Rather than keep them in lodgings outside, he said, it had seemed better for them all to be together; and in the brave smile which Mrs Bidmead gave John on his entering, there was a silent plea for him to agree, and not to show by the slightest look that he suspected Tom of thinking more of his own comfort than his family's in bringing them to join him.

Tom, at any rate, declared that it was just like old times. Over breakfast he took a doleful sort of satisfaction in going over John's affairs, and going over his own affairs, and finding them both to be quite hopeless; John meanwhile sparing a thought from his own troubles to consider those of the Bidmead children, in particular the infant who styled himself Murphy Burble. None of them was likely to thrive in this confined spot where epidemic diseases must be rife, and Murphy least of all; and when Tom, finishing his breakfast, cheerfully invited him to a game of quoits in the yard, John had a job to disguise his impatience, and made an excuse that he had letters to write. Not at all put out, Tom suggested that they meet later. 'We have a little social club in the prison – Tuesday evenings, conversation and cards, refreshments as available. You'll find the club-room on the third floor at the end of the gallery. I'll be glad to sponsor you for membership, old chap – glad to.'

John thanked him, as he could see nothing else to say; and went to take a turn about the yard, and breathe such fresh air as was to be had in that stony spot. He had walked to and fro a few times, looking up at the strings of ragged washing hanging from the galleries above, and wondering how long it would take before he too slipped into the degraded prison way of thinking, when he found that an old lady, neatly dressed, had stolen over to him, and placed a coin in his hand before he knew what had happened. In a moment she had slipped away again; but he now saw that there were several such – not only relatives visiting inmates of the prison, but various charitable ladies and gentlemen who busied themselves in the temporary relief of debtors. He saw also that a number of inmates had turned out in the yard, and were hanging about in a drooping, self-conscious way, in the hope of receiving these impromptu donations. John's first reaction was a tremendous burst of shame, which sent the blood rushing to his cheeks; and he looked about him for the old lady, so that he might give back the coin, which was a florin. But she had made herself scarce; and after a moment he put the coin in his pocket. He felt miserable and sick, but he had to acknowledge that a debtor's prison was hardly the place for pride. 'All very well for you to be disapproving of Tom Bidmead,' he told himself, 'but in what way are you any better?' Still, his sense of humiliation would not leave him, especially when he thought of Catherine and all his fine words to her before he left Norfolk; but he might as well face the fact that he was going to have to live on charitable bounty, if he was going to live at all. The thought of Catherine reminded him that no one knew where he was; so he purchased a sheet of notepaper and a pencil from the basket of a little street-seller who had come into the prison and, returning to the room where Mr Rose still snored under his heap of rugs, wrote a letter to Miss Thimblebee, giving particulars of what had happened to him and where he was, and asking that his correspondence be forwarded care of the King's Bench prison, the Borough.

'Care of the King's Bench prison, the Borough!' He seemed to recognize already the authentic debtors'-prison note of deluded and shabby pomposity in those words, and his heart sank. He gave a boy who was going out of the prison threepence to take the letter to Fetter Lane, and as he watched the boy go, waved through the gate by the turnkey and trotting off to the outside world as he could not, his heart sank lower. And when, that evening, he was admitted to the club by Tom Bidmead, and joined in some rowdy songs and applauded some incoherent speeches in a room full of smoke and torn playing-cards, his heart sank so low that he felt it was somewhere in the coal-cellars of the King's Bench prison, and would never rise out of their grimy darkness again.

CHAPTER TEN

Unaccountable Behaviour of a Bluestocking

Verity was vainly trying to establish some common ground between arithmetic and the turgid brains of the little Spikings, one cold January morning, when she was interrupted by Mrs Spikings, who swept into the schoolroom with these words, delivered in a piercing soprano:

'Well, my angels, here is the most delightful surprise! Your dear great-uncle Pomeroy, of whom you are always talking so fondly, has paid us an unexpected call, and he wished to come upstairs and see you at your studies, like the little busy bees you are!'

Verity, with a swift kick to the leg of his chair, woke Knight in time to greet Uncle Pomeroy, who was a little slow in coming up the stairs; and who, when he entered the schoolroom at last, could only stand wheezing and blowing for some moments, staring around him with all his great snuff-coloured teeth on display, and presenting such an alarming appearance that Seraphina uttered a little sob of terror at the spectacle, which her mother was forced to pass off as a demonstration of tender emotion at the sight of her beloved relative.

'Mr Spikings and I were only saying this morning, were we not, Miss Deene,' said Mrs Spikings, 'that we positively longed for news of dear Mr Pomeroy, and that he was so seldom out of our thoughts that – that it was a wonder we ever thought of anything else!'

'Yes, indeed, ma'am,' said Verity, observing that Mrs Spikings was a little flustered – for she and the companion of her joys had been quarrelling that morning, calling a few pieces of crockery into service to underline their arguments, and Verity suspected that Mrs Spikings could have wished for a little notice of this delightful surprise.

'Well, now,' said Uncle Pomeroy, having regained his breath, and rearranged his stuffing so that it gave him a chest rather than a stomach, 'well, now, so this is where the little scamps sip at the fountain of knowledge, is it?' He was in good spirits, plainly having been too much under the influence to take any offence from the children's unfortunate lapses on the night of the dinner; and his dreadful liverish eye alighting on Verity, he went on boomingly, 'Well, well, here's a face I don't recognize. I think I can say I've a pretty fair memory for faces, you know, and—'

'Miss Deene, Uncle,' said Mrs Spikings hastily, 'of course you remember Miss Deene. Well, my dears, is this not charming of your great-uncle to visit you in the schoolroom? I'm sure you have all been attending most dutifully to Miss Deene's instruction . . . They are such little thirsters after learning, Uncle, that I have had to prise their books from their little hands as they lay down in bed at night, and beg them to take a little rest, many times before now!'

'So, my pretties, you are diligent about your lessons, are you? Good, good. And what are you studying today?' Uncle Pomeroy advanced to the table, and seizing on a book that was being used to prop up a slate, opened it with a flourish. ' "*The Anti-quary*," by Sir Walter Scott." So, Miss Deene, you teach them to read novels, do you? Rather a soft curriculum, I would have thought!'

'No,' said Verity, 'we are studying—'

'PARdon?'

'We are studying arithmetic today,' Verity amplified.

'Now Scott, you know,' pursued Uncle Pomeroy, ignoring her, 'is pretty well the only novelist that can be read with profit. Still, novels are novels, you know. Now you may put me amongst the Old Fashioneds: I don't mind it – I've been put there before; and as an Old Fashioned, and a man who has done pretty well by respecting the traditions of our fine old country, I say this: there is nothing to beat the classical curriculum. When I was at school, I learnt nothing but Latin and Greek, from seven in the morning till seven at night. And do you know how I learnt it, my little man?'

Tancred, to whom this question was addressed, said he was sure he didn't know, and was only prevented from adding that he didn't care by his mother's giving his hair a sharp tug, under pretence of ruffling it fondly.

'It was beaten into me!' said Uncle Pomeroy, with such a clap of his great teeth together that Verity was irresistibly reminded of the crocodile in Punch and Judy. 'If I did not get my lessons by heart, they were beaten into me with a rod, my dears. And do you think it hurt me, my little man, to be beaten with a rod?'

Tancred, in the act of saying that he hoped so, was given another fond tug by his mother, who answered for him that he hoped not.

'It hurt a great deal, my dears – a great deal! But I was grateful for it, and I am grateful for it to this day. And do you know why – Miss Deene?' said Uncle Pomeroy, swivelling his stuffed carcass to face her.

Because you're a fool, thought Verity, looking at him with an expression of devoted attention.

'Because it is the best of all ways to learn. *Amo, amas, amat* – I don't suppose you know what that means, do you, my little man?'

Tancred, with his mother's fingers playing forebodingly in his hair, said no, very gracelessly.

'It means love. You see? I've never forgotten those lessons that were beaten into me, my dears; and what's more, those beatings built character. I was at the club the other day when Bullimore came up to me – Major-General Bullimore, you know, old crony of mine, stood godfather to his son – and said to me, "Pomeroy, I'm going to say something to you that I've never said to any man in my life. It's this, sir. You've got character, Pomeroy; enough character to lead a regiment, if you'd chosen: that's all." His words, not mine – I wouldn't mention it otherwise.'

'Well, Uncle,' said Mrs Spikings, after expressing her enthusiastic agreement with this estimate, 'Tancred is to go away to a public school this year; and if he only turns out half as well as his great-uncle, of whom he always speaks so admiringly, Mr Spikings and I will be well pleased! But, Uncle, you will stay for luncheon, won't you? We see so little of you, that I simply don't want to let you go. I know you don't normally indulge, but Alfred has some excellent hock in his cellar, and he simply wouldn't forgive me if I let you go away without trying it.'

'Well, now,' said Uncle Pomeroy, creaking and smirking, 'on any other day, I would decline the hock, my dear; but it so happens that today is my birthday, which is partly why I had a sentimental fancy to refresh my old eyes with the sight of these cherubs, and on account of my birthday I won't say no.'

'Oh, dear Uncle Pomeroy! Oh, I didn't know it was your birthday! Oh, good heavens, Uncle Pomeroy, I didn't know!' Mrs Spikings was so overcome by not knowing that she seemed all but ready to fly about the room like a bird on the strength of it, and repeatedly declared, in the midst of her ecstasies, that if she had known she would have done something, without giving any clear idea of what she would have done.

'Aye, aye – another year older, and a little wiser perhaps: who's to say?' said Uncle Pomeroy. 'And how old do you suppose I am, my little fellow?' he added, presenting his frightful teeth to Knight.

'A hundred,' said Knight.

'Ah-ha-ha, what comical ideas they have, to be sure!' trilled Mrs Spikings, transferring her fondness to Knight's spiky head, and treating it so very fondly that she came away with a clump of hair in her fingers. 'The prime of life, Uncle Pomeroy, the prime of life is the expression Alfred admiringly applied to you just the other day!'

'Ah, perhaps I haven't worn so badly, my dear, perhaps so. But I shan't see seventy again, Mrs Spikings – nor seventy-one, I fear!'

'But you will see many, many more years yet, dear Uncle Pomeroy,' said Mrs Spikings, with a little prayerful gesture of her hands, as if she were beseeching nothing short of eternal life for him.

'It may be, my dear, it may be,' said Uncle Pomeroy; and plainly growing impatient to sample the hock, he clapped his hands together and went on, 'Well, now, what do you say to giving these little pretties a half-holiday from their studies today, by way of celebration?'

'Uncle Pomeroy,' said Mrs Spikings, summoning a tear, 'I have said it before, but I do not hesitate to say it again. You are a saint, and nothing but. My dears, do you hear? Great-uncle Pomeroy says you shall have a half-holiday, and I should think you must love him even more on account of it, if that were possible, which it isn't – so kiss your great-uncle, my dears, and run to nurse!'

The Spikings brood, though glad enough of a release from lessons, were rather chary of kissing Uncle Pomeroy's carmine cheek, which had something of the open coffin about it; but Mrs Spikings urged them to it very firmly, saying to Verity in the meantime, 'Miss Deene, I suppose you may have the half-day too. I dare say you can find yourself something to do?'

'May I go out, ma'am?'

'Oh! Miss Deene, the very idea of asking such a question, when you invariably do as you please!' said Mrs Spikings, with an airy wave of her hand. 'Quite the bluestocking in her behaviour, Uncle Pomeroy – always gadding about on her own, an unaccountable creature: but there, what can I do? She absolutely lords it over us, Uncle, and we haven't the heart to be severe. Yes, off you go, Miss Deene, whatever you wish!'

Verity never thought she would have occasion to bless Uncle Pomeroy, but bless him she did, from his pointed head to his pointed shoes, for this half-holiday came very opportunely. She needed to go out very badly, for she had a pressing matter on her mind.

Pressing matter on her mind, indeed, she reproached herself as she got ready in her bare little room. More truthful to say that the matter was pressing on her heart. The old matter! London had not offered an escape after all. Her first impulse, when Catherine had written her to say that John Twopenny was coming to London and begging her to be their go-between, had been to refuse. She simply could not allow herself to be exposed to that infection again, especially when she had felt herself beginning to be cured – it was too much! But reflection had pointed out the impossibility of refusing Catherine anything, and especially a refusal such as this, which would surely betray her secret. So she had agreed. But another motive had been lurking under the surface, and she admitted it, and hated herself for it, and knew she was not cured after all. She longed to see him: under any circumstances and at any cost to her peace of mind, she longed to see him again. And he had come to London, and they were in communication, and Catherine wished for a first-hand report of him.

So she had proposed that first meeting in St James's Park. Just the one meeting, she told herself: just the one, as a kind of test for her fortitude. And after all, it might prove beneficial: it might show that the memory was more beguiling than the reality, and start the cure again. She went along in the hope that she would wonder what she ever saw in him. The hope was disappointed. She came away wondering, instead, how she could ever have borne to leave him.

'Damn and blast,' said Verity, putting on her bonnet. 'Blast and damn.'

She had shied away from a second meeting. Whenever she found herself even thinking of it, she set herself a stiff task as a punishment, in true governess fashion; and within a week had made herself net several purses, read half a volume of Goethe in the original German, and memorize the Roman emperors from Augustus to Constantine. But then he himself had proposed the second meeting, and with part despair and part joy she had commended herself to the hands of fate, and gone.

The second meeting, however, had left her with no doubts about the dangerous game she was playing. She had come close to betraying herself to him, and had rebounded into ill-humour as a result. This must stop: for even as a resentful part of her had outwardly protested that she was no more to him than a convenient go-between, inside she had known that an intimacy was establishing itself between the two of them, whether either of them wished or contrived it; and it must not be.

And yet . . . The days that had succeeded that meeting had seen Verity rehearse it a hundred times in her mind, and grow more uneasy each time. She had been sharp-tongued indeed – excessively so. 'Just because you love him, and shouldn't,' she told herself, 'is no reason to behave as if you hated him instead!' And as the days multiplied, and became weeks, and as after one letter there was no further word from him, either for her or for Catherine, Verity's unease became concern.

Catherine was concerned at the long silence too – she wrote to say so. But Verity hoped she was not being disloyal to her friend when she observed that Catherine's concern did not seem overwhelming. It was not that she did not care; but Verity perceived that she had only the vaguest idea of the struggles John was undergoing, and in the same letter in which she expressed her concern over him, Catherine also gave a full and excited account of a ball that had recently been held at Buttings Court. 'No doubt he tells her that everything's going swimmingly with him,' Verity thought, 'and instead of reading between the lines, she believes him!'

But Verity's mind could not be put at rest so easily. And as the weeks still went by, and the old year died and the new came frostily in, she became so anxious that all her old wranglings about her feeling for John and what she must do about it ceased to matter. She must see him, and that was all; and when Uncle Pomeroy's birthday decree granted her a good part of the day to herself, she knew she must seize the chance.

A shawl over her grey wool walking-dress completed Verity's preparations for going out, and she left the house by the servants' door. She had John's address for letters; and though he had told her of his domestic circumstances, and his landlady's discouragement of visitors, there was no help for it in this case. She had reached High Holborn before it occurred to her that at this time of the day he would be at the counting-house where he was employed; but after a moment's hesitation she concluded that that did not matter either. If the landlady would let her wait for his return, she would wait: if not, she would leave a note and ask him to meet her somewhere in the vicinity.

She found the little green door in Fetter Lane: she found the landlady, Miss Thimblebee, very ready to summon her up to her apartments when John's name was mentioned, though Miss Thimblebee's lips tightened somewhat when she saw that Verity was a young woman, and unaccompanied.

'I wish I could answer your inquiry about Mr Twopenny, Miss—?'

'Deene,' said Verity, giving her a straight look. 'I am governess to the family of

204

Mr and Mrs Alfred Spikings, of Montagu Place, and I am an old friend of Mr Twopenny's.'

'Indeed? From the country, perhaps?'

'From the country. We were friends in Norfolk, and we have exchanged news once or twice since both coming to London; but I have heard nothing from him of late, and was concerned.' Verity's straight look and straight answers seemed to satisfy Miss Thimblebee, who moderated her rigid propriety a little, and invited Verity to sit down. Verity relaxed a little too. She usually got on well with strong-minded, stiff-backed, independent ladies, having something of that make-up herself, and did not doubt her capacity to get on cordial terms with this one.

'Miss Deene, Mr Twopenny is no longer the occupant of my single gentlemen's lodgings. But I have not rented them out to any new occupant; for the fact is . . .' Miss Thimblebee's lip suddenly trembled, and Verity had already seen enough of her to know that this was not a common occurrence. 'Miss Deene, something dreadful has happened to Mr Twopenny.'

Verity's heart stopped.

'He – I regret to say, I profoundly regret to say that he has been arrested for debt,' said Miss Thimblebee.

Verity's heart started again. 'Oh, is that all?' she burst out in relief.

'It is no small matter, I think, Miss Deene,' said Miss Thimblebee, drawing herself up. 'It is certainly not a thing I would wish to happen to any of my single gentlemen.'

'I beg your pardon,' Verity said. 'For a moment I took you to mean something . . . mortal had happened – that's all.'

'Oh, gracious heavens, not so bad as that,' said Miss Thimblebee, softening again. 'But still a most dreadful occurrence – I was obliged to hold a burning feather under my nose for half an hour afterwards, and I am not a person given to emotional infirmities by any means.'

'Where was he taken?'

'I have had a note from him,' Miss Thimblebee said, 'asking me to direct any correspondence to the King's Bench prison in the Borough. I cannot look with favour on financial improbity, you understand, Miss Deene; but if I show a little partiality towards Mr Twopenny, it is because he always displayed the most scrupulous delicacy in his residence here, and I – in short, I cannot think ill of him. I have been on the point of going to the King's Bench to see him several times; but besides the consideration that he may not wish to be seen in such degrading circumstances, there is the question of an unprotected woman, mindful of her reputation as I must be, going about to such places.'

'The debtor's prison . . . however did he end up there?'

'I regret to say that Mr Twopenny lost his position in the City; and he was in consequence, I believe, somewhat distressed for money. As I have said, I have not let his rooms; but other than that, I freely confess to you, Miss Deene, I do not know what to do!'

John in prison! After the first relief that it was no worse, the thought of it smote her like a blow; and she was hard put to it to conceal her feelings from the button eyes of Miss Thimblebee. Feelings, however, were all very well: they would not get John out of the King's Bench. As far as she knew, that could only be achieved by some composition with his creditors, or by direct settlement of his debts.

'Have you any idea, Miss Thimblebee, of the sum that was owing?' she said.

Miss Thimblebee shook her head. 'I cannot believe it is a great sum. Mr Twopenny's habits were not dissipated, that I can engage for.'

Verity thought. She had been paid her first year's wages, and had the money about her. Providing it was enough, she would use it to settle John's debts, and free him: there was not the slightest hesitation about that. What concerned her was how it was to be done, and whether it could be done today; also, whether it could be done anonymously. Miss Thimblebee had spoken kindly and truly when she had said that John would not wish to be seen in the prison: Verity knew his pride. She would not put it past him to refuse all help, out of some stubborn idea that only he was responsible for his predicament, and only he should get himself out of it. Verity was not so fastidious. If her money could set him at liberty, without him knowing where it came from, then her money should do it. And there was no time to lose.

'Miss Thimblebee, I'm grateful for your confidence,' she said, starting up, 'and I won't intrude on your time any longer.'

'You are going to the King's Bench, Miss Deene? Alone?'

'Not to the King's Bench. I am not sure how it is to be done, but I am going to settle John – Mr Twopenny's debts. The Insolvency Court is the place to apply to, I presume: if not, then surely one of the other Courts of Justice.'

'Miss Deene, I applaud you,' said Miss Thimblebee, 'but no one understands better than I the risks to the reputation of a single woman who must go about alone. Miss Deene, will you allow me to go with you?'

Verity was glad of the company, especially of so brisk and businesslike a woman as Miss Thimblebee, who, after placing a bonnet on top of her two smooth wings of hair, pronounced herself ready at once; and so they went out together, and walked the short distance to the drowsy, crumbling old quarter of the city where sat the majesty of English law. Such delays and referrals, such forests of legalistic verbiage as she had to penetrate to get any sense out of anyone, such a heartbreaking game of tennis as was played with her by various legal representatives of this court and that court, and this jurisdiction and that jurisdiction, who thought that perhaps it was Serjeant's Inn, or perhaps it was Palace Court, or perhaps it was Common Pleas, or perhaps it was Serjeant's Inn after all, and who batted her back and forth from one dreary citadel of justice to another, would have worn out the patience of anyone less determined than Verity. But she had her reward at last. At last she stood, with empty purse, before an attorney who was empowered to record that the liability of Twopenny, J., for the above sum under the writ of the aforementioned court as was executed on the afore-cited date, et cetera et cetera, was fully absolved by an anonymous benefaction; and she managed to prise out of the same attorney an assurance that, some fees and formalities being settled, Twopenny J. was eligible for immediate release from the King's Bench.

A good day's work, if an exhausting one; and Verity still had to get back to Castle Spikings before the drawbridge was pulled up, and so regretfully declined Miss Thimblebee's invitation to have tea with her. Miss Thimblebee extracted a promise that she would come as soon as she had time; and having observed Verity with some admiration through the long battle with the law, looked at her closely on parting and said, 'Mr Twopenny is fortunate in his friends, my dear.'

Luckily Verity was not the blushing type, else she might have blushed now. But she merely said that she was glad to be in a position to help, and gave Miss Thimblebee a cordial goodbye.

'A good friend to him – yes, I suppose I am,' Verity thought as she made her way back to Montagu Place. 'I couldn't help myself, and I'm glad that I've done it even though it leaves me with precisely three shillings in the world, for now I can put my mind at ease about him; but still, yes, it was the act of a very good friend, and I hope he appreciates it. But there, he won't know it was me, for Miss Thimblebee has sworn secrecy, and so it doesn't matter. And he doesn't know, either, how much more than a friend to him I would be, and how much more than a friend to me I would wish him, if it could only fall out so . . . Oh! John, you are not the only one in prison, indeed you are not!'

206

CHAPTER ELEVEN

Mr Chipchase Shoulders a Burden

The new year saw a significant change in the appearance of the little port of Hales-next-the-sea. The huge boastful signs reading S. TWOPENNY & SON were taken down or whitewashed over; and in their place equally boastful signs reading TWOPENNY & CHIPCHASE went up all along the quayside.

Yes: Saul had taken his son-in-law into partnership. 'Well, he've spited that poor son of his from top to bottom now, and I hope he's satisfied,' remarked Mr Addy to his wife, in reference to Saul's motives for this innovation. The motives that Saul chose to acknowledge, however, were more practical. He had been feeling his age this winter; he needed someone to share the responsibility of running the business. And Edwin Chipchase, since becoming Saul's son-in-law, had shown himself to be as indefatigable as he was astute in managing Saul's extensive enterprises. He had quite justified Saul's confidence in him. He was the very man Saul had been wanting all these years.

Still, the partnership was a grand gesture, and perhaps Mr Addy was right in his estimate of what had really prompted Saul to make it. No one, at least, doubted Mr Chipchase's ability to live up to his role; and if anyone drew the comparison with a kingdom, and doubted the capacity of a kingdom to have two kings, at least without civil war breaking out sooner or later, no one voiced it.

Mr Edwin Chipchase was not a man to be brash about his new authority. It was notable that when he entered a room, he only opened the door just wide enough to admit him, and closed it immediately he had insinuated himself inside. When Mr Chipchase took a chair, he took the very edge of it, from a sort of combination of modesty and a frugal desire to spare the upholstery. As for his raising his voice, one might as soon fancy a lamb roaring like a lion. He was indeed a very different sort of master from his father-in-law. Not that anyone took him for a fool; but one or two of the workmen about the maltings and warehouses quite reasonably supposed that his mildness of manner was matched by leniency of temper, and they relaxed a little accordingly. Bobbs, the carter who had driven John to Norwich on one memorable morning, was the first to find out that this was a mistake.

He was driving a load back from Fakenham one day, and took the unusual step – unusual for Saul Twopenny's employees, anyhow – of stopping off at a country tavern to refresh himself. The diversion was not long, and Bobbs was not much disguised with drink when he arrived in the yard of the maltings – no more than a red face, a hummed tune, and an aroma of beer amounted to; but Mr Chipchase, who was awaiting the delivery, did not miss the signs, and he summoned Bobbs to him.

'Have you been drinking?' he demanded in his little, clipped voice.

Bobbs looked at him, and hesitated, as if debating what would go down best. At last he said, with a shame-faced sort of chumminess, 'A drop, sir – you know.'

Mr Chipchase did not launch into a violent tirade. Instead he sacked Bobbs on the spot, and went to tell Mr Addy that a new carter would be needed as soon as possible.

Saul, when he heard, approved entirely. 'You did right, Edwin,' he said over supper, 'quite right. These fellows mustn't suppose that things have changed here, and start taking liberties. You did right, too, in not delaying to consult me. That would have looked as if you hadn't the authority, you know, and these fellows would have seized on it.'

'Just what I thought, father-in-law,' said Mr Chipchase, methodically eating. 'Just what I thought.'

By now Saul had redrawn his will in favour of Sar'ann, which was as much to say in favour of Mr Chipchase; and this, together with the partnership, gave the impression of a man who was relinquishing his hold of his affairs, and turning to retirement and contemplation. So said Saul's solicitor, an elderly man who looked as if he had a permanent stitch in his side from anxiously placating his terrifying client.

'Contemplation?' said Saul, looking up from the will with his eyebrows all a-bristle. 'Contemplation of what, sir?'

The stitch in the lawyer's side seemed to grow worse. 'Religious contemplation, sir, perhaps . . .?'

'Religious contemplation has always been my habit,' said Saul. 'And I have always combined it with work. The active life and the religious life are not to be separated, sir; they are one and the same.'

The lawyer wore the smile of a man who is beginning to wish he had never said anything.

'And I certainly do not intend surrendering my active life, not until it pleases the Almighty to deprive me of it,' Saul said; and appended his signature to the will.

But fine words, as Sar'ann was fond of remarking, buttered no parsnips, and though Saul might declare his intention of holding on to the reins until death loosened his grip, it was a different matter in practice. In practice there was a slow, sure, inevitable erosion of his power, not only where the business of Twopenny & Chipchase was concerned, but also in the domestic affairs of the jail-like house.

At first there was not much evidence of this. Saul still had his private office leading off the hall from which he could watch every coming and going; he still went on the prowl in the servants' quarters looking for irregularities; he still officiated at long grim prayers morning and night. And he still apportioned Sar'ann her fortnightly housekeeping money, summoning her into his private office on Monday morning to perform the ritual. But one Monday, when he rose from the breakfast table and commanded Sar'ann to follow him into the office, he was surprised to hear her say, 'What for, Pa?'

'For the housekeeping, daughter,' Saul said, pulling down his brows.

'Oh! There's no need, Pa. Edwin gave it me earlier. So you needn't trouble.'

'I did not know of this.'

'Well, you know now, Pa.' There was a slight change discernible in Sar'ann's behaviour towards her parent just lately. Saul would almost have called it pertness.

'I might, daughter, have been informed first,' he said.

'Oh, but Pa, we don't want you to be troubled. When I say we, I mean Edwin and me, of course,' Sar'ann added with a coy giggle. 'You've always had to manage everything yourself, and you ain't getting any younger, you know. So we – meaning Edwin and me, tee-hee! – we don't want you to be troubled any more than you need. You deserve a long rest – that's what Edwin says.'

'Very well, daughter. As you say.' Saul was perplexed to find that Sar'ann was not looking at him: she was pouring herself a second cup of tea and humming under her breath. If it was a hymn tune, he did not recognize it. 'Edwin has supplied you sufficiently, I suppose, for the housekeeping?'

'Oh yes, Pa! Edwin know what he's doing, don't you fret. He knows all about the cost of things.'

There was no doubting that. Mr Chipchase kept the strictest record of his expenses; even if he paid a boy a penny to hold his horse's head, he would note it down on some little tablets he carried about with him for the purpose; and at night, after supper, he would carefully write them up in a large calfskin notebook. The smell of this notebook seemed to please Mr Chipchase, for when he had finished writing he would often sit with the closed book held to his snub nose, his magnified eyes blinking in the candlelight, and go into an abstraction for ten or fifteen minutes at a time. Sar'ann meanwhile, would sew, and listen out for the snap of mousetraps, and Saul would sit with his Bible open before him, occasionally glancing up at his son-in-law, and wondering what he was thinking. And just occasionally Saul would nod – very angry with himself when he did so, for it was not his way at all – and jerk awake, and find, even if Sar'ann and Mr Chipchase were in exactly the same positions, that he had a strange sensation of something having happened while he dozed, that he could not put a name to.

It was an example of Mr Chipchase's admirable economy that caused the first slight friction between Saul and his son-in-law. Mr Chipchase had occasion to reprimand one of the servants over her liberality with coal on the kitchen fire, and the servant proving insolent in her answers, Mr Chipchase summarily dismissed her. He decided, moreover, that she need not be replaced, and that two housemaids were quite enough. All this, in its narrow, merciless promptitude, was sufficiently Saul-like: but Saul's complaint was that he had not been consulted. In fact, he only found out about it by accident several days later, when he happened to ask Caleb whether the missing maid were ill.

'I don't quarrel with your action, Edwin,' he said. 'But I'd have you remember that this is my house, and that I wish to be consulted before any such decisions are taken.'

'Oh, but Pa,' said Sar'ann, 'you said you'd have done the same yourself – so where was the point in consulting?'

'Be silent, daughter,' growled Saul.

'Oh, my stars, Pa, where's the point in being silent when I'm only speaking the truth? And I do wish, you know, that you wouldn't call me "Daughter". It's not very becoming for a married woman to be addressed in that fashion. And I am a married woman, Pa – oh my stars, I am! Oh, my word, I'm very much married, and that's a fact! Ah, ha-ha-ha-ha!'

'The point is, father-in-law, that I didn't want you to be troubled with the matter,' said Mr Chipchase, polishing his spectacles. 'You have carried the burden of such things for quite long enough. I am more than glad to take the responsibility for the household management, and free you from such bothersome necessities. "It is good for a man that he bear the yoke in his youth," as scripture says.'

Saul glowered at him. 'You must not suppose, Edwin,' he said testily, 'that I am a decrepit old man. There is a great deal of life left in me yet.'

'Quite so,' said Mr Chipchase. 'And that's why I would have you enjoy it, father-in-law, and not be troubled with these details.'

'I have always troubled with details,' said Saul, flaring up, 'and that's how I got where I am. And I was not consulted about this matter – I was not consulted for a moment, about a matter concerning the staff in my own house—'

'I beg your pardon,' said Mr Chipchase humbly, 'I thought I had acted for the best. Shall I send to her tonight, and have her reinstated?'

'What?'

'The maid, father-in-law. Do you wish to take her back? It can easily be arranged,' said Mr Chipchase, with monotonous composure. 'I can have her back here tomorrow morning, if you wish. It will rather undermine my own authority in the house, but it doesn't matter. I shall do it, if you wish it.'

'No,' said Saul frowning, 'no, I would not have her back . . .'

'Oh, my stars, Pa, make up your mind – first you say one thing and then another!' said Sar'ann. 'A person would need the patience of a saint to put up with it!'

'My dear, please . . . What do you direct, then, father-in-law? Shall we engage another maid in her place? Please say the word, if so, and I shall see to it.'

'Another maid? No . . . no, I don't see the need. Two is enough.'

'There, Pa! You've come round to exactly what Edwin said in the first place, and there was no need for any of it!' cried Sar'ann. 'But then you always get your own way, don't you?'

Saul did not know whether he had got his own way or not. Even he had to concede that he could not give Edwin authority with one hand and take it back with the other, not if things were to run smoothly in the kingdom of corn and coal. And he had to admit that things were running very smoothly without him. They were doing good business, and he could not deny either that it was a weight off his mind to have his precious creation so well managed. For he was not as sharp as he had been: sometimes when he woke in the morning he would drift off into a dream of being up and dressed, into which all sorts of oddments of memory would wind themselves, and when he woke once more he found it curiously difficult to adjust himself to reality.

Of course, he was past man's allotted span as it was set down in the Bible now, and it was to be expected. But Saul Twopenny had always tended to think of himself as different from ordinary mortals with their infirmities and weaknesses. And one morning, when he had overslept again, and had found it more than usually hard to break free of those clinging dreams and memories, he resolved that today he would be the man he had been. 'Too much fuss made about age, my boy,' he said, as Caleb helped him with his dressing. 'A man who sits on his hands all day is bound to feel old. Work's the best exercise. Now, Edwin's an excellent manager in many ways, but these fellows miss the firm voice of the master, you know. I'll take a turn over to the maltings, and ginger them up. Let's see, when did I last go over there?'

'Last Friday,' Caleb said. 'Last Friday afternoon.'

'That long ago? Thought it was just the other day . . . Anyhow, let's see how things wag over there. Hand me my stick, boy. Bah, no, I don't want your arm, boy, d'you think me a cripple?'

Attended by Caleb, Saul made his way downstairs. No one was about except one of the maids, who was clearing the breakfast table.

'What are you about there, Nelly? Didn't mistress tell you to wait breakfast for me?'

'Oh! no, sir – at least, I don't think so. But shall I lay the cloth again, sir? There's a little ham left, and—'

Saul waved her away: he hadn't much of an appetite of late. 'Where is mistress, anyhow?'

'She've gone the dressmaker's for another fitting, sir.'

Sar'ann, since her marriage, had discovered quite a taste for personal adornment, and Mr Chipchase was happy to gratify it. He was quite a doting husband when business was out of the way, and it was rumoured among the servants that he had even been seen kissing Sar'ann's bony elbows in the parlour one night, whilst Sar'ann sat bolt upright with her new lace cap on squeaking, 'Oh, my stars! Oh, my stars and garters!' Saul, for his part, only grunted at the maid's reply and went on his way. He supposed that it was usual for a married woman to have new clothes, but he hoped that his daughter was not becoming ensnared by worldly vanity; he would have to caution her about it.

Outside the sweet smell of malt lay heavy on the air. 'Ah, that's the smell, my boy,' commented Saul, 'none like it!' He put his hand on the little iron gate that led through to the yard and, finding it padlocked, drew out his bunch of keys.

'Try that lock for me, boy,' he said to Caleb after some fruitless minutes of fumbling. 'I must have the shakes or something, for it won't turn.'

Even Caleb's strength, however, could not turn the key in the lock. Saul stared a moment, then struck his fist against the iron bars. 'Damn me, they've changed the lock! Now how am I to go through to the maltings? Why wasn't I told? It's too bad, boy, it's too bad!'

Saul was breathing hard, and Caleb watched him attentively.

'Well . . . never mind. We'll go round by the quay. I shall have words with Edwin about it, mind you.'

They returned through the house, and walked the long way round to the maltings, and Saul was breathing even harder when they got there. Edwin was not about. There were several faces that Saul did not recognize among the workmen; but Mr Addy was in the foreman's office as of old, and came hurrying out to greet him.

'Well, Addy, I suppose you've had a pretty easy time of it lately, without my eye upon you,' Saul growled. 'I wonder you don't put a feather-bed in that office, and bring your nightcap to work with you. Well, don't just stand there gaping like a landed fish, man, bring me the day-book – or have you got too fat and lazy to move?'

In fact Mr Addy had looked almost pleased on seeing Saul stumping in through the front yard; but now the tell-tale flush crept over his head, and he could only give a choked murmur in reply.

'Ha! Your penmanship would still disgrace a schoolboy,' Saul said, leafing through the day-book. 'And your ciphering's no better. Some things never change, eh, Addy? Well, come along. Let's see what else is amiss.'

It was indeed like old times to see Saul striding about the maltings, beating his stick rhythmically against his leg, with Mr Addy trotting beside him and coming in for his every disparaging remark. Like old times, too, to see Saul minutely examining every part of the works as if in hope of finding something to complain of. Perhaps in this case, however, the hope was genuine: for the matter of the locked gate still rankled, and at each new evidence that the maltings under Edwin Chipchase's direction was functioning perfectly without him, the set of Saul's jaw became a little harder and fiercer, and he seemed more determined to demonstrate his superior authority.

It was the kiln that he hit upon at last, to make his point. Placing his hand over the outer brick, he cried with an air of truculent triumph, 'Why, this is nowhere near at the right temperature! I could scarcely touch my finger to it before. You old fool, Addy, you've been starving the fires!'

'Mr Chipchase found we were burning too much coal, sir – said the kiln was eating it up,' said Mr Addy, looking as if he had breakfasted on some combustible material himself. 'The fires weren't drawing well, on account of the flues being blocked with years of soot; and once we had them cleaned, we found we only needed to burn two-thirds the weight we burned before. One good stoke first thing in the morning, and then the drying-tiles stay hot enough for most of the day, and you can damp the fires instead of having 'em blazing.'

Saul hoisted his chin. 'And how long has Mr Chipchase been running a maltings?'

'Six months, I reckon.'

'And how long have *I* been running a maltings? Well, man, answer me!'

'Forty-odd year,' said Mr Addy, drawing out a handkerchief and applying it to his glowing forehead.

'Well, I'm glad you recollect it, Addy. Perhaps you'd like to recollect that I am master here, and I was master here when Mr Chipchase was still in his clouts.'

211

'Aye, sir, I know, but—'

'Don't answer me back, you idle hound! Have those fires stoked at once! In fact, you can take a turn with the coal-shovel yourself, if you haven't forgotten what hard work is.' Yes, this was Saul back with a vengeance, and with the old unholy light in his eye; but Mr Addy, instead of trotting away to do his bidding, hesitated, with a most disturbed and disturbing look on his face. Saul's voice rose to a roar. 'Get on, man! I'll not have this slackness!'

'Sir,' said Mr Addy, 'I really don't think the fires need stoking . . .'

Saul's stick swished through the air close to Mr Addy's ear. 'You'll do as I say, or I'll lay my stick across your idle back. That kiln isn't hot enough, I tell you, not hot enough to soften wax, and I'm damned if I'll start sending out green malt after forty years. You're a fool, Addy, and an insolent fool – you'd have bankrupted me years ago if you'd have had your way, and I'll put up with it no longer.'

'Neither will I.'

Mr Addy said these words in such a low, soft guttural that for a moment Saul was not sure that he had spoken. 'What did you say?'

'I said neither will I!' exploded Mr Addy. His handkerchief was by now as wet as a dishrag, and he balled it up and flung it down on the ground at Saul's feet. 'You've done it! Oh, you've done it at last, you old brimstone pepperer! You've been making such a firework out of me, all these years, and I've long been afraid that I shall go off like twenty Guy Fawkes' nights – and now it's come! It's come at last, and I can't answer for myself! I shan't break your stick over my knee, like your nephew did, nor run away, like your son did – I shall just tell you, straight out, that you're a brute, a devil, a monster, a bludgeoning, bullying wooden-headed old brimstone pepperer, and what's worse, you're a Fool!'

Saul's hard features were not normally expressive; but never was there a completer picture of astonishment than he presented at that moment.

'I say it again!' fumed Mr Addy, almost dancing on the spot in the vehemence of his feelings. 'Fool, Fool, Fool! Fifty, a hundred times more of a fool than that poor lumbering creature you keep by you! Shall I tell you why? Yes, I shall! Because you drive your own son away with your brimstone ways, and then you take this Chipchase one in his place just to spite the poor lad; and you put everything into his hands, and give him charge of the whole place – and yet you think you can take back what you've given whenever it suits you. You let go the helm, and think you can still steer! Well, you're a fool for it, and you'd find it out soon enough, if I didn't tell you – but I've got to tell you, because you've got me so hot this time there's no cooling down, not if I was to go and stand under Niagara!'

'Addy.' Saul's voice trembled. 'Addy, you have time to take that back. I give you time to take that back, Addy.'

'Bo-oohh!' was all Mr Addy could say in reply; and he snapped his fingers under Saul's nose.

'Get you gone, Addy,' said Saul, breathing harder than ever. 'You have just lost your job. Go, now. I won't have you on my property a single moment longer. Get out!'

Mr Addy glared at him, and at his stick, and seemed to be reconsidering his decision about the latter; but then he threw up his hands, took his hat from its peg, and slapped it on his head, jamming it down with a blow of his fist as if it were a bung in some danger of blowing. 'I'm going, don't you fret,' he said. 'I suppose it had to happen sooner or later. But I'd say it all again, if I thought for one moment you'd listen!' And with a little impatient twist of his lips, as if he were silently pronouncing the word Fool once more, Mr Addy turned and trotted away.

It may have been that Saul found some satisfaction in his thus demonstrating his ability to hire and fire just like his superefficient son-in-law; for though he was silent and brooding for some moments, as if he were swallowing down Mr Addy's words, and not finding them very digestible, Saul soon roused himself, and began to round on the workmen in his old way. And he had the fires in the kiln stoked up to a blaze, browbeating anyone who dared to protest with threats of a similar fate to Mr Addy's; and at last he returned to the house feeling that he had done a good morning's work.

'The hand of the master, you see, Caleb,' he said. 'The wheels don't turn quite the same without it. Very well, very well, give me your arm, boy, if it'll please you. Maybe I am a little tired.'

Saul must have been, for he slept in his armchair that afternoon, a thing he had never done; and was caught up again in strange dreams and fancies, and when he woke called out for Caleb in a tremulous voice, and hardly seemed to know where he was for some moments. But he was quite himself again that evening, and was glad of it; for that evening he had a confrontation, of sorts, with Edwin Chipchase.

It was not quite a confrontation, insofar as Mr Chipchase simply seemed to have no abrasive element in his nature at all. His temper might have been chosen as an illustration of the polar opposite of Mr Addy's: all coolness, and getting cooler the more he was provoked. All the same, he made it quite clear that he was not pleased by what he had found at the maltings when he returned from the Corn Exchange. Mr Addy, an excellent foreman and difficult to replace, summarily dismissed; and the drying-tiles in the kiln so overheated that the day's production of malt was quite ruined – scorched and unsaleable.

'It is a great pity, father-in-law,' Mr Chipchase said. 'And a great pity, too, that you don't trust me to know the business by now.'

'It's not that I don't trust you, Edwin,' said Saul, a little defensive. 'But I am still master here, and—'

'I bow, of course, to your seniority, and your matrimonial relation to me,' said Mr Chipchase, cutting him off deftly, 'but with respect, sir, there can hardly be a master in an equal partnership.'

'How dare you, sir!'

'I would hope that I was stating a fact, father-in-law, rather than venturing anything that could be described as daring. But I'm sure we don't need to have any unpleasantness about this. You know, I hope, that I have your best interests, and those of the firm, at heart; and with those in mind, I merely wish to point out that there is no occasion for you to go to the maltings regularly as you used to.'

'No need for you to go at all, surely, Pa!' put in Sar'ann, who had put up her lustreless locks in ringlets, and had added ribbons to the ringlets, to very startling effect. 'I don't know what you want to go meddling there for, when Edwin's got everything running like clockwork!'

'Daughter, this is none of your concern. Go to your room.'

'Oh! There you go with your daughtering again! It makes me quite wild, Pa! And as for going to my room – *our* room, tee-hee! – I shall only go if Edwin tells me to. I promised to obey Edwin, you know, Pa, in church! It's in the prayer-book, and not even you can go against that!'

'Father-in-law,' said Mr Chipchase, coolly pacing the parlour with his pasty hands behind his back, 'I think Sar'ann has a point. There is really no call for you to trouble yourself with the maltings at all, especially when the result is . . . so unfortunate as it was today. The malt can be written off, but I'm rather afraid we shan't get Mr Addy back, you know, for there are half-a-dozen men in Hales who would jump at the chance to employ him. No, really, father-in-law, I think you had much better leave the maltings alone. After all, it only tires you: I can tell you are tired now, and that is just what I wanted to spare you, by taking up the burden myself!'

Saul eyed him narrowly, his jaws working. 'You *spared* telling me you had changed the lock to the gate,' he said.

'Quite so,' said Mr Chipchase placidly. 'As I say, I don't want you to be troubled with such things.'

'Troubled!' bellowed Saul. 'I am not troubled by simply knowing what goes on in my own house!'

'Well, sir,' said Mr Chipchase, with his head on one side, 'I think you are. You are becoming agitated now, just at discussing it; and that is precisely what I don't like to see. You must think of your health, father-in-law – or else we must think of it for you.'

'I am not agitated. I am—' Saul struck the arm of his chair with the flat of his hand – 'I am quite in command of myself, Edwin. I will have you know I am quite in command of myself!'

Mr Chipchase pursed his lips. 'Of course, sir. As you say. I have the greatest respect for your judgement; but you will allow me to be the better observer of what you are simply not placed to observe – that is, your own self. I am concerned for you, father-in-law: I would not have you over-exerting yourself. You owe it to yourself, and to the firm, to take things a little more easily.'

There was something almost soporific in Mr Chipchase's comfortable drone: Saul found he was staring dully at his son-in-law's mouth, with its rows of little identical teeth, as if in a trance. He shook himself irritably. 'Addy,' he said, 'I will not have Addy back – under no circumstances. I will not have him back, do you hear?'

'As you say, father-in-law,' said Mr Chipchase. Was that a spark of impatience in those unreadable eyes, or just the light catching his spectacles? Whatever, it was gone in a moment. 'I shall engage a new foreman tomorrow. And as for the lock to the gate, I shall have another key cut directly.'

'There, Pa!' said Sar'ann. 'I don't think you can fuss any more, now can you?'

He might well have, once; but in spite of the sleep he had had in the afternoon he found he was weary again, and disinclined to struggle any more against Mr Chipchase's arguments, which seemed to enfold him softly and smotheringly like jeweller's cotton. 'Well, after all,' he remarked half to himself, half to Caleb, when he went to bed that night, 'there is something in what he says. I *have* earned a rest, after all these years. As for Addy . . . ah, well, no matter.'

He woke late again the next morning, and reproached Caleb for letting him sleep on. 'You were tired,' was Caleb's humble reply; but Saul said he felt as fresh as a daisy, and made his way downstairs. Two workmen – again, their faces were new to him – were just crossing the hall to the front door with bundles in their arms. Saul stared at them a moment, and then stumped over to his private office.

Inside the door he stopped, and gave his leg a thwack with his stick, as if to assure himself he was not still dreaming one of those confused dreams that had troubled him of late. His office was no longer his office. It had been stripped bare: even the desk had gone, and the print of the sacrifice of Abraham.

'What the – what the devil is this?'

'Oh, good morning, sir,' said Edwin Chipchase, appearing noiselessly behind him. 'I hope the men didn't make too much noise, and wake you.'

'What does this mean? This – this is my own private office. Answer me, sir! By what *right* do you interfere with my own office?'

'Only that right of which I spoke yesterday, father-in-law. The right to be concerned for your welfare,' said Mr Chipchase, inspecting the walls, and putting his finger to a damp place on the plaster. 'I took this liberty, father-in-law, as a precaution against you over-exerting yourself. I know you, sir, I'm proud to say. I know that as long as this office is at hand, you will always be tempted to come in here and work, till all sorts of unhealthy hours. And out of very respect and affection for you, father-in-law, I won't have it. You have been in a somewhat nervous condition of late, and poring over ledgers will not help it: so I have had

214

them all moved over to the counting-house, where they will be more convenient for me, and where you need not worry about them. The housekeeper was saying she was in need of another dark store, and I think this room will do admirably.'

'This room,' said Saul thickly, 'this room has always been my private office. My office, do you hear?'

'Oh, my word and bond, Pa, what's the fuss about?' said Sar'ann, appearing in the doorway. 'It's only a room; and as for an office, you don't need one now! I should have thought you'd be glad!'

And Saul flew into a violent passion. He had always been a man of hasty temper, but no one had seen him in a fury like this; for always previously the objects of his anger had bent like reeds before it, whereas Mr Chipchase would not budge. Against Saul's wild words he presented his little soft answers, and his unearthly patience, and Saul raged in vain. He had no allies except simple Caleb, who could only look on in mute distress; for Sar'ann supported her husband. The subtle shift in her attitude to her father had continued: the fear had left it at last. Whether it was because of bitter memories of that fear, or because of that peculiarity of temperament that made her enjoy setting mousetraps, the fact remained that Sar'ann looked on unmoved as her father ranted himself into helpless exhaustion; then she tripped off to try on a new bonnet.

Mr Chipchase, however, called in a doctor that afternoon, as Saul was prostrate, and stood by gnawing his thumb as the doctor made his examination. It was as he thought: Saul was overtired, and must have rest and no disturbance.

'Now I won't say I told you so, father-in-law,' said Mr Chipchase, patting his arm outside the coverlet, for Caleb had put him to bed. 'But I hope you'll credit me with knowing what's best for you from now on.'

And Caleb? What was Caleb thinking? He was thinking only, and as ever, of his master; and he was greatly troubled. He had given no further vent to his feelings about Mr Chipchase, because his master had told him not to, but his feelings were unchanged, and he still sometimes confided them to the horses in the stables. Carefully, though; for Mr Chipchase, Caleb had found, had a habit of stealthily appearing wherever he was least expected – and a way, too, just lately, of studying Caleb in a way the big man did not like.

No, his feelings about Mr Chipchase were unchanged, except insofar as the dislike had become stronger; and they still included that element of strange, fearful fascination. And so that evening, when he was sure Saul was sleeping peacefully, Caleb slipped downstairs and lingered about in the hall, making a pretence of trimming a candle, and peeping through the open crack in the parlour door.

Mr Chipchase had finished reckoning up his accounts, and had treated himself to a long sniff of the calfskin book, and now he looked over at Sar'ann and gave her a solemn wink.

'What do you say, my dear,' he said, 'to an early night?' And winked again, with his other eye.

Sar'ann gave a single shrill giggle, like a bo'sun's pipe, and put down her sewing. 'Oh, my stars, Edwin, you are a one! I never knew the like!'

'I should hope not,' said Mr Chipchase; and gave his drainy chuckle.

'Just let me set the traps,' Sar'ann said, jumping up, 'and I'll be ready directly. I must remember to lay one in Pa's old office. My word, what a fuss he made about that today!'

'Yes,' said Mr Chipchase with a sigh. 'I'm afraid your father's temper is . . . getting worse?'

'Oh! Much worse.'

'Dear me. I do hope his wits aren't turning, my love.'

'Oh, so do I. Hope not, I mean.' Sar'ann seemed to feel another giggle coming, and gave herself a slap to prevent it.

'Yes . . . that would be a great pity. We must watch him very closely, my dear. Very closely indeed. That exhibition today – most disturbing. We wouldn't want him to do some hurt to himself.' Mr Chipchase got up and stretched. 'Of course, I understand that he wishes still to make himself useful. Quite understandable. He would hate, I know, to think that he was a burden to us.' Something about Mr Chipchase's soft and precise way of saying that word 'burden' gave Caleb a curious shudder. He was about to slip away again, but before he could move Mr and Mrs Chipchase came out of the parlour.

Sar'ann ignored him; but Mr Chipchase, who was carrying a candle, looked up into Caleb's eyes, and then held the candle higher, so that Caleb flinched at the brightness of it.

'Well, Caleb,' he said mildly, 'and where do you fit in, I wonder? Perhaps you don't. I wonder if you don't fit in at all, you know, my dear fellow!' And leaving Caleb standing frozen in the hall, Mr Chipchase picked his silent way up the stairs.

Book Three

CHAPTER ONE

Tup'ny John

John's imprisonment in the King's Bench was not of long duration – a mere matter of weeks; and to some of his fellow debtors, that was tantamount to never having been in the prison at all. A mere matter of weeks – but in the mark it left upon John's spirit, it might have been half a lifetime.

He was in the exercise yard, begging – in his mind he would not shirk the word – when the turnkey brought him the news that his case had been settled by an anonymous benefactor, and certain legal formalities pending, he should be free to leave the King's Bench tomorrow. It was significant of how swiftly the prison taint had come upon him that his first reaction was one of bewilderment and fear. He might walk freely through the gate tomorrow – but whither? and to what mode of life? Relief and anticipation followed, inevitably, after the first shock; but the sanguine mood in which he had been accustomed to regard any new development in his life was not there, and he could not summon it. It was as if something had been permanently erased from John's soul.

His gratitude to his anonymous deliverer was shadowed too, by guilt and trouble. Who could it be? Miss Thimblebee was the only name that suggested itself, as in his shame he had had no direct communication with anyone else, and only she knew his whereabouts. If it was Miss Thimblebee, then he was placed under an agonizing obligation to her, for he knew she was not wealthy, and he owed her rent arrears besides. The thought of facing her was unbearable, at least until he was in a position to reimburse her fully – and that prospect had faded into an imponderable distance. The only other possibility was that one of the charitable individuals or bodies who concerned themselves with the imprisonment of debtors had taken up his case. But he could not think of that alternative with any lesser feeling of humiliation. Guilt, shame, self-loathing, despondency, all gnawed at John from within, and made the occasion of his release decidedly bitter-sweet in flavour.

Tom Bidmead's 'club' gave John a send-off the night before; and if he could not join wholeheartedly in the beery, rackety celebrations, he could at least take the opportunity to thank his fellow-debtors for their many small kindnesses. He also took a friendly enough leave of Tom Bidmead, though his liking for the young man was of the sort that stops some way short of respect. 'Well, you'll do better out of here, John,' Tom said, weaving his way rather unsteadily back from the club-room. 'There's some people who can take to it. Me, for example. Why, I feel as if I'm in my natural element here – which is just as well, with all the creditors who've got writs against me. But they can't come knocking on your door here, you see – that's the beauty of it!'

John refrained from wondering aloud whether Mrs Bidmead and the children were quite so appreciative of the beauty of the King's Bench. There was nothing he could do, after all – it was a measure of his depressed spirits that he could think of their plight with resignation; and he parted with Tom on cordial terms.

He parted likewise with his room-mate, Mr Randal Rose, who had entertained him for many nights with accounts of what he always referred to, with a certain pride, as his 'Chequered career'. Mr Rose, at least, took a more practical view of John's situation, and raised the thorny question of 'What next?' the night before John's release.

'I don't know,' said John. 'I hardly know where I shall go to when I walk out of the gate.'

'Lodgings lapsed, as it were, my dear sir?' said Mr Rose.

'Something like that,' John said. Whether it was Miss Thimblebee who had secured his release or not, he could not go back to her single gentlemen's apartment; it would mean imposing on her further, for he had no money but a begged few shillings.

'Well, I'll tell you what,' said Mr Rose. 'If nothing else turns up, I know a place where you can be comfortably accommodated for a very small consideration . . . I presume, my dear sir, that you will be under the necessity of, as it were, getting the cheapest roof over your head that can be found? Just so. Well, you can't do better than Jolly Butcher's Yard. That's where I resided before circumstances obliged me to retire here. A pleasant spot, all things considered, conveniently situated between Hatton Garden and Saffron Hill, and there are always rooms to be had. Mention my name, my dear sir,' Mr Rose said, taking a genteel sip at his gin, 'feel free to mention my name.'

John thanked him; and though he spent much of his last night sleeplessly trying to descry some clear way forward, and preferably upward, in his life, by daybreak he had arrived at no firmer conclusion than that he needed somewhere to live, and Mr Rose's suggestion was as good as any. So, up betimes in the morning, he washed himself as best he could, brushed his one coat, polished up his one pair of boots, packed his one bag, shook the hand that Mr Rose extended from under his heap of rugs, said goodbye to the Bidmeads, and made his way down to the lodge.

A surprise awaited him there: a packet had been left for him, containing two half-crowns. There was no written direction on the front, and the turnkey said he hadn't been on duty when it came, and could not enlighten John as to who had sent it. It could not have been more welcome, but it made the guilt and shame gnaw harder within him.

The turnkey opened he gate for him, and John stepped out into the world. The light of the winter's day seemed brighter than the light within the high walls of the King's Bench, but harsher too; and the hurry and uproar of the streets, clattering, jangling and purposeful, seemed to reproach him for having no place there. Though he set out briskly, he could not rid himself of an impression that he was skulking.

He crossed Blackfriars Bridge, and entered the City. Though he knew perhaps a dozen people in the whole of London, a settled fear was upon him that he would meet one of them amongst the throngs that he passed, and he could not reason himself out of it. And still as he walked on, his mind wandered amidst vague questionings about his future. All about him the struggle to make a living was evident. Street-sellers of every description, selling or attempting to sell every article that desperate ingenuity could devise: here, fresh turf divots for the cages of captive songbirds, there, children's horn-books; here, cat's-meat and broken sprats, there single sheets of letter-paper. A hawker of broadsheets going through his husky and mechanical patter put John in mind of Waldo Tuttle, and for a moment he was taken with the idea of seeking him out and asking to be taken on again as a sweetener. But where to find him? He might be anywhere in England. A foolish idea.

'Though foolish ideas,' John thought, 'seem to be my stock-in-trade. It would be hard to find a more foolish one than coming to London, and expecting the city to fall at your feet.' His self-loathing grew more intense as he looked back at his

220

ignominious progress. Even Dr Frank Spruce's unromantic and down-to-earth advice had proved impossible for him to follow: he had failed even to keep his place as lowly clerk. Was there any hope for him?

Not if you keep feeling sorry for yourself, he thought; but it was hard to stop self-pity stealing over him. Would he not have done better to have stayed at his uncle Saul's house? But no: at that thought the maudlin vapours dispersed, and John found a hard nugget of pride remaining to him. No, not Uncle Saul: no matter what his distress, he would not apply to Uncle Saul. he would go barefoot before that.

As for Catherine . . . There his feelings were so mixed that he could scarcely tell what they were. He could hardly apply to her for help without her parents knowing of it; and what a final seal that would put on her parents' disapproval of him! 'Papa, will you make out a banker's order to relieve Mr Twopenny – he is penniless, and has just come out of the debtors' prison.' Impossible – even if that same hard residue of pride would allow him to apply to her, which it would not.

And besides that, the darker his experience of life became, the more difficult it was to see Catherine as he had seen her when he had been an innocent boy. The words that Verity Deene had spoken about love in a cottage had their part in this; for the knowledge had slowly grown upon him that Catherine would have been greatly dismayed at the idea of love in a cottage, and that she had not contemplated any such thing when she had entered into a romance with him. He did not think badly of her; but the process of disillusionment he had undergone included her, and especially her passivity before her parents' proscription of him as a suitor, and his feelings could never be quite the same again.

His wandering mind had brought him no nearer to a conclusion, but his footsteps had brought him near to his destination. He had not expected a savoury neighbourhood, and he did not find one. Saffron Hill was a slum district notorious for crime; and Jolly Butcher's Yard, though it seemed to be trying to keep its face turned to the more respectable Hatton Garden side, was just as plainly being tapped on the shoulder by its degenerate neighbour. A 'Yard' there certainly was, in that there was a cobbled space between three frowsy tenements, noxious with refuse that had been swept into banks like filthy snow, but there was certainly nothing resembling the establishment of a butcher here; and if there had been it seemed unlikely, given the disposable income of the inhabitants, that he would have found many reasons for being jolly.

An old woman was seated on an upturned basket at the entrance to the yard, smoking a pipe and nursing a collection of thin limbs that bore a faint resemblance to an infant. She confirmed, on John's inquiring, that this was Jolly Butcher's Yard; and on his further asking if there were rooms to let, she said that there generally were, on account of people 'going off' – an expression that John chose not to have elucidated – and that he should ask for Hankey, across the way.

John knocked at the door she indicated.

To his surprise, a baby answered the door. After a moment, he perceived the very small girl who was behind the baby, and holding it aloft with difficulty. He asked for Hankey, and got him; and at first he rather wished he hadn't. Mr Hankey turned out to be a very bruised and bruising-looking mountain of a man with cropped hair and a ferocious expression. But in answer to John's faltering inquiry he replied that yes, there was rooms, in a voice as soft and small as his exterior was hard and large, and stepped civilly aside to let him in.

It further transpired that Mr Hankey was not the landlord of the tenement – 'he lives out west somewheres, and oh don't I wonder why he don't choose to live on the premises, I don't think!' – but rather a tenant who was entrusted with the collection of the rent from his fellows, a capacity for which he had obvious qualifications. On John's mentioning that the place had been recommended to him

221

by Mr Randal Rose, Mr Hankey grunted and said, 'Oh yes! I remember him. And wasn't he a pretty fellow, and didn't he smell of other things than roses, not much he didn't. But there, we've all got to live, don't we? Look at me. I turn a penny in the prize-ring when I can. The fancy nobs come to watch me; but if the p'lice and the beaks break it up, is it them who gets arrested and not me?; and if the fancy nobs saw me in the street, would they speak to me?, and would they like to try living on what I earn? Would they just, and the moon is made of green cheese, I don't think!'

Mr Hankey seemed relieved to have got these sentiments off his broad chest, and returning his attention to John said, 'There's two rooms: one two-and-six a week, the other three bob. The cheaper one's got a wery nice view over the rooftops; but I'll be truthful with you, the last tenant died in it. Mind you, he went off wery peaceful, and sang hymns all the way.'

John did not find this such a comforting circumstance as Mr Hankey seemed to, and decided on the other room. Right at the top of the building it was, and accessible through a sort of vertical maze of worm-eaten stairways, dark landings, and darker passages; and it was pretty much as John expected, being small, bare, and grimy, and lit by a skylight which the pigeon population of the city seemed to have expressly chosen as its last resting-place. But he was in no position to be fastidious. The room had the supreme advantage of being cheap, and he took it for a week. Mr Hankey concluded the business by showing John the communal kitchen of the lodging-house, where a large number of people, alike only in their poverty, were huddled about the hearth and being climbed over by an even larger number of children. John's attention was transfixed by an old man who had on his neck the largest wen he had ever seen, and so he was a little absent when Mr Hankey asked him his name. 'Oh – Twopenny – John,' he said; and the company immediately taking this for a nickname, he was Tup'ny John to them from that moment forth.

And from that moment forth Tup'ny John, or John Twopenny, resumed his battle for life. And a grim battle it was, as it was for all who enjoyed the hospitality of the Jolly Butcher. There were people there who were in regular employment, but they were not many, and their faces were permanently haunted by the thought of the employment being taken away from them; and there were people there who had no employment at all, and were either languishing until the parish should take them into its untender embrace, or else inclining to the Saffron Hill element in the Butcher's personality, and earning a crust in a covert and nocturnal manner. In between these two extremes lay the great mass of the residents of the yard, and of the adjoining heaps of decaying masonry that were linked to it by dark entries, stairways, cellars, brick passages, roof-walks, and rickety timber causeways: in between these two extremes existed the seamstresses, the odd-job men, the building labourers, the street-sellers of flowers and ribbons and gingerbread, the collectors of waste-paper and chickweed and corks and feathers and horse-dung, the makers of clothes-pegs and flypapers, the washerwomen, the organ-grinders, the baby-minders, the brickmakers, the dockyard workers, the countless shifters and scramblers who clung to the underside of the city's 'respectable' life and hoped not to be shaken off into the teeming darkness below.

Including John; but as the days following his release went by, John found that darkness yawning nearer and nearer to him. He could not get work. He was too reduced and down-at-heel now to make a showing in any position that required education, too genteel and inexperienced to be taken on by any contractor of manual labour. He searched without hope, and was turned down without surprise. By the end of the week his money was quite gone, and if one of his fellow-lodgers in the yard had not offered him a small plate of potatoes in the kitchen, he would have gone to bed without having eaten a crumb in the last twenty-four hours. He was entering a passage in his life which in his cheerful youth at Saltmarsh would have seemed a nightmare of impossible ghastliness.

And he could not rouse himself: he knew now the listlessness of poverty and humiliation, and the way energy seeped away as fruitful opportunity was denied it. The shadow of waste, of failure, and of the spiked bars of the debtors' prison lay heavy on him, and he could not pull himself away from it. And it was by an irony appropriate to his despair that the debtors' prison, or the people he had met there, furnished him at last with a degraded means of support.

A man came to the lodging-house asking for Mr Randal Rose, on the supposition that this was still his address. John was warming himself by the kitchen fire, and drowsily wondering where he would go when Hankey turned him out for not paying the rent, and was half inclined not to speak. But when the man plaintively asked where Mr Rose could be found, John stirred, and told him that he was in the King's Bench.

'Confound it, why can't he stay in the same place for two minutes at a time!' the man exclaimed. 'On the tramp all day, and now I've to walk all the way over to the Borough to find the infernal fellow, supposing they'll let me in. I don't know. It's a job in itself to find a good screever nowadays – the perfession ain't what it was!'

John recalled Mr Rose's account of his 'Chequered Career', and his detailed explanation of what a screever was; and at the same moment his stomach cramped, and growled, and generally called his attention to its emptiness. He looked round from the fire at the man, who was dressed both soberly and shabbily, and something – probably that same clamorous stomach – made his decision for him.

'You're in want of a screever, did you say?'

John did it. Having impressed the shabby-sober man with his credentials – in effect, his educated speech and manner, his understanding of the screever's craft, and a sample of his handwriting – he took him up to his room where they could be confidential, and there he composed the required screeve. The shabby-sober man had the notepaper all ready, and gave John a careful account of his particular 'lay', or dodge. He posed as a respectable tradesman – 'sometimes a grocer, sometimes a draper – I leave that to you, sir' – who had been utterly ruined by a bank failure, and was forced to beg as a consequence. The documents he required to authenticate his role were letters of reference from his wealthier customers, a petition signed by his fellow-tradesmen, a notice from the failed bank and, if it could be managed, a quarterly statement of accounts for his business.

'My last set fell apart, on account of being handled so many times by the custom,' the beggar explained. 'But bless you, they did very well – ve-ry well. Shuffle into a coffee-house or a public on the Tottenham Court Road, where all the shopkeepers are chewing the fat and thinking how nicely they're a-doing, and you make quite a stir, believe me. Specially with the documents. The documents settles it. As long as they're not too new-looking – that's why I carry the notepaper around with me, to wear it in before you write on it, sir – or too old-looking, of course. Small shopkeepers is always the best custom, because they take it to heart, sir: they know how easy it is to fall!'

They were not the only ones who knew, John thought; but he said nothing, and got on with the task in hand. This was quite a complex screeve for a beginner, but want lent him ingenuity; and from his experience as a copying-clerk he knew all the appropriate forms of address and turns of phrase for commercial and legal documents. Counterfeiting different specimens of handwriting came less easily, but the shabby-sober man, who looked over his shoulder with great interest while he worked, seemed quite satisfied; only once interjecting: 'If I might suggest, sir, mix a little water with your ink for the next letter – it makes it more convincing, if the ink differs from one to another, you see.' Only when it came to the signatures did John pause, and reflect that he was engaged in nothing less than forgery; but the beggar, supposing that his invention had run dry, said encouragingly, 'Any names'll do, sir, as long as they're middling sorts of names – not all Smiths and Browns, which don't convince. And throw in a curious one here and there – say a Higginbottom – because that's lifelike.'

He did it. He finished the screeve, and he handed it over, and he charged three shillings for it. The shabby-sober man seemed to find this reasonable, and paid up; and before leaving with his documents carefully tucked in his breast pocket he said to John, 'New to the screeving work, sir?'

'Does it show?' said John grimly.

'Oh! Not in any unpleasant way, sir. I merely noted the steadiness of the hand. Screevers, I'm sorry to say, is often topers. I know quite a few chaps on the blab who'd be interested to hear of a screever who ain't got the shakes. Shall I pass the word on?'

'By all means: just ask for Tup'ny John,' said John, again with a certain grimness; and when the beggar had gone, he sat down on his dingy bed, and held his head in his hands, and gazed at the three shillings that lay on the rickety table next to his pen and ink.

But not for long. Soon he got up, and rang the three shillings, and then pocketed them. Two of them went towards his rent, and with the rest he bought a meat-pudding at a cook-shop nearby, with a pint of ale. He let his stomach have the last word on the matter; and the opinion of his stomach was, that no matter what his pride or his conscience thought of screeving, it beat starving by a considerable distance.

And so he began it. At his wits' end, his nerve and his strength of will and his resilience sapped by all he had lately gone through, John kept body and soul together by screeving. He had slipped into the 'profession' by accident, and for a while he plied it in the same arbitrary and passive way; if someone in need of a screeve came to Jolly Butcher's Yard looking for him, having heard his name by word of mouth, he obliged, but he did not go in search of the work. Probably his pride and his conscience were still trying to shout down his stomach, and argue that this was at least better than advertising his disgrace; but stomach, again, had the last word. He could not support himself so perfunctorily: if he was to be a screever, he must go the whole hog. One of the professional beggars who came to him told him that he'd do no good hidden away here – he needed to make himself known, to 'catch the traffic'; and suggested 'Ma Dade's nethersken' as the ideal place.

A nethersken, John learned, was a lodging-house of low, if not nefarious character; and that kept by the fearsome old woman known as Ma Dade was in an appalling slum district hard by St Giles's Church. The vast criminal rookery of St Giles was no longer intact: slum clearances had broken it up in recent years. But what remained was even more crammed, fetid and nightmarish than ever. John discovered this because he went there. He went there, when he had gone several days without any screeving work coming to him, and his stomach had begun to complain of its wrongs again, and would not be silenced.

Ma Dade's nethersken was a hideous heap of crumbling bricks held together more by soot and slime than mortar, and containing within its sweating walls a floating population of anything between fifty and a hundred lodgers. On the ground floor Ma Dade kept a beer-shop which was also a trysting-place for shady characters from a wide area; and here Tup'ny John made himself known, and for a small remission to the management, was permitted to ply his trade.

It soon became known, amongst the community who cared to know such things, that a prime screever known as Tup'ny John was to be found any day at Ma Dade's, and he did good business, insofar as his stomach held its peace most of the time; and as the weeks went by the seat he was accustomed to take in the seedy beer-shop became known as Tup'ny John's Chair, and was tacitly set aside for him.

It was an indication in itself of how low John had fallen, that he was readily accepted there – that they at once took him for no more nor less than the sort of broken-down hopeless shabby-genteel fellow who turned to screeving; and indeed, he thought, in what way were they wrong?

He was a beginner, but he was learning fast. He learned the various dodges or lays the professional beggars practised, and the documents that each required. Those who were 'on the glim' posed as tradesmen whose property had been destroyed in a fire, and the deeds of the imaginary property came in useful, especially when lightly scorched by a candle. 'Monkry' lays were those suitable to tramping in the country: soldiers' and sailors' credentials were popular for this, drawing sympathetic donations from farmers' wives with sons in the forces. The 'nubbingken' lay was particularly practised around the Courts of Justice, the beggar presenting himself as having been ruined by a long and expensive lawsuit; for this John produced legal documents, learning to counterfeit the special calligraphy known as law-hand.

He functioned, too, when the occasion required, as a gag-man – making up new dodges for mendicants who had worked their current lay for all it was worth, and needed a change. With perverse invention, he created testimonials from church-men verifying that the bearer was a missionary returned from his brave crusade in Africa to find his patrimony squandered by a prodigal brother, or from Cornish mine-captains who had been forced to close down because of flooding, and recommended the bearer as an honest and industrious man who had laboured in the tin-mines for twenty years. He conjured up all manner of names and professions, and signed himself as all manner of distinguished people: he was a rector, a commodore, a justice of the peace, a major in the cavalry, a brigadier in the infantry, a collector in the East India Company, and every species of manufacturer and merchant. And he was a doctor.

If he had not been in such a lowered and deadened state, the bitter irony of this would have been too much for John. For testimonials from doctors were much in demand; and not unnaturally, he was good at them. Beggars working the 'scaldrum dodge' – exhibiting sham illnesses and self-inflicted wounds – soon learned that there was no one to beat Tup'ny John when it came to doctor's screeves. 'So,' John would think, 'all that poring over medical texts that I did at Mr Wenn's wasn't wasted after all'; and often when that thought came to him, he would have to order a pot of Ma Dade's sulphurous beer to drive the thought away.

Thus he lived: enchained to the harshest reality that even London had to show, and yet living also in a wholly invented world, a world of wrecked ships that had never been launched, and burnt-down factories that had never been built; of imaginary lawsuits, and fictitious clergymen, and make-believe diseases. He lived thus from day to day, from trifling fee to trifling fee, and he lived under his own pretence – a pretence that this mode of work was merely a temporary aberration, from which he would soon break free.

About the lays and dodges themselves, John was neutral. A living had somehow to be made: some niche had to be found in the vast, unfriendly world; and to him it was indicative of how unfriendly that world was, that men should be driven to such elaborate expedients to support themselves on its margins. For if the labour and ingenuity of the professional beggars and cadgers was misplaced, it was labour and ingenuity still, and no one who had mixed with them could suppose they had an easy time of it. A piquant instance was provided by one of his customers who worked the scaldrum dodge: he was an 'Abram-man', who went about the streets shamming fits, carrying in his pocket a screeved doctor's letter stating that the fits prevented him from keeping a job. The Abram-man had worked the dodge so long that the fits had become involuntary, and now he was just such a trembling, jerking, twitching wretch as he had formerly pretended to be. The crowning oddity was that he still insisted on procuring forged credentials, when a conscientious doctor would have supplied him with real ones. Here was another irony to be appreciated, if you had a relish for sour flavours.

John stopped short of monetary forgery. It was not much to be proud of, perhaps, but he stuck to it. He would have nothing to do with cheques, notes, bills of exchange, receipts, share certificates, or anything that had a face value. And the opportunity would not have been lacking, had he chosen to take it. In frequenting Ma Dade's establishment, he was dipping a toe in a murky underworld that had no bottom, and that had sucked many honest men under; and he was more than once approached by the accomplices of a 'shofulman' or counterfeiter who had watched him work. Coiners and fences were likewise *habitués* of that pestilential spot; shabby confidence tricksters who planned their deceptions of provincial visitors over a glass of Ma Dade's fiery gin; pickpockets, mostly wretched undersized youths who were barely kept alive by their activities, but some with aspirations to join the 'swell mob', who dressed well and could mingle with a respectable crowd unnoticed; prostitutes of the most haggard kind, who sold themselves against a darkened doorway for a few coppers; petty thieves and cheats and sharpers of every sort. Feverish vitality alternating with brutish dullness; flash costume and the showily curled locks of hair called Newgate-knockers mingling with washed-out rags and lice; flaring gaslight against noisome darkness; racy sharpness and lumbering stupidity in the same breath; comradely generosity and corpse-robbing meanness; this was the world of starkness and contrast and fitful glare that Tup'ny John moved in, and lived off.

And John Twopenny? Where was he? Somewhere underneath Tup'ny John, perhaps, but buried so deep that he could not be found. Sometimes, when he leaned listlessly out of one of the landing windows at Jolly Butcher's Yard and watched the sun sinking below the crazy rooftops, his thoughts would touch upon old memories, and John Twopenny would rise up and displace Tup'ny John, for a time. And it was during such a time that he decided he must write to Catherine. The height of incongruity, inscribing her name in this place, and with the pen that he had lately used to write a false letter of recommendation; but it must be done.

It must be done, because whatever dream the two of them had been living in was over, most definitely over. He was not only unfit for her, he was unfit for anybody. He did not state it so baldly in his letter; he did not specify the lengths he had been driven to in order to keep himself alive; but he told her that he had come to poverty, that he had no prospects, and that he could not see the time when he would again be the man she had known. In the light of this, he said, she must feel free, if it was her wish, to absolve herself of any obligation towards him. He could not hold her to any sort of promise, spoken or unspoken, under such circumstances. Whatever she chose, he would abide by it.

He did not give the address of Jolly Butcher's Yard, which was not a place the postman ever called at; instead he asked for letters to be directed care of a coffee-house in Hatton Garden, and said likewise in his covering letter to Verity Deene. For some reason the thought of Verity's keen dark eyes beholding him in this condition appalled him more than anything, and he was thankful that the haunt of the Jolly Butcher was at a good distance, both literally and metaphorically, from the whitewashed façades and neatly swept mews corners of Montagu Place.

And so it was done; and John Twopenny sank out of sight beneath Tup'ny John once more. He might have stayed there for ever, but for one circumstance at Jolly Butcher's Yard that raised him instantly, and continued to revive him at frequent intervals.

It began with Mr Hankey, whom John found in the kitchen one morning drooping over the fire, with his left arm fiercely clutching at his right shoulder, as if he were trying to hug himself to death. The huge man's face was beaded with sweat, and he wore the dog-like grin of extremest pain.

Done it at a prize-fight last night, he said – not in the ring, but fending off some toughs who had bet against him, and took it ill when he won. When John asked if he could help, Mr Hankey said, unconvincingly, that it wasn't nothing and didn't hurt a bit; but he submitted to John's exploring fingers.

It was plainly a dislocation. John hesitated. He had seen it done by his father, numerous times; and once or twice his father had taken his hands and placed them on the affected shoulder, carefully explaining what he was about to do. But John had never done it himself.

'Mr Hankey . . . will you trust me?'

Mr Hankey replied, through gritted teeth, that it couldn't hurt any more than it did now, so he might as well go in and win.

John gripped: wrenched. Mr Hankey yelled, and almost leaped out of his chair, and John thought swiftly 'I've broken his arm – I've broken this man's arm, and he is going to tear me apart with the other one.'

And then he realized that Mr Hankey's shout had been the usual one of shocked surprise at the sensation of the joint clicking back into place, and he experienced a surge of relief and triumph that seemed to carry him back on its uplifted crest to happier days, and dreams that had not died.

Mr Hankey was working his shoulder. 'Well, hang me if that don't feel easier, and do I know how you did it, of course I do, I don't think! Well, hang me!'

'I should think it will still give you pain,' John said. 'There may be torn ligaments. You'd best wear a sling, I think, and give it complete rest until it's healed.'

Mr Hankey, mopping his forehead, gave vent to some more explosive sentiments, descriptive of his being hanged, damned, strapped, and blowed if he ever saw the like; and then gave John a curious look, and said, 'Tup'ny John, let me shake your hand, if you don't mind my left. I confess I doubted you there for a minute – but then I never had any call to suppose you knew doctoring, you see. Never a hint of it.'

'Oh – well . . .' John shrugged uncomfortably. 'I learnt a bit here and there from my father.' He said no more, and Hankey, though he continued to look curious, did not press him, for that was not the way of Jolly Butcher's Yard. Though it was plain to John's neighbours that he was a man who had seen better days, they would never have dreamt of alluding to the fact. Adversity and misfortune were things they understood very well, being almost continually subject to them; and they left it at that.

And it was from that day onward that John Twopenny was regularly called upon to emerge from the shadows of Tup'ny John, and perform wonders upon the infirmities of the dwellers in the yard and its environs. It was a fame that he would readily have disclaimed; for though he was always willing to lend a hand and use what little medical skill and knowledge he had, he was strongly conscious that he was completely unqualified for such a task, and continually apprehensive that his inexperience, coupled with the almost reverential trust that the people placed in him, might result in his doing harm rather than good. He could see why it was that they regarded his basic ministrations with superstitious awe: the simple fact was that they had never had any medical attendance whatsoever, and probably could never expect any until the parish surgeon examined their dying bodies in the workhouse infirmary. And now here was a man living amongst them who undertook to cure and relieve pain – or at the very least to look and reassure – and did not require paying. For John would not hear of taking payment for such untrained services as he could provide, even supposing the Yarders could afford it. There was also, perhaps, expiation for the screeving in this. He never, at any rate,

227

refused a summons, no matter what the hour.

It began fortuitously. Mrs Winch, a woman lodging in the same tenement, who made a sort of living from stitching gunny sacks, and whose husband made no sort of living at all from selling lime, was thrown into panic by the illness of her youngest child, which she suspected was the cholera. Mr Hankey, who heard her wailing from the kitchen, told her of the miraculous operation that Tup'ny John had performed on him; and the next thing John knew he was being begged to look at her baby, and see what he could do. John, desperately uncomfortable, insisted that he had no such abilities, but the beseeching look Mrs Winch gave him was not to be resisted. Feeling an imposter, but determined to summon up all he knew, he examined the child; a large number of the Yarders crowding into the room to watch, though they were respectfully silent, with the exception of Mr Hankey, who appropriately enough had made a rabbit out of his handkerchief, and kept wagging it over the head of the infant's bed whilst exhorting him to 'Buck up' – a treatment that was more kindly than effective.

John could not be certain – he did not dare to be certain – but he was strongly convinced that the child's ailment was not the cholera. The old days spent haunting the Norfolk and Norwich Hospital stood him in good stead here. The 'rice-water' diarrhoea was not present, and though there was fever, it was not following the hectic course associated with cholera. Of course even if it were, as he thought, some milder intestinal infection, the child might well not survive it; but the assembled Yarders, and the parents especially, were looking to him so solemnly that he decided to put his head on the block. He gave it as his opinion that it was not cholera; prescribed no food for the child and – though this was something of a counsel of perfection in the Butcher's environs – only clean water; and composed himself to wait. He would soon know if he was right: for if it was cholera, the child would very probably be dead by the next morning.

The child lived. Its body successfully resisted whatever gastric fever had entered it, and within a couple of days the little boy was well enough to eat, and to be amused by Mr Hankey's indefatigable rabbit. John knew that he had done little or nothing, and said so; but the Yarders refused to accept that. A confused but firm idea took hold amongst them that he had cured the cholera, or as good as, and he could not persuade them out of it. From then on he was the medical oracle of the district. The consciousness of being desperately ill-equipped for his role was with him every time he was called to a sickbed or an accident. But with him, too, was the undying desire to relieve and heal; and all he could do was apply the knowledge he had gained from his father and from his own studies, and stand by his medical beliefs – let nature take its course wherever possible, be strict about cleanliness, ventilation, and sanitary arrangements, and avoid the fashionable 'heroic' treatments with their massive doses and purges. He did not dare prescribe anything beyond common remedies like castor oil and Peruvian bark, and he had not the means to dispense; but he could bandage and splint, and advise and encourage, and act as a night-nurse; and though he sometimes reproached himself that he was no better than some village wise-woman with her herb teas and charms, he could at least say that no one whom he attended actually died.

He was certainly kept busy. The cessation of winter did not diminish the frequency of illness amongst John's neighbours; for spring was not much in evidence in Jolly Butcher's Yard, except inasmuch as the smell from the choked gutters and privies and heaps of rubbish became even more lively in the warmer weather. On one such mild and fly-blown day, John walked over to the coffee-house in Hatton Garden to see if there were any letters for him. He had omitted to call there lately: he had been sitting up at nights with a family in a neighbouring court who were all sick with enteric fever, and he felt permanently tired and listless.

There was a letter, from Catherine, with a covering note from Verity. John read them both in his garret room, which felt chill to him despite the mildness of the day – damp in the walls, perhaps. The covering note from Verity was very short. It read simply: *John, where are you living? Please let me know.* The letter from Catherine was longer.

A sort of vague dismay characterized it. She was enormously sorry to hear of his misfortunes, and hardly knew what to say or think, but she was sure that somehow things would turn out all right. She was afraid that it had been a great strain on them being apart for so long, and of course they had met when they were very young, and young people could be very solemn about things, too solemn perhaps . . . Again she didn't know what to say or think. If he thought it advisable that they should consider themselves released from any engagement, then perhaps that would be for the best, though she would never cease to think fondly of him, especially as he was in difficulties. Though surely things could not be so bad as all that. Perhaps things would resolve themselves if they met . . .? Papa had taken a house in London, and he kept promising to take the family there for the season, though it had been put off on account of Mama twisting her ankle on a molehill, and how on earth did one twist one's ankle on a molehill, he might well ask, but poor Mama managed it somehow . . . Anyway, they were surely coming up to London sooner or later, perhaps he might call? Mama and Papa might have softened a little by then, and perhaps if he left a card . . .

John laid the letter down. Call! Leave a card! He looked around at his room, at the blackened grate, the shelf with half a stale loaf standing on it, the lame table and the crippled chair, the skylight with its burden of dead pigeons. 'Oh, Catherine, Catherine,' he murmured. The last ember of understanding had winked out and died.

There was a pan of cold coffee in the grate; he decided to take it down and heat it in the kitchen, where there was always a fire. Mr Hankey was there, broiling a slice of rusty bacon, and a handful of the shock-headed children with which the tenement swarmed. John heated his coffee, but found he did not fancy it any more, and instead sat huddled close to the fire. He ought to go out in search of work; but somehow today he could not face Ma Dade's, or the roaring, racketing streets. All he wanted to do was sit by the fire, and he could not even bring himself to draw animals on a piece of slate for the children, an accomplishment for which he was highly prized by the nurslings of the Jolly Butcher. He gazed into the flames, and he thought of Catherine, and he thought of Verity; he thought of his dead parents, and of Saltmarsh and the house on the cliff, and the drawings of sailing-ships carved on the church pews; and he huddled closer to the fire, and let his thoughts take him where they would. They were curiously swift and vivid, these thoughts, in contrast with the aching weariness of his body: they passed in rapid procession through his mind, a jumbled pageant in which the distant past and the day before yesterday marched together arm-in-arm, and showed strange similarities; until at last they became so mixed up that he could not separate them, and Mr Bowerman was the headmaster of Mr Wenn's Academy, and Tom Bidmead was a parlour-boarder there; and the Soldier was digging bait on the marshes in company with Miss Thimblebee, who was holding the bucket; and Admiral Fernhill was driving a cheap-jack's cart, and Dr Spruce was buying a teapot from him.

John heard himself chuckle. What odd conjunctions! He was finding his thoughts rather entertaining, and he wondered what they would come up with next. Ah! Dear old Philip Revell, friend of his boyhood, wearing a turban and riding an elephant into Jolly Butcher's Yard! Good, very good! And Uncle Saul, dressed in a coster's neckerchief and velvet waistcoat, swapping dirty stories with the toughs at Ma Dade's! Good, indeed! What next? Why – that was surely Mr Addy, perching atop Temple Bar, and letting off fireworks into the sky to the astonishment of the populace! Excellent! And good heavens, Mr Flowers the solicitor in the yard of the King's Bench prison – now how did he ever get in there? In good spirits, though, and playing at skittles with Waldo Tuttle in his best white hat: of course, of course, why not? Capital!

And now what is this, emerging but slowly from the flames, and carrying darkness with it? Ah no. No, no. Not his poor father – not like that. If he must see his father, let him see him as he was before the fall, not wrapped in the shadows of the Hanged Man's House. Push him away! There – better. But here is Mr Goodway instead – God's curse on him! – sailing a boat up to the quayside at Hales-next-the-sea. And what is that he is dragging out of the boat on to the quay? Dear God, a mermaid – not a mermaid in a bottle, but a real mermaid – dead, alas! That infernal man has caught her, and killed her! See – no life stirs her beautiful features. Those features . . . they resemble Catherine's. They strongly resemble Catherine's . . . Oh, God in heaven, no!

John wiped his brow with his sleeve: it came away wet. The fire was communicating its warmth at last. Unusual for Mr Wenn to allow them such a fire as this, so early in the day; he wondered if Stuffins had remarked on it. Come to think of it, where *was* Stuffins? Had Mr Bowerman called him up to his office, perhaps? But then the office was downstairs, across the hall, right next to Uncle Saul's. And what was that noise? One of Sar'ann's mousetraps? He looked frantically all round him. How dingy the place was looking! Tetty must be ill – she would never allow the house to get like this. And wasn't that Murphy Burble over there? The poor child should be in bed at a time like this, it must be past midnight. How swiftly that darkness had come down . . .!

Somebody was saying something about Tup'ny John. A child's voice. What was she saying? 'Tup'ny John has fallen down!' Curious coincidence. He had fallen down too – at least, he supposed he must have, because he was face down on the floor, and his lip was bleeding. Someone was lifting him up, gently. Immensely strong someone – ah, Mr Hankey, of course. Obliged to Mr Hankey – felt faint for a moment there – better now. Can stand. No, can't stand. Embarrassing, foolish. Feel like weeping, also laughing. Bad head, dreadfully bad head.

Going upstairs. How? Carried. Dizziness, stairs for ever, stair upon stair, hundreds upon hundreds, thousands upon thousands . . . Bed. Bed, good, good, rest, but can't rest. Bed feels as if on fire. Oh dear God. Need drink. Water, brackish, but good, good, from huge gentle hand of Mr Hankey. Face of Mr Hankey looking down, troubled. Must thank Mr Hankey – if only could speak. Other faces appearing. Voices. What saying? Something about Tup'ny John again. Tup'ny John is ill. Poor Tup'ny John. Just let him rest a minute, and then he would go and see Tup'ny John, see if he could do anything for him. Wait, though. He was Tup'ny John, though he didn't see how he could be, because he was John Twopenny too. Which? Which was he? Tup'ny John, John Twopenny . . . Ah, but it didn't matter, let them both climb aboard this black ship of oblivion that was coming for him, climb aboard and sail away, beyond the farthest horizon, for ever and ever.

CHAPTER TWO

The Bluestocking Is Called to Account

Miss Honoria Spikings was the prize pupil of a dancing-academy in Oxford Street. That she was the prize pupil was frequently asserted by Mr and Mrs Spikings to their friends, though the assertion was unsupported by any physical evidence, as Miss Honoria had the grace of a duck, besides being, as Verity knew, congenitally unteachable. But no matter: the dancing-academy furnished Verity with an opportunity that she could not neglect, so profoundly troubled in her mind had she become. It was her fortnightly duty to escort the vacuous dumpling thither, deliver her into the hands of a worn-looking gentleman with a glass eye and kit-fiddle, and pick her up again after two hours. And when the day for this fortnightly excursion arrived, Verity decided she was going to use it to try and find John.

In theory she could have waited until her own half-day, a week hence – but that was just it: she could not wait. Sceptical as she was of intuitions, instincts, presentiments, creeps, horrors, and all such, she could not deny that her anxiety about John had reached such a pitch that she could no longer live with it.

Her secret feelings for him, which she often sent sternly into a corner only to find them stealing up to her and wrapping her in a sad embrace, did not bear the whole responsibility for this. Even considered as a friend, or a sparring-partner, he was in a situation that she could not regard with either indifference or optimism. Securing his release from the debtors' prison was one thing, feeling that she might now consider him as permanently provided for was another. His job was gone, and he was alone in the city: these were not encouraging circumstances for a man emerging from the King's Bench, which was why she had sent him an anonymous gift of money – almost the last she possessed – on his release. After that she had thought, having made a friend of Miss Thimblebee, to keep in touch with him that way. But John had not returned to Miss Thimblebee's apartments, as that lady had informed Verity in a plaintive note; and for weeks upon weeks there had been no communication from him except that one letter to be passed on to Catherine, and which gave only a coffee-house as a forwarding address.

What was he doing, and how was he living? Perhaps he had told Catherine in his letter to her, but Verity was above peeping into it to find out; and besides, knowing John's pride, she suspected a similar reticence there. 'He must be in trouble,' she said to herself a hundred times as she laboured in the schoolroom. 'Something must be wrong'; and at last, when the day of Honoria's dancing-lesson allowed her a degree of free movement, she resolved that she would use it to track John down.

There was one difficulty. All four children went with her on these days. Having deposited Honoria with the dancing-master, it was Verity's further duty to take the three younger children for what was called an 'airing' – just as if they were musty items of laundry; though Verity, pursuing the analogy, felt that they would be more benefited by being pounded on rocks, and then put through a mangle. However, aired they must be: Hyde Park was the usual place. But as there was no choice but to have the brats dragging along behind her, Verity decided that she would present the very different route she meant to take today as an educational

231

expedition. Though they lived in the capital of the Empire, she said, they saw very little of it except the squares of the West End: today's outing would change that.

The coffee-house in Hatton Garden, where John had instructed his letters to be sent, was her destination. If it was his habit to go there to pick up his post, then someone there might know something of him – perhaps where he was to be found. It was a long walk for the pampered and pudgy-legged Spikings, and they were already complaining as they traversed High Holborn.

'I want to go to the park. I want to see the squirrels,' grumbled Tancred.

'Hush. Now see here – Lincoln's Inn. And over there, Gray's Inn. This is where English law sits in majesty. And perhaps if you study hard, you may be called to the Bar yourself one day, and have a set of chambers there.'

'I don't want to be a lawyer. I want to be a sportsman, and shoot bags of game every day. Bang!'

'If you please, Miss Deene,' whined Seraphina, 'Knight is putting his tongue out again.'

'Well, if he catches flies, I hope he likes the taste of them. Now, let's see . . . this is it, I think . . .'

A drab area, and a drab coffee-house. She hesitated on the threshold. The children were staring at her as if she were mad; but she must go in.

'Now here is a typical example of an old London coffee-house. The first coffee-houses came into existence about two hundred years ago, and were originally meeting-places for City merchants, who used them to transact business, and – and so on.' It would do: she hustled them in. Dusty old gentlemen drooping over their newspapers looked up in surprise, while the Spikings, with their innate good manners, stared back at them.

A waiter, in answer to her query, said he knew the gentleman she meant: very tall, fair hair, more bone than meat? Hadn't seen him lately. Called over waitress: gentleman name of Twopenny, had his letters here, seen him lately? Waitress thought he'd been in the other day, but couldn't be sure. There were no letters waiting for him, anyhow. Waitress begged to point out, by the by, that the small child in the short jacket and tight white pantaloons was a-pulling the cloth off that gentleman's table, and that gentleman didn't like it overmuch . . .

Verity hauled Knight away, and apologized. Quite all right, said the gentleman, who was sitting seedily over coffee and hot roll, and had five teeth, three black and two yellow. Couldn't help overhearing – was it a young man name of Tup'ny John the lady was looking for? Only there was a Tup'ny John over at Jolly Butcher's Yard, he thought. Tall, fair hair . . . Same chap, said the waiter: never knew he lived in Jolly Butcher's Yard – did you, Sal? Sal, the waitress, supposed he had to live somewhere – a little snappish on account of Knight's playing at quoits with the mustard-pots right under her feet. Well, said the gentleman with five teeth, Jolly Butcher's Yard was the place, he was sure of it. Not a very select spot, the waiter said when Verity asked him to direct her, but if she wanted to go there, that was her business. Go left here, then cross over, turn right and right again, and then – well, follow your nose, and he meant that literally.

Verity thanked them, discouraged Tancred from tying the waitress's apron-strings to the fender, and marched the brood away. Despite this success, her misgivings multiplied as she came to the entrance of Jolly Butcher's Yard. John must be in dire straits indeed . . .

'Miss Deene, Miss Deene,' squeaked Seraphina in horror, 'I think *poor* people live here!'

'Yes, Seraphina, they do,' Verity said, looking around her in dismay as they crossed the yard, 'and it is – it is very instructive for you to see them. You also, Tancred. If you go into parliament when you grow up, as your Papa hopes, it will be your job to set all this right.'

'Why should I?' said Tancred, ostentatiously holding his nose. 'They're just lazy and dirty. They like it that way. Papa says so.'

'Oh, Miss Deene, I shall get nits and fleas!' cried Seraphina.

'Oh, nonsense. You wish to be a lady, do you not? Well, ladies make charitable visits, so you should get used to it.' Verity was far from easy about bringing the Spikings here; but it couldn't be helped. A youth was leaning in a doorway smoking a clay-pipe, and she asked him if he knew John Twopenny.

'Tup'ny John? Over there. Top floor. Want a screeve, do you? You won't get one. He's sick, they say. Mortal sick.'

Verity ran, dragging the children after her. They were too astonished to protest, and too afraid of the contagion of poor people to leave her side; and by the time they reached the top floor of the tenement, too breathless even to utter a word. A hollow-eyed little girl pointed out the room to her, and she burst in at once.

A huge crop-headed man was seated at the foot of the bed, and a scrawny woman in a shawl at the head. Both looked up in surprise; but the wasted figure in the bed continued to turn its blond head restlessly on the patched pillow, and the hazy eyes did not look her way.

'Dear God – John . . .' Verity advanced to the bedside and looked down at him. His eyelids fluttered, and there seemed to be a moment of recognition before the fever carried him away again. The presence of strangers, not to mention the children, was fortunate: it brought her back from the brink of betraying herself.

'Friend of his, miss?' said the big man, in a little husky voice.

'I . . . yes.' Verity steadied her voice with difficulty. 'I didn't know he was ill . . . How long?'

'Two days. He came down with it all of a sudden, and we put him to bed. He ain't been left alone a minute since. I keep telling him to Buck up – I say, Tup'ny John, Buck up! – But I don't reckon he can!'

'He's like a hot coal, poor creature,' said the scrawny woman, putting back John's damp fringe with a gentle hand. 'And loose as anythink. He's quiet now, but he's been talking fifteen to the dozen, and none of it sense.'

Verity looked round at the little Spikings, who were all eyes and open mouths. 'Is there somewhere I can leave the children for a while?'

Mr Hankey – for it was he – said they could wait in the kitchen; so Verity deposited them there, promised she would not be long, and flew back to John.

'Has he been seen by a doctor?' she asked, resisting an impulse to hold John's hand, which was groping and clasping at the air.

'No, miss,' said the woman, who was Mrs Winch. 'We don't have doctors here, as a rule – no money to pay 'em; and whenever anybody's sick, it's generally Tup'ny John they send for. He saved my little 'un from the cholera, you know. That's the pity of it – he can't cure himself, you see!'

John broke out in a low muttering, both urgent and incoherent.

'There he goes again,' said Mr Hankey. 'I can't bear to hear him somehow. Buck up, Tup'ny John! Buck up, ole chap!'

'He must have a doctor,' Verity said, gazing on John's writhing form with a dreadful oppression at her heart. 'He must. Is there no doctor within reach?'

Mr Hankey didn't know of any: Mrs Winch didn't know of any; but just then the youth with the clay-pipe put his head into the room 'to see how the screever was coming along', and it turned out that he did know of one. 'There's only Dr Appleyard I know of, as concerns himself with poor folks, and don't mind getting his hands dirty. I used to live over Seven Dials way, and you'd see him a lot there; only surgeon who'd come anywhere near us. I say, Tup'ny John looks terrible bad, don't he?'

'Do you know where this Dr Appleyard can be found?' Verity said.

'Yi-is, bless you. Lives in Great Russell Street,' said the youth, smoking unconcernedly. 'Why?'

Verity turned in appeal to Mr Hankey. 'Please, would you try and fetch this Dr Appleyard? I will pay his fee. I really think John should be seen by a doctor.'

Mr Hankey was off in a twinkling; and Verity, after running down to the kitchen to make sure the young Spikings were all right, and finding them happily absorbed in examining a dead rat proffered as a mark of comradely hospitality by one of the infant residents of the house, joined Mrs Winch at John's bedside. It was only now that she took in the full squalor of John's room, and saw how desperately reduced his circumstances were. But then, what did she expect? He was a fortuneless orphan, like her; like her, adrift on the cold bosom of the world, and dependent on a permanent situation. In such a vulnerable position, it did not need much to go wrong for everything to go wrong.

'He wants water again, poor soul,' Mrs Winch said, bending close to John's murmuring lips. 'Would you like to give him a drink, miss?'

Verity did so. Again recognition seemed to flit through his eyes, and then he fell back into his stupor.

'We'd have sent for somebody if we'd ha' thought he'd got anybody,' Mrs Winch said, looking at Verity with discreet curiosity, 'but we never supposed he had anybody.'

'I suppose he hasn't, really,' said Verity.

She was aware that her two hours were rapidly slipping by, and that soon Honoria would be waiting to be collected; but she simply could not leave until the doctor had called. Fortunately she had not long to wait. Mr Hankey had found Dr Appleyard at home, and came breathlessly up the stairs with the physician in his wake, panting out, 'Here he is, sir – Tup'ny John we call him – cures all manner of complaints – whenever there's someone took bad hereabouts, it's Tup'ny John they call for, and he never refuses – and yet can he cure himself lying there? Of course he can't, and I'd like to see the man who could!'

Mr Hankey fell silent, quite winded, and found a vent for his overheated feelings by manufacturing rabbits from his handkerchief. Dr Appleyard, however, showed no signs of shortness of breath, though he was not young. He was a tall, lean, sere, dry man of sixty-odd, dressed in severe black, with iron-grey hair combed austerely back, a long bony face, and deep-set, uncommunicative eyes, which took in the room and the people in it with a single glance, and then applied themselves to the patient.

He looked grim as he made his examination; but that, Verity told herself, was merely due to his general gauntness of feature. Surely.

'He doctors people, you say?' Dr Appleyard said abruptly.

'Oh, yes, sir,' said Mrs Winch, 'regular. He's a wonderful way with it. My youngest got the cholera, but Tup'ny John brought him out of it.'

'Rubbish,' said Dr Appleyard, opening John's shirt and examining his chest. 'Cholera cases live or die, practically always die. Ach, the man's a mess . . . Well, he had no business doctoring people, unless he's qualified in any way. Is he?'

'No,' said Verity, as the others looked to her. 'No, he isn't. His father was a doctor, and he was to follow in his profession, but – but circumstances prevented it.'

'Well, he did *me* a power of good,' said Mr Hankey, recovering his breath, and indignant at these aspersions. 'And there's plenty of folk round about the yard who'll say the same.'

Dr Appleyard merely raised his eyebrows, which were still black in contrast with his grizzled hair, and made him look harsher than ever. 'Has he been dosing himself with anything? No? Well, that's something.' He covered John up again, then placed his long, lean hand on his damp forehead. Something about the very dryness and untenderness of that hand reassured Verity: she trusted Dr Appleyard far more than if he had been jolly. 'He looks as if he could do with dosing with food, at any rate,' he went on. 'However, we must see if we can pull him through this first. I confess I don't like the look of him.'

Mr Hankey, still in a state of resentment, muttered something to the effect that he didn't like the look of *him* either, and then made another rabbit.

'Are you going to bleed him, sir?' Mrs Winch asked.

'What, and kill him off? I can't do anything for him, except relieve his symptoms. China-clay mixture will bind his stomach. Give boiled water, and keep the room aired. The rest is up to dame Nature. He'll need nursing, constantly, even if the fever remits. Who's to do it?'

'We'll all take turn and turn about,' said Mrs Winch. 'I don't think there's anyone here who'd see Tup'ny John go without a nurse to watch over him.'

Dr Appleyard nodded, and threw Verity his sunken, piercing glance, which plainly said, *And what do you do here?*

'I shall settle your fees, doctor, if you will be good enough to submit your bill to me,' she said.

'No you won't,' said Dr Appleyard shortly. 'I don't draw fees from such places as Jolly Butcher's Yard. Any man who would, ma'am, is a hound.' There was a little alteration in his colourless tone here, as if he had poured out a frugal measure of feeling, and then put the bottle away. 'I shall call again tomorrow if I get time, but don't expect me. Doctoring the neighbourhood, eh?' he added, looking down at John with an unreadable expression. 'Well, I shouldn't approve, and I don't, but I dare say there are worse things.' He flung on his hat with an impatient air, as if he found the mere business of clothes an irritating distraction, and then surprised all three of them by shaking hands with them vigorously in turn before stalking out.

'That's all very well,' said Mr Hankey when he had gone, examining his own hand dubiously, 'but he didn't cure him, did he?'

Verity fumbled in her purse. 'He said china-clay mixture, I think. Will you get that for John? And anything else you think he may need.'

'Can't you stay, miss?' Mrs Winch said.

'I wish I could,' Verity said, looking down at John, who had subsided into an unrestful stillness. 'I wish . . . But I'm late as it is. I shall try to come again as soon as I can. Thank you for looking after him. I'm . . . I'm glad he's amongst friends.' To her horror, she found she was about to burst into tears, and had to call up her considerable reserves of self-control to prevent it.

'Why, there's not much use in being enemies, in the yard,' said Mrs Winch laconically. She gave Verity a speaking look – a pretty face, Verity thought, buried underneath the care and poverty – and without making any sound, formed the word *Sweetheart?* with her lips.

Verity shook her head, or nodded it, or – she didn't know what she did: quavered like an idiot, probably. But she managed to thank them again, and got out of the room, and hurried downstairs to collect her charges.

The little angels had not, alas, been stolen away by chimney-sweeps or gipsies. But the interval of waiting had not been without event. Tancred had challenged the young Yarder for possession of the dead rat; and the affair coming to blows, Tancred had been soundly beaten. He had the bruises to prove it, even if Seraphina, in her usual tale-bearing fashion, had not related the whole story, supplemented by Knight, who whirled round and round like a dervish, ecstatically crying: 'Tancred got whapped! Tancred got whapped!'

Tancred himself was very quiet about the whole business. Verity took his silence as a sportsmanlike magnanimity – a mistake, perhaps; but she was preoccupied, and anxious to get them home.

She hurried them on, therefore; and they arrived at the dancing-academy only ten minutes after the appointed time. By dint of grovelling apologies, Verity got Honoria's tantrum at their lateness down to manageable proportions – only two horses bolted at the sound of her screams echoing down Oxford Street – and feeling that she had managed pretty well under the circumstances, Verity ushered the whole litter back to Montagu Place.

And there, very willingly, she surrendered them to their nurse, the unfortunate Tripp, who went down before their onslaught like a deer pulled down by wolves. Verity was enjoying a respite in her own room prior to dinner, and alternating between a practical consideration of the question of when she could see John next, and an entirely unpractical impulse to burst into tears again, when a maid came to inform her that Mrs Spikings wished to see her directly.

Mrs Spikings might have wished to see her, but it was only Mr Spikings who was in a position to do so, as Verity found Mrs Spikings prostrate on the drawing-room sofa, with her hand covering her eyes, whilst Mr Spikings stood before the fireplace, pluming his whiskers, and undecided whether to look stern or fascinating, or both at once.

'You wished to see me?' Verity said, as neither of them spoke.

Mrs Spikings gave a sort of groan, in which only the word 'Serpent' was discernible, and pressed herself into the cushions.

'Felicia, be calm, I beg you,' said Mr Spikings, still exploring his whiskers. 'Exert yourself, Felicia, for my sake.'

'I cannot!' wailed Mrs Spikings. 'Alfred, I cannot! It is too much for me. I cannot stir. You must deal with her. You must speak for both of us – I am quite unable to say a word! If my life depended on it, I could not say so much as a word!'

'Very well, my dear.' Mr Spikings ceased preening, and tucked his gingery hands under his coat-tails. 'Miss Deene, it has been reported to us—'

'You have behaved like a perfect Serpent, Miss Deene, and I shall go to my grave regretting that I ever allowed you into my household!' cried Mrs Spikings, making such a sudden recovery that she fairly bounced off the sofa. 'You have played upon the good nature of my pretties. You have taken advantage of their generosity of spirit – which has always been our family failing. Dear Uncle Pomeroy was saying just the other day, was he not, Alfred, that we are too generous. Alfred, was he not?'

'Hm?' said Mr Spikings, who seemed to have become absorbed in contemplation of the Serpent's waist. 'Oh yes! Of course. Generosity, certainly.'

'Generosity, alas, is always liable to be made the prey of designing natures,' said Mrs Spikings, very fluty and melancholy. 'Did not Uncle Pomeroy warn us just the other day, Alfred, that Lambs cannot be trusted with Serpents?'

Mr Spikings appeared to have but an indistinct recollection of this unlikely piece of zoological advice; but said yes, to be on the safe side.

'Miss Deene,' said Mrs Spikings, grandly, 'speak. Did you take the children to the park today?'

'No, ma'am,' said Verity, 'we went on a different walk today – towards the City.'

'Miss Deene, speak. Were you authorized to make this unseemly innovation?'

'No, ma'am. But I thought it would be a change for the children, and educational.'

'Miss Deene, speak,' said Mrs Spikings, repeating this impressive formula even though Verity was speaking, and very lucidly. 'Did you take the children into low and unwholesome places, and expose them to indignities not at all consonant with their breeding and station?'

Though Verity had an idea now of just how much trouble she was in, she refused to be cowed. 'Ma'am, we made a short visit to a place—'

'Enough!' cried Mrs Spikings, sweeping over to the door that led to the dining-room. 'The poor dears themselves shall testify.'

236

She flung open the door to reveal the children waiting in a row on the other side of it; and even her apprehension of what was to come could not prevent Verity from finding this theatrical tableau rather ludicrous.

'My dears, I am sorry indeed to subject you to this ordeal, especially when I fear your little hearts are already quite breaking with all you have been through; but it will soon be over.' Mrs Spikings beckoned them in. 'Miss Deene, look upon these infants.'

Verity looked, and the children looked back, with the mingled smugness and furtiveness of informers down the ages; and a mighty hateful exchange of looks it was, all in all.

'Do you see these innocent little faces? And can you look upon them without shame, after what you have done? Seraphina, my dear, please tell us again where Miss Deene took you today.'

'She took us to horrid places,' said Seraphina, her face all flushed with the joy of tattling. 'She took us into a public-house, and talked to waiters and waitresses, and then she took us to a dreadful place called Jolly Butcher's Yard, and into a horrid house full of fleas and poor people, and she left us in a horrid kitchen—'

'And Tancred got whapped! Tancred got whapped!' put in Knight, who had still not got over his delight at this.

'And she left us there,' Tancred said, taking up the theme, and aiming a sideways kick at his brother, 'while she went to visit a man.'

'A man!' Mrs Spikings had been rather restrained for her, thus far, but now there was no holding her. 'A man! I had hoped that my ears might have been deceiving me, but now I hear it again from my own child's lips, and I must believe the unbelievable. A man! Gracious heavens above! Oh, Miss Deene, a man! A man!' Mrs Spikings went on exclaiming 'A man!' in various tones of horror and outrage, just as if Mr Spikings, frowning at himself in the pier-glass over the mantelpiece, were a horse, a dog, a parrot, or anything but a man; until Verity cut her off by saying, 'Yes, Mrs Spikings, I confess that I made a short visit to a man. A very sick man, in wretched circumstances, and in need of medical attendance. This I engaged on his behalf, and then I came away.'

'Indeed, Miss Deene? And was this man – ' Mrs Spikings nearly went into hysterics again at the word, but managed to control herself – 'was this man related to you?'

'He is not. He is an old friend.'

'And when you say old, do you mean that he is an old man? Or is he, Miss Deene, a young man?'

Verity swallowed. 'He is a young man, ma'am.'

'He was in bed, Ma,' said Tancred. 'We saw him.'

'My child!' sobbed Mrs Spikings, pressing Tancred's pointed head to her bosom. 'And those bruises, my poor boy – are you in great pain? Were there many of these ruffians who assaulted you?'

Tancred said six: and then, after a moment's reflection, added that it might have been twelve.

'Mrs Spikings,' Verity said, 'I realize that this may appear rather irregular, but I assure you—'

'You mean to say that you deny none of this? You mean to say, Miss Deene, that it is true?'

Mrs Spikings was so snappish here, and so venomous in her look, that Verity lost her composure. 'What else can I say, ma'am?' she said. 'Would you have me call your children liars? In this case, they are not: though the public-house was a coffee-house, and Master Tancred knows quite well that he was not set upon by six ruffians, or twelve, but picked a fight and lost it. As to the rest, it is true, but I do not see a matter for reproach in any of it.'

'Hoity-toity, Miss Deene!' put in Mr Spikings. 'You do not think dragging your charges through haunts of vice and idleness a matter for reproach, then, I take it?'

'Such places exist,' Verity said, 'and it is as well that they should know about them.'

'*You* know a great deal about them, it appears, Miss Deene,' said Mrs Spikings. 'How many other times have you resorted to these places, when we in our blessed innocence have supposed you visiting great-aunts and such? How many times, Miss Deene?'

The game was up, and Verity knew it. 'I decline to answer that question, ma'am, because it is a very unfair one, as you well know.'

Mrs Spikings' lips tightened; and, finding she could not stare Verity down, and that the Serpent was biting back, she flung herself on the sofa and, covering her eyes again, groaned: 'Alfred, I can only assume that it gives you pleasure to see me attacked and traduced by ill-bred chits in my own drawing-room, and that you are enjoying the spectacle too much to even think of defending me.'

Mr Spikings darted hastily forward, very red about the forehead, and clasped his wife's hand. 'Felicia, be calm! You will bring on your megrims, my dear! Miss Deene – ' he gave her his bullying look – 'you will apologize to Mrs Spikings at once.'

'It is too late for apologies,' muttered Mrs Spikings through gritted teeth, giving his hand a jerk.

'It is too late for apologies!' said Mr Spikings, taking his cue. 'And the very next time—'

'There will be no next time,' said his wife, impatiently tossing away his hand and rising. 'I think the time has come, Miss Deene, for us to part. I had my doubts about your suitability from the beginning, but I erred, as usual, on the side of generosity, and felt that you should be given the chance. Well, my doubts have been dreadfully confirmed. A week's notice will suffice, I hope, Miss Deene?'

'I shall not need a week,' said Verity coolly; and, having taken a last look at the children, and refreshed herself with a vision of their being shot out of a large cannon one by one, she presented her straight back to the family, and went upstairs to pack.

CHAPTER THREE

A Sea-Change

He had been down at the bottom of the sea, and he had seen ghastly things there, and for a long time it had seemed that he would never see the sunlight and breathe the air again. He could feel the deathly currents sucking him down, and more than once it had seemed easier to submit to them, and have done with the sickness and pain. But somehow he had fought his way to the surface, or had been pulled thither. He knew that willing arms had been there to drag him back to the land of the living, though the identities of his helpers had been indistinct to his fevered mind, and he had often confused them with the weird merfolk of his delirium. But now he was lucid, and he gratefully recognized those who had stayed by him while he wrestled with death: Mrs Winch, whose child he had treated; Mr Hankey, huge and stalwart; several Yarders; a doctor whom he did not know, gaunt and taciturn, but wonderfully skilful; and also Verity.

About this last figure he still had his doubts, even as he sat up against his pillows and took his first solid food. *Was* she real, or was she a last lingering phantom of his fever? She had been often in the room – had even, he thought, put back his tangled hair with her cool hand – and she was here now, along with the doctor. *Was* she real?

'John, you look at me as if you think me a ghost,' she said smiling. 'Even if you do, be a Hamlet, and speak to it.'

'Verity,' he said. 'It's you. You're here.'

'Well, you have lost none of your scintillating conversational powers, at any rate.'

'You're not allowed to provoke me,' he said feebly smiling, 'I've been ill. At least – I presume I have. Have I? I feel as if I've been . . . far away somewhere.'

'You've been very ill,' said the gaunt doctor, 'and it's a mercy you don't remember most of it. My name is Appleyard, and I'm glad to meet you, as it were, at last.'

John shook the long lean hand. 'I am greatly obliged to you, Dr Appleyard. I'm afraid I haven't been a good patient – one thing I do remember is shouting the house down, and throwing the blanket about.'

'Your nurses have had to put up with that, not I,' said Dr Appleyard. 'You're a lucky man, Tup'ny John or John Twopenny, whichever you may be. The fever was mighty virulent, and you will be weak for some time yet. But of course, I hardly need tell you this, as you seem to be something of a medical practitioner yourself.'

John coloured. 'I hope no one's been telling tall stories. All I do is—'

'Never mind: I won't tax you with it now. But we shall have some talk when you're stronger, nonetheless. I confess my curiosity is aroused, which is not to say that I approve of uncertificated men meddling with medicine. However, I'll leave you now: you're in good hands.'

Dr Appleyard's departure, like most things about him, was swift and abrupt. John, having eaten as much as he could manage, lay back and regarded Verity.

'How did you find me?'

'It wasn't difficult, once I had established that Tup'ny John and John Twopenny were one and the same.'

'And you called in Dr Appleyard for me? I thought so. I – I can't say how grateful I am to you.'

'Well, you had dropped out of sight rather, and I was a little concerned. It wasn't the same without someone to quarrel with. You know what they say – you even miss a headache when it's gone.'

'We didn't part very good friends when we saw each other last, did we? What an age ago that seems!'

'You certainly seem to have been through the mill since then. Would you like some more water?'

'Please. I've never known such a thirst. Thank you. Yes, things didn't . . . didn't go entirely to plan. I suppose they're hardly better now, in a way.' He waved a hand at the dingy room. 'How do you like my commodious quarters? Yet you know, there's something to be said for being at death's door, if that's where I've been. Everything looks brighter, more hopeful. Even Jolly Butcher's Yard. Though the people here have been enormously kind to me. It's true what they say about the poor looking after their own. Verity, what day is it?'

'Friday.'

'And was that one of my imaginings, or have you been here every day?'

Verity nodded, setting down the water-jug with excessive care.

'Very forbearing on the part of the dreadful Spikings. Am I still your great-aunt, only a sick great-aunt this time?'

Verity sat down and folded her hands in her lap. 'The dreadful Spikings and I have parted company. Which is just as well, as I would probably have committed multiple infanticide before much longer.'

She spoke with characteristic briskness, but John saw unease behind it.

'When was this?' he asked.

'A few days ago.'

John levered himself up, impatient at the slowness of his wasted muscles to respond. 'Verity . . . I have a horrible feeling that I have something to do with this. The yard is no place for a respectable governess to be frequenting – is it? I can imagine what those Spikings would think. Oh, Verity, you haven't lost your position because of . . .'

'As I said, the Spikings and I have parted company,' Verity said firmly. 'And lie down at once, John, you're not strong enough. Yes, I have lost my position, for what it was worth. It was my free choice to come here and help you, and the exercise of free choice is precisely what people like the Spikings would deny to that unfortunate automaton called a governess. And so they have lost a governess, and I have kept my self-respect.'

He looked at her soberly, with both trouble and admiration. In this shabby place, and against the dismal wreckage of his life, she showed up like a gemstone, bright and sharp and clear-cut, amongst mud and dross. She returned his look, then lowered her eyes and said, 'Am I turning into a ghost again?'

No ghost – rather, the truest, most splendidly real thing the world contained: so he thought, with new lucidity. 'I still can't be easy about it . . . Have you a new situation in view?'

'Not yet. But you needn't worry about me. I have a comfortable berth now, with an old acquaintance of yours. Miss Thimblebee. Yes, she has let me have your old single gentleman's apartments, John – I hope you don't mind!'

'Miss Thimblebee! I didn't know you knew each other.'

'Oh, yes, we became good friends. When I heard nothing from you – after that last time – I went to Fetter Lane, in my scandalous way, to look you up, and so I met Miss Thimblebee. It was through her that I found out about your being taken for debt, and . . .'

She bit her lip, but it was too late. John saw it all, and hauling himself upright exclaimed, 'It was you! Oh, Verity, my debts . . . That was you, wasn't it? You settled my debts, and had me released!'

She could not speak, and her struggling silence was evidence enough. John ran a hand through his tousled hair, and tried to take in this startling and humbling revelation. 'And now on top of that,' he murmured, 'you've lost your situation . . .'

'I have lost nothing: the Spikings have lost the best governess they will ever have, that's all,' said Verity smartly, rising, and making John lie down again. 'Well, I had hoped you would never find out about this strange freak of mine. Why I should decide to have you at large in the world, and generally being such a thorn in my side as you have always been, I can't think. A very regrettable decision, no doubt, but there, it's done now—'

He stopped her by seizing her hand and pressing it. 'I don't know what to say,' he said. 'All I can do is – is heap my gratitude on you, and that, I'm sure, you won't like.'

'Just a small heap, perhaps,' she said. 'It was nothing so very tremendous, John.'

'It was to me. And it must have been to you too. A governess's stipend is no fortune, I know that – I'm on much more familiar terms with hard reality nowadays. The reality of money especially . . . My God, Verity, I must pay you back! You've all but ruined yourself helping me – I must, I must pay you back . . .!'

'What on earth are you doing?' said Verity, as John pushed back the blanket and swung his legs out of the bed.

'Doing? Why, getting up,' he said. 'I can never pay you back lying here. The sooner I start earning, the sooner I can pay you back – dear God, Verity, I don't want you ending up in my old room in the King's Bench.'

'John, don't be a fool. Get back in bed at once.'

'Oh, nonsense, I'm recovered now. After all, the fever's left me, and I'll be better up and about.'

'You are the stubbornest of men!' said Verity; but she did not try to stop him. She stood back, and watched him. He put his feet to the floor, and went through the simple actions that since his infanthood had been associated with getting up, but he found they did not answer. He was still sitting down. What had happened to his legs? He would have sworn that they had no bones at all, if it were not for the fact that he could see them staring through the skin.

Still, John at last got himself upright by pushing with his arms, like some curious seal; and stood swaying there in momentary triumph. 'There,' he said, 'see?'

'Yes, I see,' said Verity, and just had time to dart forward and catch him round the shoulders as he toppled.

'Now,' she said, when she had got him back into bed, 'will you at least admit the necessity of a little convalescence?'

'Well,' John said, 'today, perhaps. But truly, Verity – I can't lie easy here, knowing what you have done for me, and knowing that I'm doing nothing to repay it. It would still be a great obligation if you were wealthy – but as it is . . .!'

'Don't worry about that,' Verity said, sitting down, but giving him a sharp look as if to say she was quite ready to wrestle him down if he should try to get up again. 'I manage. Miss Thimblebee invites me to dine with her every day, and is very good to me; and in return I help her out with her work.'

'Her . . . hairdressing, of course.'

'Her hairdressing, precisely. And if it is a mode of hairdressing that does not require the presence of the client, that is no concern of mine.'

They exchanged a smile, and then a laugh.

'But really, John, what on earth is this work you were going to sally forth to do? I certainly hope it isn't coal-heaving, having seen your legs, and I mean that in the kindest way.'

John sighed, and regarded the trim, amused figure sitting by the bed. How lie to Verity? To someone so clear-eyed and unequivocal, a lie was not only an insult but an impossibility. 'I have been scraping a living,' he said, 'in a manner which is scarcely more savoury than my surroundings . . .' He told her about his life as a screever, omitting nothing, and she listened with interest; and he concluded by saying, 'So much for grand ideals, eh?'

'Well, it's hardly like being a housebreaker, John. You might say, in fact, that it's very little different from being a novelist. You create convincing fictional characters and situations on paper, and receive a not very generous remuneration for it. Why, in effect, you're a sort of unsung Dickens or Thackeray!'

'But no one is deluded into mistaking novels for reality.'

'Oh, I'm not so sure about that. After all, readers of novels are very quick to protest if they are denied a happy ending, just as if the people in the story were real instead of inventions. If the hero and heroine don't get married at the end, the readers feel as piqued as if they hadn't been invited to a wedding of their friends.'

'Precisely my point. In a novel, people expect everything to turn out all right: but in real life, it almost never does.'

'John,' said Verity, 'you are not allowed to be pithy and sceptical. That is my role. If we are to have our old regular knock-down quarrels, you must observe the rules. Now let us have no more of it.'

They laughed again; but then John, lying back and feeling the weary debility of illness creeping over him, said with a sort of drowsy urgency, 'But we're not quarrelling, Verity – are we? Not really.'

'No,' she said. 'Disputing, perhaps. But not quarrelling, John.'

'Because I couldn't truly quarrel with you. This is, I'm afraid, the maudlin tendency consequent on a prostrating illness, so forgive it or ignore it, whichever you will. But I will say it again. You are quite the most irritating woman I have ever met—'

'Have a care, sir, I may stifle you with a pillow at will.'

'—But you are also the kindest person it is possible to imagine.'

'Compliments, as I live and breathe! Now I know you're ill, John. A relapse, I think. Let me send for Dr Appleyard—'

'Good God, you're impossible! I shall only keep saying it, Verity, so you might as well hold your peace. You won't stop me saying how grateful I am; and once these infernal legs of mine begin to do their job again, I shall pay you back, I swear.'

'John.' Verity seemed to consider taking his hand, and then to think better of it. 'John, how did you get into debt? I may as well add that I will know if you're not telling the truth. So tell me.'

John hesitated. 'I backed a friend's bill.'

'I thought as much. Well, I backed your bill, John – think of it as no more than that – and I don't expect recompense. I didn't think of being paid back when I made the decision, and I don't think of it now. We have both been thrown on the bosom of the world, you and I, John, and a very cold unwelcoming bosom it is, with a good deal of whalebone about it, and very little softness . . . Dear me, my metaphor is becoming indecent. But you see what I mean. As you said, it's the poor that help the poor – and the rich that help themselves, I'm afraid. All of which will not prevent you, I know, from planning every means you can think of to pay me back. Well, I can't stop you. But please at least wait until you can stand upright without falling over. Now, is there anything you would like me to do before you go to sleep again? A letter, perhaps?' She paused. 'To Catherine?'

'I'm afraid there's not much to say. The understanding between us is . . . not as it was. It's best not to tell her how things have been, because it will only distress her needlessly . . . Apparently the Fernhills are coming to London soon, anyhow.'

'Yes . . . apparently.'

'Life is . . . not what one expects, is it, Verity? I'm not going to sleep, by the way.'

'Yes you are. No, life is not what one expects; but the curious thing is, one goes on expecting . . . Stop trying to prop open your eyelids, John, and sleep.'

'I'm awake . . .'

John slept.

His recovery was not swift; for his constitution had been lowered even before his illness, and he privately suspected that it would never be quite as elastic as before. He still needed careful nursing; but the inhabitants of Jolly Butcher's Yard were always willing to lend a hand, and Verity came every day, often bringing little gifts of fruit and pastries sent by Miss Thimblebee – for that very correct lady could not think of entering a room in which a gentleman lay in bed, even with others present.

Dr Appleyard was often there too: more often than John's illness warranted, as the doctor admitted. For John interested him. 'It's singular to find a patient who likes to make a study of his own case,' Dr Appleyard said; and whenever he had time – for he was a tireless worker – he would take a chair and talk with John, getting to know his history. He was much of an age with John's father, and it was curious to think, he said, that they might have studied at the same time, and perhaps rubbed shoulders in the dissecting-room.

'It's probable: it's probable indeed,' he mused. 'But I was not a clubbable student, and knew hardly anyone.'

That was easy to believe, for Dr Appleyard was far from clubbable now. The inner spring of the man was tightly wound, and it had produced something disproportioned in his manners which was rather intimidating until you came to know him. When his face was merely at rest, he looked stern: when he was simply listening attentively to what you were saying, there was such a knotty intensity to his gaze that you could suppose him thinking 'What nonsense is *this*?' All such social niceties as greetings, farewells, and polite inquiries, he had virtually dispensed with: he could be out of the room so quickly you felt you must surely have offended; and one morning when he arrived wet from a shower of rain, and Mr Hankey civilly commiserated with him on the fact, Dr Appleyard looked at him as if he were mad, and said, 'What the devil has the rain to do with anything?' This was genuine surprise more than rudeness, for the doctor simply did not notice such things, and could not understand it when people called his attention to them.

It was just as well, perhaps, that he was so indifferent to comforts and inconveniences; for he habitually visited worse places than Jolly Butcher's Yard. The teeming slums of St Giles and Seven Dials were his chief haunt. 'Would you believe,' he said to John one day, 'that some damned fool asked me this morning why I practise there? Because there are sick people there, for heaven's sake!'

'I suppose the damned fool was wondering how you profited by it,' John said.

'Well, he's even more of a fool, then. I *don't* profit by it. How are those wretches to pay for doctoring? I have a little money of my own, enough for my needs and those of my mother and sister; and I receive a small allowance for acting as poor-law surgeon, and as consultant physician at Newgate. Oh, but there's no talking to fools. I suppose he thinks you'll be robbed the moment you set foot in these places.'

John, from his experience of the clientele at Ma Dade's, knew that this was not an unnatural supposition; but he could not imagine anyone choosing to tackle

Dr Appleyard as he strode his impatient, grim-jawed, beetle-browed way through the courts and alleys – and if they had, he would probably have withered them with a look. Or, perhaps, told them to stop their nonsense. Nonsense was Dr Appleyard's enemy; nonsense was everything that stood in the way of his single-minded and austerely dedicated pursuit of his profession. Only once did he give a hint that his life contained anything else. He asked John one day, quite out of the blue, whether he played the violin.

'I'm afraid not. I love to hear music, but I've always regarded the reading and playing of it as something akin to sorcery.'

'Ah? Pity.' Dr Appleyard, most unusually, looked downcast.

'Miss Deene is a fine musician, though. She plays the piano most wonderfully.'

'Indeed, indeed?' Dr Appleyard rubbed his jaw, and a little light kindled his sunken eyes; but he said no more about it, and they returned to their abiding topic, which was medicine. It was so long since John had the opportunity to talk of his old passion to someone who shared it, and he was afraid sometimes that he babbled out of sheer eagerness. He was afraid, too, that Dr Appleyard might take him to task for his presumption in applying rudimentary medicine to his neighbours in the yard, for he questioned John closely about his proceedings in this regard, and took careful note of his answers; but the old physician never once gave an opinion on anything John had done – merely knitted his black brows, and grunted 'Hm, hm,' in a way that John was not at all sure how to take.

Dr Appleyard was, however, interested in Verity too, and talked much with her when their visits coincided. It was not difficult to see that he approved of Verity's downrightness and independence, and he listened with great attention to her own story, which she told with some reluctance and a good deal of wit.

'You are a curious pair altogether,' Dr Appleyard pronounced one day, when John was at last up and about. He and Verity were celebrating the fact with a cold fowl and a pint of wine courtesy of Miss Thimblebee, and the doctor agreed to join them. 'A curious pair indeed. You interest me. There could hardly be a more striking instance of the nonsense with which the world is filled, and the fools who run it, than the situation you two find yourselves in. There are men and women aplenty who wish to do nothing whatsoever with the lives that God gave them. They hunt fortunes, they make good marriages, they scramble for the favour of some titled nonentity; they build themselves monstrous great houses, they dress themselves up finely as if they were not precisely the same as us all underneath, they go into Society as if there were something there worth the having. And they are eminently successful in it. And yet here you are, two people whose capacities would be eminently useful to the world, and who have not neglected to nurture and improve them; and you have nothing!'

'Not even self-respect, in my case,' said John.

Dr Appleyard eyed him narrowly. 'None at all?'

'Well . . . it's strange. I thought my self-respect had died altogether, a while ago, before I fell ill; and yet it must have been there somewhere, because I never felt that life was not worth clinging on to.'

'Well, that's something. I would not have you be a self-hater, John, even though in your fall from grace you may feel you deserve your own contempt. I have seen self-hatred used as an excuse for giving up the fight. *Are* you ready to give up the fight, John Twopenny?'

John hesitated. 'Again, a month ago I'd have said yes: now I say no.'

'Hm, hm. And what about you, Miss Deene? Have you resigned yourself to unlucky fate?'

'I resigned myself to fate long ago,' said Verity quietly, 'but as to whether it is lucky or unlucky, I have never formed a clear opinion.'

'An answer worthy of a Jesuit. Hm, hm. Well, a mad world, my masters. The

244

pair of you could have followed the fashion, and looked after number one, and then you might have been promenading in Hyde Park Ring now: I wonder why you didn't . . .? Now, look here. My mother and sister would like to meet the two of you. Come tomorrow. Come to dine.'

Both were too startled for the moment to thank him; and John's thoughts flew anxiously to his wardrobe, which was down to one of everything, and as threadbare as it could be without actually being in rags. Seeing that something was amiss, Dr Appleyard demanded in his short way, 'Well? You've no objection to dining, I hope?'

'No – it's very kind of you, Dr Appleyard – it's just the matter of dress . . .'

Dr Appleyard gave John his what-the-devil-are-you-talking-about? look. 'Why, what's wrong with what you're wearing?'

'Well, I'm afraid it's shabby. If Mrs and Miss Appleyard—'

'Pah! You don't know them. Come tomorrow.' And Dr Appleyard flung on his hat and walked out of the room with his usual suddenness.

It felt strange to both of them to be going out to dine – 'just as if we were real people!' as Verity put it – and for John especially the return to the world where such things went on was disorienting. It was the first time, too, that he had been out of the yard since his illness, and the hurry and press of the streets was bewildering at first, until he found a feeling stealing over him so long forgotten that it was like experiencing it for the first time – the feeling of exhilaration.

'I feel as if I've been brought back to life,' he said to Verity as they walked together. 'Or – or rescued from drowning, is the closest I can come to it. Pulled up out of the deep.'

'Well, they say that a man once rescued from drowning can never be drowned,' Verity said. 'A comforting superstition; and let's hope there's a parallel in your case, John, and that you've had your last sight of the sea-bed.'

'I hope so too, and I shall do my best to ensure I never sink again – so that none of your trouble will have been wasted. For it was you who pulled me out, Verity: if it weren't for you, I really would be at the bottom of the sea.'

'Oh, nonsense, as Dr Appleyard would say. I . . .' She cleared her throat. 'I wonder what his mother and sister are like? Will they peer at us in that alarming manner, and walk out of the room when we least expect it?'

They did not: for Mrs Appleyard and Miss Jemima Appleyard were not so scornful of social convention, and were highly formal in their bearing. They were tall, stately ladies, as befitted the tall, stately house they inhabited. The house was also a little run-down, and did not appear to have had a lick of paint in twenty years; and though the ladies did not resemble it in that regard, being very neatly and soberly turned out, there was perhaps a similar air about them of being defiantly behind the times, and not much concerned with worldly show.

Miss Jemima Appleyard was a strong-nosed lady of fifty, with large, capable hands like her brother's, pious, and indefatigable about various charitable works, from making up baskets for poor expectant mothers to charity-schools in the slums. Old Mrs Appleyard, eighty if a day, was straight-backed enough for forty, and big-boned enough for a saddle-horse: a very grand personage altogether, in yards of black marocain, with her fine old face presented to advantage in a cap of a fashion that would have been considered quaint in Napoleon's day.

'I should like, Mr Twopenny,' she said to John at dinner – which was served beneath a tremendous brown portrait of the late Mr Appleyard – 'I should like to have been a bowman at Agincourt. I fancy that would be an experience worth the having. What do you feel? Would you like to have been a bowman at Agincourt?'

John said that he was sure it must have been very stirring.

'I think so too. I am strongly of that opinion. I am an active person, Mr Twopenny. The only lived life is an active life. I am dogmatic on this point. But my son tells me, Mr Twopenny, that medicine has always been your aim. Perhaps then you would rather have been a surgeon to the troops at Agincourt, if surgeons there were in those times.'

'I believe there were,' John said, 'but their methods, I think, were very rough and ready.'

'It was so in my day,' said Mrs Appleyard, majestically munching. 'I recall a surgeon in my youth who claimed to have sawed off a round gross of legs in the course of his career. I use his own phrase, which is vivid, if coarse. But people in my day were hardier than now. I am firm on this point. In my youth nothing was thought of walking to Hatfield and back in a day. The stiles alone constituted an exercise that would exhaust a person in these times. My daughter Jemima, Mr Twopenny, is an active person; but she has never climbed a stile, sir, in her life.'

'Mama, I have climbed many a stile in the country,' said Miss Jemima.

'Jemima,' said Mrs Appleyard weightily, 'in my day, a daughter who contradicted her parent would have been sent upstairs, and required to wear a stiff backboard until permitted to remove it.'

'That cannot have been very healthy, I think, Mama,' said Miss Jemima, not at all put out.

'It was extremely healthy,' said Mrs Appleyard, 'and I would recommend it to every young woman as an aid to her posture. Miss Deene, you have been a governess, I understand. What is the prevailing view on the use of the backboard, in these times?'

'I don't think there are many families who encourage it now, ma'am,' said Verity.

'Then they should,' said Mrs Appleyard. 'That is my firm opinion. James, let us hear what you have to say, as a physician. Is the practice injurious, or is it beneficial?'

'It is sheer nonsense, Mother,' said Dr Appleyard, 'and if I caught any patient of mine at it, I would tell them to stop it at once.'

'James, I find this very strange. You are not normally a friend to slackness, moral or physical. My son, Mr Twopenny, has always cultivated the strictest self-discipline. As a boy his diligence at his studies was exemplary. He was at his Latin grammar when the other boys were out bird-nesting. In fact, sir, this was so much his custom that he did not know what a bird's nest was until the age of twenty, when he happened to observe one in a tree, and wondered greatly what it could be.'

'Mother, Mother!' said Dr Appleyard, shaking his head and laughing; and Miss Jemima smiled too. It was already noticeable to John that Mrs Appleyard was in the habit of telling the most prodigious fibs about her son and daughter; but she was solemnly indignant when they protested at them, as now. 'James Appleyard,' she said in a sepulchral tone, 'do you mean to suggest that my memory is at fault? If so, I must reprove you severely. If proof were needed of its powers, I need only instance the fact that I can remember every word your late father said, on the afternoon in which he proposed marriage to me. He began by talking of hazelnuts. How he proceeded from hazelnuts to a proposal of matrimony I shall not elaborate: suffice it to say that the late Mr Appleyard was possessed of uncommon originality of mind.'

John instinctively looked up at the vast portrait, which in its brownness was eminently suited to the dinner he was eating; for this, though perfectly wholesome, was distinguished by its quantities of brown gravy. The soup was brown too, and the wine was brown, and the very chicken-breast looked as if the bird had died a natural death at a great age, and then been slowly stewed for a week. The whole brown and gamey collation was brought to table, appropriately, by the oldest maid in the world, who like everything in the household seemed to be valued for being old and serviceable; and to whom the Appleyards, in their eccentric way, gave formal thanks at the end of the meal.

It was in the drawing-room after dinner that Dr Appleyard's question about playing the violin was elucidated. The Appleyards were devoted amateurs of music. Dr Appleyard played the violin, Mrs Appleyard the viola, and Miss Jemima the cello; and they had long been looking, they said, for a second violin so that they might play as a string quartet instead of a trio. However, the presence of Verity offered the possibility of an exciting new combination, for there was a piano, and Verity could play; and soon the instruments (very brown) were being brought out and Dr Appleyard was hunting through boxes of old sheet-music (browner still). John formed the audience for the impromptu concert. The music favoured by the Appleyards was of a stern and lugubrious sort; and as John sat back and listened, he was struck by what a curious contrast this made to his late manner of living. Dr Appleyard cradling his violin with an expression of rapturous severity, Mrs Appleyard's venerable cap nodding and wagging as she plied her viola-bow, Miss Jemima drawing forth the gloomy soul of her cello with vigorous motions of her large bony elbows, and Verity at the piano trying not to drive the funereal music too fast, all formed a picture that John felt he would not soon forget.

'How very refreshing!' Miss Jemima said when the music was concluded, smiling like a handsome horse. 'Miss Deene, you are quite what we have been waiting for – I do hope you will oblige us again on a future occasion. I can hardly wait to tackle Mozart's G minor with you!'

After the music the ancient maid brought in tea, which of all the brown things that had been produced was the brownest yet. Miss Jemima did the honours at the tea-table, whilst Mrs Appleyard fell asleep in her chair. Even to this action the old lady lent a certain stateliness, remaining rigidly upright despite the nodding of her head; and she maintained her propriety even through a nightmare, pronouncing, 'Help. Help. I am pursued. Gracious me. Help,' with grave decorum.

'Hush, hush, Mama,' said Miss Jemima, 'you're dreaming.'

Mrs Appleyard woke with a jolt, and at once stoutly denied that she had been asleep; then tasted her tea, and complained that it was cold.

'Well, Mama, that's because you've been asleep,' said Miss Jemima.

'Jemima, in my day such impudence to a parent would have been severely reproved. Several of my youthful acquaintances were tied down upon ottomans, and beaten with the straps of a valise. Others were required to remain for long intervals in a broom cupboard.'

'Really, Mother, such barbarism!' said Dr Appleyard.

'As to falling asleep,' Mrs Appleyard continued, more lofty than ever, 'I may say with perfect confidence that I have never once done so outside my own bed in my entire life. Whereas, Jemima, it was a matter of common report in your infanthood that you once fell asleep on the garden-seat at the height of a thunderstorm, and failed to wake even when lightning destroyed the weathervane on top of our roof, which was in the shape of a fish, and universally admired.'

Presently Dr Appleyard invited John to look over his consulting-room. It was a large, high-ceilinged room at the back of the house, overflowing not only with medical volumes, drugs in various powdered and liquid forms in all manner of flasks, jars and bottles, and chemical retorts, but with the apparatus of Dr Appleyard's other interests – cases of entomological and botanical specimens, shells, and a microscope. There was also an articulated skeleton which, when Dr Appleyard lit the gas, looked dreadfully pleased to see them.

John was passionately interested in all of it, and gladly took up Dr Appleyard's invitation to forage around at will; and he got so absorbed in looking into a fine

247

folio anatomy that he suddenly realized he was quite forgetting his manners. He turned to find Dr Appleyard steadily regarding him with his arms folded across his chest, and the skeleton looking over his shoulder, scarcely more gaunt and fleshless in its aspect than the doctor himself.

'Dr Appleyard, I do beg your pardon, I was quite carried away—'

'John,' said Dr Appleyard, ignoring this, 'are you proud? Because if you are, you won't do. I don't mean proud in the sense of taking a pride in yourself, because that's good, and I want it. I mean stiff-necked proud, too-good-for-this-world proud. Because when I say I want an assistant, I don't mean anything very choice. You'd be little more than my servant, and you'd be paid little more than a servant, and you'd live under my roof like a servant. You'd be disposing of purulent bandages and mixing drugs and running errands, not living it up with the medical students at Bart's. I've taken careful notice of you, John: of what you know, and what you don't know; and I think you could do the job well. I need someone whom I can trust, and who thinks as I do; because I'm getting up in years, and I'd be a fool if I didn't admit that I need the help. But the question remains, do you want to do it? It really depends if you're serious about medicine. If you're not serious about medicine, I don't want you anyway.'

The skeleton might have been grinning at the spectacle of John's astonishment, which was so great that for some moments he simply could not speak. Dr Appleyard, however, calmly waited, arms folded and cavernous eyes burning into John's.

'I am . . . I am very serious about medicine,' John said at last.

'Serious enough to take on a gruelling, unremunerative hack-job, just to be involved with it?'

'Yes, indeed. Oh, Dr Appleyard, you cannot conceive what this offer means to me . . .' John swallowed an obstruction in his throat: gasped; felt he could have shouted aloud, if it were not for that he might startle the ladies in the drawing-room.

And that brought back to him the thought of Verity. Verity, and all she had done for him – and at such cost to herself. He could not rejoice at the opportunity being offered him, when Verity was in a position quite as reduced and precarious as his. He was not at all sure that he deserved the helping hand being extended to him: he was quite sure that she did.

'Well?' said Dr Appleyard. 'There is a reservation, I can tell. Name it.'

'Believe me, Dr Appleyard, there is no reservation about the job, or my wish to do it. But . . . you know my history, and that of Miss Deene. You know what I owe her – God knows what would have become of me if it had not been for her, but I would certainly not have been here to hear your generous offer. You have taken an interest in both of us, I believe; and of the two of us, I would wish . . . I would wish that Miss Deene should benefit from any help you should be kind enough to extend. I would love to be your assistant, but if there were anything you could do for Ve – for Miss Deene instead, I would just as willingly take my chance with the world, knowing she was secure. I would feel selfish to take hold of this piece of tremendous good luck, when Miss Deene was still at the mercy of fortune . . . I'm afraid I sound ungrateful.'

Something like a smile was hovering about Dr Appleyard's thin lips. 'One forgets the earnestness of youth,' he said, 'and thank heaven for it. Well, John, you *are* the man I thought you were, and it's a satisfaction to be proved right. I have, indeed, taken quite an interest in both of you – as I have said, I see waste when I look at you and Miss Deene, and I detest waste – and it so happens that Jemima is at this moment laying a similar proposition before Miss Deene. It turns, similarly, on pride. Our idea for Miss Deene does not involve purulent bandages, but it would be considered just as unsavoury by a certain fastidious type of lady – which I do not think Miss Deene is, but we shall see. You have heard of the Ragged Schools, John? Jemima is much involved with the running of the Field Lane Ragged School. It is a charitable institution concerning itself with the very poorest of the poor, and it is not overburdened with funds; but Jemima is sure Miss Deene could secure a teaching position there – if, I repeat, she is not too proud. So you see. We have anticipated your objections, John. Let Miss Deene give Jemima her answer, and now let me have yours.'

The prospect of leaving behind the ignoble struggle to live by screeving; the prospect of earning his bread through medicine, and assisting Dr Appleyard in the sort of work that had long been his ideal aspiration; the prospect above all of knowing that Verity was befriended too; all these swam dizzily in John's mind, and made his answer Yes – not once but a thousand times, and with a thousand expressions of gratitude. Dr Appleyard cut him off in about the third or fourth, however; and, saying in his curt way, 'Very well. Come tomorrow, and we'll begin,' fell to talking of the use of chloroform in childbirth, just as if nothing had happened between them.

It was a mild and starry night when John and Verity left Dr Appleyard's, and what with exhilaration, anticipation, and the light-headedness of fatigue, John felt as if he were walking with his head up amongst those stars, and his feet scarcely touching the pavement. As for Verity, it was not her way to make much of her feelings; but John knew her well enough by now to perceive that her summary dismissal by the Spikings, and the hazardous position in which it placed her, had been preying cruelly on her mind, and that her relief was scarcely less than his.

'Miss Jemima was very careful to point out that the children I will be teaching will be somewhat different from those in my last situation,' Verity said. 'She was too proper to say it in so many words, but I think she means lice, nits, and foul mouths. I didn't like to mention that in comparison with the little Spikings, any amount of infestation and profanity would be a positive pleasure. Why it should be considered less genteel to teach in a school than to be a sort of glorified servant in someone else's household I don't understand, but it's not a question that I shall allow to trouble me. I shall be independent, I shall be able to provide for myself, and I shall be doing something far more useful than trying to insert French verbs into spoiled brats. That sounds very pious and bluestocking, does it not? But I don't care. I'm just so thankful and relieved, and . . . well, I'm rattling on. Not like me at all, you'll agree, John. And I haven't even congratulated you on *your* good fortune. Well, I do so. If you can bear me saying something nice to you, I think you deserve it, even though I can't help wondering what your room at Dr Appleyard's will be like, and whether *everything* in it will be brown. John, could it be that the wheel of fortune, to be poetic about it, is turning upward for us at last?'

'I believe it is, Verity,' he said. 'I do believe it is – though I know saying such a thing is practically an invitation to fate to drop a thunderbolt right on our heads.'

'Cynical, John, very. That's associating with me that's done that.'

'Whoever called you cynical?'

'Oh! Mrs Spikings, for one. But I'm pretty certain that you also called me it, at some point.'

'Never. I've called you all sorts of names, but never that.'

'A strange omission!'

'Not really. Because I don't think you *are* cynical – in fact, I'm sure of it. Though you once gave me a thorough telling-off for claiming to know all about you, and I realize I'm risking another.'

'I'll be lenient with you this time . . . John, you look tired. You needn't walk me to Miss Thimblebee's – go straight home.'

'Indeed I won't. I'm not tired, Verity: I feel as if I could walk all night, with . . .' *With you beside me*, were the words that came into his head: for a startled moment he even thought he had spoken them. 'With no trouble at all,' he concluded lamely.

Rescued from drowning: pulled up from the bottom of the sea, and set on dry land again, and with the sweet air in his lungs, and the sun on his face; all these, certainly. But whose the figure that waited upon the golden shore, and welcomed him back to the land of the living, and stood revealed as the most beautiful and precious thing within its bounds? Ah, whose, indeed!

CHAPTER FOUR

The Admiral Weighs Anchor

There were several motives behind Admiral Fernhill's decision to close up Buttings Court for a year, and take his family to London. The first was a self-seeking one, not untypically. The outbreak of war between Russia and Turkey had placed the Navy in a state of readiness; and Admiral Fernhill had been in correspondence with their lordships at the Admiralty, and found there was a possibility of his being put at the helm of a desk again – a prospect that was more enticing as there were whispers of a knighthood as an inducement. To be able to style himself Admiral Sir George Fernhill was, he felt, worth a good deal of inconvenience.

Then there was Augustus, who had completed a less than dazzling career at Cambridge, and whose future as the bearer of the Fernhill name was now to be considered. The Bar, a commission in the services, parliament, and a good marriage were all possibilities that revolved in the admiral's mind. Whichever it was to be, the fond father saw no better way of advancing Augustus's prospects than taking him to London, and thrusting him in the faces of as many influential people as possible.

Emulation played a part too. The Fernhills had got on very good terms with the Goodways of Beacon House, and they had maintained a friendly correspondence since the Goodways had removed to London late last year. Mr Marcus Goodway was a wealthy and well-born gentleman, and Mr Marcus Goodway had a town residence: therefore, should not Admiral (soon to be Sir George) Fernhill do the same? The renewal of the friendship in London would be useful also, for Mr Goodway had lots of connections worth cultivating. He had already expressed a cordial pleasure at the prospect of meeting the Fernhills again in London; for, he frankly admitted in a charming letter, he was lonely. Mr Goodway was a widower now. His wife's health, after seeming to rally, had broken again irreparably, and she had died that winter. It would be a consolation to him, he said, to see their familiar faces again, especially as the late Mrs Goodway had known them too, and had spent many pleasant times in their company. The admiral had no doubt of it; and had such a sense of his own merits, indeed, that he felt the sight of his face could console anybody for anything.

And then there was Catherine. She seemed to have got over that entirely unsuitable youthful attachment she had formed, and she was prettier than ever; and it was high time, her parents agreed, that she was properly introduced to society. Or, thrown upon the marriage market, to put it coarsely; though the admiral deplored such coarse expressions. If any person had suggested to him that he was preparing to auction off his daughter just as surely as his son, he would simply have turned lobster-red, and accused that person of not glorying in the name of Briton.

And so the shutters went up at Buttings, and the admiral in oils, saving his country by putting his hand in his breast-pocket, was consigned to temporary darkness, and the admiral in marble – wearing a toga for no discernible reason whatsoever – was shrouded in a dust-sheet; Mrs Fernhill superintended the

251

packing of her many gowns and hats, with as tender a concern for their safety in transit as if they were beloved pets; Augustus appeared resplendent in a new travelling-coat, which was so heavy and enveloping that the porters at Norwich station had to lift him up to the railway-carriage like an upright trunk, and squeeze him through the door sideways; and steam whisked the Fernhill family away from Norfolk and towards the city whose streets were paved, as far as the admiral was concerned, with honours, places, titles, advantageous connections, and every gratification that his vanity could require.

As for Catherine, she was sorry to be leaving behind the old home and its associations, for every sort of leave-taking affected her profoundly; but the thought of a London season was exciting too. Though she had less than perfect confidence in herself, she was a gregarious person, greatly disposed to meet people, and to like them when she met them. She had remained unspoilt by her parents' vanity and pretension, for she had a peculiar simplicity of heart which was proof against all worldliness; but her beautiful eyes were of the sort that are easily dazzled. Being wholly without duplicity herself, she could not conceive of its existence in others. To be admired and complimented was a perennially fresh and new experience to her, because she always believed the compliments to be sincere. Her enjoyment of dances, levees, dinners, promenades and calls was genuine and unaffected; she had no notion of the social world as a great pool in which the circling fish were continually on the alert to eat or be eaten. And so she took her place beside her mother in the railway-carriage with a fluttering in her stomach that was half nervousness, half anticipation, but all pleasure.

The knowledge that John was in London too, and that she might see him, was with her, of course. But she was not sure what she felt about that. He had become something of a vague figure to her – though in truth he had never been entirely substantial to Catherine's perception. An ardent young man had come into her view, and had vowed love for her; and being Catherine, she had been astonished and flattered, and would no more have thought of being disrespectful towards his love than she would have been disrespectful of his religion. Indeed, she had returned it – but her nature was in general so loving that this was not the soul-wrenching experience that it was for people who were differently constituted. And then there was their physical separation, which would have told upon many a stronger vessel than Catherine. A John consistently present might well have pinned her wayward and impressionable heart down: a John almost continually absent had little chance of doing so.

Which was not to say she did not think fondly of him, even now that they had released each other from any formal undertaking; her feelings were still warm, if confused, and she was curious to see him again, and discover what effect a meeting would have on those feelings. Beyond that she did not look. She certainly did not look so far into herself as to see what an unprejudiced observer might have seen – that if the two of them had drifted apart, she had certainly not made any effort to swim against the tide.

To London, then, and to the house that the admiral has taken, in a shady street off Portland Place. Everything in readiness for them: nothing in readiness for them, according to the admiral, poking his lustrous head into every room from cellar to garret, and finding something to fuss over in every one; Mrs Fernhill unpacking in a frenzy, and finding none of her clothes fit for town wear, and declaring that she cannot show her face until she has new ones; Augustus amiably peering into vases and under tablecloths, and murmuring that the place is jolly well tip-top; Catherine looking out from her bedroom window, and seeing the gaslight moving like a glowing sprite about the neighbouring streets, and the further rooftops that ring the horizon melting into the dusky sky, as if the whole city were up in the clouds.

252

Which is very much how she feels, and continues to feel over the next few days. The Admiral has had his own carriage brought down from Norfolk, and soon it is wending its way about the squares, and Admiral and Mrs Fernhill, Mr Augustus Fernhill and Miss Fernhill are leaving cards on a wholesale basis, to alert the world in general to the fact that they are 'At Home' on Tuesdays. The carriage displays its spurious crest about the parks too, and about Bond Street and Regent Street, where Mrs Fernhill shops herself into exhaustion, and leaves behind her a trail of weeping drapers' assistants. The first 'At Home' is held, and is a resounding success, inasmuch as a steady stream of people follow the footman upstairs to the reception-room, and no one contradicts the admiral, and no one is better dressed than Mrs Fernhill; whilst Augustus goes round in his friendly, drooping way, introducing himself to people he has just met, and unwittingly fetching the seated ladies great clouts on the head with his dangling monocle. And Catherine is introduced to a great many people, some very pleasant, some rather forbidding; and finds it at last just a little overwhelming, like walking at great speed through a picture-gallery and looking at each picture for five seconds; and is heartily glad, therefore, when a familiar face surfaces amongst all those strangers.

It is Mr Marcus Goodway. He is still in mourning, a sight which always moves Catherine whoever it may be; and in her impulsive way she at once says how sorry she was to hear about his wife. 'Oh dear – I didn't think, perhaps you don't like to be reminded of it . . .'

'Not at all. It's some eight months now since Grace died, and people rather tend to avoid mentioning her, as if she never existed; but I would rather she be remembered. Thank you, Miss Fernhill.' Mr Goodway seems as pleased to see her as she is to see him; and his manner is so direct and candid that she feels she can be confidential, and says in a lower voice, 'Do you know, I have already forgotten the names of half the people here, isn't that terrible, and Papa wants me to have what is called a wide circle of acquaintance, but I have never quite understood how people with a wide circle of acquaintance manage, unless they write all the names down in a pocket-book with little descriptions attached like policemen do, which would seem rather a cold way of going about things though I'm sure very effective. That's why I was so relieved when you walked in, Mr Goodway, because I don't have to make an effort with you . . . Oh dear, that doesn't sound very nice—'

'It sounds charming,' says Mr Goodway laughing, 'and you echo my feelings exactly. I would exchange a wide circle of acquaintance for a few intimate friends any day. So come: let us pretend we are not in London at all. Tell me all the news from dear old Norfolk.'

She tells, and a nostalgic look crosses his face. 'What a sad fellow I am! When I was there, I missed the city; and now I am here, I hanker to smell that clean air again. Perhaps it would have been better if we had remained there permanently, but Grace's health seemed all but restored, and so we came up to town, and then . . . But that's vain talk. Forgive me.'

'Oh, but of course you would think that, Mr Goodway, it's only natural – but I'm sure you have nothing to reproach yourself for. Will you go back to Beacon House some time, do you suppose?'

'Perhaps. Though it might be better to take another residence in the district. Even leaving aside the memories, Beacon House is very large for a single man. But I shall certainly not sever my connection with Norfolk, where we spent so many happy hours, and made such good friends. Indeed, my thoughts have been running a good deal in that direction lately, and – well, you are the first to hear of this, Miss Fernhill, but I am having a pleasure-yacht built. There's a piece of extravagance for you! My excuse is that I have felt a little dull and liverish of late – too much confinement, I fancy – and my physician recommends sea-breezes. When she's finished, I hope to find a berth for her at Hales-next-the-sea or thereabouts, and sail her myself. In fact, once I get my sea-legs, you and your family have a standing invitation to be my first shipboard guests – though I shall be a little nervous of exposing my seamanship to your father's expert eye.'

The admiral's expert eye alighting on Mr Goodway at that moment, he comes over, and there are cordial greetings on both sides. Mr Goodway congratulates the admiral on the house he has taken, and the admiral wags his head as conceitedly as if he had built it with his own hands, and soon he is inviting Mr Goodway to dine. Mr Goodway says he would be delighted; and then Mrs Fernhill bears down upon Catherine, and parades another set of strangers before her, and Catherine struggles to commit another dozen names to memory, somewhat on the principle she laughingly suggested to Mr Goodway, so that a litany runs through her mind thus: 'Mr Bumpus, large head and small body, curled hair, ring on finger; Mrs Wincey, frosty lady with green eyes, Miss Wincey frosty likewise but eyes blue, Miss Florence Wincey, ringlets; the Rev. Dr Puce, hair growing out of his ears, Mrs Puce rather stout, maiden sister of Mrs Puce, no identifying marks whatsoever . . .' But she becomes so preoccupied with this that she ceases to notice the people she is speaking to, and calls Mrs Wincey Mr Bumpus, and calls Miss Wincey Miss Frosty, and gets so thoroughly muddled that she gives it up at last.

The dinners, at least, are less bewildering than the 'At Homes', in that there are only fourteen faces to memorize, and some are familiar to her from the family's previous residence in London, back when she was a girl: Admiralty connections of her father's – knotty, grainy men all, who look inclined to try ramming each other stern to stern when they disagree. Equally recognizable at the dinners are the India men, civil and military, who share a common burnt complexion, and a common propensity to glare at the servants as if they wanted to give them a good whipping; the City men, who use a lot of starch in their dress and a lot of exaggeration in their talk; and the parliament men, who distinguish themselves with a weighty silence until asked their opinion of something, whereupon they make a great noise of clearing their throats and pronounce, 'Now let me first say this . . .' Less readily distinguishable are the wives and daughters of the same, though they all have bare shoulders and flowers in their hair, and they all fall into two camps when confronted with Catherine's beauty and charm – those who love her for it, and those (the greater number) who smilingly hate her for it.

Many faces, then, passing in and out of view at the dinners and the carpet-dances that sometimes follow them; but not the least notable among them, to Catherine at least, is that strong-nosed, fresh-coloured, maturely handsome one belonging to Mr Marcus Goodway. Bereaved, alone, reminiscent of home, and wonderfully easy to talk with, he is much in her thoughts. There are plenty of agreeable people to be met here, of course, but she does not think any of them are quite as agreeable as Mr Goodway; and occasionally when she finds the whole social business rather fatiguing and ridiculous, she catches Mr Goodway's eye across the room, and sees there an answering glint which establishes, with a peculiar cheery confidentiality, that he understands, and finds it so too.

Many new faces, then; but there are two familiar faces that she is eager to see. She has a letter from Verity telling her that that incorrigible girl has left the Spikings' and is a teacher at, of all places, a Ragged School; and inside it, a letter from John. He has found a position as an assistant to a physician, which pleases Catherine not only for his sake, but because it indicates that he is on a respectable footing again, and that they might be able to meet on easy terms, as friends if nothing more. Well, it will be good to see both of them again, even simply for old times' sake. So thinks Catherine – subjecting herself to no more searching scrutiny than that, and allowing herself to be carried along by the pleasant tides of life, towards whatever shore awaits her.

CHAPTER FIVE

The King Goes Into Exile

'He is on the mend, I think,' said the doctor, walking downstairs with Mr Edwin Chipchase, 'but I cannot guarantee he will not suffer such an attack again, unless he avoids all exertion and lives very quietly. I am rather afraid the gentleman has a . . . choleric temper, and he would do well to master it, if possible.'

The doctor was a young and diffident man whose practice in and around Hales-next-the-sea had greatly increased since the death of Dr Robert Twopenny. He was more than a little nervous at attending on such an awesome local personage as Saul Twopenny; but he was relieved to find Mr Chipchase, Saul's devoted son-in-law and partner, so pleasant and accommodating. 'Yes,' said Mr Chipchase with a sigh, 'I'm afraid my father-in-law does have a temper, sir. I often urge him to moderate his feelings, out of regard for his health; but he is used to having his own way, and my wife and I really have very little influence over him.'

'Well, I would advise quietness, air, a plain diet and, as far as possible, freedom from cares and excitements. I rather fear, Mr Chipchase, that Mr Twopenny's mind is not as lucid as it was, and is inclined to wander.'

Mr Chipchase's little spectacles glittered mildly as he turned his face to the doctor. 'My dear sir, not at all, I'm grateful to you for your frankness. I have observed a similar . . . deterioration in my father-in-law's mental robustness; but my respect and affection for him have tended to blind me to the distressing fact.' Mr Chipchase gave a meek, sad smile. 'I shall of course do as you recommend, sir, and make sure that he is never disturbed. Indeed, I shall make it the first claim on my attention, and watch over him most carefully. Most carefully . . . I am afraid I do not keep liquors, sir – perhaps some cordial before you go?'

'Thank you, but my time is short. Please do not be overly anxious about your father-in-law's condition, Mr Chipchase. He has the remains of an extremely strong constitution, and may well live comfortably for some years yet.'

Mr Chipchase had taken off his spectacles to polish them, and it struck the young physician that his eyes did not gain in expression at all when naked, as was usually the case. 'For some years yet,' repeated Mr Chipchase in a murmur, and then gave his little smile again. 'Sir, I thank you, You have put my mind at rest. Let me show you to the door. As for my father-in-law's immediate condition – should he remain in bed, do you think?'

'Oh, I don't think so. Let him be up and about as soon as he feels well enough, as long as he doesn't do too much. And don't hesitate to send for me again, if you should feel any anxiety. Good-day, Mr Chipchase.'

Mr Chipchase gave the doctor his soft little plaster-cast of a hand, and thanked him again. He stood at the door to watch him go, and then turned and went cat-footed into the parlour, where Sar'ann was trying on a variety of astonishing caps before the mirror.

'Well? What did his lordship have to say?' shrilled Sar'ann, who did not like the young physician for curious reasons to do with his having very soft, dark and lustrous hair.

'Your father,' said Mr Chipchase, rubbing his hands together as if to try and coax some blood into them, 'is on the mend, my dear. On the mend.'

'Pooh! And what does his lordship know about it, I'd like to know! He don't have to live with the aggravating old creature!' Sar'ann plucked a cap off her dusty locks, and tried another.

'Very true, my dear. Very true. However, the doctor says he must be carefully watched. I'm afraid his wits are turning, my love, and we must take the greatest care of him.' Mr Chipchase stole up behind his wife, and placing his flat face against her cheek, insinuated his pink tongue into her ear.

'Oh, Edwin! Oh, my stars, you Caution, you!' cried Sar'ann, with her neck stretching to new lengths. 'Eleven o'clock in the morning! Oh, my stars, it's enough to make a cat laugh!' It was also enough to make Sar'ann laugh, apparently, for she went into a shrieking fit that lasted some minutes, while Mr Chipchase, smiling in his lipless way, removed himself to the hearthrug, and watched her from there.

'Well, and what did his lordship say we should do with him?' said Sar'ann, coming to herself. 'Is he to get up, and start plaguing us again? Because upon my word, Edwin, I don't care who hears me say it – it's been nice without him – ain't it?' She gave another shriek, as an epilogue to the laughing-fit, and then repeated with her eyes fixed on her husband's, 'It's been nice without him – ain't it?'

'Life has been a little easier while your father has been confined to his bed, indeed,' said Mr Chipchase, 'there's no denying it. But that's because he's not the man he was, my dear. He is really not the man he was, and we must – adjust our attitude to him accordingly.'

'Oh, I've got no attitude to him at all, Edwin, I assure you! I've got no attitude to him at all – except that he's an aggravating old creature, and that's about all there is to say! I sometimes wonder if it wouldn't be better if he . . .' Sar'ann stopped, just as she was about to place another cap on her head, and regarded her husband with a look at once startled, furtive, gloating, and excited.

'Yes, my dear,' said Mr Chipchase in his unhurried way. 'I do understand what you mean. But we must simply be patient with him, you know. "In your patience possess ye your souls", as scripture has it. Did you not, my dear, express a wish to go shopping this morning?'

Sar'ann jumped up, and expressed it again; and Mr Chipchase, with various uxorious attentions and caresses, filled her purse, and bade her goodbye. When she had gone, with her personal maid – another innovation – in tow, he remained for some minutes in the parlour gazing into the cold fireplace; then tried on one of his wife's caps, and chuckled at the spectacle he made in the mirror; and went forth at last to tour the premises of Twopenny & Chipchase.

All was well: it was coming to the end of the malting season, but the maltings were working at full capacity, and the workmen – virtually none of whom would have been recognized by Saul – gave him respectful greetings as he passed through with his little measured step and his mildly observant eye. At the warehouse on the quay he paused awhile to watch the builders at work renovating the old flint walls that had been so susceptible to damp and infestation; and then, settling his spectacles on his nose and giving his weak tufts of hair a twiddle, returned to the house to see his father-in-law.

Saul was sitting up in bed, with his Bible unopened on the coverlet before him. His servant Caleb was seated at the bedside, with his great blond hands clasped between his knees, and a shadow crossed his face when Mr Chipchase entered the room, which was answered, it seemed, by an extra glitter from Mr Chipchase's spectacles.

'Well, Edwin, the doctor gave a good account of me, I think?' said Saul, in a voice that seemed to try for his old thunder, but to fall some way short of it.

'Not *so* good, father-in-law,' said Mr Chipchase, making a circuit of the room, and seeming to take a mental inventory of its austere furnishings. 'Not *so* good. You will do pretty well if you calm yourself; but the question is, whether you will calm yourself, or whether you will persist in being unreasonable.'

Mr Chipchase, having completed his tour, came and stood by the bed. He looked at Saul; and Saul, who appeared more grizzled and Mosaic than ever in consequence of having no haircut or shave in a long while, looked back at him, whilst Caleb watched them with pale eyes. They both knew, and even Caleb knew, what Mr Chipchase was referring to. There had been a violent quarrel between Saul and his son-in-law – or rather, Saul had become violently quarrelsome, and Mr Chipchase had quietly let him be so. The occasion was Mr Chipchase's decision to sell the half-share that was owned by Twopenny & Chipchase in a couple of coastal ships that plied between Hales-next-the-sea and London – a decision prompted by Mr Chipchase's conviction that the coming railway would make the ships redundant. Saul had learnt of it by accident, and had raged wildly both at the decision and the fact that he had not been consulted. All his furious demonstrations had run off Mr Chipchase's perfect blandness like water off wax; and the end result had been that Saul had suffered an apoplectic collapse, and had been ill in bed for some time.

Just how ill he had been was plain at least to Caleb, who had heard his master cursing and rambling through the nights, and had seen a fearful, agonized vacancy pass across the old man's face, in the intervals of his old cussedness. But to Caleb's mind, firm and clear enough where his master was concerned, there was more than illness to be feared in Saul's situation. The apoplectic stroke was only an incident in the process of change being wrought upon Saul, and Caleb had no doubt of who was responsible for it. He had long regarded his master's will as an awesome force of nature, impossible to challenge; but now his devoted eyes saw it joined in battle with another, and losing.

'I shall be reasonable, Edwin,' Saul said. 'I know that a man of my age should be . . . careful of himself. So I shall be reasonable. And besides, I've no wish to lie mouldering here for ever. I wish to be strong again.'

'Of course, father-in-law, of course.' Mr Chipchase picked up Saul's stick from where it lay on the bedside table, and studied its polished head with amiable interest.

'So, Edwin. Up and about tomorrow, say? I feel quite strong enough to come downstairs, you know.'

'No, father-in-law.' Mr Chipchase spoke, and continued to speak, as if he were addressing the stick and not the old man in the bed. 'I think not. The doctor advises that you remain in bed for some days yet. A week, perhaps. You may think you're better than you really are, you see. And we wouldn't want you to be set back by trying your strength too soon, now would we? So it's best that you remain here quietly for the time being.' Mr Chipchase gave the head of the stick a playful tweak, as if it were someone's nose, and then laid it down at last and turned to Saul. 'Please be guided by us in this, father-in-law. Out of sheer duty and respect, we cannot permit you to endanger yourself by any further rashness of behaviour.'

Saul's brows contracted in their old stern frown, but his lips moved uncertainly. 'Well . . . if the doctor . . . But I am not used to such inactivity, Edwin, I have never left the running of the business for so long. It irks me that – that I am rendered useless in this way, I have never been idle in my whole life, damn it, never—'

'Father-in-law,' Mr Chipchase held up a warning finger, then wagged it with his little inward smile. 'You are over-exciting yourself – remember? It's not good for you – really it isn't.'

Saul, who had pushed himself up in the bed, subsided again, his eyes on Mr

Chipchase's archly wagging finger. 'No,' he murmured, 'you're right, of course, Edwin.'

'Now will you give me your promise, father-in-law, that you will not over-excite yourself again? I ask it, sir, because I am concerned for you: nothing but the deepest anxiety for your well-being could prompt me to take the liberty of binding you to a promise. I wouldn't even dream of it, if you were yourself. But you're not yourself, I'm afraid. So: will you give me your promise?'

After a moment, Saul nodded. Caleb breathed out a long breath.

'I'm so glad we've come to an understanding, father-in-law,' said Mr Chipchase brightly. 'Well, now, is there anything you require? I should think you're pretty comfortable here – ' with a birdlike glance about the cheerless room – 'but do say, if there's anything you require.'

'No,' said Saul, 'no, thank you, Edwin. But I'll send Caleb down if there is.'

'Ah, yes, Caleb.' Mr Chipchase fixed the birdlike look on Caleb, and, as if calling to a man across a broad street, accosted him: 'Well, my friend, and how do you do? I'm sure we can trust you, can't we?'

Caleb, his great shoulders hunched, did not answer, and raised his eyes no higher than Mr Chipchase's waistcoat.

'Hm.' Mr Chipchase put his hand to his wisps of hair. 'Very well, father-in-law. I'll leave you now. No rest, as they say, for the wicked.' And he gave his little gurgle of amusement, and scarcely seeming to open the door at all to do it, slipped out of the room.

For three days Saul was quiescent. He remained in bed, taking light meals, sleeping, and reading his Bible; but more often he would lay the book down, and gaze about the room for long periods at a time, his grim old face motionless except for the slowly moving eyes. Mr Chipchase came to see him briefly in the mornings and evenings, but most of the time Saul was completely alone except for Caleb. And it was on Caleb's great shoulders that a terrible burden of foreboding fell, as he watched his master's eyes roaming about the room and listened to the sporadic mutterings that punctuated his rest.

'William,' Saul suddenly said on the third night, just as Caleb was settling him down and about to snuff the candle. 'Where's William? Caleb – go fetch him. Fetch the boy to me directly. How dare he neglect me like this!'

'He's not here, sir,' Caleb said. 'He went away.'

'What are you talking about, boy? I want him here now. Fetch him, or you'll feel my stick.'

'Sir, Mr William went away a long time ago, sir,' said Caleb, who in his distress seemed to become more large, cumbrous, and agonizingly gentle than ever. 'He went quite away – sailing the sea, sir. He don't live here any more.'

Saul's eyes searched the big face bending over him in the candlelight. 'How . . .? Why, what nonsense am I talking, boy? Of course he went away. I remember.' His hands plucked fretfully at the counterpane. 'How could I forget it? I never used to forget things, boy – never!'

Caleb gave him an anguished look; and then said with sudden animation: 'I know what it is, sir. You've caught it off me. That's what it is. Why, I've always forgotten things. Ever since I got sick, and father got took by the angels . . . Ever since then, I've been forgetting things. You've caught it off me, sir.'

Saul turned his head restlessly, patting Caleb's arm. 'Ah, you're talking nonsense, boy. Never mind.'

'No, sir, that's what it is. You've caught forgetting off me.' This formula seemed to reassure Caleb greatly, and he began tucking in the bedclothes and plumping the pillows with new energy. 'That's what it is. Nothing to worry about – you've caught it off me, that's all.'

Caleb's mind was eased by this, if Saul's was not; but the old man presently went

258

to sleep, and Caleb tiptoed into the little room adjoining, and laid himself down in his clothes, as was his custom since Saul's illness. It was at some time in the small hours that he woke, to the sound of heavy footsteps in the next room.

Caleb sprang up, lit a candle, and hastened into his master's bedchamber. Saul was out of bed, and half-dressed, and was roaming about the darkened room as if in search of something.

'There you are, boy!' Saul said. 'I think you'd sleep your life away if it weren't for me. I want my stick, boy. Where's my stick? I can't find my stick. Damn it, I want my stick!'

He continued his restless pacing; and Caleb, after a moment of indecision, crept forward and took the stick from the bedside table.

'Here, sir – here it is. What's the matter? Shall I help you to the stool? Is it—'

'Damn you, Caleb, am I an invalid? Don't be a fool, boy. It's time we were up.' Leaning heavily on his stick, Saul stumped to the door and flung it open. 'Where's William? Is he home yet? I'll thrash him, I'll thrash him well if he's been down to the waterside again – he'll play those tricks no more, d'you hear, I won't stand for it . . .'

He stood swaying on the landing, as if uncertain which way to go, and bellowing about William and his tricks, until the noise brought forth Mr and Mrs Chipchase, dressing-gowned and slippered.

'William!' Saul cried on beholding Mr Chipchase. 'You reprobate, sir, what do you mean by it? Come here and take your punishment, boy!'

'Oh, my stars, Pa, whatever are you rambling about?' cried Sar'ann. 'Don't you know Edwin when you see him? I should think you'd know him anywhere, you aggravating old Pa, you!'

Mr Chipchase in his night attire was not, indeed, a sight readily to be forgotten, and Caleb averted his eyes from his white hairless ankles after one glance. Saul's look, however, betrayed only puzzlement.

'William . . .?'

'No, father-in-law,' said Mr Chipchase, in a very pinched manner. 'Not William. Please, sir, moderate your voice. You'll wake the whole household.' He shuffled forward and took hold of Saul's arm. 'I think you've been having a dream, father-in-law. That's what it is. Just a dream. You remember me now?'

'Edwin,' said Saul flatly, his shoulders sagging. 'I – yes, I dare say I . . . I dare say I was having a dream. A bad dream.'

'Of course. It happens to all of us, sir.' Mr Chipchase, with a remarkably strong grip for such apparently boneless hands, steered Saul back into his bedchamber. 'You'll take cold, father-in-law. I suggest you go back to bed. Come.'

Saul shambled obediently back to bed; but as he undressed and lay down he threw another distracted look around him and murmured, 'I thought William was here. I thought—'

'Well, he isn't, father-in-law. But I am,' said Mr Chipchase, looking down at him. 'I'm here.'

'Dreams,' muttered Saul as he laid his grizzled head down. 'I never used to have dreams. Never before. Now I seem to live in them!'

Caleb, greatly troubled, had followed, and took his place by his master's bed, determined to sit up there all night. Mr Chipchase took no notice of him; but Caleb heard him say to Sar'ann, as he went out to the landing, 'Dear me! I really do not like being roused in the middle of the night!' Sar'ann gave a muffled squeal in reply, and muttered something Caleb did not hear; but there was no further word from Mr Chipchase, who seemed much aggrieved, and the two went back to bed.

Saul slept again; and Caleb, though he struggled manfully to keep awake, fell into a doze at last in the bedside chair just as the sky was lightening. He woke late with a guilty start, to find Saul sitting up in bed and regarding him.

259

'Oh! sir, pardon me, I didn't mean—'

'Hush, boy,' said Saul, with a patting motion of his hand. 'It's no matter. You shouldn't wear yourself out with watching, Caleb, you'll be ill. Well, well, a restless night for both of us, eh? Dreams, Caleb – curious waking dreams . . .! How do you account for a man like me having such things?'

'Sir, I know what it is,' said Caleb eagerly, recalling his former explanation. 'You've caught it off me, sir. I've always been like that, ever since that bad time. You've caught dreaming off me, sir – that's what it is.'

'Ah, you mean well, boy,' said Saul shaking his head. 'Anyhow, I'm better now. I've rested well, and I feel better all ways; and I think it's time I got up. Oh, I'll take things steady – but it's doing me no good, shut away here in this room. Go fetch me my clothes, boy.'

Caleb jumped up with alacrity, and opened the closet door; then stood gazing in for so long that Saul said impatiently, 'Well, boy, what's amiss? Any suit of clothes will do – I'm not going to a ball.'

Caleb turned with a face of vacant dismay. 'Your clothes aren't here, sir.'

'What? What are you maundering about?'

'No clothes in here, sir. Only night things.' Caleb opened the closet door wide and stepped aside so that Saul could see in.

'What the devil . . .?' Saul's hand groped out to the bedside table; but his stick was gone too. He stared, and then thumped the table with his fist. 'Caleb, go fetch Edwin to me. Fetch him here at once. I won't have it, by God, I won't have it! Tell William . . .' Saul struck the table again, breathing heavily. 'Tell Edwin I want to see him at once!'

Caleb hurried off; and presently returned with Mr Chipchase – a very composed Mr Chipchase, licking breakfast butter off his fingers and humming under his breath.

'Good morning, father-in-law. I hope you're feeling better today. The weather is quite uncommonly warm—'

'Edwin,' growled Saul. 'Where are my clothes?'

'Your clothes, father-in-law? In the cedar closet downstairs. Sar'ann put them there early this morning, with some lavender. They'll be all nice and fresh when you're ready to get up. You were sleeping so comfortably this morning, we didn't want to wake you.'

'I want my clothes now.' Saul's hands clutched convulsively at the counterpane. 'I am ready to get up now, and I want my clothes.'

'Now, father-in-law, you promised to be guided by me, you know. The doctor said you might fancy yourself better than you are, and try to do too much, and set yourself back. He said we might have to be strict with you in that regard. I will not have you knocking yourself up, and suffering a relapse: I couldn't forgive myself if that happened. You were a little disturbed last night, you know, father-in-law. You can't have rested well. I simply wouldn't hear of you getting up today, and neither would Sar'ann, I'm sure. Now please excuse me, sir, while I finish my breakfast. I'll have yours sent up presently.'

Mr Chipchase gave his miniature bow, and walked out of the room.

'Don't you turn your back on me, Edwin!' cried Saul. 'How dare you turn your back on me! Come back!'

But Mr Chipchase did not appear to hear, and went noiselessly downstairs.

The flush that suffused Saul's grim face was terrible to see, and Caleb struggled to say something soothing, without knowing what. 'Sir – sir, please – please, sir—'

'Don't stand there gibbering, boy!' bellowed Saul, with spray escaping from his lips. 'Fetch my clothes! You heard him – they're in the cedar closet. Below the back stairs, damn it. Go on, boy – look alive! I'll not stand for this, by God I will not stand for it!'

Caleb took off at a lick. He had an ill feeling about today – a horrible fearful feeling – but his master was still his master, and he would not disobey him. He found the cedar closet and turned the handle. Stuck . . .?

Not stuck. There was a lock on the door now. He was sure there had not been one before. He was still tugging at the handle in helpless confusion when a soft finger touched him in the small of the back.

'What are you about there, my friend?' said Mr Chipchase, and as Caleb whipped round he transferred the soft finger from his back to his chest, and tapped twice with it. 'What business do you have here?'

Caleb stared into Mr Chipchase's owlish eyes, and could not stop trembling. 'Master,' he stammered, 'master's clothes – master wants . . .'

'I'm the master here, my friend,' said Mr Chipchase. His little pink tongue emerged and licked some breadcrumbs from his lips; while the soft finger tapped twice more. 'What am I?'

Caleb trembled, and could not speak. Somehow the tapping of that pasty finger terrified him – terrified him utterly.

'Who runs the household, my friend?' said Mr Chipchase patiently. 'Who has the charge of everything that goes on within these walls? Who gives the orders here?'

Caleb gasped out, almost inaudibly, 'You.'

'Well, it might be a little louder, my friend, but it will do. Yes, me. I'm glad you know it. Now, come away from that closet.' Mr Chipchase moved a few paces away, and pointed to a spot in front of him. 'There. That's it. Now, do you know what I want you to do? I want you to go down to the kitchen, and collect your old master's breakfast-tray, and take it up to him. Do it now, my friend, and I won't get angry with you.'

For a moment Caleb did not move; but then Mr Chipchase lifted his forefinger again, and pointed it at Caleb; and in horror of receiving any more of those soft taps, Caleb bolted.

There were tears in his eyes as he ran down to the kitchen, half blinding him and almost sending him tumbling down the steps. But the servants there were all new ones recruited by Mr Chipchase, who knew little and cared less about Caleb Porter, the half-wit who waited on the invalid old man; and the cook merely clucked her tongue at his clumsiness, and pointed to the breakfast-tray set out ready. Caleb picked it up, and carried it as carefully as he was able up to Saul's room; occasionally choking back a sob, for he felt that he had failed his master, failed him dreadfully, and the feeling was agony to him.

Saul was sitting on the edge of the bed, studying his own hands as if they were unfamiliar to him; and when he looked up on Caleb's coming in there was for several moments no expression on his face at all. Then his eyes hardened as he saw the tray.

'What's this, boy? What the devil are you about? I told you to fetch my clothes. Have you lost what little sense you have? Get out and—'

'Sir, please, I can't,' sobbed Caleb, 'I can't, sir – he won't – Mr Chipchase won't let me . . .'

Saul stared at Caleb for a moment. Then he got up, seized the breakfast-tray from his servant's hands and, dressed only in his nightshirt, marched stiffly out of the room carrying the tray before him.

He was halfway downstairs when Caleb caught up with him, and shouting at the top of his voice for Edwin and Sar'ann. The voice lacked the old pipe-organ power, but it was still enough to bring Mr and Mrs Chipchase hurrying out to the hall from the dining-room.

'Oh! Saints alive, Pa, what a spectacle you look!' squealed Sar'ann. 'Get back to bed at once, you aggravating old Beast, you're positively indecent! Oh my stars, what a sight!'

'I want my clothes!' bellowed Saul. 'I sent for my clothes, and I will have them! I *will* have them, do you hear me?'

'Father-in-law, really, this is very curious conduct,' said Mr Chipchase. 'Now go back to bed, do.' He had just set his foot on the bottom stair when Saul with a wild grunt hurled the breakfast-tray into the air. There was such an almighty crashing and smashing of tray, plates and teapot hitting the hall floor that Caleb covered his ears, and did not hear Sar'ann shrilling: 'Oh, you've done it now! Oh, you've done it good and proper now, Pa!'

'I will have my clothes! I will have my clothes, I will, I will . . .' Saul's raging had become a helpless weeping, and Caleb saw him slump heavily against the banister. He darted forward and grasped the old man about the shoulders; and, driven to daring initiative by his distress, he turned him forcibly about, saying, 'Sir, come back to bed. Sir, I think you should come back to bed. Come on, sir.'

'Quite right, Caleb,' said Mr Chipchase, who had ascended the stairs without a sound, just as if he had floated up, and was right beside him. 'You're not well, father-in-law. Really you're not. You must acknowledge it yourself. You were always such a sensible man, and would never have made a fuss about a little thing like this.'

Saul, between tears and fury, tried to wrench himself away from Caleb, but he lacked the strength. 'I want to get up, Edwin. I want to dress and get up . . .'

'So you shall,' said Mr Chipchase. 'You shall get up tomorrow, father-in-law. Tomorrow, eh, my dear?' – to Sar'ann, who had followed him up and was now craning over his shoulder, intently studying the tears on her father's cheeks.

'Oh! I dare say. Whatever he likes, as long as it stops him being such an aggravating old Donkey. I declare, Pa, there never was such a stubborn old Donkey as you, not since the blessed Flood!'

'But for today,' said Mr Chipchase, 'I really must insist that you rest. Bed-rest is the only thing for you today, father-in-law, and I'm sure you know it.'

Saul, impatiently brushing the tears from his face, consented to be led back to his room, and to lie down again; but once he had recovered himself a little, something of the old firmness came back to his jaw and, fixing his eyes on Mr Chipchase he said, 'Tomorrow, then. Perhaps I am a little tired.'

'Yes, father-in-law. Tomorrow.'

'Your word on it?'

'Oh, my stars, Pa,' cried Sar'ann, 'how many times do you need to be told?'

Saul ignored her. 'Your word, Edwin?'

'My word on it, father-in-law,' said Mr Chipchase, blinking. 'Of course.' He turned to Caleb. 'My good friend, will you go down to the kitchen, and tell them Mr Twopenny's breakfast is spoiled, and have them make up another tray.'

'I want no breakfast,' Saul muttered.

'Oh, Donkey, Donkey!' said Sar'ann vehemently, clenching her fists. 'Hee-haw, hee-haw!'

'Please, father-in-law, take a little breakfast. We want you well again. You want to regain your strength, do you not?'

Saul's eyes narrowed. 'Aye, aye. Very well.' He waved a hand at Caleb. 'Off you go, boy.'

After a moment's hesitation, Caleb did as he was bid. Saul continued to stare into Mr Chipchase's eyes, or what there was of them.

'I'm glad you're seeing reason, father-in-law,' said that nerveless gentleman, tucking his hands under his coat-tails. 'I was sure you would.'

'Aye, Edwin, you're right. I must get my strength up, if I'm to be up and about tomorrow. It's an age since I've been about the maltings or the warehouse.'

'So it is, sir, so it is.' Mr Chipchase made a little chirping noise with his lips, or what there was of them. 'Well, my dear, that's all pleasantly settled. Let's leave your father to enjoy his breakfast in peace.'

They left Saul alone, and Mr Chipchase closed the door behind him. And then he took out his bunch of keys, and held one up before Sar'ann's goggling eyes.

'My dear,' he said softly, 'I think we had better lock his door. For his own good, my dear. I'm a little fearful for him – his mind is most definitely going. He might do some hurt to himself, if we don't lock him in; and we wouldn't want that, would we?'

Sar'ann, with her neck at maximum length, and her eyes straining out of her head as she looked from the upraised key to her husband, and back again, let out a single, breathless, piercing: 'Tee-hee!'

'Does that mean yes, my dear?' said Mr Chipchase, tapping his nose (or what there was of it) with the key. 'It usually does, I find.'

'Oh, Edwin! You devil, you – you rascal – you absolute downright Caution, you! Whatever next!'

'And after all, as you said, my dear – it's very nice without him. Isn't it?'

Sar'ann nodded: stared at the key: stared at her husband: let out a hissing 'Tee-hee!'; and gave herself a slap across the face, as if to ward off any laughing fit that might be coming.

'Very well.' Mr Chipchase quietly turned the key in the lock. 'It's for his own good, of course. He's our responsibility, my dear – no one else's: no one else, you know, cares whether he lives or dies! – so we must take care of him.'

'Oh! But ain't he got keys of his own?'

'I took the precaution,' Mr Chipchase said, 'of removing them this morning,' and having finished tapping his own nose with the key, tapped Sar'ann's, which was a far more substantial instrument for the purpose.

'Oh, Edwin, you're a one! That's what you are – you're a one!' Sar'ann did a little jig on tiptoe; and then placing her hands on her hips (or what there was of them) addressed the locked door in a fierce whisper. 'There! What do you think of that, you old Donkey! I should like to see you get up to your tricks now! Hee-haw, hee-haw!'

Mr Chipchase observed his wife's performance with admiration, and then, taking her arm, led her downstairs, remarking that he believed she was going shopping today.

'Yes, Edwin,' she said; and peeping slyly out of the corners of her eyes, pronounced the word: 'Underthings!'

'My, my,' he said with a gurgle, pecking her on the cheek, 'my, my,' and he was still gurgling like a water-spout when he came across Caleb, emerging from the kitchen with a second tray.

'Oh, you needn't trouble about that, my friend,' Mr Chipchase said. 'Your old master's changed his mind, and doesn't want any. He's sleeping. So take it back, and then go make yourself useful in the stables.'

'But—'

'Do I need to tell you twice, my friend? I don't think I do, do I?' Mr Chipchase lifted his forefinger, and Caleb retreated. 'Good fellow. Be quick about it, now.' And humming under his breath, Mr Chipchase went forth to the maltings, and about his father-in-law's business.

Fear of Mr Chipchase sent Caleb to the stables for the rest of the morning: but devotion to Saul brought him slinking back to the house at last, and to Saul's bedroom door. He knocked, and jumped as a voice on the other side of the panelling cried, 'Who's there? Caleb, is it you?'

'Yes, sir.' Caleb's heart lifted at the eagerness in his master's tone, and he tried to open the door. When he found it locked he began to wail like a heartbroken child.

'Hush, boy, hush, he'll hear you,' came Saul's voice.

263

'Who, sir, who?' moaned Caleb, his wits quite scattered by this new and terrible development.

'Why, the demon, of course. That's what he is, boy: a demon, such as scripture warns us of; none but a demon could have done it! Locked in, boy, locked in like a prisoner!' Saul's fingers scratched weakly at the door. 'Be careful of him, Caleb. If he dares to subject me to this, then there's no trusting him. Oh! I shall have the beating of him yet, boy, I swear I shall, I swear to that God I have always faithfully served. He'll learn that he can't treat me like this – oh, he'll learn! He shall be chastised – corrected – there will be such punishments . . .!'

'Sir,' gasped Caleb, gripping himself about with his great arms in an effort to restrain his weeping, 'sir, what shall I do? I don't know what to do. Shall I break down the door?'

'Nay, boy, you'll not break this lock. He'll hear you besides. Do nothing, boy. I'll take him to task for this little trick. He's mistaken if he supposes he has me under his thumb. He thinks I'm decayed, a foolish decayed old man, rambling, rambling in his mind . . . What do you say, Caleb? What do you think? *Am* I so? Speak, boy, speak!'

'Sir . . . oh, sir, I don't understand . . .'

'Answer me, Caleb, or I'll thrash you! Speak! Or are you in his pay too? Are you not faithful – have you deserted me like all the rest?' Caleb flinched as Saul suddenly began pounding on the panelling. 'If you've turned against me, boy, I'll have your hide, I'll make you regret the day you were ever born . . .'

The pounding grew harder and faster, and Caleb shrank back from the door, half expecting to see his master's bloody fists come splintering through the woodwork; but suddenly it stopped, and there was the sound instead of Saul weeping desolately.

Caleb put his lips close to the door. 'Sir . . .?'

'Forgive me, boy. Forgive me. I don't know what I'm saying, I don't know what I'm doing . . . God have mercy on me . . .'

The beaten, whimpering note in Saul's voice was so unlike anything Caleb had ever heard from his master's lips that it brought him round like a slap in the face. He thought of his love for Saul, and his fear of Mr Chipchase; and finding the love greater than the fear, Caleb told his master that he would be back, and ran downstairs.

He found Mr Chipchase at last in the yard of the maltings, overseeing repairs to the grain hoist. He had a pencil in his hand, and was vigorously sucking the end of it as if it were some delicious sweetmeat; and he did not trouble to remove it from his mouth when Caleb appeared panting before him.

'Mr Chipchase . . .' Caleb had never addressed him thus before; and that, together with the expressionless way Mr Chipchase was regarding him while his lips sucked at the pencil, almost broke Caleb's fragile nerve. He had to summon up the thought of Saul weeping behind the door to recover it. 'Sir, my master's locked in his room, sir. He wants to be let out. It's not right, sir. He shouldn't be locked in. He wants to come out. Please, sir, you must let him out.'

Mr Chipchase withdrew the pencil with a last satisfied slurp. 'My friend,' he said, 'don't you remember what I said to you earlier?'

'Sir – please—'

'If my memory serves me right, I said to you,' Mr Chipchase went on blandly, tucking the pencil behind his ear, 'that I am the master here.'

'I know, sir, but—'

'You *don't* know,' said Mr Chipchase with a chuckle, 'because you have gone fussing about Mr Twopenny, instead of making yourself useful in the stables as I directed. That's one.' Mr Chipchase held up a forefinger, a couple of inches before Caleb's face. 'And now you come to me and say the words *you must*. You have the impertinence, my friend, to use the words *you must* to me. That's two.' Mr

Chipchase held up both forefingers, and then with a little chuckle abruptly pinched Caleb's nose between them. 'Two is too many, in my book. Do you know what employment is, my friend?'

Caleb, obedient to questioning even in his distress, murmured, 'Job.'

'Excellent! And you have just lost yours. Get out.'

Mr Chipchase retrieved his pencil; then, as Caleb continued to stand before him, staring and open-mouthed, he said with a sigh, 'Dear me, are you even more stupid than you seem, my friend? I told you to get out. Your employment here is at an end. You are no longer wanted. Pack up your clothes, and whatever else you possess, and get off these premises. If you are not gone by – let's see . . .' Mr Chipchase consulted his watch. 'Say half-past two. If you're not gone by then, my friend, do you know what I shall do? I shall have you taken before the magistrates, as a vagabond and a lunatic, and they will put you away in the workhouse asylum. There: what do you think of that?' concluded Mr Chipchase brightly.

The wild terrors that this threat held – long abolished by Saul's protection – thrust themselves upon Caleb's mind with all their old force and more; but even in the midst of whirling horrors, something stiffened within his loyal and childlike nature, and he burst out: 'I think – I think you're as ugly as sin! That's what I think! You're as ugly as sin!'

Mr Chipchase's mouth went as small and tight as if it had been pulled by a drawstring: and Caleb knew a moment of tremulous triumph.

'In fact,' said Mr Chipchase, fumbling in his pocket, 'never mind your possessions. They were all bought for you here, I should think, and precious little you've done to earn them. You get out this very moment, my friend, or I'll have my workmen throw you out. Here.' He tossed two half-crowns at Caleb. 'That should pay you off. And if I ever see you anywhere near these premises again, I'll do what I said. Do you hear?'

Mr Chipchase turned away. He had still not raised his voice; but the back of his neck was red, and the hand that he put up to twiddle the strands on his scalp was not quite steady.

But Caleb, after that little thrill of defiance, was more wretched than he had ever thought it possible to be. Not just at being dismissed from the post and the place that meant everything to him: he was miserably conscious that he could not even say goodbye to his beloved master. He knew in his bones that Mr Chipchase was not a man to make empty threats; and though he longed to steal back to the house, and place his lips against the locked door and hear Saul's voice again, the fear of the asylum was too strong. Mr Chipchase had drawn off to the other side of the yard, and was watching him askance; and after a moment Caleb put the coins in his pocket, dragged his hand across his eyes, and shambled off towards the yard gate.

Mr Chipchase continued to twiddle, and to stroll about the yard, and to watch everything that went on; and there was such a sharp glitter about his spectacles that his workmen were more inhibited in his presence than ever, and were driven to trying to hammer nails silently, and make the carthorses walk on tiptoe, and other impossibilities. At length, however, Mr Chipchase left them, remarking under his breath, 'Well, and now for *you*,' and much freshened in his aspect.

He had unlocked the door of Saul's room, slipped inside, and set down the tray of food he carried, in his deft way, almost before the old man knew he was there. Saul roared, and heaved himself off the bed, and advanced on his son-in-law; but he lacked his stick, and he felt the lack. He could only swing his arms ineffectually at Mr Chipchase, whilst Mr Chipchase gently put him off: the old bullish strength was gone.

'Please, father-in-law – I don't know what you're trying to do, but all you're likely to do is hurt yourself . . . There,' said Mr Chipchase, as Saul's stumbling feet caught in the rug, and he fell heavily against the bed. 'Now that's what I was afraid of. Come.'

Saul was winded, and could not speak. Mr Chipchase gripped his arm, and half lifted him on to the bed.

'There, that's better. You see? I declare you're your own worst enemy sometimes, sir. I really do not understand why you are being so awkward.' Mr Chipchase brought the tea-tray to the bedside; Saul, making another feeble struggle, almost upset it. 'There – now look! Really, father-in-law, if you don't act in a rational manner, I can't see that I shall have any alternative but to take the tray away. Greatly as I respect you, sir, I shall not trouble to bring your meals if it means taking my life in my hands every time – I'm far too busy. Now, let's see, what's here.. calf's-foot jelly, some cold bacon, coddled eggs, bread and butter – what will you take, father-in-law?'

'Where's Caleb?' said Saul, lying back and watching Mr Chipchase as if he were some venomous lizard not to be startled by sudden movement.

'Gone, sir. I had to dismiss him. He was impudent – intolerably impudent. Besides, I think it was doing you no good, father-in-law, having a half-wit about you all the time. Your own mind is . . . troubled, sir, troubled and tired.'

'Poor Caleb . . . poor boy. You might have left me him, Edwin. What's to become of him? Poor boy!'

'Old affection blinded you to his failings, father-in-law,' said Mr Chipchase. 'Well, no more. I have provided for him amply, so you need not worry about that. And from now on I shall look after you myself, father-in-law. I shall take your welfare exclusively into my own hands.'

'And keep me confined in this room? Is that your *care*?'

'Certainly,' said Mr Chipchase, 'when it is necessary. My dear sir, you must acknowledge that your reason is somewhat disordered just now. That is no cause for shame. I remember reading an account of the illness of King George the Third. There he was, the highest in the land: but when his mind temporarily gave way, it was necessary to put him under some restraint, for his own safety; and like the great man he was, his late majesty accepted the necessity. I choose this illustration, because it is so apt to the high respect and reverence I have for you, sir.'

'They put him in a strait-jacket,' muttered Saul. 'They put the old king in a strait-jacket – I know that! You shall not do that to me, Edwin: I shall turn my face to the wall, and die, before you do that to me!'

Mr Chipchase forked a morsel of bacon and placidly ate it. 'There now,' he said, 'that is precisely what I mean. No one said anything about strait-jackets, father-in-law, and yet you take off on this curious flight of fancy about them . . . Ah, there's nothing like the taste of home-cured. I'll leave you to enjoy your dinner, father-in-law. I'll be back for the tray. Now I beg you, don't go rushing at the door, because all you'll do is injure yourself. You are old, sir – remember that you are old.'

Saul did not move; and Mr Chipchase was just about to close the door behind him when the old man growled, 'Edwin.'

'Sir?'

The glowering look that Saul gave him had petrified many a mortal; but Mr Chipchase exhibited nothing but mild attention.

'You gave me your word, Edwin,' said Saul.

'I beg your pardon, sir?'

Saul's breast heaved, and the restless hands grasped and clutched. 'You gave me your word! You gave me your word that I might get up tomorrow, Edwin!'

Mr Chipchase's smile was melancholy. 'I'm afraid, father-in-law, that you've been dreaming again. It would have been very foolish of me to have said any such thing, given your condition. Never mind. Get some rest, and you'll be better presently.'

Mr Chipchase closed the door, and locked it.

The sultry weather broke that night with a thunderstorm. Not a wild and raving storm, but a slow pageant of gigantic power that passed right across the purple heavens. The thunder was like the drum-rolls preceding some gargantuan cosmic event; the lightning was like the first awesome flashes of some unthinkable revelation. Sar'ann was so excited that she stood out in the yard behind the house, with her head thrown back and her chin pointing at the sky, and squealed her delight and clapped her hands at each tremendous manifestation from above; and when the rain came down at last, warm and thick as spilt blood, it was only through reminding her that her new frock would be spoiled that Mr Chipchase persuaded her to come inside, and watch the remainder of the spectacle from the parlour window.

And in the close-packed streets of Hales-next-the-sea, whence everyone had withdrawn behind closed shutters and bolted doors, Caleb Porter wandered: too desolate even to fear the storm, or feel its drenching violence. From time to time a chink of light at a window would arrest his attention, and he would stand wavering before it, thinking vague thoughts of warmth and comfort; but these were as nothing beside the thought of his lost master, and they would fall away, and he would shamble on again.

And in the great house by the quayside that had always resembled a jail, the fierce old man who had made it so was wandering too. The locked door of the bedchamber allowed him but a few square yards for physical motion; but in his mind he roamed unending corridors, and traversed open spaces dreadful in their vastness, and knew the sublime horror of infinity. Shapes of things that had been, and shapes of things that might have been, accosted him in his journeyings: shapes of things that never had been and could not possibly be, too; for his tortured mind, long denied the exercise of imagination, was making up for its deprivation, and conjured monsters in its distress. From time to time the old indomitable will would rise up in his labouring breast, and he would fume and rage at the subtle web of humiliating subjection that had been spun around him; yet he feared his own rage too, for it was no staff of righteousness any more, but a liability that sapped his strength, and made havoc in his brain. From time to time, conversely, he was wonderfully peaceful; for in his wanderings he came to a time and place that was familiar, and so reassuring in its solidity that he knew that all the rest was a dream – Sar'ann's marriage, Twopenny & Chipchase, the Demon and the cold ascendancy that the Demon had gained over him: all these were fancies, and instead the old days were in place, and William was here, and his nephew John too, and Mr Addy bustled about at his bidding, and the lamp burnt in his office beside his neatly ruled ledgers, and his stick fitted comfortably in his firm hand . . . Yes, it was here – the good old time was here: something so vivid to his perception could not be other than real! And then the light would fade from the scene, and the dismal truth would return, and he would find his pillow wet with an old man's tears.

And as the thunderous night gave way to a succession of bright serene days, and as Saul languished in a careful neglect, confined to his locked room, denied his clothes, denied everything but mere sustenance, so he wandered further, a mental pilgrim bowed down with a burden of sorrow and bewilderment, and searching for he knew not what refuge. He carried with him a chafing, wearying question: how did he, Saul Twopenny, come to be under the thumb of the man he could only think of now as the Demon? How had it happened? And once or twice, his ramblings brought him face to face with an answer – a stern and stony knowledge that he had done it himself. But he could not behold that knowledge for long, and would turn

267

away from it again, and wander off into wild dreams of revenge and vindication.

Mr Chipchase, meanwhile, applied himself to business with his usual thoroughness, interrupting it only twice a day to visit his father-in-law, taking with him a faithful servant of his own employ to carry the tray, empty the commode, and ensure that the patient did not become obstreperous. Sar'ann, however, did not appear to feel herself under the necessity of visiting her invalid father, contenting herself with asking her husband the daily question, 'Well? How's the old Donkey today?'

'I'm afraid his mind really is going, my dear,' Mr Chipchase said on one such occasion, creeping behind her, kissing her shoulder, and peeping down the front of her bodice.

'That's plain enough. I wish his body would go the same way!'

'Ha-ha, you're quite a wit, my dear. But I know you don't mean it. You're as fond of him as I am; though he makes it more and more difficult to be fond of him, alas!'

'Mr Bream called this morning, and asked after him,' said Sar'ann. 'I said he was poorly, too poorly to come down or see anyone.'

'And so he is, my dear,' said Mr Chipchase. 'So he is – alas, alas!' This word seemed to amuse them both enormously; for they burst into a simultaneous fit of laughter, half squealing, and half gurgling, to very singular effect.

One burden that Mr Chipchase no longer had to bear, and which he pronounced himself heartily glad to be rid of, was Caleb: sentiments echoed by his charming wife, who opined that 'he wasn't fit for normal company, and he might lie in a wet ditch for ever more, as far as I am concerned.' Mrs Chipchase's amiable prophecy, unbeknown to her, showed some signs of coming true; for Caleb was having a hard time of it. Ill-equipped by nature to fend for himself, and rendered even more helpless by his bemused grief, Caleb loitered about Hales-next-the-sea, perpetually drawn back to the premises of Twopenny & Chipchase, but fearful of going too close, lest the Demon see him and fulfil his terrifying threat. He slept in doorways; he bought loaves and bruised fruit with the money that Mr Chipchase had tossed at him, chewing them listlessly as he roamed, and when that was gone he ate quayside leavings, or did not eat at all. His one thought was of Saul, and how he might be reunited with him; and he was dwelling on this subject, and quite heedless of where he was going, when he turned one of the tight little corners of the tight little town, and bumped straight into Mr Addy.

'Now then, now then, plenty of room on the pavement, I hope—' began Mr Addy; then he recognized Caleb, and stared in astonishment, for living on the streets had soon left its mark on the simple man, and his crop of fair hair resembled a birds' nest. 'Why, Caleb Porter! What the deuce have you been up to?'

The sight of Mr Addy was so intimately bound up with his thoughts of Saul, and of the old days before the advent of the Demon, that tears sprang at once to Caleb's eyes, and he blurted, 'Oh, Mr Addy, sir, I ain't been up to anything, and I never would, I swear, if only I could have him back!'

'Have him back? Why, who, what, which?' said Mr Addy, becoming like a grammar-book in his surprise.

'Master, sir. I been sent away. I been turned out of my 'ployment, sir.'

'What? How, when?' cried Mr Addy, continuing grammatical.

Caleb, however, was so overcome by his feelings that Mr Addy presently decided that there was nothing for it but to take him home, dry him out, feed him up, and find out what was the matter then. Accordingly the little man took hold of the big man by the hand, and led him briskly through the streets to the little bow-windowed house; and there, having put a veal-and-ham pie into Caleb, Mr Addy tried to get some sense out of him – employing Mrs Addy for the purpose, as that rosy lady had a comfortable way with her.

'Why was you turned out, poor soul?' Mrs Addy gently inquired of Caleb, who was so very large as he sat in the couple's little parlour that they were obliged to push their chairs against the wall and peep at each other over his great knees. 'What happened?'

'Mr Chipchase turned me out,' said Caleb. 'He said I weren't wanted there, and I wasn't to come back no more. He give me two half-crowns, and I went away.'

'Ask him what his master had to say about it,' said Mr Addy, over the knees.

'And what did your master have to say about it, Caleb?'

'He don't have no say,' said Caleb. 'He don't have no say in nothing nowadays. Only Mr Chipchase. And besides, master ain't well. He – he has to stay in bed.' Caleb stopped short of stating the whole facts of the case. It seemed to him, knowing how proud his master was, that it would be a base betrayal to say that he was confined to his room like a troublesome lunatic. 'It's only Mr Chipchase as gives the orders now. Master can't do anything.'

Mr Addy spoke under his breath, though with great distinctness, the single word 'Fool'; and it was not to Caleb that he was referring. 'Ask him what missis says to it all,' he went on.

Mrs Addy relayed the question, and Caleb's fair cheeks burned. 'She don't say nothing. She don't care for me, and she don't care for master neither. All she care about is Mr Chipchase, and dressing up in things.'

Mr Addy sat back, and breathed the expressive monosyllable 'Fool' once more. 'Well, my dear, it make me hot just thinking about him, and that's a sensation I'd almost forgot. It's a cool position I've got now, and it pay twice as well – but even so, I can't be indifferent to the old pepperer, somehow. I'd never wish him ill . . . And yet I can't but say it: he made his bed, and he'll have to—'

'But I made his bed, sir,' said Caleb, imperfectly understanding. 'I always made his bed with my own hands, every day . . . and I knew just the way he liked it and no one else did . . . and now it's all gone!'

'There, there, poor soul,' said Mrs Addy, as Caleb showed signs of renewed distress, 'never mind. Eat a bit of seed-cake.' And Caleb, obedient to the last, grasped a piece of cake the size of a house-brick, and stifled a sob by cramming it whole into his mouth.

'I don't know,' mused Mr Addy, filling his pipe. 'He've done it to himself. There's young John gone away to London, Lord-knows-where, on account of his peppering ways; and there's young William likewise, aboard ship betwixt the Port o' London and Holland most of the time, they say. So who's to say that Chipchase one nay? No one. The master don't hear from his son or his nephew, I suppose? Ask him that, my dear.'

No, was Caleb's emphatic answer, in amongst the seed-cake: not a word. 'But he talk about them sometimes, when he's . . . well, when he's not quite himself.'

Mr and Mrs Addy exchanged a significant look: then Mrs Addy patted Caleb's hand and rose. 'Well, poor soul, you shall stay here with us tonight. I don't suppose you've slept in a bed since you were turned out, have you? And I'll see if I can find any old clothes to fit.'

'I wonder if I might be able to get Caleb work at our place,' said Mr Addy, puffing thoughtfully. 'He's as strong as an ox, and honest as the day is long. I shall ask tomorrow. I reckon I might contrive it, you know. As for that old brimstone pepperer, I don't know what can be done. He've made his bed, and – well, I'll say no more.'

Caleb stayed that night beneath the Addys' roof, and was as grateful as his halting tongue could allow him to be. He was given the spare bed in which John had once slept, and which was even less accommodating to one of his size; but Caleb was wakeful anyhow. He kept thinking about Saul's house, and how in the old days its nocturnal quiet would sometimes be riven by William coming drunkenly home; and that in turn set him thinking about the house as it was now, and how strictly regular were Mr Chipchase's hours of retiring and waking. And that was how Caleb had his idea.

He mulled it over all the next day, while he helped Mrs Addy with pounding the washing in the dolly-tub and turning the mangle, and he was mulling it over still when Mr Addy came home from work, and told him that there was a fair chance he could get him a job on the morrow, and that he must stay with them again tonight. Come nightfall, Caleb had finished mulling over his idea, and was ready to act on it. Opportunity came when Mr and Mrs Addy turned out in their little pocket-handkerchief of a back garden for a breather before bed. Caleb wished to leave some acknowledgement of their kindness, and explanation of where he had gone, but though he could with great pains read a little, he could not write; and at last he settled on plucking a flower from the window-box, and laying it in the centre of the table where the Addys would see it when they came in. These preparations completed, he left the house by the front door, closing it softly behind him, and hurried off in the direction of his old home.

Caleb knew Mr Chipchase's routines, and those routines were inviolable: there was his advantage. If he could get inside the house and find the right hiding-place, he was confident that he could stay out of Mr Chipchase's way until the household had gone to bed. He did not fear the servants, or even Sar'ann: only Mr Chipchase. For that little blinking gentleman was a Demon – Saul had said so, and Saul's word was good enough for Caleb.

First, however, he must gain access. He slipped into the yard that gave on to the kitchen door, and secreted himself behind the woodshed. Crouching there he could see into the kitchen, the door being left open in the warm evening, and discerned the figures of the cook and the scullery-maid within. The cook, he knew, would not be long going to bed, leaving the scullery-maid to clear up; but tonight she seemed to be in gossipy mood, and he waited for a full half-hour before he saw her stretch, take up a candle, and leave the kitchen.

Still Caleb waited, while the figure of the scullery-maid passed and repassed the open doorway, burdened with pots and plates. He saw several moths flutter in, attracted by the light: the door would surely be closed soon. Dare he steal forward, and try to slip into the house the next time the figure of the scullery-maid disappeared, in hopes that she might be in the pantry or the store-cupboard and would not see him? Caleb whimpered to himself. He was wholly unused to having to make decisions, and the sensation of it was like a pain in his breast.

He held his breath: the scullery-maid was coming outside. She crossed the yard, passed a few feet away from Caleb, and entered the earth-closet next door to the woodshed.

Caleb sprang up. He could move swiftly and quietly for all his size, and he was in the kitchen in an instant. A glance round: no one here. He went stealthily to the door that led into the hall. Empty likewise. There was a chink of light from the parlour door: Mr Chipchase, he knew, would be in there going over his accounts, while Sar'ann sewed or tried on new garments, for another half-hour yet – unless they decided to have one of their 'early nights'. The thought of that, and the revulsion that the thought occasioned in him, spurred Caleb forward. He crossed the hall to the stairs, and paused with his hand on the banister. No hiding-places down here: his master's old office, a storeroom now, would have been perfect – but Mr Chipchase kept it locked. Likewise the cedar-closet where his master's clothes were. Mr Chipchase locked practically everything.

Even the broom-cupboard upstairs? Caleb could not remember a lock on it, but then he never wholly trusted his observation. If it was locked, then he was in a fix. Caleb heard himself whimper again. What to do, what to do?

The sound of Sar'ann's shrill laughter from the parlour jolted him into movement. He hurried up the stairs, wincing at each faint creak, and along the landing. He had to pass his master's room, and was sorely tempted to try the door-handle. Just to see him again . . .! But he knew it would be locked, and feared that his master might call out. He hastened on down the long passage, past the Chipchases' room. The broom-cupboard was at right-angles to it, at the end. Tremulously, Caleb grasped the handle of the door, and it came open at once.

In his relief he wanted to shout aloud, and he had to drag his mind forcibly back to an appreciation of the gravity of the situation. The broom-cupboard was dark, and he suspected there might be spiders, of which he had a mortal terror; but he made himself squeeze inside, and pulled the door to behind him, leaving the thinnest crack through which he could observe the corridor.

It was not one of Mr and Mrs Chipchase's early nights, and Caleb, very cramped in the broom-cupboard, had gone stiff and numb in half his joints when at last a light flickered up the stairwell. Here came the Demon down the corridor, with his arm about his wife's waist; disengaging it only to open the bedroom door and usher her in. Sar'ann, however, did not go in. She turned her head almost three hundred and sixty degrees, like an owl, and stared directly at the broom-cupboard.

'Wait a moment, Edwin,' she said; and Caleb stifled a cry as Sar'ann, with narrowed eyes, came straight towards his hiding-place.

And stopped, just before it, and picked up the mousetrap by the skirting-board. 'Pooh! Nothing,' she said with a disappointed sniff; and laying it down again, turned and stalked into the bedroom, Mr Chipchase following her and closing the door.

Again Caleb had to resist the impulse to shout aloud; but he was coming now to the most dreadful part of his idea, and that sobered him. His master was locked up; his master's clothes were locked up; the whole house was locked up as if to resist a siege. If he was to take his master away from here – and that was the whole aim of the idea – then he would need the keys. And to get the keys, he would have to enter Mr Chipchase's bedroom.

Caleb's fear of this was so great that it paralysed him for some time. But that, he told himself at last after fighting down a fit of whimpering, was all to the good. For he knew, without knowing how he knew, or what it was exactly that he knew, that Mr and Mrs Chipchase did not go to sleep straight away, as he did when he laid himself down. It was as well to wait as long as he could, before embarking on his desperate venture. So he waited – he had great bodily endurance, and could as easily have waited on a bed of nails; and it was only after what his feeble grasp of time told him must be two hours, that he crept out of the broom-cupboard, and approached the bedroom door.

Someone was snoring within; and from the timbre of the snores, and a curious conviction that Mr Chipchase would never be so unguarded, Caleb guessed it was Sar'ann. He could not, in fact, imagine Mr Chipchase ever sleeping at all; and he was immobilized again by a vision of Mr Chipchase sitting up in bed with his spectacles on, coolly waiting for him to enter. 'I'm not brave enough!' thought Caleb distractedly: but he was. He opened the door with stupendous care, and sidled in.

Finding the keys turned out to be the easiest part: for there they were, a great bunch of them, laid on the washstand beside the bed, and glinting in a faint ray of moonlight that penetrated the window-curtains. But the same ray of moonlight showed Caleb Mr Chipchase's face on the pillow, with the little eyes ready – so it seemed to Caleb – to open and behold him, and the little thin lips ready to part, and display the little teeth in a mocking smile; and even the sight of Sar'ann in her nightcap with her mouth open was as nothing beside the horror of this. Caleb came very near to bolting, and giving up the wonderful idea altogether. But something fortified him – perhaps it was the feel of the soft rug underfoot, so different from his master's spartan quarters – and he stepped forward, reached out his hand, and closed his fingers around the bunch of keys.

No: he had got hold of something else. With a shudder of loathing Caleb realised it was Mr Chipchase's spectacles, which were folded up behind the keys, and which were curiously warm to the touch, so that it was as much as Caleb could do to prevent himself hurling them away in disgust. But he managed to lay them down again, and then took hold of the bunch of keys by the ring, praying that they would not jangle, and lifted them up. A sideways glance at Mr Chipchase, which revealed that that enigmatic gentleman was slightly smiling in his sleep, and then Caleb had the keys in his great fist, and was away, as fast as he dared.

To Saul's room. A despairing hunt through the keys in the dark passage. None of them fitted! Don't begin crying, Caleb: try again. Yes: a click of tumblers. The door swung open.

Agony, lest Saul make some noise that would reach the Demon's ears. A bad smell in the room: they had let the old man become unclean. Caleb's heart ached as he saw a white head stir in the dimness.

'William? Is that you, William?'

Caleb stepped forward. 'Sir—'

Saul raised his head. 'Why, surely not John . . . John, have you come back?'

'Sir, it's me, Caleb, and you got to be quiet, sir, in case the Demon hears you,' said Caleb in an urgent whisper, bending over the bed. 'Hush now – I've come to take you away, sir.'

'Caleb, my boy . . .! Oh, but which are you? Are you a waking dream, or a sleeping dream? I haven't learned to tell between them yet, but I shall. An old dog can learn new tricks, my boy, no matter what they say . . .'

'Hush, hush, sir, please!' whispered Caleb, searching for his master's hand. But what was this . . .? There were bands of linen knotted about Saul's wrists, and tied to the bedposts.

'Aye, boy, aye,' said Saul, his head drooping. 'I was naughty today. I did not behave myself today, and so I was restrained. But listen – ha! I upset the Demon, I think. I was in such a passion that I threw something at him, and he didn't like it. Oh, not he! The old dog can get in a few nips still, boy – he has a few teeth yet, though they collar him and tie him up – hey?'

Caleb's agony of feeling was beyond expression. All he could do was untie the linen bands, and when his master's gnarled hands were free, press them against his face.

'Why, that's flesh,' said Saul wonderingly. 'Am I not dreaming after all? The Demon sent you away, Caleb – I know. How do you come here?'

'I couldn't leave you, sir,' said Caleb. He held up the keys before Saul's eyes.

'Ha! A pretty stroke, Caleb, very pretty! What do you say to that, Demon? Worsted by a simple boy! Oh, but a loyal boy, a faithful boy – let's see you inspire such faith, Demon!'

'Hush, sir, please, we must—'

'Aye, boy, you're right,' said Saul, dropping his voice. 'The Demon has ears everywhere. Many tongues, many ears. His name is Legion. Your Bible, boy, attend to your Bible, for it is all there. Give me your arm, boy. I am weak, but the Lord shall make me strong. I am dirty, Caleb: can you bear to touch me?'

'I don't mind, sir,' said Caleb. 'We'll get you clean, once we're away.'

'Away! Yes, away, while the Demon sleeps. A good thought, Caleb! The world is wide, and he cannot pursue us for ever. Away, ha! Aye, boy, good, good, away, away!'

Away, then: downstairs, in darkness, the sick and distracted old man following his servant obediently, eyes darting to left and right lest Demons and their minions cry out upon their flight. Cedar-closet unlocked, Saul's clothes retrieved, a hasty dressing. Away, away! But wait: there, at the bottom of the closet, Saul's stick.

Tears in his eyes as he took it in his hand; and then a savage light in his eyes.

'Ha! Let me try falls with the Demon now: let us measure our strength now!' But the hand that tried to raise the stick was weak and palsied, and he saw it, and the tears dropped.

'Come, sir, quick,' Caleb urged him. 'Quick, in case they wake up.'

Away, away! Terrible moments at the front door, where the many bolts ground and rattled, and Demon-ears must surely hear . . . Open, at last. Out, into the night.

'Sir, what shall I do with the keys? Will you have them?'

'Throw them on the midden, boy. He has touched them. What use have I for them? Worldly goods, Caleb. "What is a man profited, if he shall gain the whole world, and lose his own soul?" There – throw them away, boy. Good, good!'

Away, away – away from the Demon: this was the only thought in the two injured minds adrift in the starry night. But when they reached the outskirts of the town, and Saul rested himself on a low garden wall, Caleb saw how weary he was.

'Sir, we must find you somewhere to rest. You'll be ill.'

'I have been ill, boy,' said Saul, wheezing. 'I have been under the Demon's enchantment. A cunning enchanter, boy! Beware of him! But no matter. We have left the Demon far behind, and we shall leave him yet further behind, boy, you and I. That is . . . if you will go with me, Caleb. I cannot reward you, if you do: see, here's money in these pockets that the Demon missed, but I have no more. The Demon has devoured my substance. May it choke him!'

'I don't want any reward, sir,' said Caleb. 'But you must have rest . . . I know, sir! Mr Addy! He was kind to me, when I was turned out. Let's go to Mr Addy's. He'll look after you—'

'No, no.' Saul grasped Caleb's sleeve, and threw crafty glances around the darkness. 'Remember the Demon, Caleb. He is too close. If Addy shelters me, the Demon might come to him. I would not have Addy endangered because of me. What can the Demon do to Addy, you ask? Oh, much, boy, much. You don't know him as I do . . . No, Caleb, we must go further away.' Saul breathed deep, and closed his eyes for a moment. 'Sweet air! It has the sea in it . . . Boy, there is somewhere I wish to go. Will you help me there?'

'Sir . . . yes. Yes, I will.'

'Then give me your arm. I am rested now, and it is not so very far.'

The route that Saul wished to take was eastward, along the coast. He would not take the cliff road, lest the Demon track them down; instead they struck the lower path that crossed the marshes. Caleb, after a long interval of silent puzzlement, at last recognized their route just as dawn was sketching the first colours across the flats, and cried, 'Sir, this is where Cousin John used to live!'

'It is,' said Saul, pausing to catch his breath, and eyeing the great tower of Saltmarsh church rising from the mist that still clung about the cliff slopes. 'Come.'

Fearfully hard on the old man's weakened constitution was the climb up the winding path to the church above the village, after the long tramp from Hales to Saltmarsh, and several times Caleb begged him to stop, and sit down on the grass; but in the wreck that had been Saul Twopenny the old stubbornness, at least, remained. The church was reached, at last; and only then did Saul sit himself down on the churchyard wall and rest.

'Caleb,' he said at length, 'stay here a moment, boy. There is something I must do.'

He entered the churchyard, and stood bareheaded before two neighbouring graves in the far corner. Caleb was sure they were the graves of Cousin John's parents, whom those greedy angels had taken away just like his own; but when Saul finally returned, his face was grim and withdrawn, and Caleb chose not to say anything about it. Instead he urged his master to eat and drink something – he could see an inn-sign down in the village; and Saul agreeing with a single nod, they set off down the cliff-path again.

It was too much for Saul: Caleb had feared so. The old man gave a groan, and put a hand to his head, and sat heavily down on the grass bank beside the path. For some time he could not or would not speak, and Caleb was almost beside himself with anxiety, when he saw a strange tattered figure coming up the path towards them. The figure's face was all but hidden by a wild tangle of hair and whisker, and it bore a sack over its shoulder, and it wore a bright red coat like a soldier.

The tattered man hesitated when he saw Saul and Caleb, and seemed about to pass them by; but then he stopped, and spoke, not as it seemed to either of them, but quite audibly.

'Here's an old gentleman took poorly, mice, by the looks of things. Is there anything we can do for him? Just what I was wondering. We'll ask, shall we?'

'Oh, can you help, please?' Caleb cried. 'He's sick, and worn out, and he needs to rest terrible.'

'Ha! And how did *you* come to be brought so low, my good fellow? Did you fall victim to the enchantment of a demon too? You have a wild look. Your looks are very like the thoughts in my head – very like!' cried Saul, who seemed fascinated by the shaggy figure bending kindly over him, and roused himself to grasp the man's hand. 'You have been demon-rid, I am sure of it. What appearance did your demon take, my friend? Did he wear spectacles, and speak soft?'

'My master's suffered terrible in his mind,' said Caleb in anxious explanation. 'He've been poorly, and not treated well.'

'So we can see, mice, can't we?' said the Soldier, releasing Saul's hand gently. 'I'm of the opinion that we should offer the old gentleman our hospitality, such as it is. Hm? Why, food, of course, and a bed to rest himself on. And an arm to help him there, certainly. We'll only mention, mice, that it's very rough and ready, and hope he don't mind that.'

'The rougher the better,' said Saul, as Caleb and the Soldier assisted him to his feet. 'Better rough than smooth. I don't trust smoothness, my good friend, not I. A creeping, soft-tongued, soft-handed smoothness – ach, beware of it, fly from it, my friend! Better locusts and wild honey in the wilderness. Let us feed on those, my good John the Baptist, if you have them!'

Together they supported the old man along the cliff-path to the Soldier's ramshackle hut amongst the heather; and there the Soldier gave Saul and Caleb goat's milk to drink, whilst he cooked herring with wild herbs in a blackened pan over the fire. Saul, seated on a driftwood chest, gazed about him with an appreciative eye at the Soldier's nets and sacks and tools, and at the miscellaneous flotsam and jetsam that he had picked up and hung about the rough walls; and at last asked, 'You live here quite alone, my friend?'

'Aye, quite alone, don't we, mice?' said the Soldier, turning the fish in the pan. 'It wouldn't do for some, no doubt, but it suits us.'

'Wise – wise in you, John the Baptist! Store up no children for your old age, my good prophet, for they will betray you. They will not respect your grey hairs. Either they will desert you, or they will turn against you . . .' Saul's eyes dulled, and he fell into an abstraction from which it took all Caleb's efforts to rouse him, and get him to eat. The old man made a good meal at last, however; and his mind becoming lucid again, he said humbly to the Soldier, 'My friend, I beg your pardon, I fear I am not clean. Have you enough water for me to wash myself?'

The Soldier had not; but the sea, he said, was at hand, and it had kept him clean for many a year. Saul was greatly taken with this idea. 'Aye, what could be better? Bravo, Baptist! Wash my sins away, good St John, if you will!' So the Soldier and Caleb accompanied him across the marsh; there was no one about, and Saul and

Caleb having stripped, they waded out into the sea. 'Not too old to try sea-bathing for the first time, eh, Caleb?' Saul cried, blowing and puffing and laughing; and Caleb laughed too, delightedly, and the Soldier chuckled a little, squatting on the sand and stroking his ragged whiskers, and looking on with melancholy eyes.

After his bathe, Saul, at the Soldier's insistence, laid himself down on the Soldier's sheepskin bed, and slept at once. Caleb had little conversation, and the Soldier required none, and so all was quiet in the hut except for the scufflings of the mice and the soft communings of the sea. At last the Soldier went outside to smoke his pipe, and a few minutes later Caleb, half dozing himself, looked up to see Saul regarding him from the bed.

'How are you, my boy?' Saul said.

'Oh! I'm all right, sir. I always am.'

'I hope so, my boy. I have much to thank you for . . . Where's our friend?'

'Just stepped outside, sir. Shall I fetch him?'

'No, no. Time we planned what we are going to do, Caleb. We cannot impose on John the Baptist any more; and we must put a good distance between ourselves and the Demon, you know. He may be pursuing us even now. What do you say, Caleb? Will you come with me, wherever I go?'

Caleb could not speak for the pressure of feeling within his breast; but his expression was eloquent enough.

'That's well. I've been dreaming again as I lay here – oh! not the bad dreams, this time. I've been dreaming of William, and of my nephew John. Where do you suppose they may be?'

'London, sir.'

Saul frowned. 'What makes you say that, boy?'

'Mr Addy said, sir. He said William's a sailor, but he puts in at the Port o' London; and he said Cousin John went there too.'

'John in London, eh? I should have thought of it . . . but once he was gone, I wouldn't let myself think of him. Pride, boy – I was snared by pride. You remember John pretty well, Caleb? Remember how he wrenched the stick from my hands, and broke it in two, and thrust me down? Me – Saul Twopenny, who no man dared challenge! If he struck me no physical blow, I did not forget the blow to my pride. And yet it was a man's blow, my boy – not a smooth, sneaking, underhand blow, of the sort that's brought me so low . . . And I would wish to speak a word or two to the man who gave me that blow, before I die.'

'You're not going to die, sir!'

'Don't blaspheme, boy,' said Saul with something of his old growl in his tone. 'We must all die. And before I do, I must . . . I must settle up my accounts. Well, would you like to see William and John again, my boy?'

'Oh, yes, sir. I'd like everything back just as it was!'

'I don't know about that, my boy,' said Saul with a distant look. 'I'm afraid that can't be . . . But we shall see them, boy. While I have strength in my limbs, we shall seek them out, and see their young faces again.'

'Go to London, sir?'

'Aye, boy, aye. You have never seen the Great Wen, eh? You shall, Caleb. We shall see London together. We shall go on the tramp, my boy. Saul Twopenny, on the tramp! Ha! A wry world! But at least we are free of the Demon. The Demon's arm is long, but not that long. Well, Caleb, fetch our friend the Baptist, and let us thank him, and be off!'

The Soldier would accept no money for his hospitality; and when he heard of Saul's intention, he offered his help again. 'They'll need to get to Norwich first of all, mice, I reckon. And we know where they can get aboard a carrier's van, or a cart, going that way – don't we? Why, because we ride to Norwich on them ourselves, and the carriers know us pretty well, of course – don't say you've forgotten that. We'll just pack these apples, and this half a loaf, into this pouch for our friends to take with them, and then we'll show them the place.'

The Soldier would accept no thanks, either, for what he had done; but when he had led them to a waypost on the coast road where the inland carriers passed, he shook Saul's hand, and Caleb's; and he stood there with his strange cords and strings and tatters flapping in the wind as the carrier bore the two of them away, and lifted his hand in salute, and kept it there until they were out of sight.

'God be with you, my honest prophet!' cried Saul, waving his stick. 'I am baptized now, and a new man. Old man, but new man – there's a pretty conundrum for you, Caleb. Well, my boy, we are on the tramp now. Our Lord had no companion when he went forth into the wilderness, but I have you, and I am content. I am content, my boy: I am new-born!'

CHAPTER SIX

Nothing, and Everything

John had never worked so hard in his life.

It was not merely the physical exertion that was tiring – though it was tiring enough, for Dr Appleyard filled his days to bursting. Five was his hour of rising; and it was John's duty immediately after breakfast to prepare drugs in the consulting-room, and anything else that Dr Appleyard would require in the course of the day. At eight, unless he had patients to see at home, Dr Appleyard would sally forth with irritable briskness, outpacing hackey-carriages as he strode along – it would have been impracticable nonsense for him to have set up a carriage of his own for the places *he* visited – and with him went his assistant, who for the first time in his life was heartily grateful for the length of his legs. Throughout the long day, John attended him, going from this nightmarish pest-hole to that, and from workhouse casual-ward to jail infirmary, and from jail infirmary to hospital; and when at last they returned to Great Russell Street, there was more work for him in the consulting-room, not only writing up Dr Appleyard's notes, but studying on his own account, for his employer wanted a knowledgeable assistant, and set him some stiff tasks of learning.

But tiring as all this was, the tiredness was of a sort that could be cured by sleep. What took the heaviest toll on John, and jangled his mind awake even when his limbs cried out for sleep, were the harrowing sights he saw in the course of his work. In that dark period of his life in which he had been Tup'ny John, he had been no stranger to the grimmer side of London; but working with Dr Appleyard, he found there were depths of deprivation that he had not even guessed at when he had lurked in Ma Dade's seedy taproom.

Such places for human beings to live in! The magnificent dome of St Paul's might overlook these places, and that marvellous triumph of human ingenuity, the railway, pass close by them and shiver their decayed walls; and yet here, creatures brother to those who had made such wonders lived in conditions beside which rabbit-holes and anthills were abodes of comfort and convenience. The comparison was irresistible; for John could not help noticing, as he became acquainted with the foulest of the city's slums, that these places set in the midst of the most heightened civilization in the world tended to revert, in a grotesque way, to natural forms. The crude holes that had opened up in partition walls resembled the entrances to caves; the blackened ceilings, cave roofs; the damp unfloored cellars that might house two large Irish families each, burrows; the footworn pathways that ran from house to house and through passage and alley, the runs and boltholes of furtive animals; the warped and mossy timbers – which were all that was holding up some of the craziest piles – trees. The comparison did not hold completely. There was no parallel in nature for such wretchedness as was to be seen within certain tenements and lodging-houses, where twenty, thirty, forty people could be found crammed into one room, heaped on top of one another in a manner that would have been thought degrading for corpses, and breathing in and out such a vapour that it was a wonder anyone lived with it in their lungs.

Many did not, of course. John and the doctor were often no more than followers in the bleak train of cholera and typhus; and John quickly became so accustomed, in particular, to the sight of children tenderly laid out upon handkerchiefs and scarves, that he could not look upon a living infant without a sort of wary surprise. These were the things that kept him from sleep, and left him with a feeling that his capacities were being stretched to the uttermost. For Dr Appleyard would not spare him in this, either: he must not shirk at supporting a dying head upon his arm, however lice-ridden, or shrink from laying plaisters on the feverish chest of a child who would probably not be here tomorrow.

And John did it. It was hard, and sometimes it was ghastly; and he was not as strong as he had been, and was vulnerable to fatigue. But he was happy – or rather, perhaps, fulfilled: at any rate, he was beginning to see that for him, one depended on the other. He was beginning to see something else too. He was beginning to see Verity – true, clear, in the round, and for the remarkable person that she was.

For they were much together, as was not unnatural given their mutual obligation to the Appleyards. While Verity continued to lodge with Miss Thimblebee, she was at the dusty brown house in Great Russell Street almost every evening, either to assist Miss Jemima with work for her many charities, or to dine, or to make a fourth in the Appleyards' expeditions into the gloomier reaches of chamber music. Such free time as John and Verity had, they spent in each other's company – at first through sheer proximity, certainly, but presently by design. John found that he could not wait to see her again, even if he had only parted from her a few hours ago. He had been long without friendship, and with Verity he discovered it anew – discovered it for the first time, indeed, for in his youthful friendships there had been no depths of experience beneath the froth of personality. Now here was a person to whom he could talk freely – a person, moreover, who loved talk as much as she hated chatter.

Not that he could talk in the expectation of perfect agreement: far from it. She was quite as likely to take up something he said like a ball, and with the deftest of spins, knock down his own convictions with it like skittles. Infuriating! Yet stimulating too. In fact, he liked it, because there was life in it, and life was what he was being wonderfully restored to after his dark submerged time. And life was what he saw above all in Verity: life sometimes blithe, sometimes prickly, life with lights and shadows and tenderness and sharpness, life keen and various and contradictory – just as those penetrating eyes of hers were at once dark and bright, night and day together.

He admired her: admired the no-nonsense readiness with which she undertook the work of teaching at the Ragged School – work of which he gained an inkling when he visited her there one day with Dr Appleyard. How any teaching or learning was ever done in this huge, ill-ventilated room, with at one end a dropsical stove that in cold weather roasted the nearer infants and left the further ones shivering; how any instruction was ever got into the matted heads of the poor children drawn up on wooden forms in two vast columns; how the devoted men and women who worked here maintained the strength to keep on swimming day after day against the tide of ignorance and deprivation: these were matters beyond John's understanding. He did gain a certain insight, however, into why the more pig-headed grandees of society were so vehemently opposed to educating the poor.

For it was inevitable that the teachers at the Ragged Schools would find themselves being a little more than teachers. Sometimes children would turn up at the school desperately ill, and medical attendance would have to be called in. Sometimes they were so verminous that there was nothing for it but to take off their clothes and burn them, replacing them with garments donated through one of Miss Jemima's charities; occasionally they were so famished that they had to be fed if they were ever to walk out of the schoolroom again. Many of them, besides, worked for a living when they could, and were subject to all manner of exploitative abuses, which the teachers, as the only responsible adults that the worst-off children had anything to do with, could not ignore. And so, randomly and without concerted intention, Verity and her fellow-teachers became involved in social provision. Public health, housing and employment were no part of their brief, but there was no avoiding them, and no avoiding either – in Verity's case, at least – the conclusion that much was amiss, and much must be done.

But there were some facts that the administration of the Ragged School, well-meaning as it was, would not admit, and Verity was sometimes driven to impatience.

'Look at this, John,' she said one day, slipping into the consulting-room and handing him a pamphlet bearing the inviting title 'The Christian Child's Vade-Mecum'. 'A hundred copies, courtesy of one of Miss Jemima's charitable bodies, to be distributed amongst our pupils. Oh, well-meant I know, but this is precisely the sort of thing that makes me wild. Here are some devotional verses supposedly written by a dying child, whose deathbed agonies do not seem to have prevented it composing stanzas in perfect pentameters, and using words like "seraph" and "ineffable". And here is a long effusion urging the poor little wretches to "Remember Lot's wife", a piece of advice which will doubtless be of priceless value to them the next time they are hauled before the magistrate or turned on to the street by the bailiffs. They have been brought up in the gutter, and have seen things that would make our hair stand on end, and yet they are all supposed to be miniature curates . . .! Well, I have done now, and feel better for letting off a little steam. But you see what I mean.'

'Miss Jemima's of an evangelical turn, I'm afraid. She said to me the other day that if she could save one soul before she died, she would be content.'

'It's the children's bodies that are in danger, not their souls. Oh, but I know she means well. John, am I a sharp-tongued, censorious, cynical old scoffer?'

'Yes,' said John. 'I thought you knew that.'

'Be careful, sir. I have learnt some very good techniques for subduing impudent boys.'

'Well, before you send me into the corner, let me show you something. Something much pleasanter than the "Christian Child's Vade-Mecum". Now. Here it is.' He cleared a space on the table amongst the jars and retorts, and laid down a purse full of money. 'My wages from Dr Appleyard.'

'Very nice,' said Verity. 'Now what do I do?'

'Why, take it.'

'What *are* you talking about?'

'My debts. You paid off my debts, and freed me from the King's Bench. I've paid Miss Thimblebee's arrears. This should cover about half the sum I owe you, and with my next wage . . . What's the matter?'

Verity had turned sharply away from him, and in a muffled but vehement tone she said, 'For someone who is kindness itself, you can be uncommonly insulting, John Twopenny!'

'I can't even begin to work out what that means. Verity, please, don't go all feminine and enigmatic on me, I beg you—'

'What do you mean, feminine and enigmatic?' she blazed at him, turning around.

'Ha, it worked! I got you to turn and look at me. And now you will listen?'

'Indeed I will not.'

'Well, I'll say it anyway. I remember what you said: I know you chose to pay those debts of your own free will, and didn't expect repayment. Well, I didn't expect to be in a position to pay you back either; but now I am, and I choose of my own free will to give you this money. Now, will you take it?'

279

She frowned, but he guessed she was displeased with herself for having no quick answer ready. 'Oh . . . John, I don't want it. What am I to do with it, anyhow?'

'I don't know. Buy yourself some books, perhaps.'

'I don't have time for reading at the moment.'

'Well, buy yourself a new gown or hat or something.'

'Oh! So I look a fright, do I? I need sprucing up, do I?' she said with a lift of her chin.

'You contrary woman! As a matter of fact, you don't – you look very beautiful, but . . .'

There could not have been more astonishment in the room if a chasm had suddenly opened up in the floorboards where they stood; and it was impossible to tell on which side the astonishment was greatest. But it was Verity who recovered first, quickly saying with a light laugh, 'Oh, you needn't think to win the argument with compliments, John. Anyhow, I truly can't think what to do with the money – and besides, you've earnt it.'

'Well, I can't think what to do with it either,' said John, following her lead, and studiously ignoring that chasm in the floor, though feeling rather hot about the cheeks on account of it. 'I have . . . I have everything . . .' It really was a very large chasm, and tremendously deep. 'What was I saying?'

'You have everything, apparently,' said Verity, her eyes not quite lifted to his.

'Oh yes! I have everything I want here, my bed and board and so forth, and Dr Appleyard made me a present of a suit of clothes, us being pretty much the same size, and so . . . what a pair we are, Verity!'

'How so?' she said, rather faintly.

'Well, disputing over who should have this money. When both of us spend our lives amongst people who would be glad of a tenth of it.'

'Oh, I see . . . Yes, a good thought. So, how shall it be spent?'

'Well, if you absolutely will not take it . . .?'

Verity narrowed her eyes at him, and pointed to the corner.

'Very well – I'll say no more of that. But suppose we were to pay it over for the relief of debtors in the King's Bench – how would that be? I would feel that I had made you some sort of restitution then. Rather illogical thinking, but never mind. Shall I do it?'

'An excellent notion,' said Verity, scooping up the money and pressing it into John's hand, a contact which produced a certain awkwardness in both of them, for some reason. 'Well, my dear illogical one, I am to tell you that your presence is requested this evening, as audience to the latest performance by the Appleyard quartet.'

'Oh, Lord,' said John in a low voice. 'Aren't you going to play something cheery?'

Verity shook her head with a devilish look. 'Certainly not. Only the driest fugues and canons. Don't worry, John – I'll play a *forte* whenever I see you nodding off.'

He did not nod off that evening, however; for he was in a curious state of tension, and when he asked himself why, could only answer that the chasm seemed to have followed him and Verity into the drawing-room, and he could not ignore it. As for Verity, she was adroit at hiding her feelings; but he suspected that she was aware of that gaping hole too, from a certain absent-mindedness in her usually impeccable playing – an absent-mindedness that manifested itself when she was accompanying Dr Appleyard in a particularly arid violin sonata, and dropped into a few bars of 'Gee up Dobbin', to general surprise.

All was strange, and John was deeply perplexed. He had come, he thought, to a period of equilibrium in his life, and very welcome it was; but when he lay down to sleep that night, the image of a chasm returned to him, along with other curious images of precipices, tunnels, and bridges, and he found that he was clenching his fists in bed, as if nerving himself for some sudden enterprise. This restless sensation, he felt, could only be referable to some approaching crisis in his life; and yet his mind would only circle warily, endlessly, round the matter, as if it were indeed some yawning hole down which he hesitated to look.

And his confusion was so great that he did not know whether the crisis had come, or whether it lay somewhere else entirely, when the very next day Catherine Fernhill reappeared in his life. Or in Verity's life, at first; for when Verity came to Great Russell Street in the evening, she told him that she had been visited at the Ragged School by Catherine and Augustus.

'I had a note from her saying the family was in London; and almost before I knew it, my monitor was tugging my sleeve and saying there was a lady and gentleman to see me. I thought at first it might be these gentlefolk visitors we are always having, who look in out of patronage, and so I was a little short when I turned round – and there were Catherine and Augustus, not changed a bit.'

John knew he ought to say something, but for long, long moments he could not think of a single thing. 'And – what did they think of the school?' he got out at last.

'Oh, Augustus was his usual amiably surprised self, and Catherine – well, I fancy she was a little shocked to find a Ragged School so very literally ragged, but she was very sweet, and even the hardest little rogues there took to her, and kept writing shaky ABCs on their slates to show her . . . John.'

'Hm? Oh! sorry.' He had been gazing abstractedly out of the window, and had not noticed that Verity had drawn close to him, and was holding out a letter. 'What's this?'

'Catherine asked me to give it to you.'

'Oh . . . thank you.'

Her expression was unreadable as she handed him the letter and remarked, 'Playing postman again for you . . . just like the old days, isn't it?'

'Just like the old days,' he agreed.

But it was not just like the old days, and he knew it.

The letter was brief and friendly, telling him of the house the Fernhill family had taken in London, and how they all were, and what they had been doing. Catherine concluded by saying that she and Augustus were to go to Drury Lane Theatre tomorrow night, and Augustus had an extra ticket, and they would be delighted if he could join them. A friendly meeting, for old times' sake.

He went. Despite the thousand conflicting thoughts and emotions the prospect aroused in him, the idea of not going at all was untenable somehow; but why this should be he did not know, any more than he knew why he *was* going, or what he expected to find when he got there. It was in a sort of fatalistic trance that he dressed for the theatre, having been not only permitted a night off by Dr Appleyard but lent a tail-coat for the purpose, and set out for Drury Lane.

And here was Catherine, inviting him to a seat next to her in the theatre box; and it was true, as Verity said, that she had not changed a bit. As freshly and luminously beautiful as ever: the same brilliant blue eyes, and heart-shaped face, and charmingly uncertain mouth, and quixotic manner. All the same. Why, then, did she look different?

No change in Augustus, at any rate, who only needed his memory jogging three times before he recollected John. They had last met in the garden at Buttings, when Augustus had played the go-between; and once Augustus's mind had fairly got hold of this remembrance, he would not let it go, and periodically throughout the evening would nudge John, and wink, and say, 'I think I was pretty fly that day, eh, Twopenny? Pretty discreet, eh?' or 'Remember the garden, old fellow? Mum's the word, eh?' and look very knowing, and then turn back to his opera-glasses, and bump his nose on them dreadfully.

'You look well, John,' Catherine said, as they waited out the overture.

'Thank you,' he said. 'So do you.'

'Town seems to agree with you,' she went on after a few moments' silence. 'I know it's supposed to be unhealthy, and people go out into the country for their health and so on, but I've never found it so, and the worst colds and chills I have ever had have been in the country, I think it's something to do with the rain, it seems to come down harder and wetter in the country which is very unscientific I know. But then I should ask you that question, about the health I mean not the rain, because I understand you are all but a doctor yourself now.'

'No, no,' he said, 'a doctor's assistant merely – not qualified at all. Sort of servant, really; but engaged in medical work, anyway.'

'Oh, dear! And you had such high hopes when you went away!'

There was genuine sorrow for him in her words; and he could not find a way to convey to her how very fortunate he was to have gained the position with Dr Appleyard. He saw how the word 'servant' affected her; and he felt another sort of chasm open up. They were sitting in the same theatre box, but in terms of experience they were on opposite shores of a great sundering sea.

'I must confess I greatly wondered how we . . . how we would meet each other, when we did meet, if you see what I mean,' Catherine said, doing balancing tricks with her fan, and colouring. 'I was afraid it would be very awkward, because they always say that people simply can't meet as friends after they . . . well, after they have been more to each other. And yet I think we've proved them wrong, you know, because we're not awkward, are we? – and we are quite friendly, aren't we?'

'Very much so,' said John. 'I should hate to think that we couldn't be.'

'Oh, so should I! Because then it would seem as if – as if one had made a mistake in ever coming to an understanding, even though that understanding is no more. As if one regretted it. And I don't regret anything, do you, John?'

If there was an answer to that question, it must be a complex and subtle one, and he did not have it: in spite of all the tortuous reflection that had constantly occupied him since yesterday evening, he could not come up with an answer. But a reply, at least, was expected from him; and he saw from her anxious look the reply that she wanted. She wanted to be reassured: she wanted – and after all, why not? – to be made comfortable. And so he smiled and said, 'No, I don't regret anything, Catherine.' She smiled too, the smile that had once wrought prodigious havoc upon him; and then the curtain came up, and they turned their attention to the play.

Or at least, Catherine did. John watched and listened, but he found he was not taking much in. It was something about a set of misunderstandings at an inn in Gretna Green, with two pairs of young lovers, a misanthropic uncle, and a drunken soldier who, in the theatrical manner, only needed to raise a tankard to his lips to be rendered immediately insensible. Easy enough to follow, no doubt: but John found himself undergoing the curious experience of seeing only the actors, and not the roles they were playing. For some reason, he could not suspend his disbelief, and wanted to cry out: 'But it isn't real! They're only pretending!'

Strange indeed, for he normally loved a play; and Catherine was enjoying it, whilst Augustus was practically the ideal audience – guffawing at the mildest of jokes, turning mighty grave at the touches of pathos, and responding to the misanthropic uncle's cruel separation of the lovers with an audible exclamation of 'Cad – beastly cad!' John kept quiet, and gave nothing of his impatience away; but still these sham sentiments irritated him. Why so? Why did the sight of people playing at being in love discomfit him? Ah, why!

The interval came, and Augustus left the box to go and make himself sick with a cigar, and John and Catherine were alone. If either were conscious of how they would once have prized this opportunity, they did not refer to it: instead they trod a narrow bridge of bright, casual conversation which was all about the present, and not about the past at all. Perhaps this was the bridge that he had dreamt of . . .?

'. . . I beg your pardon?'

'John, you're quite a dreamer tonight! I was saying that we're at home on Tuesdays, well, that's rather nonsensical, as if for the whole of the rest of the week we drive round and round in the carriage and sleep on London Bridge and daren't go home at all, of course we're at home a lot of the time but we're "At Home" in the social way on Tuesdays – if you wanted to call, that is. I know there was that trouble with Mama and Papa, but after all that was a long time ago, and after all it's not as if you're anything but a friendly caller now, rather than a – well, a suitor as you used to be. Suitor, good heavens, what a word, it makes me sound like some lady from the Middle Ages, leaning out of a castle window in a pointed hat with a veil on it . . .'

'Yes, it was a long time ago,' said John. 'Well, I don't know how your parents would feel about it, but if you think . . .' He tailed off. He was wretched company tonight, and he knew it. Fortunately Catherine had conversation to spare. She was obviously loving London, and was full of the places she had been and the people she had met, all very amusingly described and, typically, with never a hint of malice. It was a pleasure to listen to her; and if sometimes she asked him if he knew Lady So-and-so, or whether he had ever been to one of Lady Tother's soirées since coming to London, and generally assumed a familiarity with a world that Tup'ny John would never have been allowed to enter – well, what of that?

Yes, what of it? And what of the fact that as he sat beside Catherine in the box, he was seeing his love for her as a boy's love, with all the poignant pain that such a perception must inspire? And her love for him likewise – a girl's love, the love of an affectionate nature that could never turn away tenderness – what of that?

What of it, indeed? For here they were on a new footing. They were both in London, and he was at least on his way to respectability again, and they might form up in the elaborate dance of calls and at-homes and theatre-going and all the rest of it. They had met up again on friendly terms, and this was an unlocked door that might be opened or left closed. He saw as much in Catherine's demeanour. There was not an actual flirtatiousness: rather, she was welcoming him to her crowded, sociable, dancing, dining world, and would not be indifferent to the figure he would make in it, if he chose. They must get to know each other all over again, but that was no great difficulty, if he was willing.

Nothing was wrong, then. Nothing should worry him. There was nothing to prevent them being friends, and seeing if the friendship would lead them down the old ways to something more. Ah, that Nothing! It was that Nothing that pursued him home after he had parted from her outside the theatre; and it was that Nothing that made him decide, after all, not to go straight home, but to walk the darkened streets awhile, and try to resolve the ferment in his mind.

For that Nothing, he was afraid, was everything. Throughout his meeting with Catherine, Nothing was there. Cordiality was there, kindly feeling was there; affection, perhaps, was there; some shared memories were there, certainly; and the pale ghost of a spent emotion was there, in its nebulous way. And yet Nothing was there. That was the one unanswerable conclusion the evening had left him with. He had seen and spoken with Catherine, admired her beauty, sat close to her in a darkened theatre box; and yet . . . 'Nothing there!' John spoke it aloud, as he crossed Covent Garden. 'Nothing there!'

And had he supposed there would be anything there? Probably not. If he had not been subject to the common lover's complaint of lying to himself, he would have admitted long ago that the light had died. A pity, a great pity; and it would have been a pity indeed if he had seen any evidence that for Catherine the light still burned. Happily, not so; and he could accept without pain the knowledge that for her the light had never burned with a *very* great intensity.

Very well: here were some sad reflections, but no tragedy. Indeed, the whole thing was eminently civilized. He might go home, and take up his new, industrious, fulfilling life, and think no more about it: no one would be hurt. Why, then, these wanderings, these echoing footsteps about the night-time streets? Was there some other element to the conundrum – was there an Everything, to balance the Nothing?

John gave himself up. He gave himself up to the clockwork motion of his legs, which took on the responsibility willingly, and let his mind be still while they carried him over Waterloo Bridge and along the drab thoroughfares of the Borough. The King's Bench prison: what curious distortion of nostalgia had made his legs bring him here he could not guess, but he obeyed, and lingered a while before the high spiked walls, and thought of the people within. And then his legs said that was enough of that, and took him back across the river, by Blackfriars this time, and after a long wearisome tramp stationed him in front of Jolly Butcher's Yard.

The Yarders kept late hours, and when he went in he found several old friends up and about, including Mr Hankey, who excitedly went round knocking on doors declaring that Tup'ny John was back. John was there a good while, for there was much news to exchange, and many new babies to be thrust into his arms, and many highly unlikely anecdotes to be told of the medical wonders he had performed during his residence there; but he was glad that his legs had brought him to the yard, and gladder still when the Yarders, gathered about him in the old kitchen, asked after the young woman who had come here and took such care of him when he was poorly.

'Miss Deene – Verity – yes, she's very well, and I see a good deal of her,' he said: and suddenly felt as if he were extremely drunk.

'Ah! I remember her,' said Mr Hankey, with a blissful look over his clay-pipe. 'There's a face a man could forget in a hurry, I should think not, and do I remember those dark eyes, like two bright berries, and that smart look she had about her, and the way she stayed by Tup'ny John's bed when he was raving, and is the queen in her palace a-dining off wenison, I should say so . . .! Why, Tup'ny John, what's the matter?' – for John had suddenly leapt out of his seat. 'I ain't said a word out of turn, I hope?'

'Not at all, not at all,' said John, feverishly shaking Mr Hankey by his beefy hand. 'You have – well, whatever is the opposite of saying a word out of turn, you have done it. I must go . . . What did you say those eyes were like, again?'

'Two Bright Berries,' said Mr Hankey distinctly, with a doubtful look, as if he feared he had dreadfully committed himself.

'Exactly. You've put it exactly. Well, goodbye, goodbye! And thank you!' John shook hands all round, and then shook hands all round again; and ran out of Jolly Butcher's Yard.

He would have carried on running all night, probably, if a remnant of reason had not asked him where he was running to, and pointed out that at this hour Verity was likely to be safely asleep within Miss Thimblebee's gilded fastness. True, true . . . He must have still felt drunk, because he fell into a great despondency at this thought, and trudged his way back to Dr Appleyard's house very gloomy in the knowledge that he must wait till tomorrow.

Wait for what, by the by? Why, wait to tell her the truth. And supposing she did not like that truth? Very probable, but it didn't matter. Nothing mattered beside this wonderful, sublime, ridiculous, unbelievable, irrefutable truth that had been working its way towards the surface of his nature, and had now burst forth into the light and flowered, most unexpectedly, most beautifully.

The Appleyards' house was in darkness, even the servants having gone to bed; but John had a key for the servants' entrance at the back of the house, which was reached by a long brick passage much favoured as a battleground by tom-cats. He was hunting in his pocket for his key as he walked down this passage, and his head was lowered, and so when the figure loomed out of the darkness in front of him he practically leapt a foot in the air.

'John . . .?'

It was Verity: pale, and wrapped in a shawl, and looking up anxiously into his face.

'Verity – whatever are you doing here?'

'I waited for you. I've felt quite felonious lurking about here . . . I played some highly resistible Beethoven with the Appleyards till late, and you still weren't back; and then I left to go home, but I had only gone half-way down the street when I knew that I couldn't go until you were back. I would have knocked at the door again and asked Dr Appleyard if I could sit up and wait in the parlour, but they'd gone to bed and I thought it would seem strange and so I . . . I waited here. I don't know why. I – I was just worried about you.'

'Oh, Verity,' he said softly, 'you've done a good deal of worrying about me, one way and another.'

'Have I? I suppose I have. You're a very worrisome person, John Two-penny . . .' She stepped closer. 'You look tired.'

'I don't. I mean, I'm not. At least, I mean I am, I've been walking half across London, but inside I'm not. Tired, I mean – that is, I . . .'

'John,' she said, 'what *do* you mean?'

'I mean,' he said, and then swept off his hat and spread out his arms, 'Oh, Verity, I mean that I am most desperately in love with you. I can't help it. I'm sorry.'

The little sound she made might have been a gasp, a laugh, a stifled cry of reproach or scorn – he couldn't tell; and he could not read her expression in the dimness either. But there was light enough to show him how lovely she was: what darkness could hide that!

'John,' she said, 'will you say that again?'

'Say what again?'

'That you love me, you idiot!' she said, lifting her hands towards him.

'Very well. I love you, Verity. I love you. I love you. I love you . . .'

She was laughing, or crying, or both together, as she put her arms around his neck and with her cheek against his said breathlessly, 'Oh, it's about time, John! Oh, my dear John, it's about time . . .!'

CHAPTER SEVEN

Another Portrait

A holiday! It was the sheer fact of it that they could not get over. It kept occurring to John and Verity throughout the day, so that they would stop short and gaze at each other in amazement. Everyone else was going about their business so deedily. The skipper of the little steamer that took them down the river to Richmond – he was in such a state of bustle, bestirring himself from stem to stern with a clay-pipe clenched between his lips and puffing mightily, that one might have supposed that the engine was redundant, and he was propelling the ship himself. The waiter at the Star and Garter on Richmond Hill, where they had dinner – he laid the cloth with such a whisk and a flourish, and made such a swordfight out of sharpening the carving-knife, and darted so briskly about even when burdened with a dozen dishcovers, that it was quite exhausting to see him. And even when they were left to dine in peace at last, in a snug bow-window with a delicious view across the park, a diligent gardener kept appearing in their view, and raking up leaves in quite a furious manner. It was as if everyone was in a conspiracy to remind John and Verity that they were at leisure: and very delightful it was too, even if they still could not quite believe it.

But then, delighted disbelief was pretty much the customary state of John and Verity now, even though three months had elapsed since they had startled each other in the brick passageway beside Dr Appleyard's house, and the scene at the bow-window was an autumnal one. The fact of their being in love came up like the sun each day, fresh and radiant and never commonplace; and often when they were walking together Verity would stop and turn to John and say, 'John, stand still and take off your hat.' And he would do so, and she would laugh and kiss him. 'That's it – that's precisely the way you did it on that night in the passage. I just can't get over it – the way you had to take your hat off to declare your love for me.'

And even as they dined together in the bow-window of the Star and Garter, Verity could not forbear picking up John's hat from the window-seat and saying, 'Go on, John. Put it on and take it off. Please.' And he obliged, very gravely; and then they both went off into such fits of laughter that the industrious gardener suspended his rake and stared for a full minute, with the unfortunate consequence that the wind got hold of his neat pile of leaves and scattered them all over Richmond Hill.

A holiday! Only one day: but John and Verity were both so accustomed to unremitting activity that the one day assumed vast dimensions. And the opportunity to be loverlike was similarly unprecedented – loverlike in the sense of devoting themselves wholly to each other for an appreciable length of time. Everything thus far had been snatched in the intervals of either duty or social formality, and it had been a strain at times. Not that they had neglected such opportunity as there was, Verity proving particularly resourceful in this respect – frequently volunteering, when she was at the Appleyards' house, to carry messages to John at work in the consulting-room, and performing her errand by the novel means of bursting into the room, slamming the door behind her, and wordlessly seizing John in such a

286

fierce embrace that he was frequently flung back against the articulated skeleton, who grinned tolerantly over their shoulders throughout the passionate episode. And it always filled John with amused admiration on these occasions to see the way Verity corrected her dishevelled appearance, and returned upstairs as if nothing had been in her mind during the interval but Miss Jemima's Fund for the Relief of Distressed Apothecaries.

However, something about their changed relation must have been evident to the eccentric family who had taken them under their dusty brown wing; for one day when John was assisting Dr Appleyard with one of his chemical experiments, the abrupt old physician, without raising his eyes from the murky test-tube into which he was peering, suddenly said, 'John, there is an attachment, I presume?'

John thought at first that Dr Appleyard was referring to the blow-pipe he was holding, and looked about him for anything that might be an attachment to it. And then a dreadful consciousness came over him, and he found himself licking his lips over and over again, and wilting under Dr Appleyard's parching gaze.

'There is, I see,' said Dr Appleyard; and then he said no more about it until the experiment was concluded, when, drying his hands on a towel, and fixing John with a look more penetrating than ever, he resumed: 'Well, is it a strong attachment?'

John could only be candid. 'It is a very strong attachment indeed, sir,' he said.

'Is it indeed? Hm, hm. And is it so strong, now, as to be unbreakable?'

'It most certainly is,' said John hotly, thinking he detected a certain scepticism in the doctor's tone.

'Then,' said Dr Appleyard, giving John his lean firm hand, 'allow me to be the first to congratulate you. I have the highest regard for Miss Deene, and I consider you a fortunate man, and I know that my mother and sister will be as pleased about this as I am, as they have talked about nothing else for weeks. Oh, you thought you were being very discreet, did you? No, no, John: there are certain things that cannot be hid.'

'I – I was afraid you might be angry,' said John, shaking his hand.

'Angry, why? Perfectly natural development. Which is not to say that I haven't considered the matter with regard to your position here. You don't, I hope, think to slip away tomorrow and marry, on what I pay you?'

They had scarcely given the matter a thought, being directly absorbed in each other to the exclusion of all past and present; but he hoped they had both learned to be practical, and he said as much to Dr Appleyard.

'I hope so too. Not that I am imposing terms on you, John; you are a free agent, and not bound to me by indentures or anything of that sort. But I have invested a good deal of time and trouble in training you up in the work I do, and I would not see it jeopardized by one romantic impulse.'

'I must confess I have been a prey to romantic impulses in the past,' said John. 'But they have not done me much good. If I say that I retain the romance, but not the impulsiveness, will that sound like equivocation?'

'It's good enough,' said Dr Appleyard, with one of his rare, wintry smiles; and immediately returned his attention to his chemicals, as if dismissing the subject for ever. That was not the end of it, however. Verity was invited that evening to take a share in the Appleyards' brown dinner before making some brown music with them, and as soon as she came into the parlour from taking her bonnet off, Dr Appleyard pounced on her, shaking her hand and drawing her into the centre of the room.

'Well, well, Miss Deene, all is known now, and I think it an excellent notion, and let us announce it formally straight away. Mother, Jemima, I think you have an inkling already of what I am going to say.'

Verity, still having her hand vigorously shaken, looked questioningly at John, who, as far as he was able, shrugged with his eyes (which wasn't easy).

'Mother, Jemima, our Miss Deene and our Mr Twopenny have formed an attachment,' said Dr Appleyard. 'I have spoken to Mr Twopenny about it, and everything is plain and straightforward, and it only remains for us all to add our congratulations, as the attachment is an excellent notion, and thoroughly to be approved.'

That word 'attachment' was repeated all through the subsequent congratulations, and was somehow typical of the Appleyards. They felt that the attachment required a tribute, just as they always gave grave thanks to their ancient domestics for their trembling service; but there was no fuss about anything so worldly as an engagement. They were not orange-blossom people: the mutual feelings of Miss Deene and Mr Twopenny were what engaged their attention and respect. Miss Jemima said that earthly love was a reflection of the divine; while old Mrs Appleyard said she had always approved of Miss Deene on account of her posture.

'A woman's posture is an infallible guide to her character,' the old lady pronounced. 'I well remember Miss Pockleton, an acquaintance of my youth, the straightness of whose carriage at a very tender age was universally remarked upon. It was no surprise that she went as a missionary to the Punjab, for her piety was as notable as her bearing; and it was reliably reported from there that she would not countenance the indignity of breaking into a run, even when pursued at quite close quarters by a tiger on the banks of the Indus.'

'But didn't the tiger eat her, Mama?' said Miss Jemima.

'The tiger most certainly did *not* eat her,' said Mrs Appleyard, quite indignant. 'That I can vouch for, because Miss Pockleton retired, full of honours, and having personally converted three native princes and a Begum, to St Albans, where I saw her with my own eyes, and where it was a matter of common remark that even at the age of ninety-two she could not abide a cushion.'

'Dear me – I think she deserved a little comfort, after all that,' said Miss Jemima.

'Pardon me, Jemima, no,' said Mrs Appleyard loftily. 'If you had offered her a cushion, she would have been insulted. I would go so far as to say she would have thrown it at you with no little force.'

'Then she would have been a very disagreeable old woman,' said Miss Jemima.

'On the contrary,' said Mrs Appleyard, 'I applaud her for it. I hope I would do the same myself. Indeed, I hope you would too. I brought you and James up to disdain bodily comforts. You may be interested to know, Mr Twopenny, that at the age of two my daughter's sense of altruism was so admirably developed, that she begged me to cut off all her hair, and give it to the poor.'

'Mother, really, such nonsense!' laughed Dr Appleyard.

Mrs Appleyard, in a stately huff, asserted that she would stake her life on the truth of what she said; and added, as an afterthought, that when she herself was young, her hair was so long she could sit on it. However, the old lady soon reverted to the subject of the attachment, and said there should be a toast to it; and so there was, at dinner, the happiness of Miss Deene and Mr Twopenny being pledged in some very brown wine, and the ancient maid being so overcome with emotion at the occasion that she fell over in the fireplace, and served the rest of the meal in a very sooty condition.

And in further tribute to the attachment, Dr Appleyard granted John a day's holiday, and Miss Jemima likewise secured Verity leave from the Ragged School; so that this day was very much a celebration of the two of them, and entitled them, as Verity said, to be as spoony with each other as they liked.

'For example,' she added as they sat at dinner in the bow-window of the hotel, 'drinking out of the same wine-glass – so. Also twining our fingers across the table – thus. Also . . . what else do couples do in these situations?'

'The man gazes in a dreamy, moonstruck way into the lady's face,' said John.

'Oh, is *that* what you're doing?'

'That's what I'm doing.' And so he was: for to see her sitting there, so trim and smart, with that keen intelligence lurking in her every play of feature, and with it that unsentimental, unstinting tenderness which had bound his heart to hers so wonderfully these months, was a holiday in itself.

It was untrue what they said about first love, and also true. It was untrue insofar as this, his second love, was immeasurably more profound in its effects upon soul and body, in its intensity of expression, and in its mutuality. And it was true, insofar as he could not regard this as anything but his first love, because of that very profundity. That was not to despise what had once existed between him and Catherine Fernhill, only to see it for what it was: a boy-and-girl romance which uncommon circumstances had prolonged beyond its natural life.

Of course it would have been difficult for Verity to see it in precisely those terms. Very early on she made a joke about being assured she was not poaching on Catherine's preserves; and though the friendly indifference into which relations between John and Catherine had sunk could not have been plainer, he knew it should be put to visible proof; and accordingly they called on Catherine and Augustus one evening when the elder Fernhills were out. Catherine was warmly affectionate at meeting with Verity again, a little shy and arch with John; and all of these things to the many other people who called in the course of the evening, amongst them many gentlemen, young and not-so-young, who hung longingly about her butterfly beauty, and amongst whom she divided her attention equally, as much out of innate fair-mindedness as flirtation.

Nothing more needed to be done or said; and John's mind was set at rest quite as much as Verity's, for he wished to be sure that not a trace of uncommon feeling, either warm or embittered, remained on either side, and the evening had amply demonstrated that. Still, Catherine was a subject that neither John nor Verity tended to refer to if possible. It was past, and they both had a certain mistrust of the past. 'The things I love most in the world,' Verity said to him once, 'are you, books, today, and tomorrow, in that order.'

And this today was well worth loving. After they had dined they took a walk along the river as far as the lock at Teddington, and got themselves so absorbed in contemplation of some rather bedraggled ducks that they nearly missed their steamer back to the city, and had to run for it, and got there just as the gangplank was about to go up. Not that they could possibly have missed it on a day like this, they agreed: it just wasn't in the scheme of things.

Down-river, then: London, like a grand and shabby dame in her great shawl of smoke and November fog, with a few jewels here and there where the gas had been lit, and cold colours coming and going in the darkening sky. Up Hungerford Stairs from their mooring, and through the market amidst a smell of grease-lamps and sprats and a massed growling of costers' voices. The day drawing to its close, yet not precipitately, and with something still to be savoured in every minute of it.

' "I wonder, by my troth, what thou and I did, till we loved?" ' Verity said softly as they made their leisurely way through the streets; and gave John a sly smile. 'There, you never bargained for me quoting poetry at you, did you? You thought you were getting a no-nonsense sort of woman who would never be embarrassing. Sorry, my dear. I've lots more where that came from. Oh, John, are we turning into one of those appalling spoony young couples of whom I have always thoroughly disapproved?'

'Well, let's see. Quoting poetry is a bad sign; but on the other hand, we don't have coy pet names for one another. I have never, to the best of my knowledge, addressed you as Mouse, Duckling, or Piggy-wig.'

'Or Chicken Lumpkin,' said Verity parenthetically.

'Or indeed Chicken Lumpkin. So that's something on the credit side. I – Good Lord.'

They were passing down a side-street off the Strand, and John had stopped dead before a shop window.

'What's the matter?'

'Well, talking of quoting poetry – you remember I told you how it was I made my way to London?'

'In a cheap-jack's cart, with typical eccentricity.'

'Well, this establishment – unless there are two Waldo Tuttles in the world, which seems unlikely – belongs to that self-same cheap-jack.'

It was a little squeezed old shop with a narrow frontage, but newly painted and refitted; and there was an extravagant sign in the window, with practically every word in a different type: 'Waldo TUTTLE: *Photographic PORTRAITURE*, incorporating the *newest* and most convenient PROCESSES. *Reasonable Rates*. SITTINGS *always* to be had.' Below it were several specimen photographs mounted on card, and featuring various ladies and gentlemen presenting that petrified and glassy stare that the marvellous invention always seemed to call forth.

'It must be him,' John said, peering in. 'What a change from selling butter-dishes with roses on!'

Verity's curiosity being as great as his, they went in, and found themselves in a small studio which, as Verity remarked, resembled a bad cheese-dream. On one side was a waterfall tumbling into a gloomy grotto; on the other was a Tuscan hillside in tremendous perspective, with an excessively ruined temple in the distance. Supplementing these painted backdrops were a Corinthian column made of plaster, a quantity of ferns, and a table bearing a stringless violin, an hour-glass, a human skull, and an inkpot. A bell had rung above the door on their entering, and a voice called from an inner room behind a curtain, 'I come, sir or madam, I come directly!' The voice was followed by the appearance of Waldo Tuttle himself, who whisked back the curtain with a certain courtly grandeur of gesture that could have belonged to no one else.

'Sir, madam, you honour me. Speaking as a connoisseur of the photographic art, I may say that the capturing of such likenesses will be as much a matter of pleasure as of – Good heavens above! Not Mr T.?'

'How do you do, Mr Tuttle,' said John, offering his hand. 'You're not in need of a good sweetener, I take it?'

Mr Tuttle was more soberly dressed than in his cheap-jack days, but he retained the great colourful banner of a pocket-handkerchief, and he was obliged to fan himself with this in his surprise, in the intervals of heartily shaking John's hand, exclaiming that he would never have believed it, being introduced to Verity, shaking her hand, exclaiming that he still would never have believed it, and shaking hands with them both all over again; at last pressing them into chairs, and taking one himself – a curious affair with iron clamps attached, suggestive of an instrument of torture – remarking that he was quite overcome.

'Ah, Miss Deene, just to see Mr T. sitting there wafts me backward straightway on a silver cloud of reminiscence!' Mr Tuttle said, with a lyrical smile wreathing his great long face. 'There never was such a sweetener. The stickiest crowds was meat and drink to him. While memory holds a seat in this distracted globe, remember thee, and wipe the table while you're about it, et cetera – I quote from memory. Ah, gone, gone, Mr T! But not a matter for regret, I think, after all – for you came to London to make your fortune, sir, and ten pounds says you've done it!'

'I have found the greatest good fortune I have ever known here, certainly, Mr Tuttle,' said John, 'and could not be happier.'

'Is that so, is that so?' said Mr Tuttle with a twinkling look, and a graceful flourish of his handkerchief. 'I must say it would appear so, from where I'm sitting

– it would certainly appear so. But here is a curious coincidence, Mr T.! Do you know why I gave up the cheap-jack line, sir – leaving aside the difficulty of getting a sweetener to come up to you – can you guess why?'

'Wished to settle down?'

'Part of it, sir, part of it – but come! Bid a little higher! What of all things in the world, would make me want to settle down?'

'Not marriage?'

'Done!' Mr Tuttle slapped his knee. 'Sold to the gentleman with the charming lady at his side. And now, Mr T. – bid a little higher, sir – who do you suppose, in all the world, could tempt Waldo Tuttle into marriage?'

'Not – not your lost Arabella?'

Mr Tuttle slapped his knee so hard that he was obliged to rub it for some moments afterwards. 'Done! Sold to the gentleman who has plainly not forgotten those colloquies under the stars, when he and I travelled the green lanes of old England together, and he was good enough to lend an ear to a tale of thwarted love. Mr T., the lost Arabella is found! She is more – she is Mrs Arabella Tuttle! She is more – she is in the back room a-measuring out the chemicals – and you shall meet her!'

So saying, Mr Tuttle darted behind the curtain again; and John just had time to give Verity an account of Mr Tuttle's search for his lost sweetheart, before the ex-cheap-jack returned, ushering before him a laughing lady who declared that they must excuse her, but her hands were all of a muck.

'Mr T. – which is to say Mr Twopenny, only old habits die hard – and Miss Deene, allow me to introduce that ineffable She with whom I plighted my infant troth under the flowering chestnuts, twenty-five years ago and more, and this very June permitted me to fulfil it at last, and make her my wife. Arabella!' Mr Tuttle made a low bow and, seizing his wife's hand, succeeded in kissing it in spite of her laughingly protesting that it was as black as a Newgate knocker on account of the chemicals.

Arabella Tuttle was a blooming, buxom, sloe-eyed young woman with a certain likeable asperity about her: her response to Mr Tuttle's declaration that a photograph of her hands alone, placed in a public place, would break the heart of every man who beheld it, being a cheerful, 'Oh, it would, would it? Very nice I'm sure, and will it get the pots washed and the beds made, I wonder?' She listened with a sceptical smile to Mr Tuttle's account of how he had tracked her down at last, which involved overhearing her name mentioned in a public-house in Maidenhead, and which she could not help interrupting with the observation: 'Yes, and what were you doing in there, I wonder, and was the barmaid dark or fair, that's what I'd like to know!'

'The barmaid, my sweet,' said Mr Tuttle readily, 'resembled, if memory serves, nothing so much as one of those three weird sisters immortalized by the Swan of Avon in the lamentable history of Macbeth. In other words, she was as ugly as sin. Yet I freely admit I could have kissed her, my angel, when she corroborated the information I had gleaned, and confirmed that the beauteous Arabella was near at hand – to wit, housekeeper at a villa on the river, where her flying master had been at last obliged to fold his wings, on account of the gout. Mr T., imagine the throbbing of my heart as I beat a path to that door, and knocked in the scarcely bearable expectation that the hand that lifted the latch would be – this one!' And Mr Tuttle made an amorous dart at Arabella's hand again, and got inky stuff all over him.

'And what an item he looked, with his white hat on his head,' said Arabella merrily. 'I was all ready to shoo him off with a broom, and say we didn't want no gewgaws; but then he started quoting like he does, and carrying on something unmanageable, and so I knew him.'

291

The reunion had been worth the wait, it appeared, and Mr Tuttle had proposed at once to take her away from Maidenhead and gout, and make her his own. Arabella, however, had had the gravest doubts about married life in a cheap-jack's cart, and these, it fortunately turned out, found an echo in Mr Tuttle's heart.

'I didn't want to admit it to myself,' he said, returning from the back room with a bottle and glasses in honour of the occasion, 'but the cheap-jack line ain't what it was. There's the railways; and where there's railways, there's well-stocked shops; and a man with a horse and cart, and a crate full of crocks, don't cut the figure he did in former times. And so I decided to sell up; and Arabella's master being an amateur in the photographic line, to console him for the gout and not flying any more, it put the notion into my head, and I made Inquiries. I knew that portrait photography was all the go, and that any number of people would pay sixpence for a head, and a shilling for full fig; but it was the initial outlay that worried me. The apparatus don't come cheap – ' with a sweeping gesture at an object like an enormous black spider, covered with a velvet cloth – 'and then there's rent of the premises, not to mention three rooms above for connubial relaxation, and a girl to do the laundry. I trembled – I don't mind telling you I trembled on the brink. But then, the scientific process is so fascinating in itself, that it nudged me to take the plunge.'

'*I* nudged him,' said Arabella, 'else he would have havered till doomsday. I said, if it pays, well and good; and if it don't, sell up – because if *he* was fool enough to buy it, then somebody else will.'

'So you did, my own,' said Mr Tuttle, 'and I was right to listen to you, not that I had any choice, your voice being like music, and beyond the power of mortal man to resist.' ('Stuff!' from Arabella, fondly.) 'And it *does* pay, my friends. We use the wet-plate process, which is the most practical, although it's as wet as it sounds, and liable to leave you looking inky; and we capture any number of faces every day. People are so hungry for likenesses! In fact, Mr T., and Miss Deene, let me demonstrate the photographic process with you as subjects. No – I insist. In consideration of those old times, Mr T., I insist upon taking your likeness and Miss Deene's, gratis; and if the two of you should wish to exchange the resulting portraits, and lay them under your respective pillows, I'm not the man to say anything about it.'

Mr Tuttle was all eagerness, and would accept no refusal; and Verity volunteering to submit to the strange operation first, he uncovered the giant spider, and then carefully placed her next to the table, with the waterfall behind her. 'Now, Miss Deene, I shall repair to the glass-house and prepare the plate, and when it's ready, I shall insert it in the apparatus, and expose you. As soon as I come out with the plate, be ready. You must be absolutely still while you're being exposed: I find that fancying yourself an intruder in a pirates' cave, and liable to all sorts if you move a muscle, is generally helpful.'

There was a theatricality about the complex business of photographing that was well suited to Mr Tuttle's flamboyance of character. His abrupt exit behind the curtain, his long absence, and his sudden reappearance from the glass-room bearing the wet-plate ceremoniously before him, were all worthy of a conjuror, as was the flourish with which he uncapped the lens, and the dramatically suspended attitude he held, one finger aloft, throughout the long exposure. Verity remained admirably still and poised until the process was complete, and the plate borne back into the glass-house; but when it came to John's turn to look the giant spider in the eye, he found it impossible to maintain the required immobility, and Mr Tuttle had to bring into the play the curious torture-chamber attachment to the chair, which turned out to be none other than a vice which clamped tightly to the back of his neck. 'Don't be troubled, Mr T.,' the photographer said. 'You'd be surprised how many people *can't* sit still, sir, and have to be clamped. Not to mention the elderly parties with the congenital shakes – now what a challenge *they* are to the art. Strapping 'em down helps, I find, but it has to be said that they object sometimes, and if the buckles show up on the finished portrait it don't make for a happy effect.'

Mr Tuttle had scarcely spirited John's plate away to the glass-house when the shop-bell rang, and a little woman in a chip bonnet came in. She had come, she said to Arabella, for her portrait which had been taken that morning. Arabella disappeared behind the curtain, and there were sounds of a whispered consultation in the back of the shop before Mr Tuttle emerged at his most airy and grandiloquent, bearing a photograph wrapped in brown paper.

'Your portrait, madam,' he said, 'and a most excellent specimen of the photographic art it is. I trust it will be a lasting ornament to your home; and may I add my humble hope that when your many friends admire it, you will mention the name of Waldo Tuttle as the originator.'

Mr Tuttle seemed rather eager to usher the little woman out of the shop at once; but she would not be ushered, and opened the package there and then.

'Why, this isn't me!' she cried, holding the portrait at arm's length. 'I don't look like that – never!'

'A frequent response, madam, of those viewing their first photographic likeness,' said Mr Tuttle smoothly. 'The exactness and fidelity of the process is far beyond anything that a looking-glass can provide; and it *can* be a little startling, there's no doubt of it.'

'But this is a man!' cried the little woman; and added, as if this were the worst thing of all, 'and with whiskers, too!'

'It may appear so, madam. Photography is an awesome and mysterious process. But there is no questioning such scientific apparatus as this: it simply can't go wrong. What you must understand, madam, is that this plate is as yet very new, and your likeness has yet to take fully, as it were. One might draw an instructive comparison with wine, or cheese, in this respect. You must give the chemicals time to act, madam. That lunar caustic will *not* be hurried. Hang your portrait, madam, and let the scientific process complete itself; and if any ignorant and misguided persons should raise any doubts about it, you just tell them what I have told you.'

The little woman went off at last, considerably mollified, if still a little dubious on the question of the whiskers; and when she had gone, Mr Tuttle bolted the door, and mopped his brow with his great handkerchief. 'Whew, I thought for a minute she was going to be an awkward one,' he said, 'and I'd have to expose her again.'

'Did you really give her a picture of somebody else?' John said laughing.

'No choice, I'm afraid, Mr T., in certain eventualities,' Mr Tuttle said urbanely, filling his glass. 'Sometimes it happens that the plate don't come out – happens quite often, I'm afraid; and the establishment simply won't bear the expense of taking a fresh plate, and exposing 'em all over again, for you can't charge twice, you know. So the only thing to do is give 'em a portrait from stock, and hope they'll be satisfied. But bless you, they nearly always are, even if you can't find one that's a near likeness, as in this case. People think they know what they look like, but they don't, sir – not really. And they don't understand the photographic process – *I* don't understand it myself, though I do it – and they think of it like a sort of magic. You can tell 'em it's the light, or the chemicals, or they must have moved during the exposure – anything really, as long as you give them an explanation; and they go away quite happy. Why, we had a young gentleman in last week, whose portrait didn't come out, and we gave him one from stock – picture of a fine old chap, major in the Hussars, full dress uniform. *He* went away pleased as punch, on account of my explaining that the apparatus don't just show you as you are – it show you how you *will* be; and the photograph was pointing out what a

293

glorious future lay ahead of him, serving under her majesty's flag. It so happened that he'd often thought of enlisting, but had hesitated on account of having one leg shorter than the other; but the photograph settled it for him. So, my little harmless deception may well have showed a young man his way in life, and sowed the seeds of a future Duke of Wellington, and that's good enough for me!'

Somehow it was impossible to reprehend Mr Tuttle, who had retained his capacity of believing what he wanted the public to believe. He regaled his visitors with many more anecdotes over the bottle of wine, occasionally pierced, if not deflated, by a shaft of scepticism from Arabella; and he would surely have gone on regaling all night, if the time had not at last come for John and Verity to make their way home. Urging them to come again soon, he accompanied them to the door, where Verity paused before a display of portraits mounted on the lintel. 'These are stock, I suppose, Mr Tuttle?' she said.

'Some of 'em: I keep some more out the back. It sometimes happens, you see, that a customer don't call back for his portrait after being exposed, and then there's others who just don't like the look of it – usually when it shows their wrinkles, or the line of their hairpiece, for the apparatus is a mite unforgiving that way. But some of these, Miss Deene, I take for free, as an experiment. Often if I spot odd-looking individuals in the street, I can't resist having them in and exposing them; and your fancy-pictures and curiosities show your artistic bent, and add a bit of tone to the establishment, and fetch the quality in. The fiddler with the hook for a hand, for instance – now *there's* a study for you.'

'Odd-looking individuals indeed,' said Verity. 'John, just look at this curious pair!'

John looked over her shoulder at the portrait she indicated; and for a moment he was sure he was a victim of some mesmeric trick. It could not be . . . it simply could not be . . .

'Ah, queer-looking coves, ain't they?' said Mr Tuttle, who had not noticed John's expression. 'They came by as I was unlocking the shop one morning – on the tramp, you know; and I just had to have 'em in and capture them. Fierce sort of old chap this one was, but rambling in his mind, poor soul; and the young item with him, who stuck to him just like a faithful dog – well, he didn't have much furniture in the attic, I'm afraid.'

'John, whatever's the matter?' said Verity, looking up into John's face with alarm.

'Mr Tuttle,' he breathed, 'when did you take this portrait?'

'Oh, a few weeks ago, I would say. I'm not entirely sure they knew what was going on, to be truthful; but they kept quite still, and then I slipped them a shilling, poor creatures, and Arabella gave them a bag of broken victuals, and they went wandering on their way.'

'John,' said Verity tugging at his sleeve, 'what's wrong?'

It couldn't be, it couldn't be . . . And yet there was no mistaking the strange, haunted, baleful faces staring uncomprehendingly out from the photograph. He knew them, almost unearthly though they looked in their worn and emaciated shabbiness: he knew the white-haired old man seated in the chair, and he knew the hulking creature who stood behind him with his great fair hand on his shoulder. Impossible though it was to conceive how they had come to this condition, it was equally impossible to deny that the two tramps in the photograph were Caleb Porter and Saul Twopenny.

CHAPTER EIGHT

A Ghost Story

Dreams, the intense like of which John had not known since his parents' death, ravaged John's sleep that night. The haggard and empty faces and ragged costumes of Saul and Caleb, framed and mounted amongst the curiosities of London's streets, were the disturbers of his rest, and they continued to haunt him even when he woke.

Verity had never seen John's uncle, but she knew enough about him to share at least some of John's surprise. Tentatively she suggested that he might have been reduced by some great financial misfortune – bankruptcy even. John sensed that she hesitated over this because of what had happened to his own father, and he pressed her hand as he said, 'It's a possibility, my love – indeed, it's the only one that seems to make any sort of sense. And yet my uncle is the last man in the world I would expect to go under in that way. He was so solidly established – you remember those huge signs all over Hales-next-the-sea – and so prudent . . . I just don't understand it.'

One thing was sure: he could not simply let it lie. He had left Norfolk with only the harshest feelings about his tyrannical uncle, and had sought no communication with him since. But adversity had worked a change within him, and drawn the teeth of his bitterness; and he could not contemplate unmoved that terrible image in Mr Tuttle's studio. Some unthinkable catastrophe had befallen his uncle, and he could not rest until he had found it out.

His first act that morning, therefore, was to write a letter to his uncle's old home – though addressed to whom? Had William and Sar'ann shared in the disaster, whatever it might be? In the end he directed the letter to Messrs Twopenny of Hales-next-the-sea, assuming it would be delivered even if someone else had taken over the quayside premises; and simply stated in the letter that he had seen his uncle Mr Saul Twopenny in London in very reduced circumstances, and as a near relative sought information as to what had become of him and his family.

The letter that he received in reply, three days later, was almost as astonishing to John as the photograph had been. It was from a person called Chipchase, who described himself as Saul Twopenny's son-in-law and business partner. Sar'ann married? John, ungallantly enough, gaped. Mr Chipchase thanked John for his communication, but declared that it was of little interest to him. Mr Saul Twopenny, he said, had left the bosom of his family of his own free will, some months ago, on one of the arbitrary whims that so regrettably characterized him of late; and what Mr Saul Twopenny chose to do was his own concern. Mr Chipchase had enough to do running the business, the responsibility of which had been made over to him long before Mr Saul Twopenny chose to make his abrupt and unaccountable departure. As for Mr William Twopenny, he went on, he was no longer to be found at this address. Mr Chipchase concluded his letter by repeating his thanks to Mr John Twopenny for his communication, but reiterating that it called for nothing from him but a formal acknowledgement, and this having been made, he considered the correspondence closed.

295

'In other words, he is not his father-in-law's keeper,' Verity said, when John showed her the letter. 'Which is true enough, I dare say, but it's rather extraordinary all the same. Not the slightest trace of concern! And your uncle's daughter – is *she* not concerned that her aged father is apparently wandering the streets of London like a tramp?'

John summoned up a mental image of Sar'ann inspecting her mousetraps. 'It would seem not . . . but then she's a curious creature. I don't know what to think. I suppose my uncle was eccentric in his very strictness, but that's about all. As for whims, he was the least whimsical person I ever met in my life. And to think of him voluntarily walking away from S. Twopenny and Son – or Twopenny and Chipchase – it simply doesn't make sense. Something has happened that this Mr Chipchase won't divulge. If only I could see my uncle, and find out the truth of it! But I don't know how to find him – if he's still in London.'

'Well, judging by his condition in the photograph, it would be no use placing an advertisement in the newspapers. The poor old man looked as if he would be sleeping in them rather than reading them.'

'Yes . . . I never dreamt I would think of Uncle Saul as a poor old man. Strange, strange . . . I've got to find him, Verity. He might be a tough old bird, but he can't endure such a life as that for very long.'

The task seemed, at first sight, all but impossible: how to track down two men out of London's vast population of derelict wanderers? And yet there were hopeful elements in this case. For one thing, John could hardly have been better placed to conduct such a quest. His work with Dr Appleyard regularly took him into the haunts of the dispossessed – the slums, the low lodging-houses, the workhouse infirmaries and casual wards; and what was more, Tup'ny John had been a denizen of that world himself, and knew its ways and by-ways, and could gather intelligence from it as few men in his position could. And there was, besides, the singularity of Saul and Caleb as a spectacle, which must have been conspicuous even in London's multifarious underworld. And in this regard John had one further advantage: the photograph, which Mr Tuttle willingly gave to him when he explained what he intended to do. 'Take it, Mr T., take it. If I'd known your relation to those queer-looking coves, excuse the phrase, sir, I'd never have let 'em go wandering off; but hey-ho! There's a divinity that shapes our ends, Mr T., as the Swan says, and all our yesterdays lead on to something or other that escapes me just now, the matchless Arabella and I having made a bit of a night of it last night. Take it, sir, and good luck!'

So John took it with many thanks, and bore it round with him. In every rack-rented tenement and squalid nethersken, in every pot-house and poor-house that he visited, he showed the photograph, and asked if anyone knew of the strange pair represented thereon. He even returned to Ma Dade's, that sordid establishment where Tup'ny John had carried on his trade, and touted his curious exhibit around the nefarious characters who assembled there. Those who did not know him were guarded, suspecting him to be a 'crusher' in plain clothes; those who remembered him were willing, but wanted supplementary information that he could not give. What lay were these coves on, then? Were they Abram-men? – shamming lunacy? – looked as if they might be. Or on the scaldrum dodge, maybe? – couldn't see any sores or wounds in that there picture, but they might be covered up. Or were they praters, perhaps? bogus preachers? – the old cove had the face for it, and might have preached up a thirty-bob collection on any street corner by the looks of him. Well, they'd keep their eyes peeled, but there was so many beggars on the pad, coming in from the monkry – the country – and going out again, that there was no keeping track of 'em.

John also confided in Dr Appleyard, who promised to keep his ear to the ground; and Verity made the same inquiries among her ragged pupils. No luck from that quarter; though one precocious urchin informed her that if it was a beggarly old man she wanted, she could have his grandpa, and she was welcome to him.

And as John searched, the year dwindled towards its end, with bitter weather that touched with a fell hand the haunts of the poor, and made the search more urgent. He saw many cruel sights; and it would have been hard not to have adopted a view of the human predicament as bleak as the December skies, had there not been a counterbalance to pessimism in his love for Verity, and the love she bore him. Here, at least, was something that the gropings of blind chance could not seize and choke in its malevolent claws. It was too strong; for it had all of Verity's quiet, unshakeable strength in it, and if John did not believe himself to be her equal in that respect, then he hoped at least that he was learning from her.

Christmas brought no relaxation to the Appleyard household. Miss Jemima was busier than ever, raising subscriptions to give the poor a dinner, with gospel sauce; and as sickness and disease did not suspend their activities for the festive season, but were open for business throughout, there was no let-up for Dr Appleyard and John either. And it was on Christmas Eve, on a dark afternoon when the streets were treacherous with an enduring frost like sullied glass, and the air was thick with a fog more like ice than vapour, that John at last came upon the news that he sought. A parish officer at Spitalfields recognized the picture of Saul and Caleb. They had applied for admission to the casual ward a couple of nights ago, he said, but the place had been full to overflowing, and he'd had to turn them away. The old man had been in such a poor way, however, that the officer had given him a note referring him on to the workhouse infirmary at Shadwell, where he hoped they would have room for him.

Dr Appleyard did not hesitate when John told him the news. His authority would gain them entrance to the infirmary, he said: they would go there at once. It was a dismal waterside district that they had to traverse, made more ghastly by the sputtering gaslight that was already trying to penetrate the shrouded air; and the Union workhouse there was apt for such a spot, differing from the general grimness only in its forbidding regularity of brick.

The poor-law surgeon was in attendance, and knew Dr Appleyard; and when they described the men they sought he nodded, and led them to a bed at the end of the infirmary ward, a gloomy barrack murmurous with the groans of extremity. 'He came in as a casual, and the Board don't encourage keeping them more than a single night,' the surgeon said. 'But such is his condition that it can't be helped, in this case. As for the other one, he simply won't leave his side, and as he merely sleeps on the floor by his bed, and won't touch food, we let him be.'

No: a mistake of identification, after all. Saul Twopenny was a big robust old man, and the hollow-cheeked and trembling creature in the end bed could never have been such. And yet, wait: the wretched man crouching beside him was surely none other than Caleb Porter – a gaunt, shambling shadow of the giant he had once been, but Caleb Porter nonetheless; and in the eyes of the broken old man stretched out in the pauper bed, cavernous beneath wiry brows, there was something . . .

'Dear God,' said John. 'Uncle Saul.'

Yes, he knew him: but the old man was low, and weak, and wandering, and recognition only flickered in his eyes before they closed again in a sleep as shallow and troubled as his breathing. Dr Appleyard, with the surgeon's permission, made a brief examination: John had learned to read his expression at such times, and he knew the diagnosis was not hopeful.

'His sufferings have been great,' Dr Appleyard said, 'too great for a man of his age to support. I am sorry to see this, John. And yet he was a man of wealth, you say? A strange fall!'

It was from Caleb, whose joy at seeing John quickly sank again beneath his hangdog anxiety for his master, that they pieced together the story of that strange fall. It was not easy, for privation had not sharpened Caleb's wits; still, a clear enough picture emerged of a subtly established domination leading to a calculated ill-treatment, which had surely done much to exacerbate the derangement of Saul's mind; and a clear enough picture too of their wanderings, which had had London as their aim, but which had shared in all the vagaries of the enfeebled minds that had undertaken them. They had lived pretty much as tramps, it seemed, since arriving in the capital, sleeping in doss-houses where they could, cadging a meal likewise, and all the time engaged upon a haphazard quest to find William and John.

'Well, now we've found you, at any rate, sir,' Caleb said, brightening a little. 'He don't know you just at present, but he will do when he comes to himself. He goes in and out of it, you see . . . now here, now gone. He caught it off me, but he's got it worse than me, I'm afraid; and he've been so low these past days, I don't know what to do!'

There was not much, it appeared, that anyone could do. John asked Dr Appleyard whether the old man should not be moved somewhere else; but the doctor said no, coolly. 'He is too ill to be moved, I think; and he will do as well here as anywhere else, for what life remains to him.'

Dr Appleyard left him, to have a private word with the surgeon; and John sat down on the end of the bed, tracing out his uncle's familiar features in that worn mask that tossed on the pillow, and tracing out too the complex shape of his own feelings. Here was a harsh and merciless man, who had been brought low, it seemed, by his own wilfulness, as well as by a man if anything more harsh and merciless than himself: dying alone but for a simple-minded servant, the last living mortal whose loyalty he had retained. What should he feel?

The question perished as soon as he posed it. What was there to feel but pity? The old man's hand came groping out from the bedclothes, and John took and held it. Such mulish strength, he remembered, had once been in this hand, which was now like a bundle of twigs!

Dr Appleyard was back, and was leaning over his shoulder. 'John,' he said, 'I have other work to do. The surgeon here is very capable of seeing to such wants as your uncle may require. Do you wish to stay with him? Feel free to do so.'

John felt a faint tightening of the grip in the gnarled old hand. 'I . . . I will stay, Dr Appleyard. Thank you for your kindness.'

Dr Appleyard touched his shoulder, a gesture unusual for him. 'Very well. Come home when you want. I shall tell Miss Deene where you are.'

Soon after Dr Appleyard left, the gas was lit in the ward, and threw its callous light on a score of pitiable sights in those narrow iron beds; but John did not lift his eyes from his uncle's face. The light was slowly rousing the old man from his torpor, and Caleb bending tenderly over the bed-head murmured, 'Aye – he's coming out of it again, Mr John. He's fighting up. It's all right – there's no Demon here, sir, he's far away. There's only your old Caleb – and someone else, sir. Cousin John! We found him after all, sir – we're winning out after all!'

Saul was awake: weak and feverish, but awake. His eyes looked into John's, and the gnarled old hand twitched.

'How's this?' Saul wheezed. 'Am I above or below? Has it – has it come at last, then? I didn't think to meet you here, nephew. Who brought you to the grave, my boy? Were you demon-rid too? What was yours like – sly and soft and paddy-paws like mine? Ha! Never fear, boy. He will never come here. He will be gathered to the other place, whence he came.' Saul cackled, and then winced as his ruined chest rose and fell convulsively. 'Ach, but how is it I still suffer pain, and you do not, nephew? Is it a punishment? – and dark – so dark!'

298

'Oh, sir, you ain't in heaven!' cried Caleb. 'Sir, come out and be yourself, and show cousin John you're getting better, do, sir!'

'Uncle,' John said, as Saul struggled and looked wildly about him, 'uncle, be calm. You're in the infirmary at Shadwell Union, and you're being cared for. And I shall stay by you, until – until you're well.'

Saul stared at John's face, and then at John's hand, which he still held in his own; and then he nodded. 'Aye,' he breathed, 'aye, this is the hand. See, Caleb? This is the hand that challenged me, and broke my stick: this is the hand that might have struck me! I've found you, nephew! God has not deserted me, and has led me to you at last!'

'Yes, uncle,' John said, clasping the nervous hand in both his own. 'But don't speak of that last time. That's past and forgotten. I'm just thankful to have . . . that you have found me.'

'No, no, no, no,' said Saul, trying frantically to sit up, 'past, but not forgotten. I have thought much of it these past months, whilst I have . . . Do you know what happened to me, nephew? Have you heard of the Demon, and how it was that Caleb and I went on the tramp? Saul Twopenny on the tramp – ha! But better Shanks's nag than the Demon.'

'Caleb has told me something of it.'

'Ah, poor boy! He has suffered with me, nephew, and complained less, if truth be told. Lift me, will you, Caleb? That's well. I feel the better time coming upon me – they still come, aye, but fewer now – and I must speak. Well, nephew, have you prospered?'

'Well enough, uncle. But you – I had no idea – no conception of the plight you were in—'

'Ha! No one did. Demons leave no tracks. Ah, but I regret nothing, nephew – nothing, anyhow, since I slipped away from his soft clutches. There was a stroke! Ha! Take that, Demon!' A pale shadow of the old crafty look passed across Saul's face. 'No, I regret nothing. Better the hardness of the road, than the softness of those hands . . . We came . . . we came to seek you, nephew, you and William. You don't know, I suppose, where William is to be found?'

'I'm sorry, uncle. I've heard nothing of him since I left Norfolk.'

Saul looked wistful, but waved a hand. 'Ah, well – if it is not to be . . . So, Saul Twopenny is come at last to a pauper ward, eh? Good: I have no complaints. We have met with kindness, Caleb and I, since we came to London, sick and footsore and money spent. When I have had the falling fit upon me, there have been hands to hold me up and put water to my lips – coarse hands, nephew, dirty hands, hands that may well have thieved in their time; but kind! We have moved amongst the meek of scripture, and they do not look pretty; but I have seen no Demons, nephew. Late to learn, but not too late: not quite!'

Saul's breathing rasped again, and his head lolled back on Caleb's arm, and for some moments he seemed to be dozing. But then he grunted, and his eyes were lucid as he fixed them on John. 'We were speaking of William,' he said. 'I have no right, nephew, to bind you to any sort of promise. I can only ask you to see if you can find him – some time – and give him my love. He may well laugh to hear it: he may well throw it back in your face. But no matter. Do it, anyhow, if you will.'

John nodded: he could not speak.

'You need not be discomfited, nephew: I know well that I shall not live to give it him myself. Ah, it is all I can give him! Everything was made over to the Demon and the Demon's wife: he made sure of that . . . But that's no matter either. The things that truly matter in this life are few, few and precious, when once the fancy trappings are stripped away from it.' Saul suddenly turned his eyes on Caleb. 'Well, boy? Still here? Ah, poor creature, I fear you have not eaten. Go, boy, eat: there's twopence in my pocket, I know. Take it, and eat.'

'No, sir, I don't want to,' blubbered Caleb. 'I want you to eat. *I'm* all right, sir – it's you who should eat.'

'Nonsense, boy, I'm past eating,' said Saul with his old sharpness. 'Do as you're told – nephew, help me – make this boy eat.'

John's persuasions, however, were in vain. Caleb would not leave Saul's side, even with John there; and presently the old man, having called him all sorts of names, patting his great blond hand the while, drifted off to sleep again. Poor Caleb was owl-eyed with weariness, and once he saw that his master was quiet, laid himself down on the floor beside the bed, and slept likewise; but John stayed where he was, seated on the bed with his hand close to his uncle's on the rough grey blanket.

The ward grew quieter as the evening wore on, and the sufferers therein embraced that oblivion that was the only pleasure they knew. Somewhere outside, amidst the freezing fog that was smearing its unhealthy breath against the grated windows, a party of carol-singers was abroad, and their lusty voices penetrated even to that dingy interior – of all sounds the most dolefully inappropriate here, thought John, who had quite forgotten the season; and he thought of the curtains being drawn against the night, and fires being stirred against the cold, all over the city, and the world of difference that lay between even the humblest of them and the situation of the obstinate old man coming to the end of his life in this frowsy bed. He thought of many things as night drew on; and he was just groping at an empty conclusion that life was more unpredictable and fantastical than any dream could be, when he became aware that Saul was awake, and watching him.

'How do you feel, uncle? Would you like some water?'

'A little water, nephew, if you will,' said Saul. His voice was clear, yet it seemed to issue from some vast distance. 'Thank you . . . Is that poor boy of mine sleeping? Good . . . I would not have him ill too . . . How do I feel, nephew? I am a little chary of telling you; because you always had a bent for doctoring, and I have some memory in my head of you arriving here with a doctor – is it so? And you have followed that course? That's something, then . . . Nephew, I feel as if I am breathing through a straw – not painfully; because much of this carcass of mine has gone to sleep, and doesn't seem to need the breath. And I feel clearer in my mind than for many days . . . and I have wit enough to know, without a doctor telling me so, that these are not good signs. Hm?'

John hesitated. 'The one thing doctors have in common,' he said, 'is that they all disagree.'

'Pah, don't coddle me, nephew,' said Saul, but all the old rancour had left his eyes, and his hand sought John's again as he went on, 'Again, I have no right to hold you to a promise . . . but will you see if you can help Caleb? He'll be but a poor thing on his own, though it's he who's held me up these past weeks.'

'You have my promise, uncle. But what about this Chipchase? Surely he should be brought to some sort of account for the way he has acted.'

'We shall all be brought to account, nephew. My faith in that is unshakeable. When I die, the Demon will get what he has wanted from the beginning, and let him rest content with it: it will avail him nothing, when he is called to reckoning. Besides, what did he do to me? Nothing that I did not do to myself. I placed the whip in his hands, and he saw no reason why he should not use it. No, no, leave it be, nephew. There is more I would say to you . . . things I must say before I depart this life. Do you hear me aright, nephew? – you seem fearfully far off from me, and I can hardly tell whether I whisper or shout. I would not disturb the rest of the other poor wretches in this place . . .'

'I hear you well, uncle,' John said. 'But I would not have your rest disturbed either. These things you have to say to me – do they concern our last meeting? Because if so—'

'That is one of them,' said Saul. 'I did you an injustice then, my boy; and if you cannot forgive me for it, then very well. But I freely confess it, even so.'

'There's nothing to forgive, uncle,' said John. 'As far as I am concerned, we are reconciled, fully reconciled, and there is nothing in the past to sever us.'

'Bless you for that, my boy . . . God bless you . . .' Saul turned his wild white head restlessly on the pillow. 'But there is more . . . more I must tell you. There is a burden I have carried with me these two years and more – God knows what part it played in the scattering of my wits! But I am clear in my mind now; and I must shed the burden, John, before I die. In what I have to tell you, there are things that you will not like to hear; and it may be, at the end, that you will wish to take back that forgiveness you gave. If so, no matter. It will be no more than I deserve. All I ask is that you hear me out.'

The old man drew in another whistling breath, and composed himself with his hands laid across his breast, and his eyes on the high rafters above. For a few moments there was silence in the ward, but it seemed to John that the beating of his own heart, which had begun to pound without his knowing why, must be audible all down the long room.

'John, you do not know all of the circumstances surrounding the death of your poor mother and father,' said Saul at last. 'Because you were away at school when it happened, it was not difficult for it to be hid. What I am about to tell you was told to me by your father, the day after your mother's funeral, when we were closeted together in his study, and you and William and Sar'ann were out – you recall the day? It was then that your father told me all. I was his nearest kin, and though it was long since we had been close, I suppose it was natural that he should turn to me, in his grief and distraction, to unburden himself of the terrible weight that lay at his heart, and that he could not tell to another living soul – least of all you, my boy, as you will see.'

Saul licked his cracked lips. 'You know, John, that your parents had become intimate with a wealthy man named Goodway, who had come to live on our coast for his wife's health. A sociable, high-living man; and your poor father, trying to keep up with him, got himself tangled deep in debt to the man himself. This you know. But there was more to that involvement, John, than financial obligation. Your mother, to her immediate shame and regret, allowed herself to be seduced by Goodway. Ah, John, John, I would spare you this, but believe me, I cannot! He was a winning sort of man, I hear; and your mother was very much younger than your father, and had lived a very quiet and simple life for one of her talents and spirits. It happened, John: she was won over by this Goodway, who cloaked his seduction under the appearance of a family friendship, and she gave herself to him. Her shame and self-loathing, I say, came almost at once: the involvement was brief. But by then the damage was done. Your mother found she was with child by him. No doubting that it was by him; for her marriage to your father was by that time a marriage of companionship, and it was a long while since they had lain together.

'Here was something that could not be hid; and she confessed all to your father. Her last communication with Goodway had been to tell him that she was pregnant, but that was of little account to the scoundrel. He had got all he wanted – the conquest of a beautiful woman: probably the story had been repeated half a dozen times before. What had he to fear? Was your father about to publicize his own cuckolding, and his wife's shame? For her shame, John, was great; and great too was your father's love for her, even then. There were bitter words, and many tears; but there was never any serious thought of separation. And in the end it was decided that they would keep the child, and raise it as their own, and try to put the episode behind them. You, as I say, were away at school in Norwich; and all you would need to be told was that your mother had been blessed with a late

301

pregnancy, and that you were to have a little brother or sister.

'That was not to be. Before you could be told, John, your poor mother miscarried. Your father said he had never seen a worse case; and though he said nothing of it to her – she was past hearing it, poor creature – he suspected that she might have tried taking something from his store of medicines, in a fit of renewed shame and loathing, to get rid of the child. Well, all his skill and love could not save her from the infection that set in, and her death was swift. None witnessed what had happened but your father and the servant, Tetty, who was too loyal to breathe a word; and your father being a physician, he was well placed to conceal the real cause of your mother's death, and put it down to a malignant fever, and keep your mother's reputation unspotted. He might, perhaps, have told you that she died miscarrying his own child; but he did not think he could maintain such a fiction, so fraught with pain and humiliation as the whole subject was. Better, he thought, for her passing to be presented as a sudden illness, and her memory preserved just as it had been before Goodway entered their lives.

'As for him, you know the part he played in your father's financial ruin. This in spite of the fact that he must surely have guessed what had befallen your poor mother. Another Demon, perhaps, John! For he seems to have had no more conscience than a demon. He had had his pleasure from your mother, and he would have his money from your father. Are you there, John? You seem further off from me yet. Will you take my hand . . .? But no, not yet. For now we come to my own shame, and you may well cast this hand away from you when you hear it. Ah, my eyes are not so weak that I cannot see those tears, John! God forgive me that I have brought them forth – but you will know, in a moment, why I had to tell you.

'All this, I say, I learned from your father, in that long day we spent together in his study. It's my belief that he already had it in mind then, to take the dreadful way out of this world that he did; for he spoke to me about you, my boy, and how he had ruined your prospects, knowing well that he was close to bankruptcy. He knew you would have nothing; and he begged me, though we had been but cold brothers to one another for many a year, to take care of you if anything should happen to him, and to help you to that profession you'd set your heart on. Ah, yes! Your father's dying wish, in all but name, was simply that I should set you on the road to becoming a doctor, as I had ample means to do. But I didn't, did I, my boy? Oh, John, you came close to striking me a blow once: strike now, and I would thank you for it . . .!'

John shook his head. It was all he could do. He was wrapped in darkness: he was bound hand and foot at the bottom of a fathomless pit, and silently howling.

'Well,' said Saul, with a grinding breath, 'the blow will come soon, and it will be struck by one greater than all of us . . . That is how I wronged you, boy, and that is the sin I must confess. I gave your father my promise that I would do as he asked; and it was not long after that, that the wildness of his grief drove him to his terrible end. Your poor father thought he had one consolation in death, and that was that you were provided for. Oh, God have mercy on me! I did not fulfil my promise, John – for I thought less of you, and of your mother and father in their shamed graves, than of my own bitterness. For your father and I were good friends enough once, John: we were friends when he first met your mother, twenty-five years since; and I admired her too. Oh, yes, I wished in my secret heart that such beauty and sweetness might be mine. But I knew that I had no chance, for he was the good-tempered, laughing one, and right for her, whilst I had already got the sourness of money and gain upon my tongue; and so he married her; and I hugged my bitterness to me, and polished it up along with the guineas and the rod, and fancied myself satisfied with them. Envy, John: always I envied your father, not only for what he had, but for the kind, bright soul that brought him what he had; and out of that envy, I wronged you. When I took you into my house after his death, I saw in you only your mother's fairness of face, and your father's merry ways; and instead of cherishing them, I made a tool of you, and would have had you turn into the hard dreary likeness of myself. Why should I help another mortal to the happiness and fulfilment that I had never known . . .? I had set my bitter mark on everything about me, and I would have set it on you too; but thank God, you escaped it; and William also – I pray it was not too late for William. Oh, John, you are further away yet . . .! I am answering for what I did now, my boy; but I had to confess it, before I go to a greater answering . . . Speak one word, John, if it is only a curse – this silence is like the silence of death . . .'

John sobbed, and blindly grasped his uncle's hand, and clutched it. Saul gave a long sigh; and as John wept, with bowed head, he thought he felt a hand lightly touch his hair, and then withdraw. Somewhere a clock was striking, and some part of his stunned mind counted the strokes, and registered the fact that it was Christmas Day.

'Perhaps,' said Saul with a fretful motion in the bed, 'perhaps I am a Demon too – the greatest Demon of them all. Who else but a Demon would think as I did as I took you in? – think such cruel and vengeful thoughts, of a woman taken in adultery, and a man dead by his own hand – sinners, I branded them, sinners, when I had lived all my life in fear of the Lord! If you had not risen up against me, John, I truly believe I would not have rested until I had made you as miserable a being as I . . . But you are not, John? Say you are not. Tell me I did not even begin to succeed . . . and that you walk upright in the sun as your poor parents would have wished for you . . .!'

'It is so, uncle, it is so,' said John, finding his voice at last. 'Have no fear of that.'

'And William? Has he found that happiness I would have denied him, do you think? He always wished to go to sea. I hope it has not disappointed him. Perhaps he stands on deck at this moment, beneath the stars, and tastes the salt air; and the life he once lived in his father's house seems no more to him than an evil dream, fast fading from his memory. I hope it is so! Oh, John, I hope it is so!'

Saul was much agitated now, and fighting with all his old stubborn will for breath that would not come. John hastily wiped his own tears, and made the old man lay his head down and be calm. 'Rest, uncle,' he said, smoothing the matted hair, 'you must rest now. Don't talk any more.' .

'Beware . . . beware Demons, John,' murmured Saul, his eyelids fluttering. 'The Demons inside yourself, most of all. Have I told you everything? My memory plays me false. It lets slip what passed an hour ago . . . and yet the memories of old dead years are as fresh as the morning. I even recall – ha! I even recall the names carved on the form at my first school, and the way the master wore his hair in a queue with a brown ribbon . . . Is it not morning yet? It seems to grow darker and darker . . . beware the darkness does not swallow you, John – are you there?'

'Hush,' said John, 'hush, I'm here, uncle, I'm here. Rest now.'

'Yes, rest . . . He that endureth to the end shall be saved . . . Is Caleb still sleeping there?' Saul tried to raise his head, but his strength was gone. 'Let him sleep on . . . Make him eat, when the morrow comes, John, will you? He's as stubborn as . . . ha! as me . . . Look to the morrow, John: I have raised these ghosts only to shrive my soul, and now they can be laid again . . . let the dead bury their dead . . . You were blessed in the love of your mother and father . . . hold that fast . . .'

Saul sank into silence and stillness, and only the thin keening of his breath remained, and the sickly stirrings of the other sufferers in that bleak place. John sat down at the foot of the bed, and supported his head in his hands; and there he remained through the small hours – hours that seemed, in their abysmal darkness and unendurable length, to mark not the Nativity but the birth of some ghastly new era in the world, in which the brightness and purity of dawn would have no place.

Had he slept? He could not tell whether he had slept, or had wandered so far down tunnels of anguished memory that he had left the waking present behind; whichever it was, he found he was lifting his head with a start, and looking up at the poor-law surgeon bending over the bed, with the milky morning light at the grated window making a curious angel of him. John jumped to his feet, and at the same moment Caleb stirred on the floor.

'Oh – I didn't mean to sleep,' Caleb said, scrambling up at the sight of the surgeon. 'He's better, isn't he? He caught it off me, you see. That's why he've been queer and poorly. He caught it off me. But he's getting better, isn't he . . .?'

The surgeon did not speak: only shook his head, and drew the rough blanket over the face of the still form on the bed; for the wanderings of the exiled king had come to an end, and there was no question of better or worse any more.

'What is it?' cried Caleb, brushing the sleep from his eyes with a quivering hand, and looking wildly from the surgeon to John. 'What is it? Cousin John, what is it? Not death? Oh, no, not death?'

John put his hand on the big man's shoulder; but Caleb was beyond comfort. He fell across the body of his master, and whispered desolately, 'Oh, sir, I wish I could catch it off you! I wish I could catch it off you, sir, and be the same!'

CHAPTER NINE

The Ghosts Will Not Lie Down

Saul was buried in London. Mr Chipchase, when John wrote him the news of his father-in-law's death, replied with some formal expressions of grief on black-edged paper; but added pointedly that as the late Mr Twopenny had chosen for his own mysterious reasons to die out of the bosom of his family, he might as well be buried out of it. He did, however, arrange for a supply of funds for the occasion, so that Saul was spared a pauper's funeral; but he had to leave the arrangements to John, as pressure of business, he said, prevented him making the journey to London in person – and as for Mrs Chipchase, there was no question of her travelling, as she was expecting her first confinement.

Saul's only other living relative was his son William; and though John placed an advertisement in several London newspapers begging Mr William Twopenny or anyone who knew of his whereabouts to get in touch with him at Great Russell Street, no reply came, and the funeral could not be deferred any longer. It seemed likely that William was at sea; and so the sole mourners were John, Verity, Dr Appleyard and Caleb Porter.

Mourning, indeed, was a feeble word to describe poor Caleb's condition: the big man was in a trance of despair. John was mindful of Saul's request that his faithful servant be taken care of, but in some difficulty as to how it was to be done. Though fit enough for all manner of heavy work, he was fit for nothing at the moment; and though Dr Appleyard was giving him a temporary lodging, and the charitable Miss Jemima feeding him up and fitting him out with new clothes, there could be no permanent place for him in the household.

John might have been better able to apply his mind to this problem if he had not been in a trance of his own. All normal mental processes, and all accustomed feeling, had been knocked out of kilter by Saul's momentous revelation. John resumed his life, but he went about it like a sleepwalker: he was simply not there. He had been cast again into outer darkness, such as he thought he had left behind for ever. The ghosts that Saul had raised walked by him every waking moment, and infiltrated his dreams. John was truly a haunted man.

He felt so profoundly that for some days he could not tell precisely what it was he was feeling, just as extremes of ice and heat are indistinguishable to the shocked senses. And when his feelings resolved themselves, they were so many and so contradictory that identification gave him no relief. Pity, repulsion, horror, love, hate, anger, despair, all buffeted him in turn. His mother and Goodway! Goodway and his mother! His mother bearing Goodway's child . . . his father's grief . . . his mother's shame . . . His mind could not even begin to assimilate these things logically: it could only recoil at the appalling images it conjured up, as if it would go on torturing itself for ever, like a maddened and imprisoned animal battering itself against the bars of its cage.

Nothing, he felt, could ever be the same again. He had supposed his innocence destroyed at the time of his parents' death; but now he knew better. Innocence had merely received a blow then: in the small hours of Christmas Day, in that fetid

305

pauper ward where old Saul had shed his burden, it had been brutally murdered. Life would go on, but he would never again be able to see the sun rise with the same feeling as before.

Why was it worse? His parents were no more nor less in the grave, and lost to him, than before: so why was it worse? Some plaintive part of his self posed the question, but it was scarcely worth an answer. It *was* worse – a thousand times worse. What had been a story of dreadful misfortune was now a story of tragedy and betrayal almost intolerable to think of. The house at Saltmarsh had seemed to him the receptacle of all that was true, beautiful and valuable in an uncertain world, and it had been terrible indeed to find it destroyed by untimely death: how much more terrible to discover that it had been cankered inside – that even its memory was false.

Memory: he was much concerned with it, in the bitter days and weeks following Saul's death. Where previously he had shunned the remembrance of the time leading up to the catastrophe, now he relentlessly sought it. And much of what he had hidden took on a new complexion: he saw it, indeed, for the first time. He remembered, in particular, those moments alone with his mother in the garden-room, when she had surprised him with a passionate protestation of loyalty to his father. He had supposed her then to be speaking out of defensive concern about his father's extravagant ways: ah, no! The pale face he had seen reflected in the window-glass must have been the face of agonized temptation confronting itself, and confessing even as it denied!

John could not accept what he had learnt of his parents' tragedy – accept, sigh, and turn the page: it was impossible. And yet the ghastly paradox was, there was no alternative but to accept it. No action of his could change the fact that while he was away at school, divided between puppy-love and cramming, his mother had been seduced from her marriage vows by a man who had wormed his way into his father's confidence, and become pregnant by him, and had died of it; and that his father had known all. And that it was because of such knowledge that his father had climbed the cliff to the Hanged Man's House, and put an end to knowing there, at the end of a rope.

So, buffeted by contrary feelings, and pounding a treadmill of memories that he could not change; thus the sleepwalker that had been John Twopenny drifted into a new year, and could see nothing that could be inscribed in its blank annals capable of restoring his peace of mind, or wholeness of heart.

Only one element of the turmoil within gave him a strange sort of hope – strange indeed, because that one thing was his hate. His hate for Marcus Goodway, which had already been such as to transcend every antipathy he had ever felt, now struck through him and clove his nature to the root. His hate was not transient. And there was a sort of hope in it because this, of all the multitude of feelings that assailed him, was the only one that had a living object. It was something, even though that living object might be beyond his power. For John soon admitted the fact that there was nothing he could do to Marcus Goodway – no way of expressing his hate commensurate with its intensity. Or rather, there was: he could seek out Goodway's London home, force his way into it, and either shoot him through the head or stab him through the heart.

Very melodramatic, and utterly unreal. Nevertheless, John felt that the man fully deserved it, and more. The enormity of his conduct, which had previously seemed sufficiently inhuman, staggered him now that its extent was known. Nothing was more agonizing to John, when he thought of Marcus Goodway, than the fact that he had held out his hand to that man and pulled him from the fatal embrace of the marshes; and nothing more certain than his conviction that now, knowing what he did, he would stay his hand, and watch the man drown – watch, carefully, with an unblinking eye and an unmoved heart, right to the end.

306

There was no denying that the thought of his mother surrendering herself to that man was the most monstrous blasphemy of all. And yet here a voice of reason that he might have lacked a year or two ago came to his aid. The voice reminded him that he had been disastrously mistaken in the impulses of his own heart; and it reminded him too of that curious ambiguity of feeling that had hovered in the air whenever he had met Marcus Goodway – the way that the hated man always seemed to establish an immediate intimacy, even when they were at daggers drawn. He perceived, too, why Goodway had persisted in animosity towards a young man who should have been less than nothing to him. John was an awkward leftover from a successful adventure. John knew as surely as he knew his own name that Goodway had approached his sexual conquest of Emma Twopenny in the same spirit of amused contempt as he had the material conquest of her husband; but the continued existence of John, who had never submitted to him, was an irritant, and a reminder of the incompleteness of his power.

Some relief might have been found in sharing this burden of unbearable knowledge. But John could not share it. Even to that heart which was so closely bound to his own, John could not reveal what it was that was making him a blank stranger to himself and everyone else. It would mean telling of his mother's shame and his father's humiliation; it would mean exposing what his parents had tried to keep secret even from him. He could not do it. He could not tell any of it without telling all of it, and dragging through the mud the names of those whom he would protect even in death; and so he could not tell Verity. It was his first secret from her; and if he knew in his heart of hearts that a secret – any secret – must always be a loose cannon to lovers, he ignored the danger, out of the sheer impossibility of telling it.

Of course, Verity knew something was amiss with him: she would have detected a disquiet far less significant than this. But the change in him had followed immediately upon his witnessing the death of his uncle, and she supposed him deeply affected by this – as indeed he was – and no more. If she was dismayed that he seemed to be stranded on a high ledge of experience, and to be clinging on there where she could not follow, she did not say so – not yet.

Was there perhaps some prevision, in the not entirely natural, not entirely relaxed state of calm that existed between them during those first dark weeks of the new year – weeks that in spite of the freezing weather, seemed to carry a humid heaviness as of an approaching storm? They were affectionate, they were tender, but they were not as they had been: John knew it, and could only trust to time to restore what had been lost; but had he some foreboding that that trust was misplaced, and that time had some far less healing, far more destructive work in store?

It seemed innocuous when it came. The Appleyards now allowed them two evenings a week to dispose of as they pleased; and it fell out on one of these that John and Verity were invited by Catherine to a special 'At Home' evening at the residence of the Fernhills. John, it seemed, was no longer *persona non grata* as far as the admiral was concerned, an indication in itself that the whole business was consigned to the painless past; and as neither of them saw it otherwise, and saw no reason why they should snub Catherine and Augustus, at least, they agreed to go.

A special 'At Home', indeed: the Fernhill residence off Portland Place was lit in every window, and three carriages were jousting with each other for space outside, and the footman who waited for them at the top of the steps was in a high state of powder. A special 'At Home' indeed: it seemed as if nobody else in genteel London was 'At Home' tonight, for they were surely all here, judging by the great drone as of a myriad well-bred bees that issued from the reception-rooms. A special 'At Home', indeed: for here was Mrs Fernhill herself greeting them, wearing bare shoulders and goose-pimples for the occasion, and coming commendably close to remembering precisely who they were. Such a gathering of people under the great chandeliers, which struck flashes of glory from the Admiral's head as he strutted beneath them: such a fluttering of fans, and rustling of crinolines, and wilting of flowers in headdresses, and clouds of involuntary incense from pomaded whiskers; surely some great event was being celebrated here, amongst the soft bare arms and hard laughter?

Yes: it was an engagement of marriage, though it was Augustus who came forward to give them the news – with difficulty, for he had adopted such a tight-waisted silhouette that he could only speak in little gasps, and say that Catherine, God bless her, gasp, was getting herself, gasp, spliced a month from today, and it ought, gasp, to be a jolly good send-off . . .

No need, however, for Augustus to say any more: for through a gap in the assembled drones, Catherine was now visible, seated in state beside her intended, and being heaped with congratulations. She looked shyly happy, a little over-whelmed, very beautiful, and rather glad to keep hold of the sturdy arm of her husband-to-be. Who was none other than Mr Marcus Goodway.

Yes: the intimacy between them had grown apace, and the year's mourning for his dead wife had elapsed, and a general benevolent interest had grown around the two of them. Such a handsome and charming couple! Catherine something of a tender plant, and requiring to be trained to a strong tree: Mr Goodway not yet forty, and so hearty and upright and frank, and so touchingly devoted to his late wife through her long sickness: surely it was right that he should have a second chance of happiness. And so thoroughly eligible, a man of breeding and fortune, with a town establishment and a country house, pleasantly close to her own family home, to lay at her feet: what could be better? So Admiral and Mrs Fernhill had thought, and had rejoiced in the match, and the marriage was arranged to the satisfaction of all parties.

Mr Marcus Goodway: there, just over there, smiling and chatting and laughing his manly laugh, and occasionally directing a glance of gentle reassurance into his fiancée's eyes. Mr Marcus Goodway, engaged to be married to Catherine Fernhill, a month hence. Mr Marcus Goodway, who had scarcely been out of John's thoughts since Christmas Day, but whom he had scarcely expected ever to set eyes on again, and never, never in such circumstances as this.

The intensity of his feelings was such that John felt a wave of nausea in his throat. He could find no voice to answer Augustus's amiable inquiries: he could not move: his very heart seemed to cease pumping, and he knew that the blood had drained from his face, and that he must be sensationally white.

Verity pressed his arm. 'John?' she said, watching him carefully. 'Are you all right?'

He could only shake his head, tightly; and continue to stare at the happy couple. 'It is rather stuffy in here,' Verity said – watching him, oh so carefully. 'I don't think we need stay long. All we need do is give them our congratulations, and—'

'No.' John recoiled so violently from such an idea that he flinched back, disengaging his arm from her hand in the process. 'No. No, Verity, I – I can't stay.' An image of his mother's pale face reflected in the windows of the garden-room rose up between him and the scene, and he shuddered. 'I can't stay here.'

'But we can't just go without speaking a word to them. It would look as if . . .' She stopped: watched him again.

'Congratulate them? Never. I can never . . . I can't go near them. Let me get out of this place, for God's sake . . .'

He had turned, and was already plunging his way blindly through the press of people, almost knocking over a footman carrying a tray as he burst out of the drawing-room and took the stairs at a run. He was hardly aware that Verity had followed him until he reached the street outside, and leaned against the railings, fighting down a wave of sickness. When he looked up, breathing hard, she was there, pulling her wrap about her, and watching him.

'I'm sorry,' he said. 'I wish I could explain . . .'

'I don't think you need to,' Verity said, her face a cool mask. 'I'm not blind.'

'Verity . . . you don't understand . . .'

'I understand very well, John. I understand very well, without the need of words. Your face spoke volumes, when you saw her. You saw her engaged to another man, and—'

'No. Not – not the fact of her being engaged. *Him*. To see her engaged to him. Verity . . .' He struggled: he could not, simply could not tell her the one unconquerable reason for his feeling – could not betray his mother's memory – could not resurrect the shame that had killed her. 'He . . . you remember the old time, in Norfolk. That man – my father was deep in debt to him when he died, and – and he was the most implacable creditor, and . . .'

'I remember hearing something of it,' Verity said. 'Not generous in him, I'll admit. But hardly sufficient to justify such emotion on your part, I would have thought.' She gave a bitter laugh. 'After all, it's not you who's marrying him, my dear John. It's Catherine. But perhaps that's where the emotion lies, eh? Isn't it so, John?'

He glared balefully at her; and the light from the windows of the house was quite enough to show him that Verity was coldly, dangerously angry. No trivial pets with Verity: her wrath was rare, complete, and unassuageable. But John was at white heat himself; and though he could see her well enough in that warm window-light, he was also not seeing her at all. The outraged ghosts of the past interposed themselves like a mist between him and the woman he loved, and sowed division there.

'I must see Catherine alone,' he muttered. 'I must see her alone, and – and try to dissuade her from this – unthinkable marriage—'

'Do so, then.' Verity's voice was steady.'If that is what you want, I have no influence to stop you. I thought I did have a certain influence over you, John: a beautiful and precious influence; but now I see it is not so.'

'Verity – damn it, you don't understand . . .'

'So you said. And as I said, I understand very well. I am not blind, John, and neither am I stupid. I *have* been so, perhaps; but I shan't be any longer.' There was the merest trace of unsteadiness in her voice then, but she corrected it and, gathering her wrap about her, went on, 'I'm going home, John. Don't try to follow me.'

She was gone, swiftly: leaving John grasping at the railings, and wishing that the strength of his body might equal the turbulent strength of his feelings, and that he might tear them up and hurl them through the windows of that house where Marcus Goodway was celebrating his ultimate triumph.

Love should be stronger than hate, no doubt: in John's case, that night, he found it was not so. He lingered about beneath those lit windows, gnawing and chafing within; and at last he drew out his pocketbook, scribbled a note, made his way round to the servants' entrance, and there persuaded a maid, with the help of five shillings, to pass the note to Miss Catherine when she was alone. Then he made his way back to Great Russell Street, and moodily threw himself upon the bed in his clothes, and awaited the issue of the morning. He did some desultory looking into himself during the long dark hours, and tried to impose some reason upon his disordered passions; but still he came to the same insistent conclusion. The seducer of his mother, the destroyer of his family, the man who had been the black and taunting bane of his life since that ill-omened day on the marshes, was to marry Catherine Fernhill. That gentle and susceptible girl, with the blessing of her

309

block-headed parents, was to be delivered into the hands of Goodway – hands which, to John, were marked with the blood of his mother and father as surely as if he had butchered them to their untimely deaths.

No, and again, no! His whole being revolted against it. He was able to be sufficiently dispassionate to examine his feelings about Catherine, and to acquit himself of that which Verity suspected to be the real reason for his excessive reaction – a continued love for Catherine. No, it was not that: but nor could he stand by indifferently and see so innocent a creature as Catherine, to whom he was bound at least by ties of fond and affectionate memory, unite herself to a man who had done what Goodway had done.

He was able, too, to see that Verity had ample grounds for her suspicion of him. He had given her no cogent reasons for his behaviour: what could be more natural than her hurt and indignant conclusion? And here too came the first glimmerings of another perception – that a love which stopped short of complete openness and candour was no love worth the name. But he only glimpsed this truth before the darkness closed in on him again, and extinguished it.

Catherine met him the next morning, as he had requested in his note, at the park corner of Portland Place. 'This is all very mysterious, John,' she said, aglow from cold and hurry, 'and was rather difficult to arrange. We didn't see you or Verity last night: Augustus said you left almost as soon as you arrived. Whatever—'

She stopped, taken aback by his grim look; and without preamble he said, 'Catherine, you must not marry Goodway.'

'Marcus? Whyever not? Oh! John, I know you are not friendly towards him, on account of that awful time in Norfolk. But really, it was hardly Marcus's fault that your father owed him money, and he had a right, you know, to be paid; and he was a little distracted at the time, from caring for his wife. Truly, John, Marcus is the kindest and most considerate of men; and even if you cannot be on friendly terms with him, I hope you will wish us well.'

John gazed into her bright face; and with a savage flaring of despair, he seized her by the shoulders and cried, 'Catherine, you cannot give yourself to that man! Don't ask me the reason why, it's something I cannot tell, but I swear by the feeling we once bore each other that it is reason enough for you to fly from that man and never let him in your sight again—'

'Good heavens, John, you're half mad,' said Catherine in alarm, shrinking back from him. 'If I didn't know you better I'd say you were drunk, oh dear that sounds terribly prim and disapproving and I don't mean it that way but really John I don't know what to think, I truly don't understand what it is you're saying . . .'

'What I'm saying,' said John, 'is just this. Promise me, Catherine, that you'll reconsider your engagement to that – to Goodway.'

'But John,' Catherine said, regarding him soberly, 'the time when we could bind each other to promises is long gone. Isn't it?'

John sighed, and dropped his eyes. 'Yes,' he said. 'I know.' He tasted defeat – a defeat he had known, deep down, would come. For what was Catherine to think of this extraordinary request? One thing only. As long as he could give her no reason for this extravagant behaviour, she must put it down to jealousy – either the reflex jealousy of an ex-sweetheart, or something stronger. And it was plain that she was trying to address herself kindly to this jealousy when she said, in a softer tone, 'You made reference just now to the feeling we once bore each other; and believe me, John, I am very far from making light of that feeling, or holding it in contempt. I would not be here now otherwise. But that's past, John: I thought we'd closed that volume for good and all, and with no hard feelings on either side. If I did not think that, I would never have entered upon this engagement. And I have entered upon it, John. I . . . I love Marcus, and respect him, and have promised myself to him; and truly, John, that is not something that can be dismissed simply because of what you have told me this morning. not that you *have* told me anything, really – except that you don't want me to marry Marcus. And all I can think of that is that you . . . well, that you . . .'

'Don't think that,' John said, 'it isn't that.' He was trying simply to be truthful, but in his agonized state it came out so curt and ungallant that Catherine – who was no more averse to being admired than she had ever been – was offended. 'Well,' she said, 'then I don't know what to think. It's all very strange, and I must say it's not the sort of behaviour I ever expected from you. And if this is all you've got to say to me, then I might as well go in. *Is* this all you've got to say?'

John drew a deep breath, strove to find a way of saying . . . But no. Ashes, defeat. 'Don't marry him,' was all he could say, shoulders slumping; and again, 'Don't marry him.'

Catherine studied him, her smooth brow puckered in a frown in which perplexity, fondness, and impatience were all to be seen. The latter won. 'I'm sorry, John. I truly can't see any point in listening to this. I must go.' A pause, in which she seemed to hesitate over whether to give him her hand; but then she resolved it by awkwardly smoothing her glove, and turned quickly, murmuring goodbye, and left him.

Ashes, defeat: he supposed he had tasted them to the full now, even though he knew he would get but a cold reception from Verity when he met her again. But the extent of his defeat, and the bitterness of the ashes, were not known to him until that evening; when, after being an absent-minded hindrance to Dr Appleyard all day, he was granted a grudging permission by that stern gentleman to absent himself from dinner, and go out.

With one destination in his mind, of course: Verity's lodging. Miss Thimblebee was so fearsomely correct that even he, who was well known to her, had never been allowed to call on Verity there – they had to rendezvous in the chaste publicity of the street outside. But now there was no help for it. The confusion of angry and frustrated feeling in which he had spent the day had been shot through with one urgent certainty. He must see Verity, and—

And what? He did not know: did not know what he would say to her. There might be no question of his saying anything – he might be pounded into silence by volleys of scorn and indignation. Very well, if so. The important thing was to see her.

Ashes, defeat: she was not there, and was not to be sought there. Miss Thimblebee, allowing him no further than the foot of the stairs, and standing five steps above him holding a crochet-hook which, her expression seemed to say, she would not hesitate to use, told him that Miss Deene was no longer resident in her upper apartments.

'How so?' said John.

'I must decline, Mr Twopenny, to respond to so monosyllabic an interrogative,' said Miss Thimblebee, in her most starched manner.

'Please, Miss Thimblebee . . .' John made a rash attempt to place his foot on the next stair, but was discouraged by a flourish of the crochet-hook. 'I must see Miss Deene – it is a matter of the greatest importance . . .' Why was it? No matter: it just was. 'If she is in—'

'I am obliged to repeat, Mr Twopenny, as your conduct is so ungovernable, that Miss Deene is not here, and is not to be found here. She has vacated those rooms which I was wont to call my single gentlemen's apartments, before I made her amiable acquaintance; in short, she no longer lives here.'

'But where has she gone?'

'She has gone to another place,' said Miss Thimblebee, unconsciously parliamentary in her language; and added, with another flourish of the crochet-hook, 'I am expressly forbidden to say precisely where. That is – and believe me, Mr

Twopenny, this impoliteness is very repugnant to my feelings – I am expressly forbidden to tell *you* where she has gone.'

John, his mind in a ferment, placed his foot on the next stair again, and earned a squeak of reproof from Miss Thimblebee. 'Mr Twopenny, I really must ask you to desist from this behaviour which only decorum prevents me from comparing with that of a Bull in a china shop, and be content with my assurances that Miss Deene is not here, is not to be expected here in the near future, and has removed to an address which I am forbidden to disclose. I gave my word that I would not disclose it to – pardon me, to you, Mr Twopenny; and though it is far from my habit to draw my figurative language from natural history in this manner, the exceptional circumstances force me to avow that Wild Horses would not drag it from me.' Miss Thimblebee looked so discomfited at the very idea of wild horses, that John would not have had the heart to press her – if, that is, his heart had not been so anxiously involved in this matter. But pressing her did not avail: she was firm, and at last informed him that if he did not desist she would be obliged to summon her domestic; and so he went away at last, wondering and desponding.

Desponding, but not utterly despondent: for their mutual connection with the Appleyards meant he could surely trace Verity through them. He was disabused of this notion in short order when he returned to Great Russell Street, where dinner was over, and the Appleyards were just getting out their instruments. Miss Jemima answered his inquiries with horsy asperity, tuning her cello the while. Miss Deene? Miss Deene was not to join them tonight. Regrettably, Miss Deene could no longer make a fourth in their musical evenings, and was not to be expected at this house in future: this was Miss Deene's own decision. Might he see Miss Deene at the Field Lane Ragged School tomorrow? No, he might not: Miss Deene was not to teach there any more, at her own request – she had asked to be transferred to one of the other establishments run by the Ragged Schools' Union, and Miss Jemima had been happy to facilitate her request. Might he ask to which school Miss Deene had transferred? He might indeed ask, but Miss Jemima was absolutely not at liberty to tell him, on Miss Deene's explicit instructions; and now, if he did not mind, they wished to proceed with their musical evening. And so John retired in defeat, and sat himself down, and formed the unheeding audience to some turgid scrapings which had proceeded from the laboured pen of a dreadful monster called Krumpholz, and brooded.

She had fled from him. Hurt, angry, and disdainful, Verity had rung down the curtain on their relation with typical thoroughness, and fled from him. He should have known that for all her clear-headed practicality, Verity was both ardent and absolute where her feelings were concerned. He had failed her. It was no prideful conceit, he saw, that had made her cut herself off from him thus – rather, the opposite: she had supposed herself incompletely loved, and rather than being outraged at this, had bitterly accepted it, and withdrawn. Yes, he saw it, in a flash of regretful perception: without self-pity, only harsh sadness, she had looked upon him last night, and said to herself: 'I knew it! He cares for her more than me!' and had gone away, and taken refuge in a stern citadel of pride.

And there was no blaming her. He saw that, too late.

He could not find her. There was no breaching the defences of either Miss Thimblebee or Miss Jemima; and if, over the ensuing days and weeks, he deplored Verity's ability to fence herself about with strong-minded spinsters, that was only his frustration coming out – and his despair. As for Dr Appleyard, he was far from a weak vessel, and if he knew where Verity was, it would have taken more force than John could command to get it out of him. That the old physician did not like this rift between two lovers whom he had done much to unite, was plain from his bearing, which was both resigned and unapproachable; and he was once or twice heard to remark, at the conclusion of some deathly sonata, that the music had lost its sparkle without Miss Deene. But to John all this was of no account beside the simple fact that Verity seemed lost to him. And it was the reappearance of Marcus Goodway in his life that had caused it! Reinforcement, if any were needed, to his hatred of that man. Everything in John's life that he touched, he destroyed.

And yet not so. John began to know it, in those bleak weeks that followed Verity's disappearance. The monstrous truth that he could not tell Verity squatted on his chest when he lay in bed at night, and clung to his back when he went about his work in the day; and the more insistent its presence was, the more his heart demanded to know why he could not tell it to Verity. What was Verity to him, then? Nothing? No, a million times no. Less than everything? No – another million times no. Very well then. Of all the people in the world, whom could he entrust with the secret of his parents' shame, not merely in the confidence of her not betraying it, but of her understanding it to the uttermost, and defending the sanctity of the memory to the last breath as he would?

Verity. Only she. And he could not find her – and feared that even if he could, she would not reach out her hand to him across the abyss.

CHAPTER TEN

An Example and a Warning

Newgate! The very word was like a stroke upon an awful drum. There were other prisons in London, some deserving an ill repute just as terrible as that of the grim old establishment in the heart of the City; but Newgate it was that still had the power to chill the spine, and to impress as a fearful monument to the darker capacities of the human animal.

Seventy-odd years ago, when the Gordon Riots had put a match to the gunpowdery mixture that was London's underworld, Newgate had been the principal target of the mob's wrath, and they had burnt it to the ground; but it had been rebuilt, in even more massive a fashion than before, and now its high, thick, rusticated walls, with their huge pediments and deep-set grated windows and crown of spiked bars, looked invulnerable to anything short of attack by siege-engines.

Dr Appleyard, as consulting physician to the prison authorities, was familiar with the interior of Newgate as few non-felons were; but he had never taken his assistant along on his visits there, until a day in early March, when he signalled to John that the time had come for him to pass through the great iron-nailed gates with him, and see the forbidding spectacle with his own eyes. 'There is one wretch I am to attend in particular, whom I would wish you to see as a dreadful example and warning to our profession,' Dr Appleyard remarked, as they waited for the turnkey to admit them at the door of the governor's house; but he said no more, and they were both silent as they were conducted through a succession of lodges and gates, and along a stone passage which imparted such an oppressive sensation that it might have been a vertical shaft leading directly downwards into the bowels of the earth.

It was impossible for John not to be profoundly affected by the dismal sights, sounds, and smells of Newgate; but it was impossible, too, for him to shake off his own darkness, or to see in the denizens of this place anything but a bleak reflection of a general doom. Extreme perhaps: but his sense of failure and loss was extreme too.

A month had passed with no word from Verity, and no indication of where he might find her. She had removed herself from his life; but he knew now that she was merely carrying to its logical conclusion what had begun in the Fernhills' reception-rooms. As far as she was concerned, the separation between them had been all but complete then, and physical separation was only the finishing touch.

Well: no use thinking of what he could have said, should have said, and all the rest of it. After passing through an initial phase of angry indignation that she should doubt him, he had rapidly come up against the stern truth that the failure was his. There had been a failure in trust, in confidence – in love, if you liked; however much, and however genuinely his heart might protest the truth of his love for Verity, the fact was he had failed to demonstrate it at the crucial moment.

And yet he must, must find her. It might be that it was too late – it might be that that demonstration of his love which he had omitted before was worthless coming

314

now; but he must try. Out of the very truth of that love, he must try – beat himself senseless at the closed gates of her heart, if need be; nothing less was owed to his feeling for her. But first he must find her, and he had yet to gain a single indication of where she might be. Miss Thimblebee was resolutely not at home to him: Miss Jemima was obdurate. He used such free time as he had in combing London for every charity-school he could find, but with no luck. Hope often quite deserted him; but he went doggedly on without it, because not to do so was to surrender everything.

Whether Dr Appleyard was impatient with his brooding mood, and had chosen this expedient to jolt him out of it, John did not know. Certainly the interior of Newgate prison was enough to make any man count his blessings. A whole inverted world was contained here, only a few yards from the busy streets of the City. There were great subterranean kitchens, there was a chapel, there was an infirmary, there was a schoolroom for the juvenile inmates; and there was even an equivalent to the system of social class that prevailed outside, for one ward of the building was set aside for prisoners of the 'respectable' sort. And it was to this ward that Dr Appleyard led John, to show him that cautionary sight of which he had spoken.

'This man's trial has been deferred, as there is a good deal of evidence to be collected. He is a physician, John; in his day, I would imagine, a good one. Misfortune, disappointment, drink, opium and other dissipations – all had their share, I believe, in reducing him to the creature you shall see; but he is an example and a warning, because it can happen to any of us, once we slacken our moral sinew even for a moment.' Dr Appleyard threw John one of his most skewering glances, and seemed to refrain from comment on the condition of his assistant's moral sinew. 'I cannot help feeling a certain partisan interest in one of my fellow-practitioners, even so degraded a one as this; but I need seek no excuse for visiting him. The abuses he has inflicted on his body warrant medical attention. He is improving now, but it seemed for a while as if he would not survive to be tried. His name is Spruce – the most inappropriate of names, alas, for the lamentable condition he is in—'

'Not Frank Spruce?' said John with a start.

'It is. You have heard of him?'

'I know him. At least – he was a friend and colleague of my father's, years ago; and when I first came to London, I sought him out in the hope that he might set me on the path to a medical career. He was in a poor way then, and told me to abandon the idea, lest I end up like him – but still, I never dreamed . . .' John recalled that haggard, diminished figure, uncorking his second bottle in his drab parlour as he demolished John's airy castles with a few embittered words. 'Good God, what has he done, to be confined in this place?'

'Gross medical malpractice, if you want the legal term,' said Dr Appleyard, as they waited for yet another of the iron-studded doors to be opened. 'The old story, in other words: selling drugs to anyone prepared to pay for them for any purpose, and undertaking to perform abortions likewise. Some poor wretch died from the latter, and that set the law on to him. As I say, the evidence is still being collected.'

'Dear God . . .' John breathed, 'not Frank Spruce . . .'

'I'm sorry that he should be known to you, John, and yet I am not sorry,' said Dr Appleyard crisply. 'It will make the illustration all the more forcible, for – now, what the devil's happened here?'

They had come to the ward set aside for the 'respectable' prisoners, a long bare whitewashed room overlooking its own yard, and found it in a state of utmost confusion, with the whole complement of prisoners milling round one of their number who seemed to be fainting, or at least under the necessity of being supported. The jailer wading in amongst them, and ordering them to stand away,

315

presently revealed the figure of Frank Spruce himself, who was being held up by two fellow-prisoners and made to walk up and down the room. A kindly and well-advised move, as Dr Appleyard, taking charge until the jail surgeon could be summoned, soon found; for Frank Spruce had got hold of some poisonous substance, and introduced it through a vein with professional exactness. Fortunately his jailers had been watchful of him in case of just such an eventuality, and the wretched man had not been able to procure any dose sufficient to his purpose. The jail surgeon, arriving, administered swift emetics; and Frank Spruce, who had shown himself refractory before, was consigned to a solitary cell adjoining the infirmary to recover, Dr Appleyard undertaking to watch over him.

It was a scene to sober any man: the stone cell with its single iron candlestick, its wooden bench on which Dr Appleyard and John took their uncomfortable station, and its narrow cot where the sallow, emaciated wreck that had been Frank Spruce coughed and groaned from the effect of the emetics, occasionally asking for water, but otherwise seeming to take little note of his two companions. At length, however, he sat up, and ran his hand through the matted curls that were the only remnant of the boyishly handsome man he had once been, and said in a low, exhausted voice, 'Dr Appleyard . . . you have taken a good deal of trouble over me, once again.'

'I cannot be indifferent to the fate of anyone, but least of all a brother physician, even—'

'Even so broken and contemptible a one as I.' Dr Spruce gave a saturnine smile; then focused his bloodshot eyes on John, and frowned.

'My assistant,' Dr Appleyard said. 'Mr John Twopenny. I understand that you have met before.'

'Well, well, John Twopenny.' Dr Spruce's smile grew sourer still. 'Forgive me not recognizing you, John. It comes of only associating with felons nowadays. A pretty place to meet up again, is it not? And so, you did not take my advice? John came to me, you know, Dr Appleyard, as an old colleague of his father's, all aflame with idealism for the medical profession, and wanting to know how to go about entering it. I cordially advised him to avoid it like the plague. Why did you disdain the advice, John Twopenny? Was I not a sufficiently discouraging example as you saw me that day? I certainly am now, am I not?'

'An example, perhaps,' said Dr Appleyard, 'but an example to dissuade a man from other things than medicine.'

'Ah, Dr Appleyard, you have begun to preach. That is a pity, and not like you. Well, now you have given your pupil a good sight of me, and he must be suitably chastened. Perhaps I should start charging for admission. A living exhibit that no medical student should omit from his education. Gather round, gentlemen, and see the Awful Warning in the flesh. What do you think, John?'

John felt pity for him, but he instinctively knew that that was what Frank Spruce would hate most of all. 'I – I'm glad to see you for old times' sake, Dr Spruce,' he said. 'And I did try to follow your advice, but . . . it didn't fall out somehow.'

'Well, you might have done worse. Appleyard isn't a bad old stick, though he won't thank *me* for a compliment.' Dr Spruce swung his legs off the bed, and made a gingerly attempt to stand upright.

'Be careful, Spruce,' said Dr Appleyard, 'don't overtax yourself.'

'Ah, rubbish,' said Dr Spruce, standing unsteadily. 'I know what I'm doing. You forget, my good friend, that I am a doctor. Graduate of Cambridge, licentiate of the Royal College of Physicians, and generally infallible. Better qualified, I might add, than the resident surgeon of this choice establishment.' Dr Spruce ran a rasping hand across his chin and regarded Dr Appleyard covertly. 'The buffoon will not even allow me a single grain of opium, though he must know how it will benefit me. Now you, Dr Appleyard—'

'Will not allow you a single grain of opium either, so don't ask it,' said Dr Appleyard, with his dry sniff. 'And from what has just happened, I would be a fool to supply you with anything. What in God's name were you trying to do?'

'Why, make my quietus with a bare bodkin, or rather with a doubtful potassium preparation, of course, I would have thought it was obvious,' said Dr Spruce rapidly, with a glassy look. 'What else did you suppose? A little chemical experiment, just for the scholarly fun of it?'

'*Why*, is the question that concerns me,' said Dr Appleyard, springing up and impatiently pacing the narrow cell. 'Are you a coward, man? You are to stand trial, for offences that you have as good as admitted. Can you not face it like a man, instead of hiding from it?'

'Face it? You don't know what you're talking about,' said Dr Spruce, burying his hands in his disordered hair, and frowning moodily at the floor. 'You don't know – you have no conception of what I have to face, every morning when I wake and every night when I lay myself down. What I have to face in *here*' – giving himself a violent cuff across the head. 'All very well, Dr Appleyard, all very well to face such things when you are at liberty, and there is always the bottle or the opium-pipe to make them look better; but try facing them out in such a place as this, where there is nothing to do but think of the past, and you are forever at the mercy of memory, that most pitiless of enemies to the reason and the conscience . . . If you could begin to understand *that*, you might begin to understand something, Dr Appleyard; but until you do, don't talk to me of *facing* it.'

'Give me the opportunity, then,' said Dr Appleyard, in an unmoved tone, tucking his long hands beneath his coat-tails. 'Give me the opportunity to understand. Tell me these things you have to face, and of which I have no conception. Do they differ from what I already know? For I have already heard about the malpractice of which you are accused. And about that I—'

'If it were only that!' cried Dr Spruce, with a broken laugh, and a gesture to John of a sort of terrible appeal. 'John, my friend, if it were only that! At least that could be construed, taking a *very* generous view, as not contrary to my Hippocratic oath. People desire certain drugs? Very well, they shall have them. Women desire to rid themselves of a pregnancy? Very well, I try to oblige. The intention is pure if not the result . . . Oh, I am talking nonsense, I know. Don't, I beg you, think me such a fool as to dismiss these things out of hand. It is reflecting on them, indeed, that has led me into these deeper and darker tracks, and revived memories that I had hoped to kill with the blessed opium . . . I might kill them yet, you know. I believe they are not indestructible – and if one grain – if you were to see your way to one grain—'

'In the name of God, man,' cried Dr Appleyard, whose ingrained harshness of expression had become fiercer as Frank Spruce's words had become wilder, and who now darted forward and seized the wretched man's shoulder in a strong grip, 'in the name of God, if you have some other professional crime on your conscience, let it out now: it can scarcely harm your cause, certainly not to the extent it is harming your mind. In the name of God, man, let it out.'

'What? In the name of God, you say?' said Dr Spruce, shrugging off the older man's hand. 'No, no, pardon me, I must be excused there, Dr Appleyard. I worked, when what I did was worthy of the word, in the name of man. When I attended a dying child in some dismal pest-hole, it always tended to be poor despised sinful old humanity, in the shape of some sorrowing parent or grandparent or even neighbour, who was present to give the suffering creature what comfort there was to be had. I attended many such, but I never saw God there. I never saw God stroke the hair from a burning brow. I never saw God clean the loins of a child

317

that had fouled itself in its agony, or carry away the trays of sputum and blood. Perhaps my sight was at fault, but upon my soul I never saw God on any of these occasions on which He might surely have chosen to justify His benevolent reputation. So don't, I beg you, Dr Appleyard, prate to me about God's name.'

Dr Appleyard had turned pale. 'You go too far,' he snapped. 'Really, Spruce, you go too far in this, and—'

'No, Dr Appleyard, surely not.' It was John who had spoken; and rare indeed were the occasions on which he presumed to contradict the testy old physician – as was amply demonstrated by the glare that Dr Appleyard now gave him. But John was moved, and would not retreat. 'This is surely something that any man who has devoted himself to medicine may with justice feel – I don't mean what he *should* feel, but what he *does* feel. It doesn't detract from anything Dr Spruce has to say.'

Dr Appleyard glared again; but then shrugged and said, 'Very well then. In the name of – in the name of the man and the physician you once were, Spruce, say what it is that plays on your mind.' And as Dr Spruce, after a surprised look at John, hid his face in his hands again and shook his head, the old man went on sharply, 'You are already to face stern justice, man. I don't see the necessity of concealment.'

Dr Spruce gave a long sigh, and lifted his head. 'True enough. True enough as far as my case goes, at any rate. And it is for that very reason that I have kept this secret. *Is* there justice, Dr Appleyard? John? Because what I have to tell demands it – and not just from me.'

Dr Appleyard sat down again on the bench, and fixed Frank Spruce's wayward eyes with his own. 'If you have anything on your conscience from which justice may come,' he said, 'then say it.'

Dr Spruce looked at them both in turn, slowly; then, knotting his fingers together and gazing at the stone floor, he began to talk. 'Very well,' he said. 'I am not proof against the luxurious pleasure of confession, and it can make little difference, as you said, to my case, and so I may as well let it out here and now. In truth, I'm tired of being the villain of the piece, and in this story I am not so; at least, not compared with the principal, and if it is not too late to come over all moral, he is the one who should be brought to justice. So: my one great shame is this.

'More than a year ago, I was called in to the sickbed of a gentleman's wife, over in the West End. It was sufficient indication that this was no straightforward business, and that I might be required to be less than truthful, that the gentleman called in such a broken wretch as I in the first place. He could have afforded the grandest, most carriage-driving, most fee-eating physician in London: instead he chose me – the most humiliated wretch of a doctor that the city had to offer, and accordingly open to a bribe. As I was: I do not pretend otherwise. The gentleman's wife was certainly ill; I was given to understand, and could easily conclude, that she had spent much of her life in a feeble state of health. She was more than ill, however. She was, when I was called in, on her deathbed. She was also with child, or had been shortly before I arrived; but she had lost it, and had contracted those severe internal injuries which I was very soon to diagnose as inoperable; and the reason for all this was, that she had been violently kicked in the stomach.'

Dr Spruce drew in a long breath. John, for his part, felt he could never breathe again: even Dr Appleyard's immovably stern face twitched as he gazed on the speaker.

'A drunkard and an opium-eater I may be,' went on Dr Spruce, knotting his fingers more tightly, 'but I have been a good physician in my time. I have the true doctor's eye – if not the true doctor's character. And that she had been kicked thus was perfectly plain to me. There were marks on her neck beside, which suggested she had been dragged about by the hair. She was sinking fast, and in no condition

318

to speak lucidly; but even if she had been, I had a strong impression that her fear of her husband was so great that it would have prevented her even now. The gentleman was agitated – but not very. It was clear that he knew quite well what he was about – that he had thought carefully after whatever mad passion had induced him to carry out this brutal assault. There were servants in the house, and both appearance and legal forms demanded that his wife, in her dreadful extremity, be medically attended. But it must be a doctor of a certain kind . . . my kind, in short. The kind who, though he saw, was prepared to pretend he had not seen. Who was prepared to sign a medical certificate asserting that the lady had died simply as a result of miscarrying her child, which her generally precarious state of health always made a likely eventuality. I may add that I thought it likely that the lady, in other circumstances, would have been able to carry the child to its full term, and that her infirmity did not appear life-threatening. And if the intuitions of someone like me are worth anything, I would further add my impression that the gentleman, to put it baldly, had rather expected to be rid of her before now; and that her continued stability of health, even through pregnancy, was somewhat dismaying to him. Well, the lady was past saving – I managed to convince myself that my Hippocratic oath bound me always to save if possible, but no more, and the law was not my concern; and she died in great pain that night.'

The knuckles of Dr Spruce's knotted fingers were as white as if the bone were showing through, and his jaws worked convulsively for some moments before he went on in a rush: 'The gentleman offered me a good deal of money. I was in debt, and living wretchedly; and my addictions required constant feeding. And so I took the money. I took the money, and I set down my professional opinion that the lady had died of the effects of a miscarried parturition; the lady, I suppose, was buried with her grieving husband standing at the graveside; and that was the end of it. And do you know what, out of the whole business, makes me hate myself the most? The fact that the man knew I would take the money. I do not believe he doubted, even for an instant, that he had found in me a sufficiently degraded instrument for his purpose; there was an abominable sort of twinkle in his eye as he looked at me, as if he saw right down into the depths of my heart, and cheerfully observed the corruption there.'

A terrible trembling, that seemed to begin in the pit of his stomach and spread outward, had begun to take possession of John. He did not know why. Why should this be?

'Well,' said Dr Spruce, 'there it is. You have heard all now, Dr Appleyard, and may begin to preach whenever you are ready.'

'I have heard all,' said Dr Appleyard after a grim pause, 'but it is not enough.'

'It's all there is,' said Dr Spruce with a harsh chuckle, throwing himself back on the bed.

'Not enough,' repeated Dr Appleyard. 'It is not enough for you to confess this to me and John. Don't you see, man? This must go to the law! The man you have spoken of is a murderer! He is still alive, still at large, I take it?'

'I presume so,' said Dr Spruce. 'How should he not be?'

'Then he should be brought to justice!' cried Dr Appleyard. 'Think of it, Spruce. The law can do little more to you: you already stand charged – it may even help your case if you make this confession—'

'You think so? I rather doubt it. Merely another misdemeanour to add to the list . . . However, it's true enough that I have little more to fear from the law, I suppose.'

'Very well, then. This thing has been weighing on your conscience: you have cleared it a little by telling the story to us; clear it further, by testifying to this before the law, and ensuring that the man whom you helped to escape justice is brought to account at last!'

'My conscience can never be entirely clear,' said Dr Spruce, brooding. 'I took that man's money, and signed that false certificate: that is a thing that can never be undone.'

'It can be paid for,' said Dr Appleyard. 'You are paying for it now. Put more credit in the balance, and testify to this story! Will you do it, Spruce? Will you . . .?'

Dr Spruce suddenly sat up. 'Well, the man was a vile brute; and I have long ago spent his money. Why not? Let him breathe the Newgate air, and see if he can smile then.'

'If what you tell us is true, he would not be breathing any air for long,' said Dr Appleyard sombrely. 'What is his name?'

'Goodway. Marcus Goodway. Dorset Square is his residence. Gentleman of means, whatever that means . . .'

And now the trembling had overtaken John completely, and the mortar between the stones of the cell was forming grotesque patterns before his eyes, and the bare floor seemed to be swooping away beneath him; and he squeezed his eyelids shut and pressed his hands to his temples, and seemed to hear Dr Appleyard asking him from the other end of a long tunnel whether he felt ill; and he could only nod his head, and then shake it, and murmur something that even he did not understand, whilst his mind groaned like an overburdened beast beneath this knowledge . . .

And then – he hardly knew how – he was outside the cell in the cold stone corridor, and Dr Appleyard's lean hand was supporting his arm, and a jailer was looking with a sort of professional interest in his face and saying, 'Yes, it's the air in here, sir. It *is* bad; but use is everything, and I'm used to it, and so are you, sir, coming here so often. I should come down to the lodge – it's a little sweeter there . . .'

'I'm all right,' said John, taking a deep breath. 'Just came over a little faint. I'm all right.'

Dr Appleyard studied him closely; but he said nothing until they had been conducted down to the turnkey's lodge, where he pressed John to sit down on a bench, and stood frowning down at him.

'John,' he said. 'This man – this Goodway – he is known to you?'

John nodded. 'He is known to me.'

Dr Appleyard's frown deepened. 'From what you know, then – have you reason to doubt Spruce's story?'

A wild profusion of images capered across John's mind's eye: his mother's face reflected in the window-glass, Saul grasping his hand across the rough workhouse blanket, the Soldier pulling him back from the threshold of the Hanged Man's House, Catherine shyly smiling across the Fernhills' drawing-room, a pair of strong hands reaching up to him from a creek on the foggy marsh . . .

'No,' he said, willing the visions to disperse: for his mind must be clear. There were important things to be done: vital things. 'No, no reason to doubt, Dr Appleyard. Quite the opposite.'

Dr Appleyard scrutinized him a moment longer, then nodded. 'Very well. Spruce has agreed to testify: I shall go to the police, and see to it that his deposition is taken, and anything else that may be required. Do you wish to come with me, John?'

'Yes!' said John springing up, 'yes, I will come with you'; and he would have responded with the same enthusiasm, and the same grim alacrity, if Dr Appleyard had proposed a barefoot walk to the North Pole – as long as Goodway, and the retribution he had so long evaded, was at the end of it.

CHAPTER ELEVEN

A Small Matter of Business

Sergeant Paradine is their man. He is large, fair, pink-lipped, stocky; soft-spoken, with a touch of soothing West Country in his accent; unemphatic and considering in his manner; dressed in the plainest of plain clothes, so that he might be a steady tradesman, a prosperous engineer, a grazier, a clerk in the post-office – anything almost; and similarly, might be any age between thirty and fifty.

There is also, for all his apparent blandness and deliberateness, something impressively swift and economical about the Sergeant. He knows what he wants, and he knows how to go about it, with the minimum of fuss, and requires only one word and a nod to understand you thoroughly. This is something of a relief to John and Dr Appleyard, for matters seemed to progress with a frustrating slowness at first. Their initial dealings with the Detective Force of the Metropolitan Police at Scotland Yard – a body of officers not very large, not very long established, and not very well known – involved a certain weighty Mr Inspector, who was cautiousness itself. Strongly interested in the case, certainly: but wishing to know everything about Dr Appleyard, about John, about Dr Spruce, about Mr Marcus Goodway, and not seeming to mind how long it took to know it. But now Dr Spruce's affidavit has been taken, and witnessed by a magistrate, and a warrant has been issued for Mr Marcus Goodway's arrest; and Mr Inspector, suddenly becoming as brisk as he was previously slow, has introduced them to Sergeant Paradine, with the simple recommendation, in which he conveys a world of approval and admiration, that he is their man.

Sergeant Paradine, then, is the detective officer assigned to the task of taking Marcus Goodway into custody for the suspected murder of his wife; and Sergeant Paradine accepts this assignment as coolly as if he were indeed some steady tradesman, who has been told that a parcel of linen has arrived for him at the coach-office, and he is to pick it up at his convenience. Sergeant Paradine having been acquainted with all the facts of the case by Mr Inspector, merely nods, and says that he has a pretty good idea of their man, and a fine specimen he sounds and no mistake, and let's go and take him.

And with those words the sergeant takes up John and Dr Appleyard, who have been kicking their heels for the third time in a dusty waiting-room, and fairly propels them out, and has them in a hackney-coach almost before they know they have left the police-station.

'Now then, gentlemen,' says the sergeant, 'here's a slightly curious case, with the principal witness in prison. We can't take *him* along, for we haven't a chain long enough. But you're acquainted with our man, ain't you, sir?' – patting John's knee.

'I know him,' answers John.

'And you don't sound overjoyed to have his acquaintance, sir, I must say. Never mind! I shan't want you much, sir: hardly at all, I hope, if we can find our man at home; just a nod to say that's him. And off we go to Dorset Square!' with a sudden rap upon the coach roof, that seems to communicate itself directly to the horse, so instantly are they whisked away.

No stir is caused by the arrival of a hackney-coach in Dorset Square – why should it be? – and the genteel street is quiet as Sergeant Paradine gets down, and casually tells the other two to remain there while he sees to a little matter of business. He gives a glance up at the windows of the tall house as he mounts the steps, and does not seem to like what his observant eye sees; and very soon returns to the hackney, after a few words with the old woman who answered the door.

'I thought as much by the look of the place,' says the sergeant, smoothing his light hair. 'All closed up for the summer – dust-sheets and curtains. Only a charwoman a-clearing the place up. It seems our man was married again – just yesterday; and him and his bride set off for the country this morning, the woman doesn't know where.'

'Oh dear God . . .' The words escape John's lips before he can prevent them; and for a moment he is afraid he is going to plunge into that darkness and dizziness that overcame him in Dr Spruce's cell. The thought of the gentle Catherine with that man has been the one thought, since Dr Spruce's confession, that he has striven to keep from his mind; and it is, of course, the one thought he has been unable to prevent, any more than he can prevent himself by mere effort of will from blinking.

'Ah! Not the sort of chap you'd wish to see married again, that's for sure,' says the sergeant, with a close look at John. 'But never mind! As you're acquainted with our man, sir, perhaps you know who the lady is, and who her people are, and so on. That'll help, if you can tell us that, you know.'

John knows, and tells; and with the same smart rap upon the coach roof, and the same astonishing responsiveness on the part of the horse, they are whisked away to Portland Place, where the sergeant goes through the motions as before, and presents himself at Admiral Fernhill's door, requiring to speak with that nautical worthy on a little matter of business. He is admitted, and this time he is gone longer – though not above fifteen minutes; and that might have been shorter, he remarks as he returns to the hackney-coach, if the lady of the house had not been a little agitated at the presence of a police-officer in her house, to the extent that all she could do was repeat that she really mustn't be bothered in this way, or she didn't know what would happen.

'Well, our man was married from that house yesterday,' says Sergeant Paradine, smoothing his light hair again, 'and a regular slap-bang affair it was, apparently. And this morning the happy couple set off for our man's country place, according to the admiral – now there's a fine-looking gentleman! There's a head! Anyway, Norfolk's where they've gone: Beacon House, near Hales-next-the-sea, is our man's country place; and according to the admiral (what a head!) they're going to spend their honeymoon afloat, weather permitting, on account of our man having a pleasure-yacht at a place called Blakeney. Called the boat the *Catherine*, apparently, after his bride . . . Never mind, sir!' – observing John's expression. 'We'll take our man, don't you worry. Now look here. That's where you got acquainted with our man, ain't it? Your part of the world, up in Norfolk?'

'That's where I first knew him,' says John, oppressed with dark memory. 'God forgive me, I even helped him when he was stranded on the marsh once, and would have perished.'

'Did you now? But there's never any telling, you see. I could tell you some tales – and I'd like to, but I can't, because I haven't the time. Not when we've still got our man to take. Now I'm no Norfolk man. I could find these places out, no doubt, but I'll find them quicker with you there to guide me; and you know our man, whereas I wouldn't know him from Adam. Are you ready to go with me?'

No hesitation. John is ready.

'And what about you, sir?' says the sergeant to Dr Appleyard. 'You were instrumental in a-bringing of the charges, and you may like to see it through; but it'll be a powerful lot of travelling, I advise you.'

Dr Appleyard looks at John. Though John has said nothing of it, the sharp old man has seen that this is more than a matter of abstract justice for his young assistant, and that he has reasons of his own to abominate their quarry; and, typically, he takes those reasons on trust.

'I will come,' says Dr Appleyard, as much to John as to the sergeant, 'yes, I will come with you.'

'All right: it may – I only say may – be as well to have a physician on hand. One thing I must ask of you both, and I'll sure you'll understand why, is that you act completely under my direction, until our man's taken. No acting on your own account, if you please. Very well: we're off.'

And so they are, as rapidly as before; and are set down at the railway-station at Fenchurch Street, where Dr Appleyard sends a post-boy with a note to Miss Jemima explaining their absence, and saying they may be gone overnight. For the day is fast waning now, and they are only just in time for the last Norwich train before the evening: Sergeant Paradine boarding it, however, in spite of whistles and slamming doors, quite as calmly as if he were the engine-driver, and knew that it could not possibly go without him.

Away, then: with the railway, very like the sergeant in its directness, cutting its arrow-like way straight through the city that is so tangled and laborious to the passenger by foot and horse, and soon leaving it behind, and plunging into the country, and dealing with its topographical vagaries as summarily as it had dealt with the city's: hurling itself across rivers, and ploughing its way through hills, and lifting itself up above low-lying meadows, and cutting across farm and village with the completest disregard for trespass; just as if it is bent upon its terminus as the sergeant is bent upon his man, and is going to take it at all costs.

The sergeant, meanwhile, with his characteristic economy, sees that nothing further can be done while the journey is in progress; and so settles himself comfortably in the carriage, crosses his legs, smooths his light hair, and takes the opportunity of asking Dr Appleyard some questions about his mother-in-law's lumbago, which that lady is apparently convinced has got up into her head. The sergeant rather doubts that this is possible, but wouldn't care to say so downright, without seeking a medical opinion first. And is led on thereby to a musing consideration of the ailments of various other members of his family, and such general reflections as how none of them could eat shellfish without coming up in pimples; interrupting himself only to remark casually to John – whose own haggard and baleful aspect has become clear to him from his reflection in the darkening carriage-window – that he shouldn't worry himself, as worrying wasn't going to help them take their man. 'And I *am* going to take our man, sir,' says Sergeant Paradine, tapping John's knee. 'I'm not a man to make rash promises, but I will promise you this: I shan't sleep till I've got him in custody. Not one wink. And now, being a medical man yourself, sir, or as good as, what do you reckon to my great-aunt getting a fit of the sneezes whenever there was a cheese in the room . . .?'

On, then: across the flats of Anglia, trailing a banner of fiery smuts, and glimpsing on either side what seem at first to be other fires burning in the placid fields, but quickly resolve themselves into reflections of the setting sun, blazing as it dies, in flood-meadows and meres. On, then: with three faces that, to anyone idling at a country halt who happens to see them in the carriage-window, must present a curious contrast – the eldest face narrow, almost skull-like in the lamplight, and austerely patient; the youngest face nervous and mobile, with impatience contending with resolve in its pale features; the third face, large, fair and bland and, though there is nothing secret about it, absolutely unreadable in its repose.

Oh, then: with the sun surrendering to the level horizon at last, and the landscape reduced to hints and dim shapes, and Sergeant Paradine calmly chatting on – just as he would chat on, John thinks, if that extinguishing in the sky were not mere nightfall, but apocalypse. And then very suddenly the sergeant's demeanour changes: he glances out of the window, uncrosses his legs, announces they are nearly there, and instantly becomes the detective-officer again; seeming to have divined supernaturally that Norwich is at hand – for here come the first lights of the outskirts – even though John, who knows the country, had no idea.

'Now, sirs, it's my intention, if it can be done, to take our man tonight,' says the sergeant, with a finger on each of their knees. 'We might put up here for the night, and go and take him in the morning; but I'll tell you why I'm against that. It's that sailing I don't like. A man on a pleasure-yacht's a devilish hard man to take, you see. A man on a pleasure-yacht can go anywhere he likes; in fact a man on a pleasure-yacht may well decide, if he gets wind of police-officers wishing to speak to him, to sail that pleasure-yacht clear away from old England's shores. That's why I'd as soon take him tonight – assuming that him and his bride have unpacking to do today, and so on, and ain't likely to set sail just yet. So, I propose to hire a post-chaise, or whatever's to be got in Norwich; and if you can be our navigator, Mr Twopenny, we'll light out for the coast tonight, and have him. All right, sirs: off we go!'

The train is hardly stationary before Sergeant Paradine is out on the platform, and weaving a deft way between the crowds of passengers and porters, with John and Dr Appleyard hurrying in his wake. Their best bet for carriage-hire, John says, is the Thorpe Hotel near the station, which has extensive stabling – it's that way . . . Sergeant Paradine is already halfway there. The big hotel is busy, but the sergeant, somehow, manages to be attended at once, and bespeaks a post-chaise and the freshest horses in the hotel's stables. And a man to drive? The hotelkeeper is not so sure about that; but the sergeant's bland persuasiveness is too much for him, and a driver is found. All this in a twinkling; and then the sergeant is steering John and Dr Appleyard into the coffee-room.

'They're bringing the chay out to the yard, and they'll call us when it's ready,' he says, beckoning a waiter with his eye. 'And in the meantime, I think we should fortify ourselves. What do you say to brandy-and-water? Brandy-and-water all round, my friend, and whatever you've got cold in the kitchens, that we can eat quick and convenient. There'll be another shilling on top of that one, if you can bring it in two minutes.'

The waiter can, and does. The sergeant disposes of his portion of the viands before John and Dr Appleyard have barely started, and, taking pity on their non-constabulary frailty, gives them a minute or two to finish, while he goes to consult with the hotelkeeper about the roads to the north coast. There is a diamond-paned window in the coffee-room, overlooking the yard, and John looks out to see if their post-chaise has been made ready yet. There are several equipages drawn up there: one with the horses in the traces, and ready to be off. Theirs? No: a private carriage, by the looks of it, and a well-appointed one. A gentleman in a travelling-coat is there, giving instructions to the coachman. And as he speaks, the gentleman turns and presents his profile for a moment.

Is it the fumes of the brandy? Is it the fact that that man has never been out of John's thoughts all day, and his mind is playing tricks accordingly?

It is not. The gentleman in the travelling-coat, about to step into his private carriage, is Mr Marcus Goodway.

A hasty word to Dr Appleyard, and then John is scrambling out of the coffee-room, and into a passage with a dismaying number of turnings. Where,

where is the sergeant . . .? Hastily he turns, and runs straight into him.

'Steady, sir, what's amiss . . .?'

Goodway, Goodway. John is shaking, but the sergeant is if anything more calm and swift than ever. 'Now, sir, point him out to me,' he says, steering John back to the coffee-room window, 'just a moment for formal identification – that's our man? Very good. Waiter, what's that room there . . .? Private supper-room? I want it, if you please, and there's another shilling for you if you *run* out to that gentleman, Mr Goodway, and say there's a gentleman wishes to see him in the supper-room, small matter of business, sharp now! Mr Twopenny, Doctor, stay out of the way if you please, and with luck it'll all be over in a trice—' and even as he finishes speaking, the sergeant is slipping into the private room, and pulling the door to behind him.

John has strong misgivings, remembering those large powerful hands that had gripped his when he had pulled Goodway from the marsh; but Dr Appleyard insists that the officer is used to dangerous men and knows what he is doing, and makes John come to the other end of the coffee-room with him and pretend to look over some newspapers there. Still, John cannot help but turn his head when the door opens, and Marcus Goodway enters the coffee-room with a look of faintest impatience on his handsome face. Dr Appleyard puts a warning hand on his arm, and John nods; but it is with difficulty that he suppresses those images of his parents' graves, which have been joined now by a vision of the wan, pretty face of the late Mrs Grace Goodway; with difficulty that he prevents himself from flying at that fresh-coloured, curly-haired man crossing the coffee-room with his confident stride, and laying his hand on the door of the private supper-room.

It is opened; closed: he is in. John shuts his eyes a moment, hardly breathing; and thinks of that carriage outside, and the newlywed Catherine surely within it. What will she think, what *can* she think when her husband's crime is revealed – when she learns what the man whose bed she has shared, though so briefly, is capable of? Will her mind be able to bear it . . .?

Confused sounds from the private room: a heavy, dreadful noise. John shakes off Dr Appleyard's hand, and starts forward as the door is flung open.

Goodway, face wild and contorted, running at full tilt, knocking a potboy sprawling, and out into the yard. John leaping, shouting in pursuit; but too late. A shout from Goodway to his coachman, and he is into the carriage, the door swinging shut behind him as the vehicle lurches and buckets out of the yard gate, and rattles pell-mell away into the night.

Dr Appleyard is in the private room, and is lifting Sergeant Paradine from the floor. A pair of open handcuffs lie there: and there is blood too, amongst broken glass. Blood in the sergeant's hair. Serious hurt? Not serious hurt, though a less sturdy man might have felt it so. They help the sergeant to a chair, and send the potboy, who has picked himself up, for water and bandages, and Dr Appleyard attends to the sergeant's head.

'The devil!' says the sergeant, who is agitated, though not as much as most men would be. 'The damned, double-dyed devil, pardon my language! I've never been caught like that before. Phoo! I should have been ready for him when he snatched up the lamp – but it's as if he knew me almost before I spoke, and he had a start on me . . . Well, it's no use talking. He's off, I suppose? Ah. Never mind! I shall still take him. I wanted to take him before, and I very much want to take him now, and I shall. He knows he's pursued – that's a pity; it's so much neater to take a man when he don't know you're after him; and we shall have to take care, on account of the lady with him. But there – he can't run for ever. If our chay's ready, let's be off at once. Is that all right up there, Doctor?'

'Well, I've patched it up,' says Dr Appleyard. 'The gash is quite deep, and will need treating; and it will pain you.'

'Never mind – I'll have the pain later, when we've got our man.' Sergeant

Paradine is already on his feet, and making for the door. 'Much obliged, mind you, Doctor – capital chap to have along. Mr Twopenny, are you ready? This'll be a bit of a bone-shaker, I'm afraid, because we'll have to go like the wind. I've an idea where he'll be heading for. How far to Blakeney, Mr Twopenny?'

'About twenty miles.'

'Dear! Pity the horses. Never mind. In you go, sirs. We're off!'

And so, on again; but with no calm talk of great-aunts and shellfish this time – the sergeant crouching forward in the confined space of the post-chaise, and craning his head out of the window every few minutes, and bringing it in again with his hair all wild, and occasionally giving a smart rap on the roof to encourage the coachman. On, out of the narrow streets of the venerable city, and on to the post-road, with the coach-lamps momentarily catching trees and hedges and gateposts in weird sentinel attitudes; on, with a thunder and a rattle, into the quiet country of John's birth; with no sound or stir in all those dark-enfolded lanes and meadows and hamlets, and yet with every last twig and leaf that bends in the wind of their passing, and every stone that spins out beneath their growling wheels, seeming to John's taut nerves to cry out: Pursue him! Pursue him! Take him, take him, take him!

CHAPTER TWELVE

Mr Goodway's Shadow

'How can I make him happy?' This had been Catherine Fernhill's chief thought, on preparing to marry Mr Marcus Goodway.

It was the way she had been taught: woman as the ever-patient, ever-solicitous helpmeet of man was an ideal that had been held up before her since her infancy. And this ideal was most forcibly recommended to her by her parents; for Mrs Fernhill, as long as she was richly dressed, had been content all her life to bask in the glory reflected off the admiral's head, and always agree with everything he said. And the day before Catherine's wedding, Mrs Fernhill had even gone so far as to speak independently to her daughter on the subject of marriage – taking her aside, and bodying forth some extremely vague hints about a woman's duty being in submission, and her pride being in her duty, except she wasn't to be proud on any account, but not ashamed either because it was ordained as a patent remedy, or something. Hints so vague, indeed, that Catherine was forced to ask her mother what she was talking about: a challenge that that lady took so ill, that she declared quite hysterically that she mustn't be questioned in this way, or she didn't know what would happen; and retired precipitately into her dressing-room, to console herself by counting her shoes.

These, then, were Catherine's formative influences, in regard to her personal destiny. They might well have been counteracted, if she had been given so broad and unconventional an education and upbringing as Verity Deene, for example. But no such enlightened conditions prevailed in the household of Admiral Fernhill. And there was, besides, Catherine's character, which quite irrespective of convention, was uniformly trusting, gentle, yielding, unthrustful, and considerate. It was her nature to think more of giving than of receiving; and this tendency had come strongly to the fore when she had begun to be courted, not long after their arrival in London, by Mr Marcus Goodway. For she knew his circumstances: knew that he had nursed a sickly wife for years, a duty which he had performed with exemplary tenderness, and which must have been hard indeed upon a man of such vital spirits, robustness and sociability. He was a man, in short, who had lived with sadness; and his general affability, and refusal to make himself a heavy-eyed object of pity, only made this the more poignant.

To a great degree it was this that had attracted her to him, and made her contemplate becoming his wife. For all his brightness and frankness of manner, she detected something about him – something hidden and suppressed, that could only be the sadness of his first marriage. If he had been more obviously a man of sorrows, her sympathies would not have been so thoroughly engaged. But the sadness, it seemed to her, was always and only in the background, just lurking behind the cheerful smile and the voice of steady bronze and the twinkling grey eyes: lurking there, like a shadow.

And so when he courted her, and at last proposed to her, that shadow had much to do with her acceptance. The love for him came easily; she had never had any difficulty in loving. And she had perhaps been faintly aware of this fact, and

327

recognized that, for her, the love should be bolstered by something more when it came to so momentous an experience as marriage. And in her relation with Marcus Goodway, she thought she had found that something more. The shadow. He was a man who had been unhappy, and it seemed to her that if she could remove the shadow of that unhappiness, she could consider herself worthy of the honour he had bestowed on her by marrying her. For her natural modesty allied with convention, in leading her to suppose that it was he who conferred the honour and not she; and out of the same modesty she was far from complacent about her ability to make him happy. But she had resolved, as she tremblingly said Yes to him, that she would devote herself to trying, and not fail for want of effort. A certain sense of the aimlessness of her life, and its lack of earnest design, added its weight to this too; and her parents were so very pleased with the match that agreeing to marry Marcus Goodway seemed to her not only the right decision, but the best decision she had ever made. And so she married him.

Again, she was modest: she had little confidence in her own judgement. And so when the unpleasant surprises began, almost immediately after their wedding, it was her tendency to assume that she was at fault in being unpleasantly surprised.

It was unexpected, for example, to find Marcus behaving towards her when they were alone in a subtly different manner from when they were in company. If she had had to put it into words, she would have said that it was like the behaviour of a firm parent to a young child – tolerant within limits, but with a smacking in reserve when the limits were overstepped . . . But perhaps this was usual: she was, she admonished herself, rather innocent. What was more, Marcus was a good deal older than her, and had lived in the great world; and perhaps the way he had replied to something she had said after the wedding-breakfast – 'My dear, don't be so stupid, I beg you' – was common in that world: a sort of Society tone, that didn't mean anything.

Those doubts she managed, at least in part, to dismiss. The doubts that assailed her in the sore and sleepless hours of the wedding night were different. She had been protected from the facts of procreation as completely as a young lady of her time and class could be – which is to say, rather incompletely, given that she could read, that she had lived in the country, and she could put two and two together. She had had one or two wrong notions, but mainly right ones, and had not thought the experience sounded overwhelmingly disagreeable. And yet the painful operations to which her husband had subjected her . . . Was this, too, something quite usual and normal, which she was interpreting quite wrongly? Not just the operations – she could think of no other word – but the fierce, exultant, and uncaring stranger they made of her husband?

In the small hours of that night, indeed, the doubts had swelled in her mind to monstrous certainties. A man who could do such things, and at one particularly excruciating point break into a bright metallic laugh as he looked down at her . . . A whisper in her heart asserted that she had been both right and wrong about the shadow behind Marcus Goodway's eyes. The shadow was there: but it was not sadness. Oh, no, it was something very different from sadness.

And yet the morning after the wedding, in the way of mornings, brought hope. Marcus was his old agreeable self again; and there was fun and excitement in the preparations for going away to Norfolk. Beacon House! She remembered attending a Christmas party there when she was a girl (for she was a woman now, she thought, with a renewed awareness of the pain and the laughter) – yes, a Christmas party, with Verity there, and John, and dear Mr Flowers the lawyer . . . Little had she thought she would one day be the mistress of that house! And then there was the yacht too, that had been finished just in time for their marriage, and was waiting for them in Blakeney harbour, and that had been named for her. Fun and excitement, and Marcus as kind and attentive as she had ever known him: she gave herself up to these things, and devotedly believed that it would be all right.

And so it was. The railway journey as far as Norwich, Marcus genial all the way; the arrival at Norwich, where Marcus's private carriage had been sent down from the coast to meet them, and where he was completely good-humoured on learning that the carriage had arrived with a cracked hub, and would not be ready till it was repaired (though why had she feared his anger at this?); Marcus's cheerful suggestion that they make a day of it in Norwich, and drive on to Beacon House later; and the day in Norwich itself, with a lot of shopping, and a stroll about the Cathedral Close, and a little dinner at a riverside inn. No sign of the shadow at all – whether the shadow was sadness, or that dreadful otherness she had feared last night – through that whole day! And thus they had repaired at last to the Thorpe Hotel, where the carriage was now ready to take them to the coast. Their luggage was loaded, and Marcus handed her in, and spoke to the driver, about to get in himself; and then he was called back into the hotel to speak to someone.

The someone had discomposed him severely – that much was clear when Marcus came hurriedly back to the carriage, and flung himself in without a word, and they shot away at speed. Catherine could not think what the trouble might be, but she supposed that Marcus would tell her. And yet the carriage hurtled on – unthinkably fast, it seemed to her; and all Marcus did was thrust his head out of the window, and shout at the coachman up on the box to make haste, and then turn his head about to try and see the road behind them, as if he expected to see something there.

Not a word to her: the miles jolted and rattled sickeningly by, yet he spoke no word to her. He did not deign to reply to her timid remarks – merely threw her a glance whenever she spoke, a lowering, hooded glance, which had none of his old kindly sparkle in it – none. She ceased to speak for a while, because of that glance, and because of what she saw in it: the shadow. Not suppressed, but fully revealed; and whatever that shadow was, it was not sadness. And still her husband kept the carriage window down, in spite of the blast of cold night air, and thrust his strong face out time and again to shout to the coachman, and crane round to see the road behind them.

Why, why this haste, which was so dangerous on the dark country roads with only the flickering coach-lamps to guide them, and which was throwing her about the interior of the carriage so roughly that the bruises from last night were aching afresh? What had happened at the hotel, to give Marcus this dreadful look of a man dwelling in some other world than hers, and what did he think to see behind them on these quiet Norfolk roads, where there was scarcely a hoofbeat or a wheel besides theirs? If the idea were not so ridiculous, she would have thought him pursued – and judging by the intent and furious way he studied the road behind them, pursued by his own shadow!

But she could not ask these questions: she feared to. And she would have maintained her silence until they had reached their destination, if the headlong jolting, bumping and lurching of the carriage had not mingled with the memories of last night, and made her feel alarmingly sick.

'Marcus,' she said, breaking her silence, and trying not to heed the hard, swift look he darted upon her, 'Marcus, I'm so sorry, but I feel rather ill. Could we not slow down just a little?'

He did not reply to her at first; instead leaning out of the window again and peering into the darkness in their wake. 'No, my dear,' he said at last. 'I want to see Beacon House tonight, don't you?'

His tone was so curt that she was silenced again; but then the carriage lifting itself with a great heaving motion over a pothole, and coming down with a crash, she had to press her hand to her mouth, and cried: 'Marcus, please, I am going to be ill, so ill!'

'Do as you please,' said her husband, with a cool, and yet a heated look; and then thrust his head out of the window again.

'Marcus – oh, please, I beg you—'

'Dear God!' he hissed, ignoring her and staring at the road behind. 'Oh dear God, I see them!'

'Marcus!' She was too ill and afraid to bear it any more, and she seized his arm. He whipped round to face her; and though she saw nothing but the shadow now, and no brightness at all, she went on with a sob: 'Please, Marcus, we must stop . . . Marcus, please! What's wrong? What does it mean? Who's following you? For God's sake, tell me!'

'Be quiet.' He struck out, and hit her across the face, deftly.

A moment of shock, and then she began to scream. She hammered on the carriage roof, and he grabbed her wrists, and pulled them roughly down; still she screamed, and tried to call out of the window. He pulled her towards him, and they struggled together in the dark and violently swaying interior of the carriage; and then Mr Marcus Goodway, staring into his new wife's terrified eyes, seemed to come to an abrupt decision and, releasing her wrists, and bracing himself against the back of the seat, he kicked open the door with both feet, and with both feet he kicked Catherine out of the carriage, thumping the soles of his boots against her body until she was pushed out of the doorway, and was whisked rapidly out into the night with a flutter of an unwinding shawl.

CHAPTER THIRTEEN

The Work of Another Moment

They spotted the crumpled figure at the side of the road only because of the white gown she wore, as befitted a bride.

They had been closing in on their man, and his carriage, heavier than theirs with luggage, was in sight; but if Sergeant Paradine felt disappointment, as they pulled the post-chaise up beside that pathetic white form on the road and let their quarry speed out of sight, he did not show it. He murmured, 'Ah! Slowed him down, no doubt, and so he got rid – God save her!' as they jumped down from the post-chaise, and as John and Dr Appleyard knelt down beside Catherine where she lay. But as soon as they had established that she was alive – she was no more than that – the sergeant was all practicality and decision again.

'Doctor, here's two questions,' he said. 'One, can she be carried in the chay, without danger to her? – I'll mount up on the box to make room. Yes? That's well. Two, if we set you down with her at the next town or village – and I think I see lights up there, through the trees – can you make shift to care for her there, in an inn or a house or whatever I can get for you – meaning, that I would leave you there with her, and go on after our man?'

'She is injured,' said Dr Appleyard. 'How badly, I cannot tell here. But yes, let us carry her to some safe place, and I will do all I can.'

'Capital,' said the sergeant. 'And now, Mr Twopenny, tell me where we are, and how far to Blakeney – quick, sir, if you please!'

John, kneeling on the ground, looked up into the sergeant's commanding eyes, and forced himself to think. 'I believe – yes, that must be Holt up ahead – a large village. A couple of miles or so to Blakeney . . .'

They had to go slowly, for Catherine cried out when she was moved – not a full-blown cry of pain, but a sort of inward whimpering even more terrible to hear. It was doubtful whether she knew who was with her, or what was happening. Dr Appleyard said nothing, and revealed nothing in his expression; but John knew enough by now to realize that there were bones broken, and that they might be the least of it.

They found an inn at Holt – a large mossy old country inn with low lintels and acres of beeswaxed floorboards, and a landlord and landlady who were all anxious obligingness when the sergeant made the state of the case known to them. They prepared a room on the ground floor, which the landlady, in between lighting lamps and calling for basins of water and closing shutters, distractedly mentioned had been slept in by Oliver Crumble's wife, as if this might be of some consolation; and here Dr Appleyard and John laid the pale form of Catherine Goodway down.

'Is there a surgeon, a licensed apothecary of any sort at hand?' Dr Appleyard asked the landlady. 'I shall need help.' He looked at John and made a soothing gesture. 'You go, John. The sergeant may need you.'

John gave the broken figure on the bed a last look, and nodded. The sergeant's hand touched his elbow. 'Very good, Mr Twopenny,' he said. 'We're off, if you please.'

The sergeant had given instructions to water the tired horses, and they were a little fresher when the post-chaise set out again. 'He's got a start on us,' he said, 'but not so very much of a one, perhaps. Of course, I'm staking it all on him going to his boat, and making off that way; but bless you, I don't imagine he's just going to head for his country place, and sit there by the fire with a pipe, waiting for us to call on him. No, no, it's got to be his boat. I wish we had an almanac of the tides . . . Good harbour at Blakeney? Easy to get out on a night tide?'

'Not from the quay to the open sea,' said John. 'There's a good stretch of water before you get past Blakeney Point, and it's a slow business sometimes . . .' He was assailed by a memory of a white form lying in the road, and the sergeant saw it, and tapped his knee. 'I know, Mr Twopenny, I know,' he said. 'Why, I don't know the parties, and I feel the same. Never mind! There's only one thing to do, sir; only one thing to fix your mind on. And that thing is, take him. Take him, sir.'

Take him! Yes, take him: though the coats of the horses steamed and their muzzles frothed, and the axles of the post-chaise squealed, and the flying wheels plunged into deep ruts, and the whole lurching vehicle seemed in danger every minute of overturning. Take him: and make him face that justice to which he thought himself superior – yes, let him face it, for that very humiliation of being publicly dragged before his fellow mortals, and judged by them on the grounds of that common humanity he disdained, would be the bitterest gall to one of his nature. Take him!

Quiet, in the little port of Blakeney: lights glowing from the tumble of flint cottages, speaking of bolts snugly drawn and bright fires stirred, and no reason to be out in the dark, windy night. There was life in the little taverns down by the quayside, but that too sounded remote and innocuous – the notes of a fiddle or an accordion, snatches of laughter, the clink of glasses floating out on the salt air like echoes from a lost and better world. The post-chaise came to a halt on the quay, and the exhausted horses hung their heads where they stood; and John and the sergeant got down.

'Boats a-plenty,' murmured the sergeant, gazing across the harbour, where a three-quarter moon spangled the water and silvered the masts of vessels at anchor there, 'but I don't see anything that looks like a gentleman's pleasure-yacht. If he's slipped away, and we've lost him, I'll be hanged!' The sergeant bit his lip, and for the first time looked discomposed; and then at a faint sound down below the quay, he darted forward and peered down into the darkness. 'Ahoy there! Identify yourself, if you please: officer of the police!'

The sound, it turned out, proceeded from two youths who were tying up a rowing-boat at the quay. They had a bull's-eye lamp which they were trying to cover; and the reason for their general furtiveness, they tremulously confessed, was that they had slipped out for their nocturnal expedition without their fathers' knowledge, and would get a larruping if it was known. They must have been startled indeed, and supposed their fathers to have gone to extreme punitive lengths, to find an officer of the Metropolitan Detective Police accosting them; and came up the steps quite hollow-eyed with terror, until Sergeant Paradine reassured them.

'Now, lads, that's no concern of mine. But I'll tell you what is. A pleasure-yacht, name of the *Catherine*: know her?'

The boys knew her: she had been tied up here for a few weeks, and they had just passed her as they sculled into the harbour.

'Ah! Where away? Smart, now: there's a shilling on it.'

The boys, stammering eagerly in their relief, pointed out to where the shingle bank enclosed the harbour. There: see her lights? She was going out on the ebb, but she was heavy-built, and the gentleman sailing her didn't know how to keep the luff, and so she was making slow going of it.

'Mr Twopenny,' the sergeant said, with the steady light back in his eyes, 'can you row? That's well. Lads, here's another shilling says you'll let me borrow that rowing-boat of yours, and the lamp, and that you'll fetch the constable of the town and have him wait here for us on the quay. That's a lot for a shilling to say – make it two – and sharp now, Mr Twopenny, into the boat, and we're off!'

It was long since John had rowed; but the feel of it came back to him as soon as the sculls were in his hands, and they slipped swiftly out on the dark water, the sergeant holding the bull's-eye out at the bows and peering ahead to where the shape of the *Catherine* could be faintly seen, close to the mouth of the harbour with her stern towards them. The dried blood on the sergeant's bandaged head looked black in the lamplight; and marking this, and recalling Goodway's animal look as he had fled from the hotel, John said, 'How is it to be done? He is a dangerous man, and has nothing to lose.'

'So he is,' said the sergeant, 'and I shall have to be careful with him: also a mite forceful.' He touched his head reminiscently. 'I'll douse the lamp, and you rest on your oars, sir, as we come alongside – the tide should carry us in to her, and we mustn't make a sound that we can help. She looks pretty low in the water, and I reckon I can board her; and if our man won't be reasonable, I shall just have to be unreasonable with him, and treat him to a little of what he gave me. I'll give you one whistle to say, All right: two whistles if things turn nasty and I need you up there. Now, Mr Twopenny, let her run, and not a word; and let's see!'

The boat glided in beneath the shallow keel of the *Catherine*. A light burned on board, but no one was visible; and there was no sound but a faint creak of rigging and a mutter of rippled sailcloth. The sergeant, crouching, scanned the whole port-side for a handhold, slowly and intently; and then suddenly he sprang up so lightly that the rowing-boat hardly swayed. John saw a rope clutched in his hand: and then the sergeant was swarming up the side of the vessel, and was over the guard-rail and on to the deck, all in a couple of instants.

Immediately he was out of sight a dreadful foreboding came over John. The sergeant was a tough customer, but he had been right when he called Goodway a devil: the man was nothing less. If he could do what he did to Catherine, then . . .

How many silent seconds had passed? Was that a movement on deck? Should he uncover the lamp? Go up there? But suppose the rowing-boat drifted away . . .?

He had started up, resolved to climb up after the sergeant whatever happened, when there was a grunt from above him, and a figure appeared at the edge of the deck close to the guard-rail. No: two figures, locked together, struggling, frantic and noiseless. A hand went up, grasping a spar – Goodway's: John's throat felt like a lock turned by a key. But the spar swept down through empty air. The sergeant had twisted away, and side-stepped, and came at Goodway low and expertly. There was a cry of rage and frustration as the officer caught him about the middle, pressing him backward against the guard-rail, and then Goodway freed himself with a hideous wrench that sent him hurtling over the rail and into the water, twenty feet from John in the rowing-boat.

The ebb tide was stronger here, at the mouth of the Point, and Goodway had hit the water flat, and it had stunned him; and the current began to bear him swiftly away. Without thought John seized the oars, sculled the boat about, and made after him. Once when he looked over his shoulder the shaggy head had gone under, but a moment later it surfaced again, some yards further on towards the Point. The sergeant was shouting something from the deck of the *Catherine*, but John could hear nothing but the splash of the oars and the pounding of his own blood in his ears. He must be close: he looked over his shoulder, and saw Goodway's lolling head some ten feet away, to the starboard side of him now. The ebb was very strong here, and there were treacherous cross-currents at the Point mouth that were dragging the stranded man all ways, and wearying him the more he feebly fought them. Goodway gave a great gasp as John approached him, his head thrown back; and their eyes met.

Their eyes met, and John's hands fell still on the oars. For what could only have been a moment, but which seemed an eternity to John's spirit, they looked into each other's eyes, and John was still, and the possibility of remaining still, and simply watching as Goodway went down, was vividly present to him through that eternity, until he seemed to have studied it from every angle, and peered into its tempting heart. And then John sculled the oars again, and brought the boat nearer to the drowning man, and the words rang through his head as clearly as if he had spoken them: *Not death now. Too easy. That is the only reason I act. I would have him suffer more.*

He was within a few feet of Goodway now: he let go the oars, and scrambled to the bows and leaned over the side, stretching out his arms. A foot or so – six inches – Goodway hardly had the strength to lift his hands, but with a last summoning of will he pulled his arms up out of the embrace of the water, and stretched them forth towards John. Six inches – three inches – their eyes met again, and John seemed to see in Goodway's something of that unholy twinkle, though it was surely only a reflection of moonlight on the sea. Two inches – an inch – their fingers, vibrating with the strain, just touched; and then, before John could take a grip, a stealthy cross-current lifted the rowing-boat away like a giant hand, and the inches became yards again in a moment; and while John was desperately trying to bring the boat round again, Marcus Goodway was quietly sucked under, an arm flailing weakly above the surface, and scattering flakes of moonlight, before the water closed over him and resumed its silver calm as if it had never been disturbed.

CHAPTER FOURTEEN

Chiefly Numerical

He was returning home, on a mild spring evening, from a courtesy call at the London house of Admiral Fernhill – now Admiral Sir George Fernhill. With the outbreak of war in the Crimea, the admiral had been induced to take command of a desk, and in reward the queen had touched the sword on either side of his polished head, and he had his desire at last. John had to admit that even the admiral's vanity had not been proof against the events of the past month or so, and that the honour did not mean a great deal to him.

Appreciating the mildness of the air after a cold slow season, and disinclined to go home just yet, he took a stroll down to Covent Garden and mingled with the people there – the market-traders, the hawkers and costers, the street entertainers. After the ghastly events in Norfolk, there was a strange, shy sort of pleasure in these simple things – much, he thought, as a man must feel who had been released from a lunatic asylum, stepping from dark into light.

Not all light, of course. But one shadow at least had vanished for ever. The world no longer contained Mr Marcus Goodway. He had cheated justice to the last, but only at the sacrifice of his life. It was long before Sergeant Paradine gave up hope of taking his man alive, that night at Blakeney; and only at noon the next day did he formally give up the search. Goodway's body was finally found washed ashore at Shipden, ten miles down the coast, three days later. John greatly wondered whether, as often happened, the body had beached first on the flats at Saltmarsh, and been thrown back: perhaps the Soldier had found him, and done it. He hoped so. Much of his bitter vengefulness had been worn away by a corrosive sadness, but enough remained for him to find satisfaction in the thought of Goodway's corpse drifting up in sight of his parents' old house on the cliff.

A little *fantoccini* theatre, with Italian marionettes, had set up in a corner of the market, and John lingered to watch. The puppet show was some Arabian Nights tale: John was glad it was not Punch and Judy. Nonsense, perhaps, but there was no smiling at those exultant beatings of squealing Mrs Punch – not when the memories that would never leave him included that vision of a woman in a white gown lying broken by the side of a country road.

A memory, indeed, that might have been intolerable. But there was another memory that had succeeded it which would also never leave him, for a different reason. He had returned to the inn at Holt in the early morning after Goodway's drowning, and found the door of that room on the ground floor closed. Dr Appleyard and the local surgeon were inside, the landlady said, and were not to be disturbed; but John had been about to knock anyway, with his heart in his mouth, when Dr Appleyard in shirt-sleeves opened the door and came out. The old physician rubbed his tired eyes, and – here was the memory that would never leave John – smiled greyly at John, and put his lean hand on his shoulder, and said: 'Well, John, he has not killed this wife. She is in a poor way – a poor way indeed; but I swear that we shall keep her in the land of the living. He has not killed this one, my friend.'

Dr Appleyard had been as good as his word. He had stayed in Norfolk, by Catherine's bedside, for another two days, until her family came, bringing with them their own physician; but John had no doubt about whose skill had saved her. Her recovery, of course, would be slow – it had been a week before she could be moved, and she had only just been brought back to London; and while the broken collar-bone and ribs would heal in time, there was a partial paralysis of the left arm which, Dr Appleyard confided to John, might be permanent; and this was to say nothing of the mental scars she would wear. He was sure that there had not been damage to the brain; he was far from sure that she would ever be the same person.

But now she was home, bride and widow: Goodway could do nothing more to her, and her parents had been shaken a little out of their complacency, and devoted themselves to her; and the honest Augustus never left her side. Salvage from a wreck, then; and it was surely not fanciful to hope that John's parents might rest easier in their shamed graves.

Salvage from a wreck. But where was the one treasure that John would have given anything to save, and take to his embrace once more? Nowhere: nowhere to be found. The deep, abiding, mournful hollowness within him that was his loss of Verity could not be filled by any incidental consolations. He longed for her, and could not find her.

He suspected that Dr Appleyard, moved by his desolation, had tried more than once to persuade his sister to break her vow of confidence, and reveal Verity's whereabouts. But Miss Jemima, with the best of intentions no doubt, would not be shaken. Sometimes, at his lowest moments, John half convinced himself that he was resigned to the loss of her; but in his heart he knew he was not. He would give anything to be reconciled with her, he would give anything to speak with her, he would give anything to see her face again for the merest instant; and from day to day, week to week, that did not change, and he felt it never would.

'Because I love her – that's why,' he said to himself as he strolled away from the *fantoccini*. 'I love her, but I gave her cause to think I did not. A simple enough riddle to solve, one would think – yet where is the solution?'

Nowhere: nowhere to be found.

Home, then. Enough of this wandering: if he were honest with himself, he would have to admit that he undertook these walks partly in the hope of spotting her in the street some day – but he had never had any luck with it, and it was hopeless. He turned the corner by the Opera House, and was instantly accosted by an ear-shattering cry of, 'Mr T.! Mr T., stand still, my friend, don't move a hair, because I am going to come over there and shake your hand!'

It was Waldo Tuttle, who came hurrying across the road to him, nearly getting himself run over by a meat-wagon in the process, and was immediately true to his word, vigorously shaking John's hand until he had all but shaken his own hat off his head.

'Now, do you know what this is under my arm, all wrapped up in newspaper, Mr T.? Oysters – that's what: I've been to fetch 'em, on account of Arabella and I deciding to have a bang-up supper tonight – twenty likenesses today, sir, and only three black plates amongst them! And do you know how many oysters there are here, sir? Why, lots; and that's lucky, because you're coming home with me to share 'em.'

John was touched by this friendly invitation, and did not wish to appear churlish in refusing; but he was afraid that he was very indifferent company at the moment, and tried to say as much. Mr Tuttle however, was having none of it. He was insistent that John join them for supper – 'just we three, sir – you, and me, and the divine Arabella: that's all, sir – just we three. So: take my arm, Mr T., and come along, because if Arabella don't mix the best shrub you've ever tasted, I'm a liar. Just we three, Mr T. – that's all!'

336

Mr Tuttle was most emphatic on this point, and repeated it several times as they repaired to the Strand; but John supposed that Mr Tuttle had simply divined his present aversion to much company, and was seeking to reassure him that no strangers would be present. They came to the little photographer's shop, and found Arabella within, sweeping the floor of the studio.

'Well, Arabella, my own, I've got the oysters, and I've assured Mr T. that it will just be we three for supper,' said Mr Tuttle, bestowing a hearty kiss on his wife. 'You, me, and Mr T., leaving aside the oysters and shrub: just we three!'

It was odd to find Mr Tuttle so emphatic on this point with Arabella too; and she, after a surprised moment, began to be quite as odd, repeating that it was, most definitely to be just the three of them, and making several more references to the fact as she took off her apron, put away the broom, locked the shop door, and invited John into the back parlour behind the glass-house; even once dropping into mime, as she and her husband laid the table – looking up at John with a secret sort of smile lighting her sloe-black eyes, and holding up the salt, mustard, and pepper one after the other, as if to say 'Three!'

They gave him a seat, and a glass of shrub which entirely lived up to Mr Tuttle's encomiums on it, and Mr Tuttle stirred up the fire, remarking that it was sometimes nice to have a fire even when it was mild, just as it was sometimes nice to have a scratch even when you didn't itch. And then there was a knocking at the shop-door. At least, Mr Tuttle said that he heard it, and Arabella said that she heard it, though John never heard a thing; and Arabella went to answer the knock that John didn't hear, and returned saying that Mr Tuttle was wanted. Apparently Mrs Tuttle was wanted as well, because they both went away – making many apologies to John, and saying they wouldn't be long; and so they left him alone there with the fire and the shrub, and with a strange impression that the Tuttles had not gone out to the shop at all, but had, for some reason, walked upstairs.

He had been sitting in perplexity for some minutes when he heard footsteps – yes, the stairs definitely; now what did it mean? He turned as the parlour door opened again, and there was neither Waldo Tuttle nor Arabella, but Verity.

'Hullo, John,' she said.

He started up from his seat, but then was paralysed by – he did not know what: shyness, love, longing, apprehension, all of them perhaps. And in the meantime she walked into the room, and sat down at the table opposite him.

'Oh, Verity,' he said. 'Oh, Verity, I've been looking for you everywhere.'

She did not speak, but nodded, her eyes lowered.

'How – how did you come here?'

'This is where I've been living,' said she. 'The Tuttles have a spare room upstairs, and I asked them, and they let me have it. They've been very kind. I thought that you wouldn't find me here.'

He gazed at her, with unspeakable pullings and tearings at his heart. 'You didn't want me to find you,' he said: not as a question.

'No,' she said, still not looking at him. 'I . . . ahem, I . . . Oh, damn you, John Twopenny, I'm afraid I'm going to cry, and I greatly dislike crying in front of anyone, please let us talk about some neutral matter just for a few moments until I've conquered it, what do you think of the Turkish war?'

'I – I don't think anything of it. Verity—'

'But you must,' said Verity, her eyes closed and her hand to her mouth, 'have some opinion, John, on this – this matter of grave concern and great interest for the student of European affairs . . .'

If she should shed tears, he thought, he doubted his ability to prevent himself seizing her in her arms . . . 'I think that there has been a certain stubbornness on both sides,' he said, 'but that, as with all such cases, there was a wrong which should have been righted and was not. It only takes a little wilful stupidity on the

337

part of one of the parties – a failure of trust and openness on his, I mean their part – for them to fall into mutual misunderstanding, and drift apart, until the situation becomes . . . becomes . . .'

'Irretrievable?' said Verity, lifting her eyes to his at last.

'Never irretrievable,' said John, 'oh, Verity, never irretrievable.'

She could not return his gaze for long, and presently dropped her eyes again, and said in a low voice, 'Do you know how Catherine is? Miss Jemima told me – about what happened with Marcus Goodway.'

'She's recovering,' John said. 'Slowly, but she is recovering.'

Verity bit her lip. 'You were right about her marrying that man, then,' she said. 'When we quarrelled about it, I thought—'

'Right for the wrong reasons,' John said. 'Oh, yes, I was violently opposed to her marrying him; but you had every right to suppose that I was so passionate about it because . . .'

'Because you were still passionate about Catherine,' Verity said. 'Yes. That is what I thought . . . Oh, John, we'd better go back to the Turkish war—'

'Damn the Turkish war. Verity, you had every right to think that, and you had every right to expect me to fervently deny it and swear on bended knee that it was not so and vow that it was you, you, you that I love and to tell you why it really was that I opposed the marriage and all of this I failed to do. I failed, my darling Verity: but I shall do it now, if it's not too late. In fact, even if it *is* too late.'

'You can omit the bended knee,' she murmured.

'No, I won't. I shall bend both if I like.' But he did not; for though they had unconsciously slipped into their old way of talking, there was no place for frivolity now. He simply told her, plainly, what he should have told her before: everything he had learned from old Saul, about his mother, and her seduction by Goodway, and her death. She was silent and solemn throughout; and when he had finished, she was silent still. And then he saw that tears were beading on her eyelashes. They gathered there, and fell, and ran down her cheeks; but she did not move or make a sound, for what must have been several minutes, until at last she gasped and groped blindly across the table for his hand.

'God forgive me,' she sobbed, 'oh, God forgive me.'

'For what?' he said, squeezing her hand.

'For doubting you. Oh, John, God forgive me for doubting you, when such a dreadful, tragic truth lay behind it all!'

'Why should you not have done? I gave you no indications to the contrary – not one. That's what I mean when I say I failed, Verity. It is me who should seek forgiveness for having doubted you. Yes; I may not have meant to, but I doubted you – by not telling you this before, I was doubting your worthiness to share my parents' secret. You – of all the people in the world – you, whom I should never have hesitated to entrust with the inmost secrets of my heart! Oh, it's me who should seek forgiveness, Verity. But it's not God's forgiveness I want: I don't care about that.'

'Blasphemer,' she said, wiping her eyes.

'Probably. I don't care about that either.'

'Quite a lot of things you don't care about, it seems.'

'Many. In fact, all of them – everything – except you. You, Verity, I love you, I love you, and I sound like a parrot no doubt and I don't care about that either! You, you!'

She met his eyes, and swallowed. 'Oh, dear, I can feel the Turkish war coming on again . . . John, this will sound very stupid and – and not at all like me who have never, as I'm sure you'll agree, said a stupid thing in my life, but anyway: I went away from you, John, because I loved you. Does that sound stupid?'

'Yes. I mean, no.'

338

'You provoking man! Well, that is the plain truth. I went away, and cut myself off from all communication with you, because . . . because I loved you, and could not bear to think that you did not love me. Can you accept that?'

'I can,' said John. 'But only if you change your tenses, and say "love" instead of "loved".'

'Pedant!'

'Pedant, and blasphemer. Anything else you'd like to call me while we're about it?'

She frowned at him, but not for long; because a smile, the old impish, glinting smile that could enslave him in a moment, crept over her face, and vanquished the frown utterly. 'Yes, John,' she said. 'There is something I'd like to call you. But first, perhaps you'd like to fulfil that promise about the bended knee.'

He did: both knees; and it brought him into close proximity with her. Such close proximity, indeed, that her arms were very soon round his neck, and her cheek was against his; and it was in that position that she called him various things, all of them extremely pleasant. And it was in that position that Waldo and Arabella Tuttle found them when they crept back to the parlour to view the success or otherwise of their kindly stratagem – 'squeezing the life out of each other!' as Arabella approvingly expressed it.

'It was Arabella, you see,' said Mr Tuttle, after they had shaken hands all round ten times over, and laughed, and done it all over again, and at last composed themselves. 'There's no microscope to beat her, when it comes to seeing close into things. We were very happy to have Miss Deene living with us, and very happy likewise to respect her request that she live in perfect seclusion, and that a certain person never be told about it; but after a time Arabella said to me in private, that Miss Deene *wasn't* happy; and that it was all to do with that certain person; and that if we could get a hold of the two of them, and push 'em together in any discreet sort of way, it would be all the better for Miss Deene and the certain person. Now this echoed, as it happened, my own thought—'

'Oh, did it indeed!' said Arabella merrily. 'And how is it that you never said anything of it yourself, I wonder!'

'My love,' said Mr Tuttle, 'I was coming to that. It echoed my own thought, I say, but I never act upon any such thought without consulting Arabella first, on account of her more-than-human perspicaciousness—'

('Stuff!' said Arabella, affectionately.)

'And so we consulted, and so it was agreed, and when I happened on Mr T. today, I knew that our opportunity was here at last; and I can't do better than call upon the deathless words of the Swan on this occasion, and remark, if you will join me in toasting the sentiment with a glass, that All's Well That Ends Well!'

And so it was not three, after all, but four, who sat down to oysters and shrub. But later, it was two who were tactfully left alone again, to rediscover their delight in being two; and to demonstrate the wonderful paradox that two can also be one, for ever.

CHAPTER FIFTEEN

A Sad Loss

Grief inconsolable sits brooding upon the house of the Spikings in Montagu Place. There is a wreath upon the front door, and within there is so much black crape that the Spikings might be supposed to have elected to corner the market in that article, and to be sitting on the whole stock while they wait for the price of it to rise. Even the mirrors with which the house abounds have been draped with black, and the letter-paper on which Mrs Spikings pens her lamentations to their friends is so deeply edged with black that there is hardly room for any writing. But then Mrs Spikings drops so many tears upon the page that the writing on these missives is hardly legible anyway; and very puzzled their friends must be to receive them.

As for the Spikings themselves, it is hardly enough to say they are in mourning. They have gone into black as if they meant never to come out of it. Beads of jet dangle at Mrs Spikings' ears, and nestle round her neck – which is appropriately crêpey to begin with – and Mr Spikings seems to shed darkness about him when he goes sorrowing into the City, and turns the thoughts of hardened old brokers to solemn things. The children are in mourning too – the sight of Knight's little fat legs in black knickerbockers being found particularly affecting by Mrs Spikings, who only has to glimpse them to go off into a watery fit from which only the strongest of smelling-salts can revive her. The servants are in mourning likewise, including Tripp the nurse, whose haggard aspect is admirably suited to the costume; and also the governess who replaced the reprehensible Miss Deene. A meek young lady, the new governess, and gratifyingly free from the bluestocking pertness of her predecessor; but nevertheless not entirely satisfactory, for she has been found on more than one occasion hiding under the nursery table, murmuring prayers in quite a mystical manner, whilst her young charges exercise their animal spirits all over the room.

Everybody and everything in the house of Spikings, in fact, has gone into mourning: even the carriage-horses that take Mrs Spikings to Oxford Street, where she shops desolately, feature black plumes in their equipage. Callers at the house know better than to intrude on such grief, and merely leave cards, and tiptoe away feeling almost guilty for being alive; and even the chimney-sweep feels apologetic for keeping his appointment there, and tries to perform his function in a hushed and reverential manner, and when Mrs Spikings attacks him like a furious terrier for getting a spot of soot on the carpet, tells himself, 'It's because of her loss, that's all: it's her loss!' – quite forgetting that she is always this vicious with him as a matter of course.

But the Spikings' loss, as they do not tire of asserting, is no common one. It is a bereavement which time has no power to heal. It is a tragedy beyond the power of words to convey. It is the fall of the sun from their sky. It is the loss of Uncle Pomeroy.

Yes: the sublime Uncle Pomeroy is no more. The inestimable, the incomparable Uncle Pomeroy has been gathered up to glory, and numbered among the bright seraphim; which is to say, his valet came in with his shaving-water three mornings

340

ago, and found him lying dead in bed with his whipped-cream hair all standing upright on the pillow. It is an article of faith with Mrs Spikings that she suffered a terrible nightmare on the very night in which Uncle Pomeroy expired, and started up in bed with his name on her lips, and an ominous feeling at her heart; and there is no one in the household – certainly not her husband – who would dare to suggest that she had actually spent most of that night quarrelling with Mr Spikings, and that at the probable moment of Uncle Pomeroy's dissolution, she had been trying to bring the companion of her joys round to her point of view by throttling him with his nightcap.

Uncle Pomeroy deceased! There would surely have been a state funeral, the Spikings aver, if Uncle Pomeroy had not always been a man of such modesty that he had eschewed that high office which would otherwise have been his (First Minister, according to Mr Spikings: Lord Chancellor, according to his wife). But never mind: the funeral which Uncle Pomeroy's affectionate nephew arranges for him is little short, in its magnificence, of that which a grateful nation would tender to a hero. No expense is spared. Chief mourners – naturally – are to be Mr and Mrs Spikings: all four children are to be present, Tancred being brought home from public school for the occasion (and so distracted with grief that he uses quite uncharacteristic language, declaring that he doesn't see why he should come away from the fellows, just because that stuffed old coot has pegged out); and numerous lesser mourners are invited to gather at the Spikings' house prior to the funeral, and to return thither afterwards, there to climb a mountain of cold meats, and swim in a lake of port wine.

Also, to hear the reading of the will. Alas, that such deplorable practicalities should intrude upon the ceremonious expression of heartfelt grief! Mrs Spikings is all for doing away with such things: for her part – and Alfred is in full agreement with her in this – she has not the slightest interest in what becomes of Uncle Pomeroy's fortune. She would gladly see every last farthing of it thrown into the sea, if she could only have that dear man back! But, convention must be observed, and Uncle Pomeroy's lawyer is a particular stickler for it, and so the reading of the will is to conclude the sad occasion. This business of Uncle Pomeroy's will must, however, have severely tried Mr and Mrs Spikings' familial feelings, for they are heard by the meek wan governess to be talking about it for much of the evening before the funeral. Though they do talk also of other things, no doubt to take their minds off their grief: things such as an open barouche, a new set of silver, and a villa in Surrey.

Comes the morning of the funeral, and the heavens open; and Mrs Spikings, waxing poetical in the intervals of requiring smelling-salts, declares that the skies themselves are weeping for Uncle Pomeroy; Tancred Spikings, meanwhile, showing that he is still quite distracted with grief, by grumbling that he isn't going to get a soaking just to see that old Dummy planted, and he doesn't care who knows it. The downpour continues as the mourners gather at Montagu Place; and Mr and Mrs Spikings turn it to good account, getting impressively rained on as they support each other out to the black-clad carriage, and climb in with grief writ large in their every dripping gesture. It is only the first, however, of half a dozen such vehicles, for nothing less than a six-carriage funeral will do for the great Uncle Pomeroy; even though the Spikings had a little difficulty in making up the numbers, and the last carriage to trundle off is occupied by various makeweights who have not the faintest idea who Uncle Pomeroy is or was, or what they are doing here.

Everything passes off well at the church, where Mrs Spikings exhibits an admirable self-command, and only chokes back a loud sob at every third word of the service. The rain is still falling when the proceedings move on to the churchyard, and the graveside – falling so hard, indeed, that there seems some danger of Uncle Pomeroy's casket simply floating like a boat at mooring when it is lowered into the hole; but the vicar, who is rather impatient to be back in the dry, passes off any such awkwardness by taking the burial service at a canter; and having got to the Sure and Certain Hope of the Resurrection in double-quick time, he lights out for the vicarage like the wind, and the mourners dash to their carriages likewise, just as if the coffin were a bomb about to explode.

Back at Montagu Place, a certain lightness comes over the company. The lesser mourners who know each other make secret jokes, and stifle their laughter in their port-glasses; and the lesser mourners who do not know each other make friends, and promise to meet up under pleasanter circumstances, and cement their alliance by murmuring sly remarks about the Spikings' decor. Even Mr and Mrs Spikings recover their spirits a little, and pick at some slices of boiled ham, and reply to condolences with brave, bearing-up smiles and allusions to Providence.

And Uncle Pomeroy's solicitor, meanwhile – a little toothy man like a watchful rabbit – keeps himself to himself, and is quietly appreciative of the attentions with which Mr and Mrs Spikings load him, and steadily appropriates his due proportion of food and drink. At last, he steps forward from his self-imposed shadow, and declares that the moment has come for him to perform that duty with which he was entrusted by their late friend, and produces from his breast-pocket, rolled up like a baton, the last will and testament of Uncle Pomeroy. An announcement which occasions a sort of trance of anticipation in the company, which is only broken by Mr Spikings' darting forward to place a comfortable chair for the lawyer, and Mrs Spikings' lapsing backward on the sofa, and murmuring 'Dear Uncle Pomeroy!' in the most nostalgic, reminiscent, and inconsolable tone.

There is a long preamble to the will, in which the authentic voice of Uncle Pomeroy is to be heard; but when the little rabbity lawyer gets to the meat of the document – that is, the legacies – Mr Spikings turns red, and begins to twitch and fume, and Mrs Spikings slowly rises from her woeful horizontal like a reanimated corpse, and fixes the speaker with a curdling glare. *No!* The Spikings, matrimonially harmonious even in this, protest with one voice; and Mr Spikings is only prevented from flying at the lawyer and smiting him hip and thigh by the lesser mourners, who are enjoying this too much to have it interrupted.

So, the lawyer hardily proceeds, and details the bequests of the great Uncle Pomeroy. Which are, the sum of five pounds, and an enamelled snuff-box, to his nephew, Alfred Spikings, Esquire; and five shillings each to the four children of the aforesaid Alfred Spikings, Esquire.

No more. That is the entire disposable estate of the man who could have been First Minister or Lord Chancellor: about as much, in total, as the cost of the young Spikings' mourning-knickerbockers. The reanimated corpse that is Mrs Spikings is thoroughly galvanized by this scandalous revelation, and hurtles about the room in quite a Frankenstein manner; but to no avail. The will held in the lawyer's hand is quite sound; and when Mr Spikings thrusts his big beefy face into the lawyer's little rabbity one, and demands to know what it means, the lawyer obliges.

And what it means is this. That Uncle Pomeroy squandered such money as he possessed, long ago, at ratting-matches in the least salubrious quarters of Seven Dials; that Uncle Pomeroy's grand address, to which the Spikings had been directing their fawning letters for years, was his address only insofar as he was permitted to occupy a room above the stables at the back for a nominal rent; that Uncle Pomeroy's circle of distinguished acquaintances was a conceited and pretentious fiction from beginning to end; and that Uncle Pomeroy, in short, was the most thorough-going liar, fraud, and humbug that ever imposed upon the greed and cupidity of fools, in the West End or the East.

A breathless pause descends on the mourners in the Spikings' drawing-room; and then Mrs Spikings turns on her husband, and hisses between clenched teeth, in an undertone audible three streets away: 'I *told* you! I *told* you, but you wouldn't listen . . .!'

CHAPTER SIXTEEN

A Beginning

The stream of the years flows on, now calm, now turbulent, and bears many things upon its breast: driftwood of many shapes, some ugly, some beautiful. What can be picked out from the flotsam, and held up to the light for a moment, before being returned to the unhurried and unrelenting tide?

The maltings and coal warehouses of Hales-next-the-sea: here they are. The great whitewashed letters have been repainted again; where once there was S. TWOPENNY & SON, and then TWOPENNY & CHIPCHASE, there is now E. CHIPCHASE & SON. The Son there represented is much, much smaller than those letters, but the hopes he bears are just as large; he is the first-born of Mr and Mrs Edwin Chipchase, and his father dotes on him. Certainly he is a true sprig of the Chipchase tree, for he has a fringe of fluffy hair round a bald pink crown, and small blue eyes without any depth to them, and soft fleshy hands with hardly any nails, and a low gurgling laugh, and a grotesque way of making much of his sex when his clouts are off; but the stream of years must flow on for a good while yet before he can patrol the maltings and terrify his workforce with bland tyranny. And in the meantime, the first-born is joined by a second-born; and the curious thing about the second-born is that he does not resemble Mr Edwin Chipchase at all. If he resembles anybody, it is the dark and brawny foreman who was taken on to replace Mr Addy, and who has slowly made himself indispensable to the business: a curious coincidence! No resemblance in character, however: for the foreman is a muted and stealthy sort of man, whereas the second son of Mr and Mrs Chipchase displays, even in infancy, a rebellious temperament that suggests he might not be averse to challenging his father, when the time comes.

Here is a curious piece of driftwood: strangely fashioned, but by no means ugly. Caleb Porter, whom John has found work for as an ostler at an inn on the Hampstead Road, and who is an excellent man for the job – not only industrious and trustworthy, but possessed of such a way with horses that people for several miles around send for him when they have trouble with a mount or a draught-horse, and are never disappointed.

And here is something rather rare, fragile and beautiful, cast up on the breast of the stream. Catherine Goodway, née Fernhill, is restored to health now, though her left arm is notably thinner than her right, and she does not use it overmuch – does not go about overmuch, in fact; and there is a certain melancholy something that strangers note in her eyes, and which when they go away they can only classify as a shadow. But her beauty is still there, and some if not all of her sense of fun; and she is a staunch ally and comfort to her brother Augustus in his courtship of the young lady from Cambridge, who besides an acid face boasts two left feet – but who is going to lead him a merry dance all the same.

And here is something pleasant to pick up from the moving stream and behold: a picnic by the river at Richmond, where John and Verity had their memorable day's holiday together. They are only two of the party gathered on the bank; for besides them there are Waldo and Arabella Tuttle, whose friendliness in bringing them

343

together has never been forgotten, and who form the loud, laughing centrepiece to the group; and Miss Thimblebee, who is seated very demurely on the grass with a sandwich in one pink hand, and who is trying her hardest to disapprove of everything that is going on, and not succeeding.

And here . . . a darker sight, and yet one that has light in it too – the bright light of human aspiration and endeavour. It is a ward at Guy's Hospital; and walking the ward, and attending the tuition of a fierce old resident surgeon, are a group of medical students. And among them is John Twopenny.

Attending very closely: for John knows that he must not shirk or fail. Dr Appleyard was very stern with him, in proposing to subsidize his studies, and see him through financially to his qualification as a doctor. He must not suppose, Dr Appleyard repeatedly tells him, that he has found a father-figure in this regard. No, no: Dr Appleyard is merely investing in the future of the medical profession, and any sentimental gratitude is out of the question. The simple fact is, Dr Appleyard does not expect to be around for ever, and he wishes to be assured that there will be at least one good physician of his own stamp to carry on his work. So John must work, and work: that is all the recompense Dr Appleyard requires. If he gets more, in the shape of a profound and abiding respect united to the warmest of affection, then that is just the way John is, and cannot be helped. So says Dr Appleyard; and only to Verity, between the movements of a fearsomely difficult violin sonata, does he confide the fact that in John he has found the son he never had; hurriedly adding that in her he hopes to find, likewise, the daughter-in-law he never had. And then he returns to tackling the gloomiest adagio ever heard, and says no more of it.

Well, there is a hope that will be fulfilled, for John and Verity have already agreed on it, joyfully. Theirs is a love of purest metal, that the fire has strengthened in the testing; and as it is carried with the rest of the flotsam along the stream of the years, amongst much that is dark and misshapen, it gives forth the brightest of gleams, ever and again; and will not cease to shine there, brilliant and untarnished, until it is gathered with the rest into the waiting sea.